SUPER DOODLES

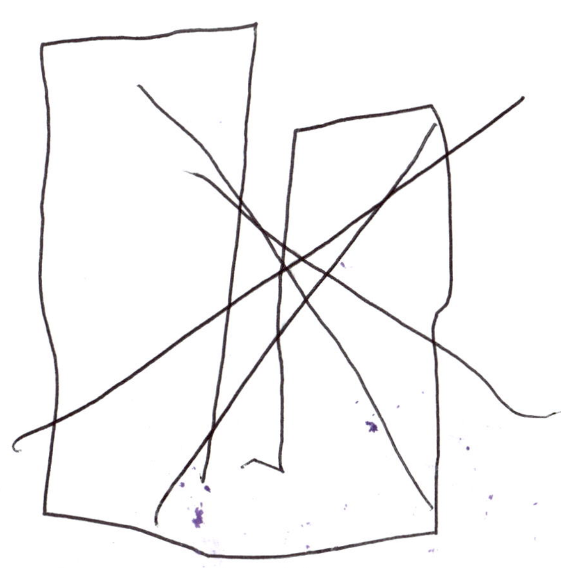

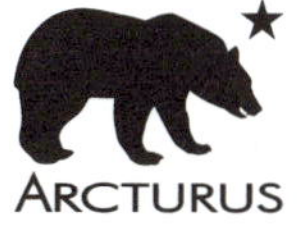

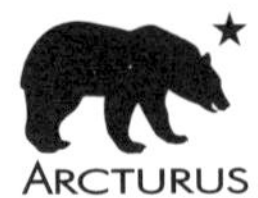

This edition published in 2009 by Arcturus Publishing Limited
26/27 Bickels Yard, 151–153 Bermondsey Street,
London SE1 3HA

ISBN: 978-1-84837-458-4
CH001329US

Illustrator: David Mostyn
Editor: Fiona Tulloch

Printed in Singapore

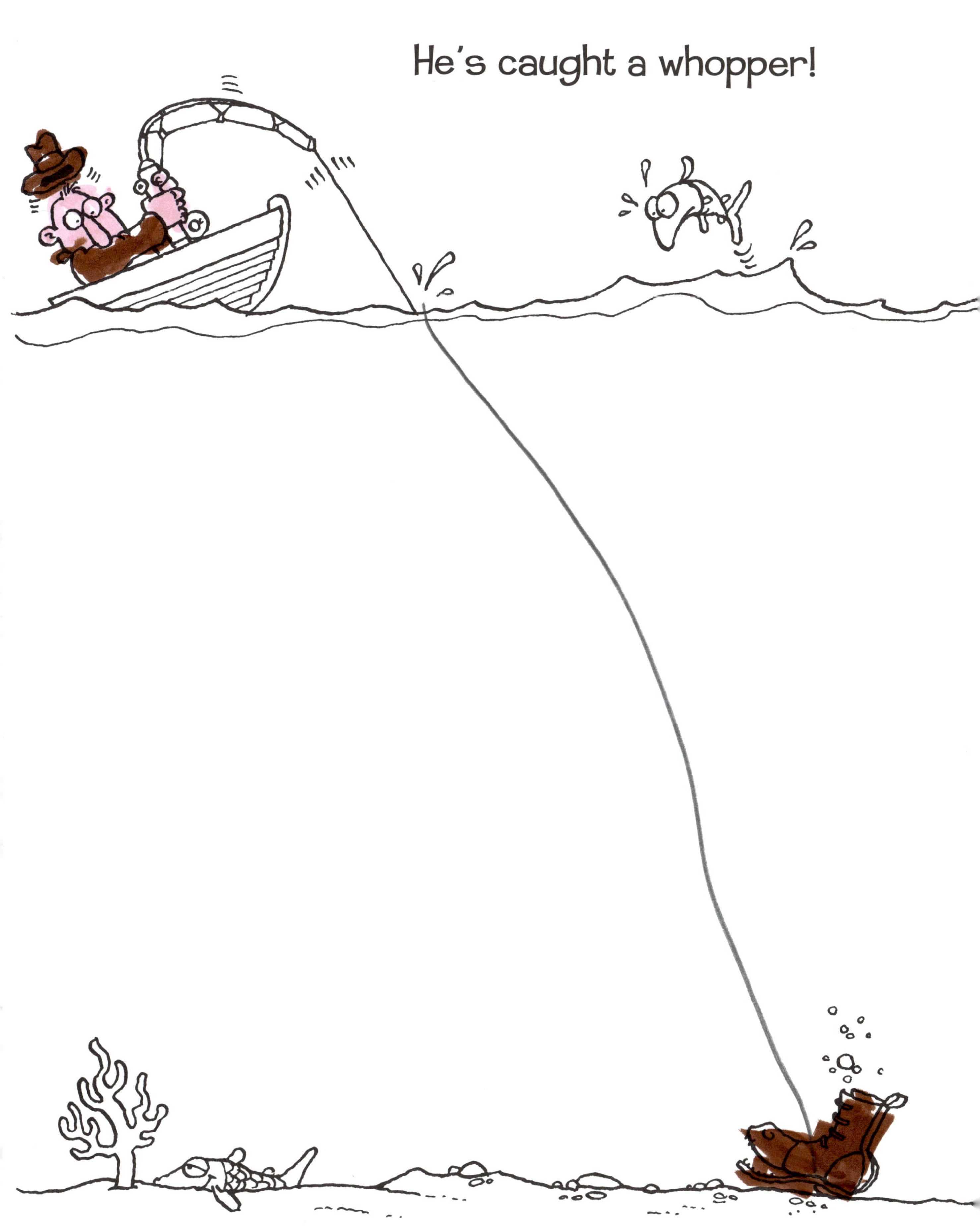
He's caught a whopper!

Give his graffiti
some color

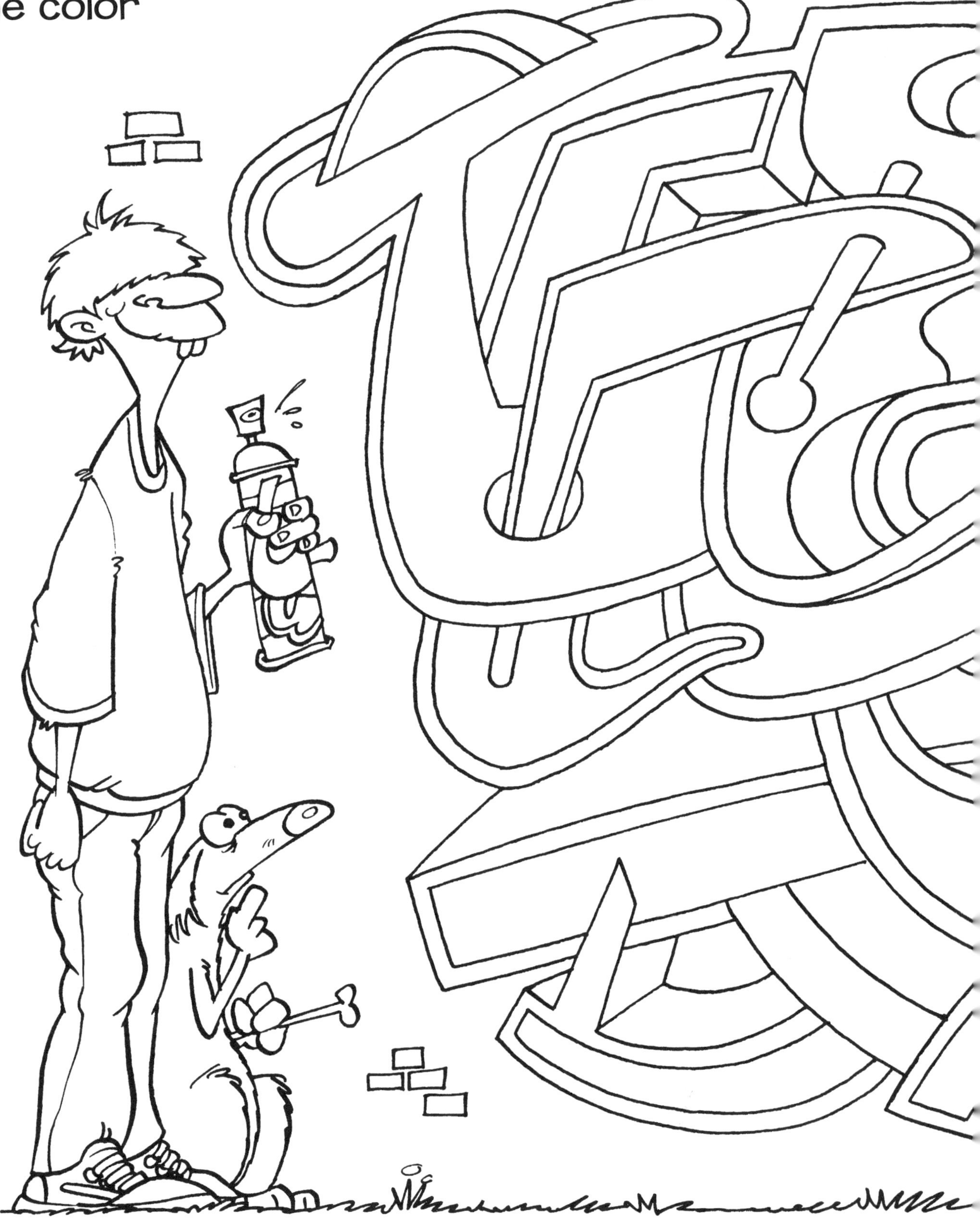

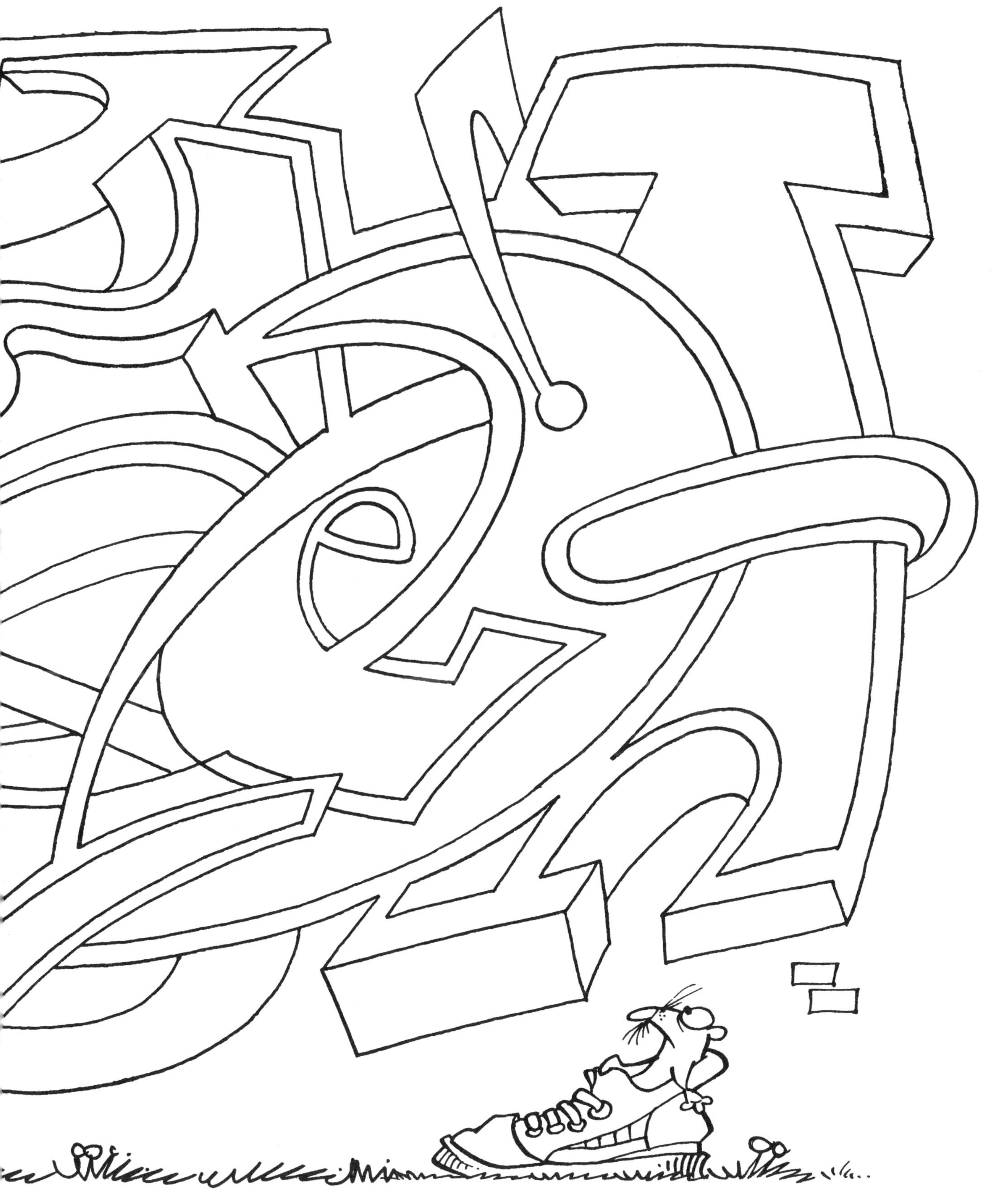

What has the monster just eaten?

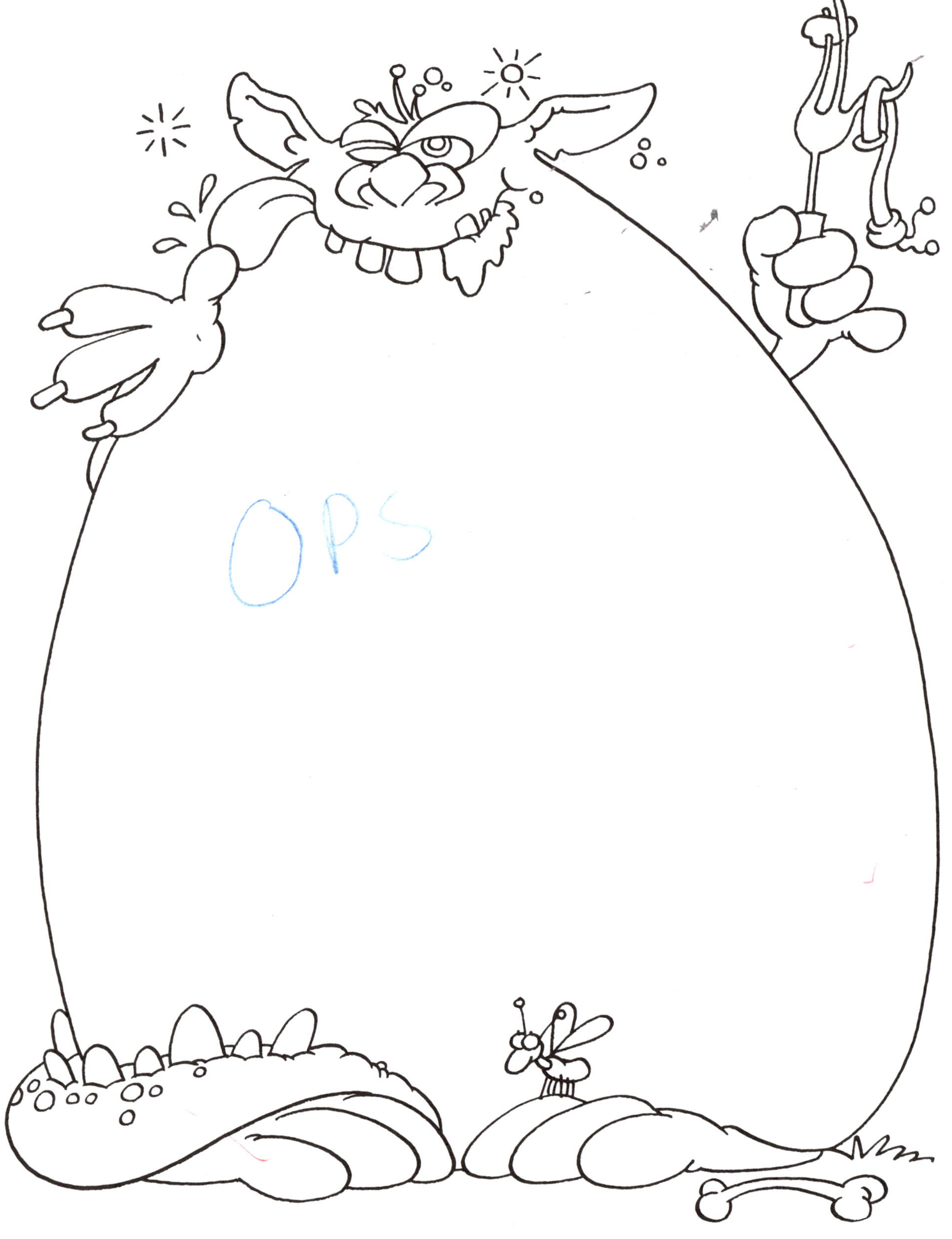

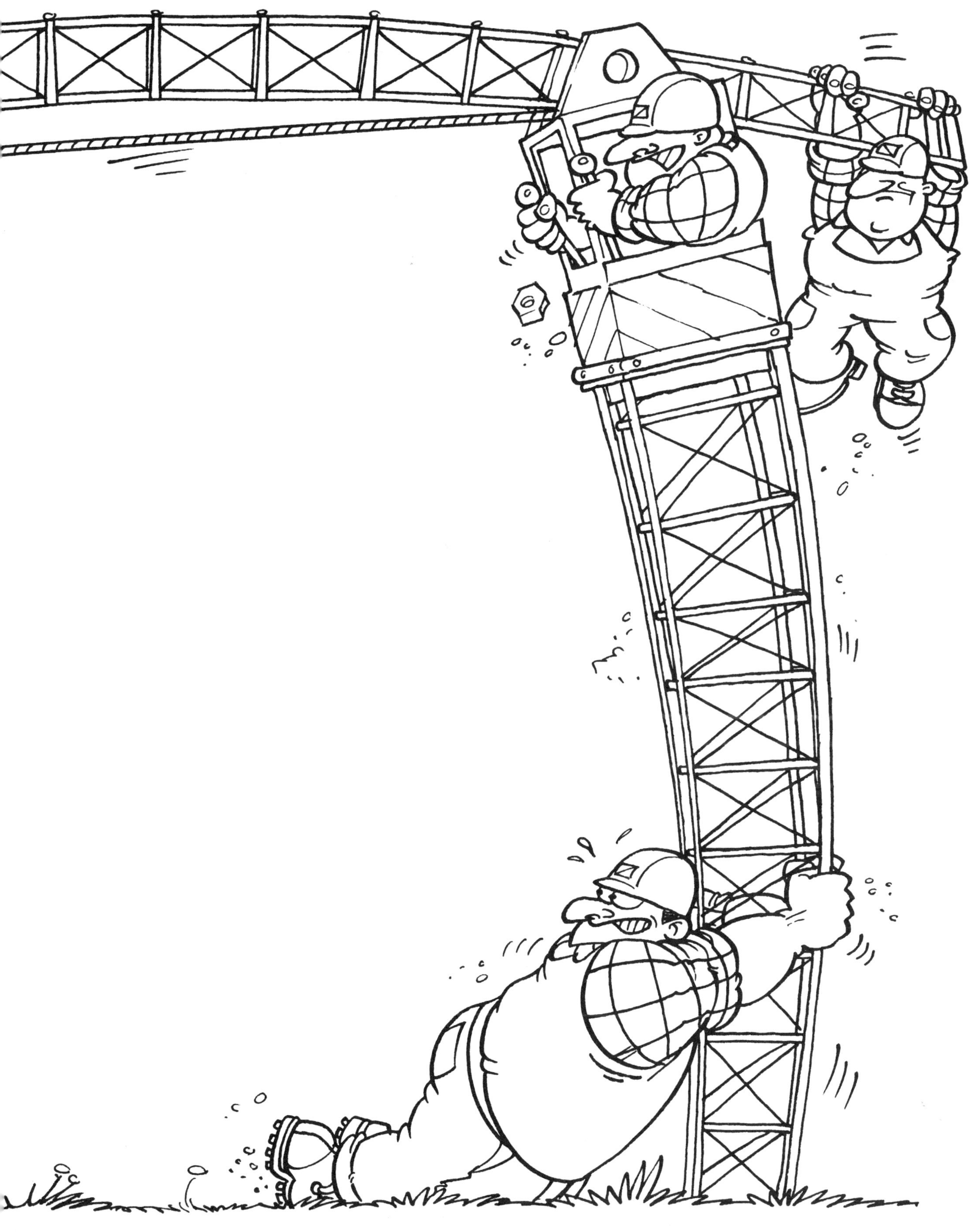

The flag of Koozbane is waving on planet Zlug

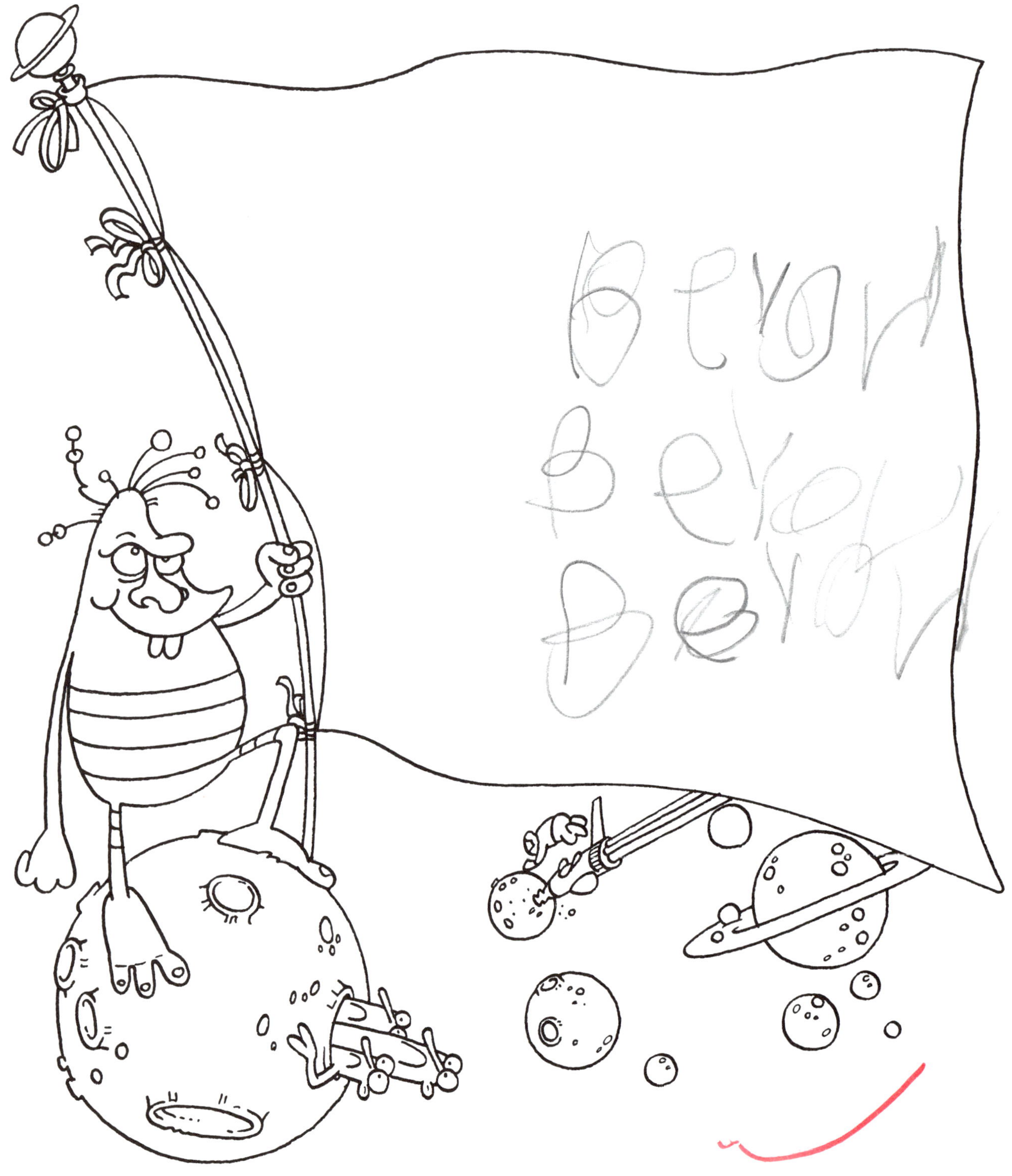

What's making that awful sound?

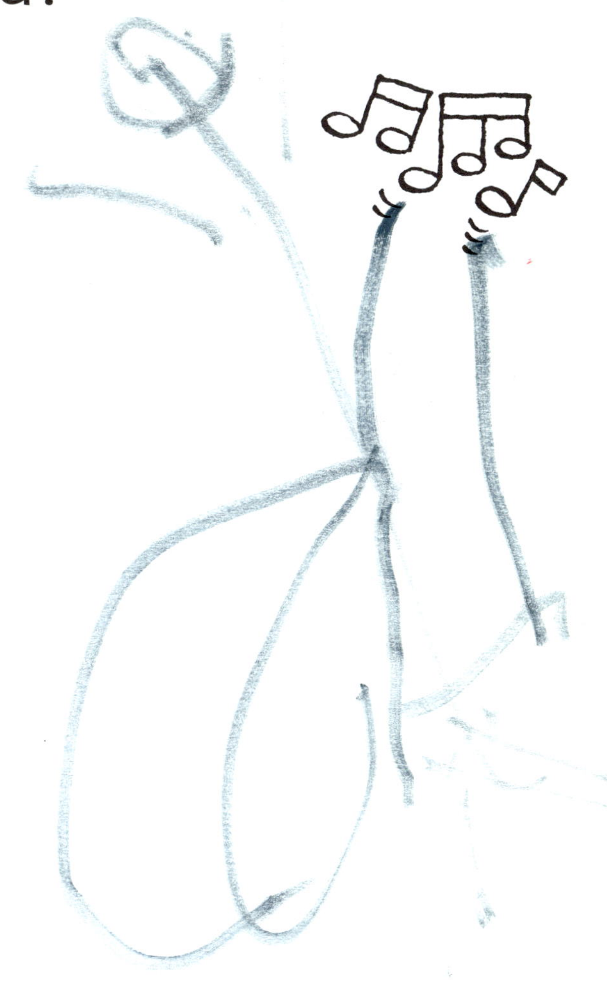

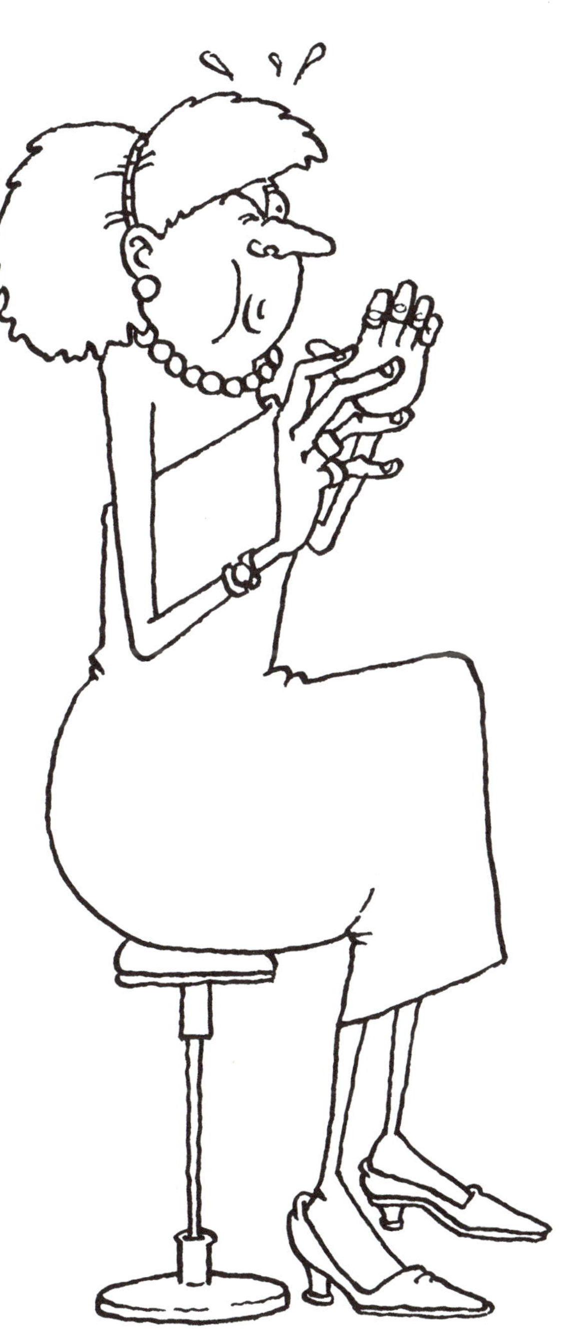

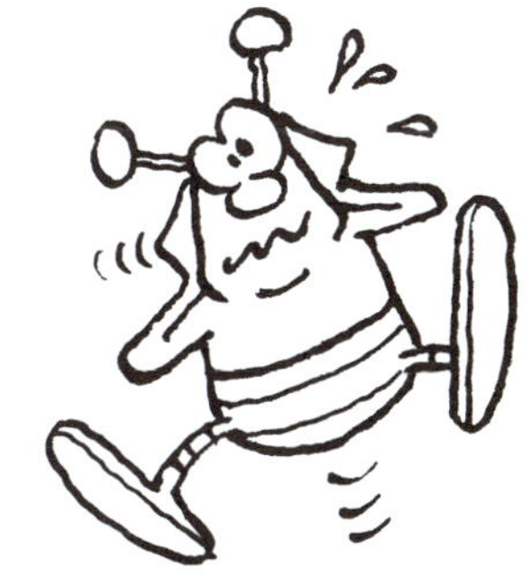

He'd never seen a genie that color before

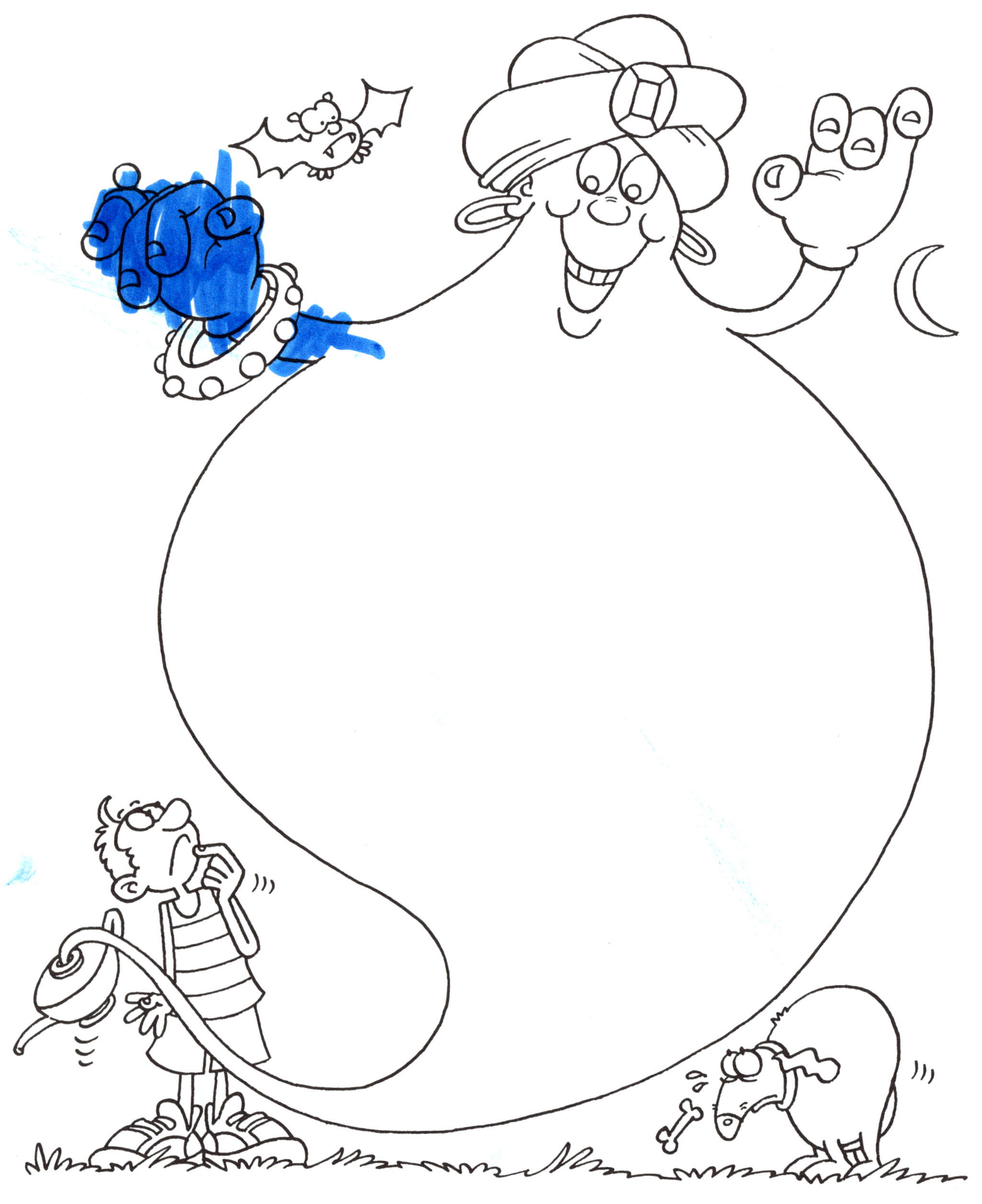

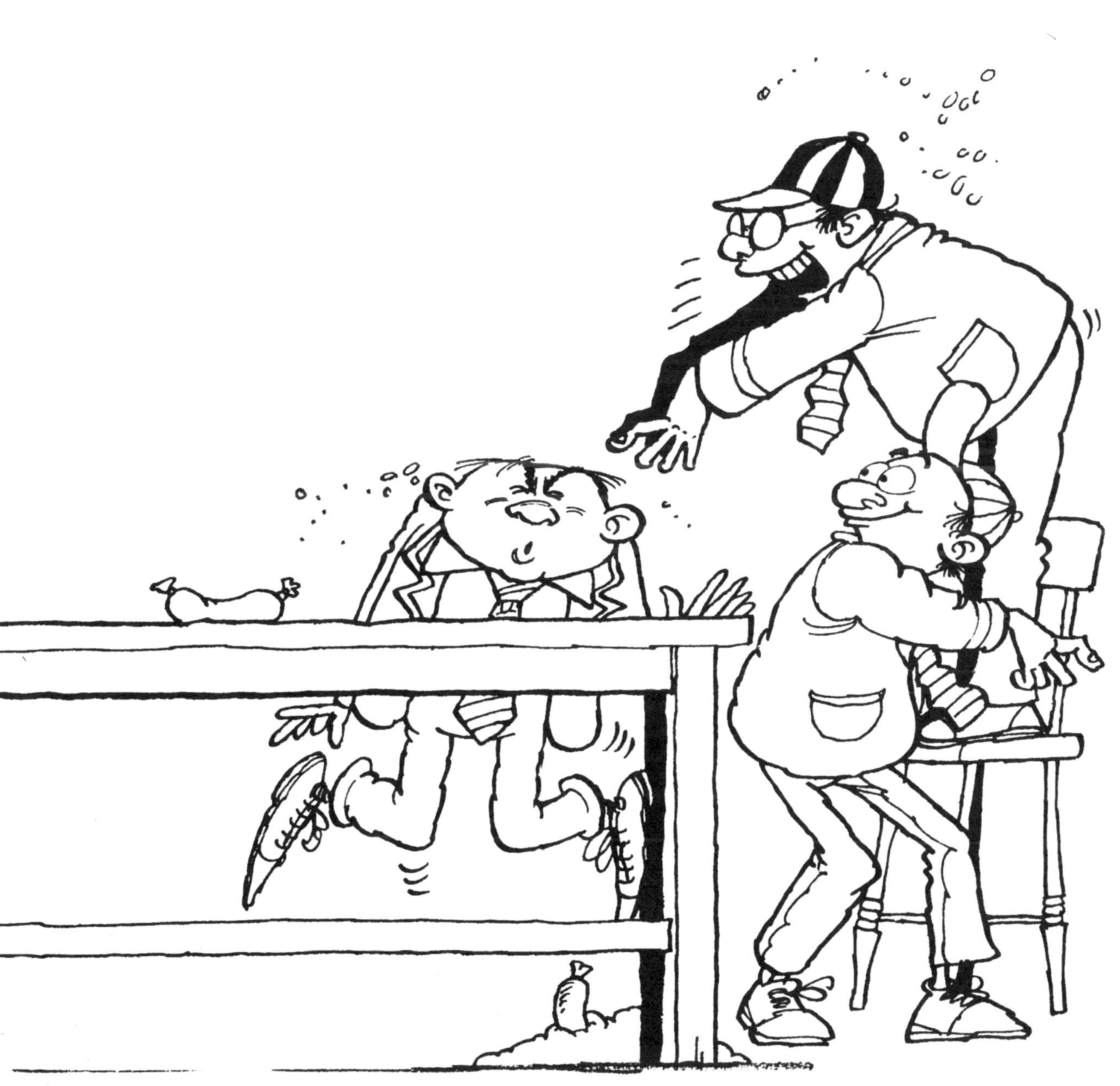

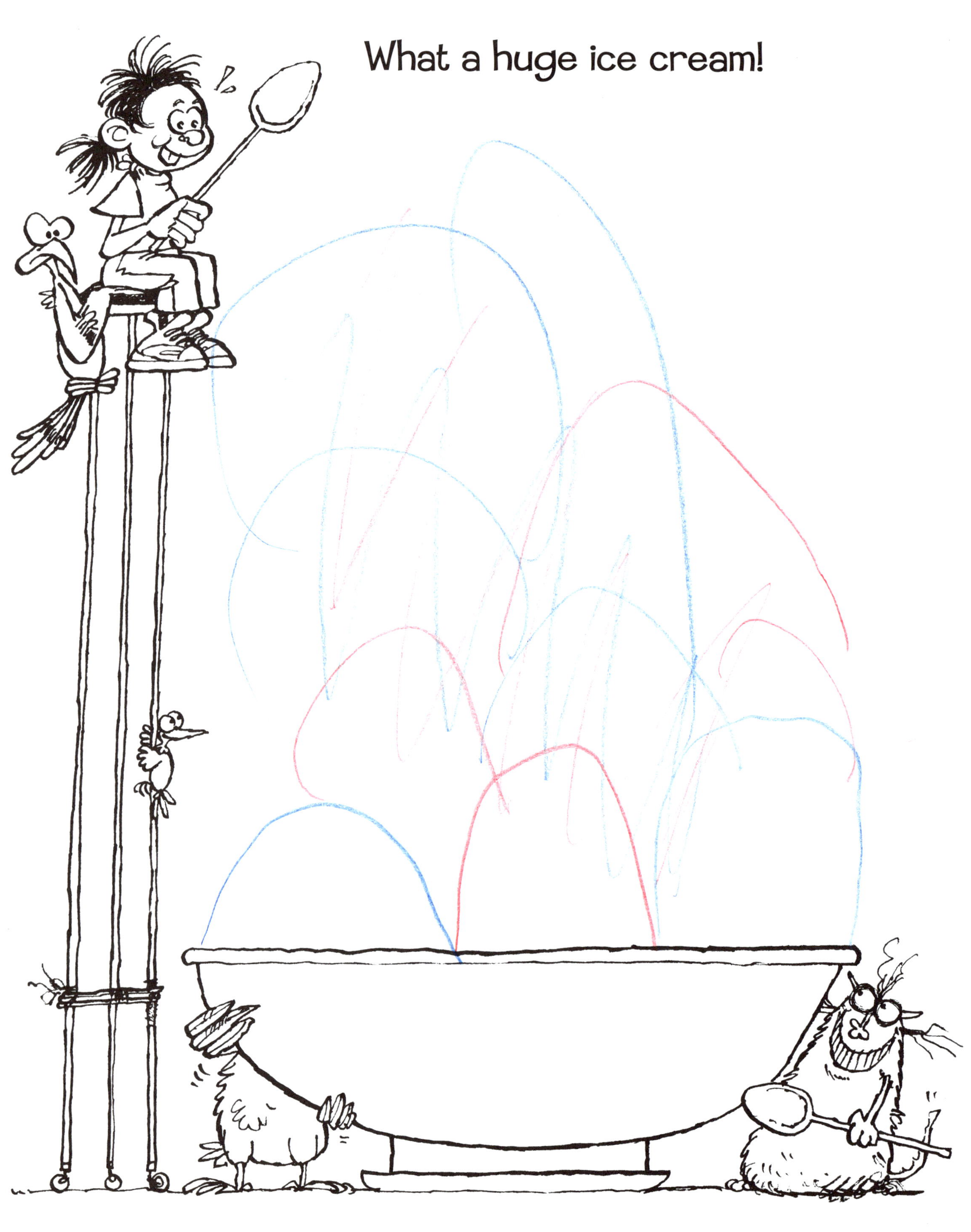
What a huge ice cream!

How do people get around in the year 2109?

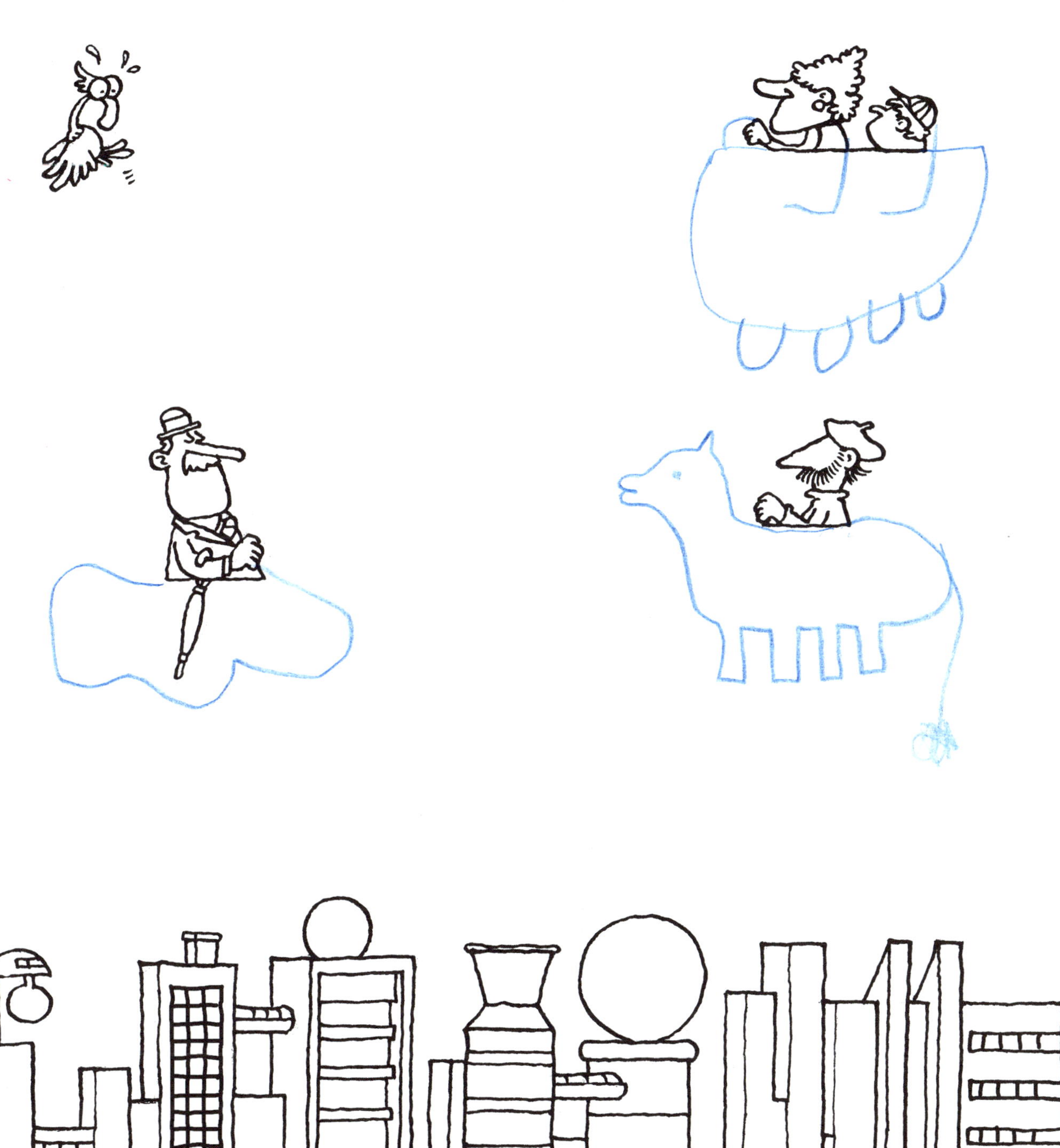

It's your favorite band

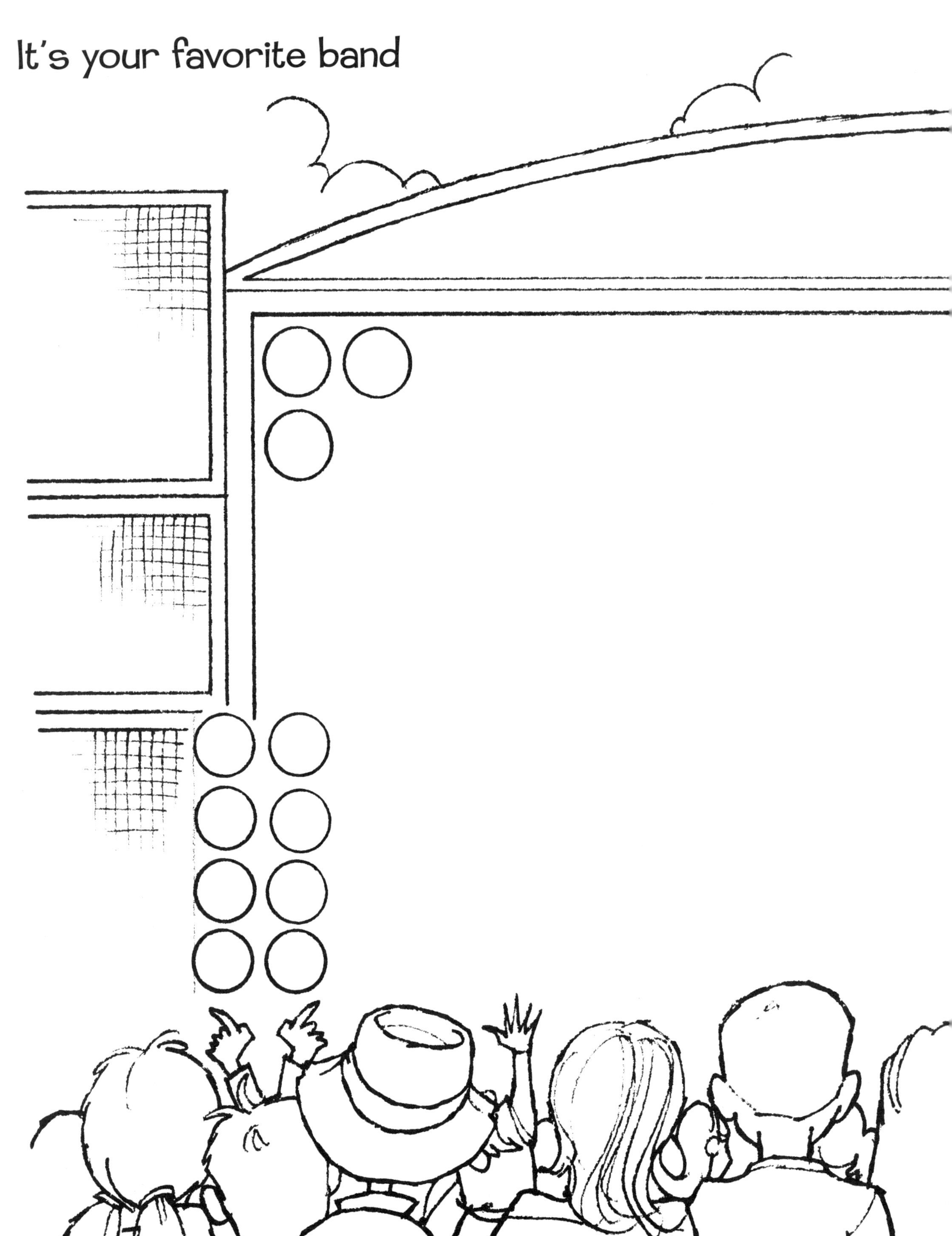

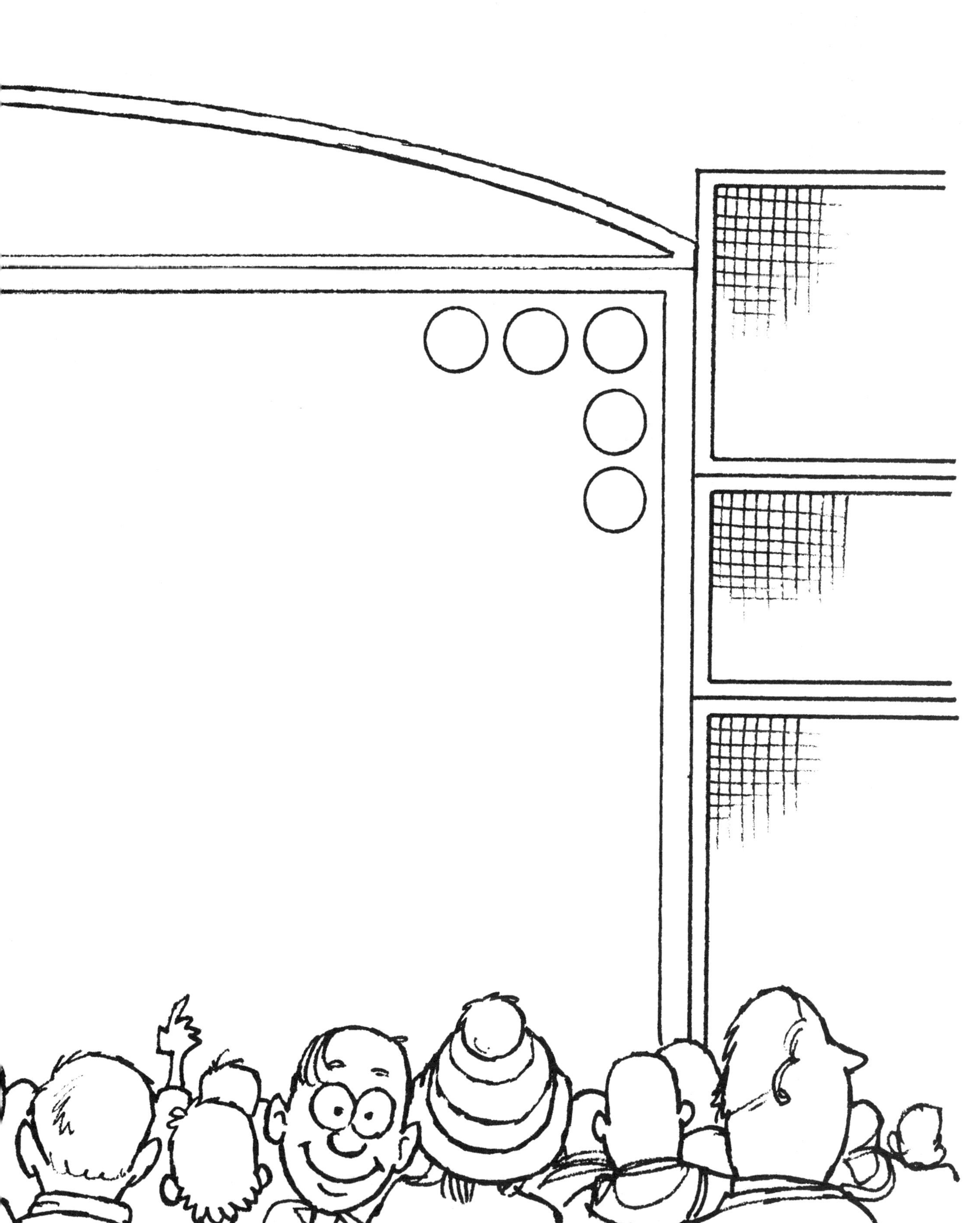

Freddie's dug up something unexpected

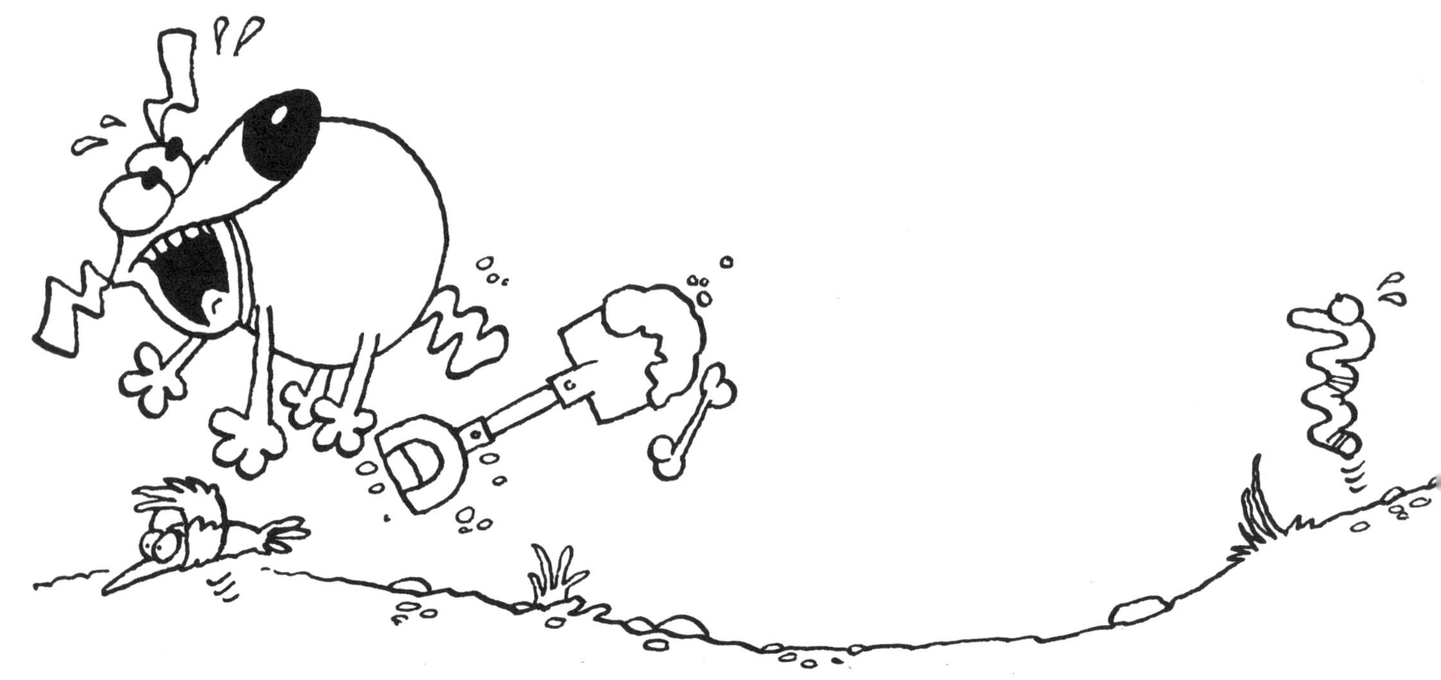

Give each layer a different flavor!

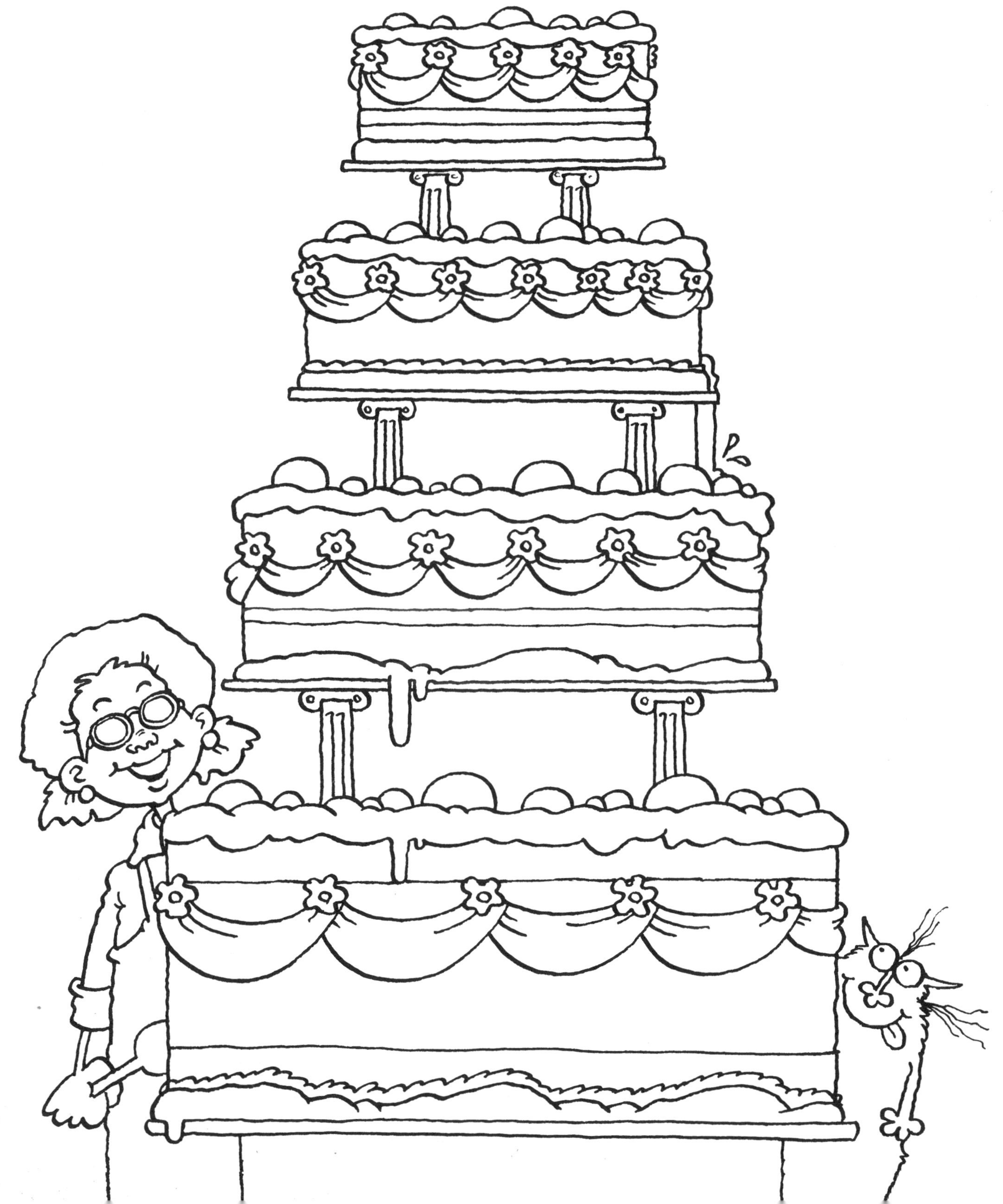

What an incredible fireworks display!

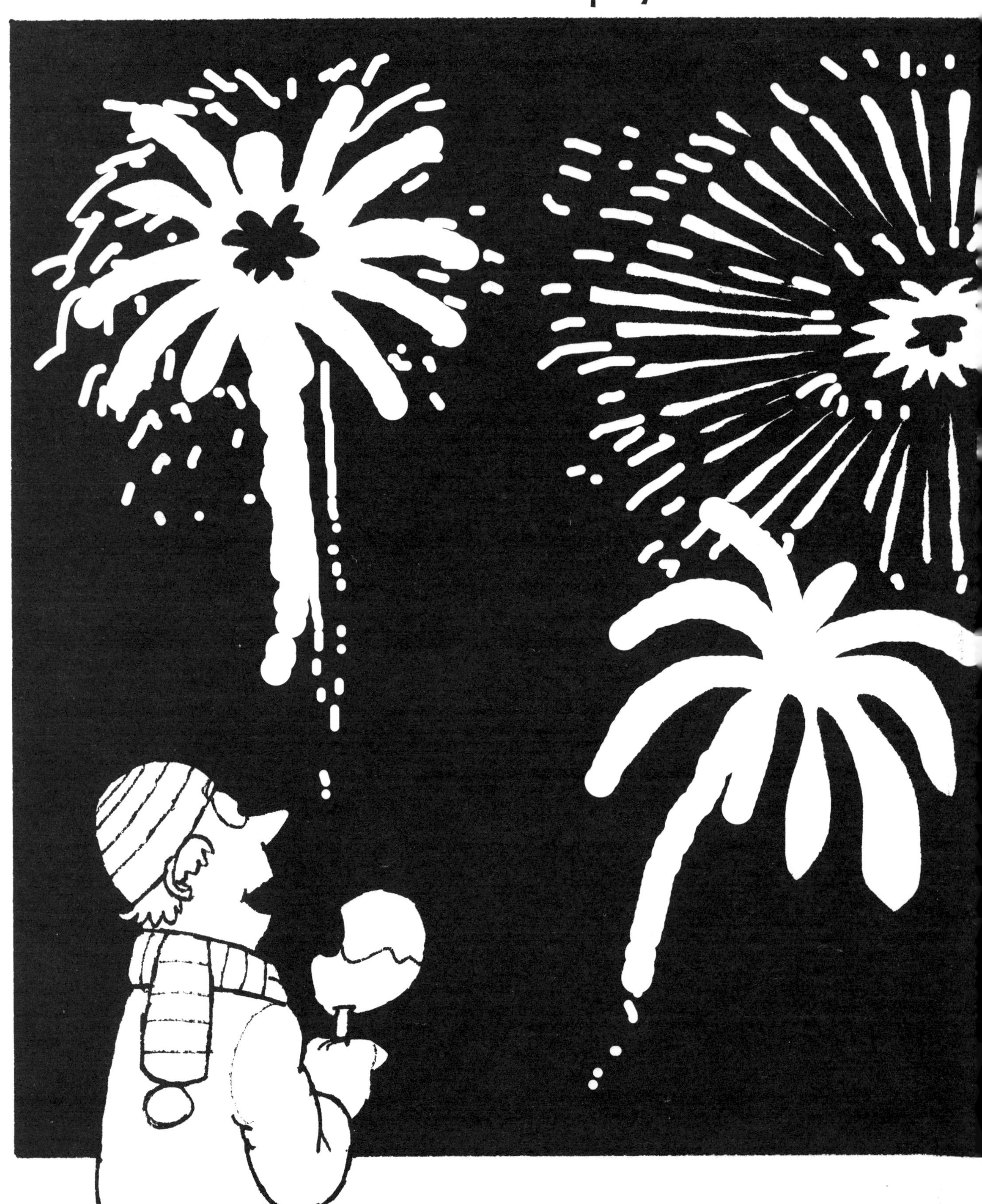

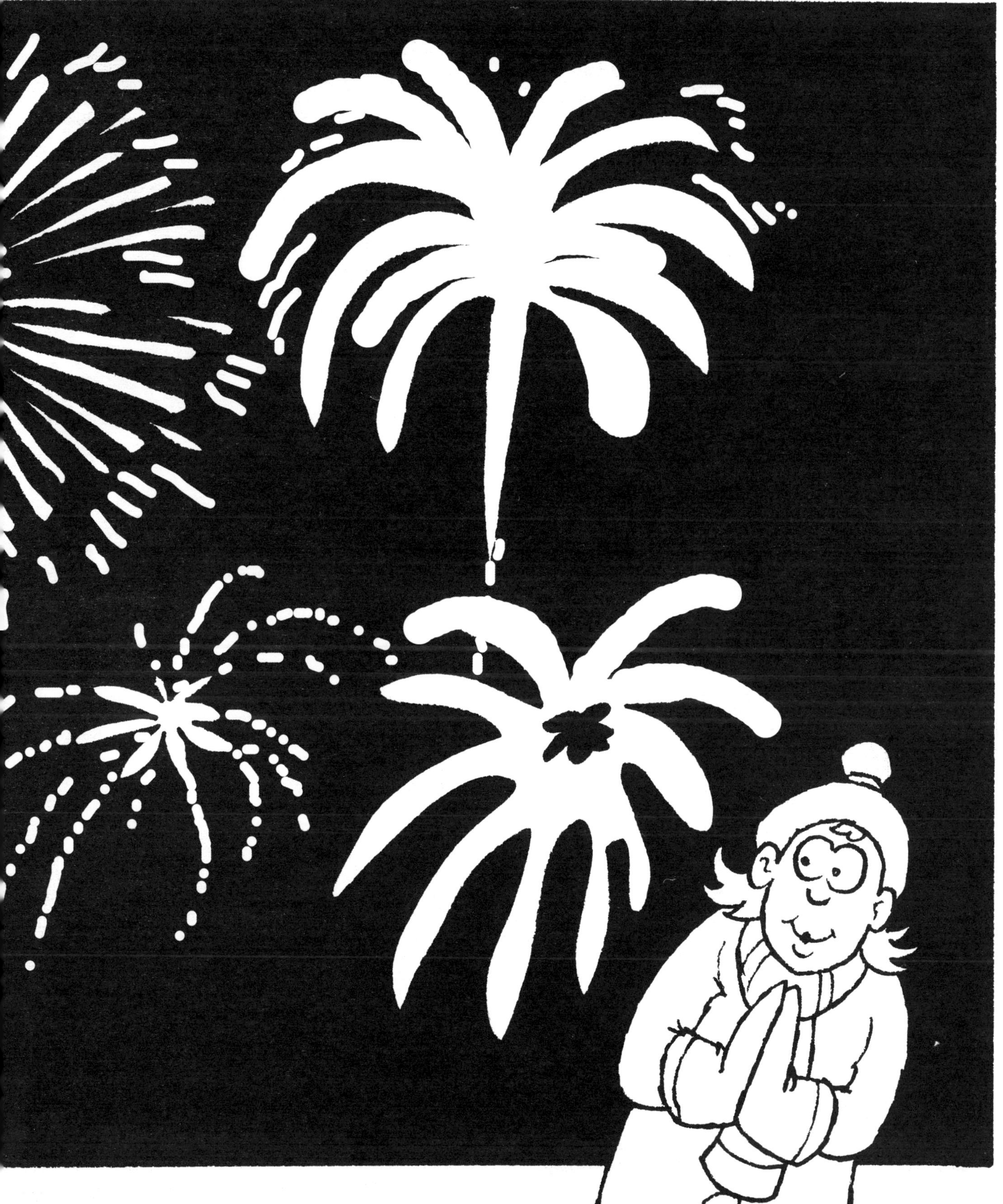

Clint's discovered gold, but where is it?

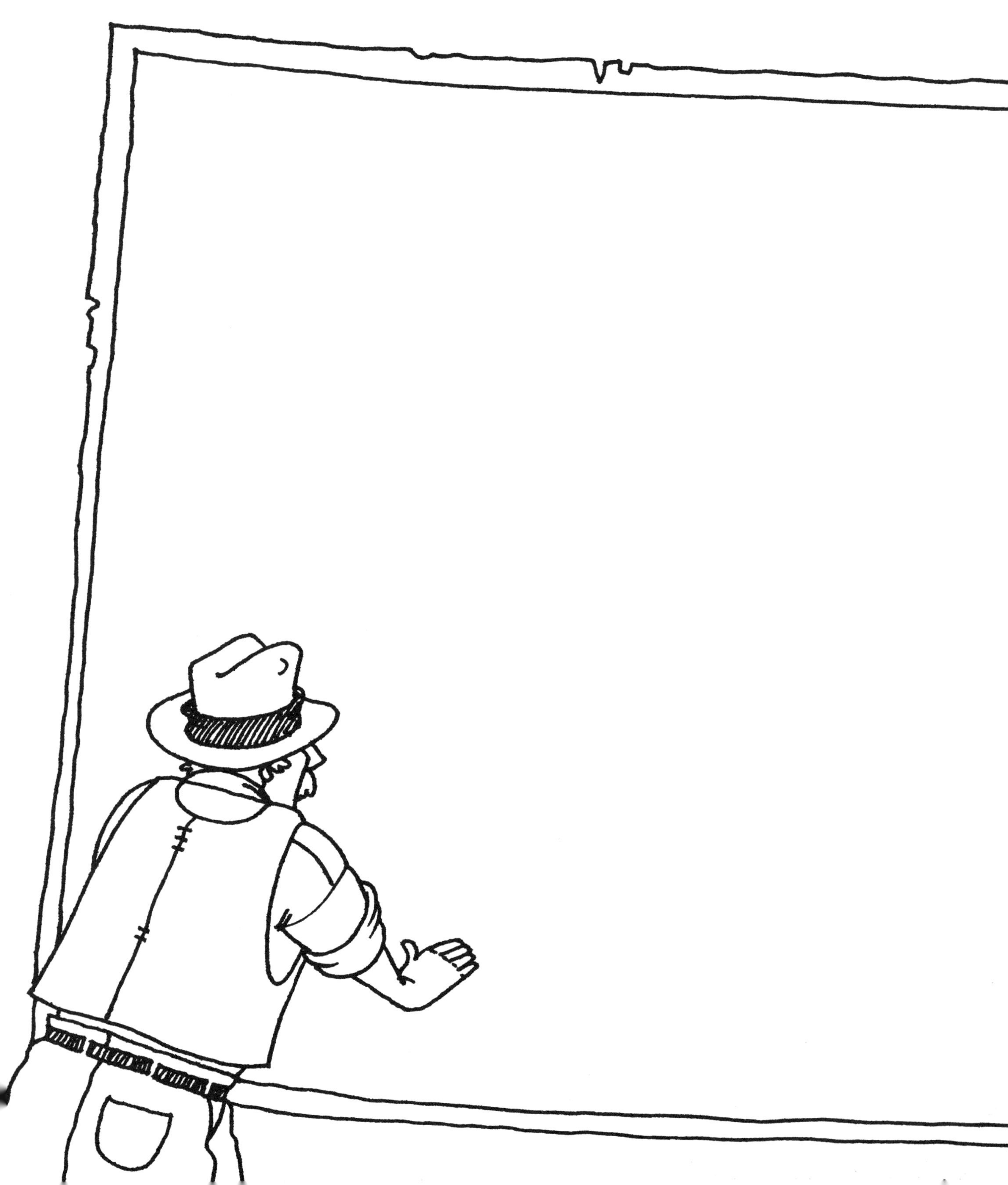

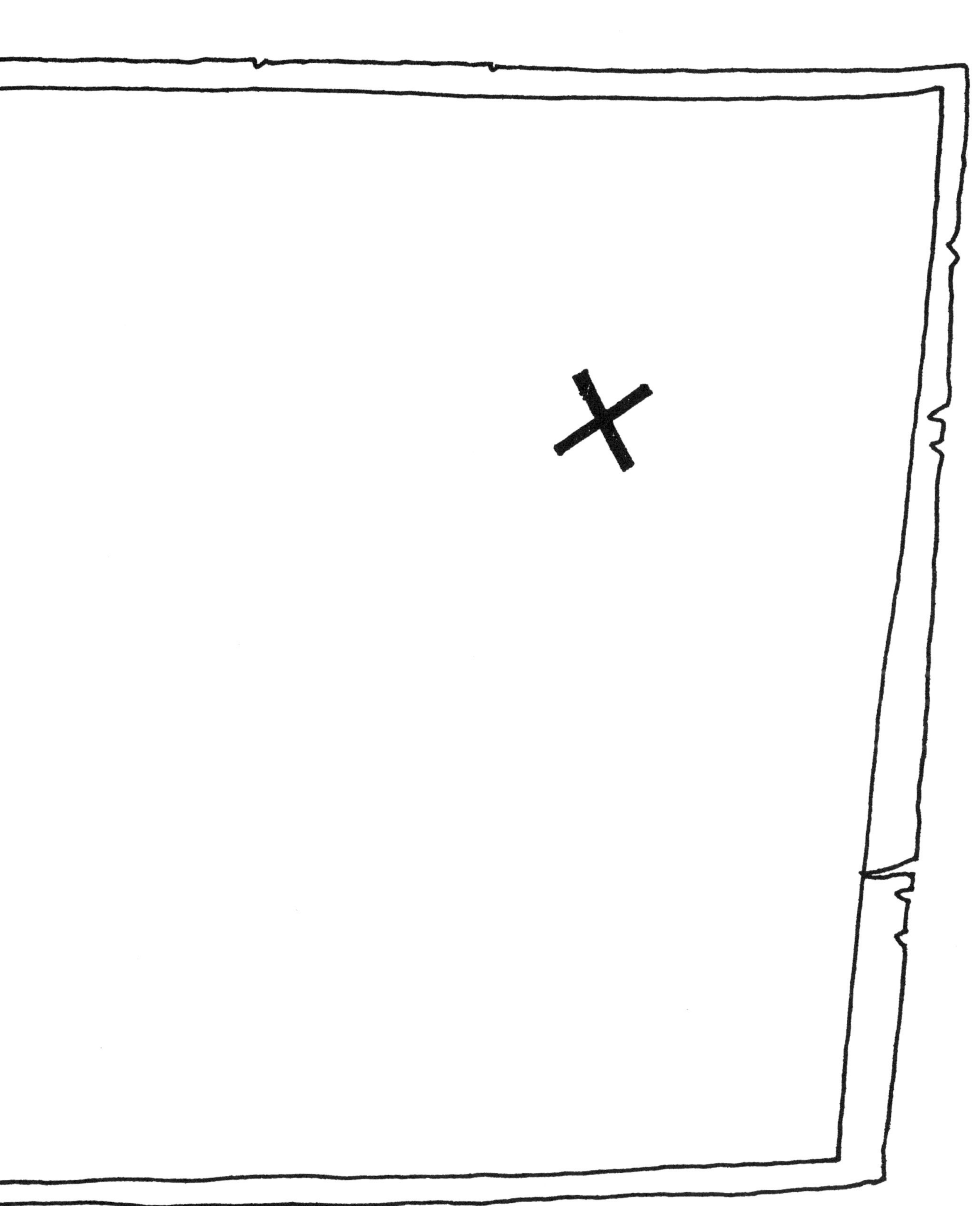

Your name in lights

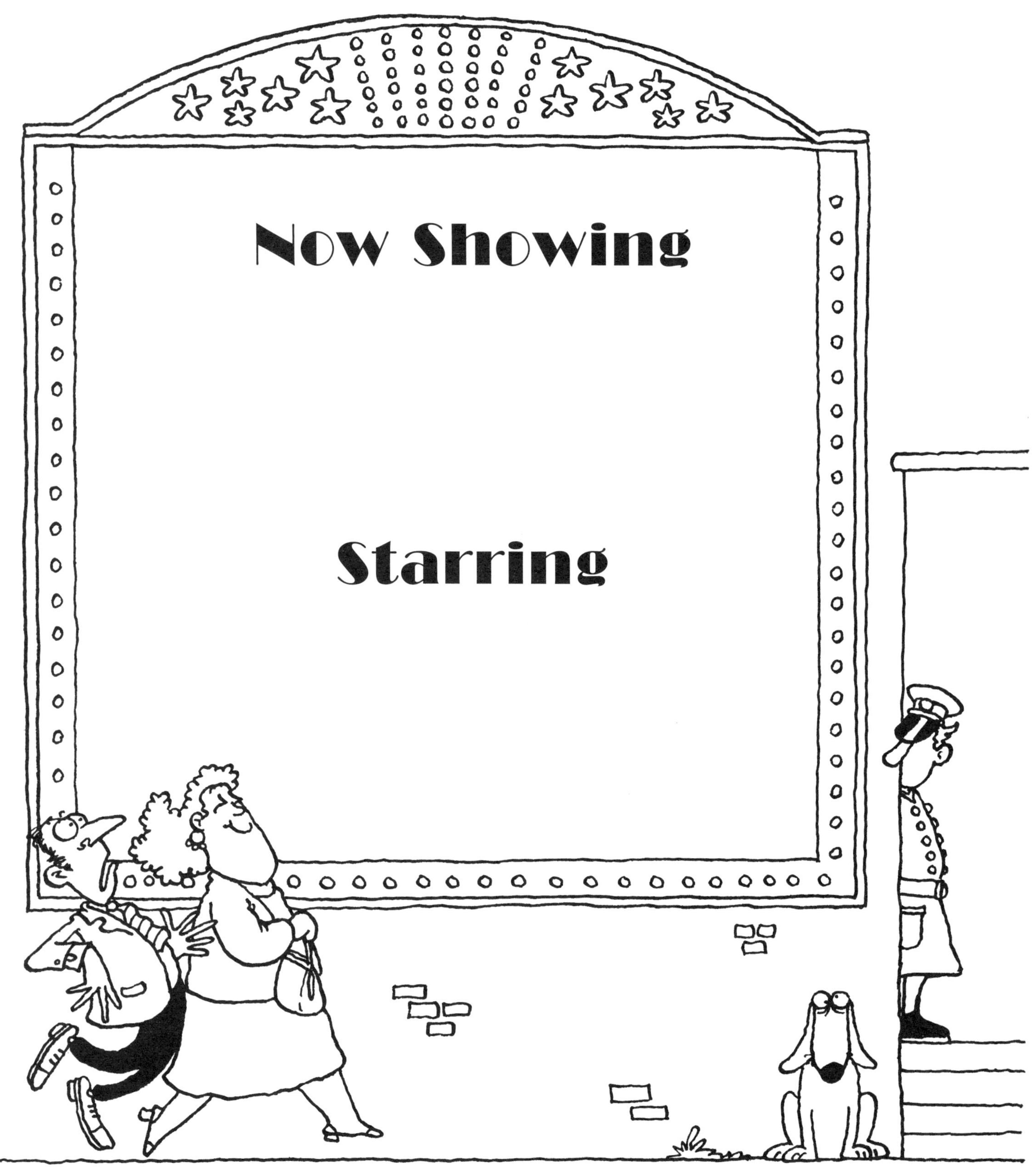

What a cocktail!

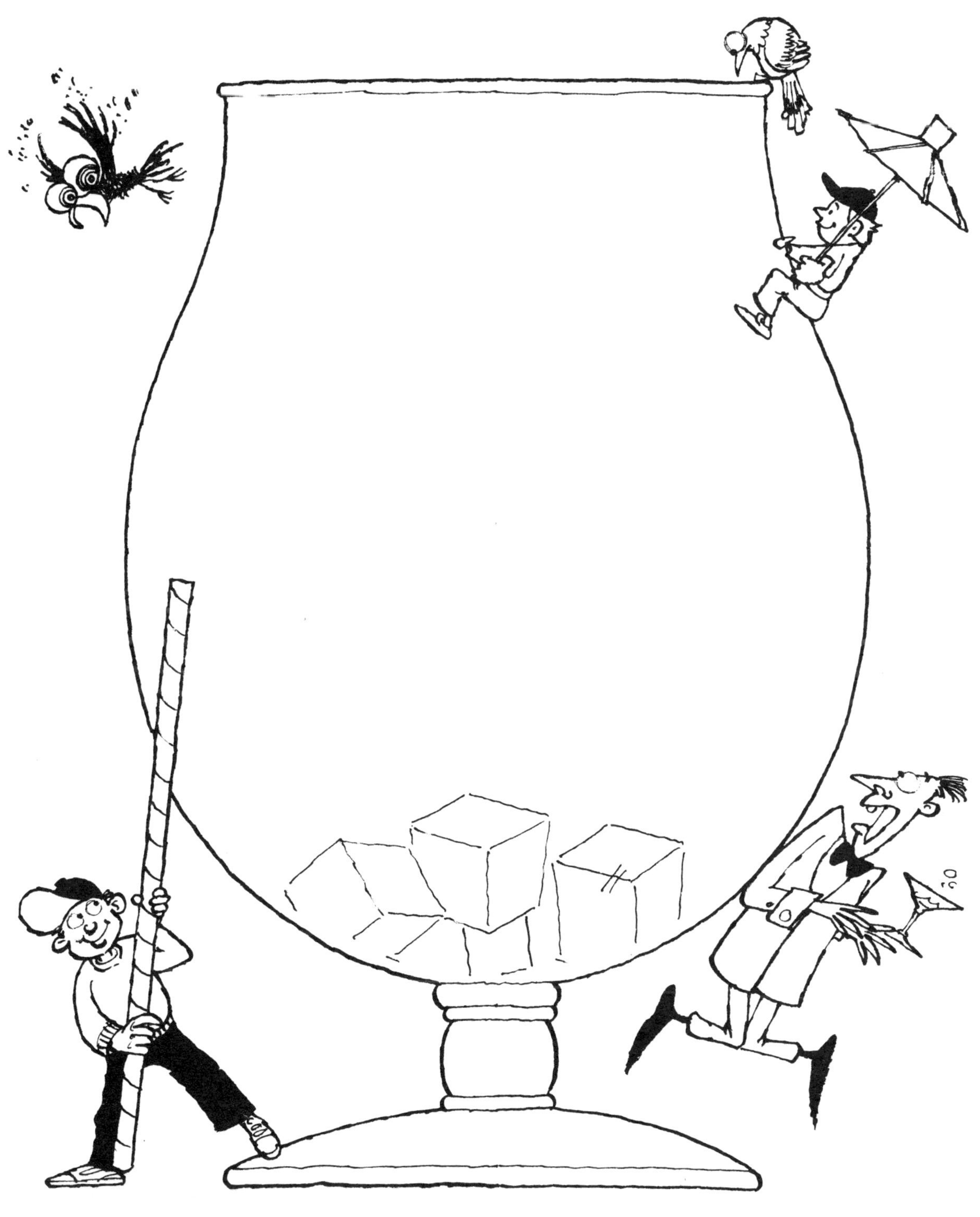

Add the colors to the paintball battle

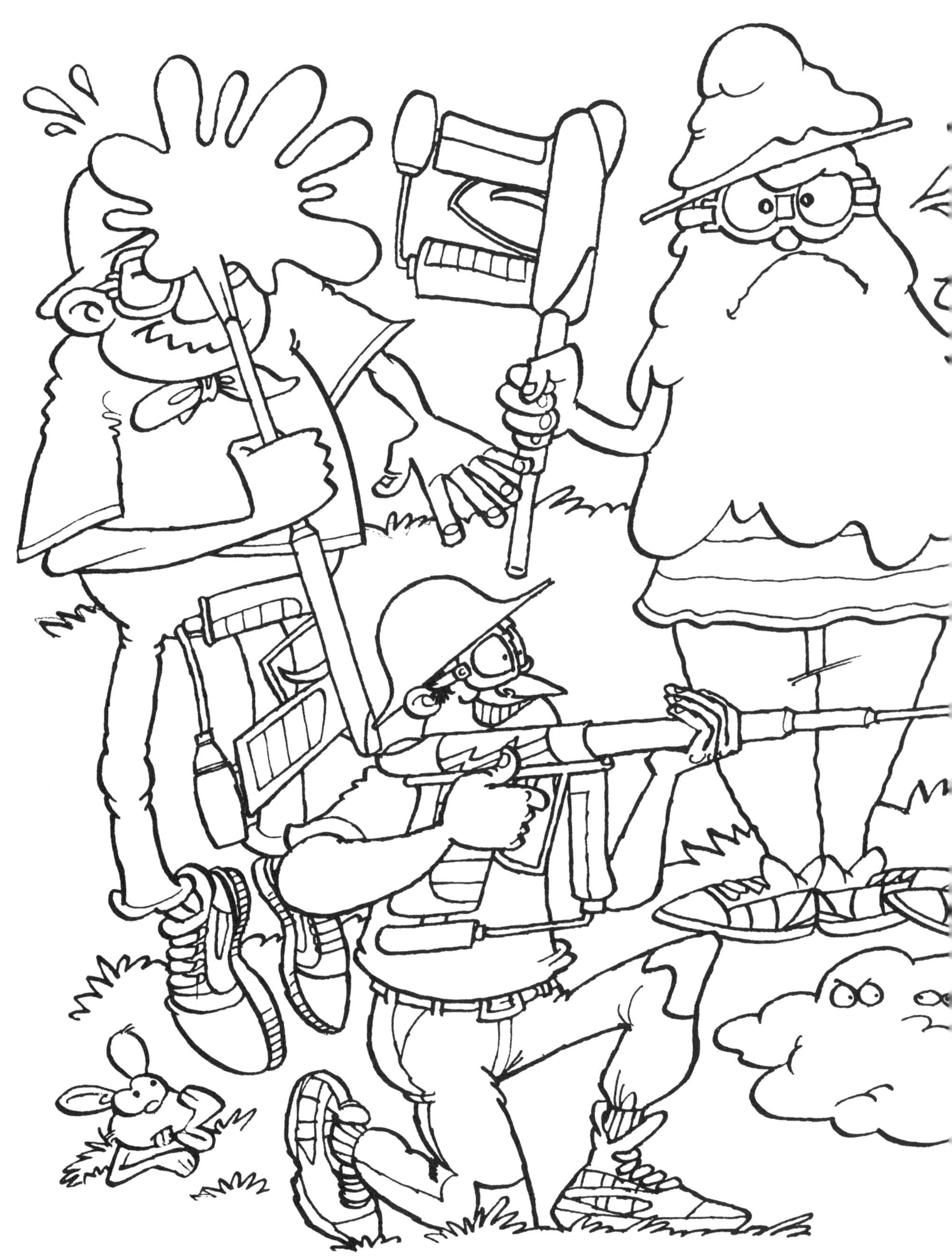

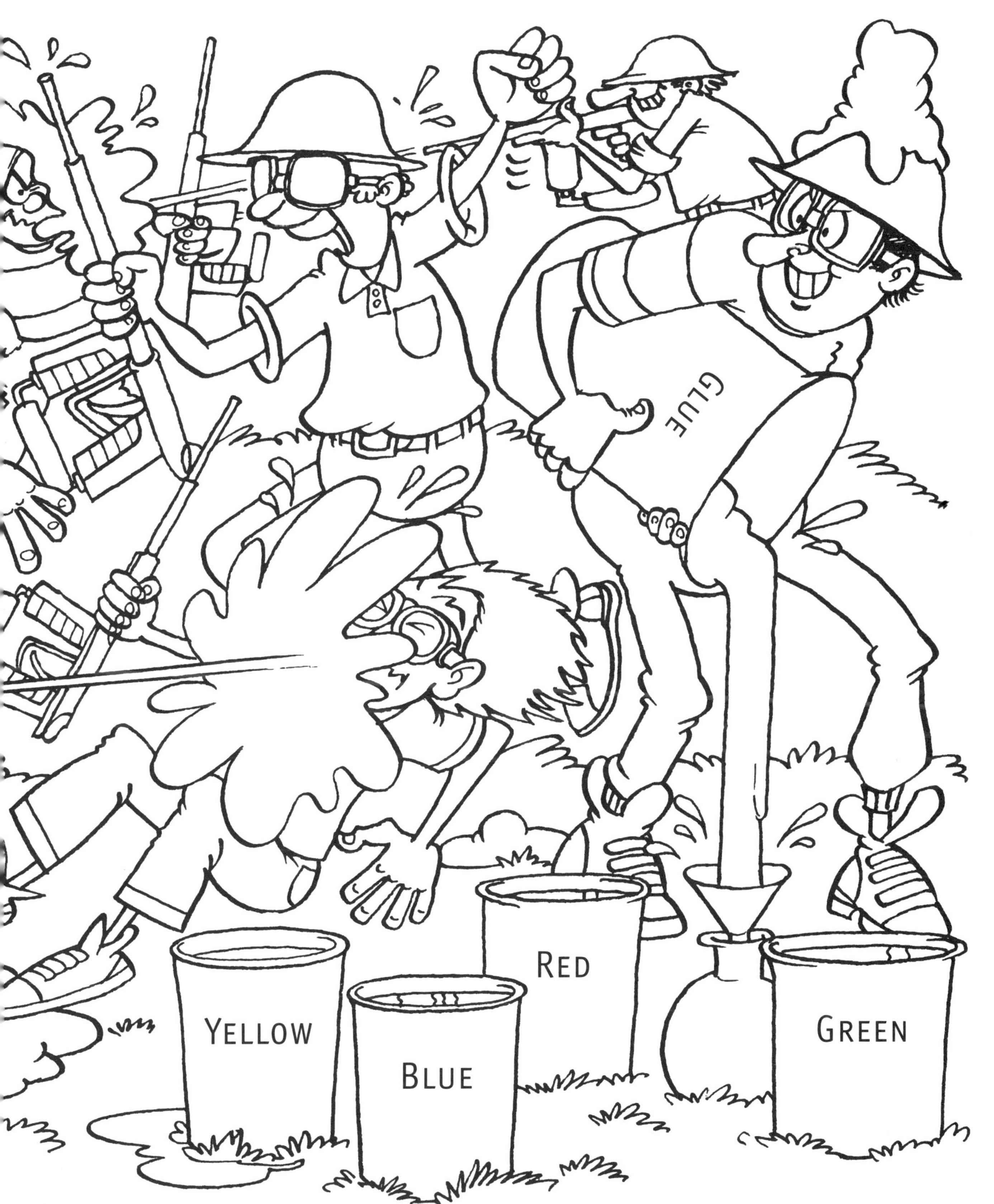
GLUE
RED
YELLOW
BLUE
GREEN

Hollywood's most glamorous star has arrived

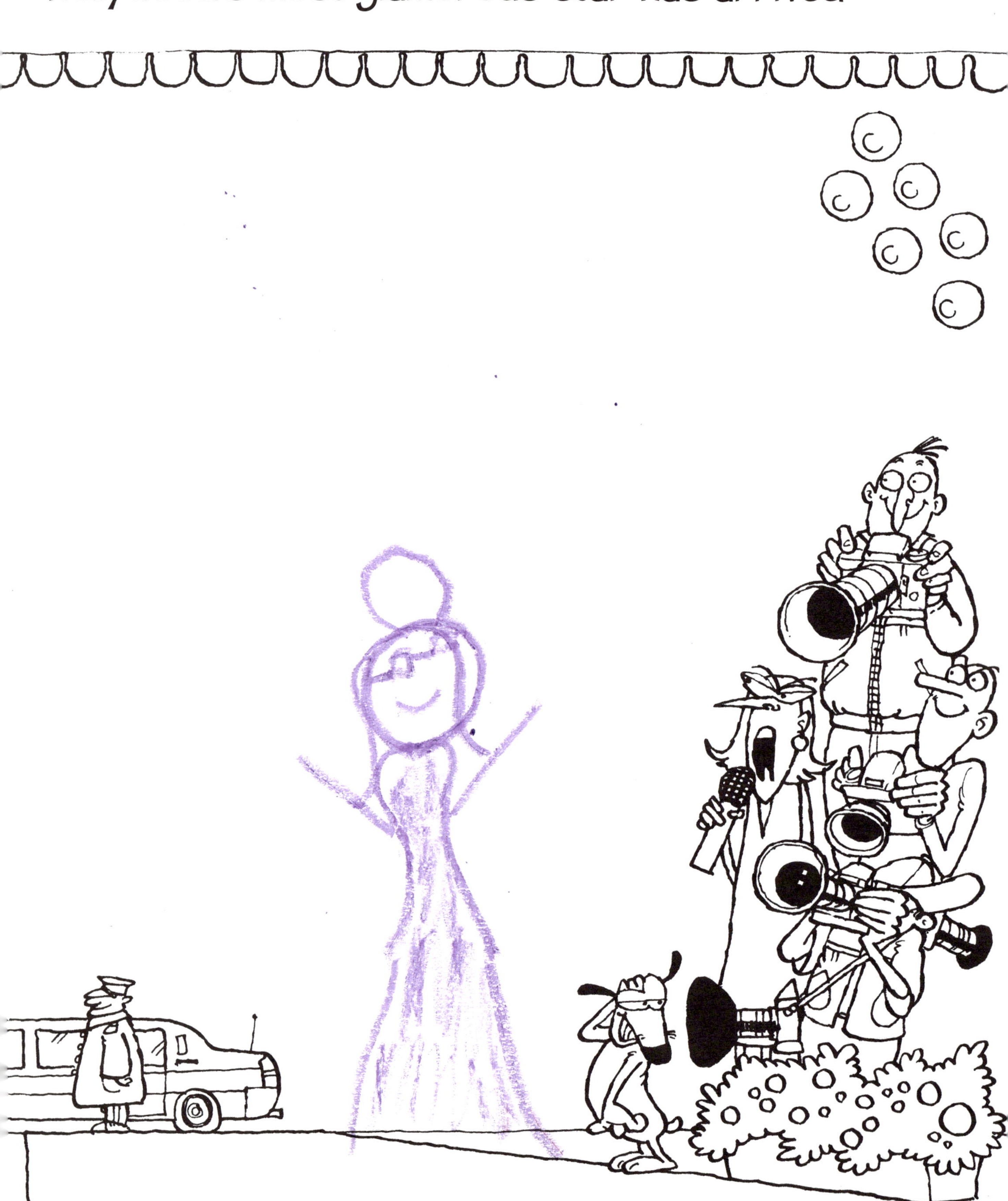

The best exhibit at the aquarium

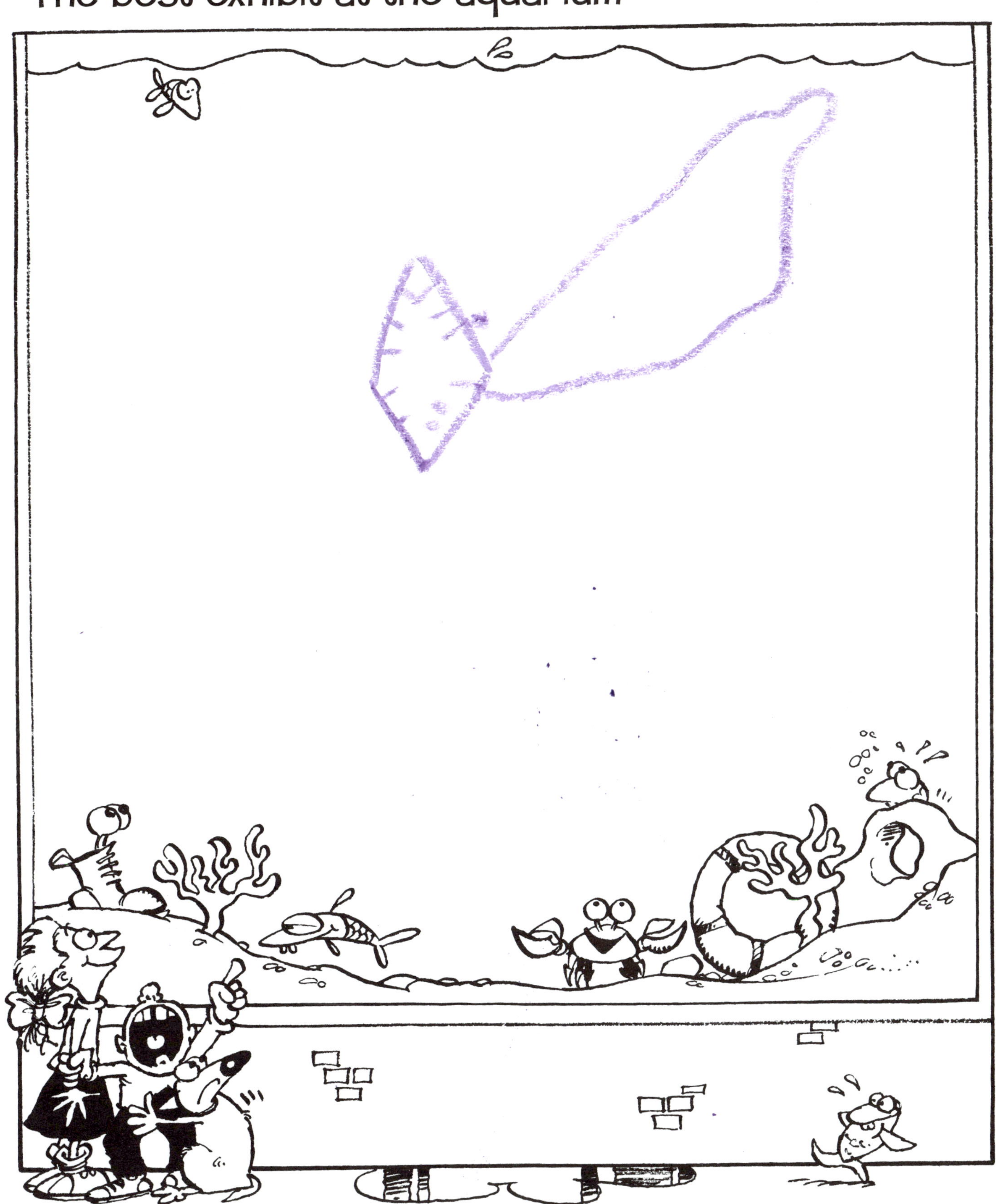

They never could agree on the same wallpaper!

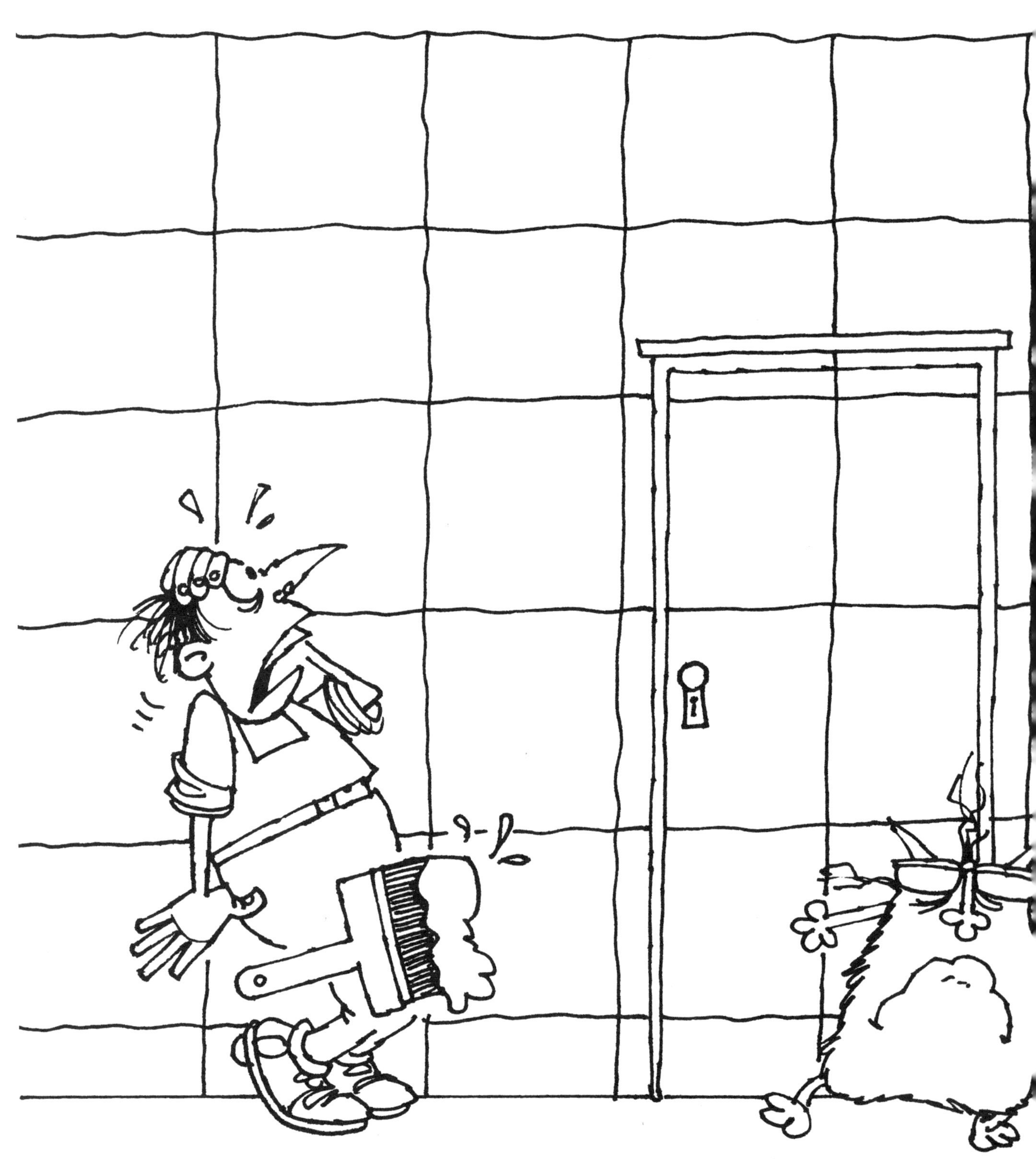

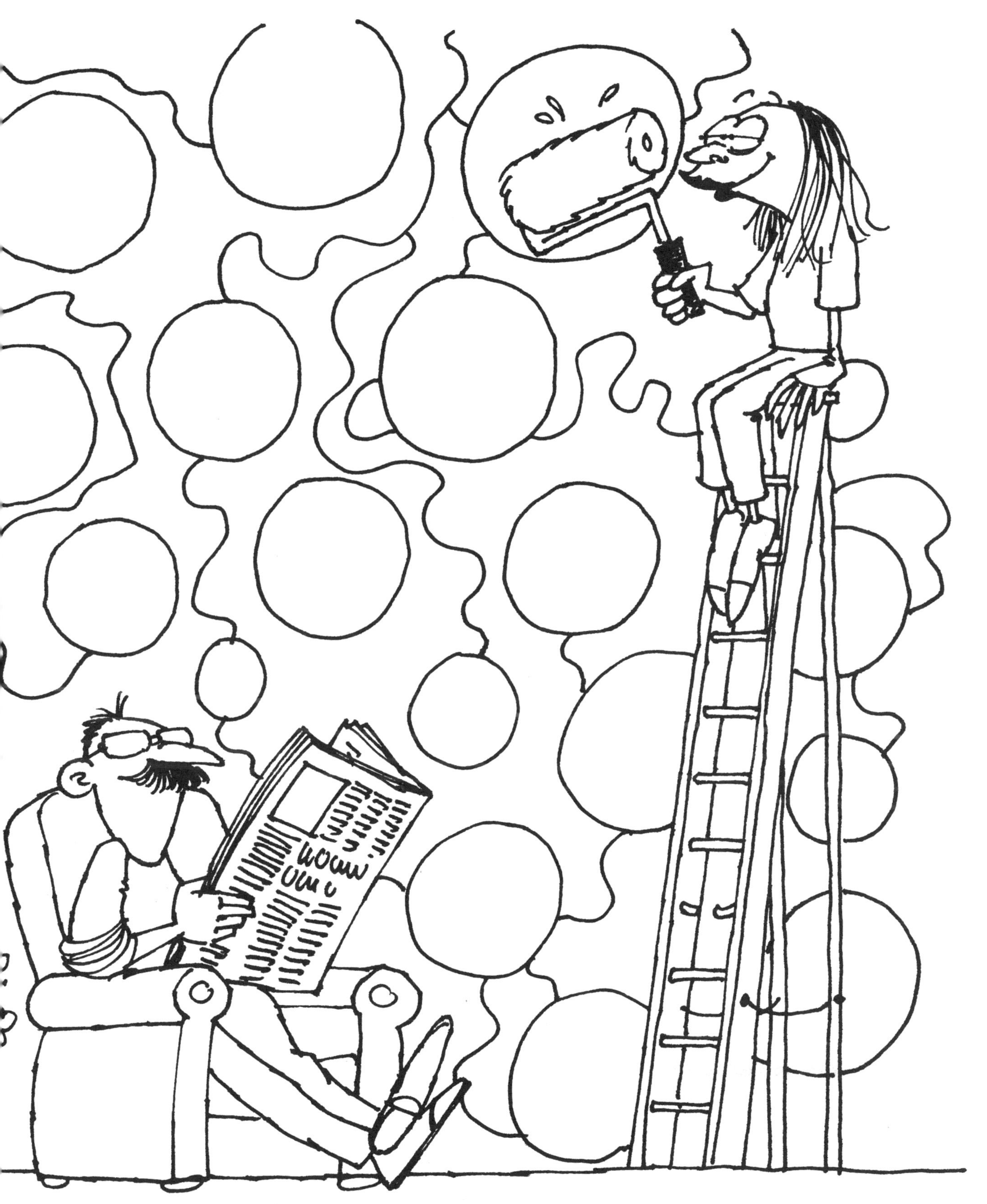

These Vikings need a warship

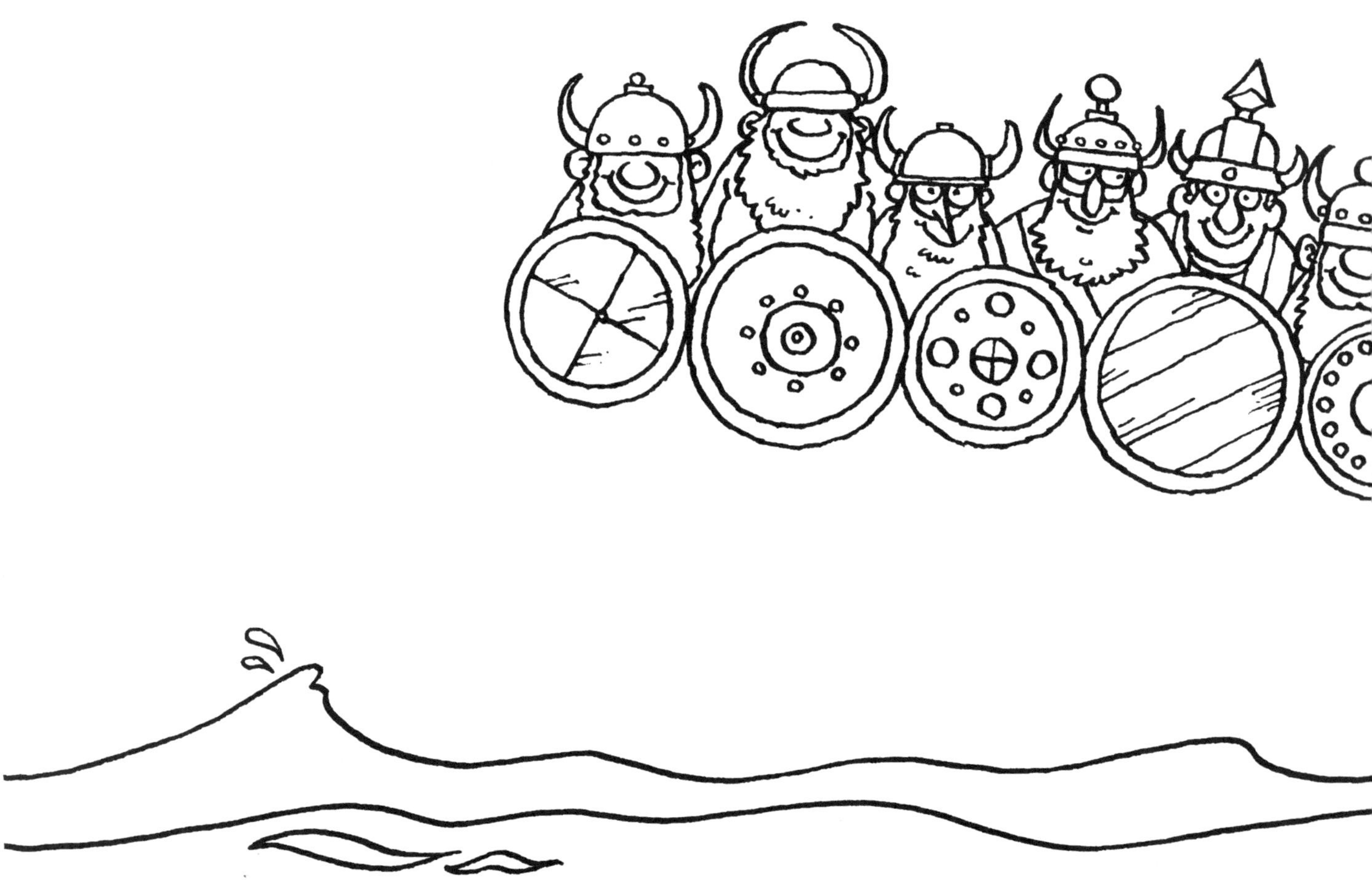

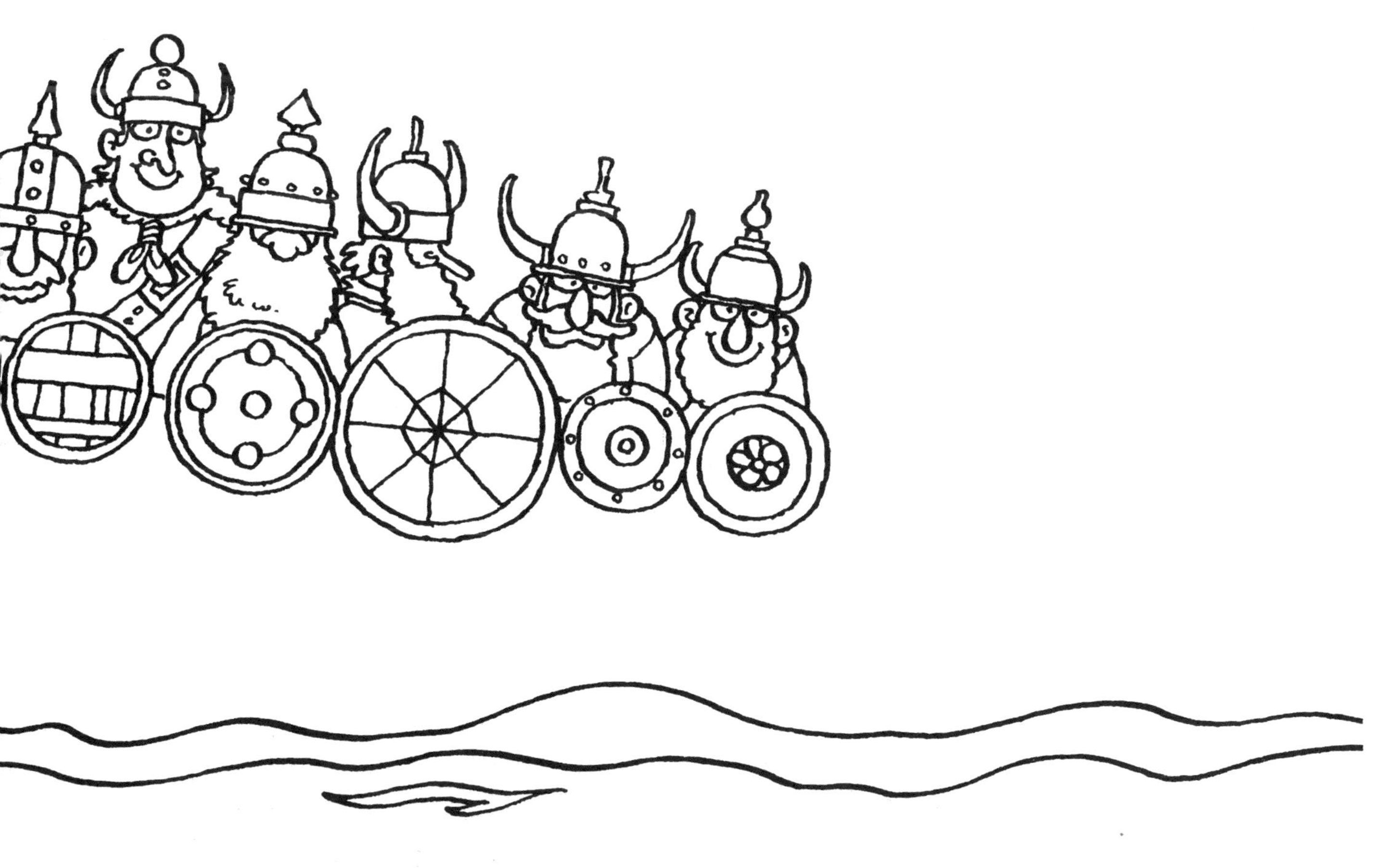

Color in their winning outfits

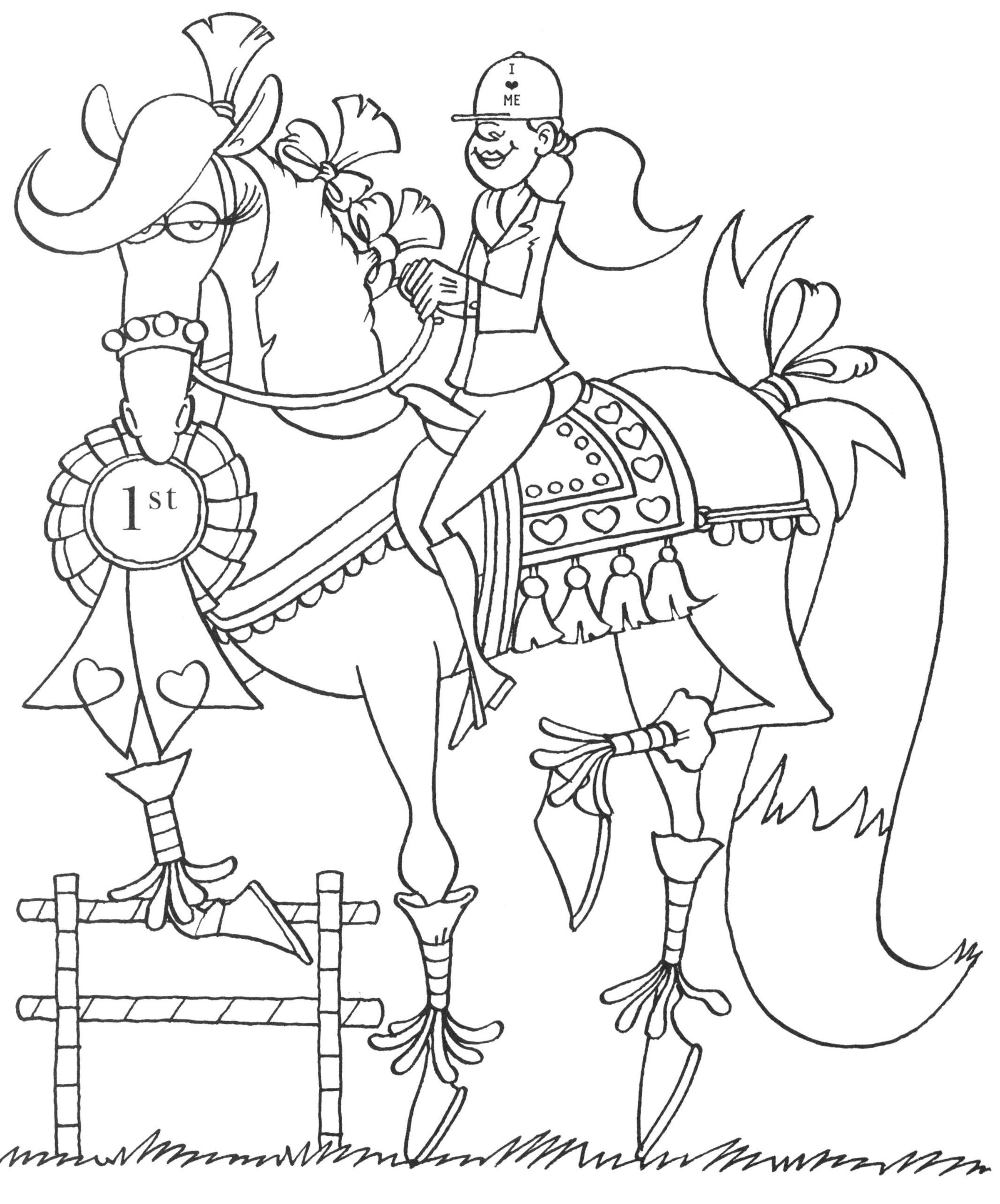

What video game are they playing?

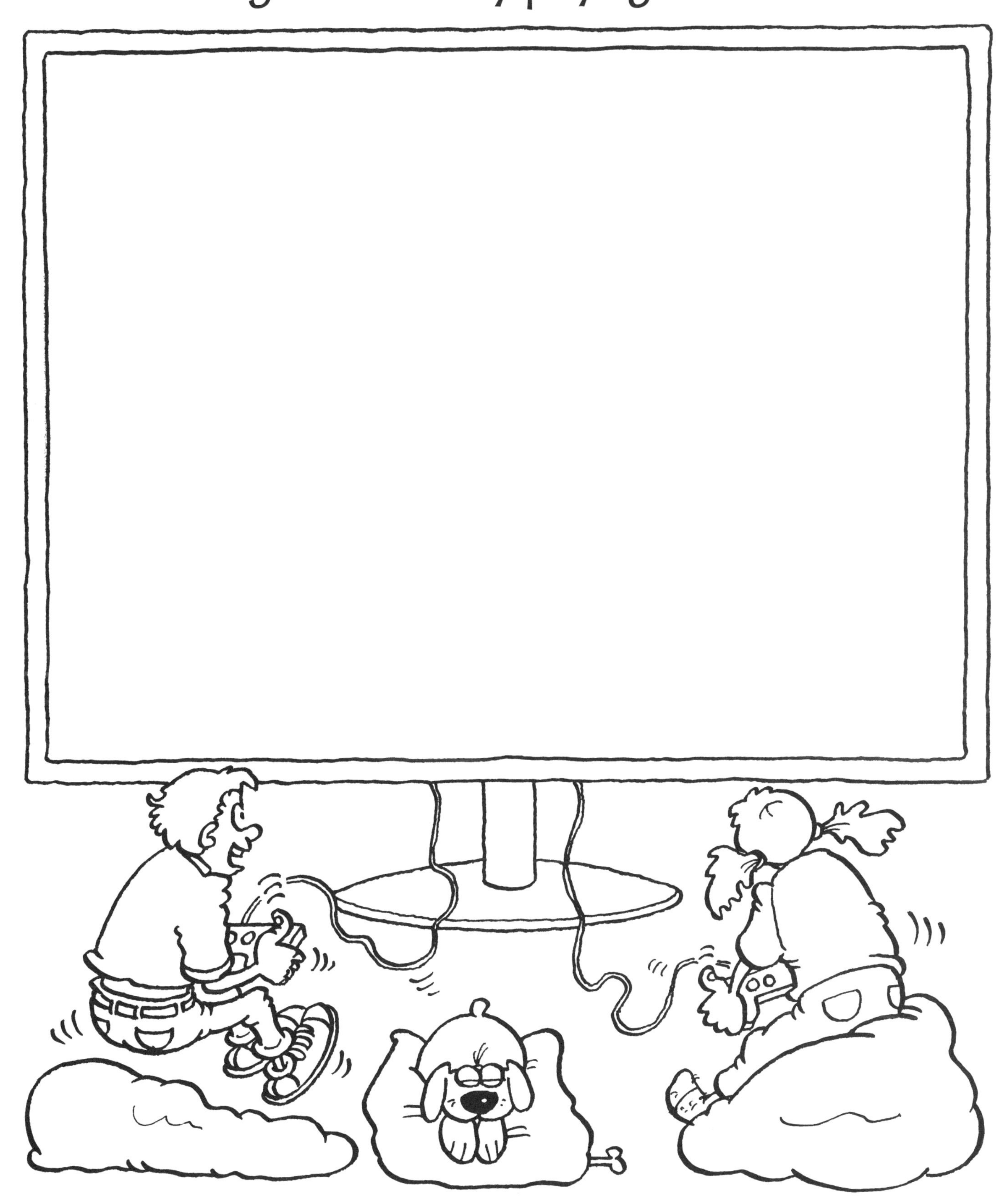

She's changed her appearance...

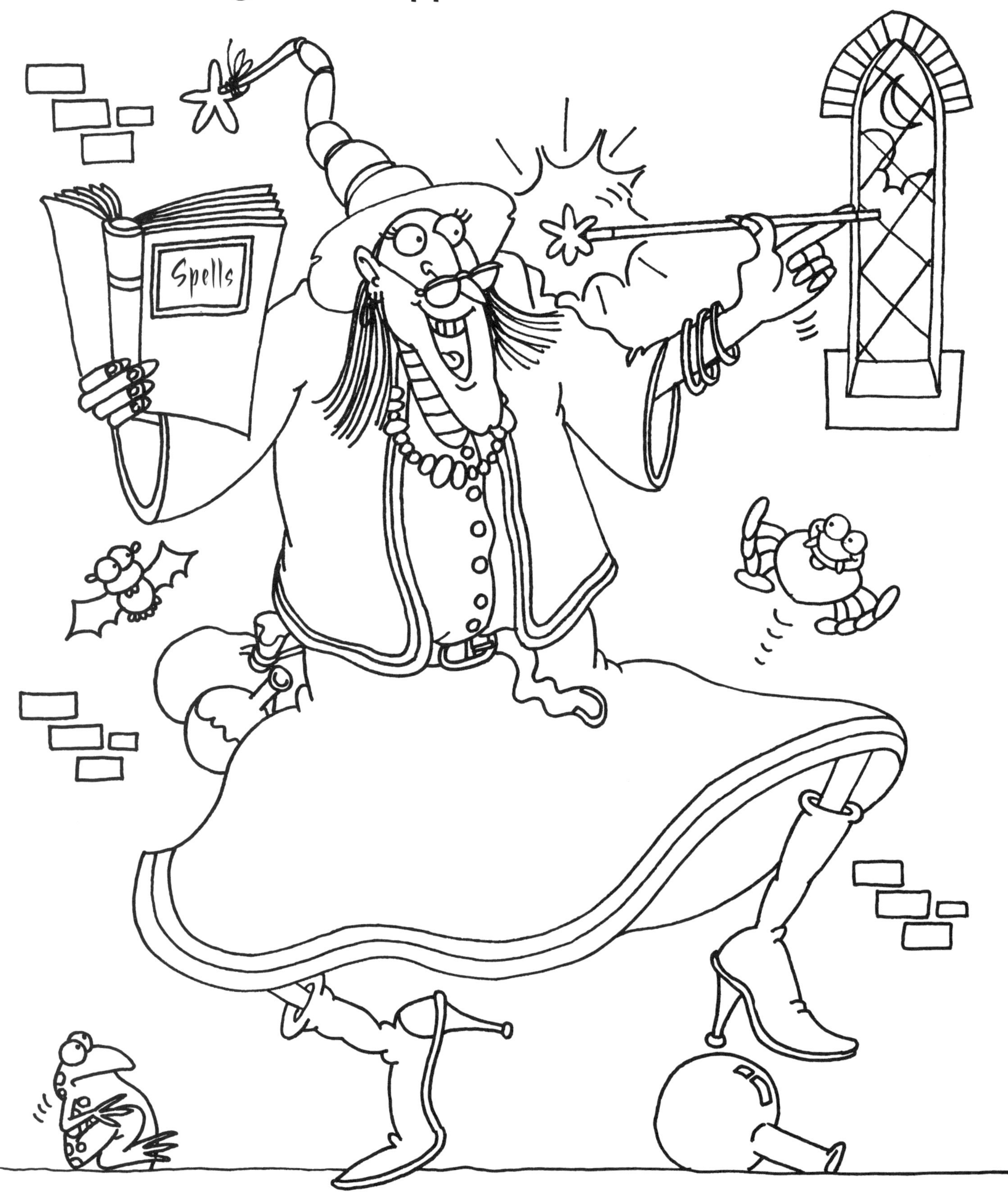

...but is it for the better?

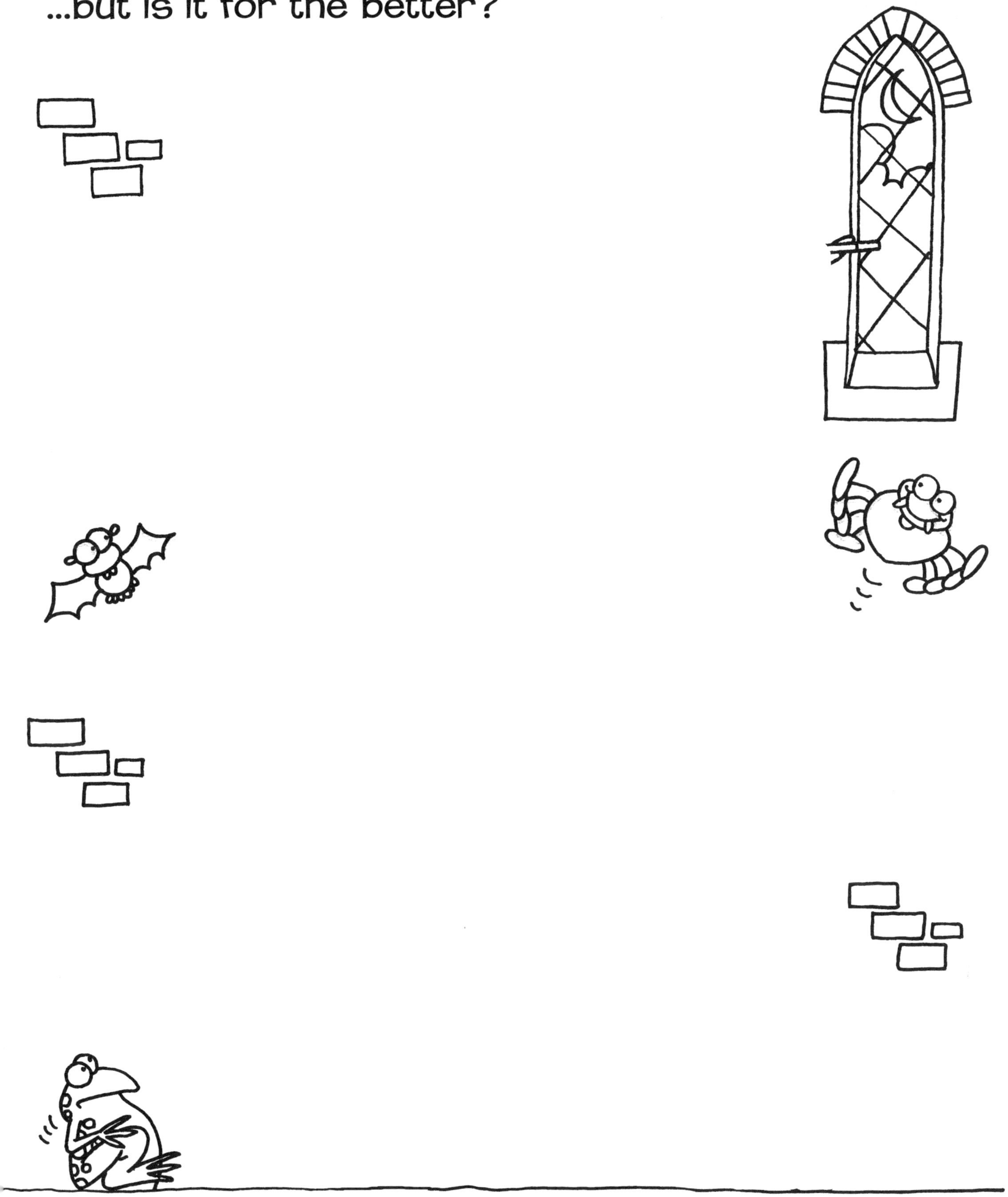

What is Dangerous Dave about to jump over?

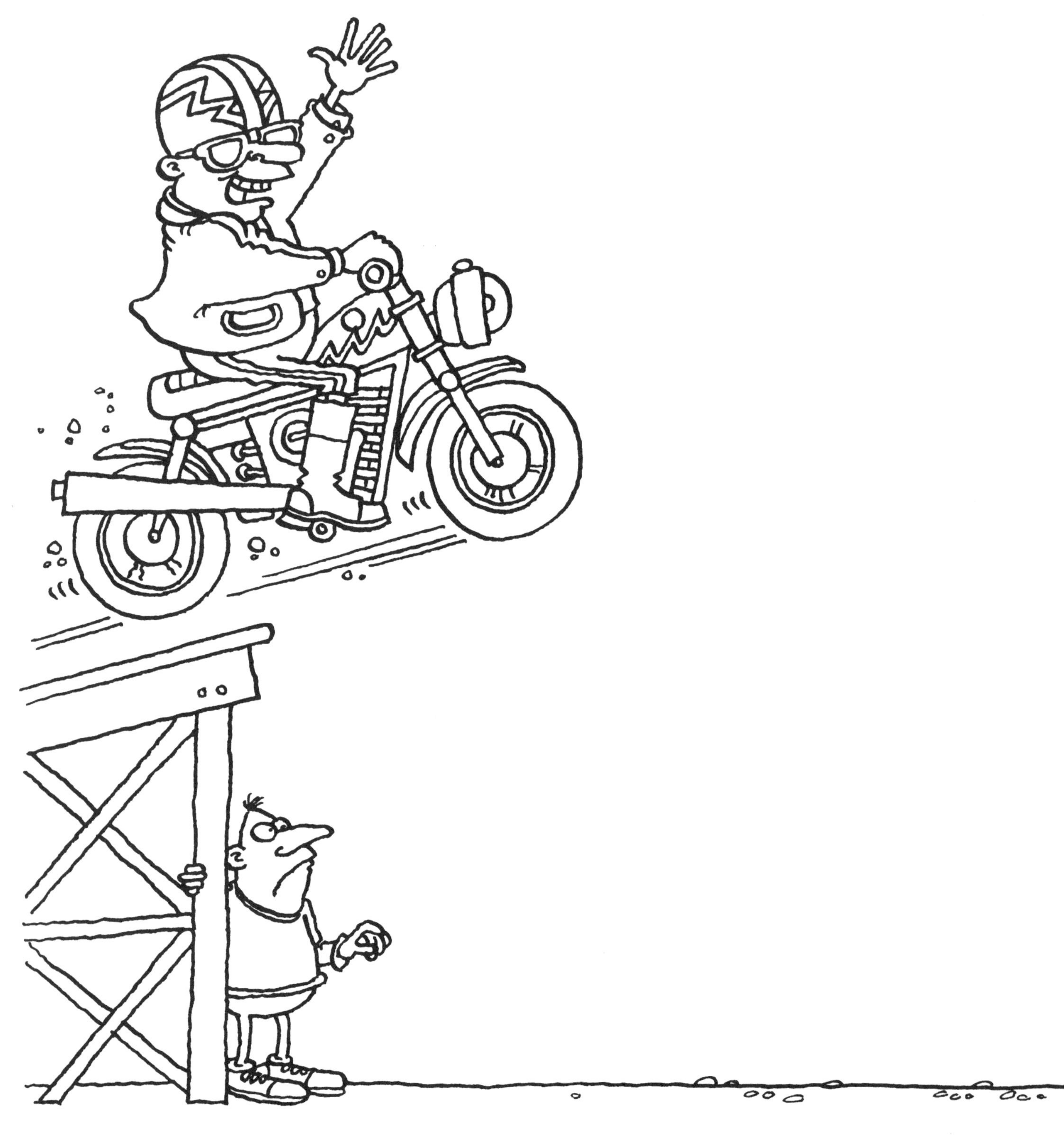

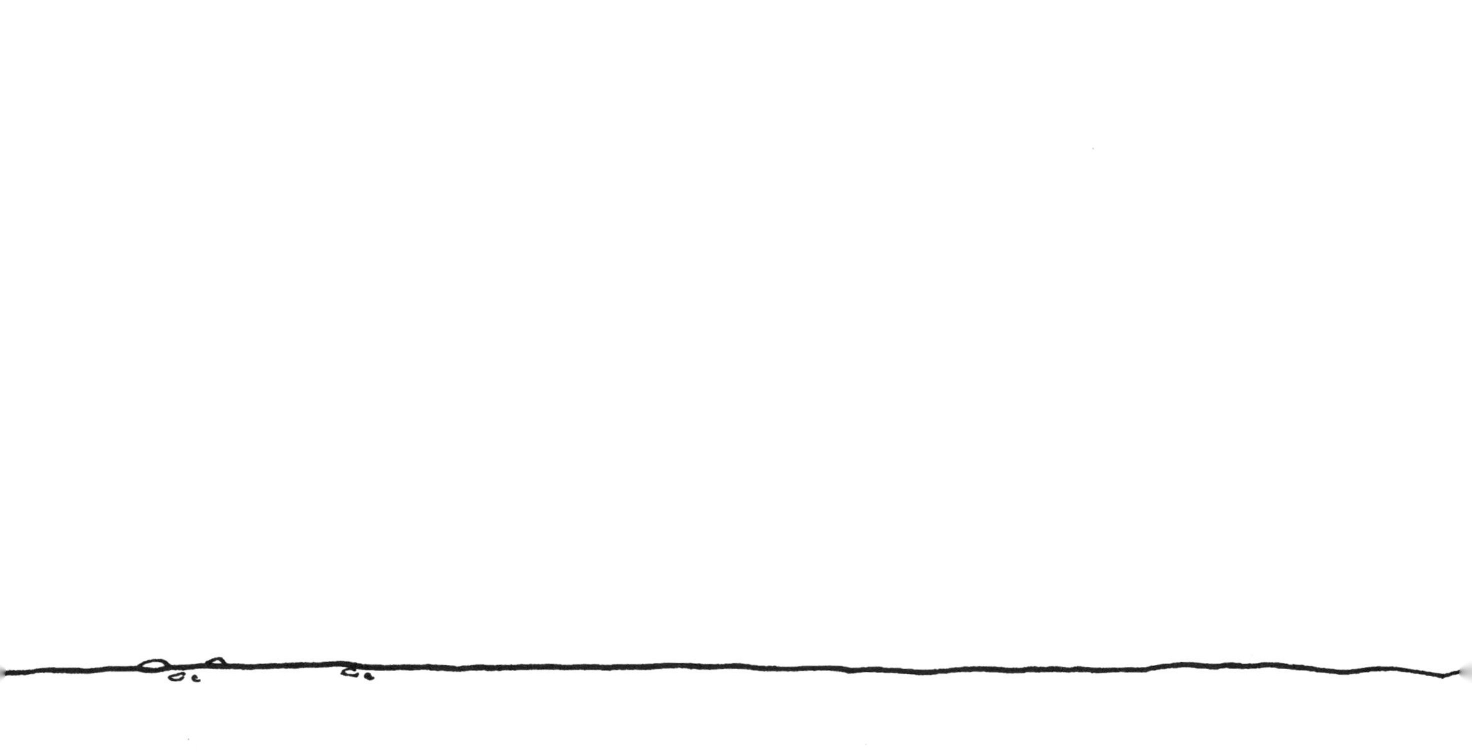

Katie loves her colorful parachute

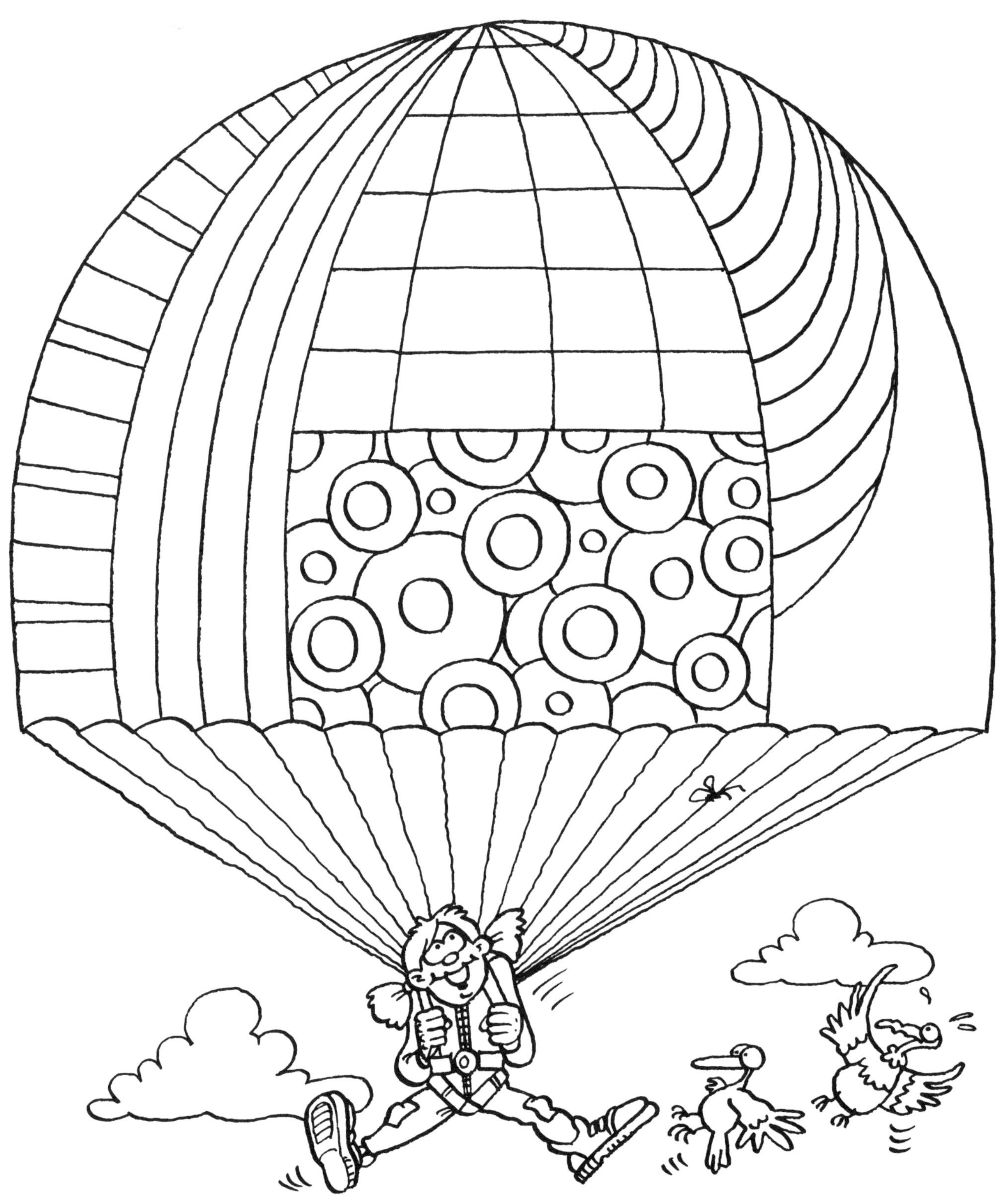

A very tasty burger

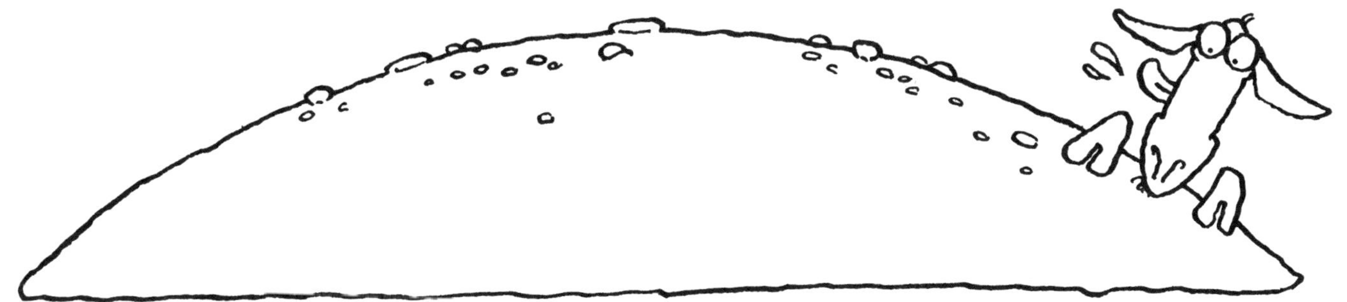

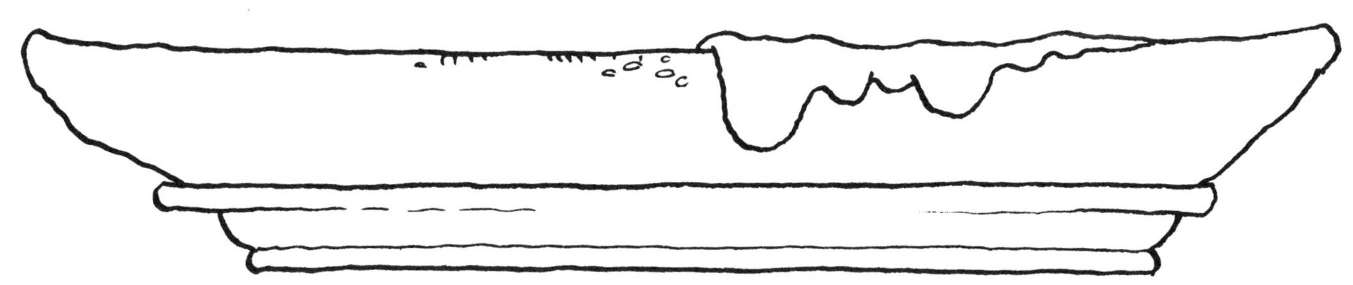

Yee-haw! He's got it this time

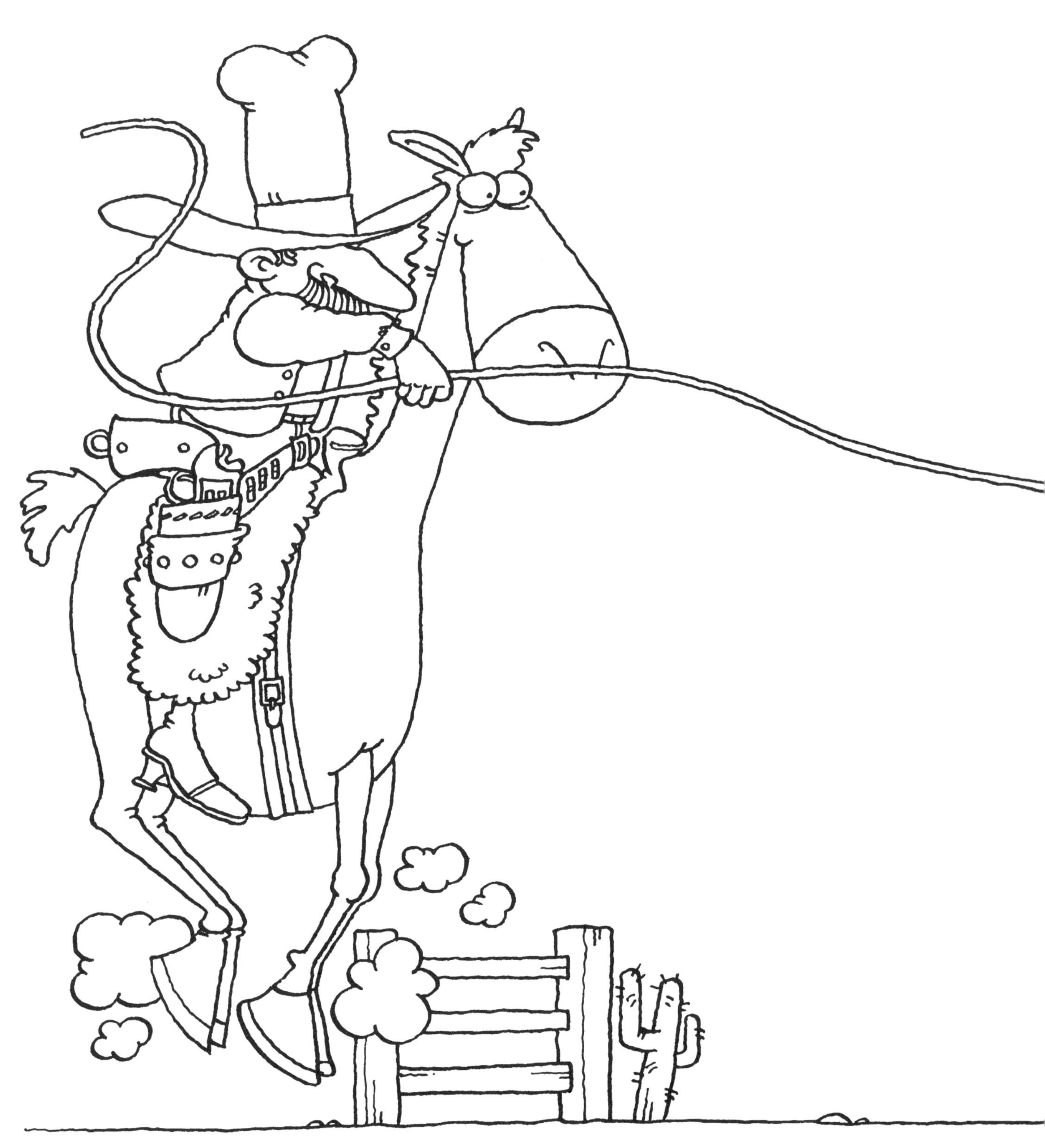

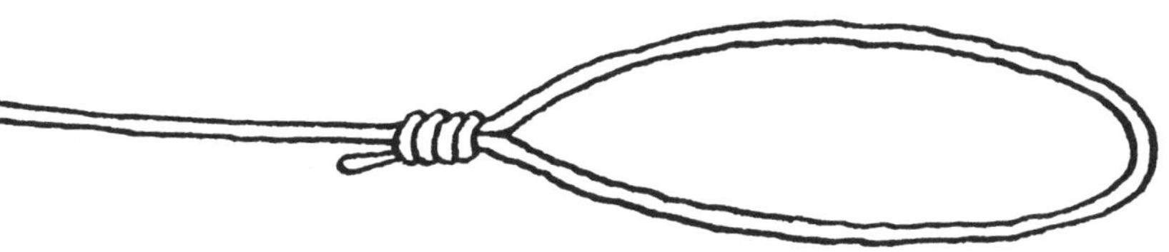

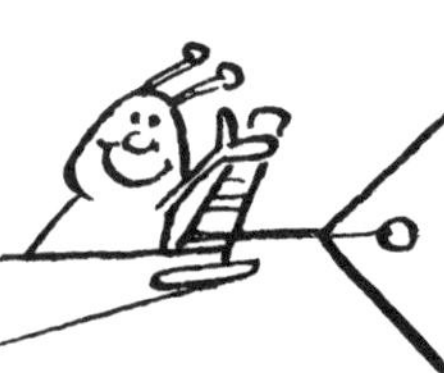

His spaceship is out of this world!

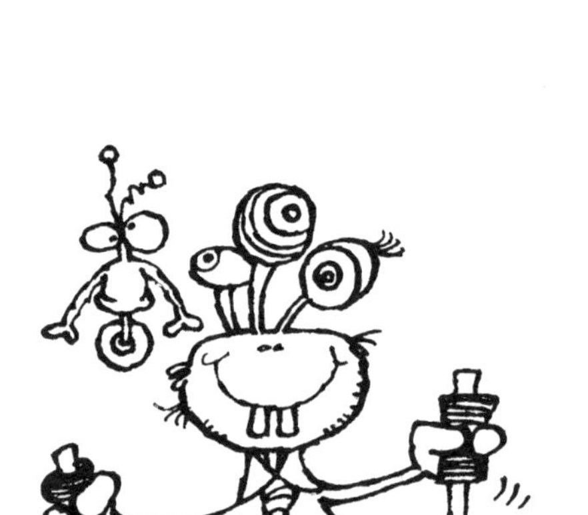

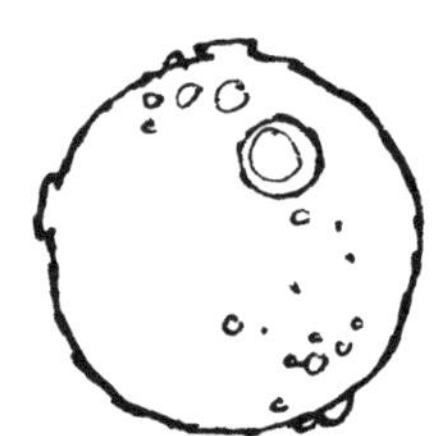

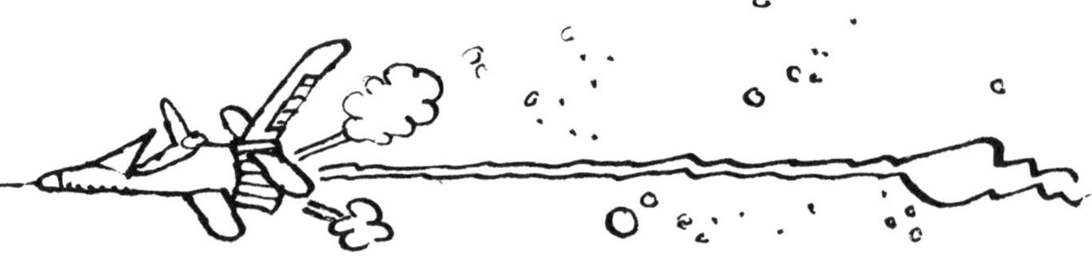

What is he stealing?

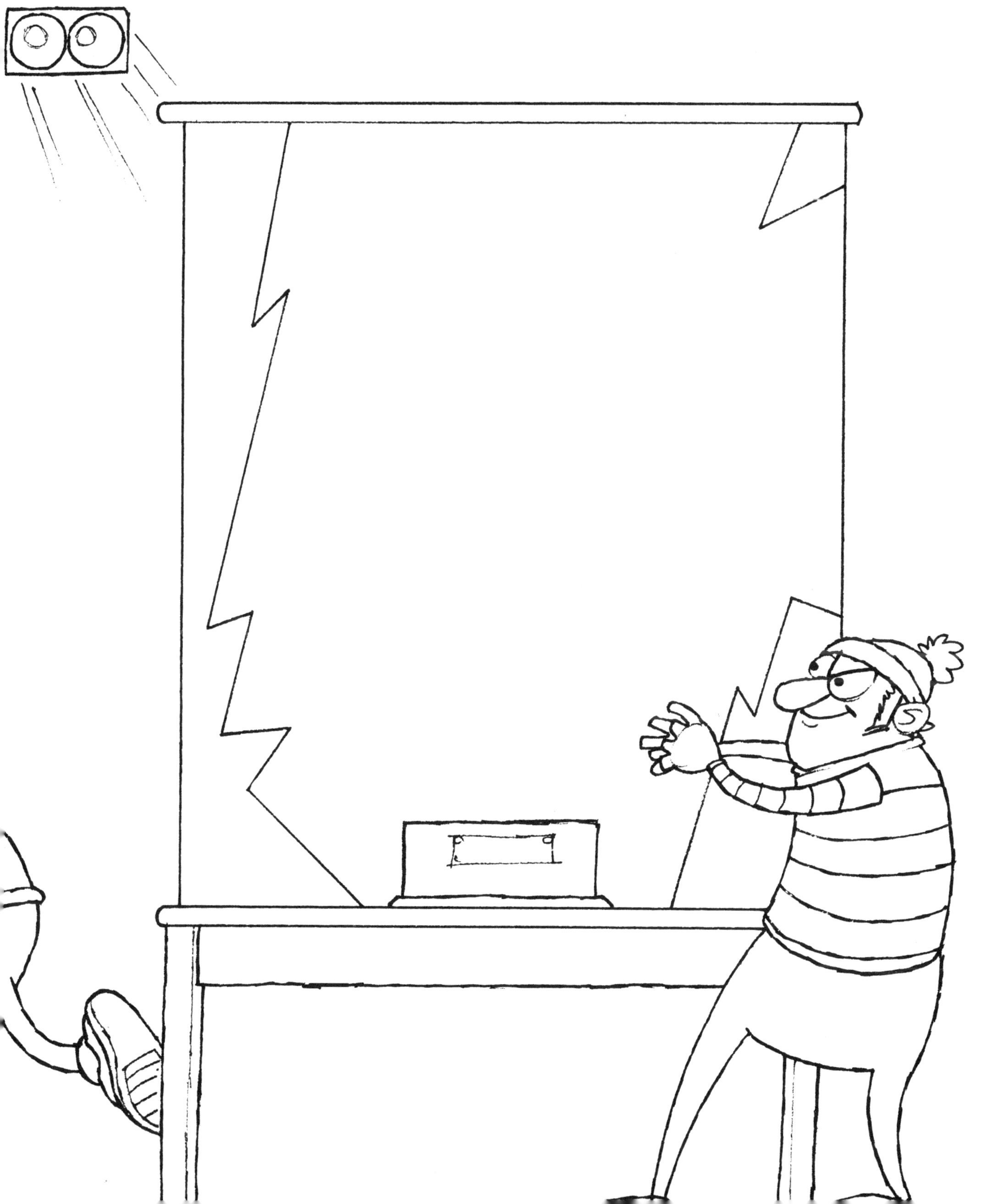

He shouldn't be feeding that to the animals

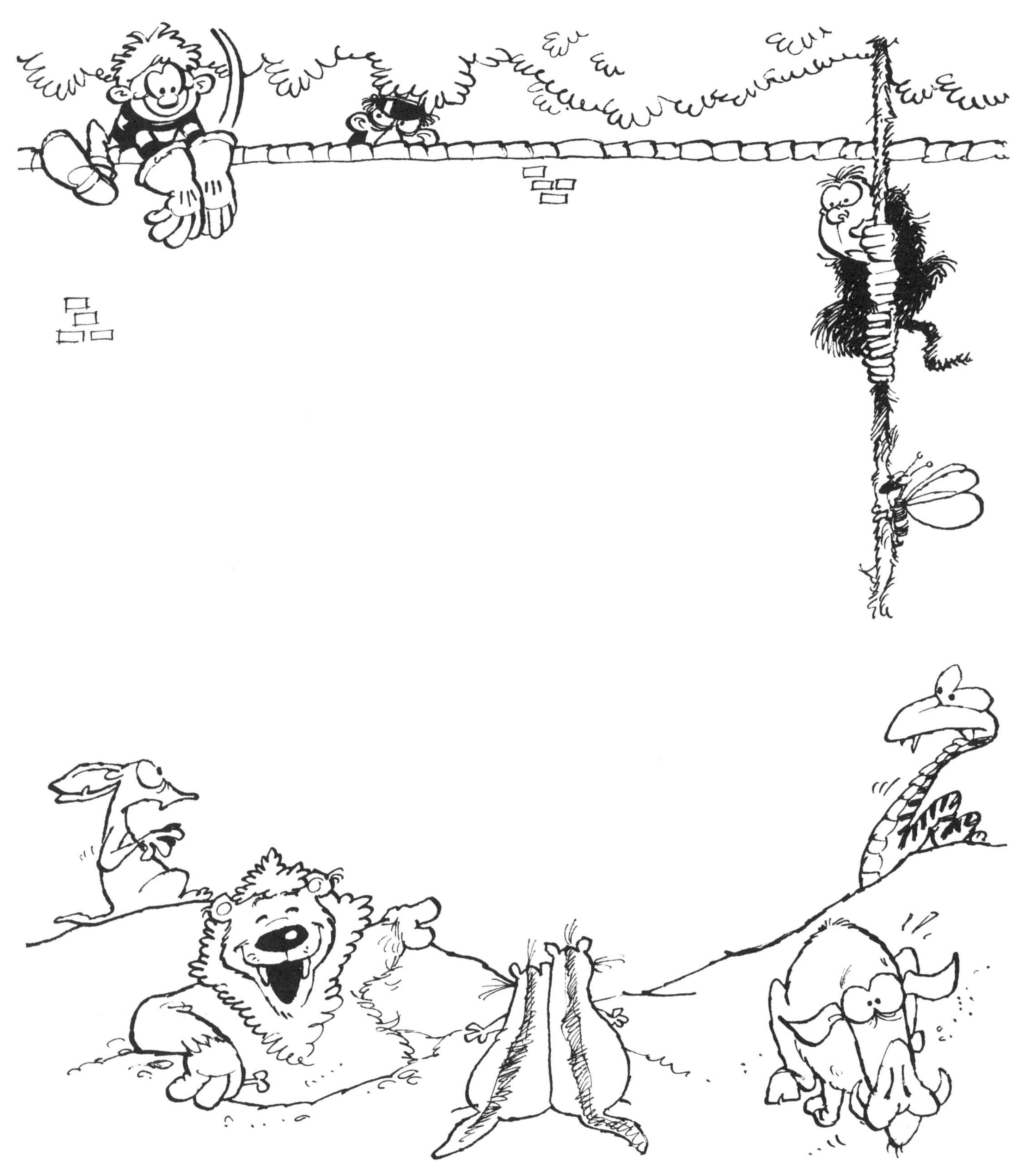

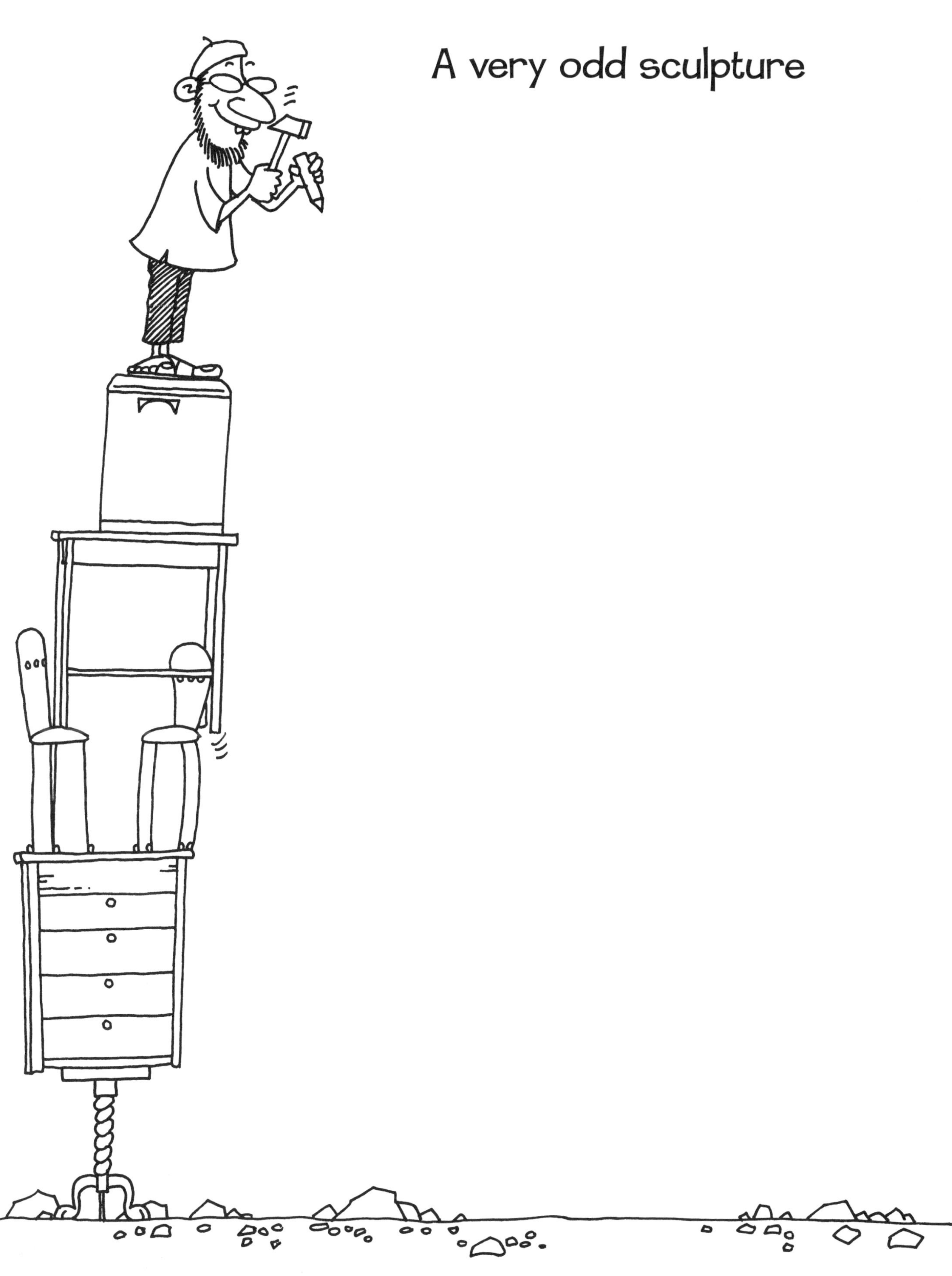
A very odd sculpture

Turn on the lights at the fairground

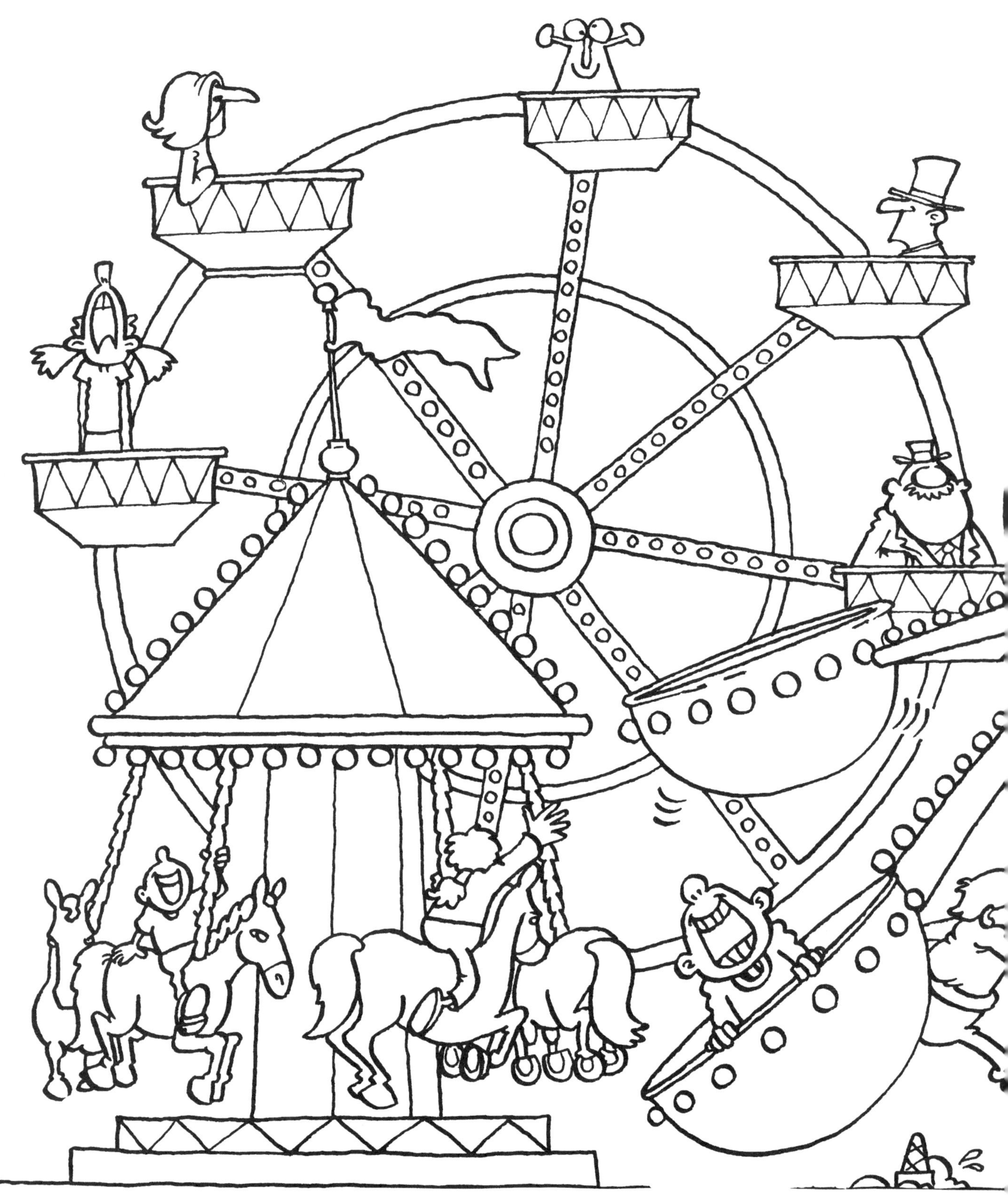

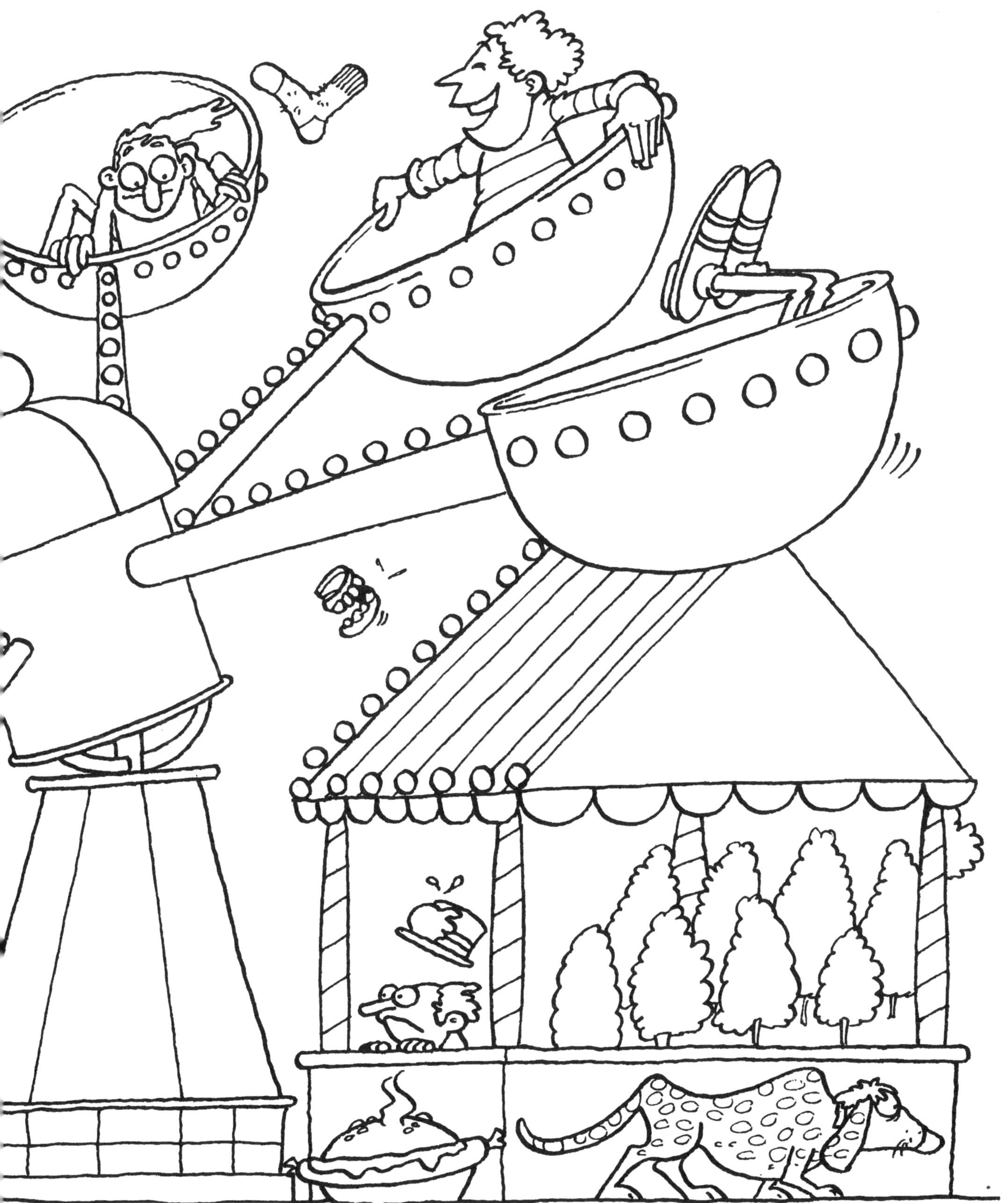

He's about to take a very important photo

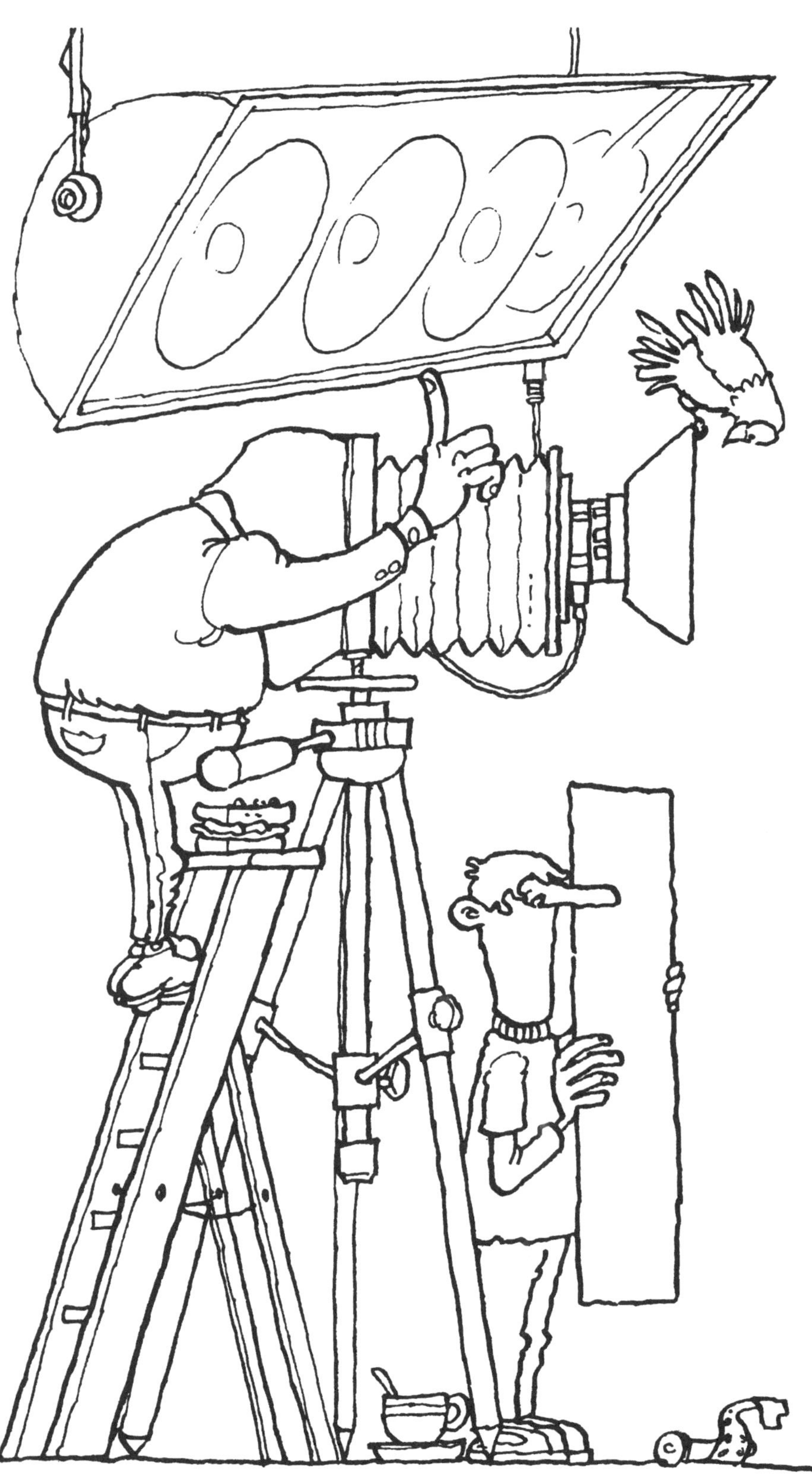

Who have the cops caught?

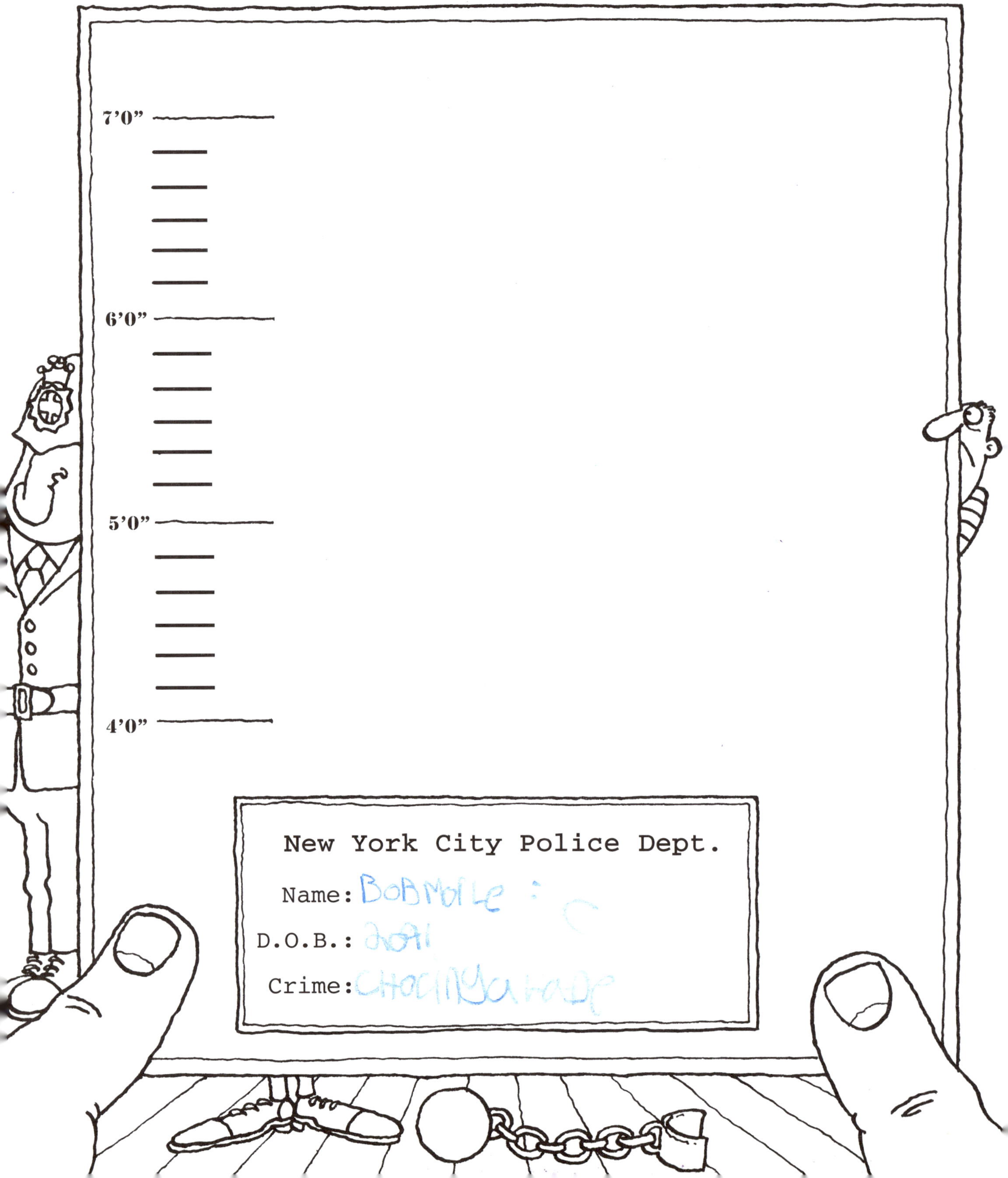

7'0"

6'0"

5'0"

4'0"

New York City Police Dept.

Name:

D.O.B.:

Crime:

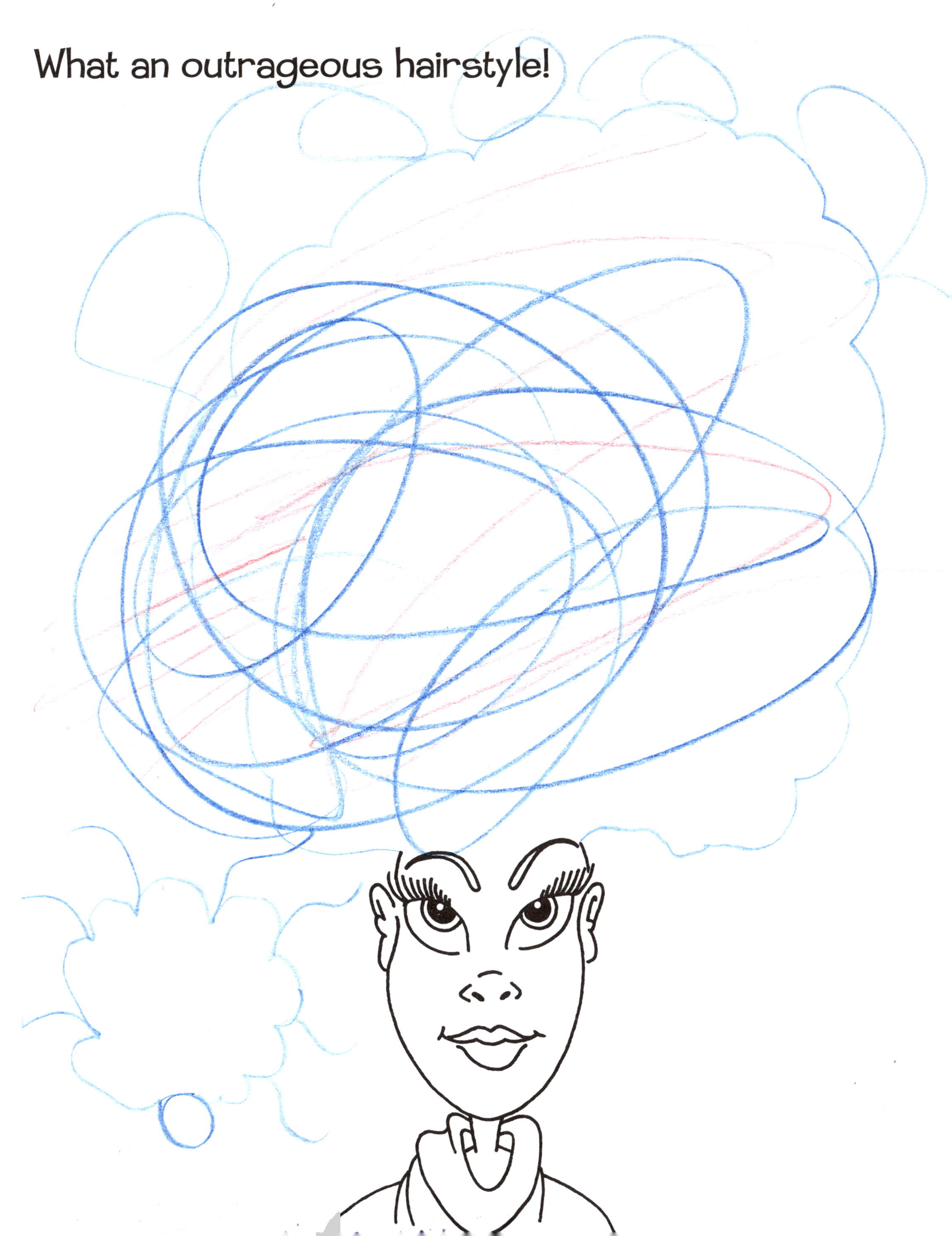
What an outrageous hairstyle!

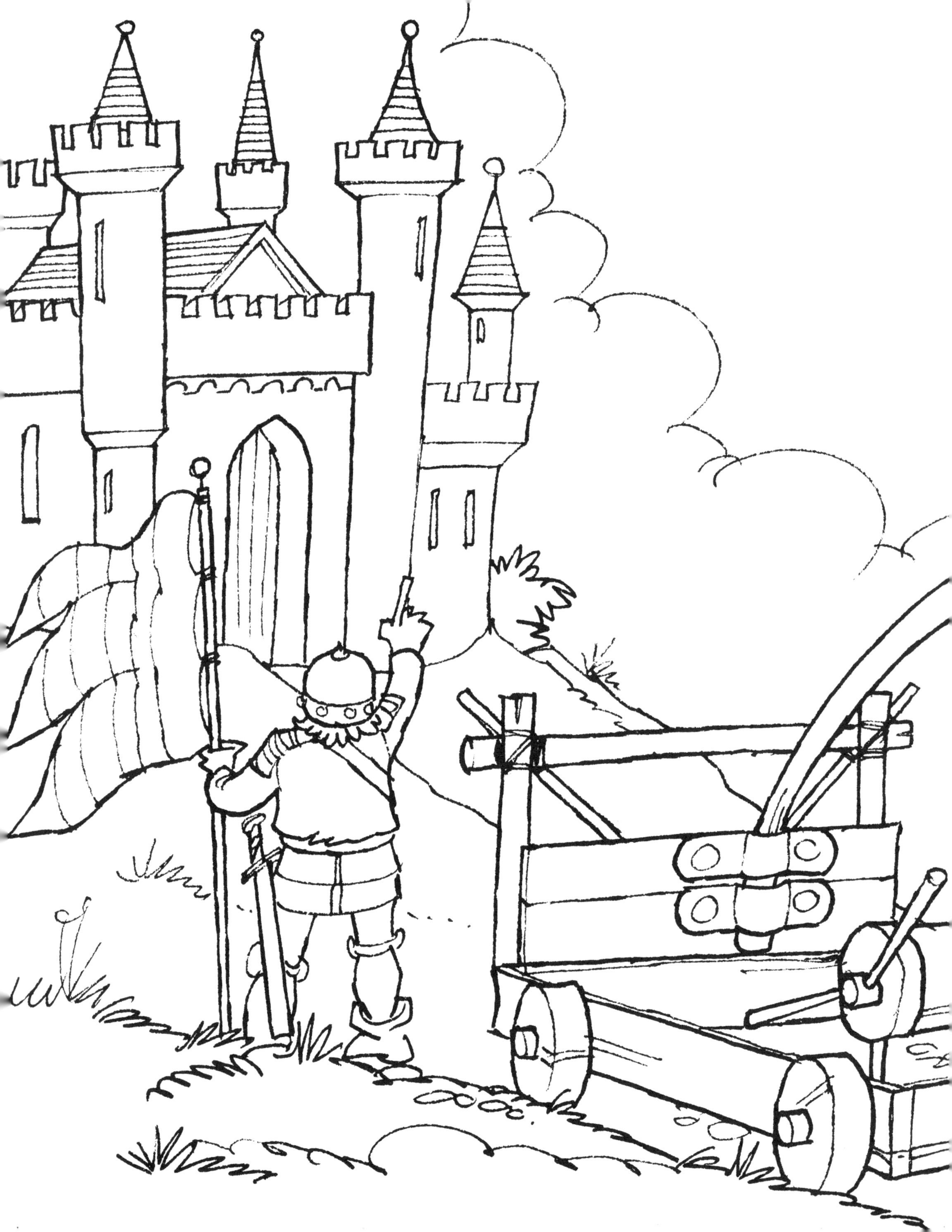

They won't see this one coming!

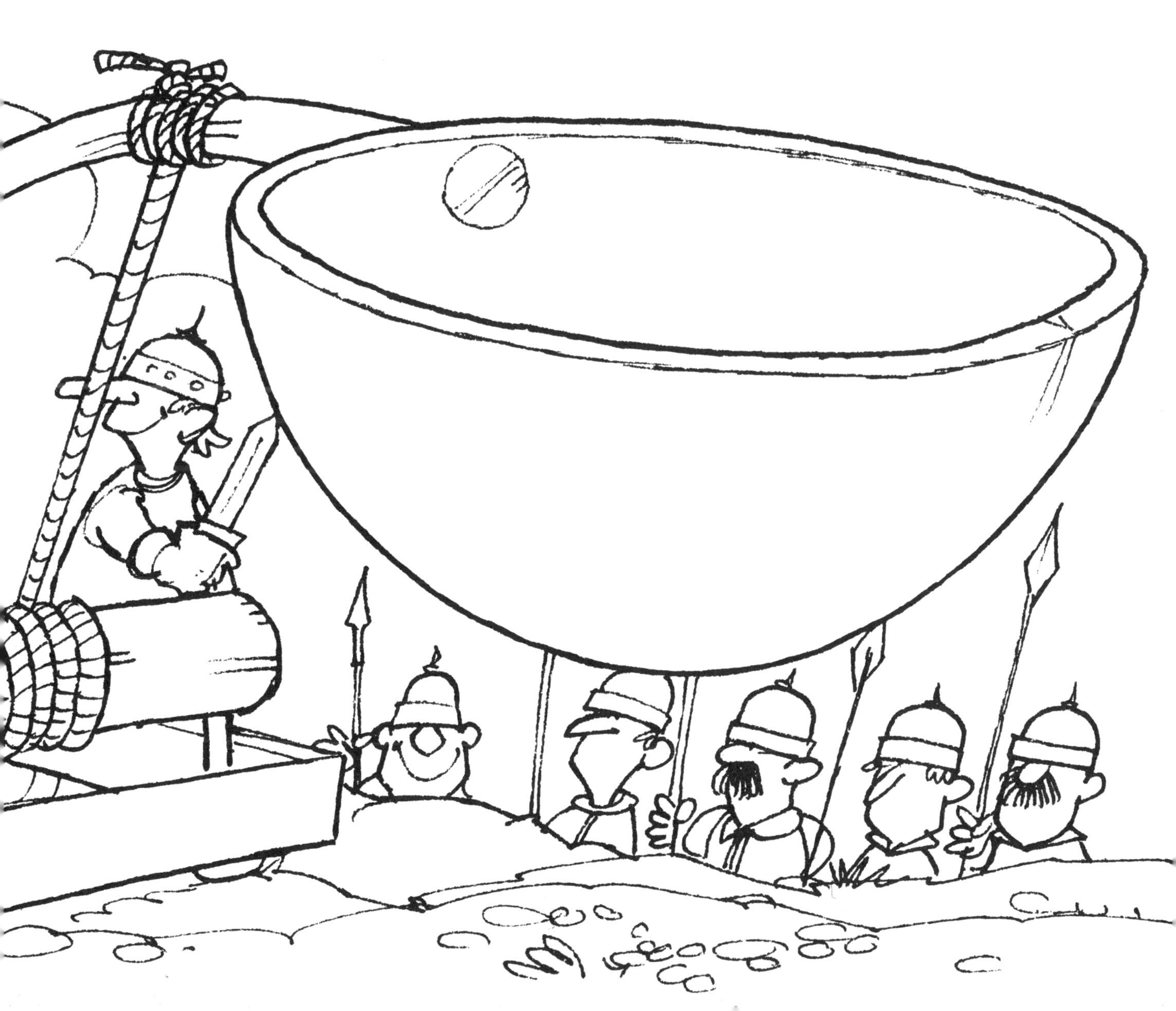

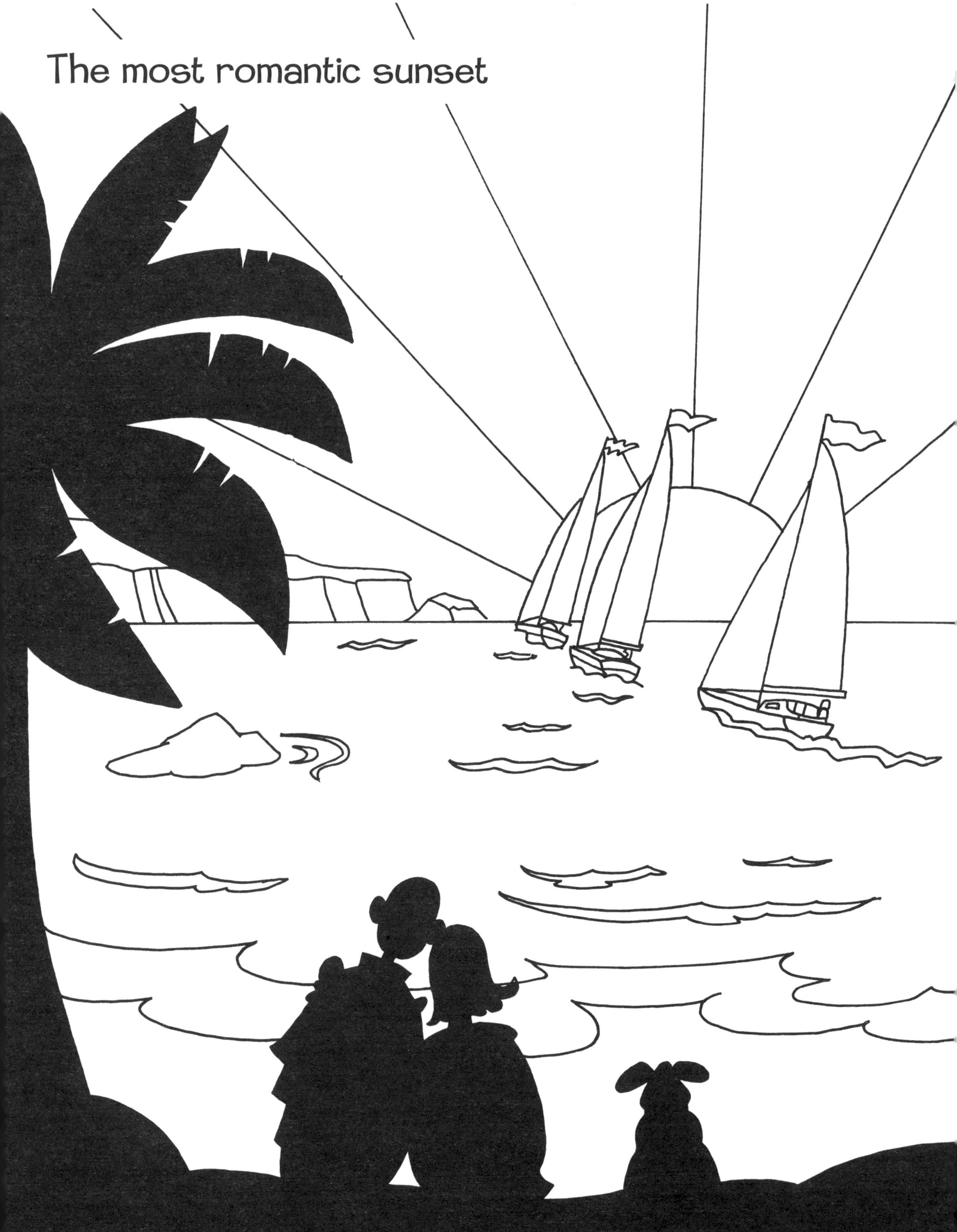
The most romantic sunset

What is Andre serving?

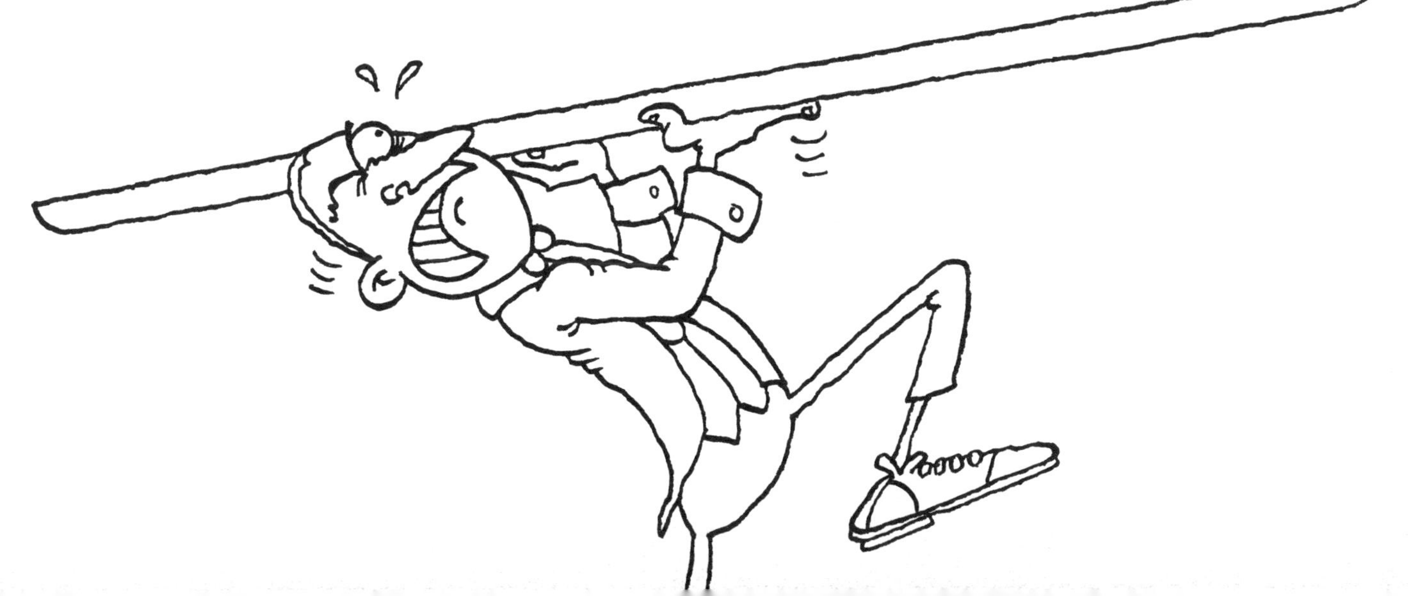

What do bears dream about?

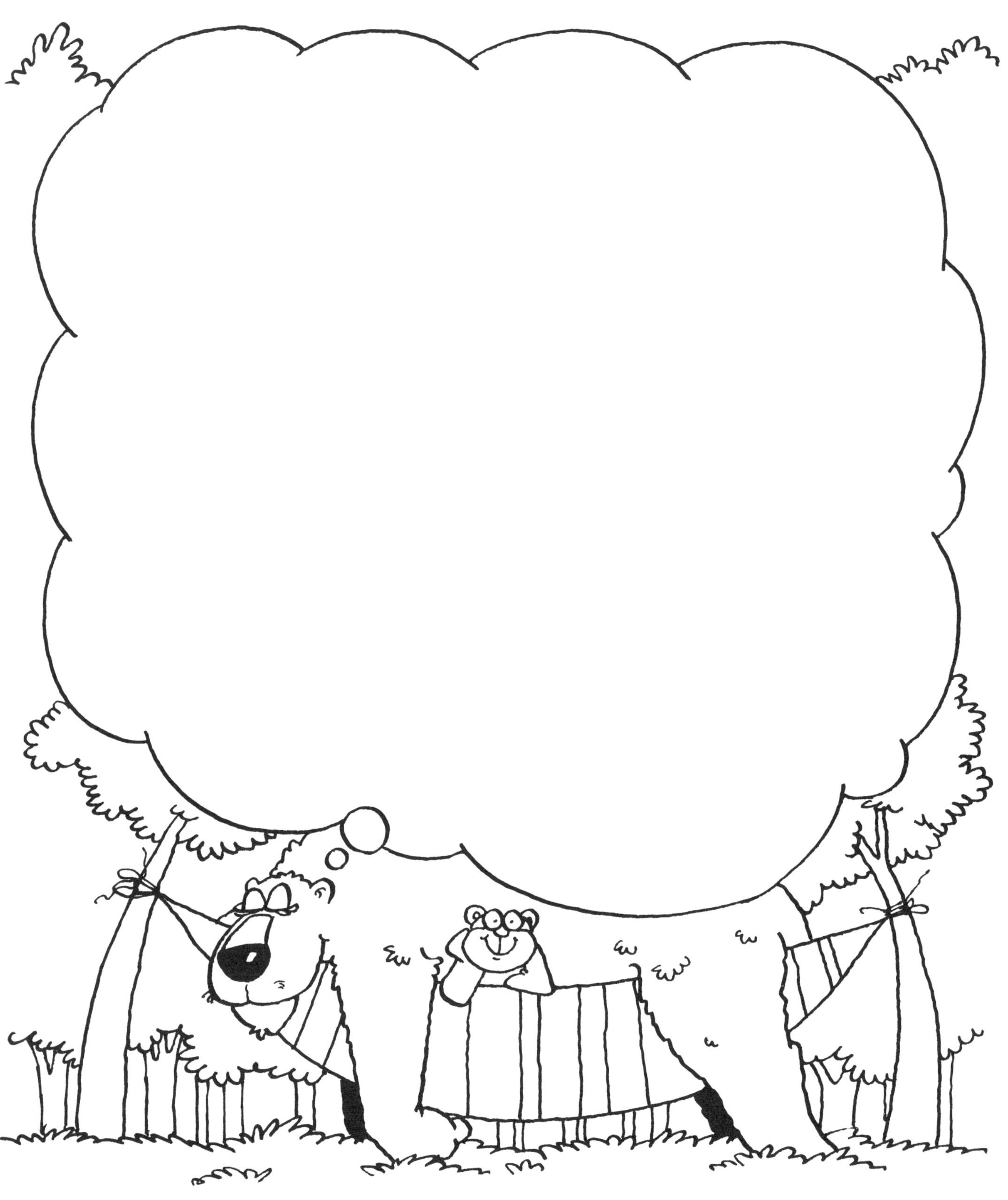

Look at all those different flavors!

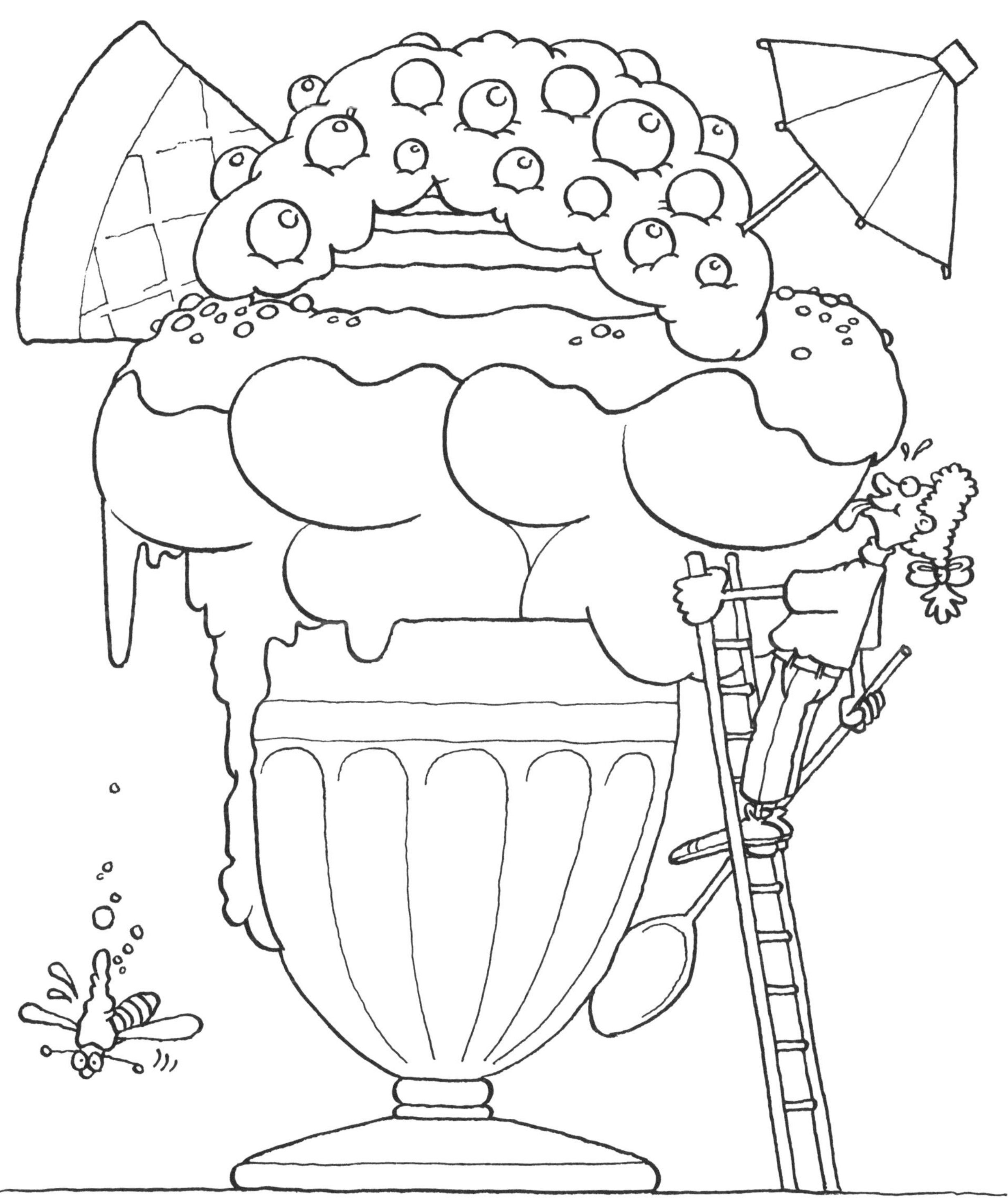

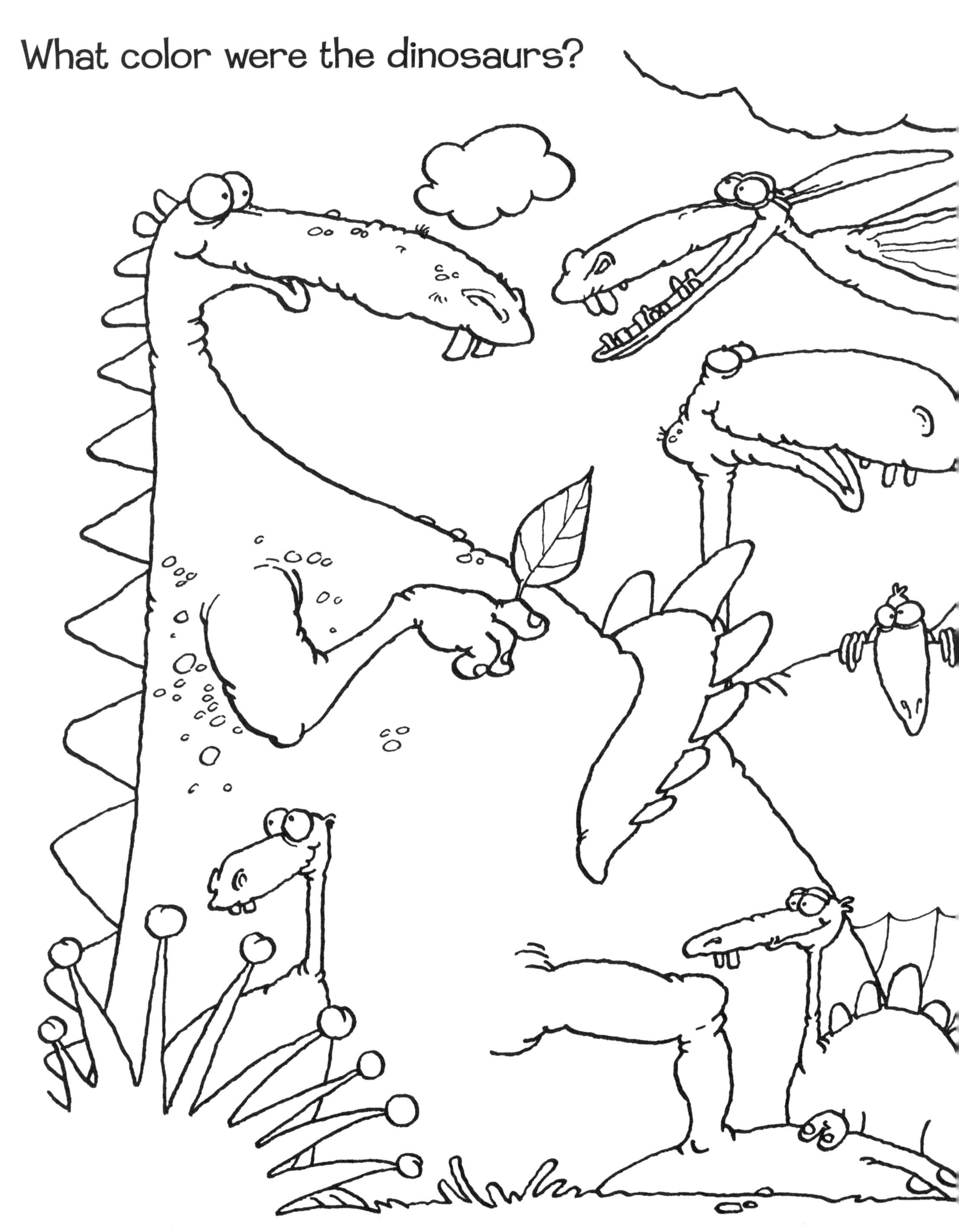
What color were the dinosaurs?

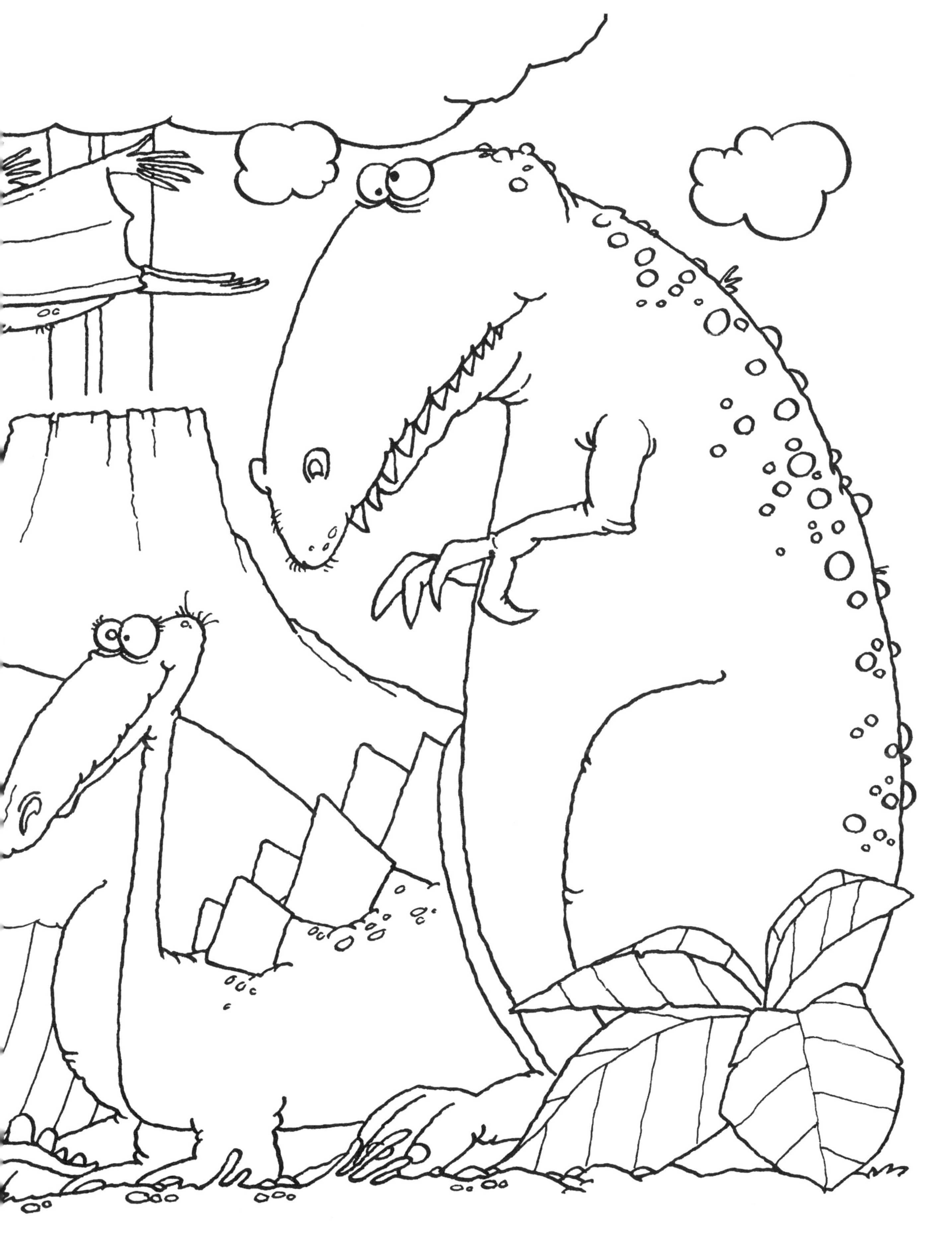

What do toys talk about when you're not there?

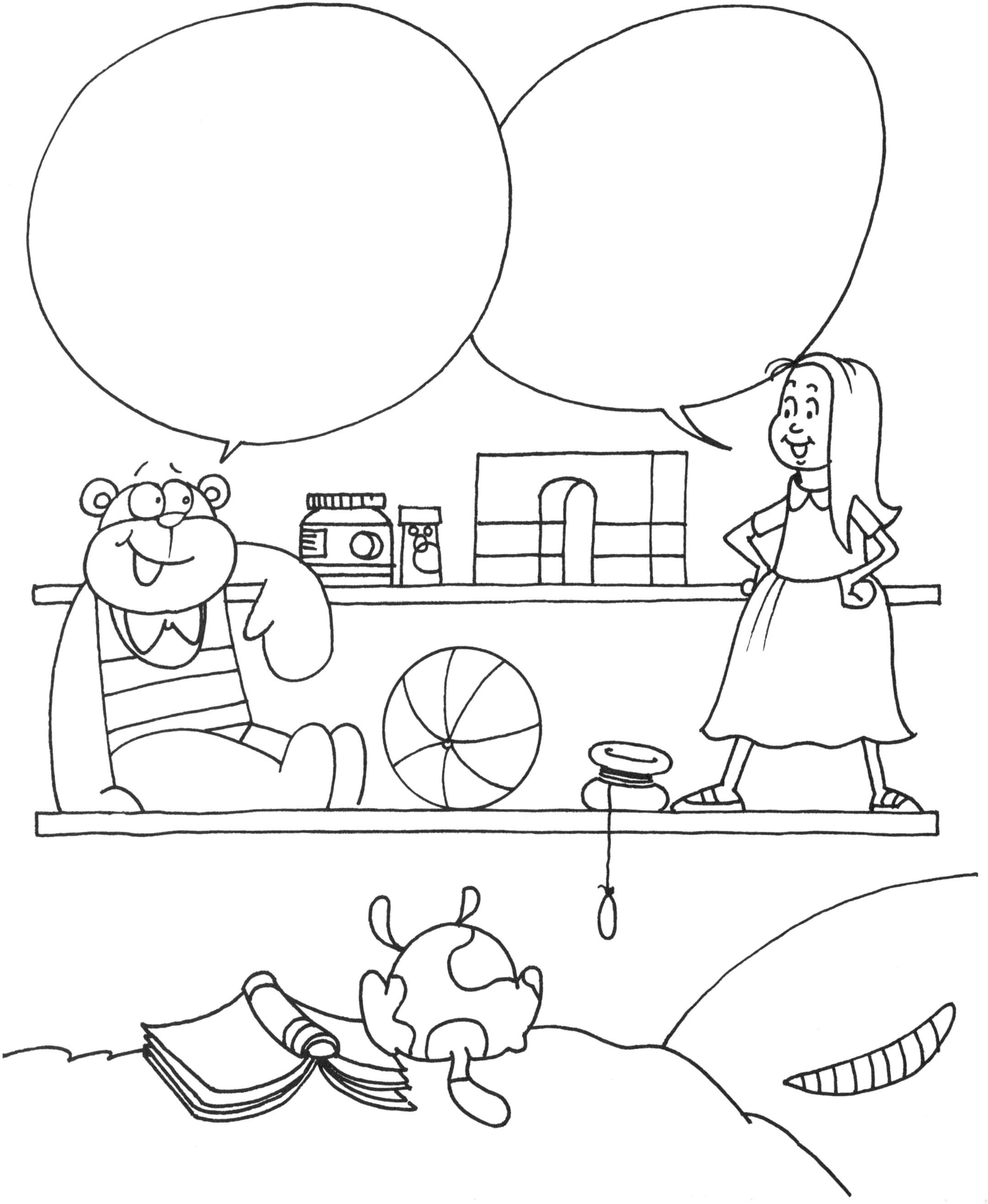

Uh-oh. It's a long way down

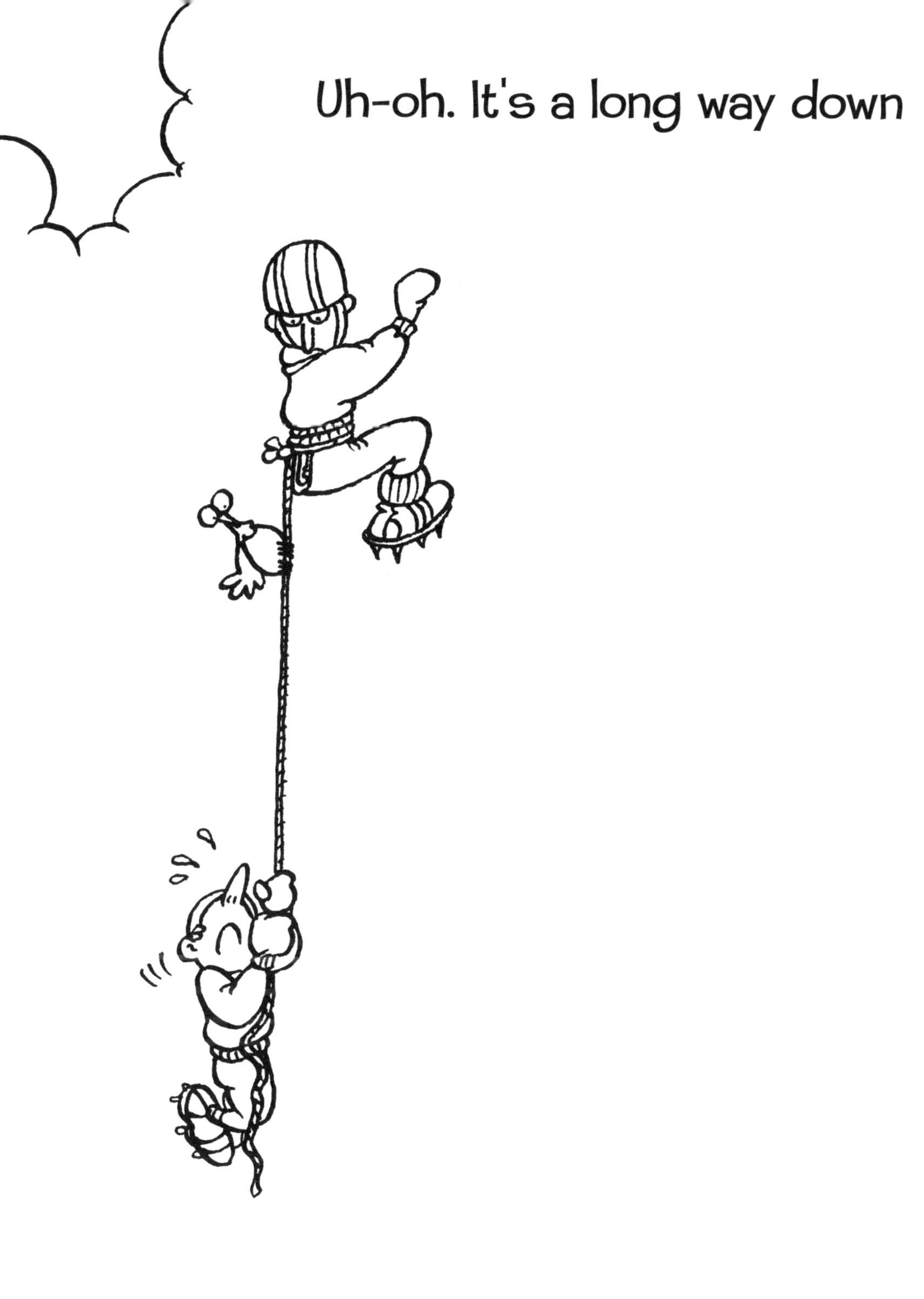

The time machine is ready

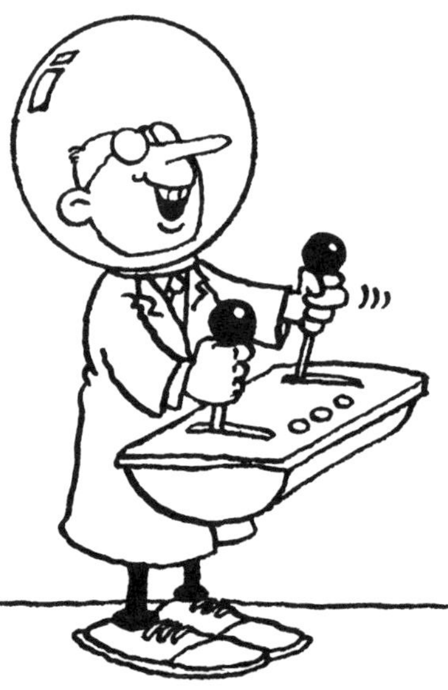

What pattern is on the alien's pajamas?

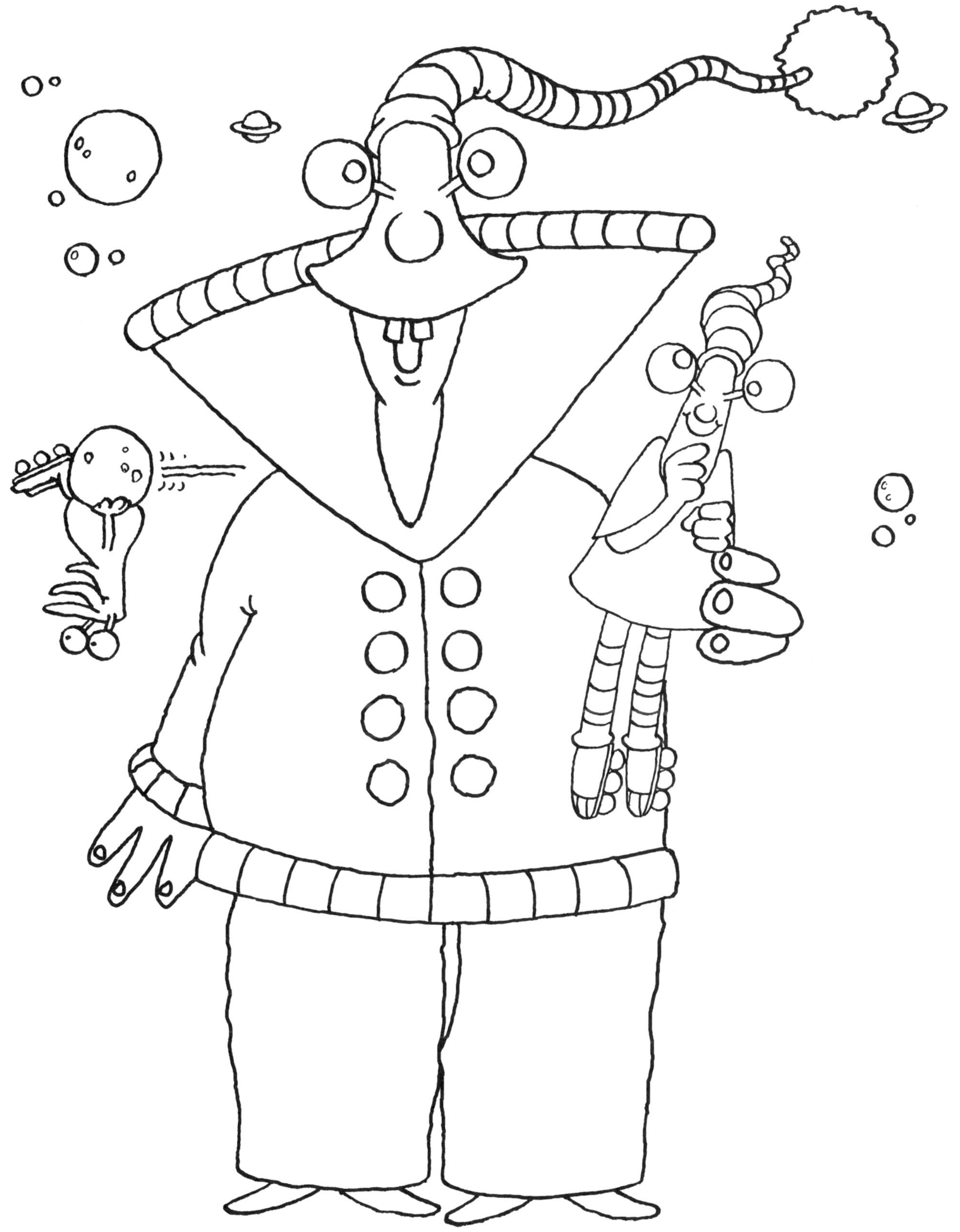

The world's biggest dog

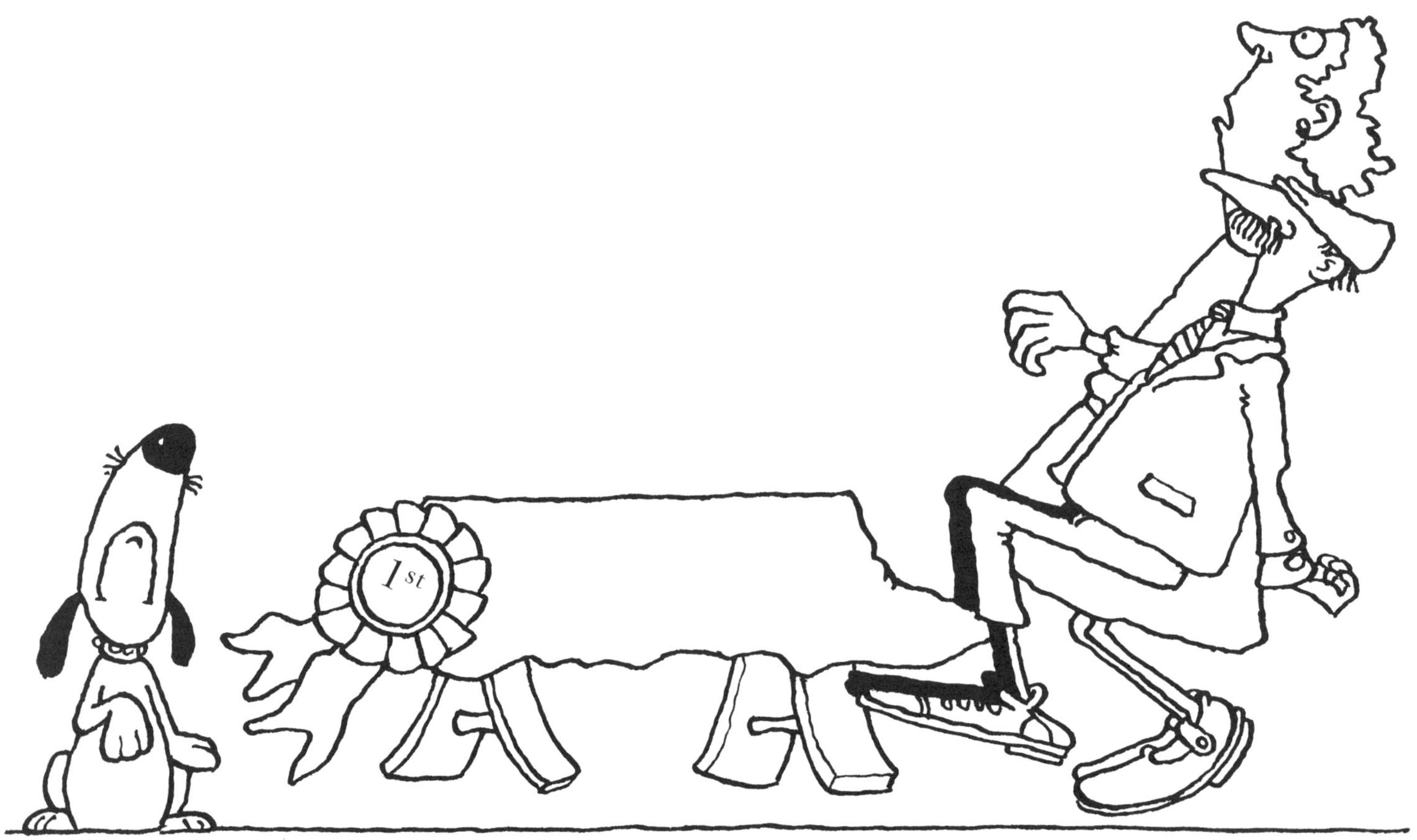

Big Bad Bob is regretting his new tattoo

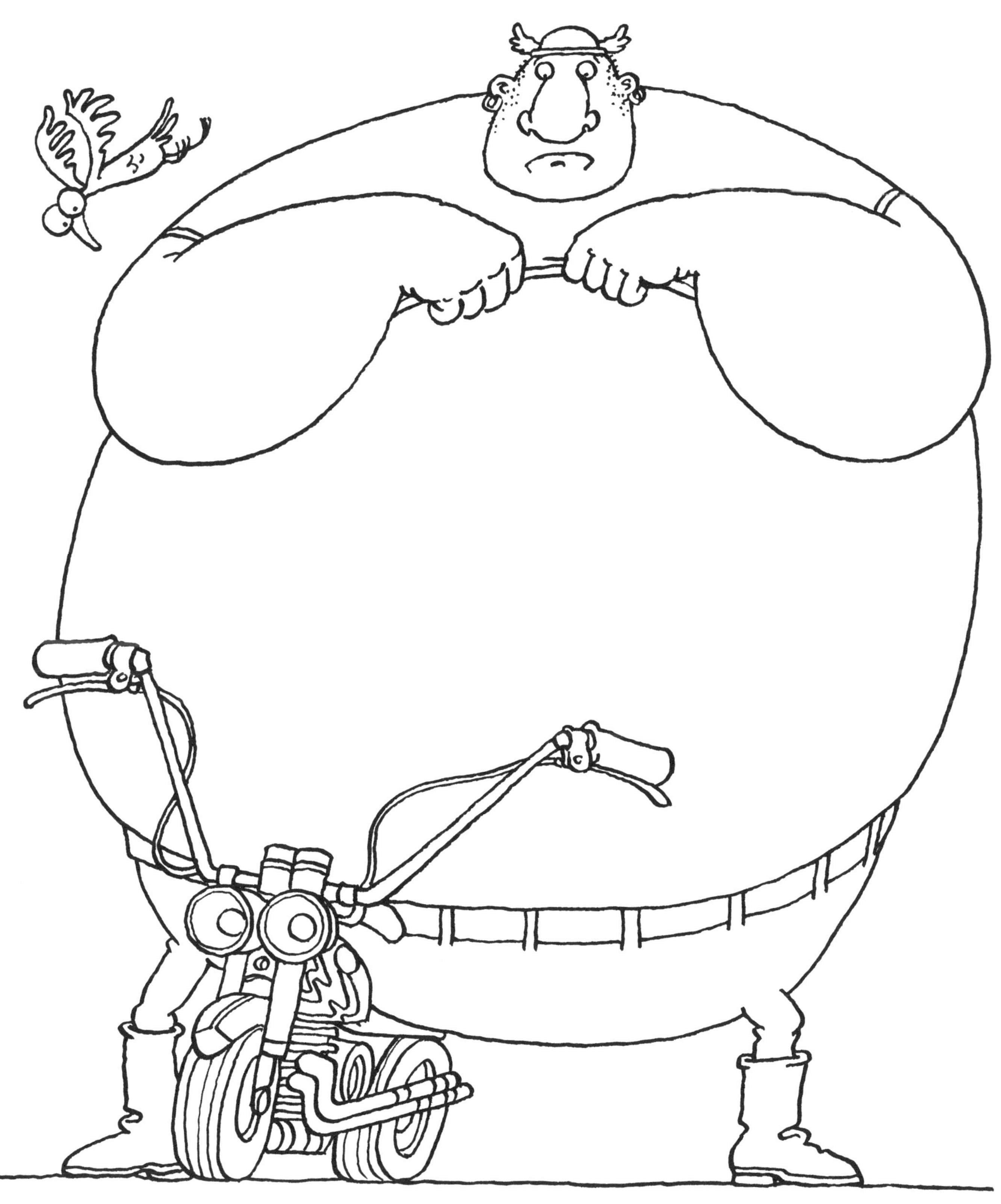

Who's delivered the knockout punch?

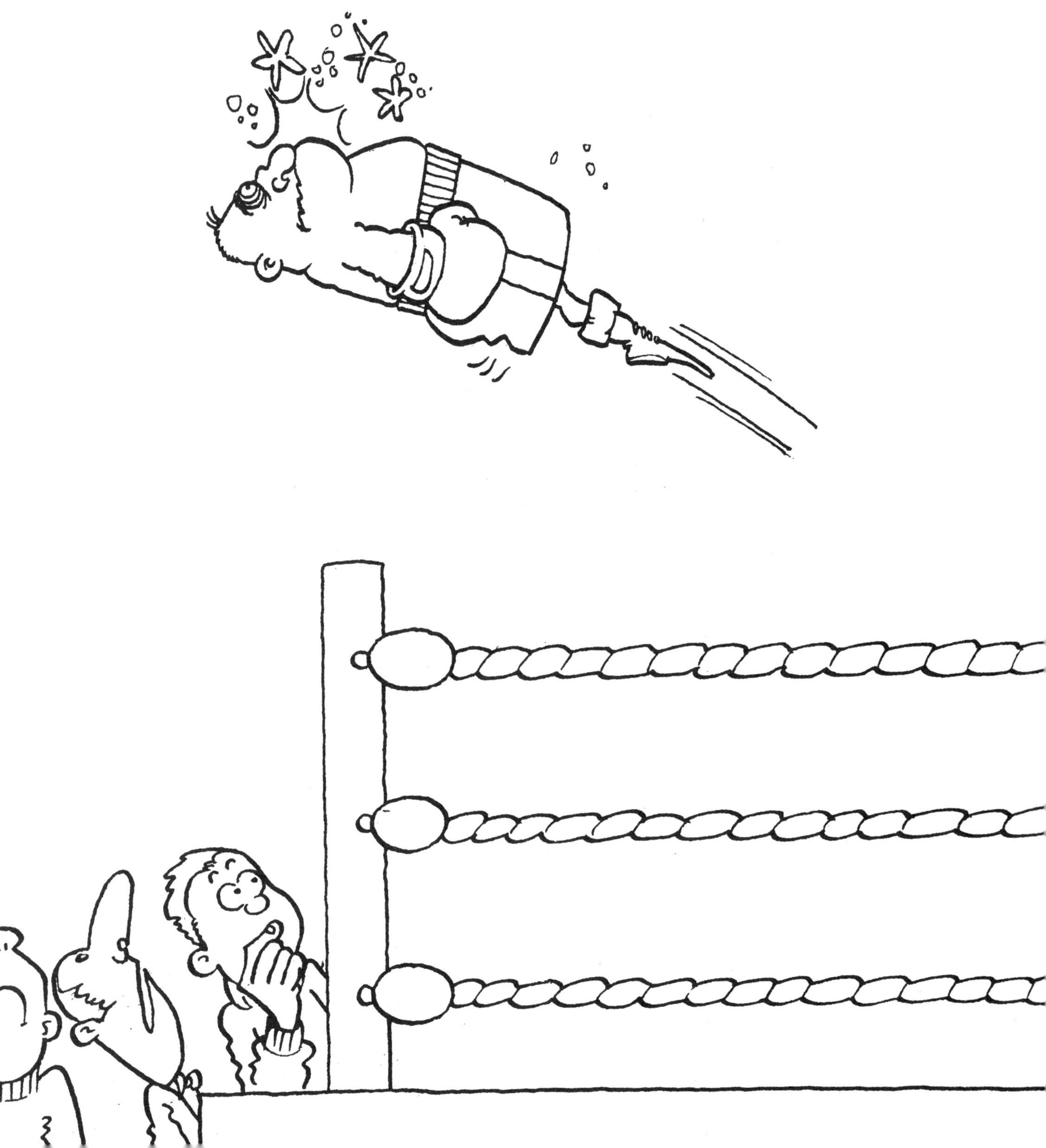

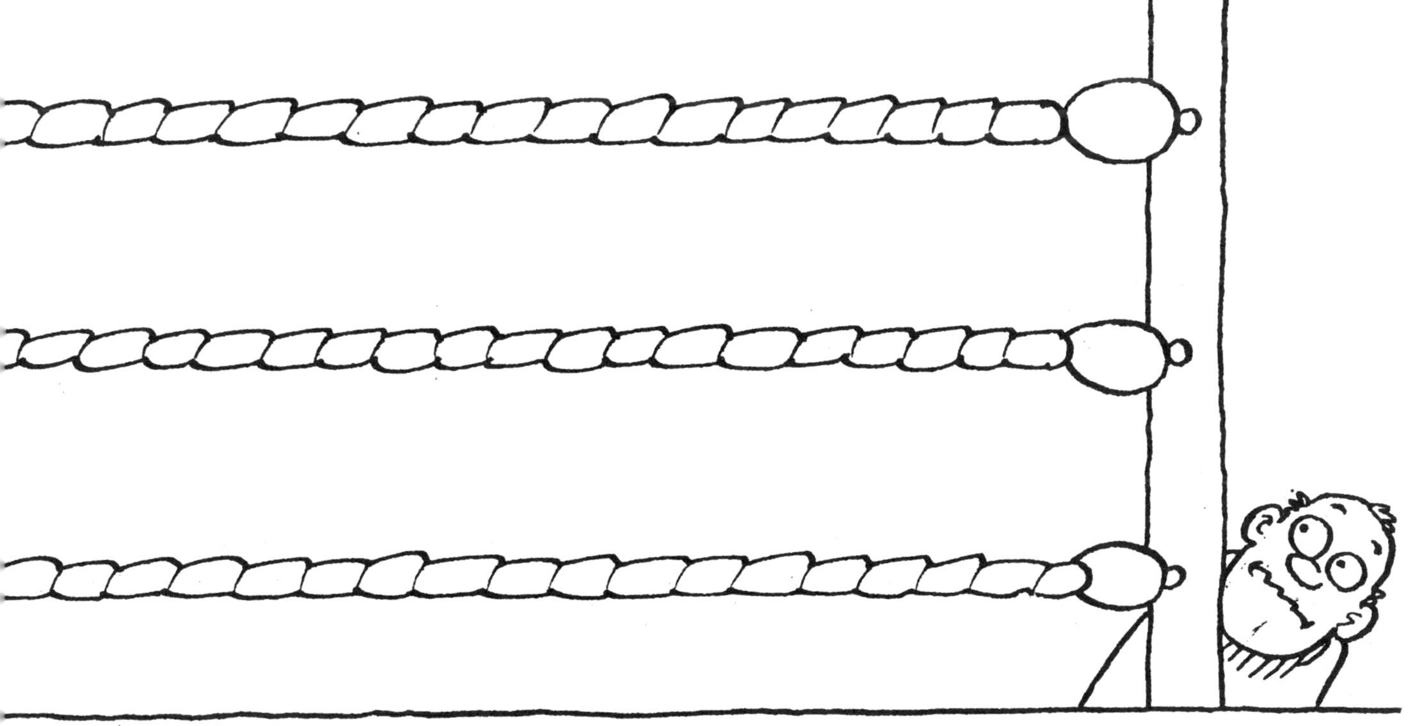

If only he'd recognized its warning colors

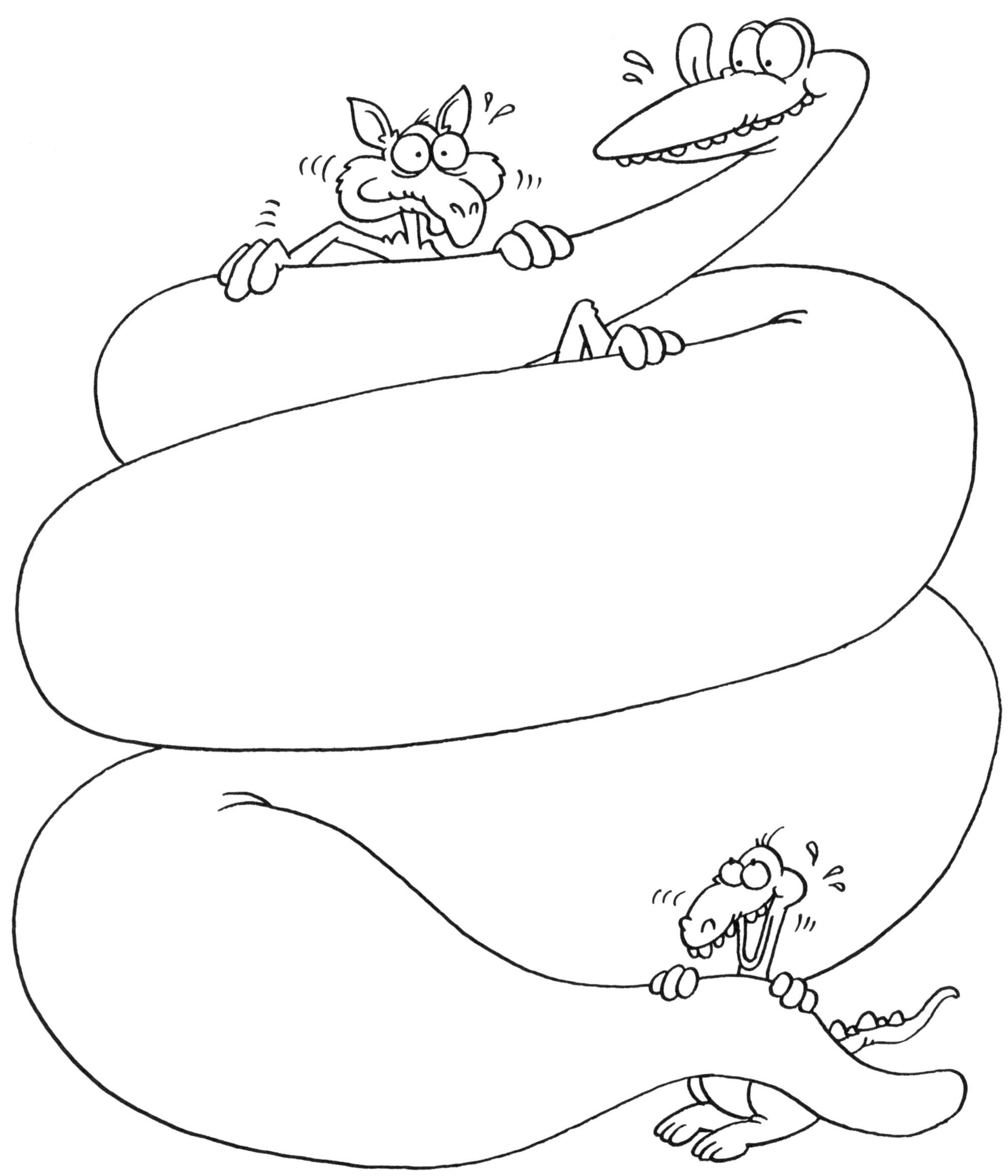

What is Joseph building?

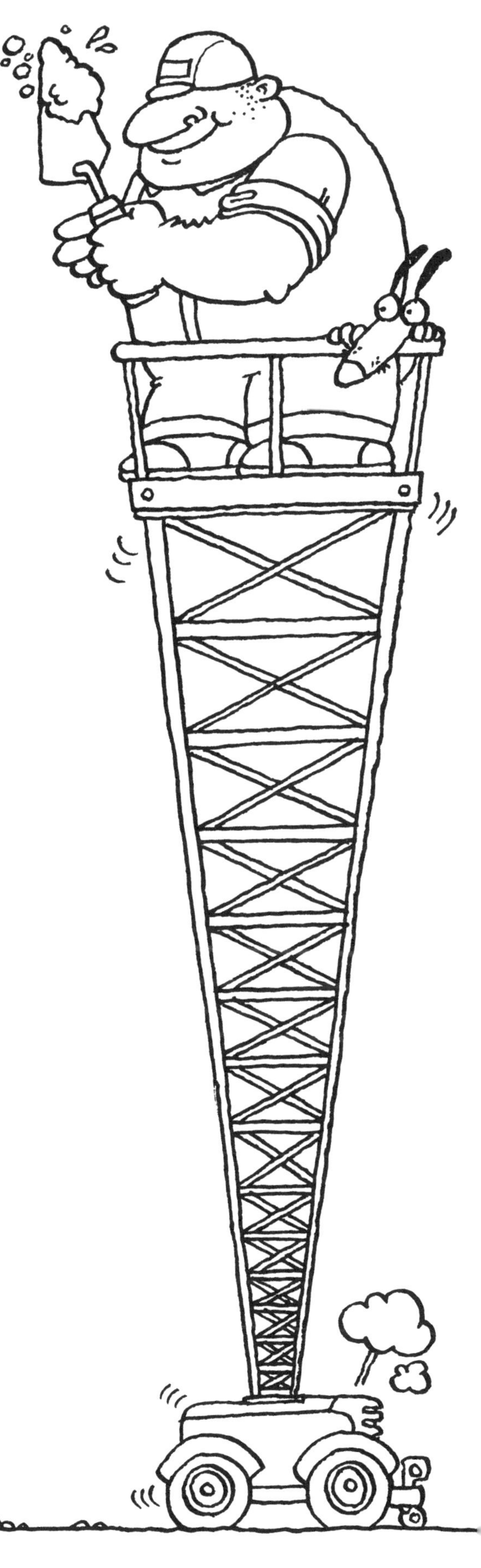

Who's beaten the champion to the finishing post?

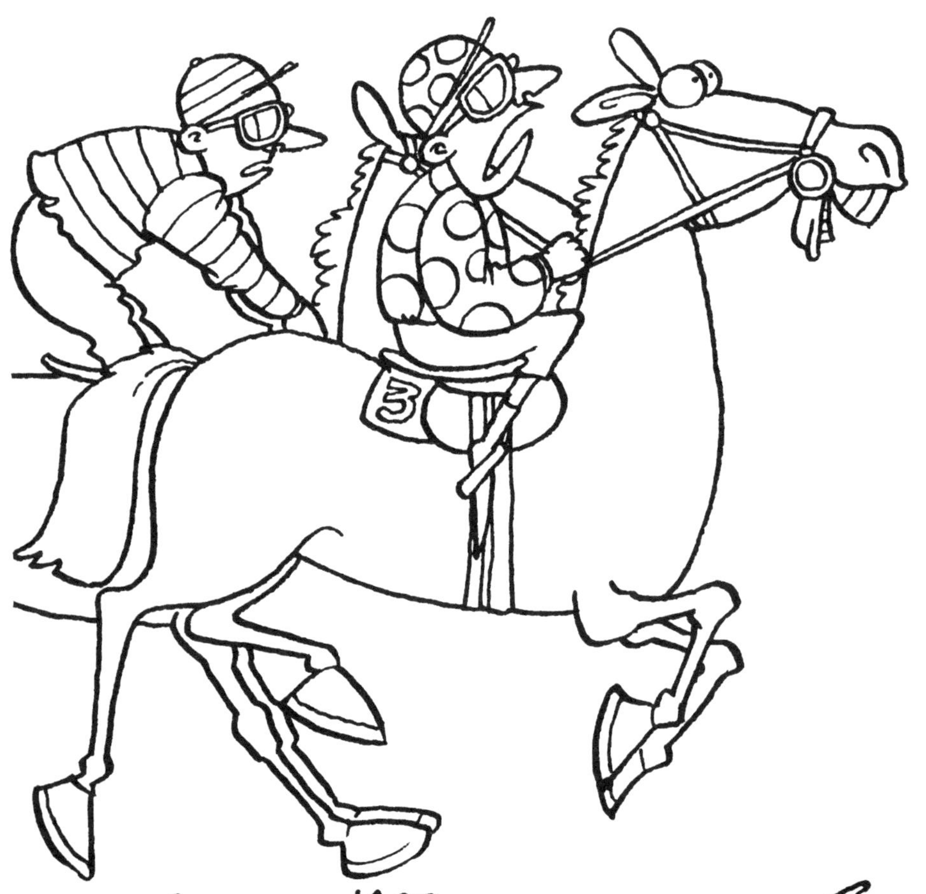

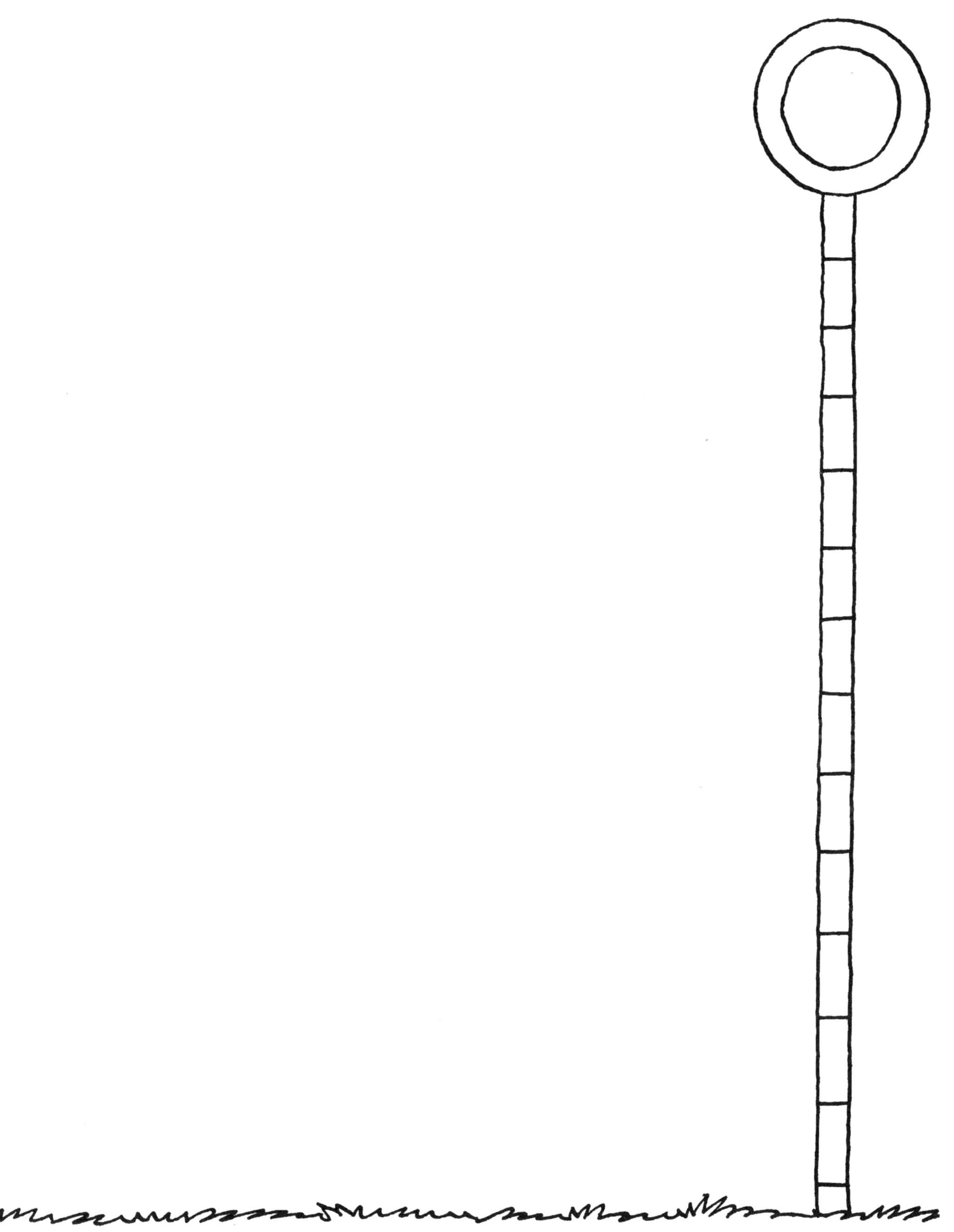

Give him some things to juggle with

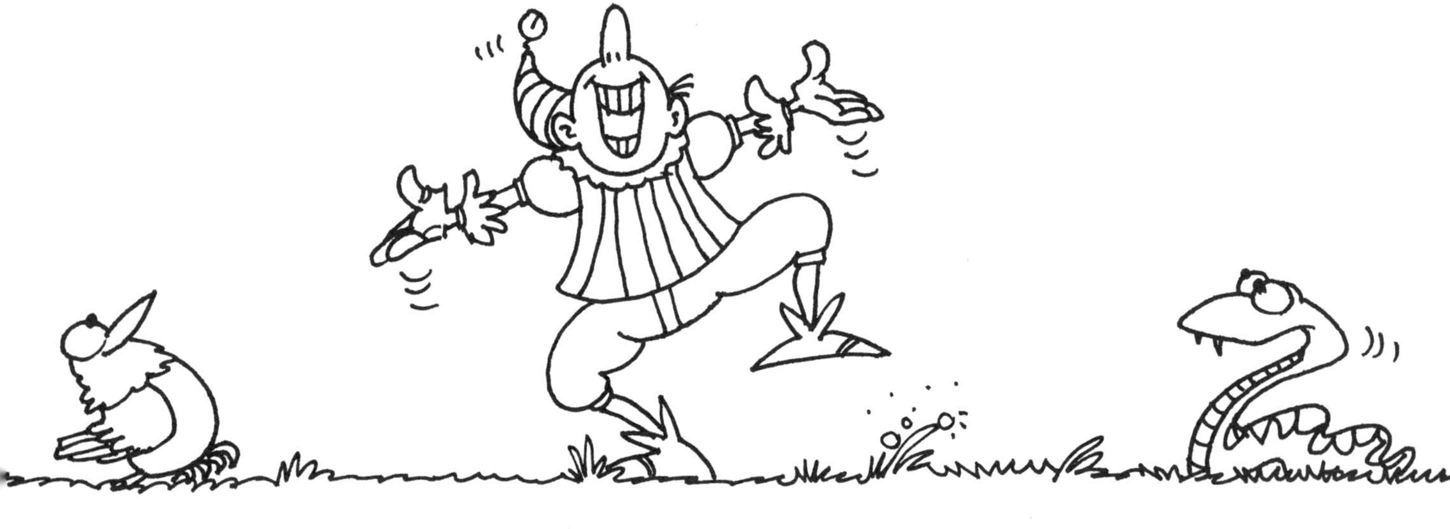

Looks like trouble just came a-knockin'

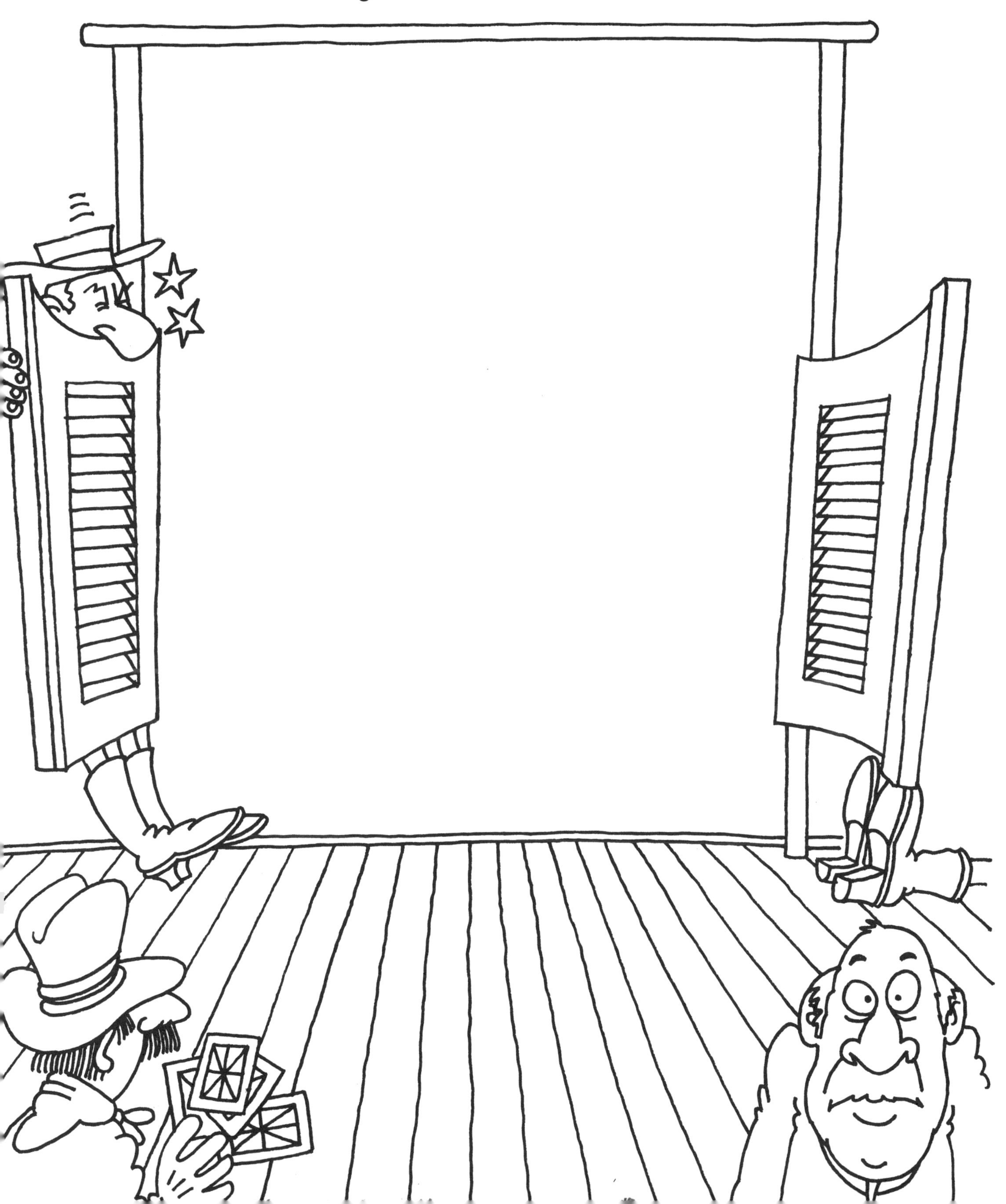

Join the art class

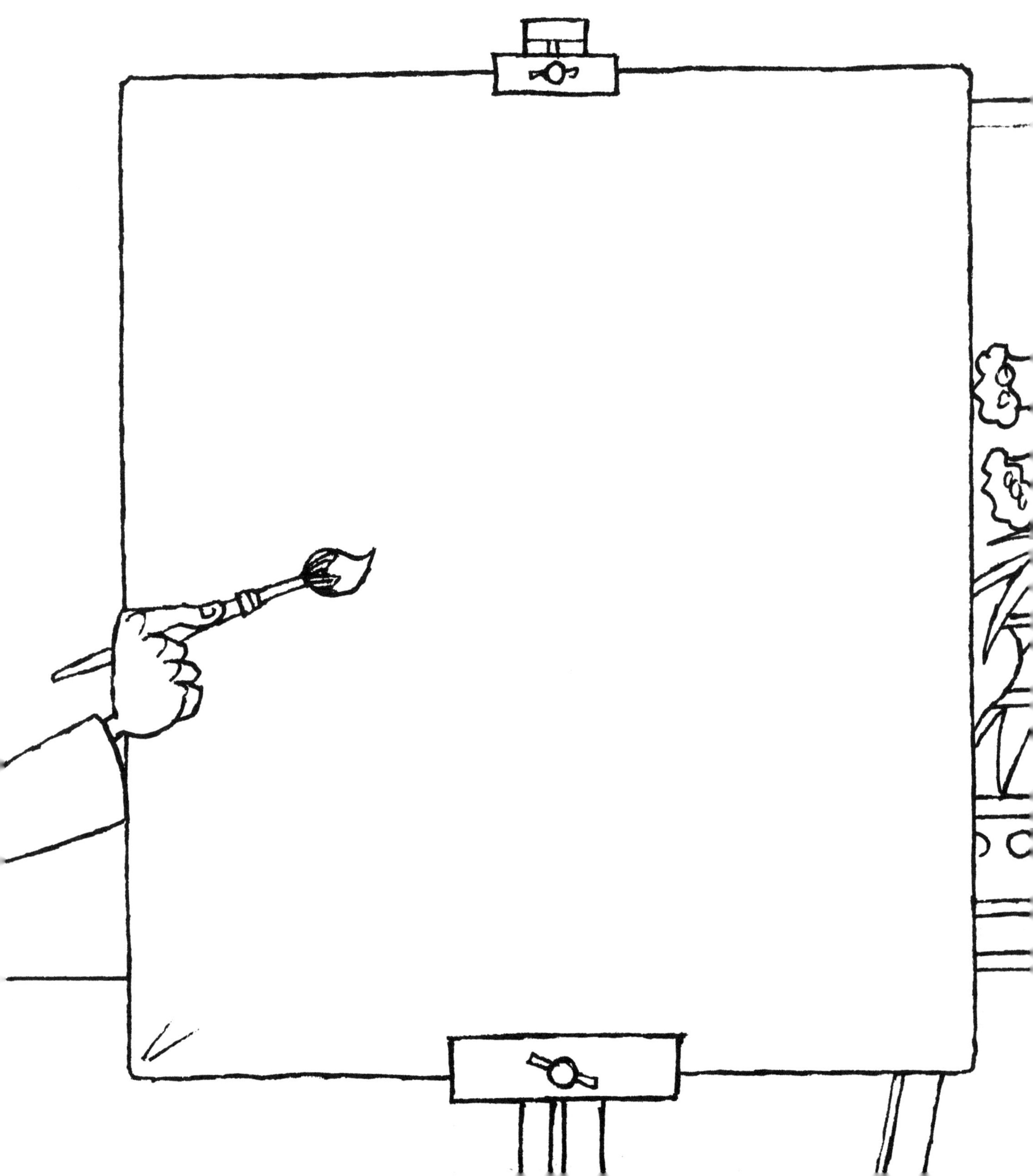

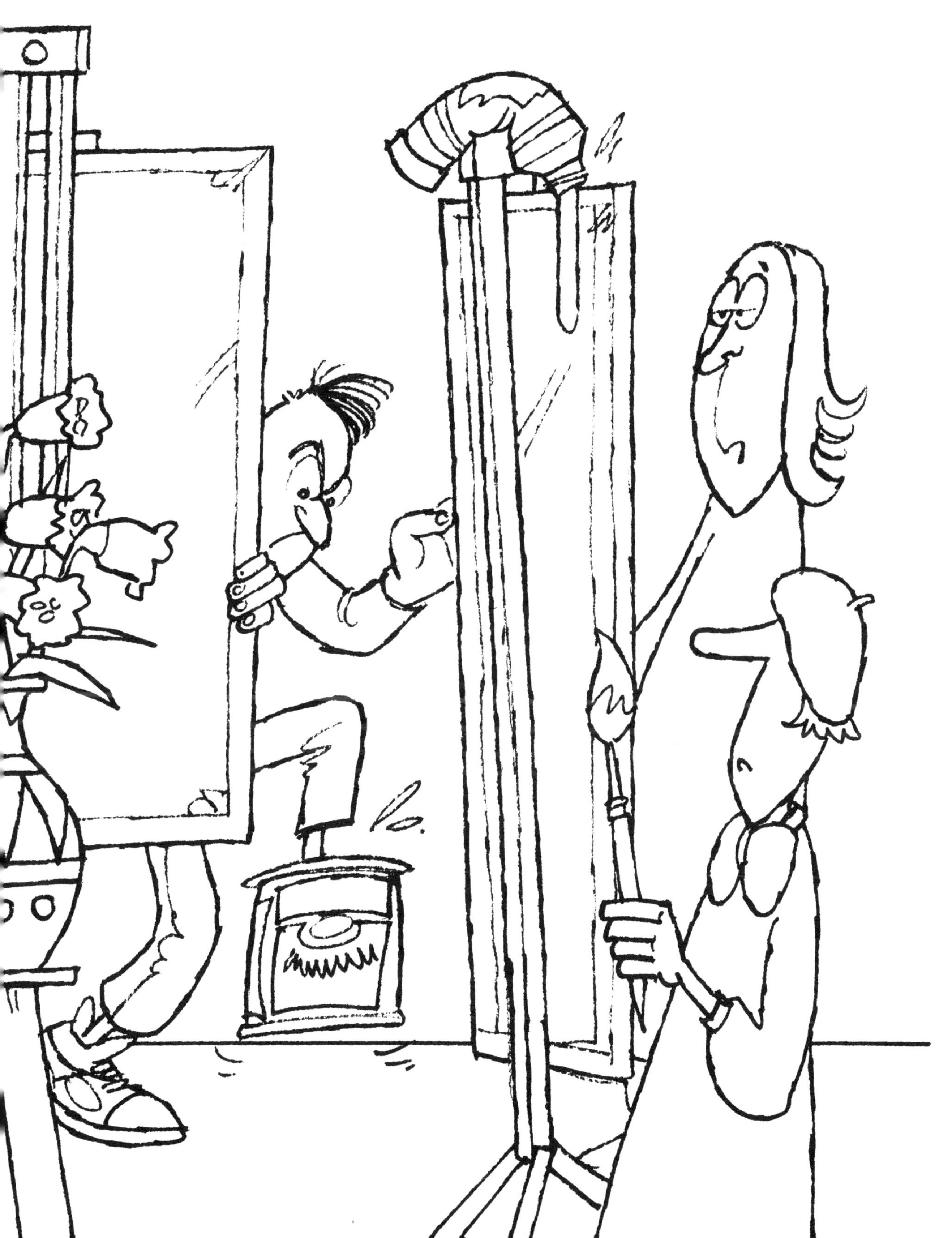

Sweet dreams!

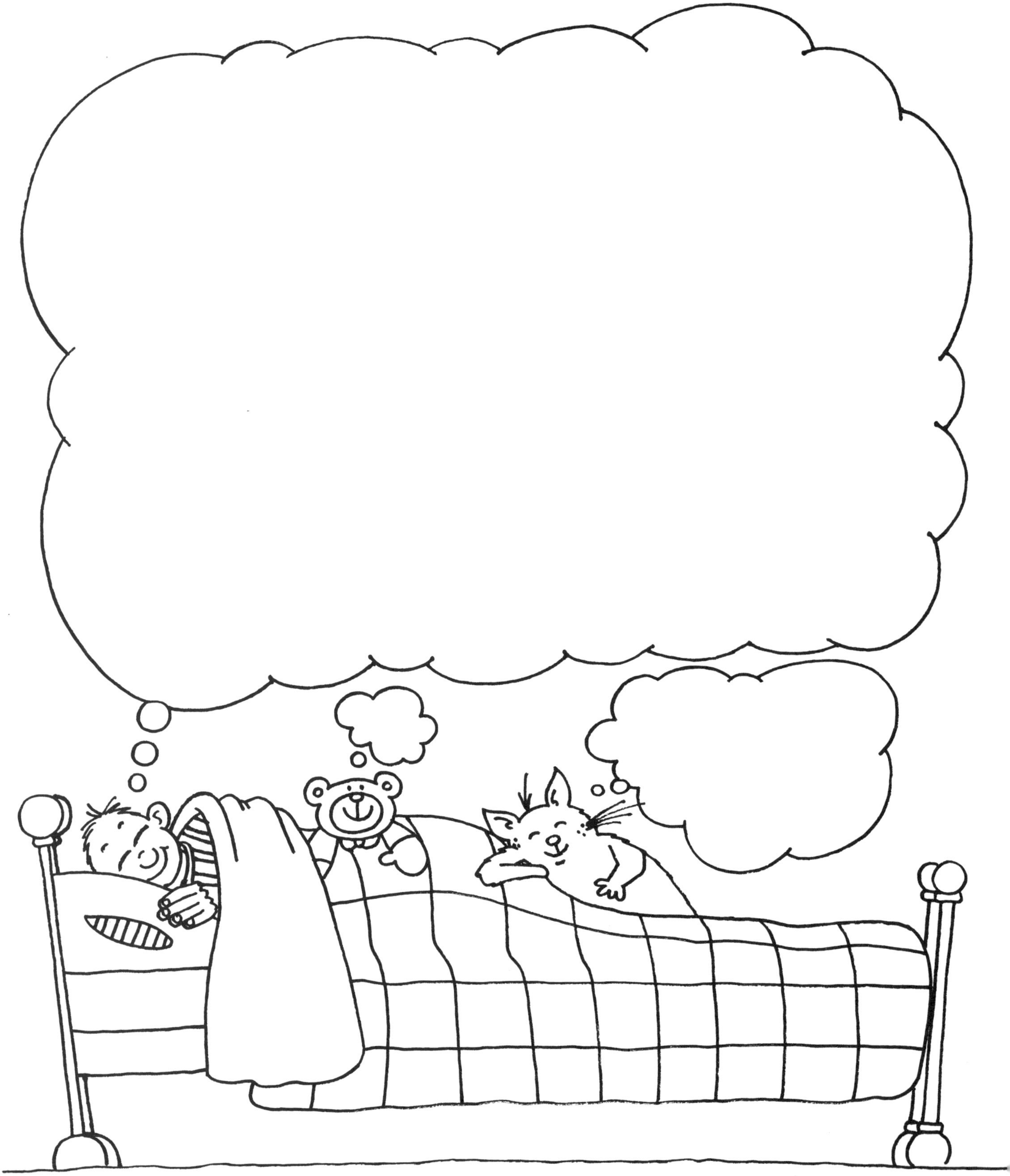

Santa's impressed with the tree this year

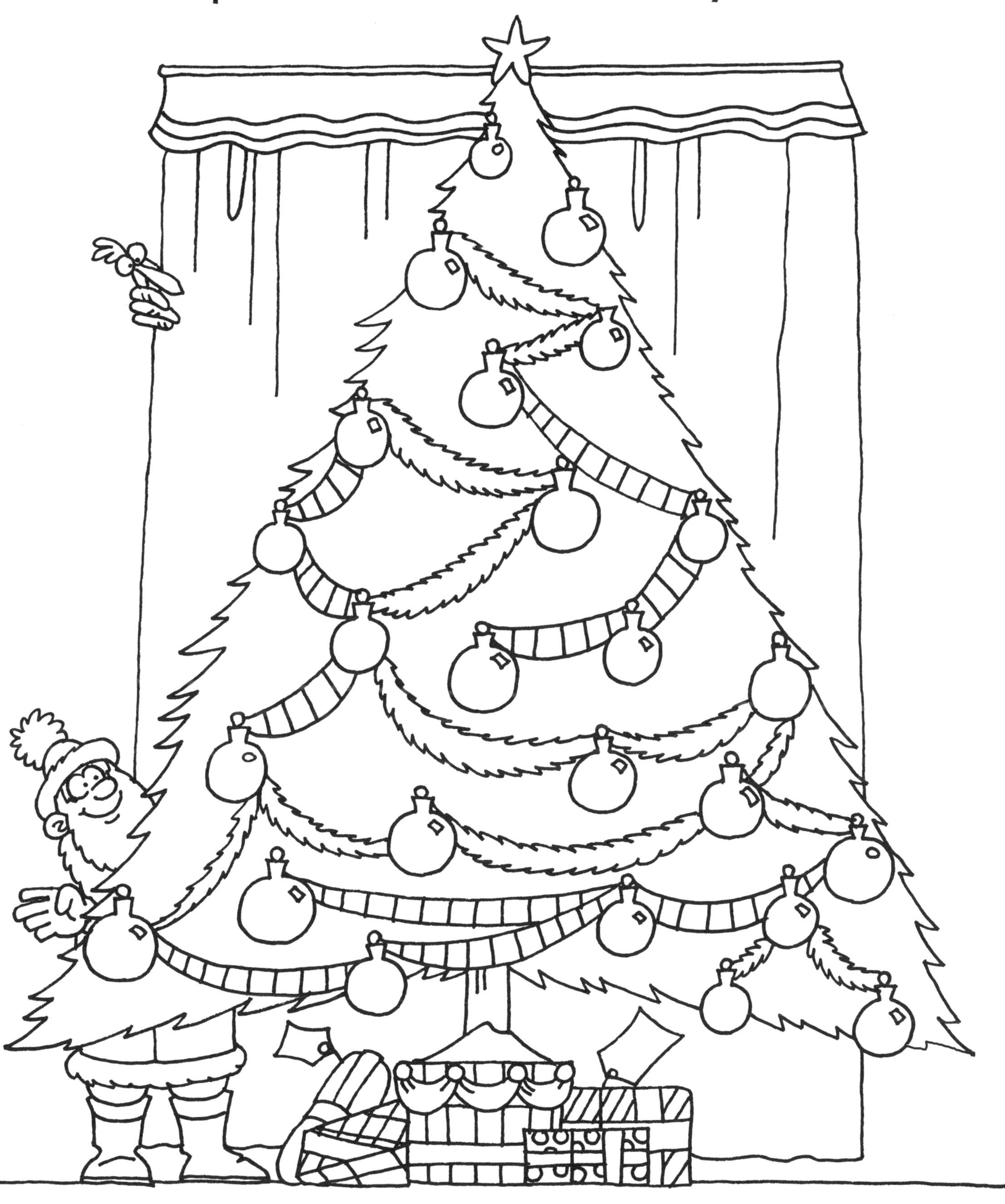

Wow! That kite's flying really high!

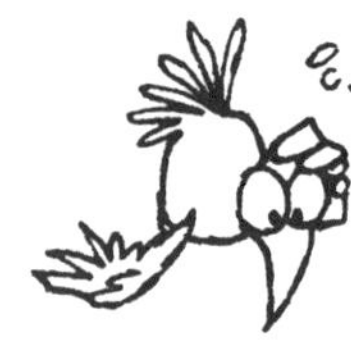

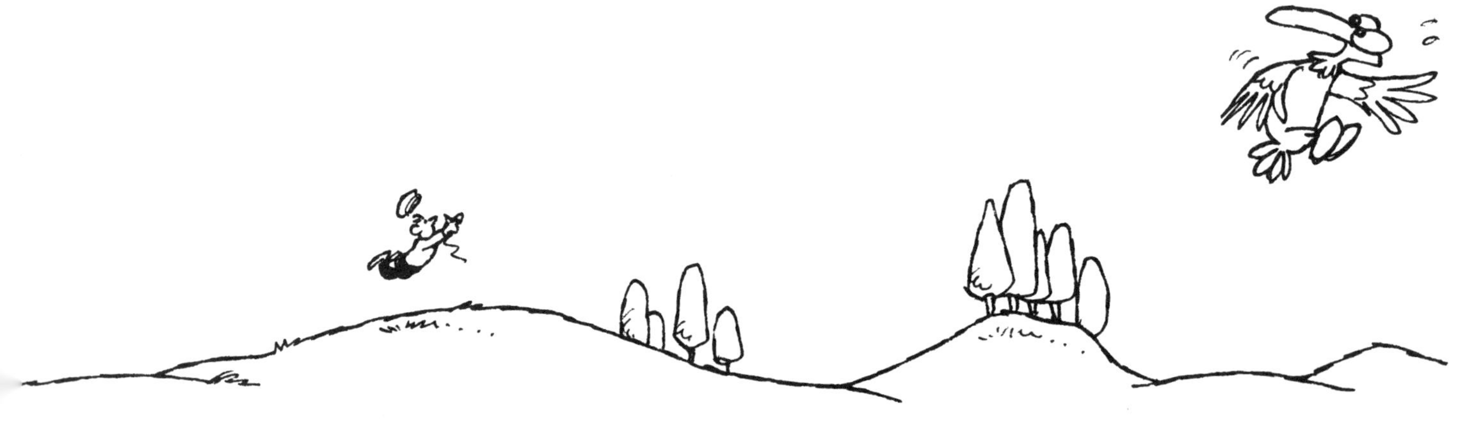

The flowers are blooming

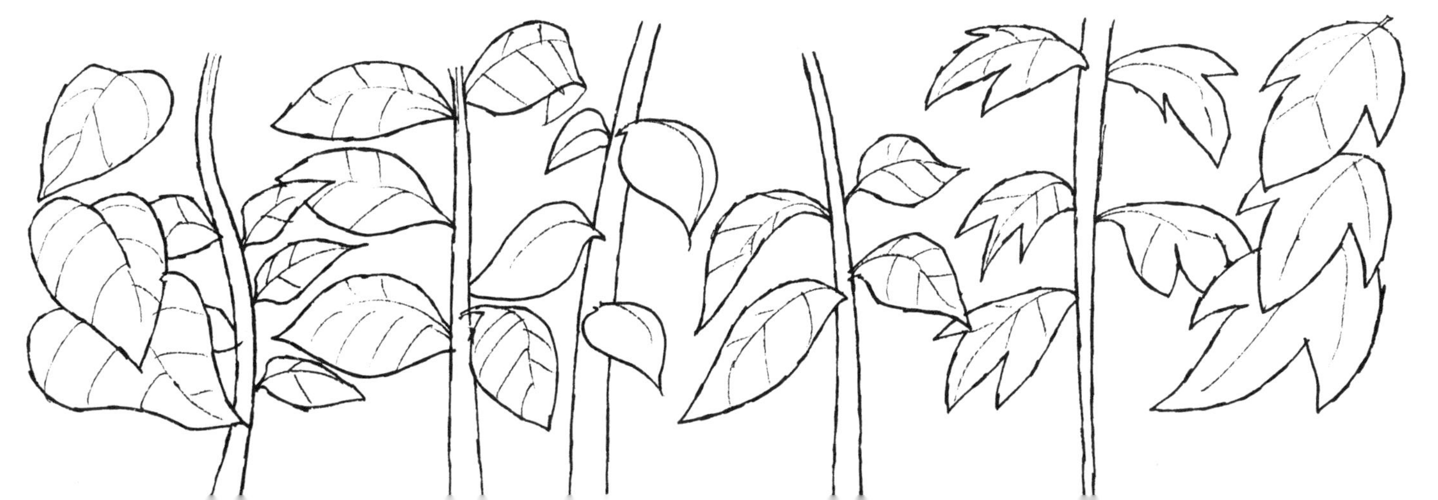

Seaside boards are loads of fun

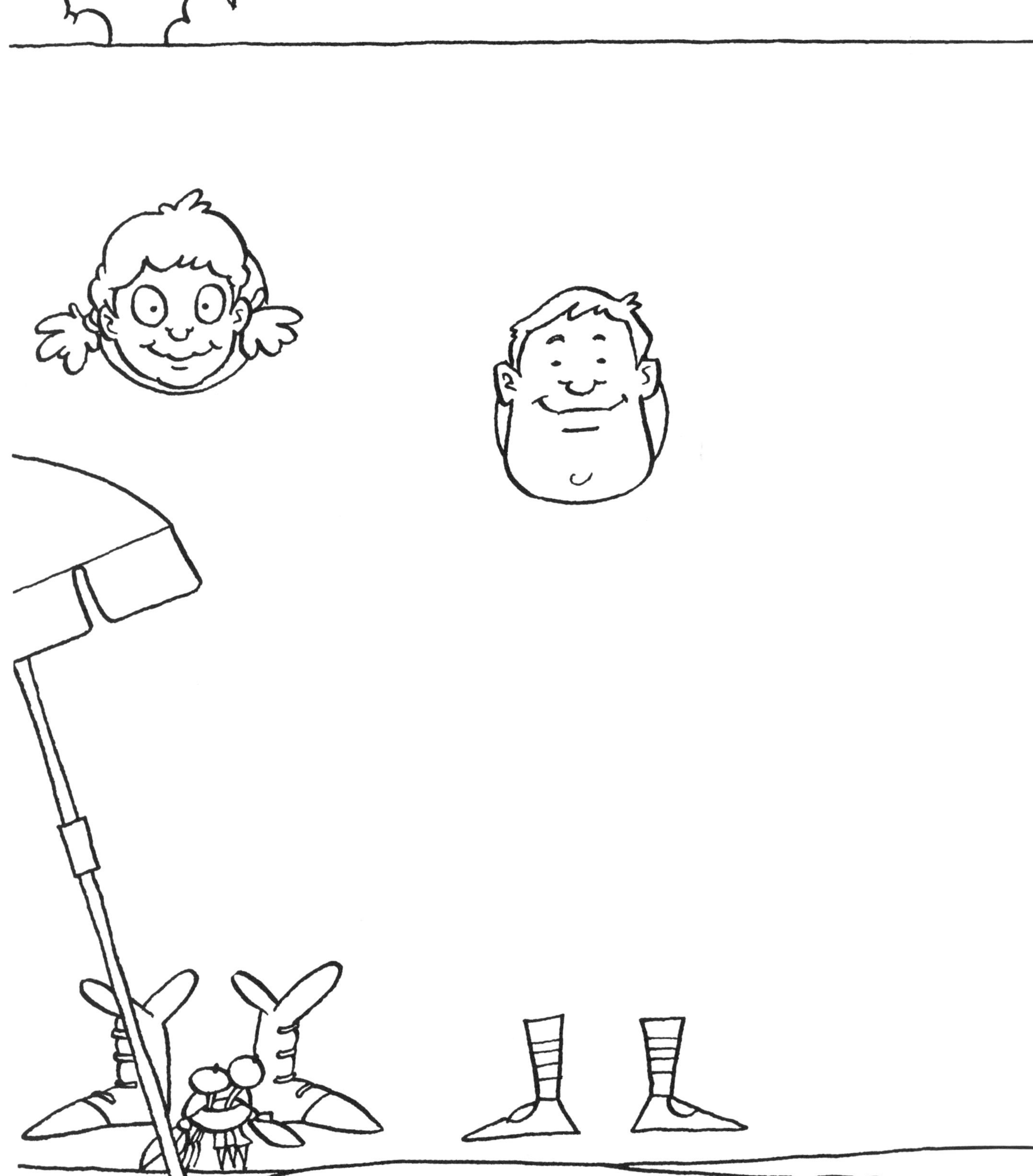

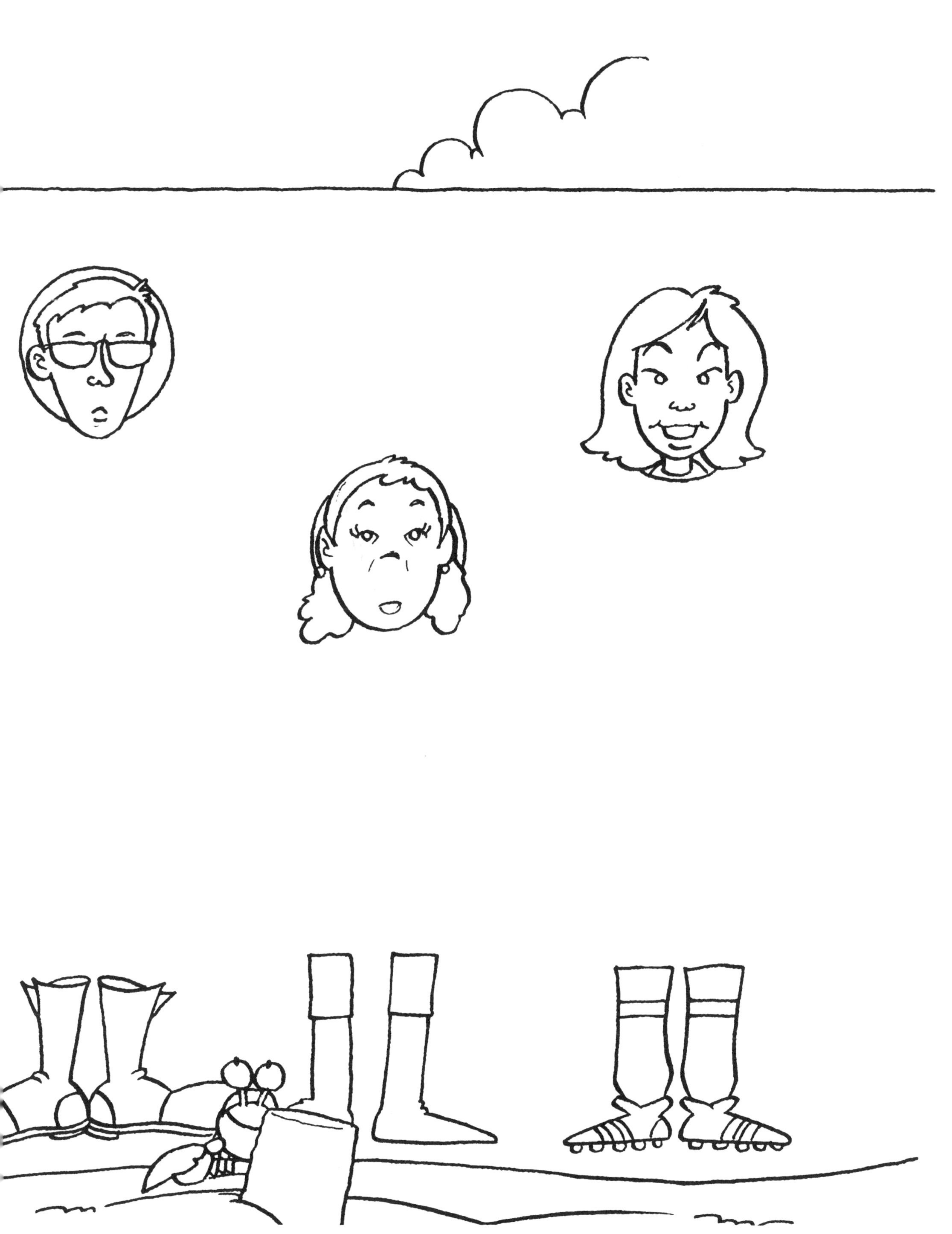

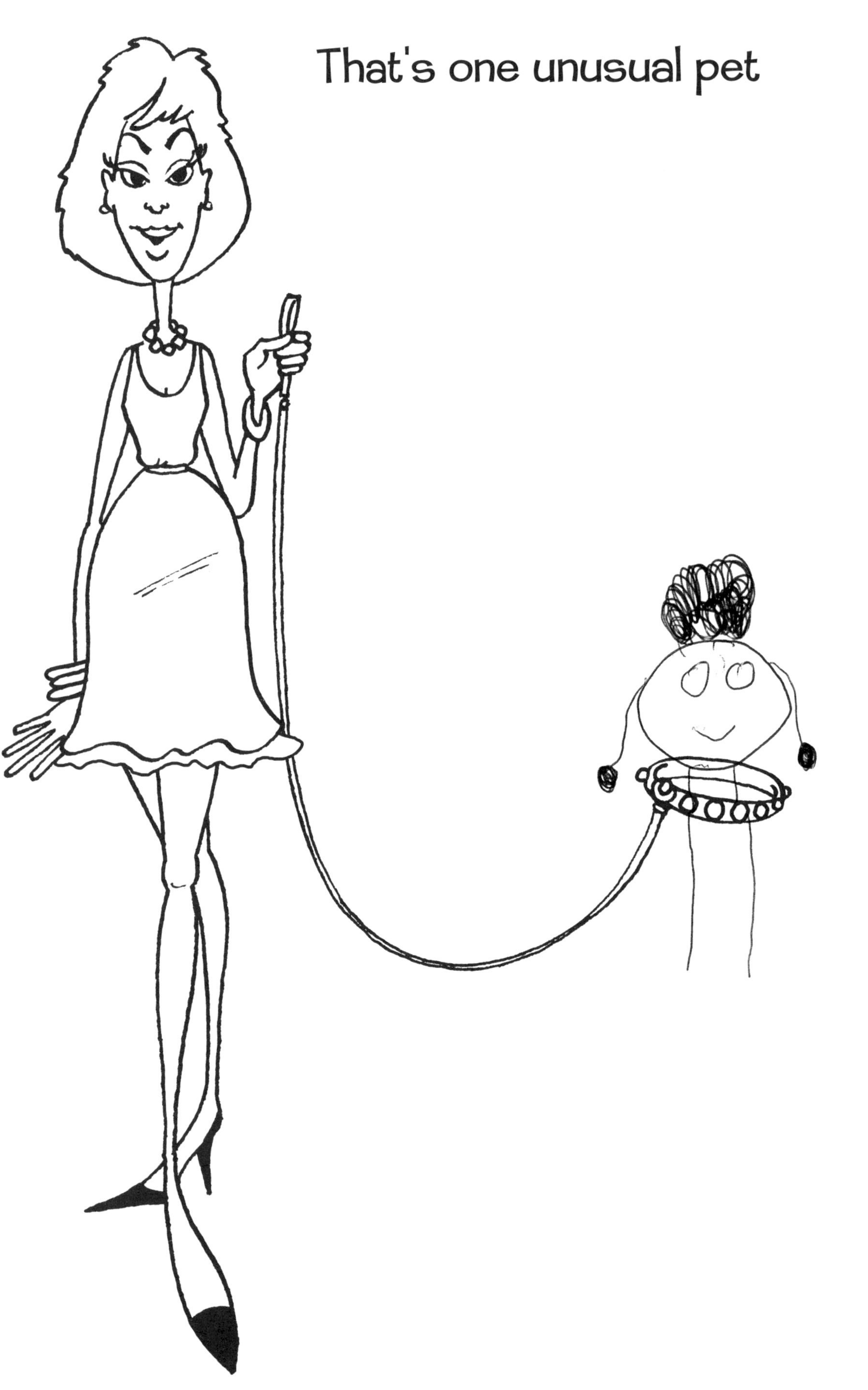

That's one unusual pet

Give the winning car its winning colors

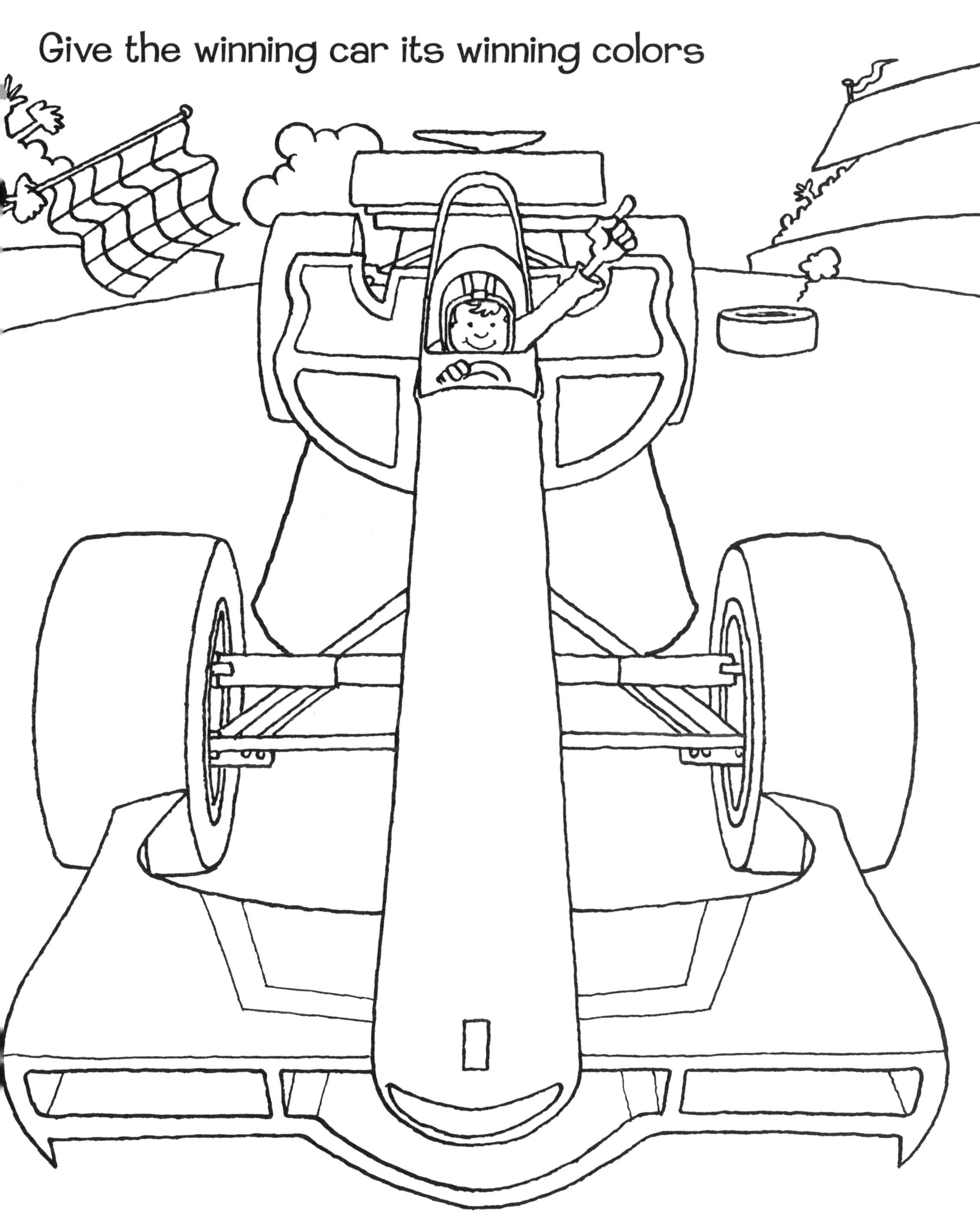

Rainbows are a funny color on planet Xoobublu

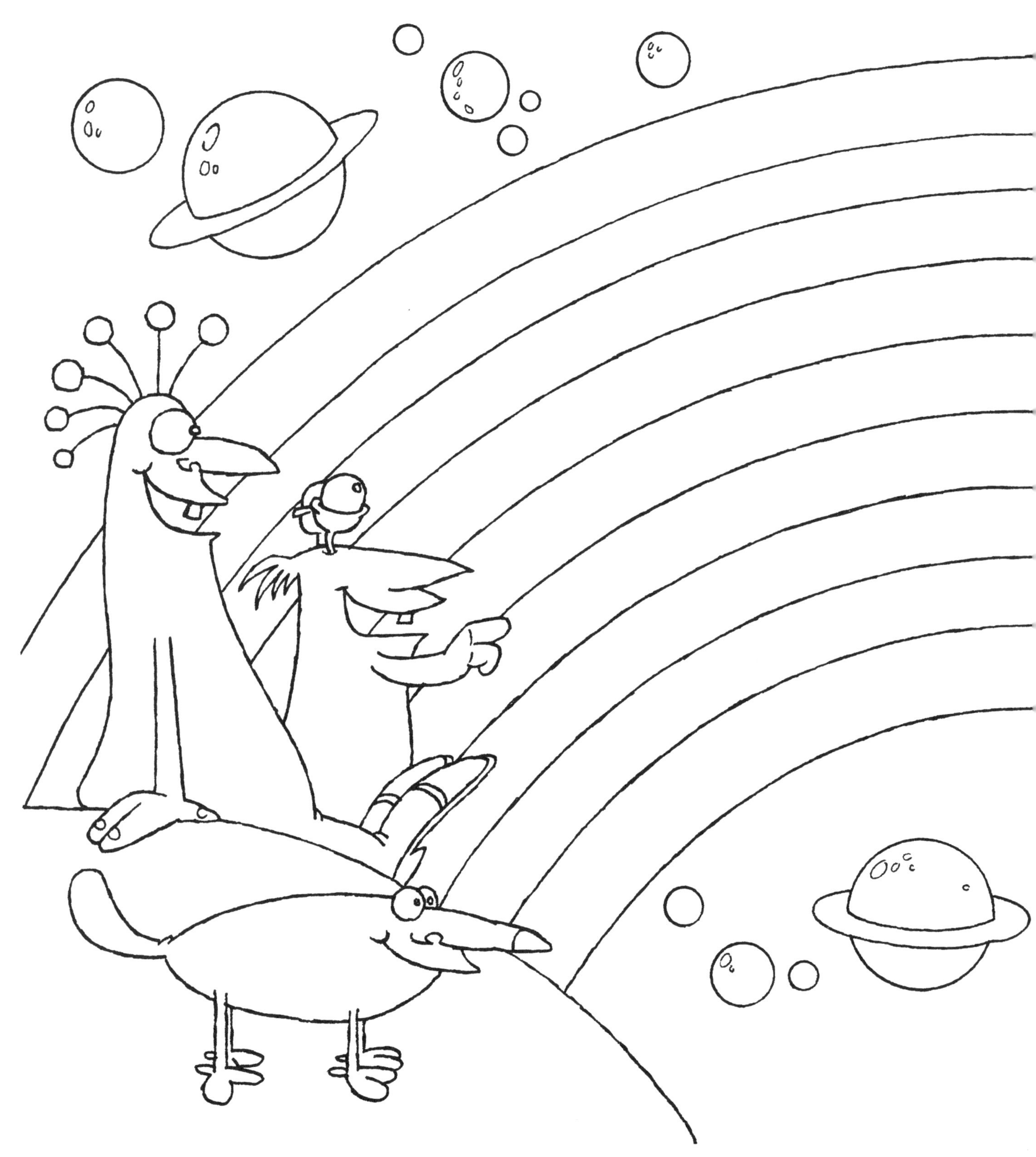

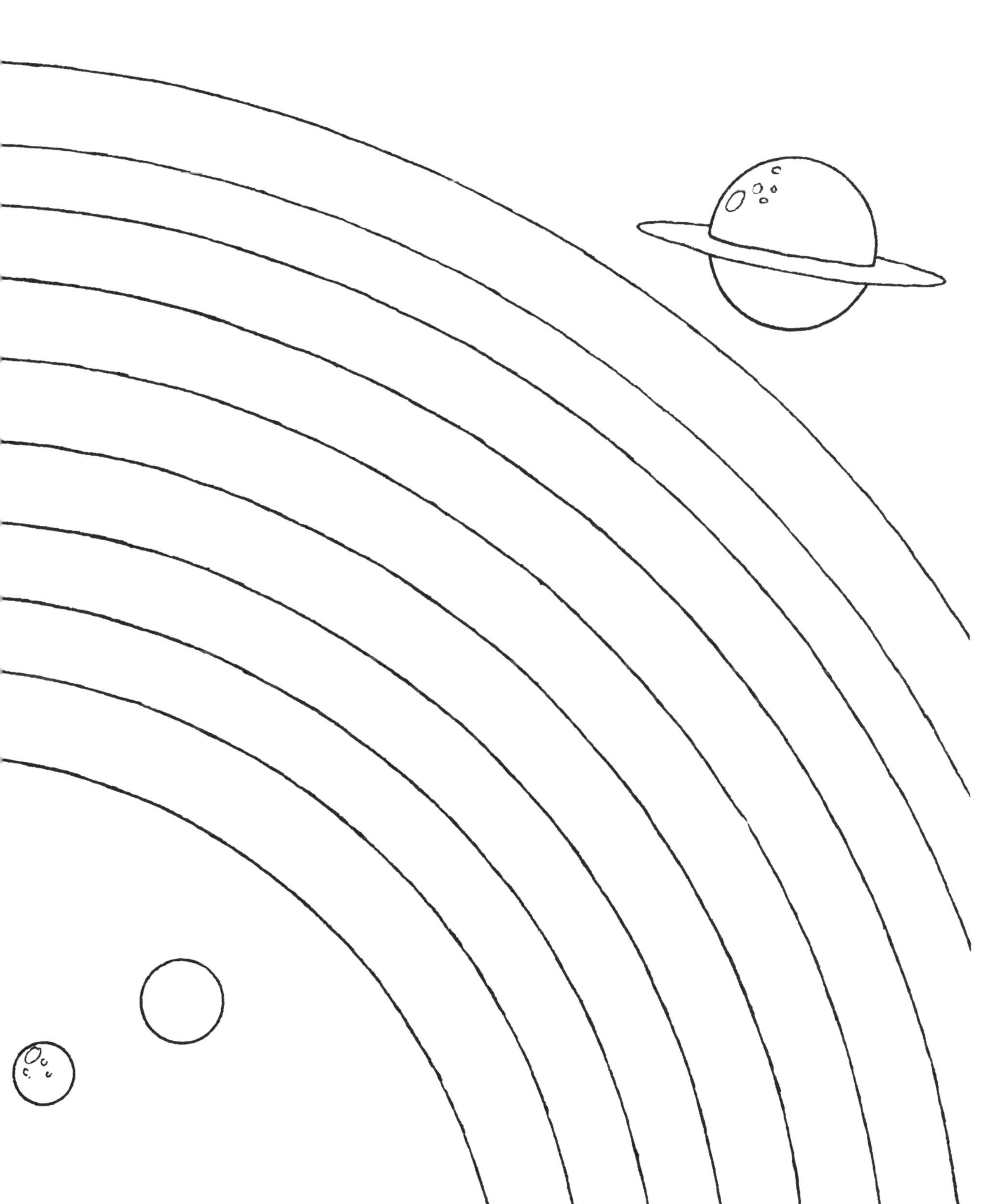

Show how Cam the chameleon is feeling today

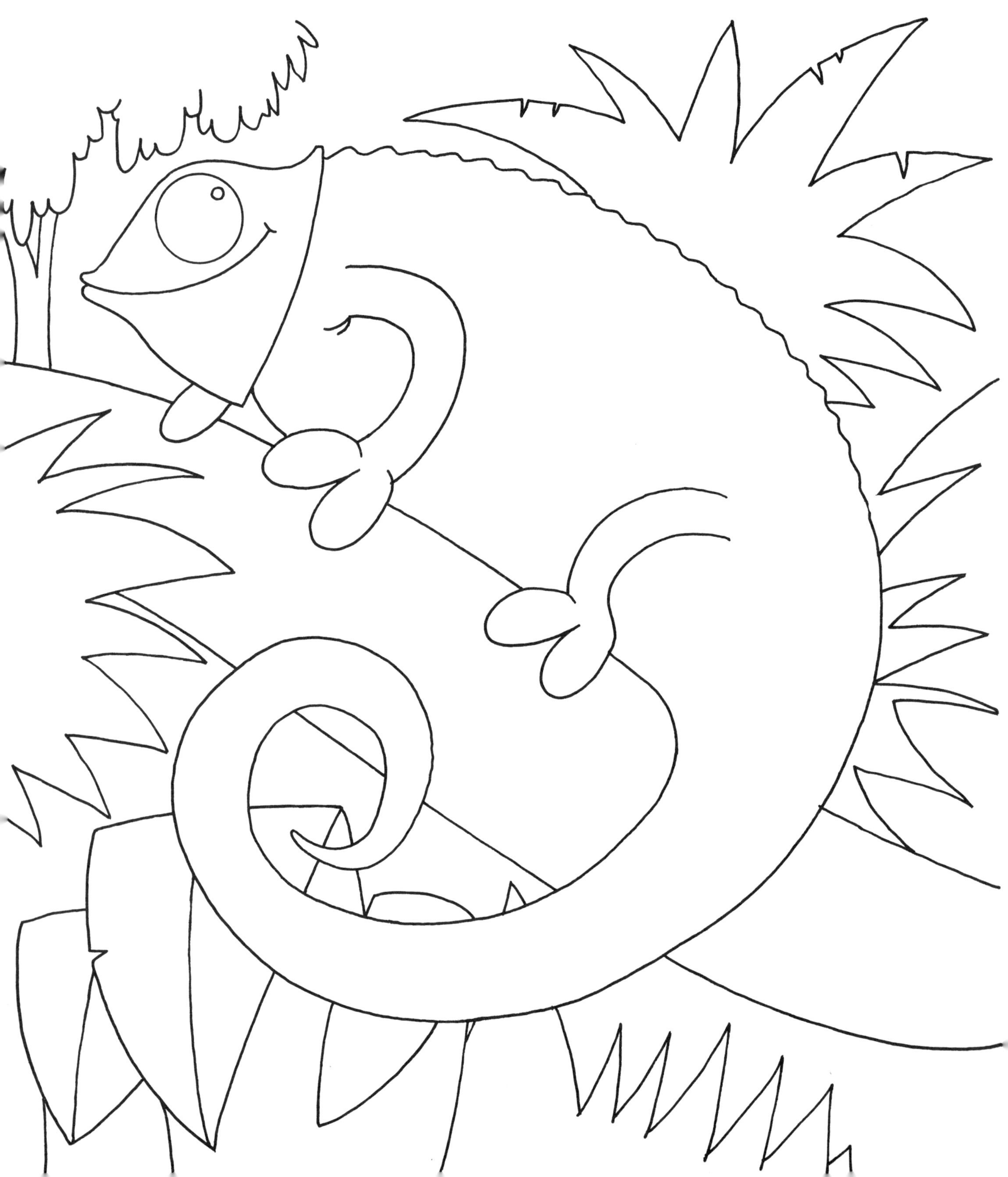

Give the pilots their controls...quickly!

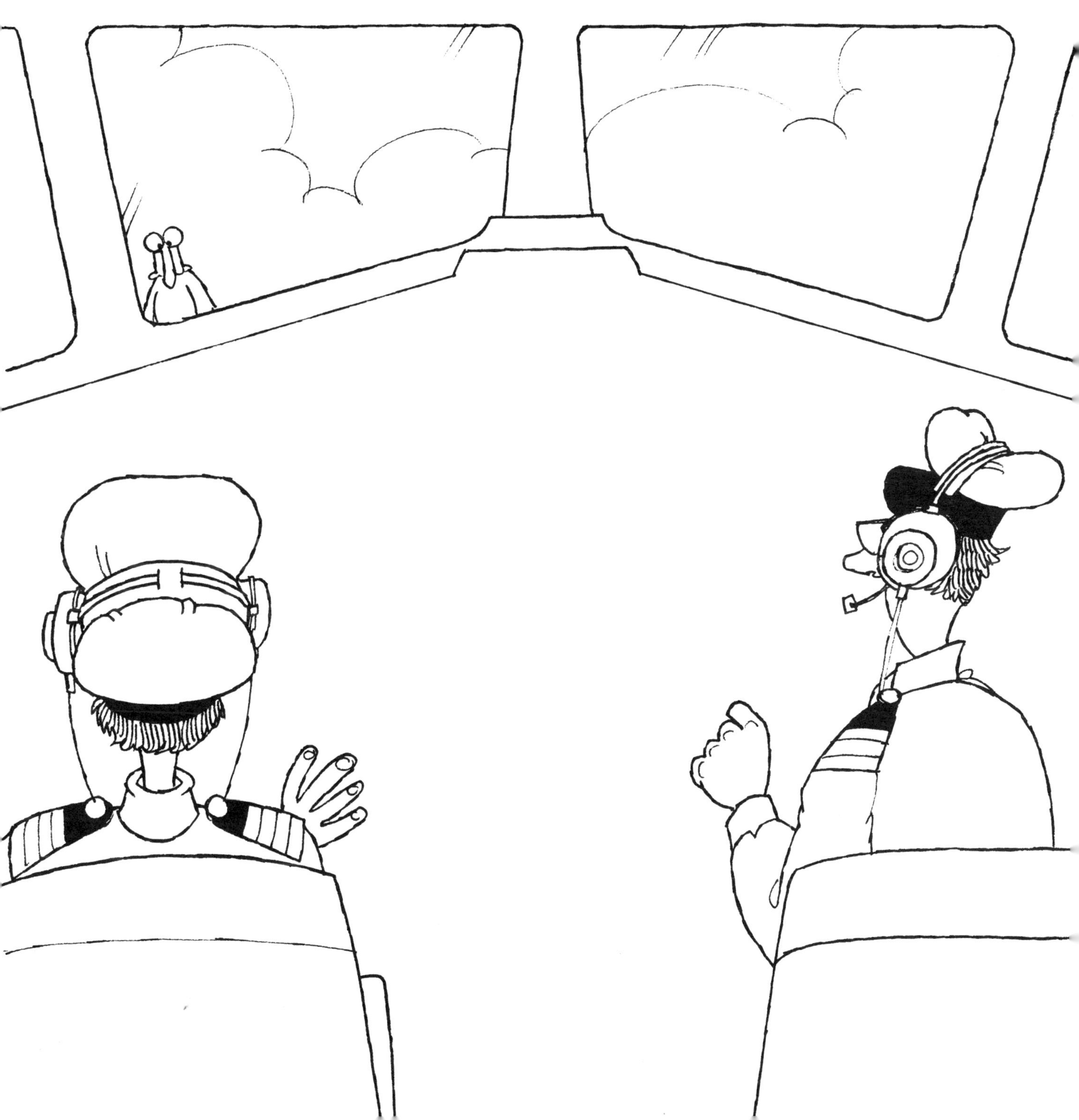

What else is hiding in the garden?

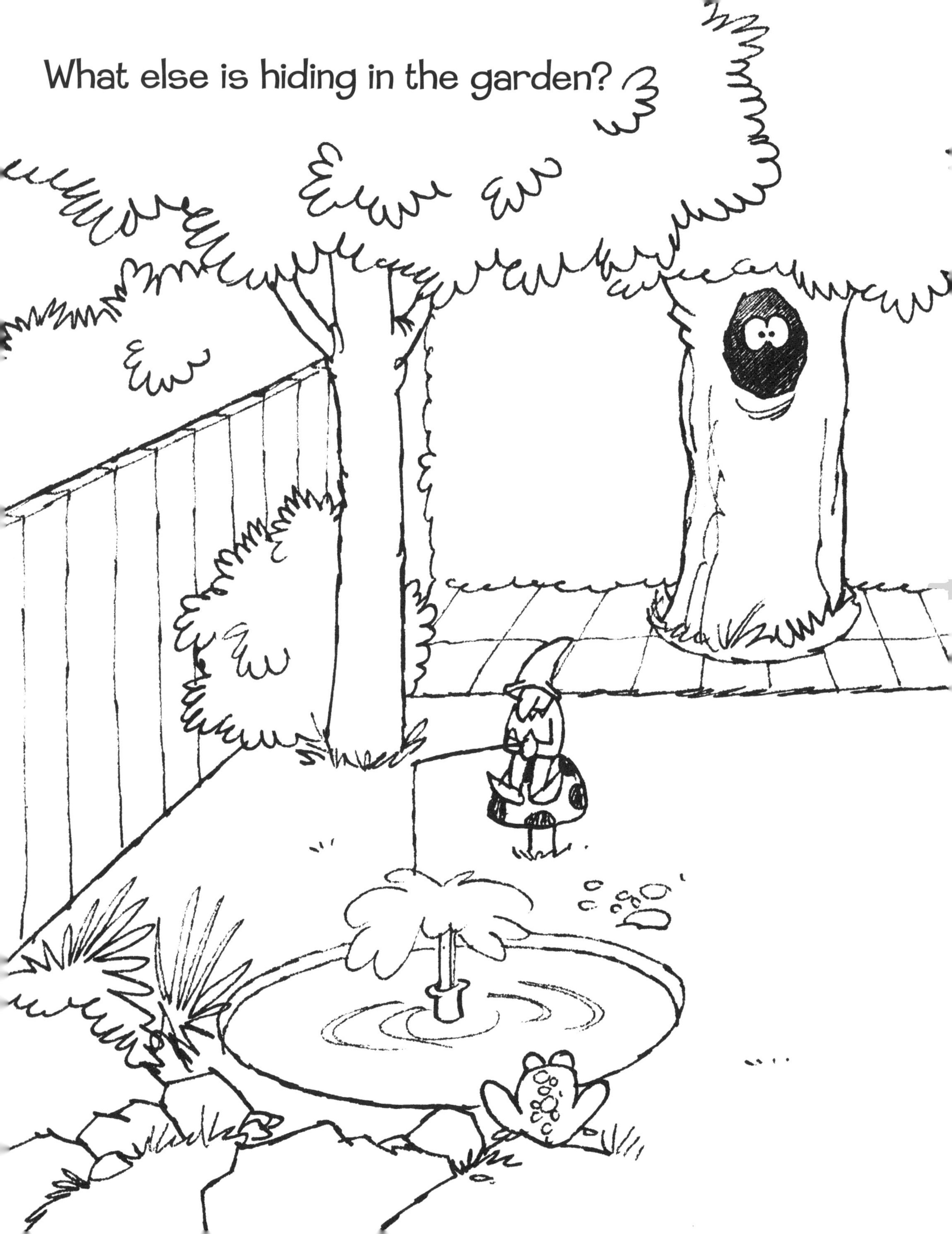

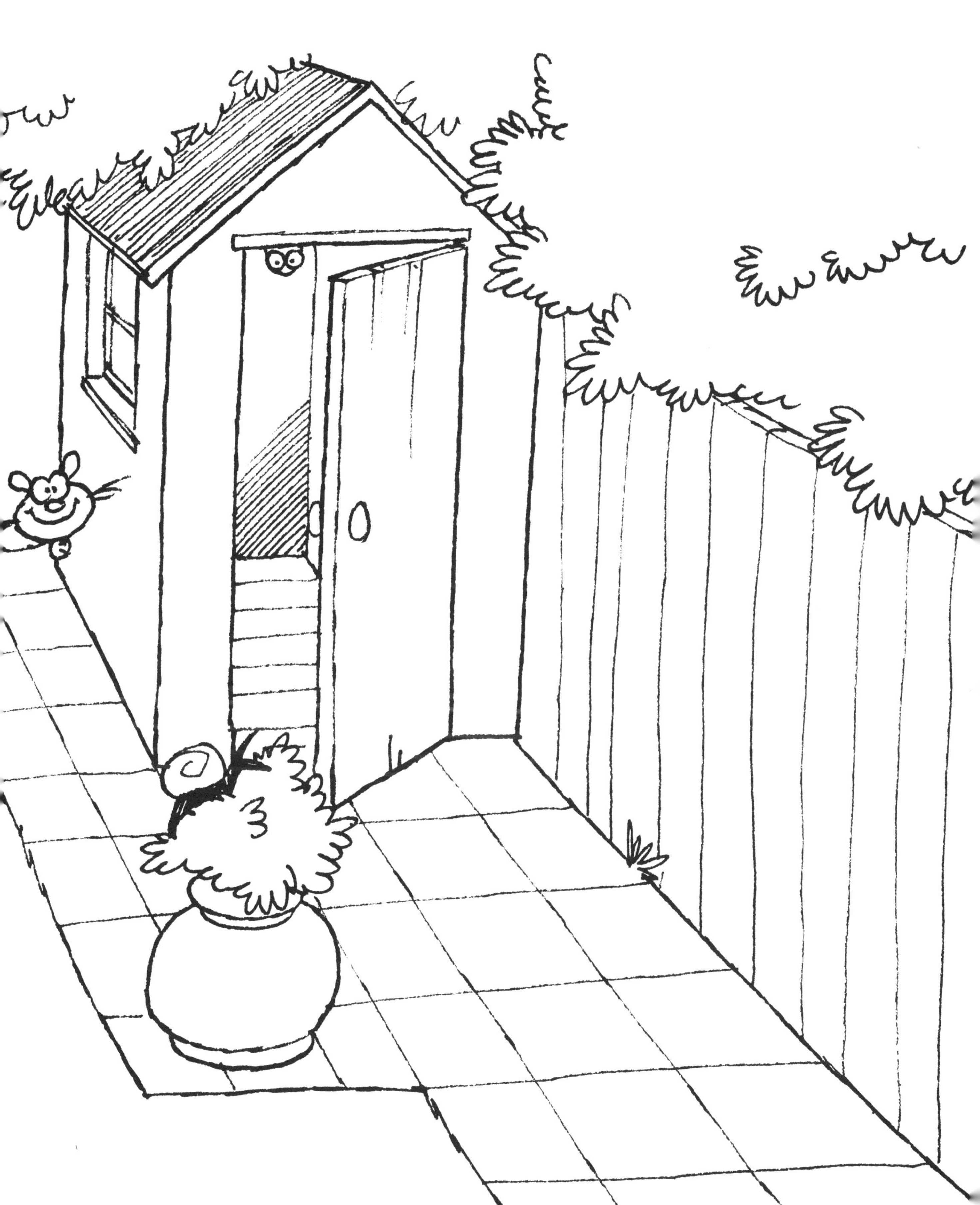

Add the rest of the vampire family

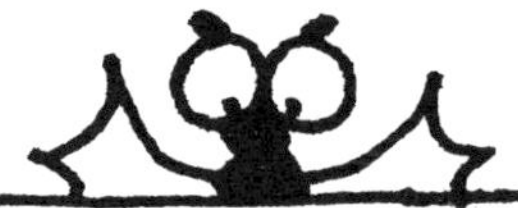

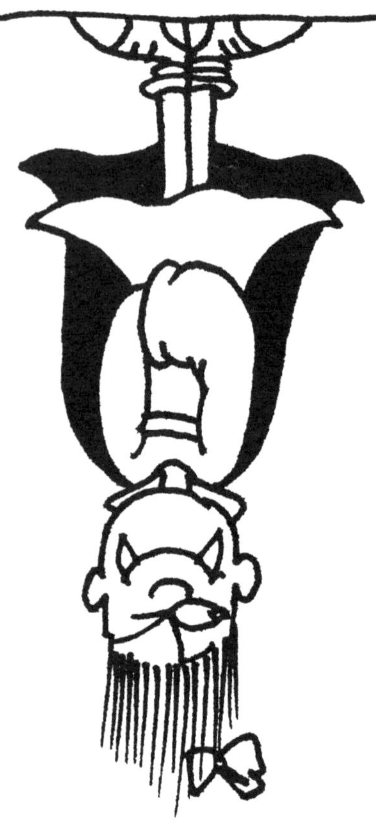

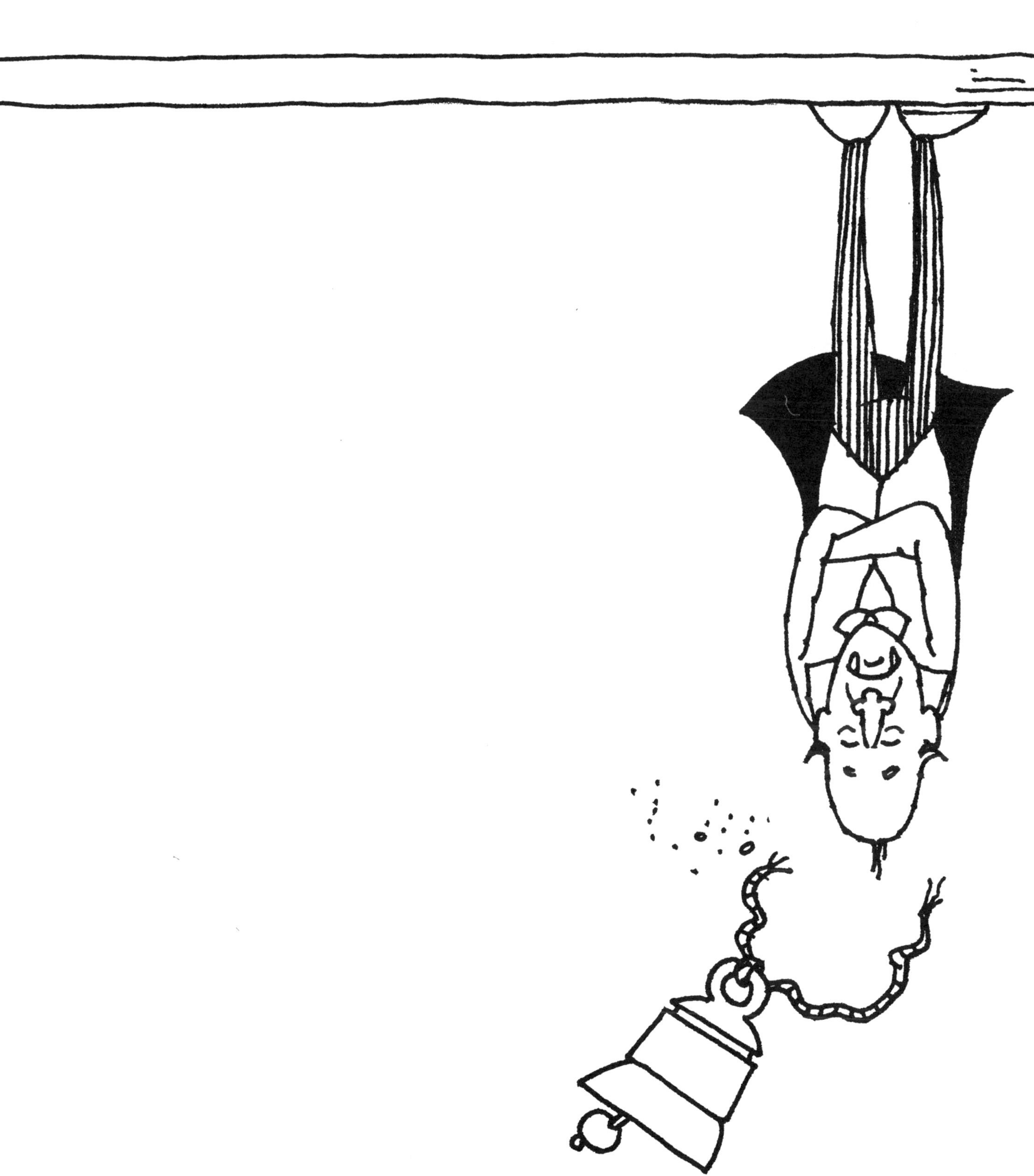

Number 3 is looking guilty

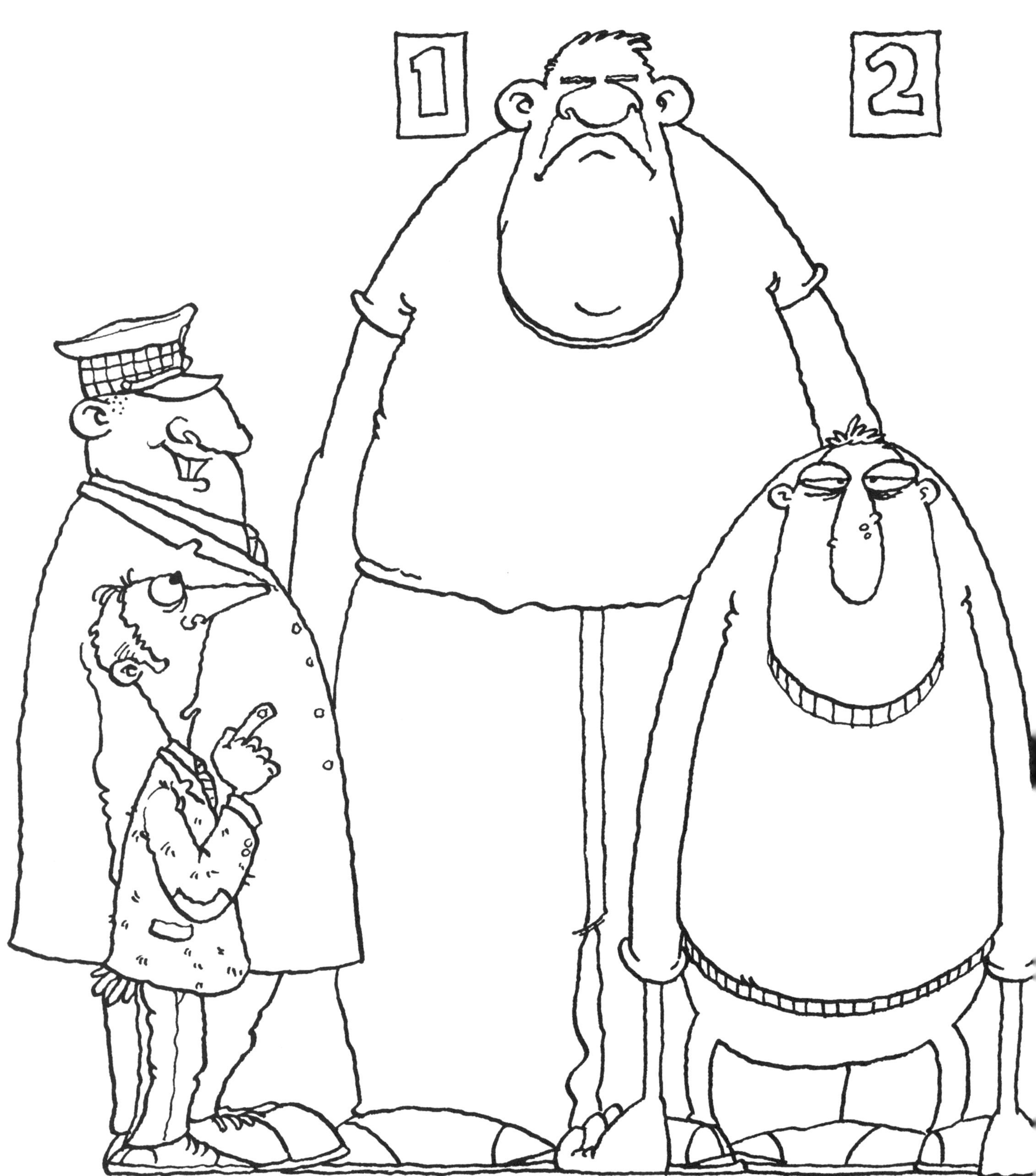

3

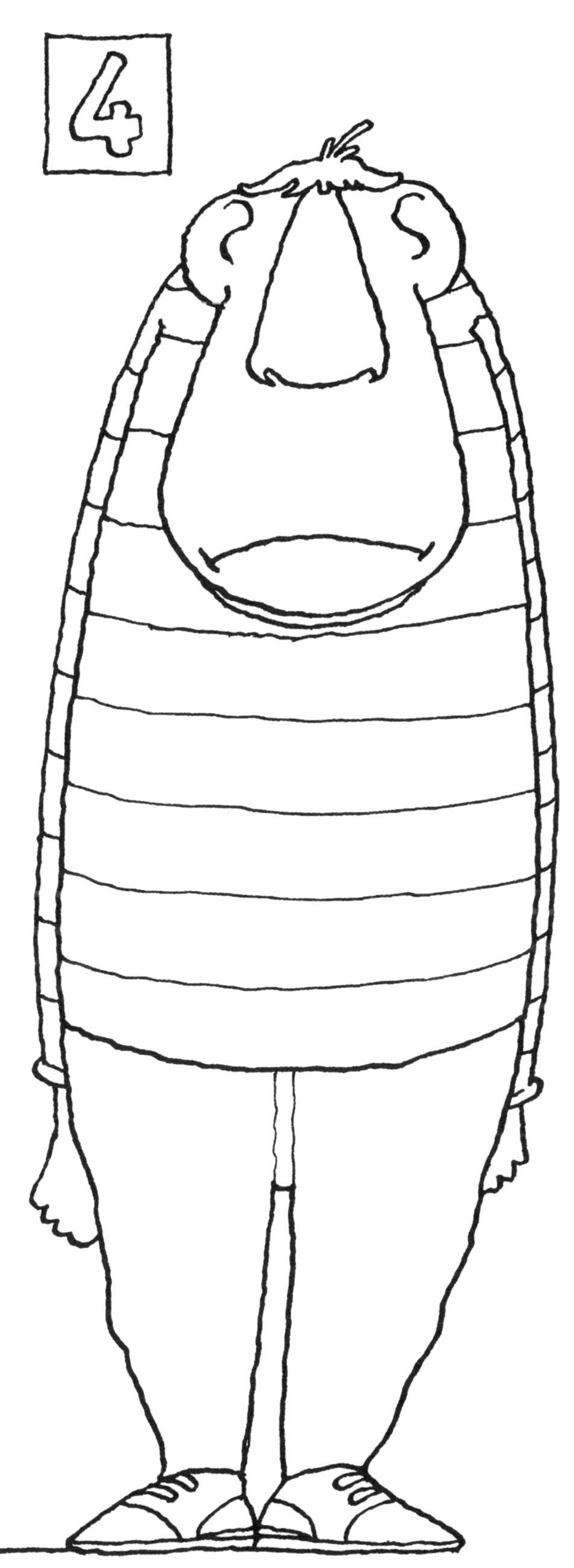

Leo's just painted a masterpiece

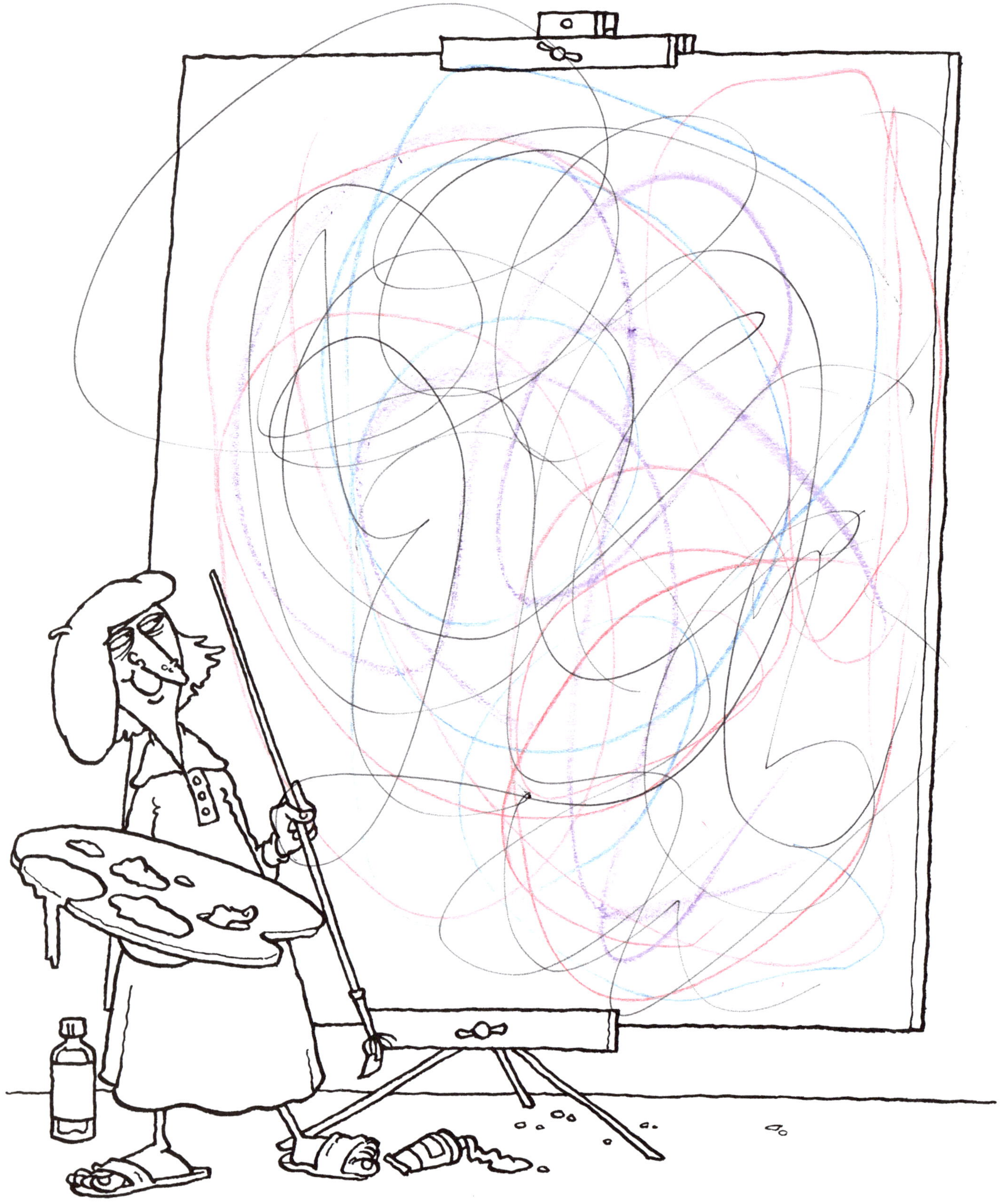

Eureka! What a fantastic creation!

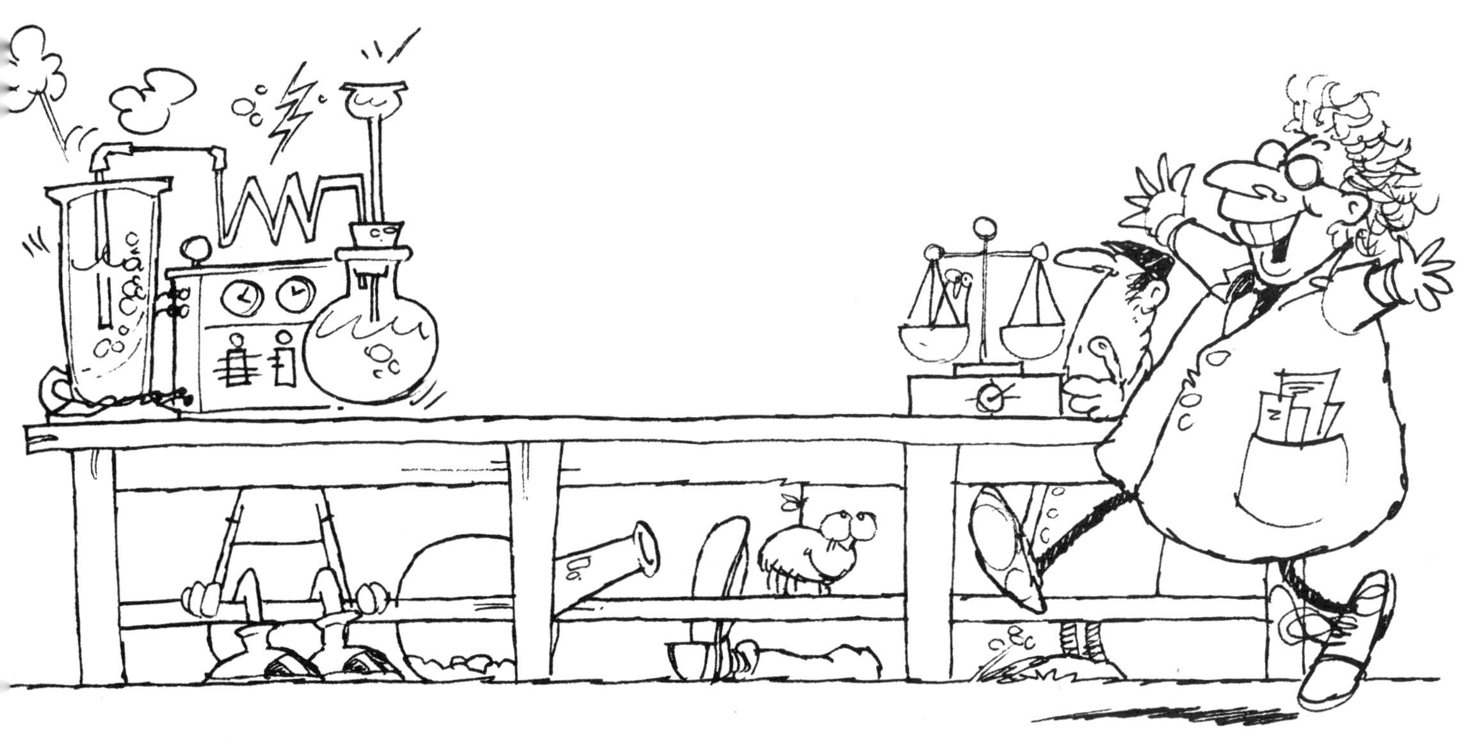

What's been eating Farmer Joe's vegetables?

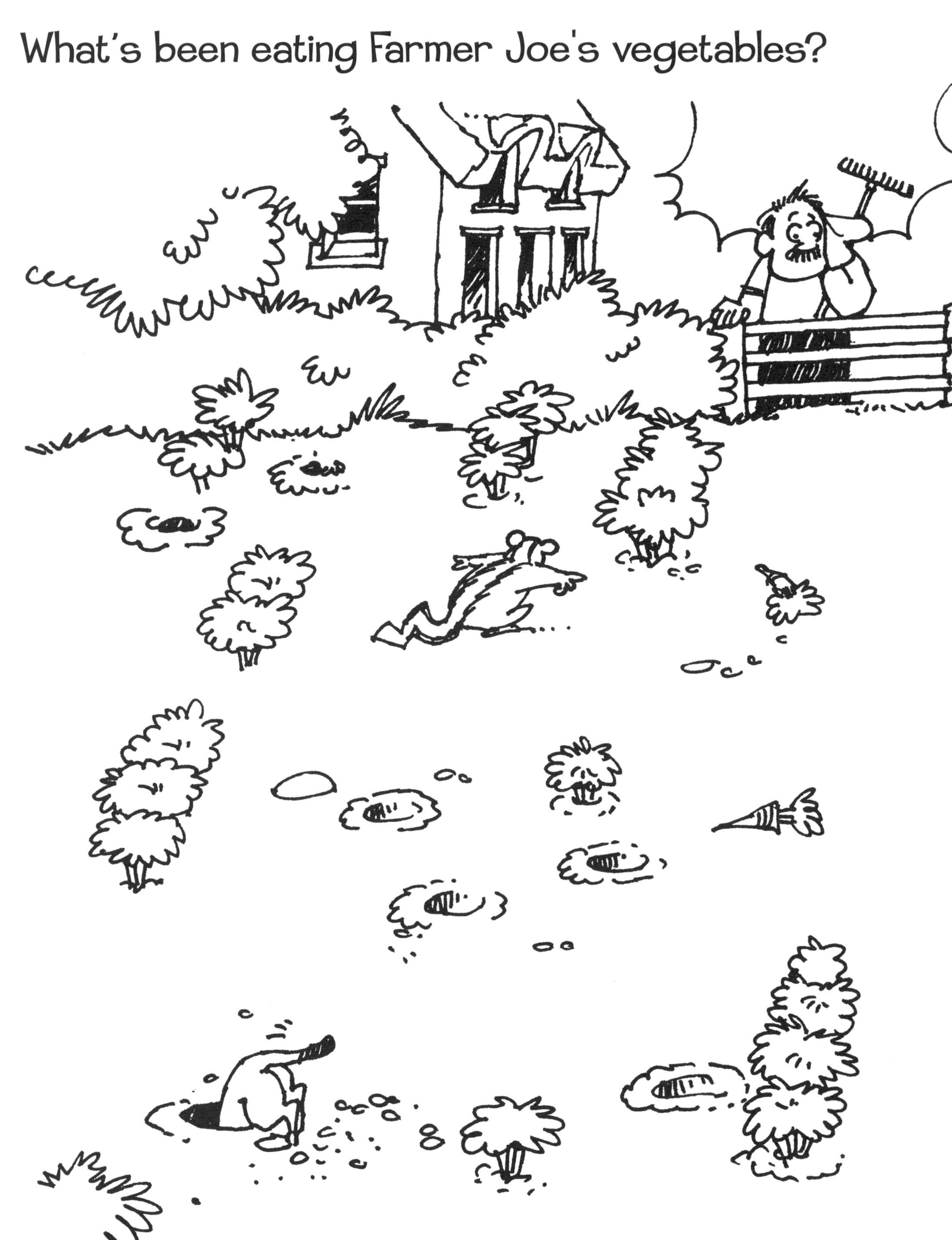

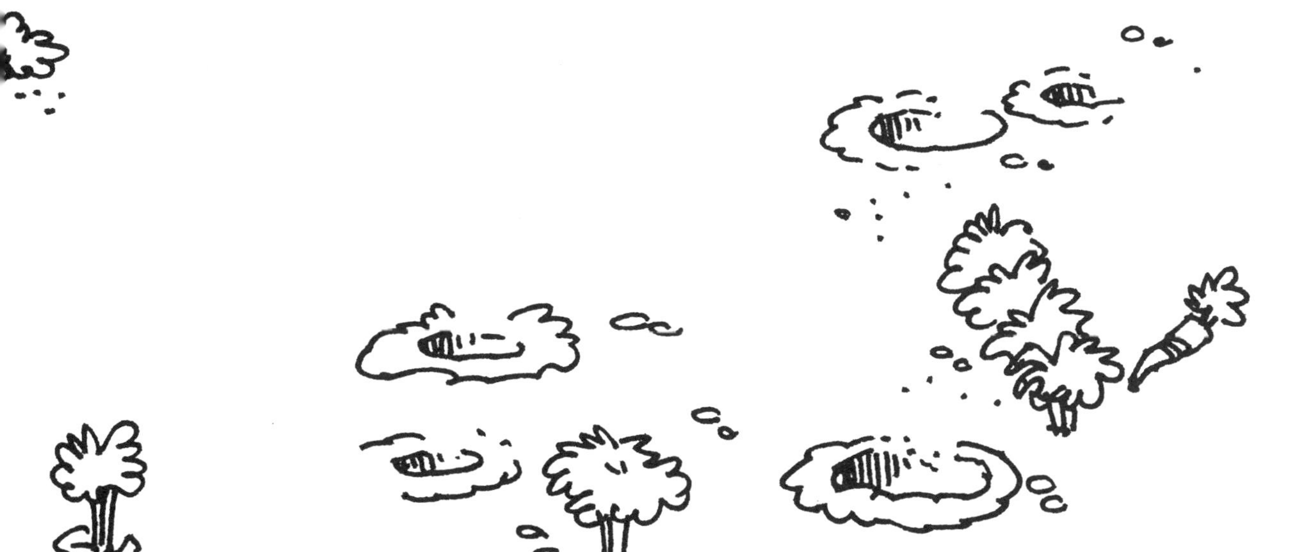

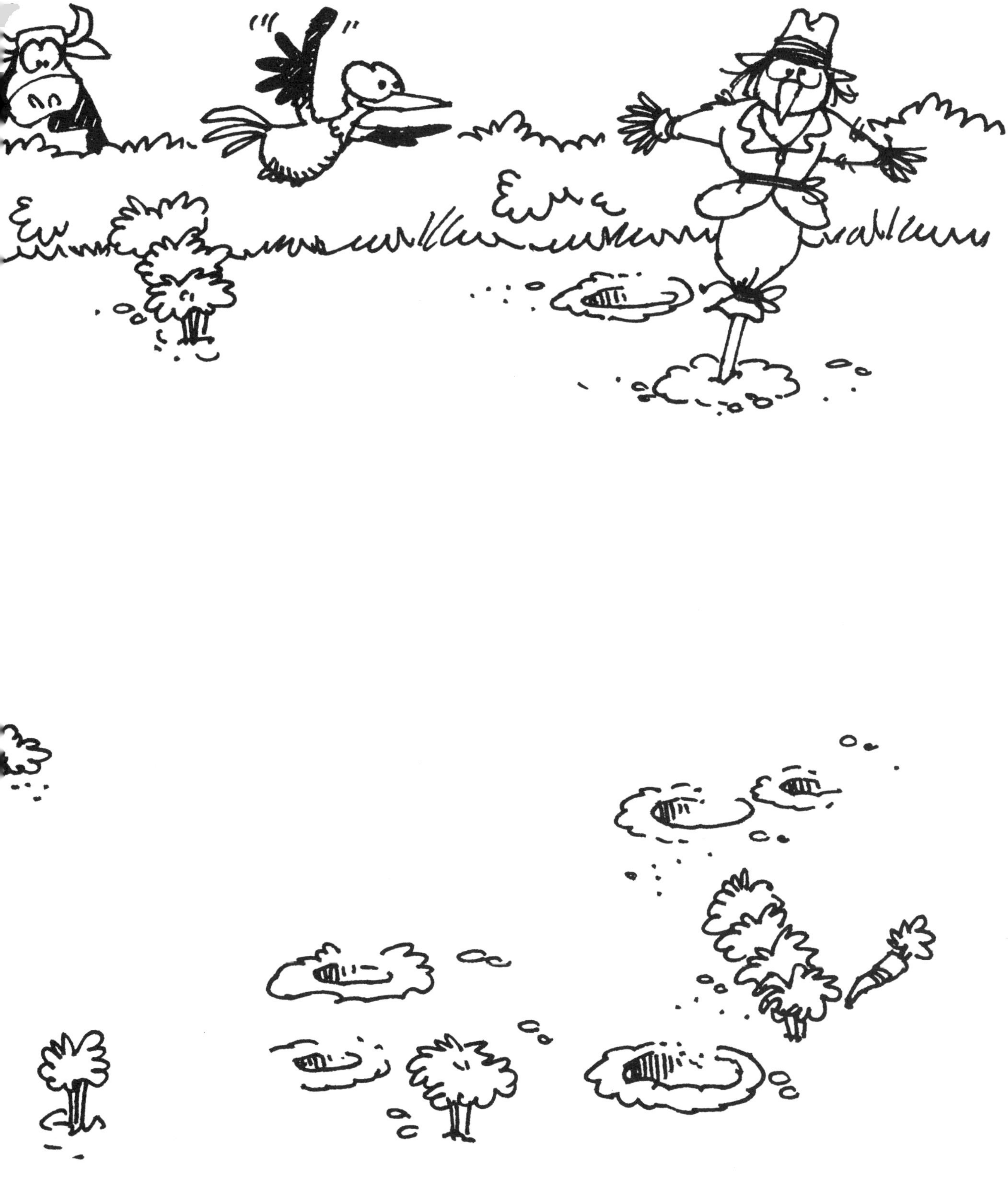

The Ugliest Dog Competition

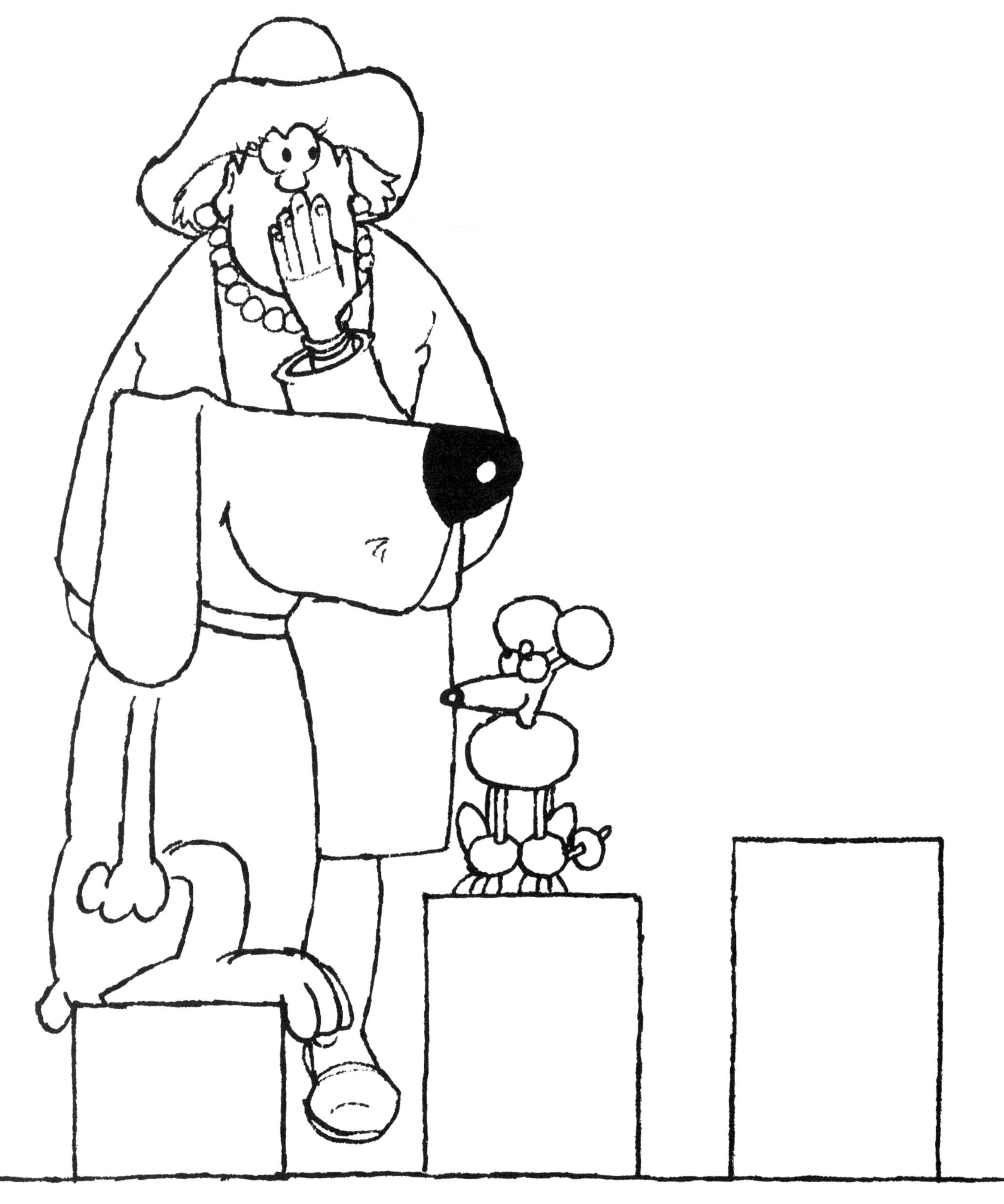

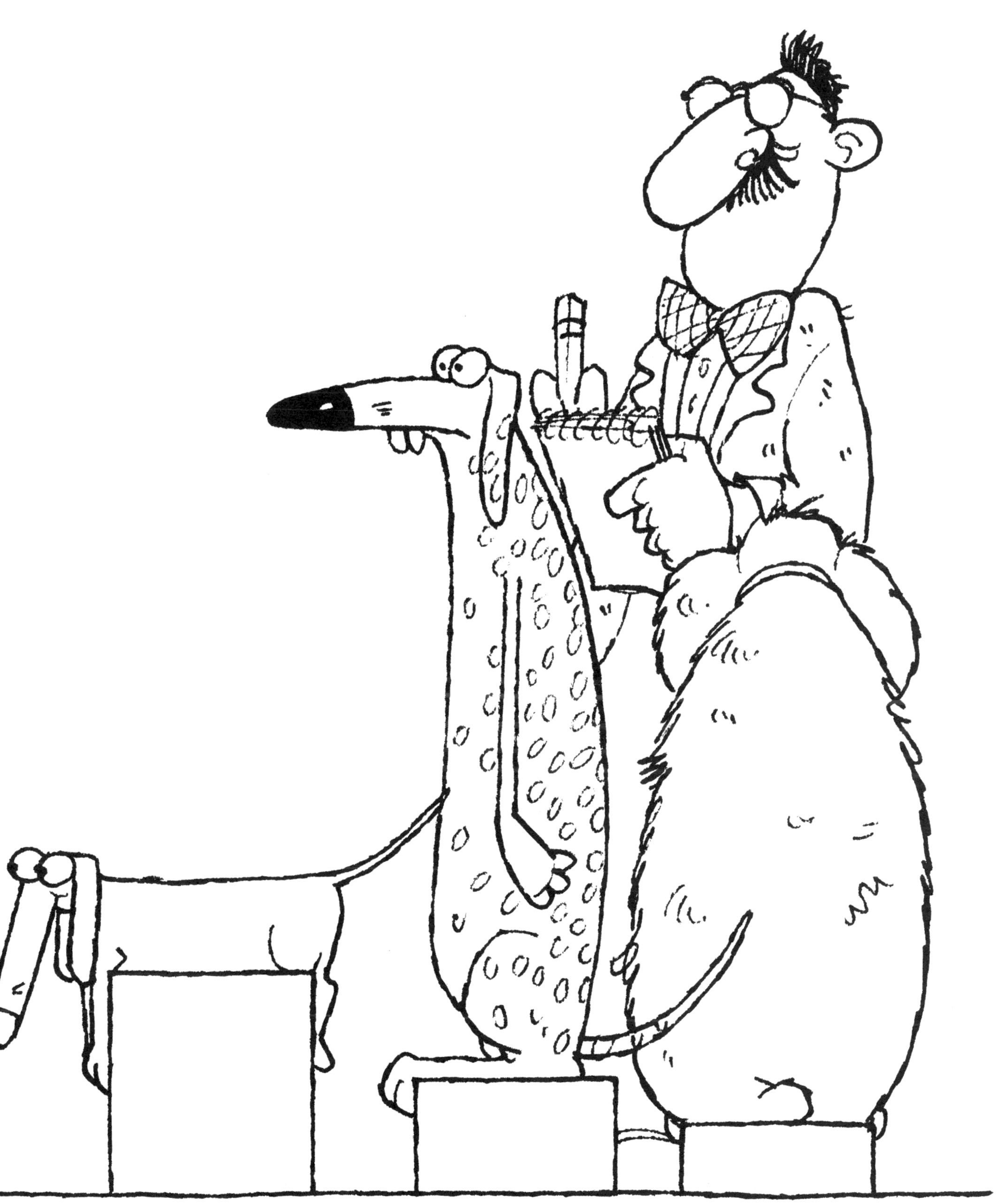

What do garden gnomes like to chat about?

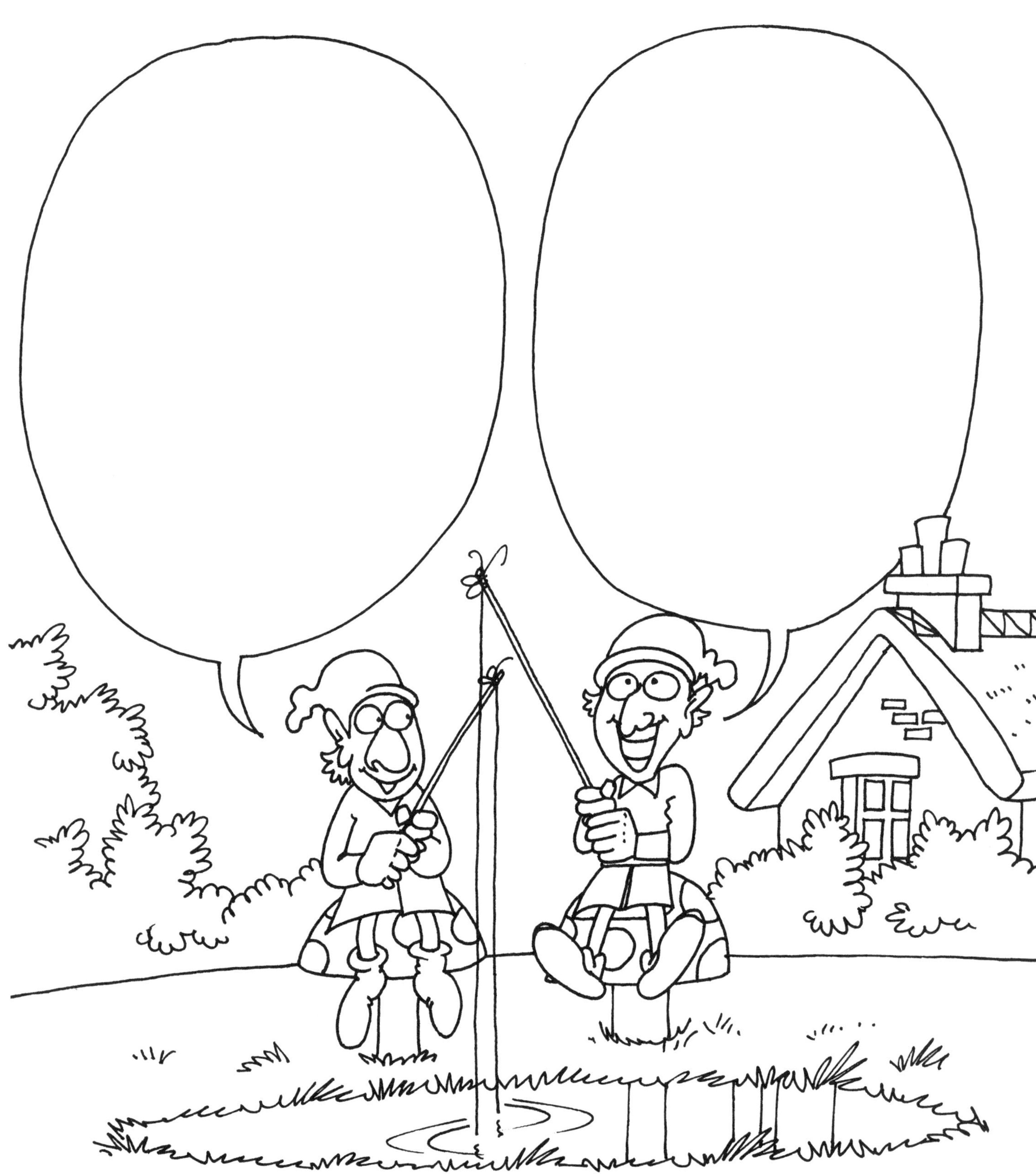

There's a monster in the closet!

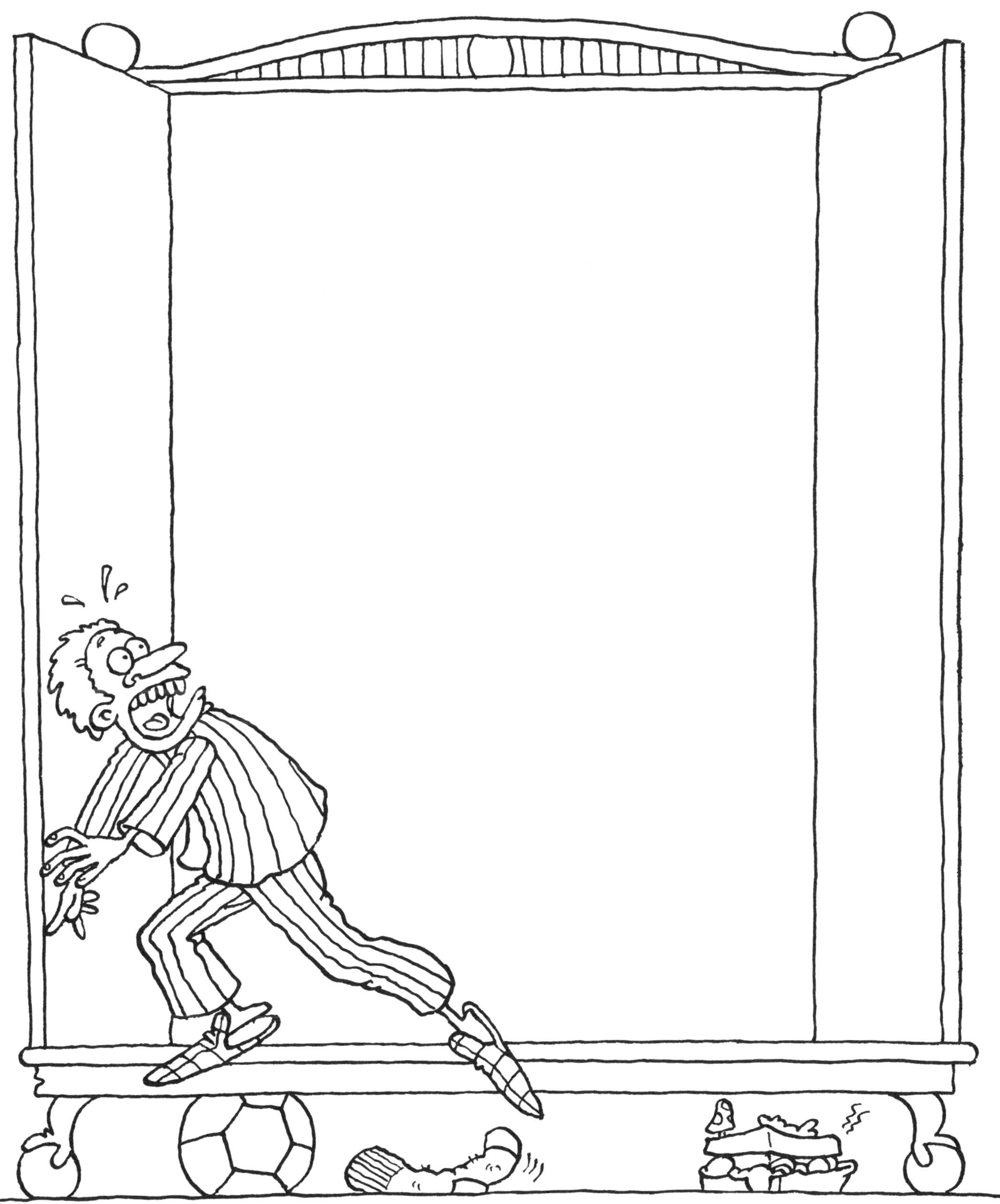

Where do these steps lead to?

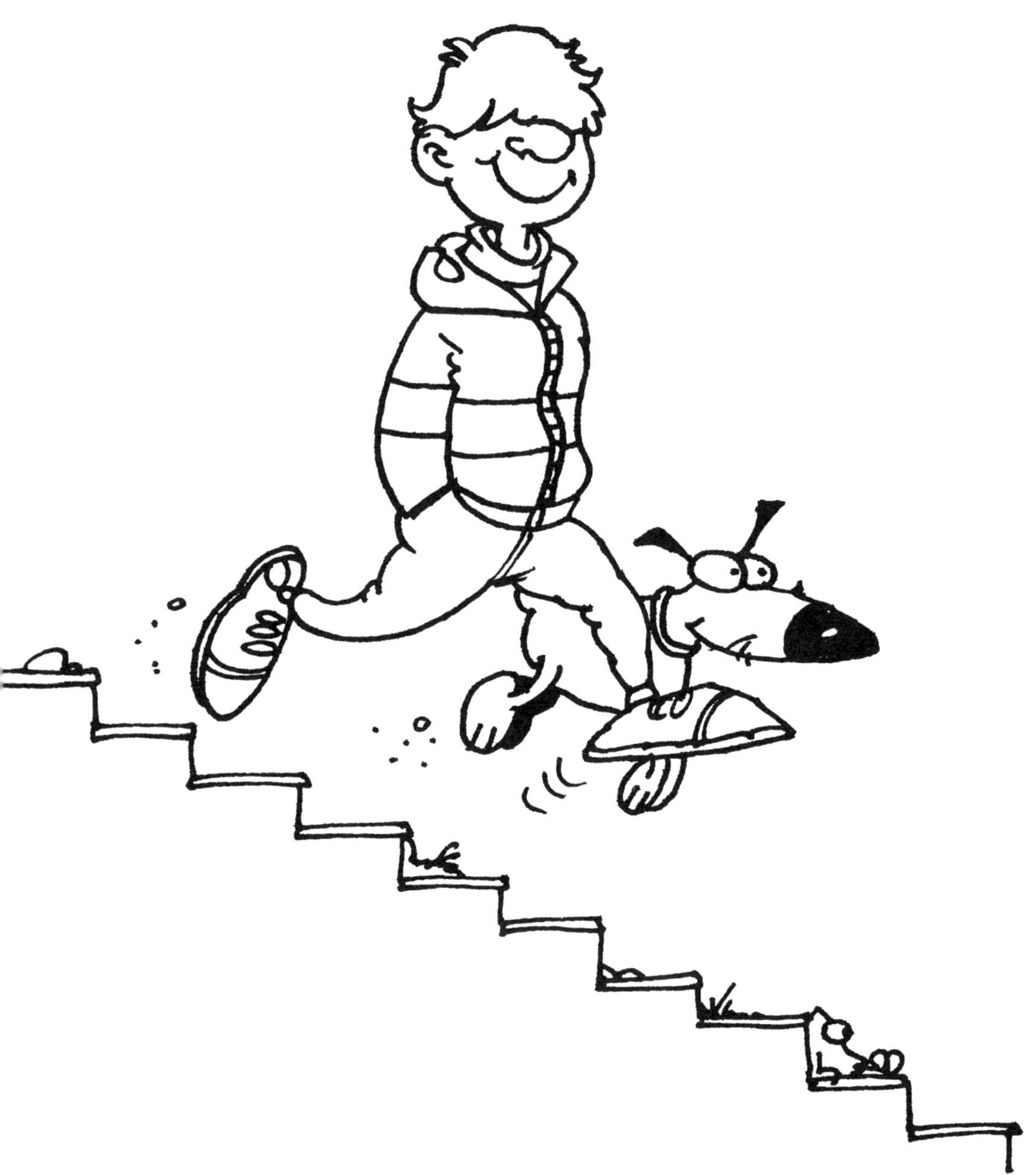

The neighborhood of the future

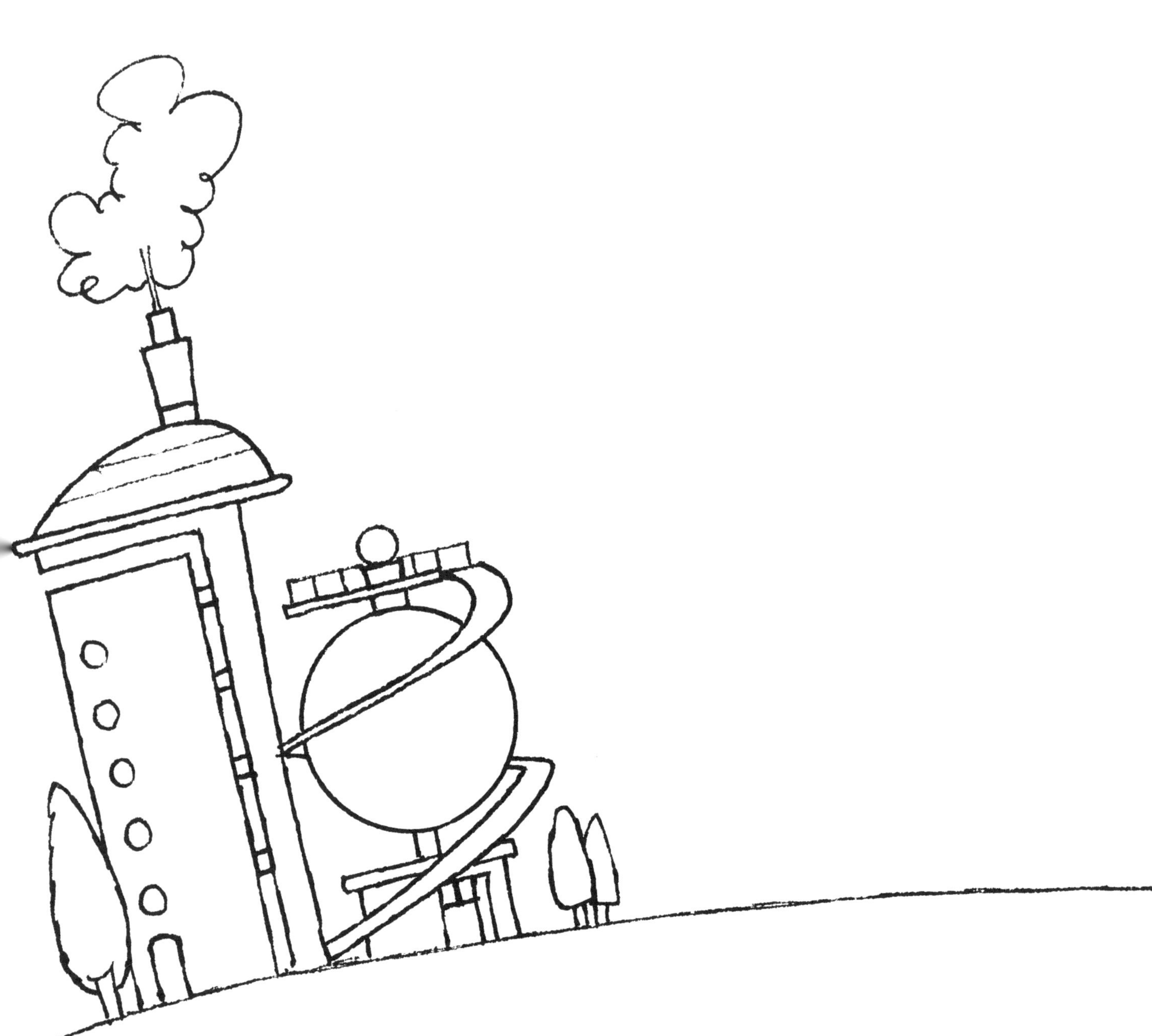

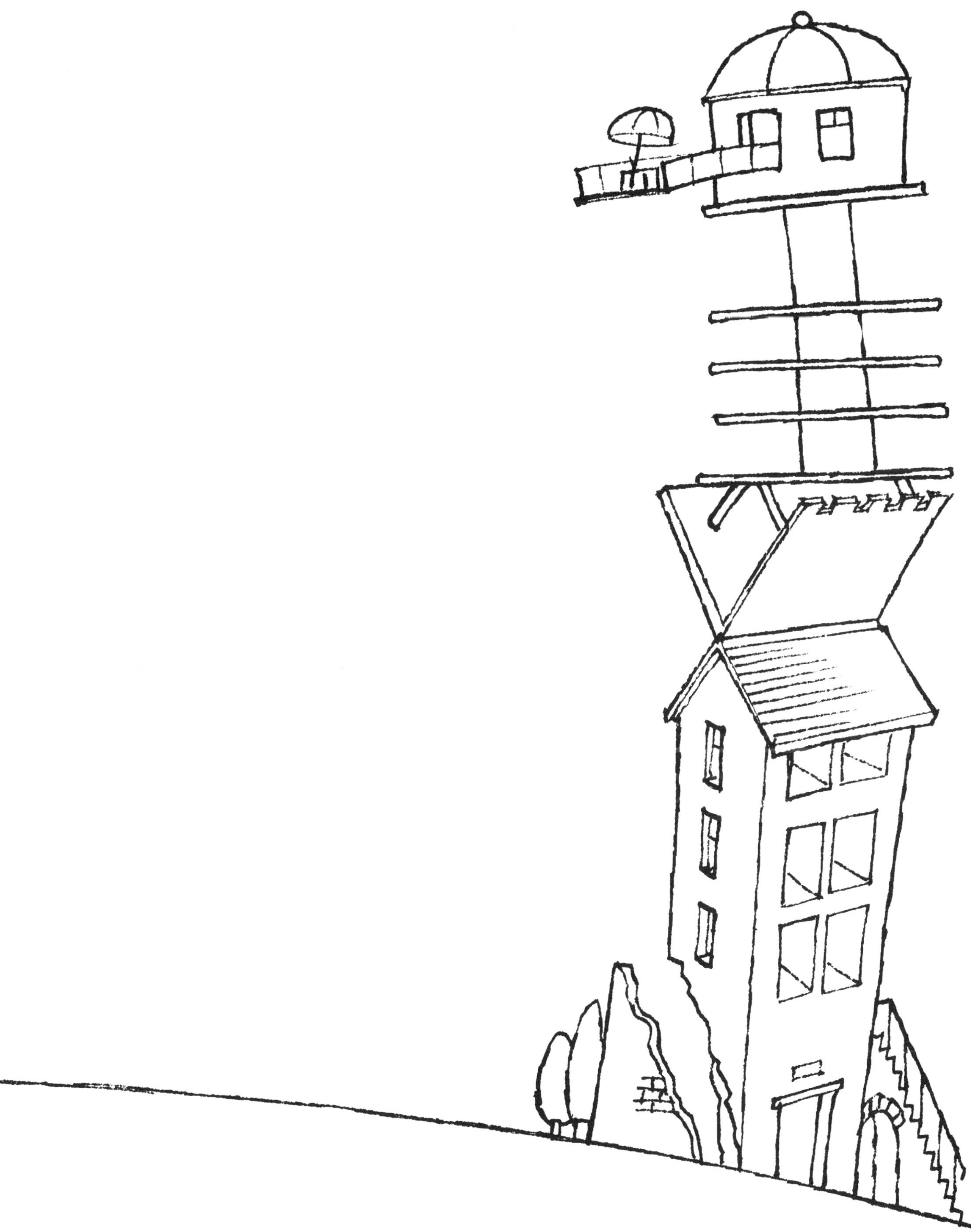

Who's your sweetheart?

Felix hates those mismatched curtains

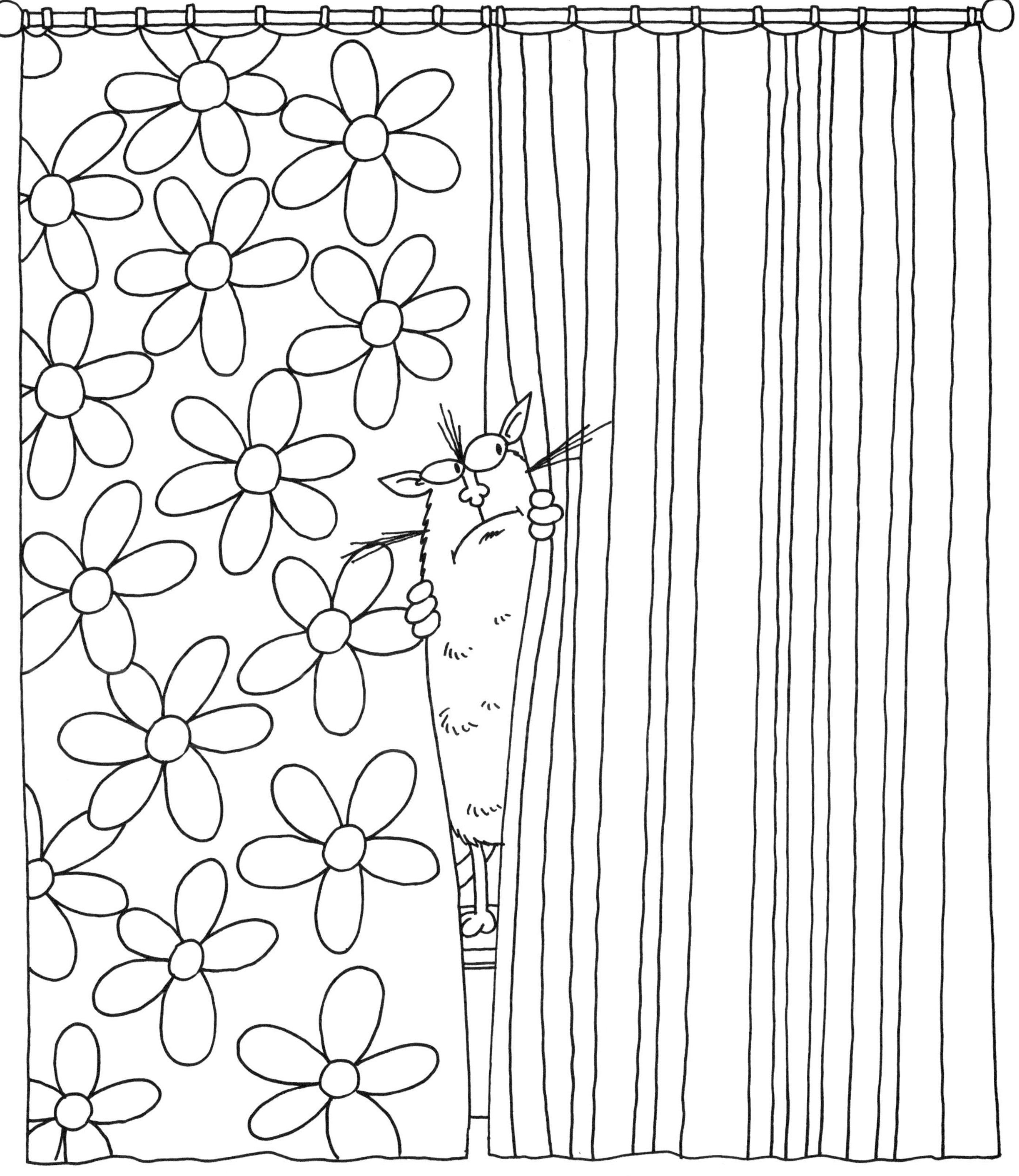

Mixed up markings!

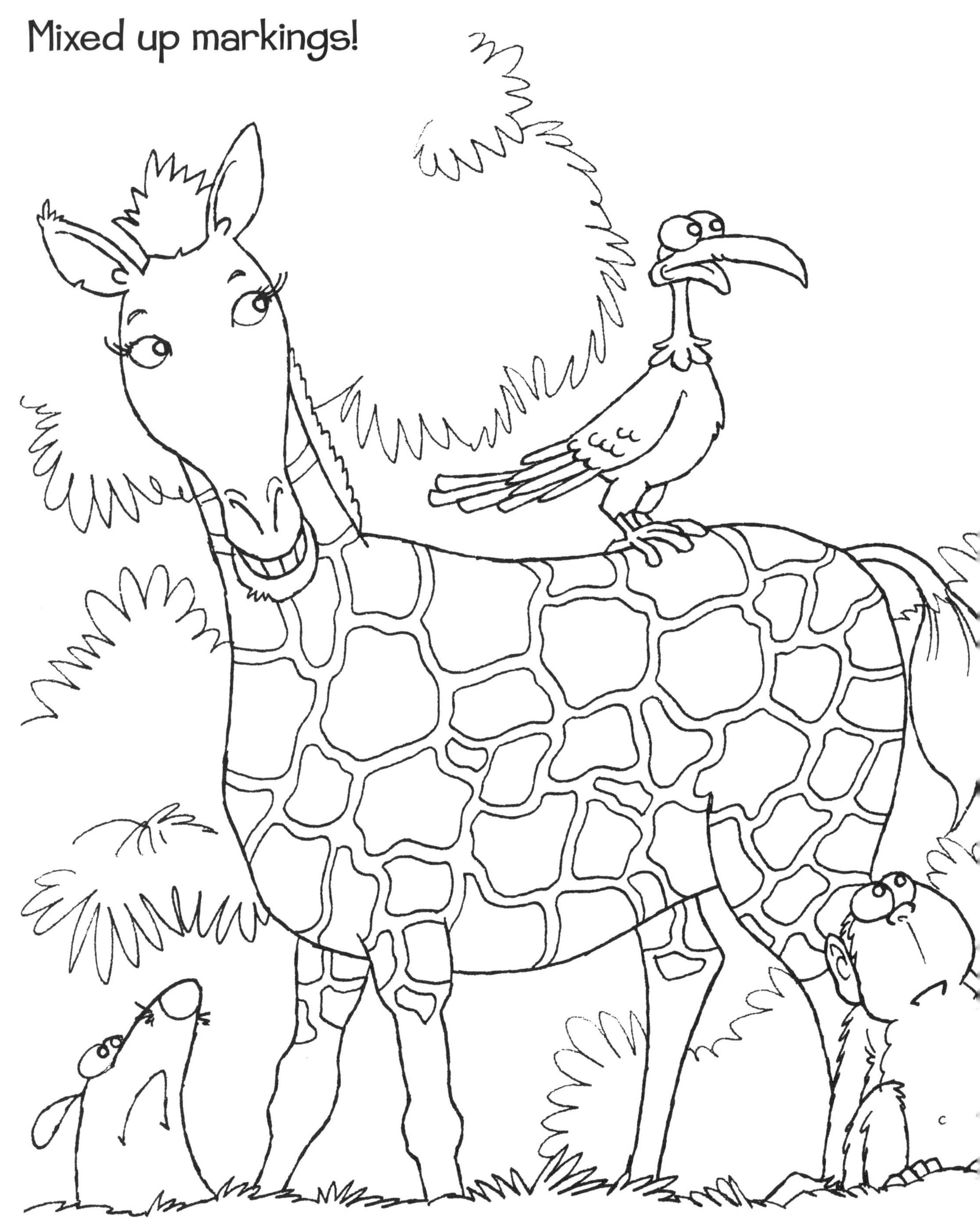

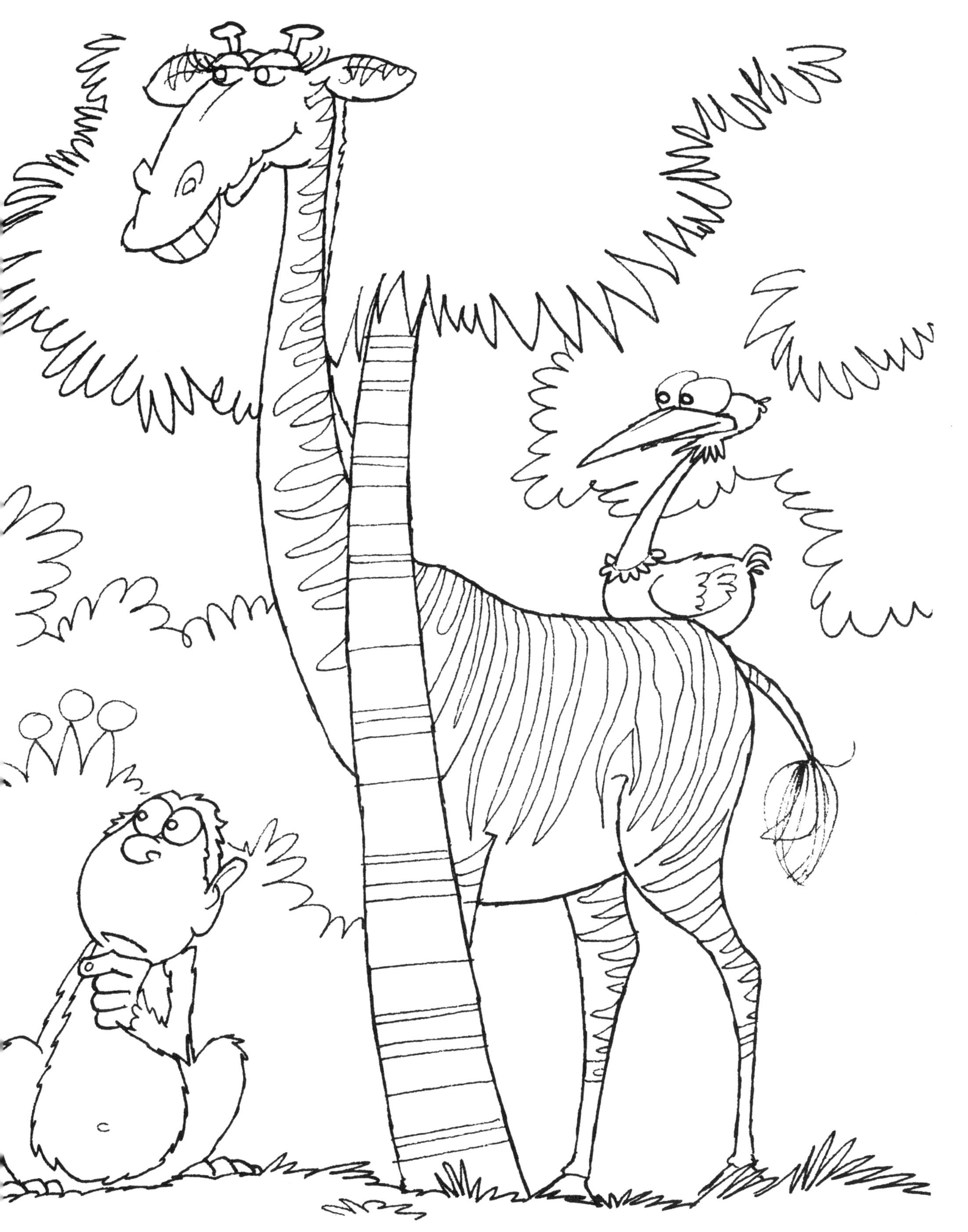

What other perils await the explorer?

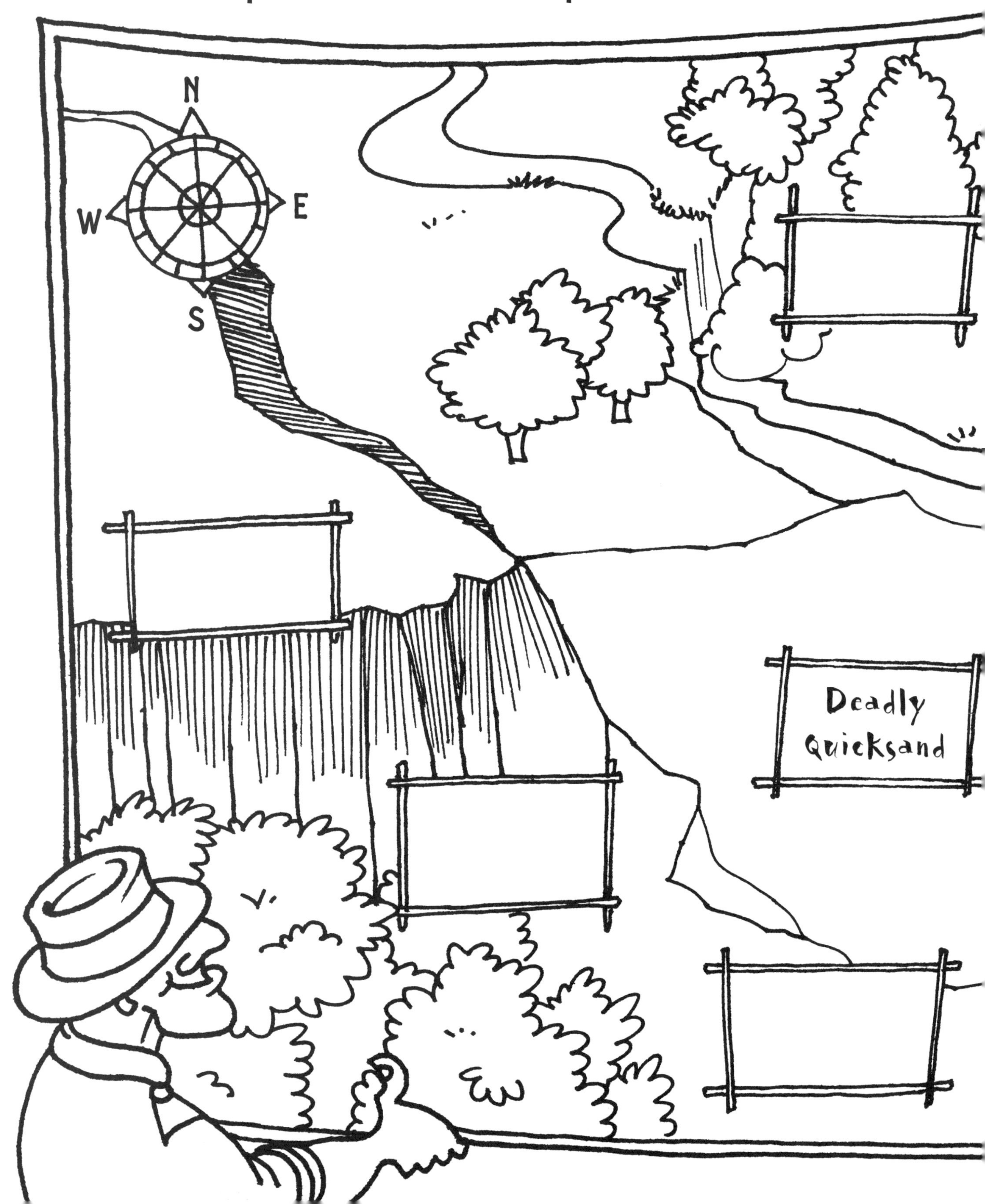

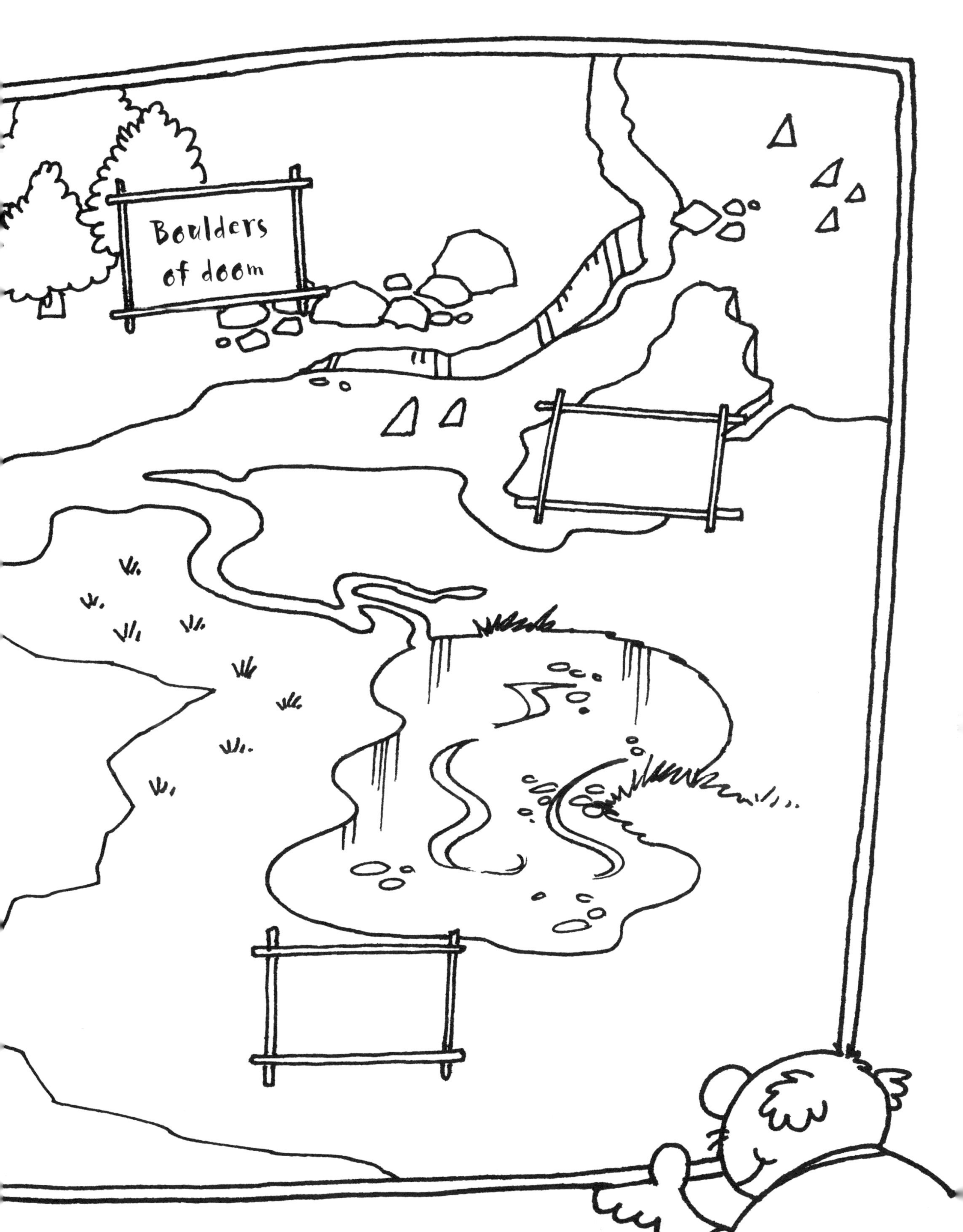
Boulders
of doom

The most fashionable colors this season

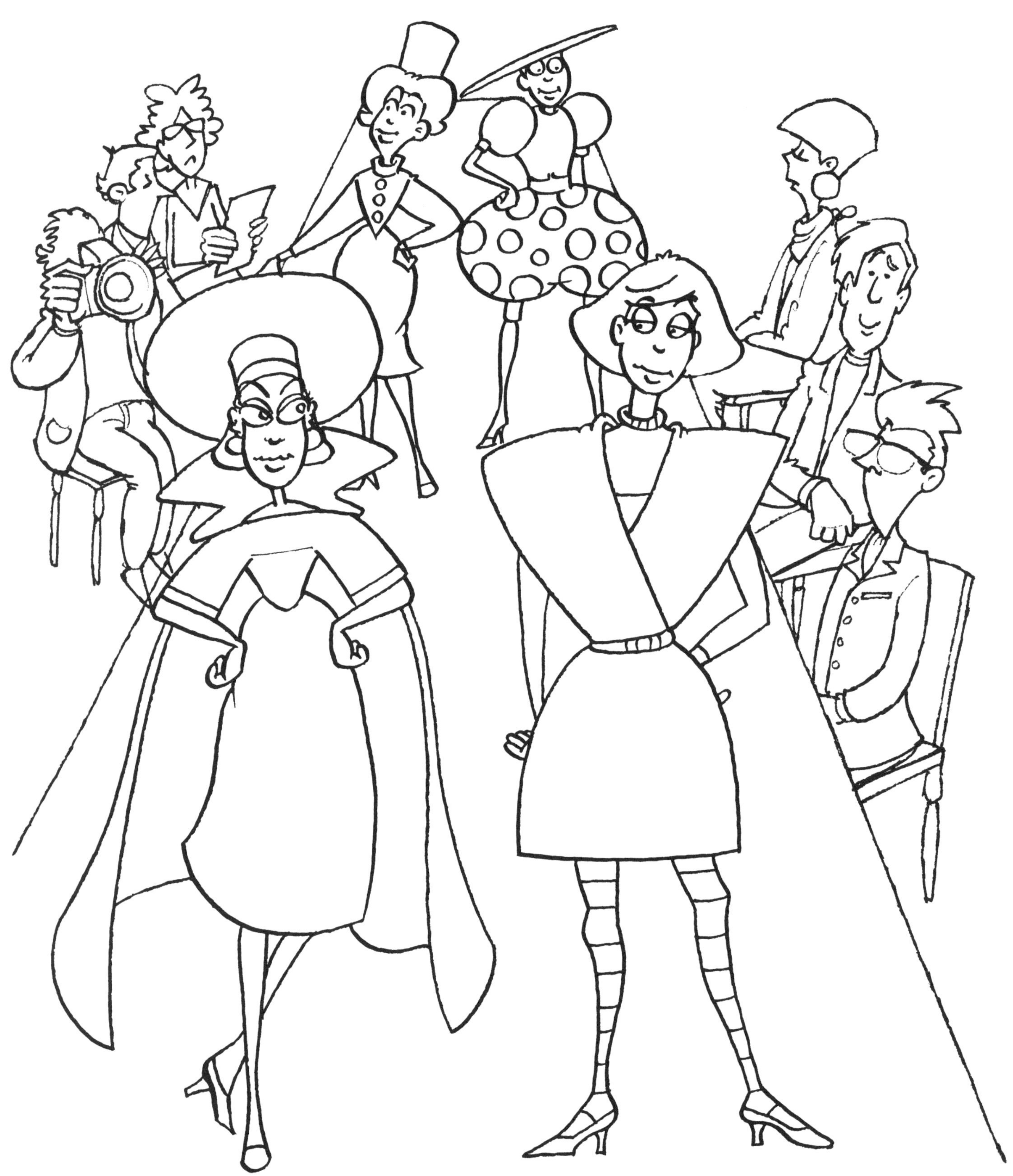

It's a surprising read for Boris the bookworm

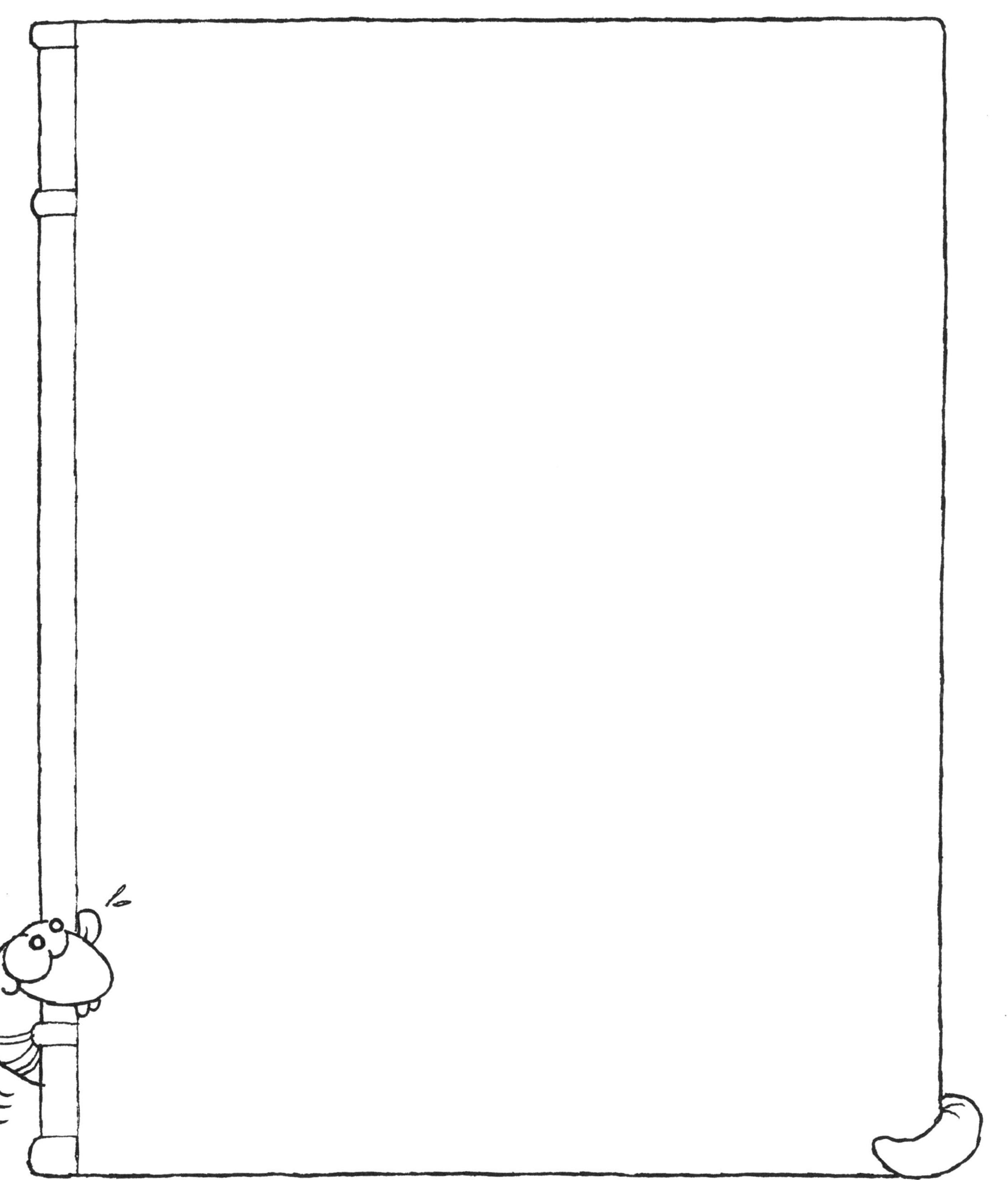

Not even the Sheriff could tame this horse

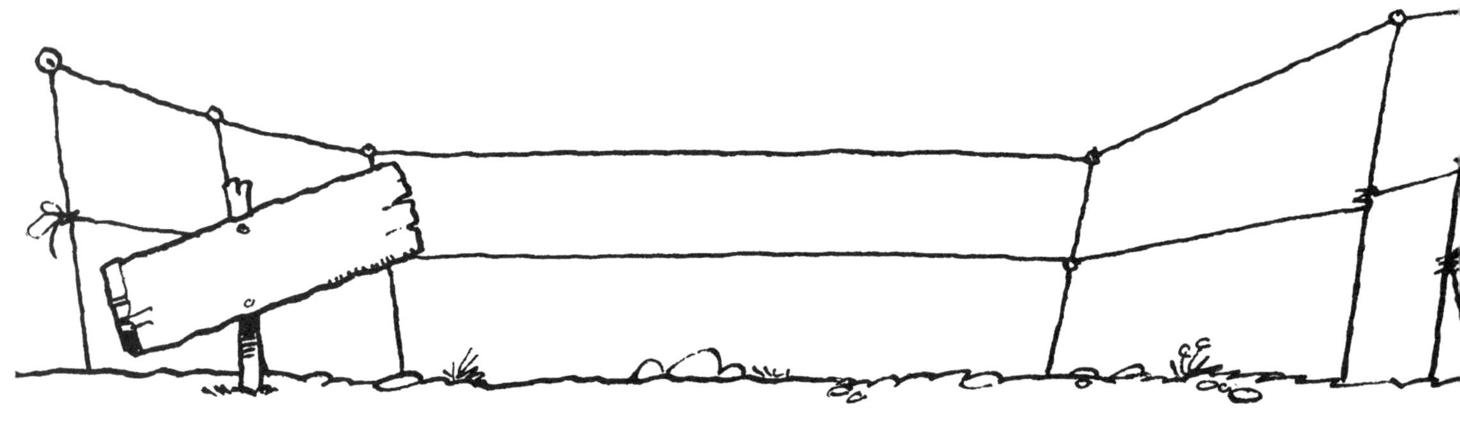

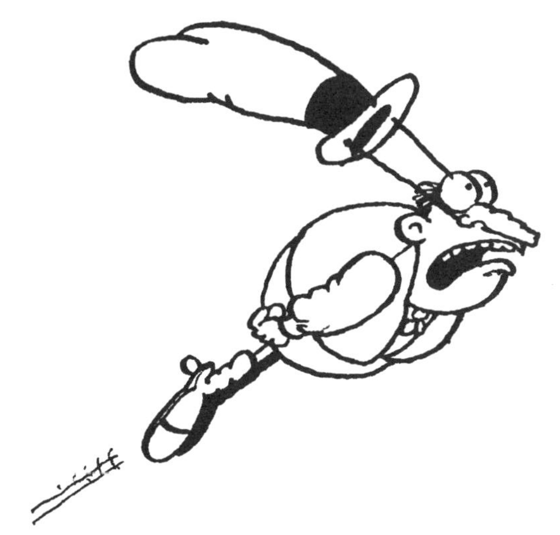
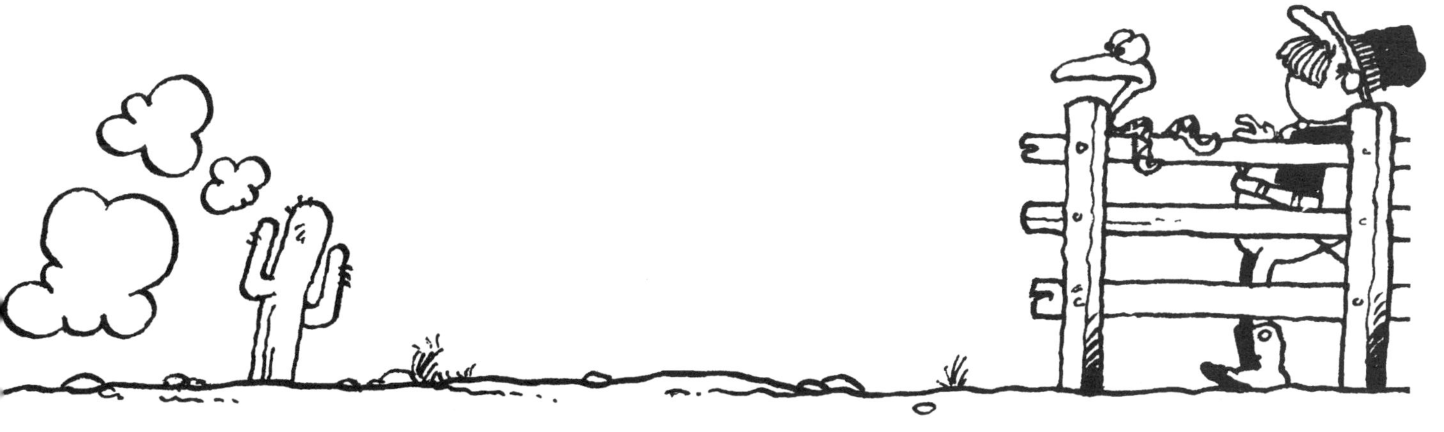

Dennis is very proud of what he's built

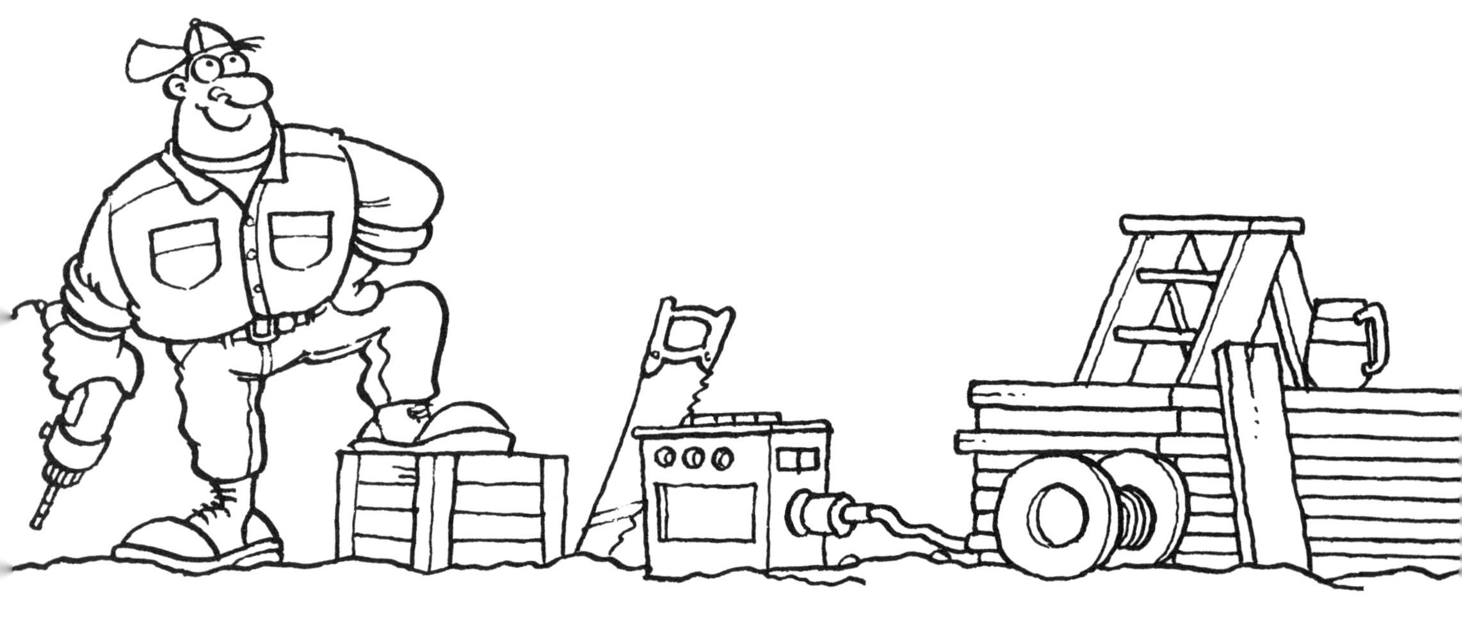

Cinderella doesn't like the color of her new dress

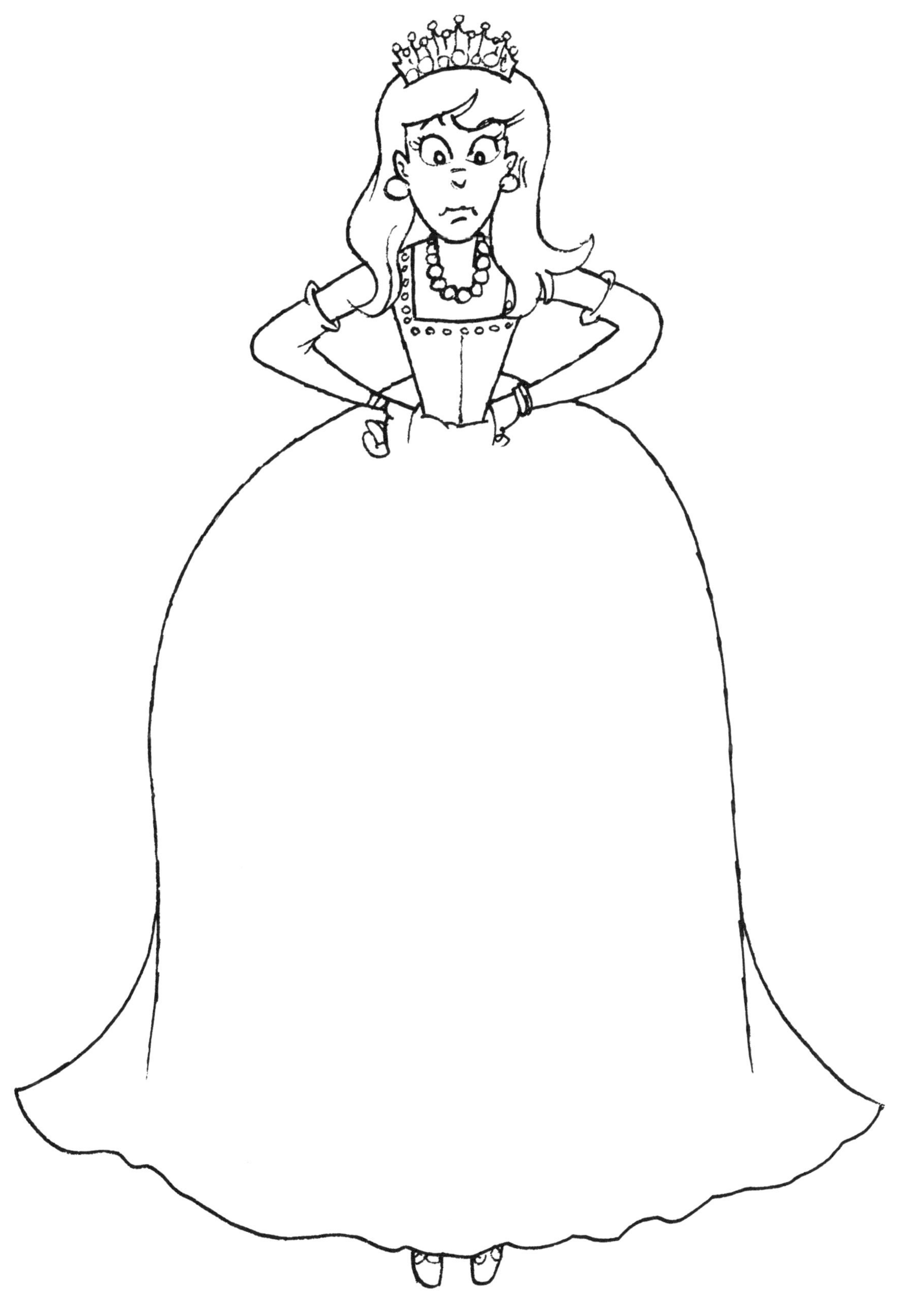

A crazy bus needs a crazy driver

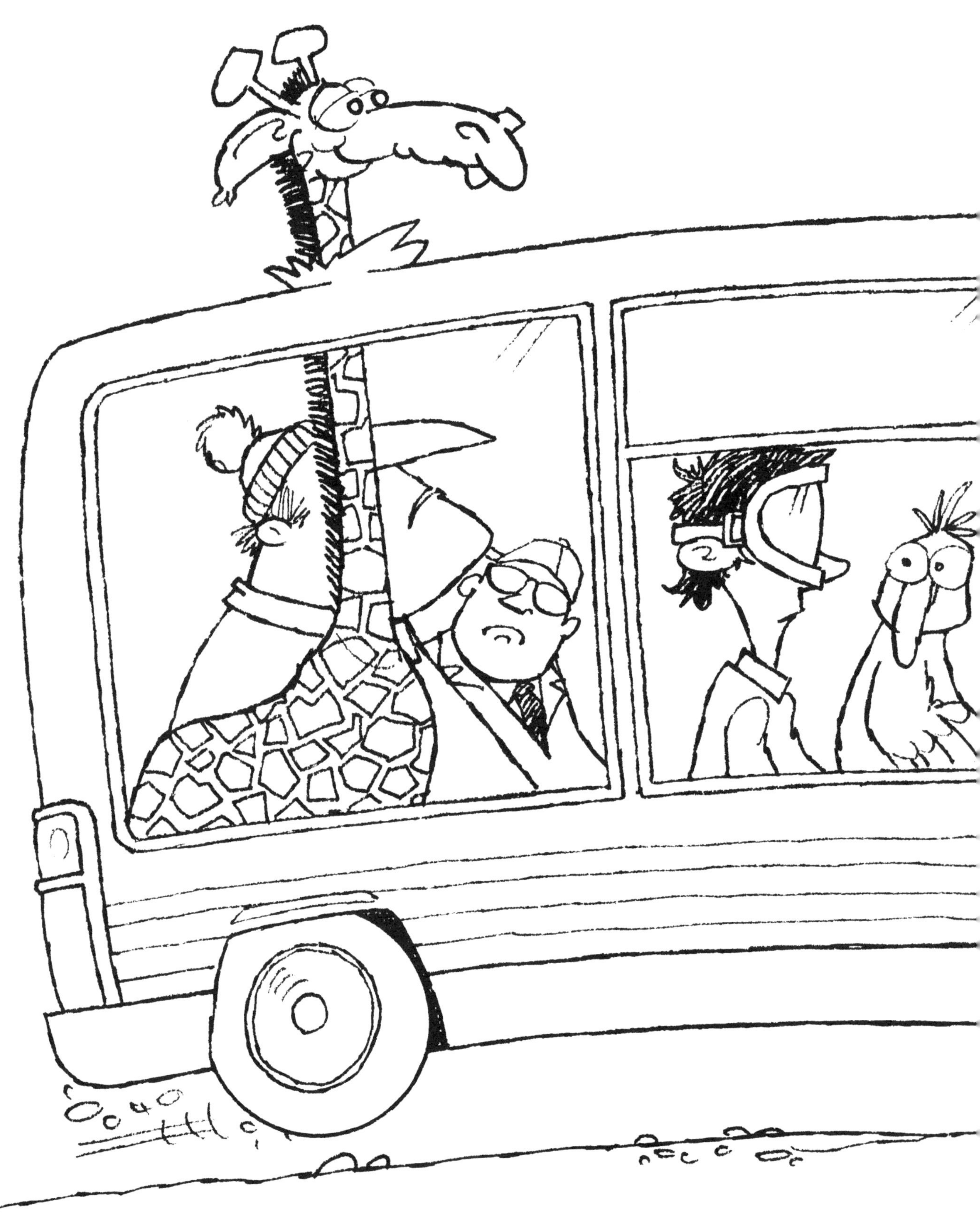

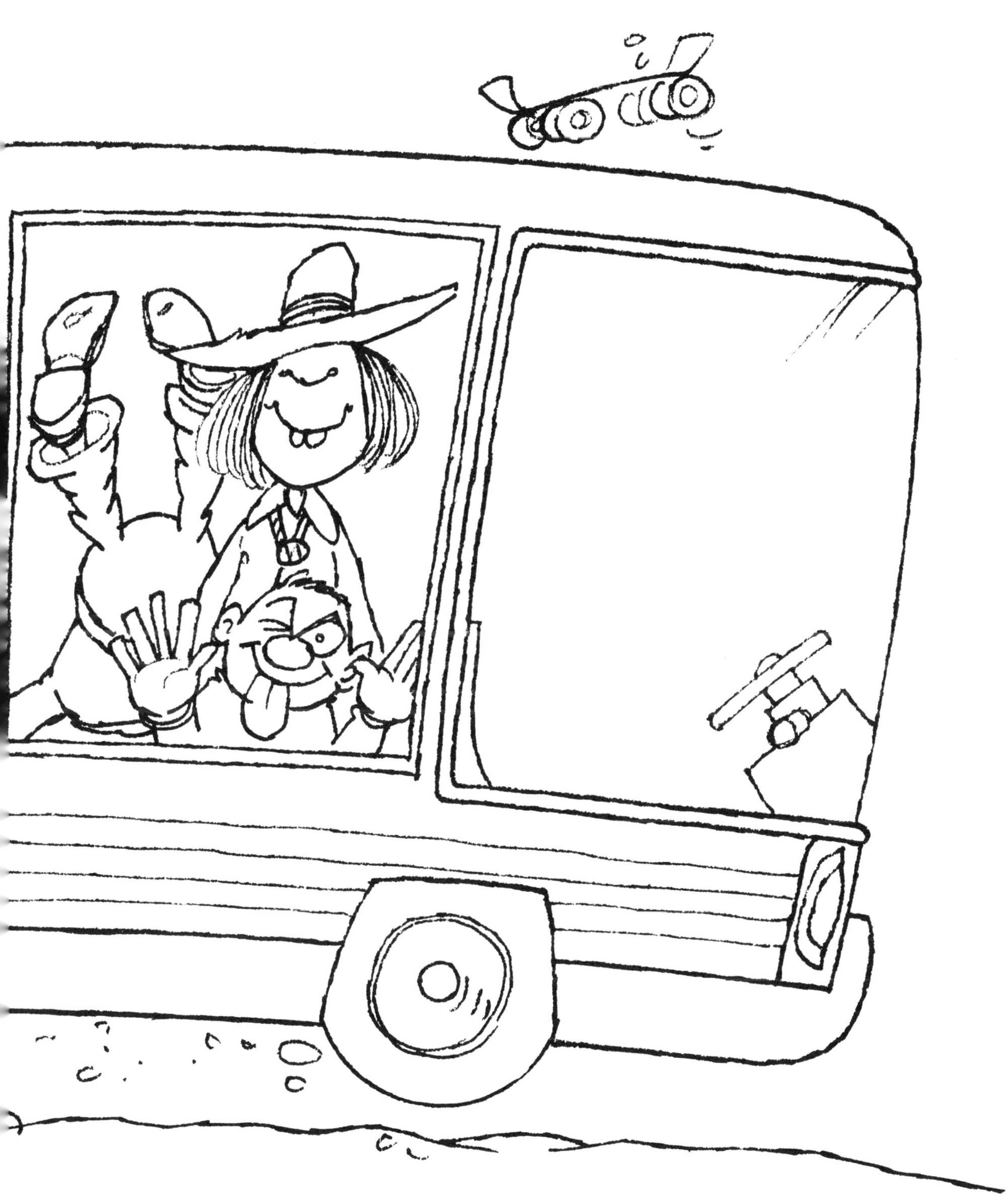

Medieval mayhem!

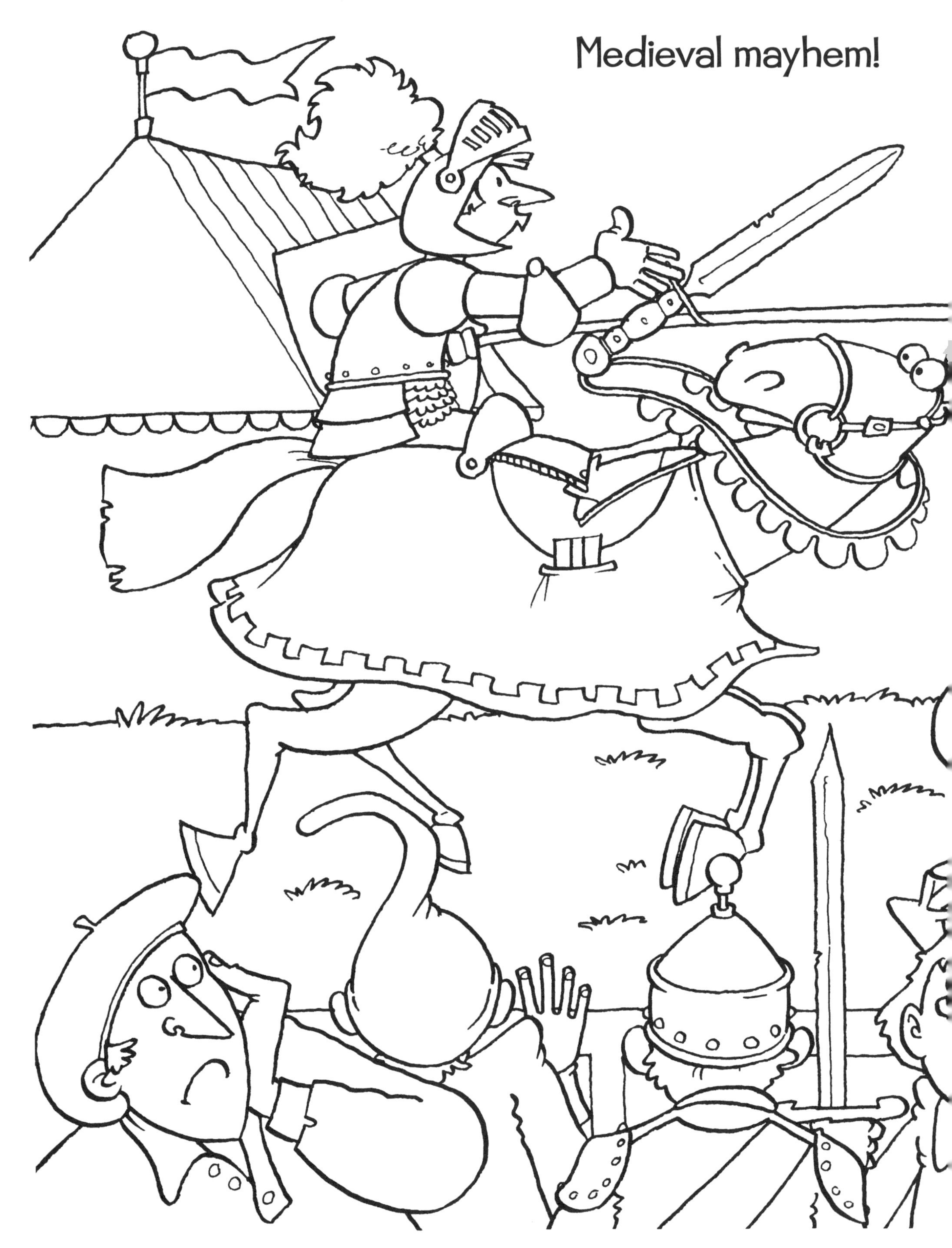

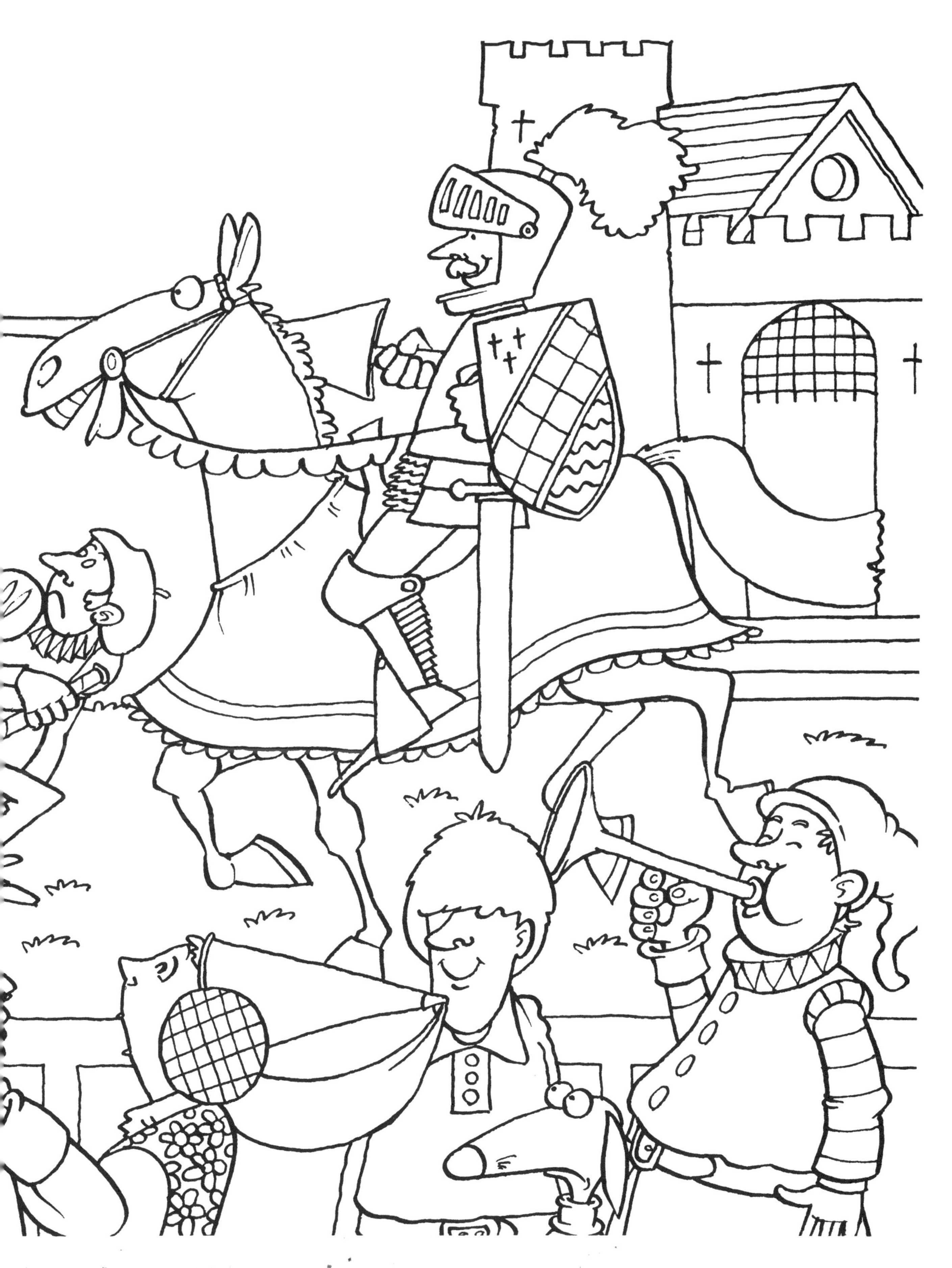

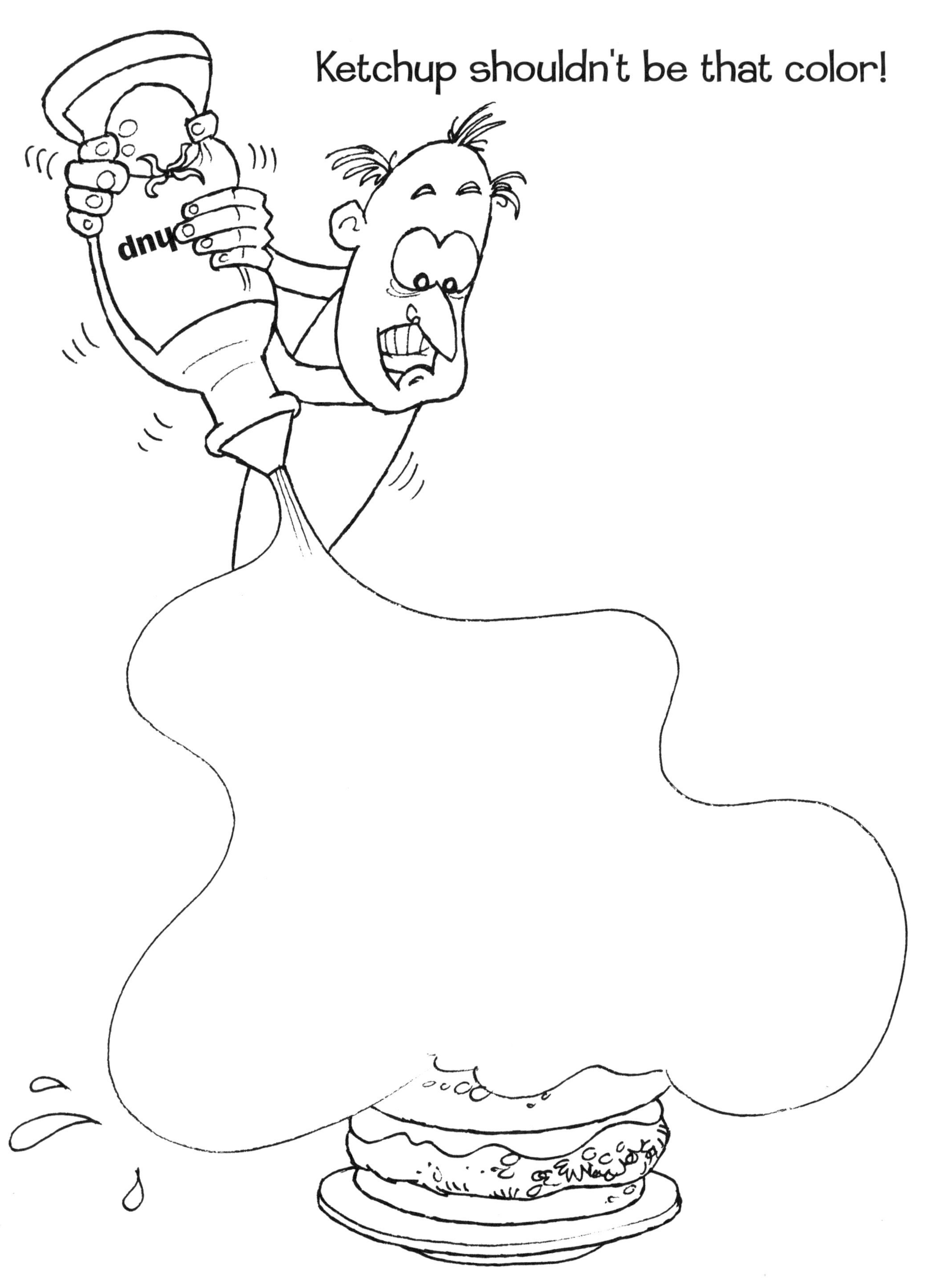
Ketchup shouldn't be that color!

It's behind you...

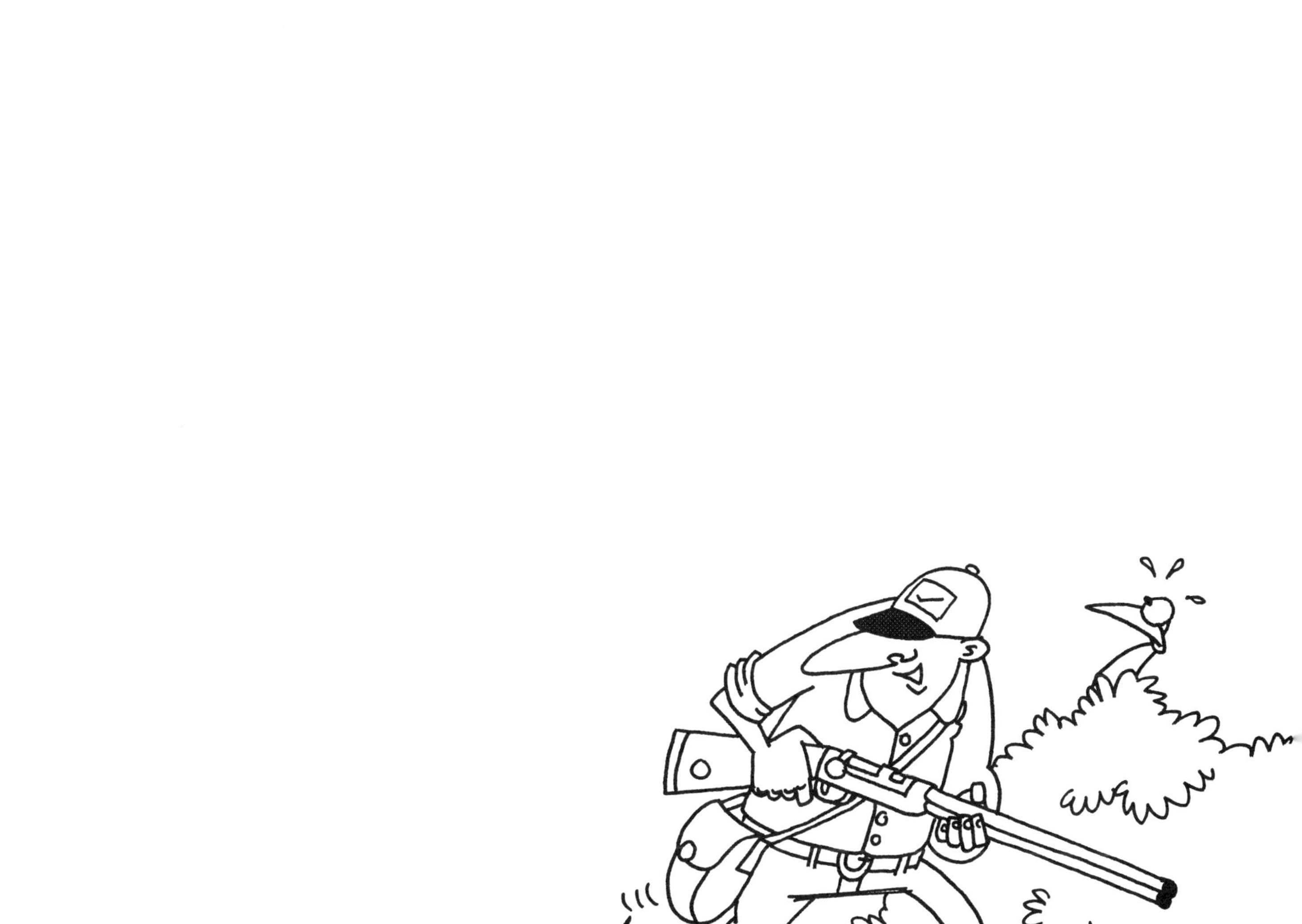

These surfers need some waves, dude

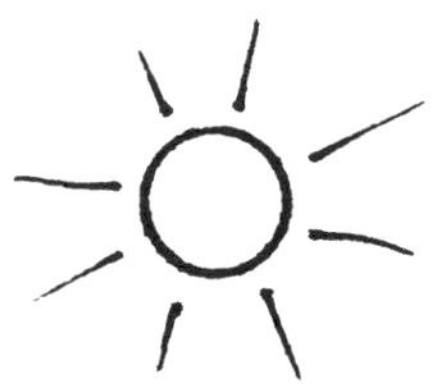

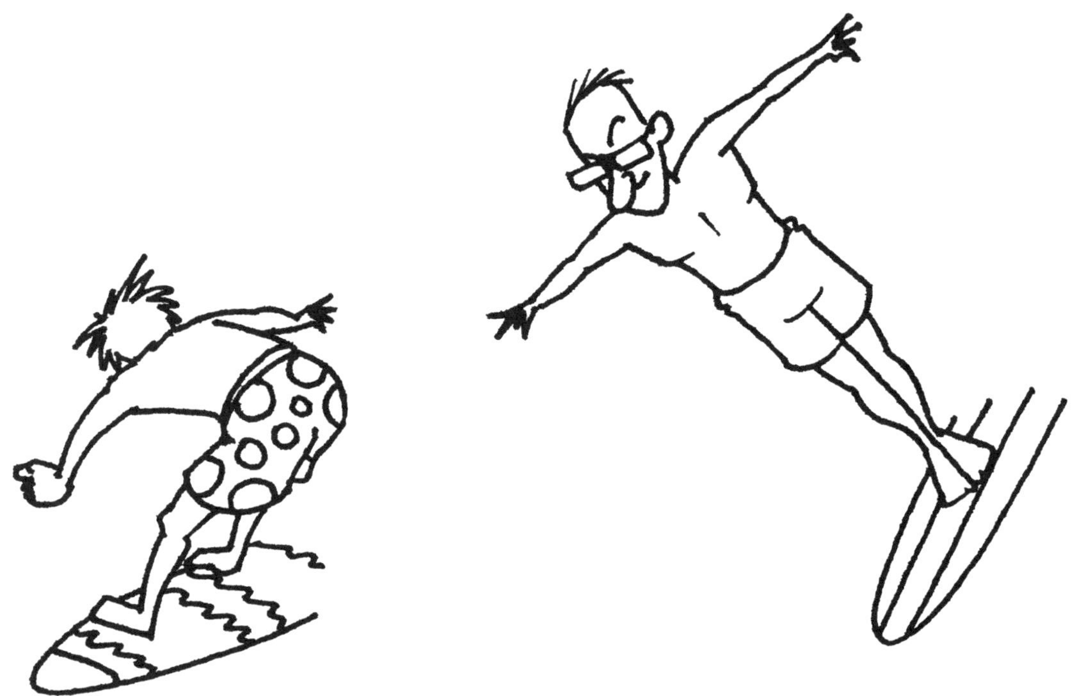

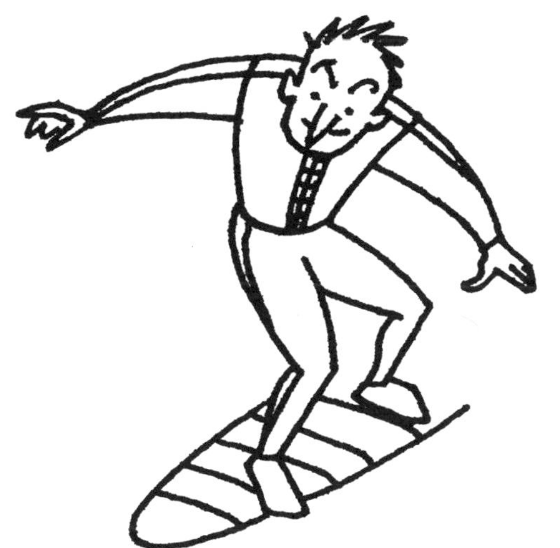

What other animals have been here?

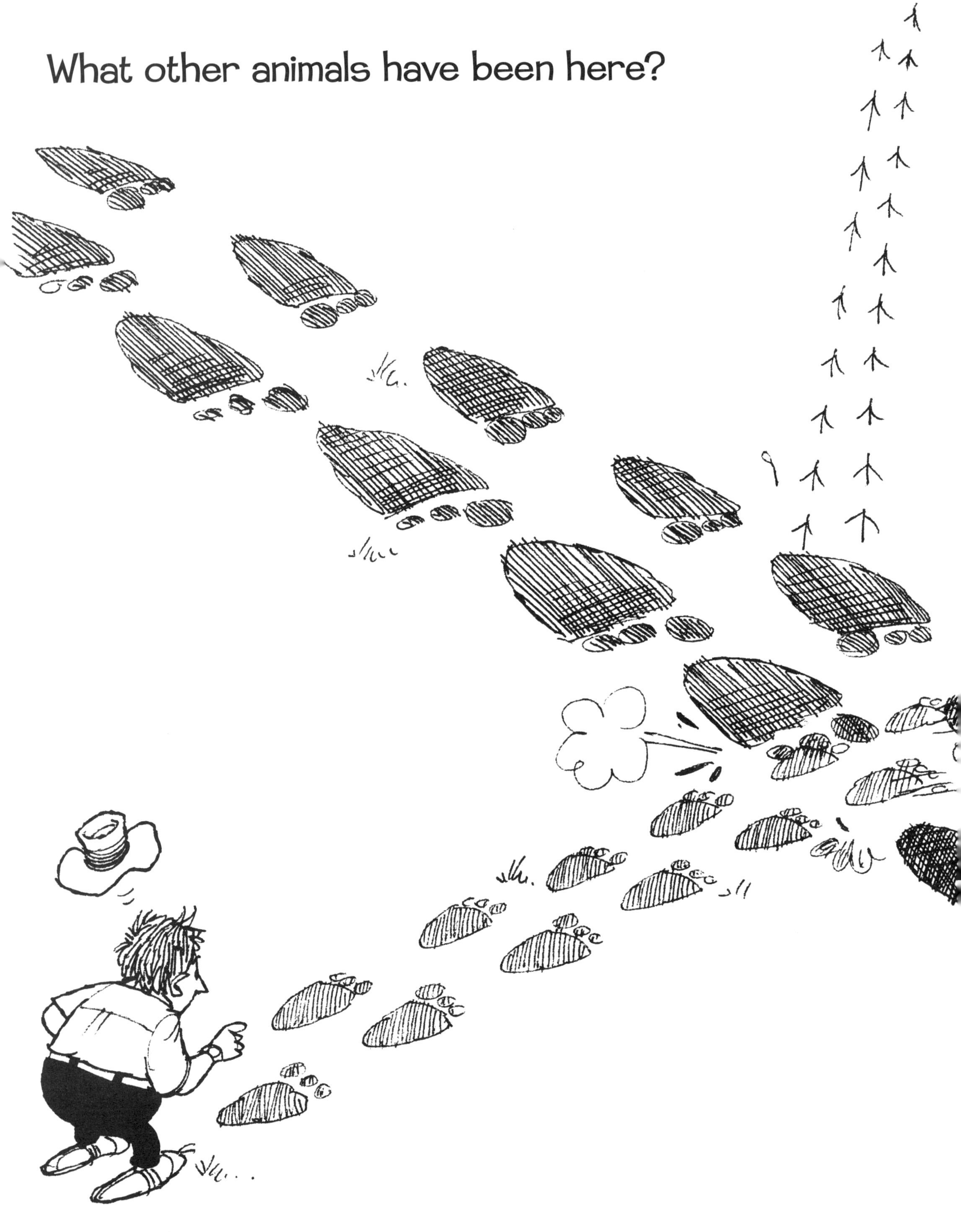

It's not the natural color she'd asked for

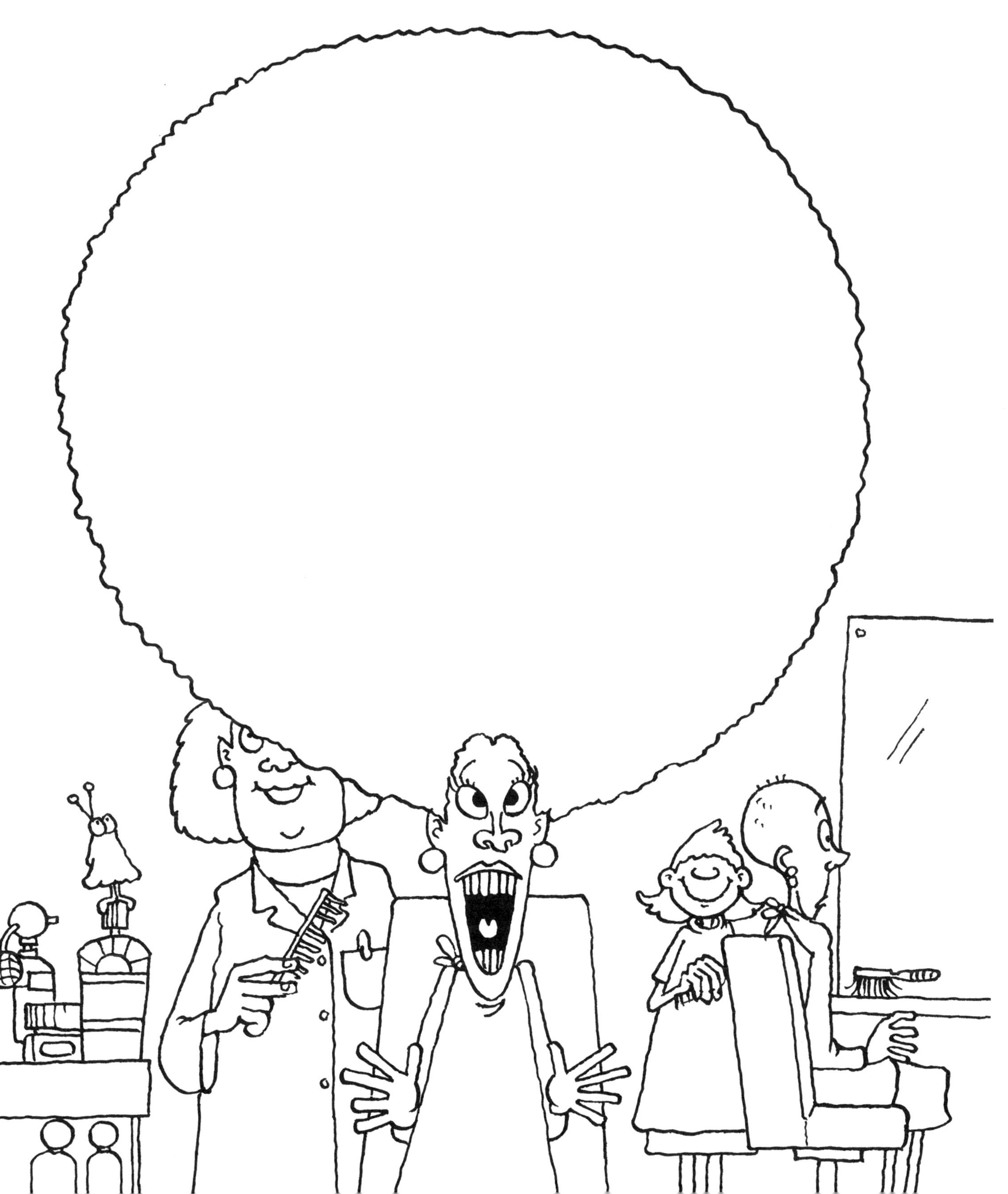

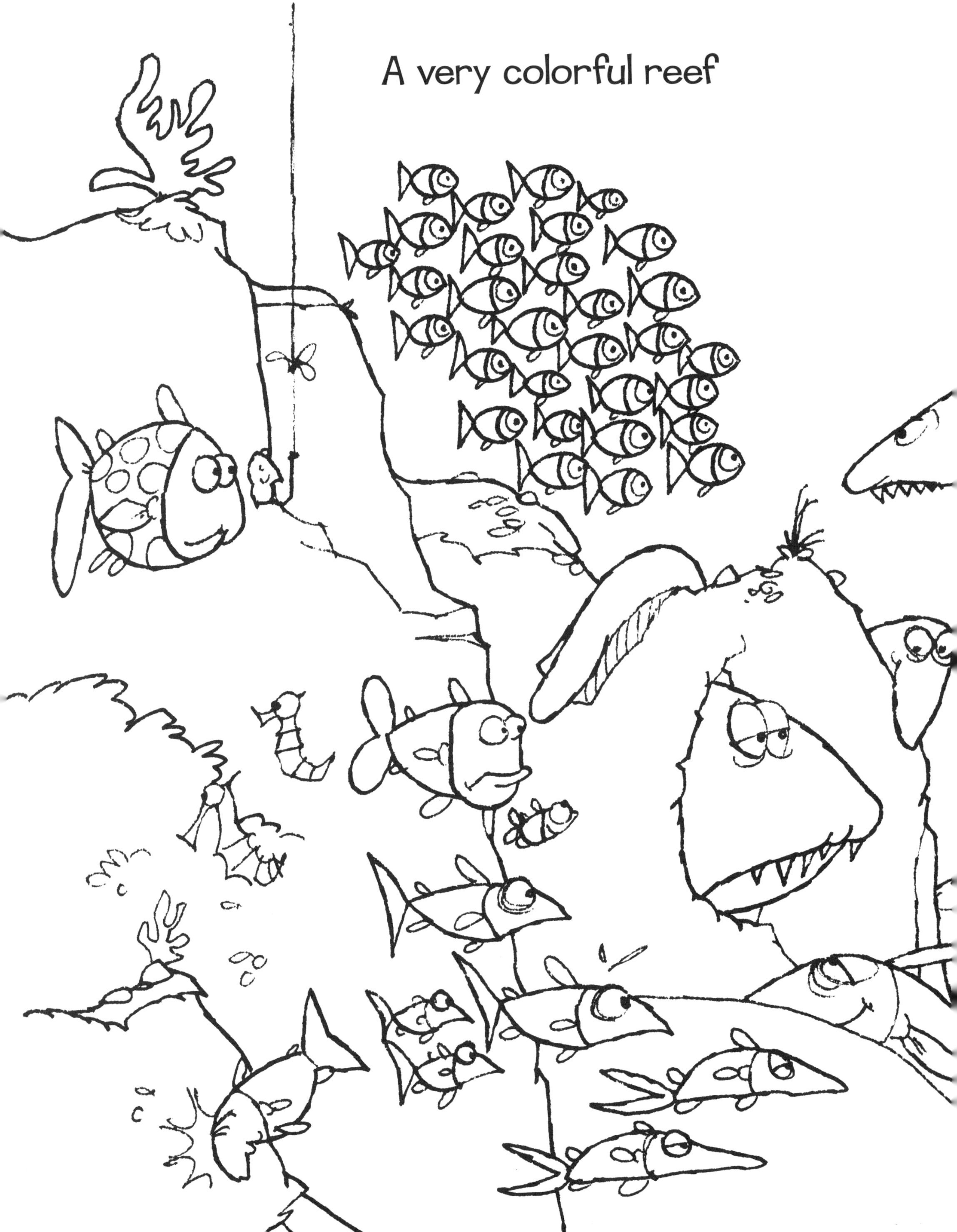
A very colorful reef

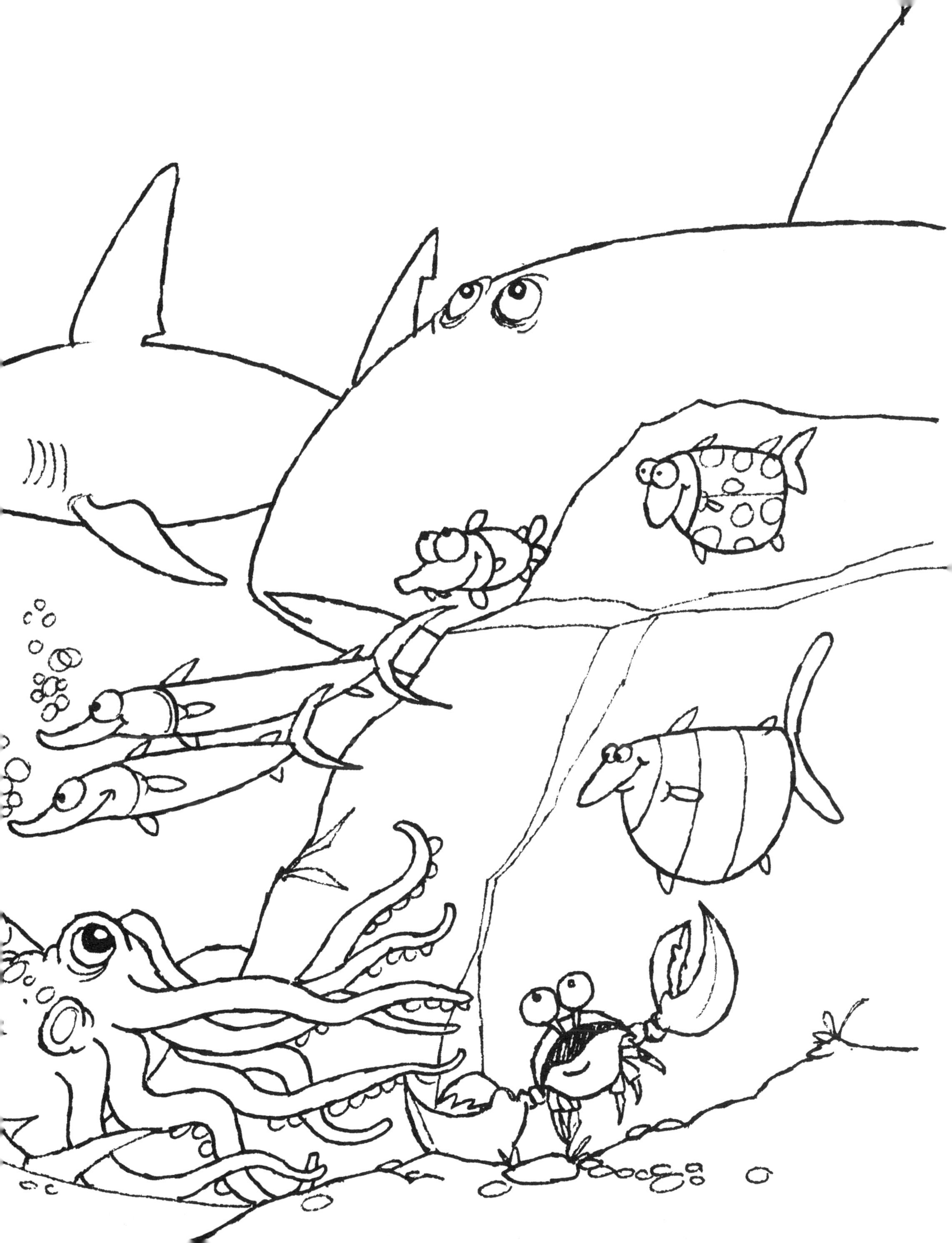

What's happened here?

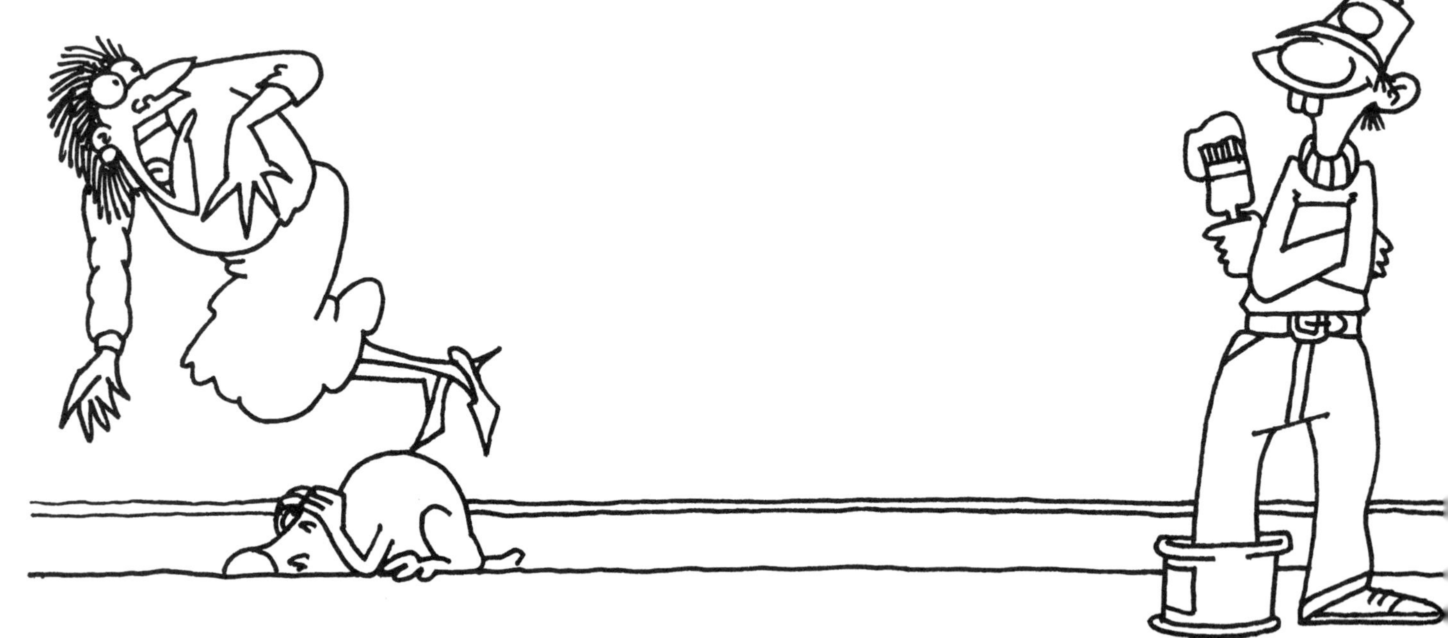

A totem-lly colorful pole

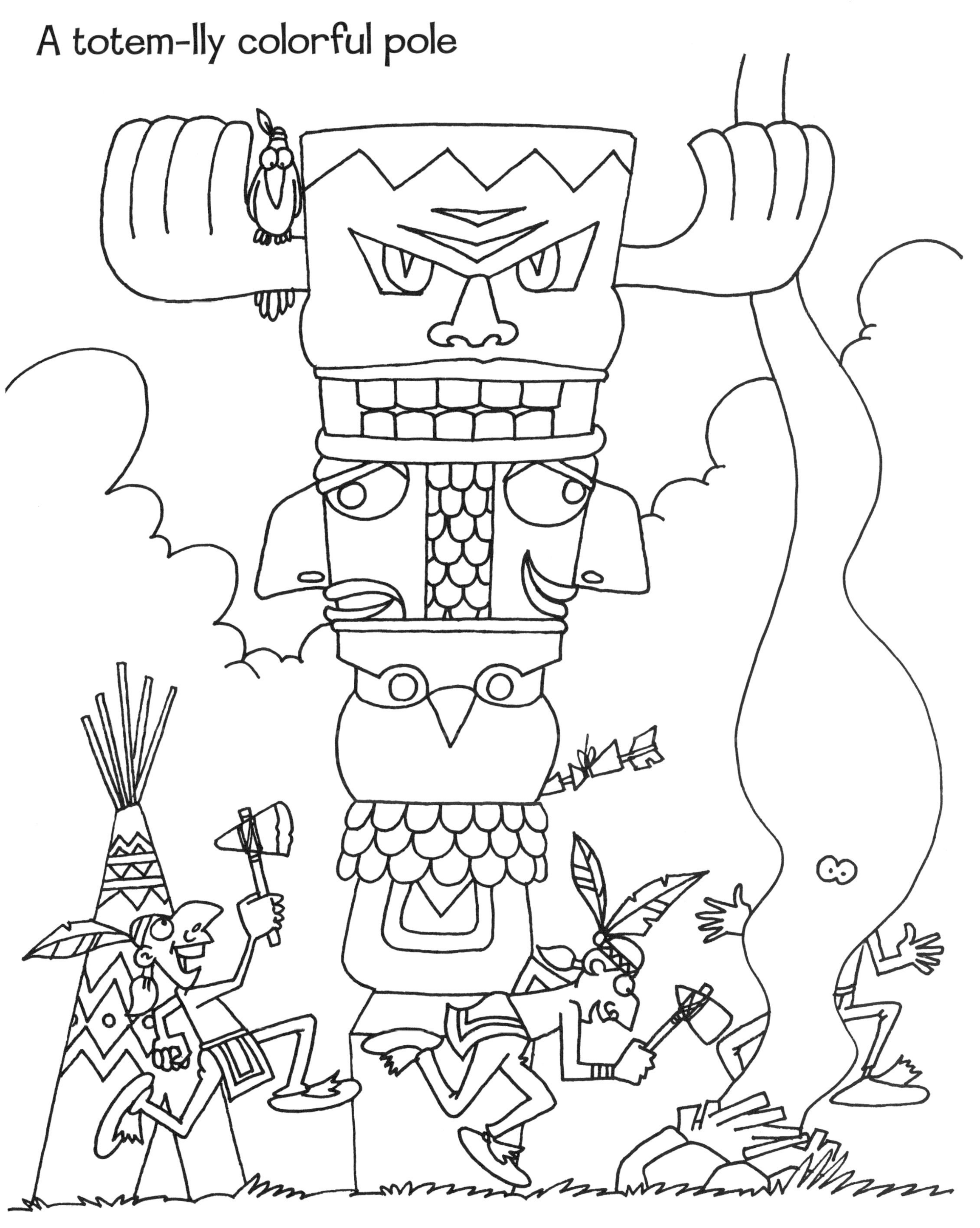

Finish off these split personalities

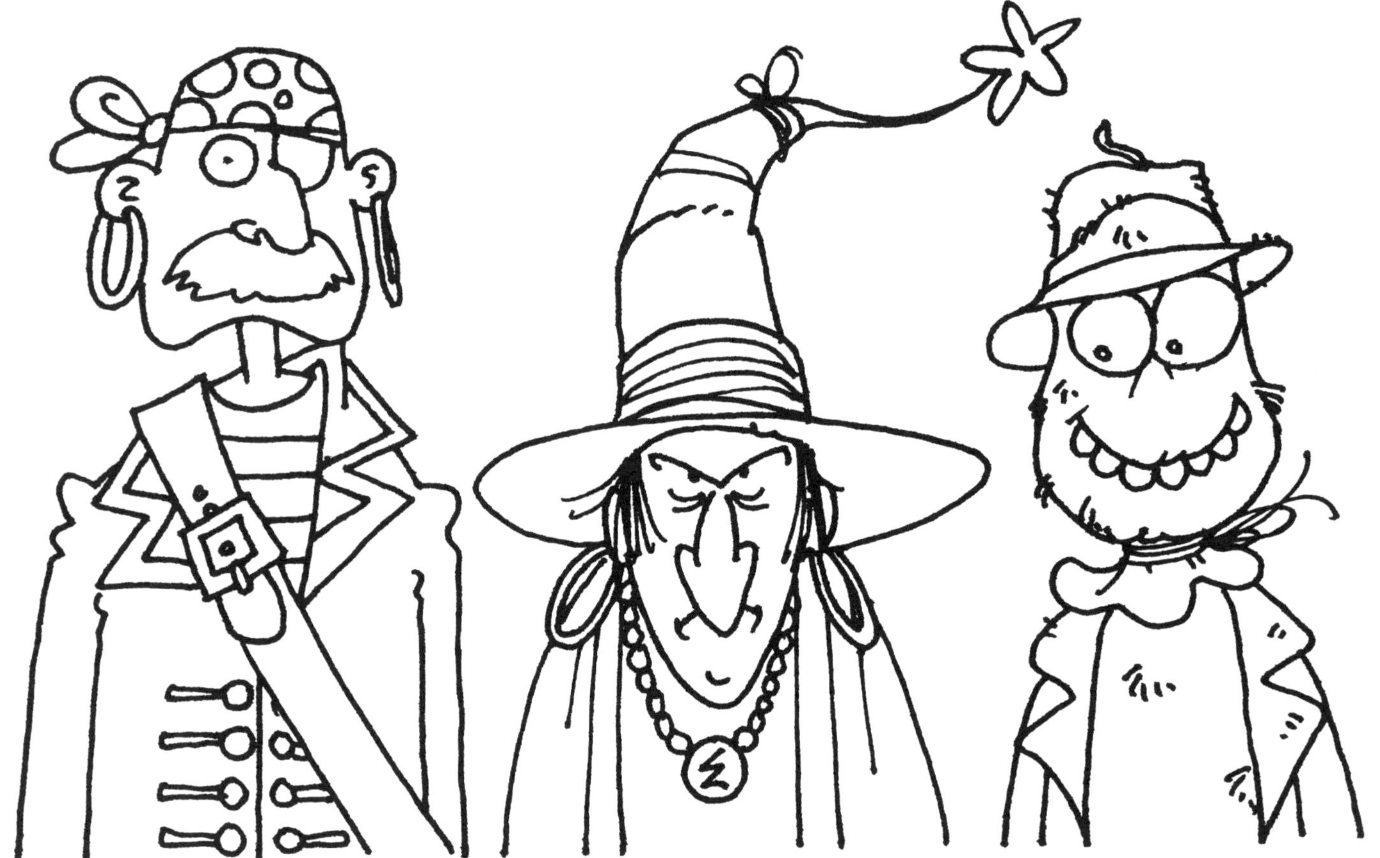

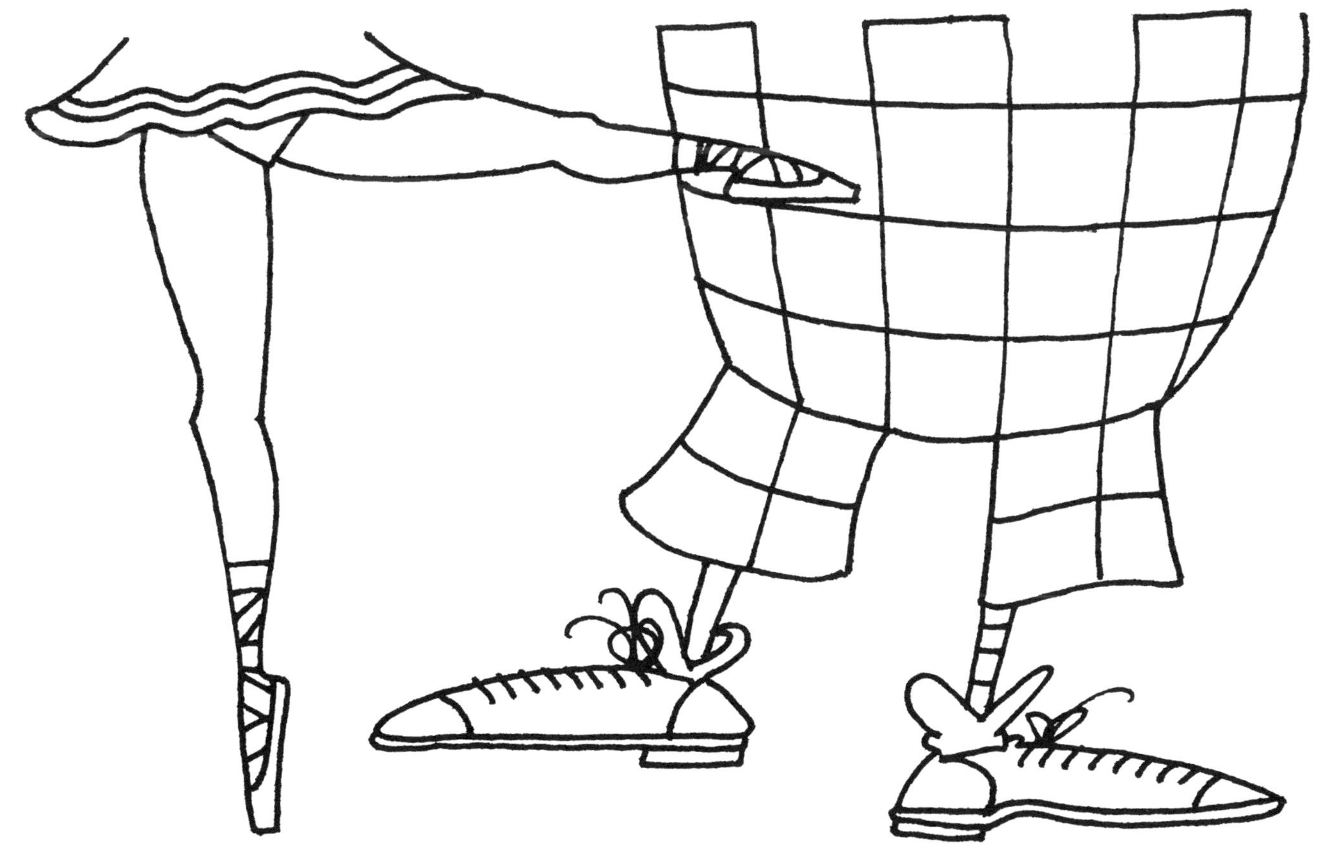

Get her to the palace on time!

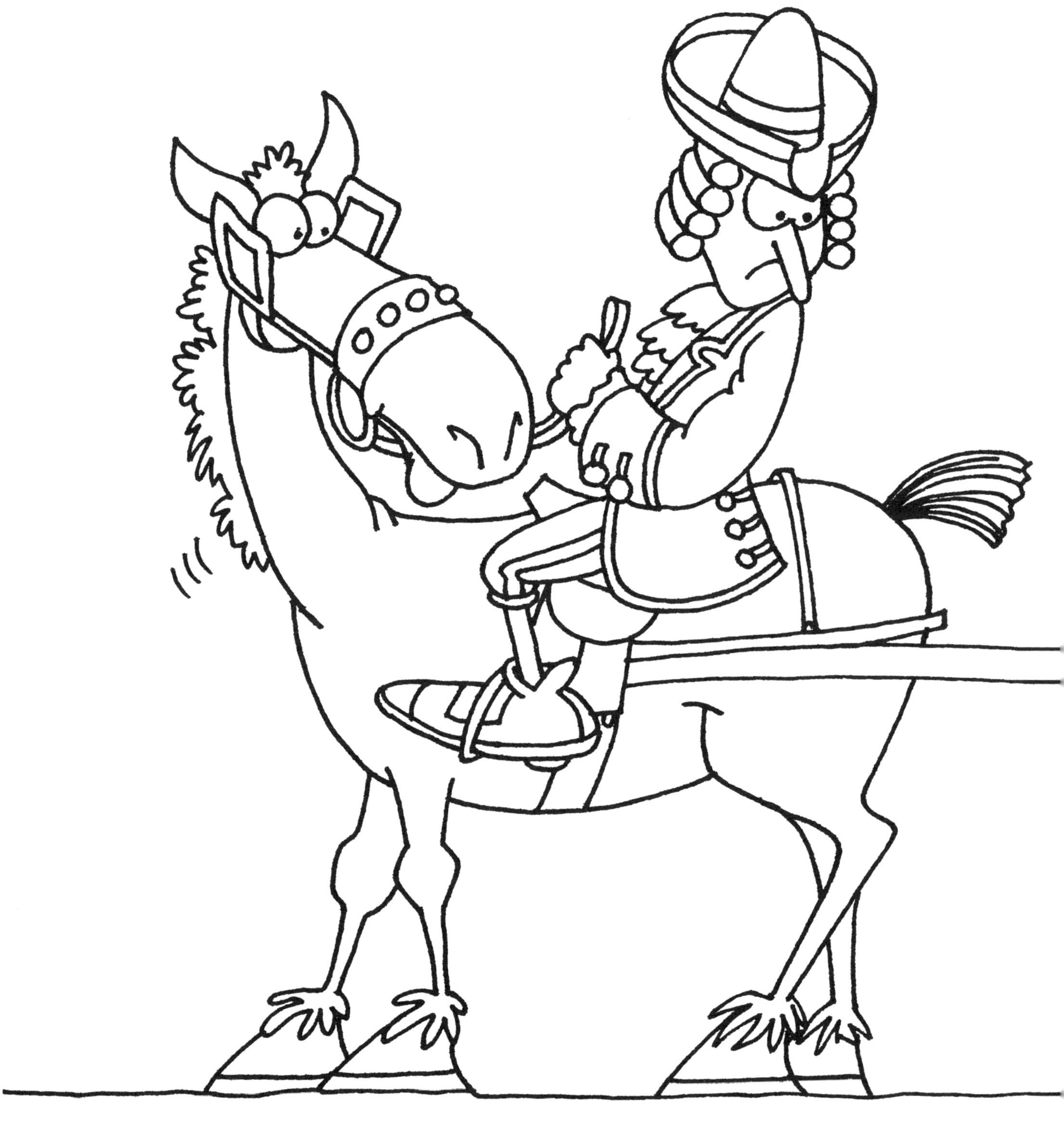

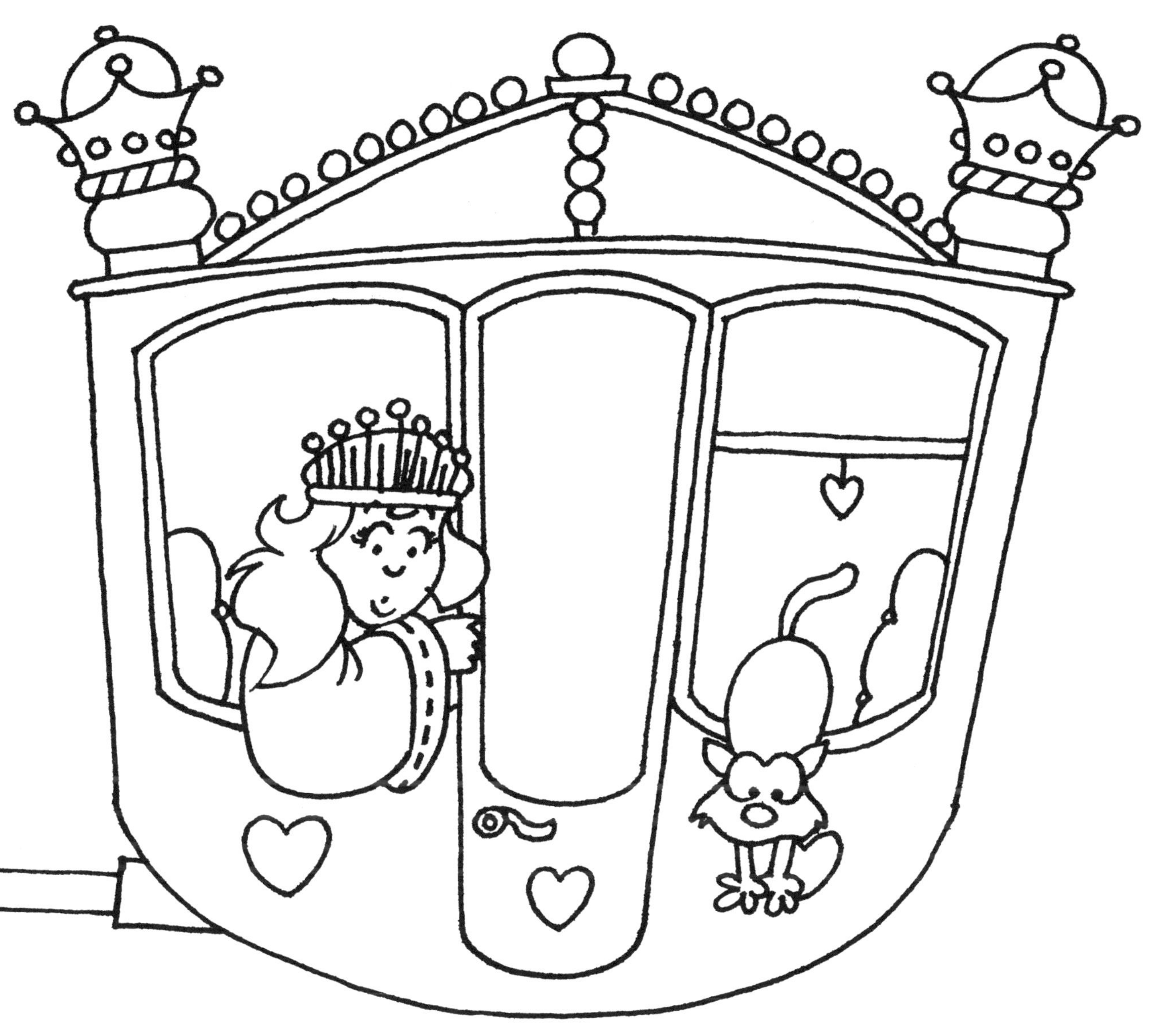

Give Henry a beard to be proud of

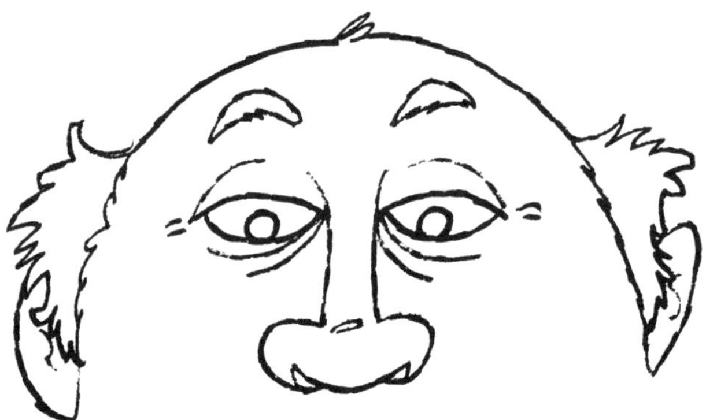

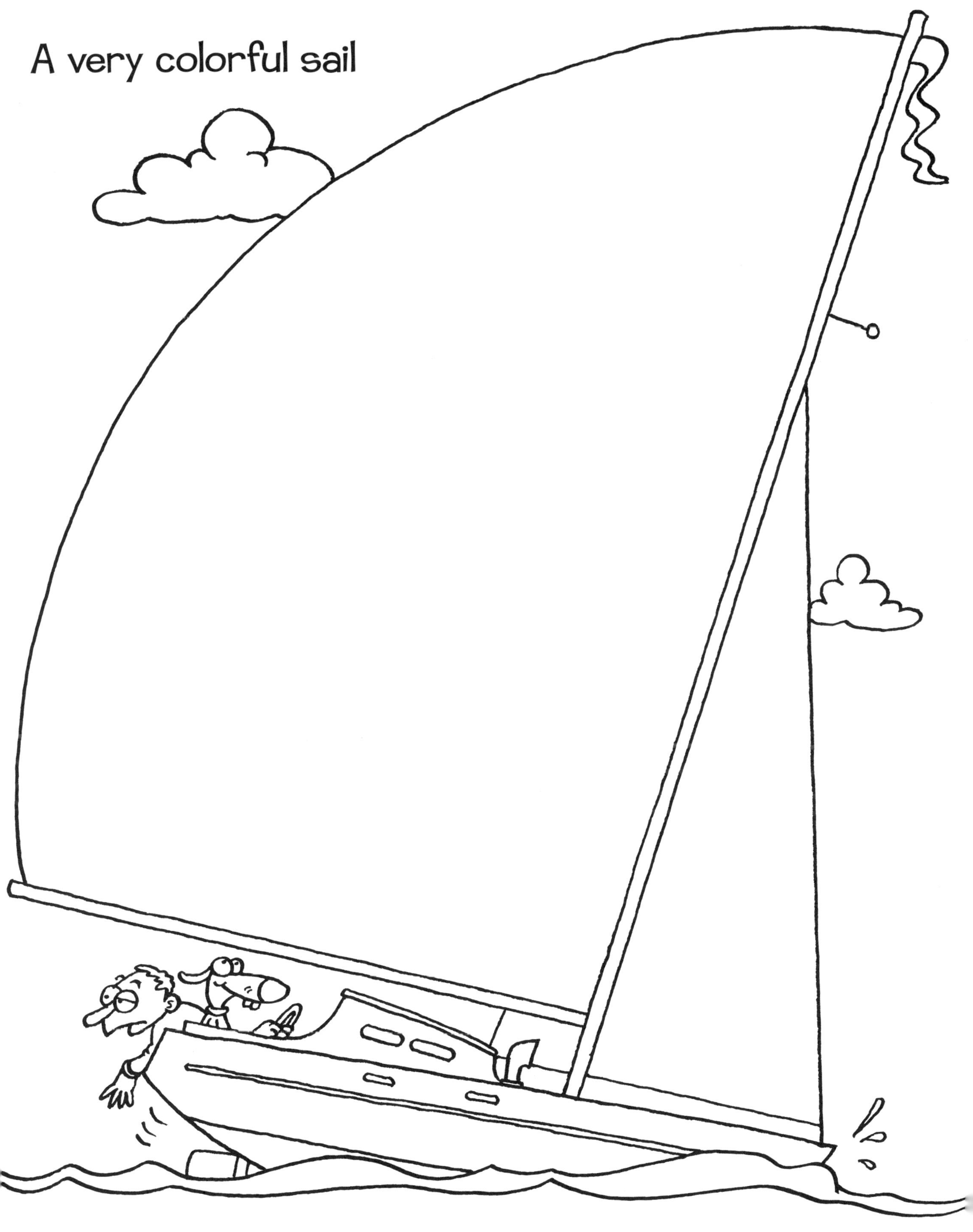
A very colorful sail

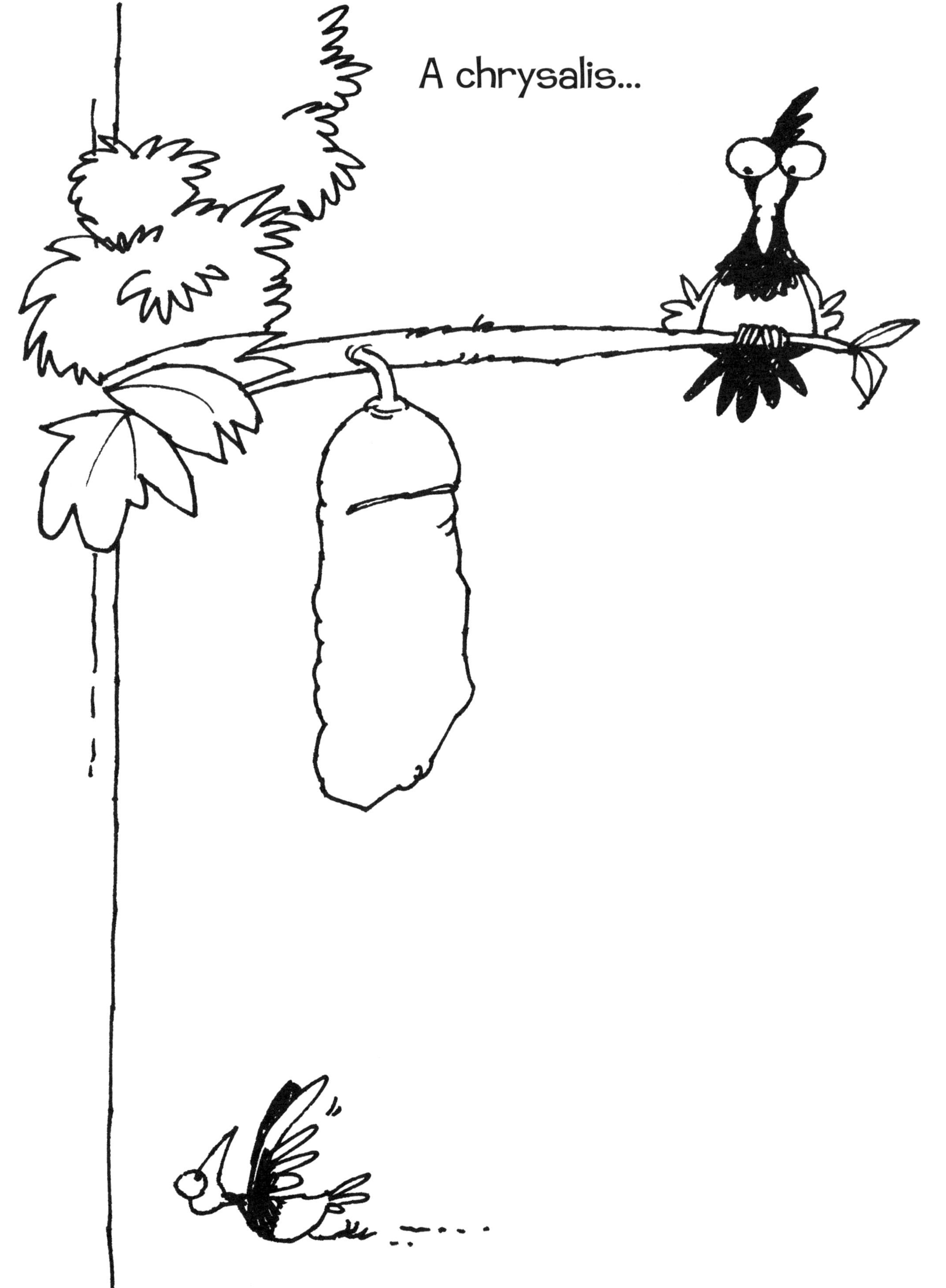
A chrysalis...

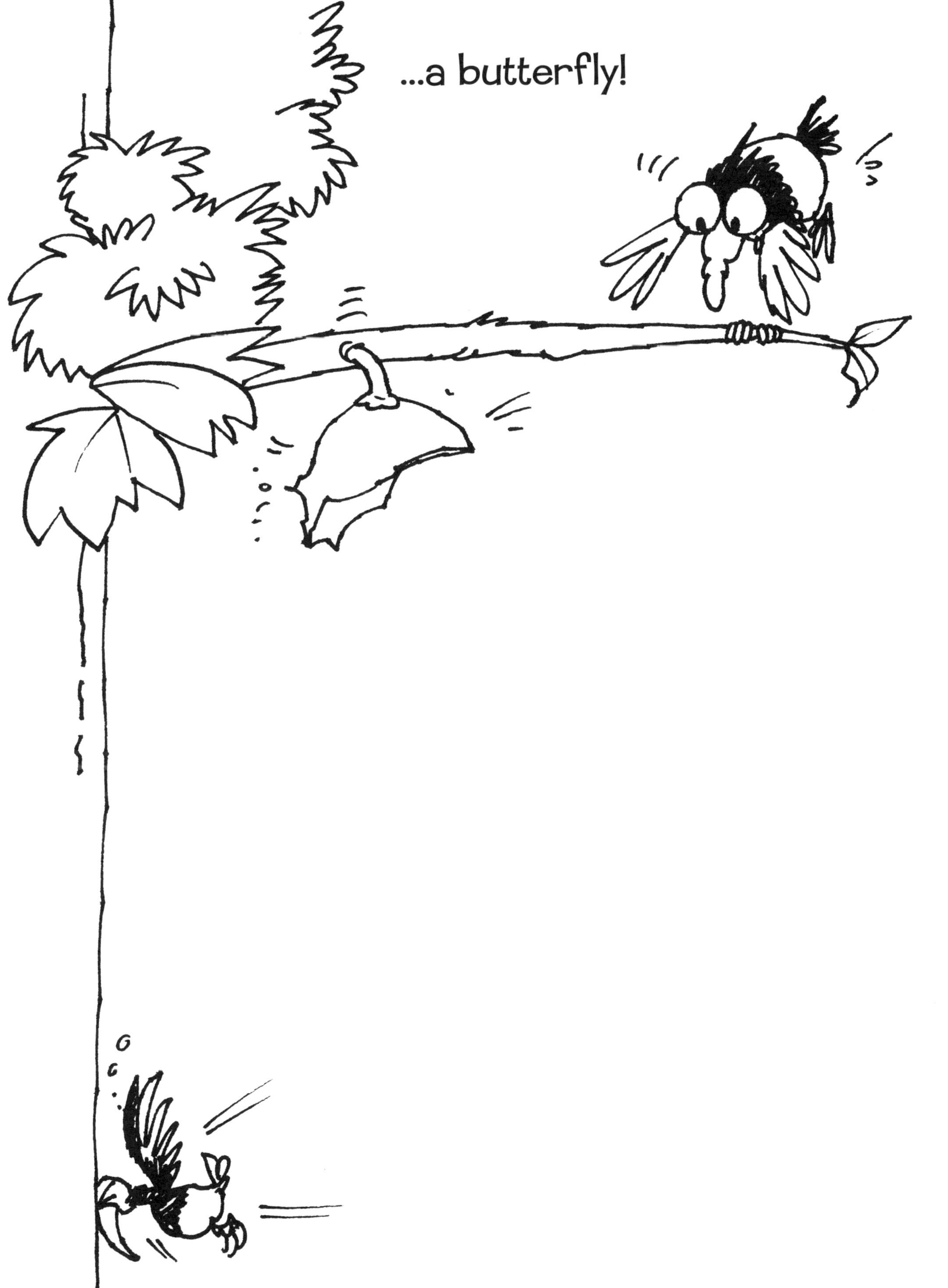
...a butterfly!

Olé!

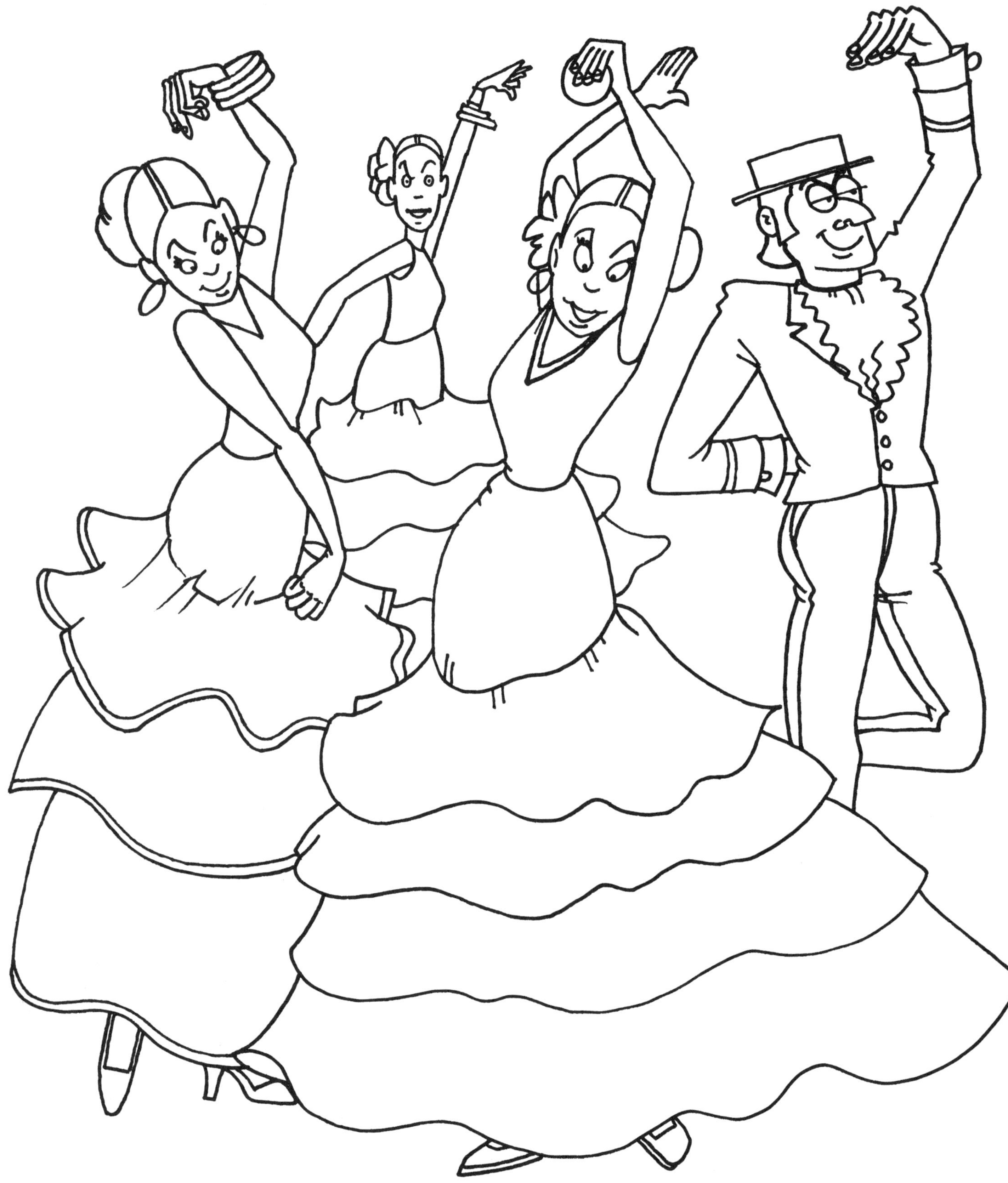

What has he lifted this time?

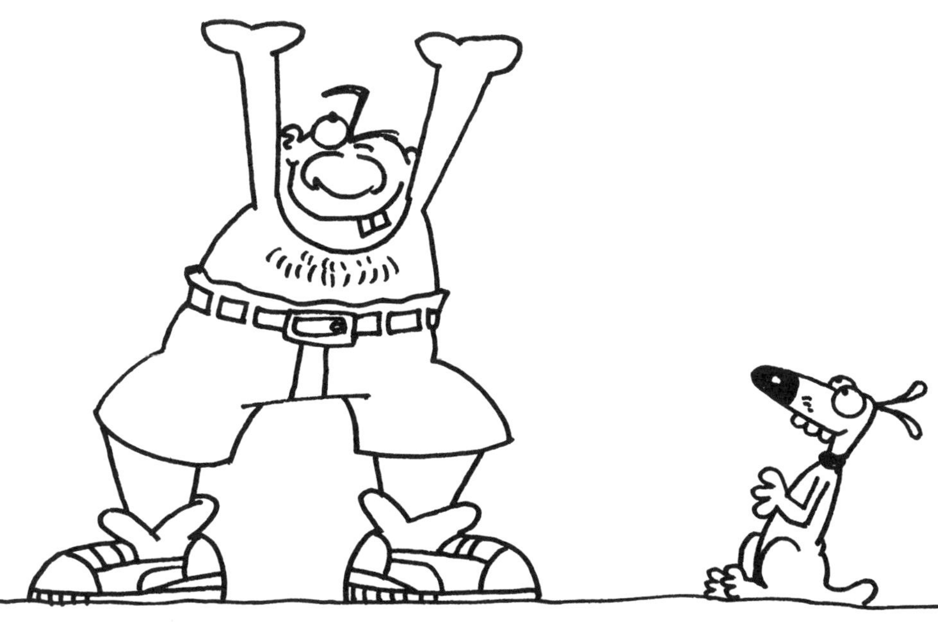

Jo Jo is jealous of Bo Bo's costume

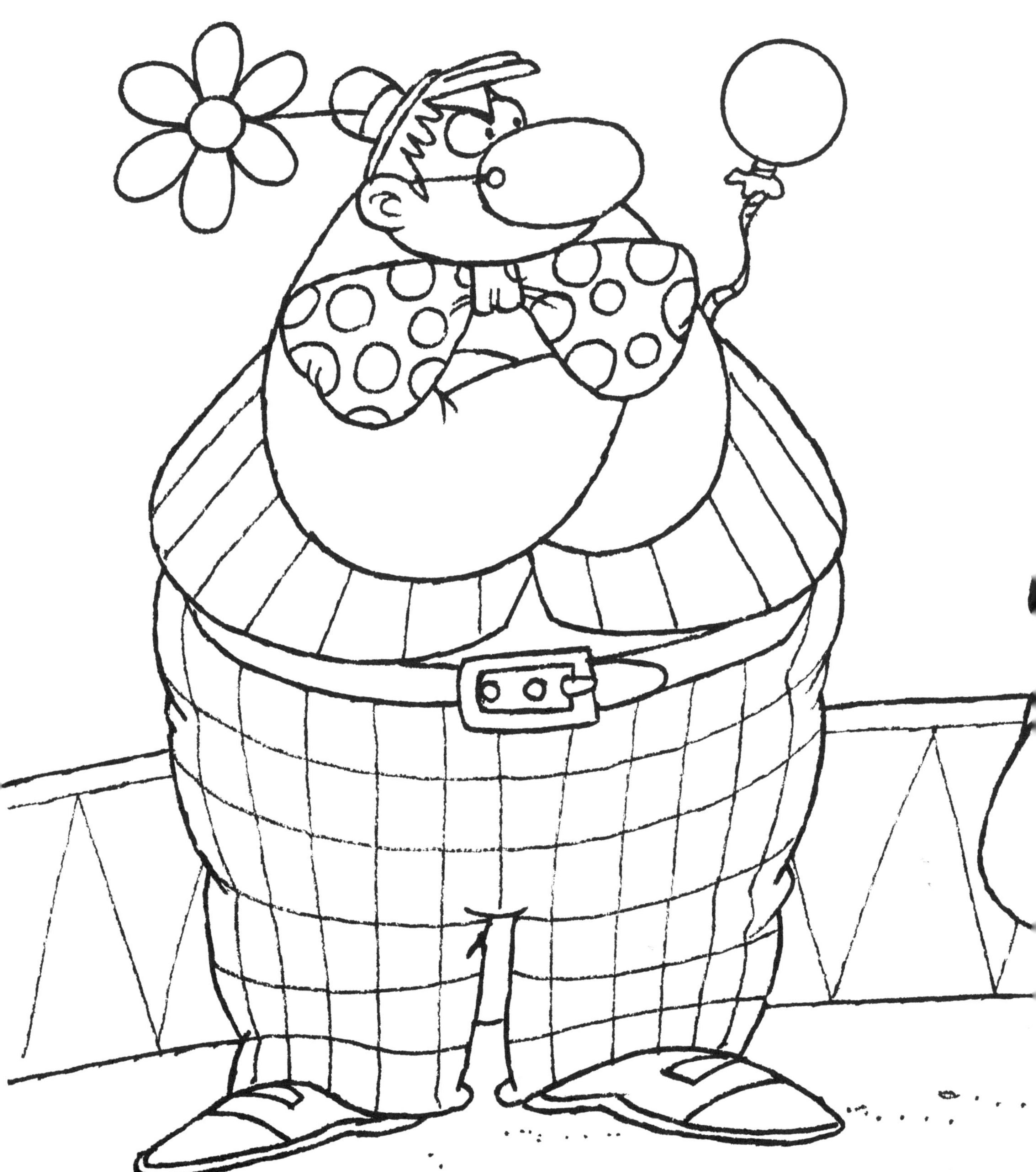

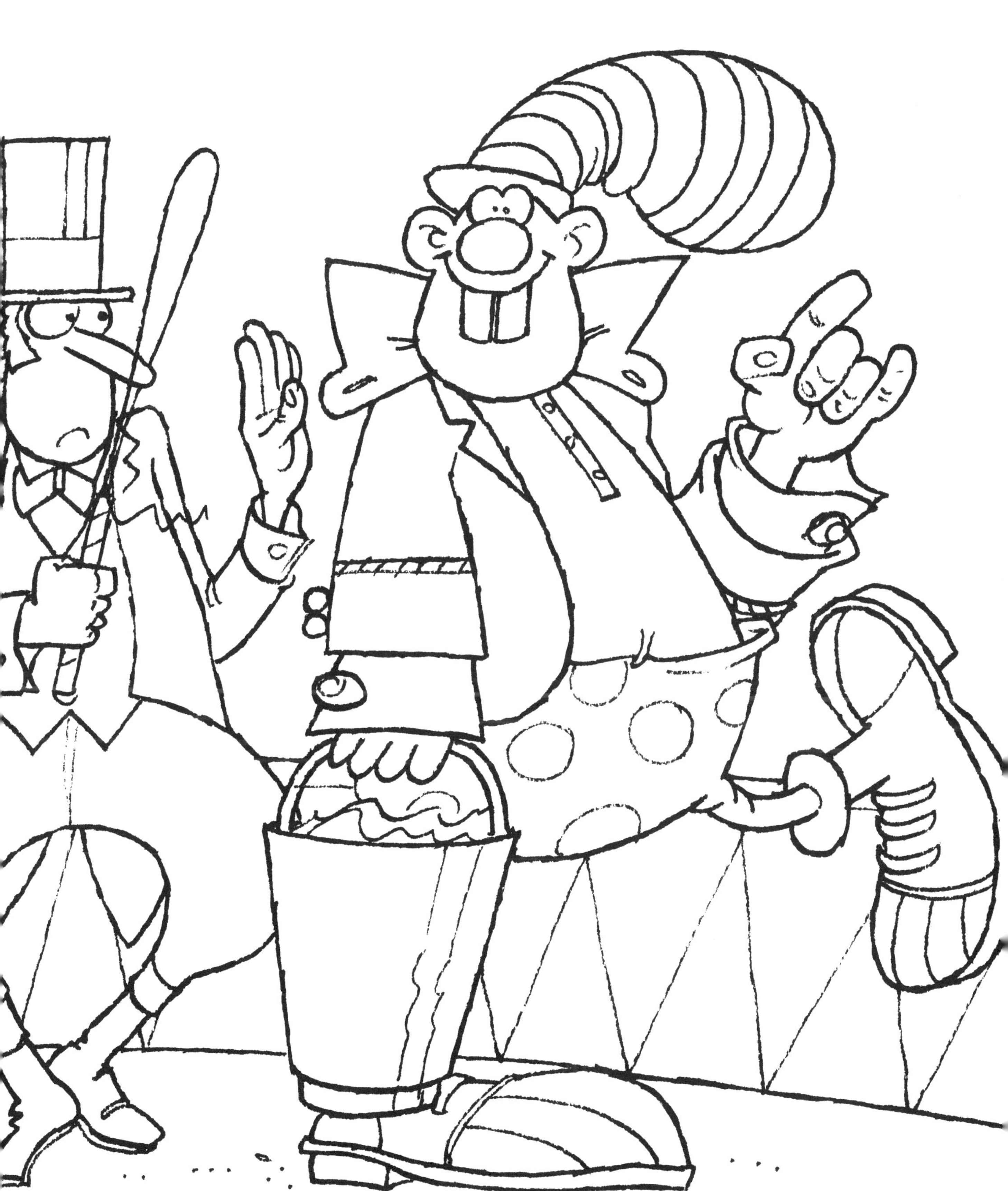

Who's winning the tug of war?

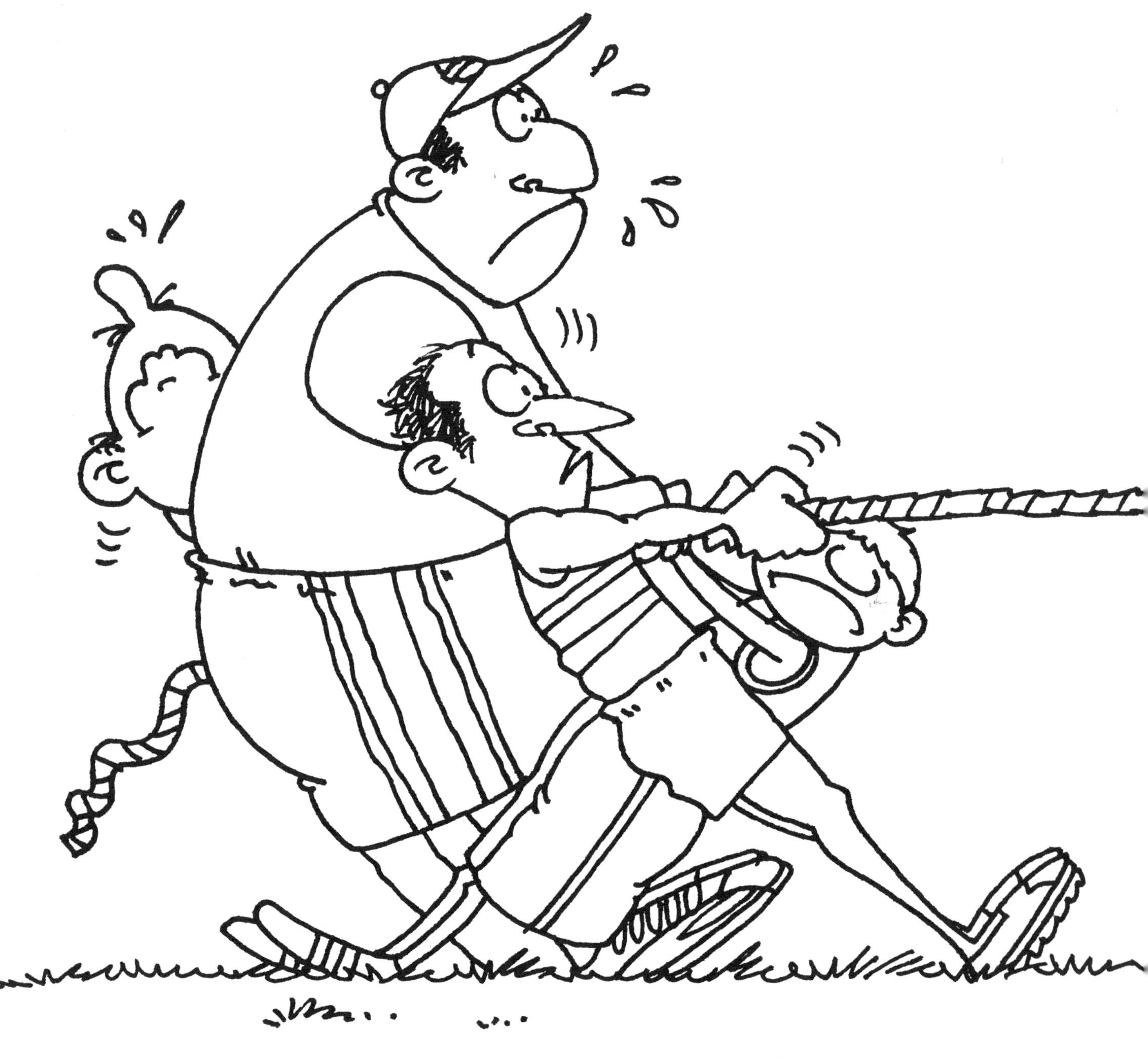

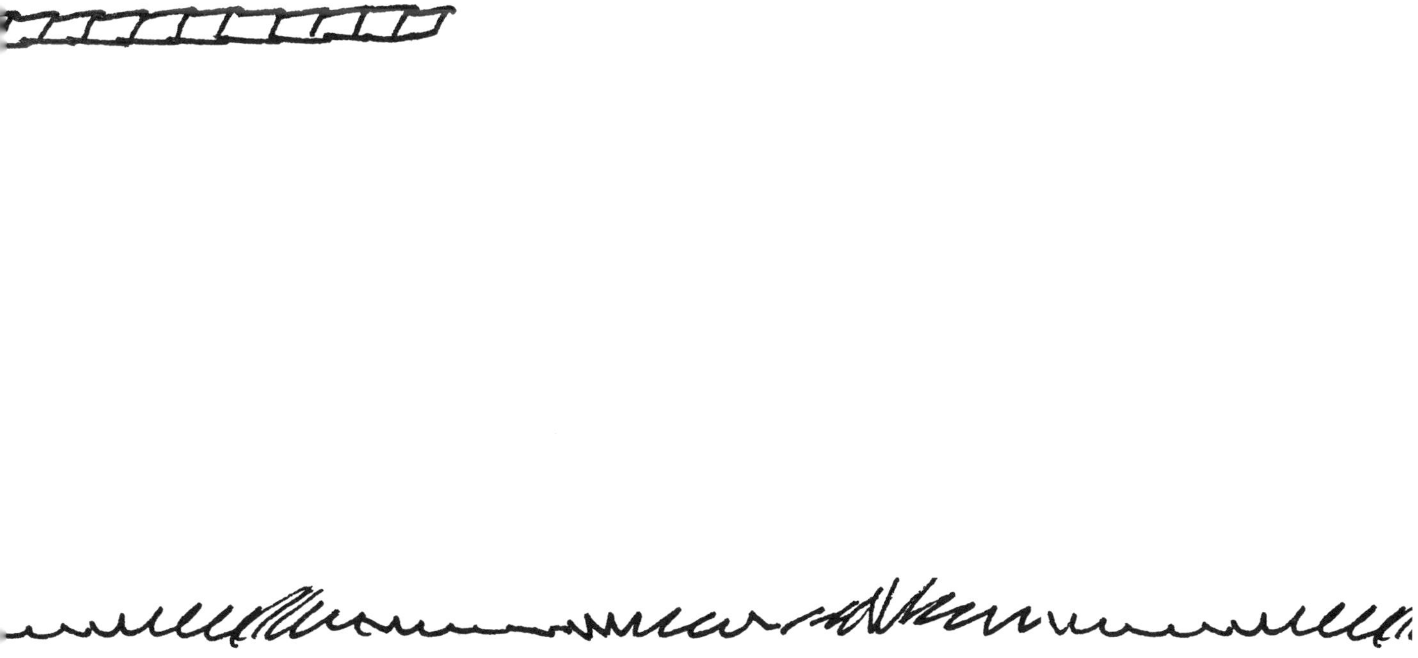

Carve a creepy halloween face

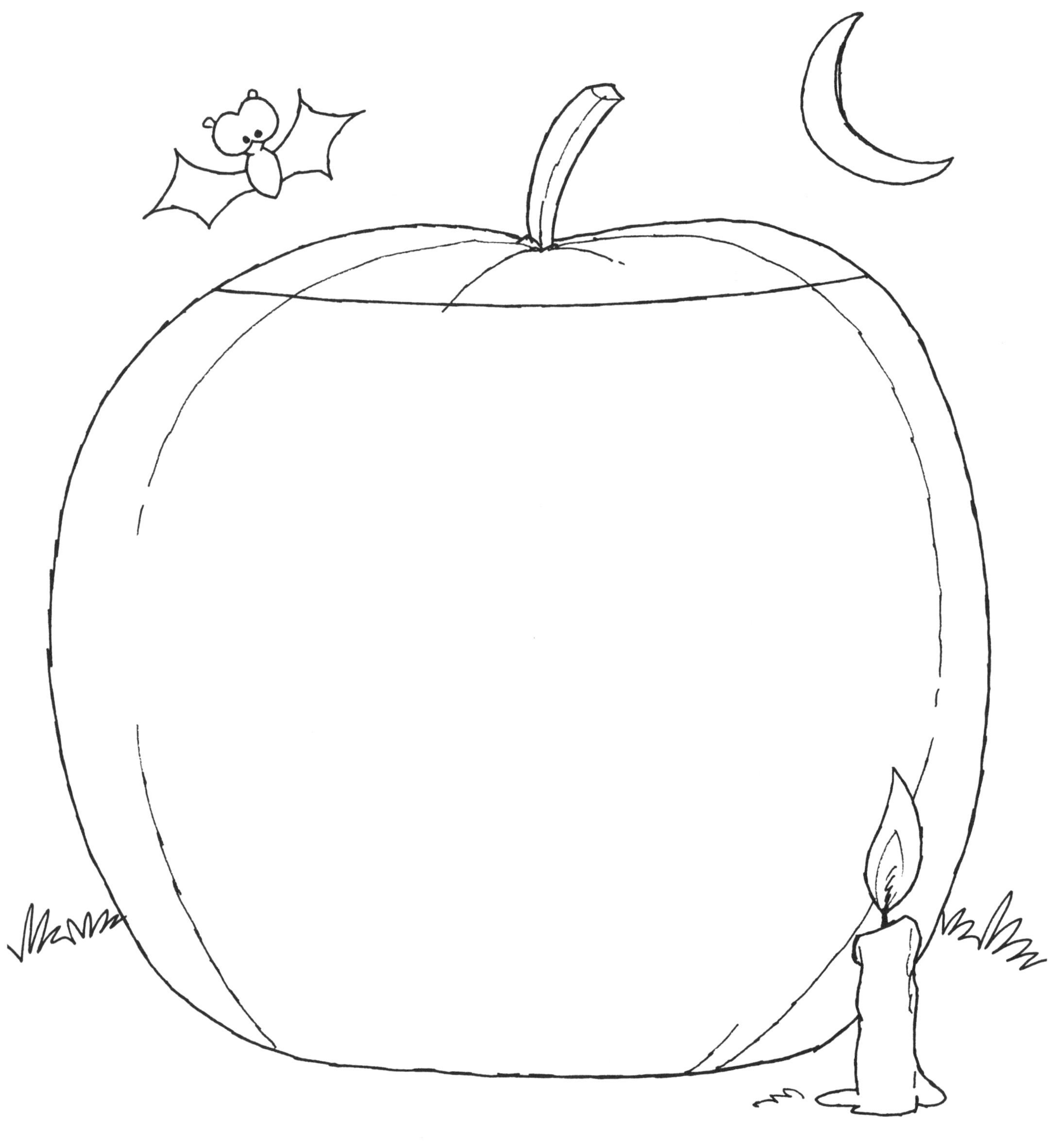

Guests always get the fancy teacups

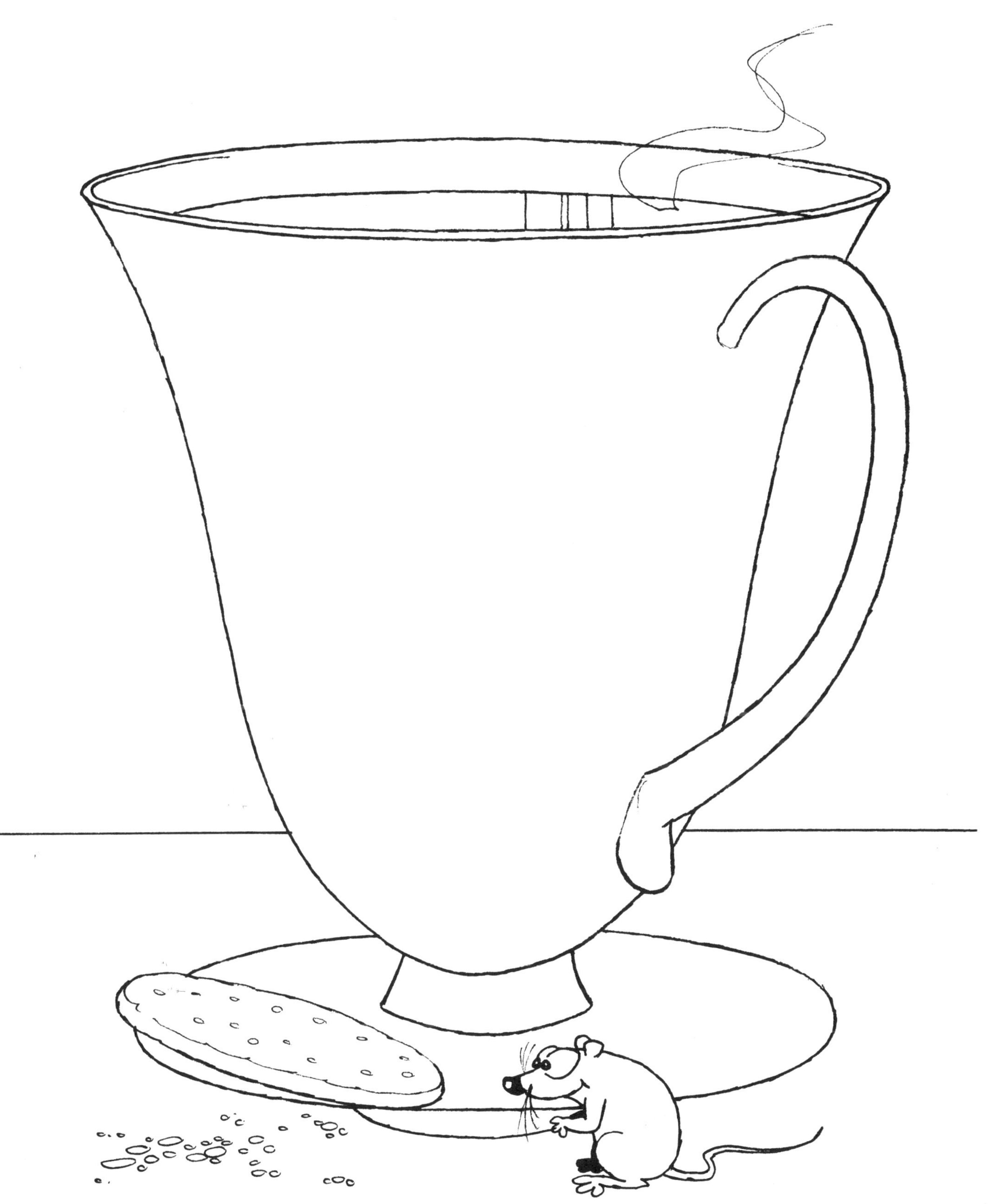

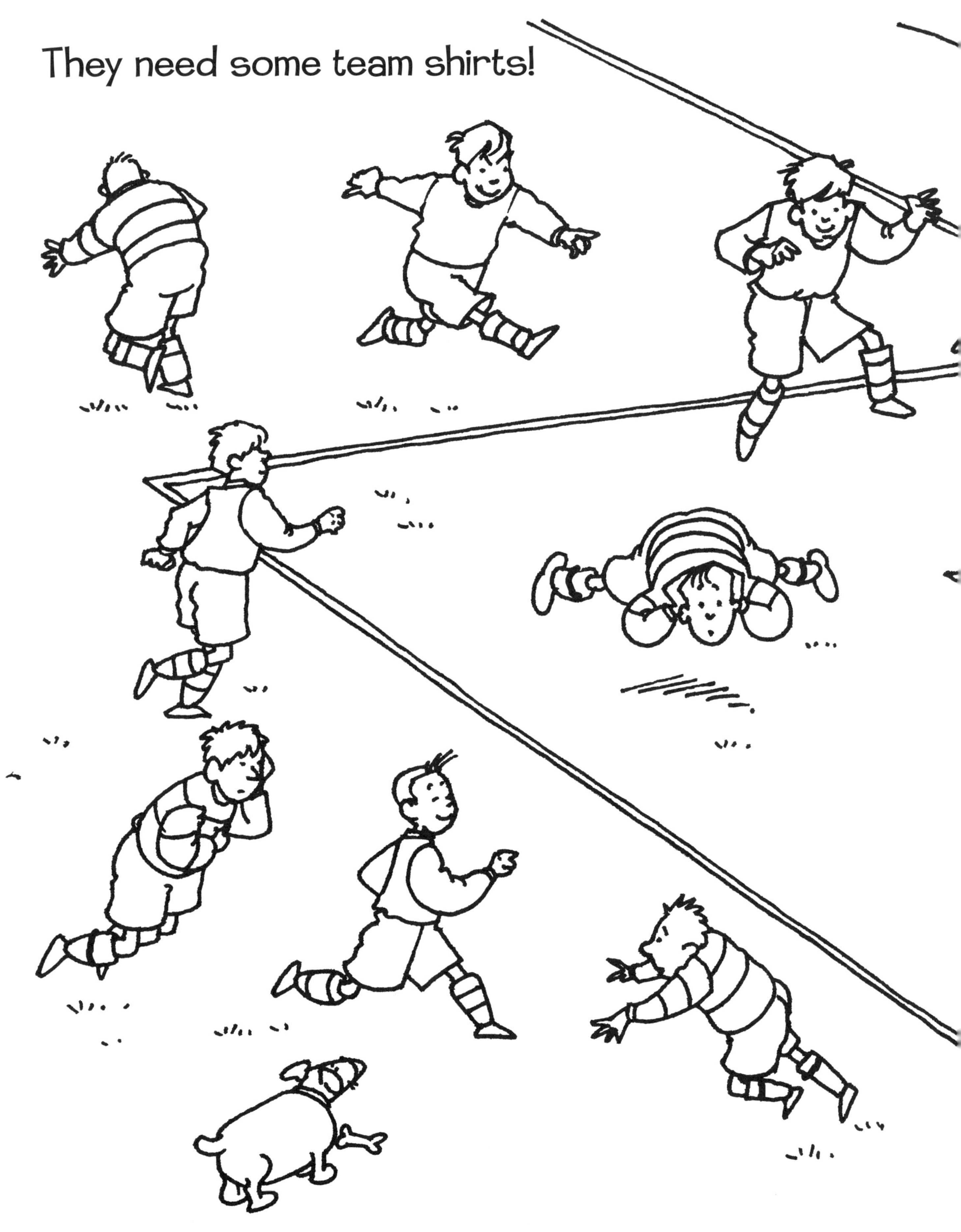
They need some team shirts!

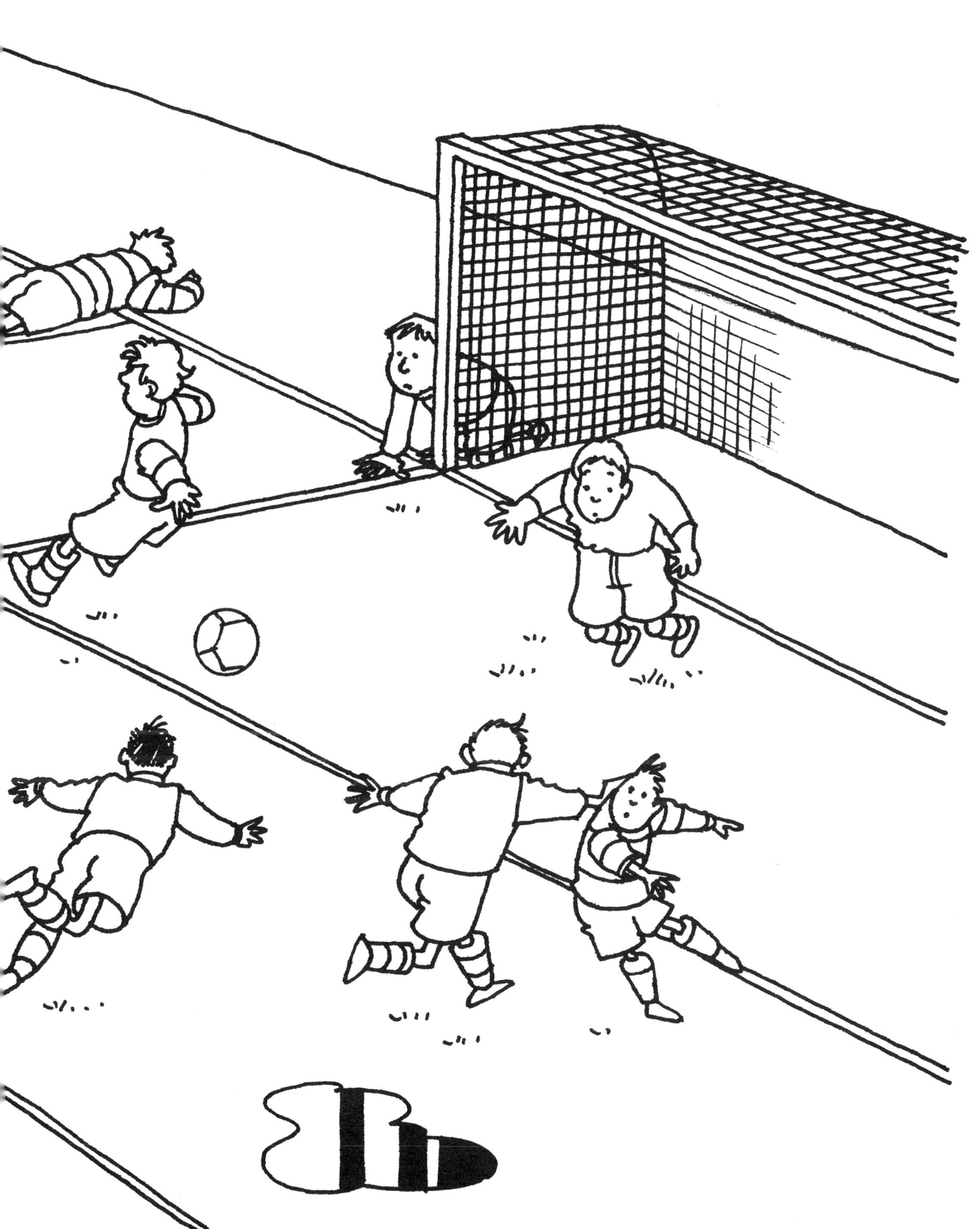

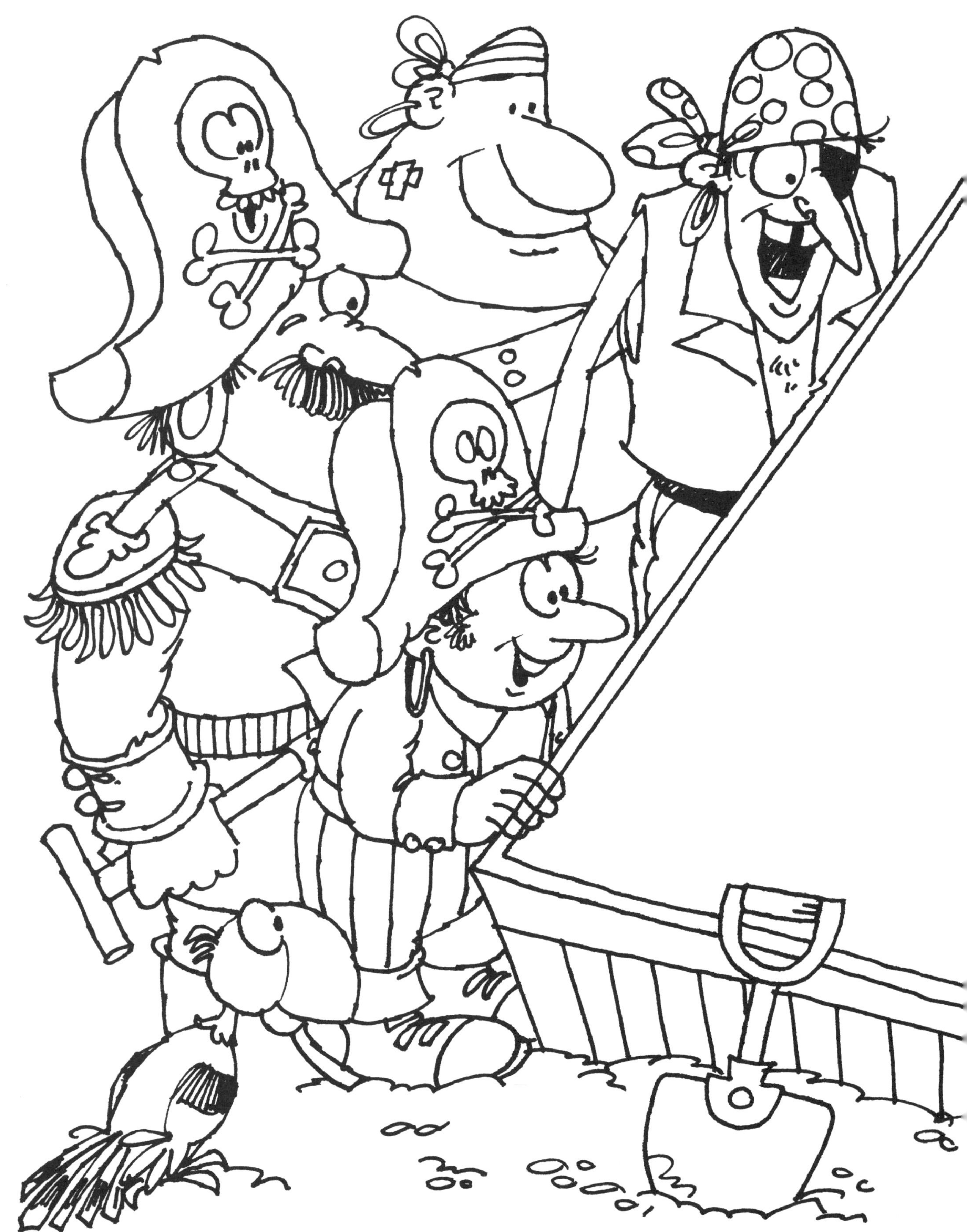

Treasure!

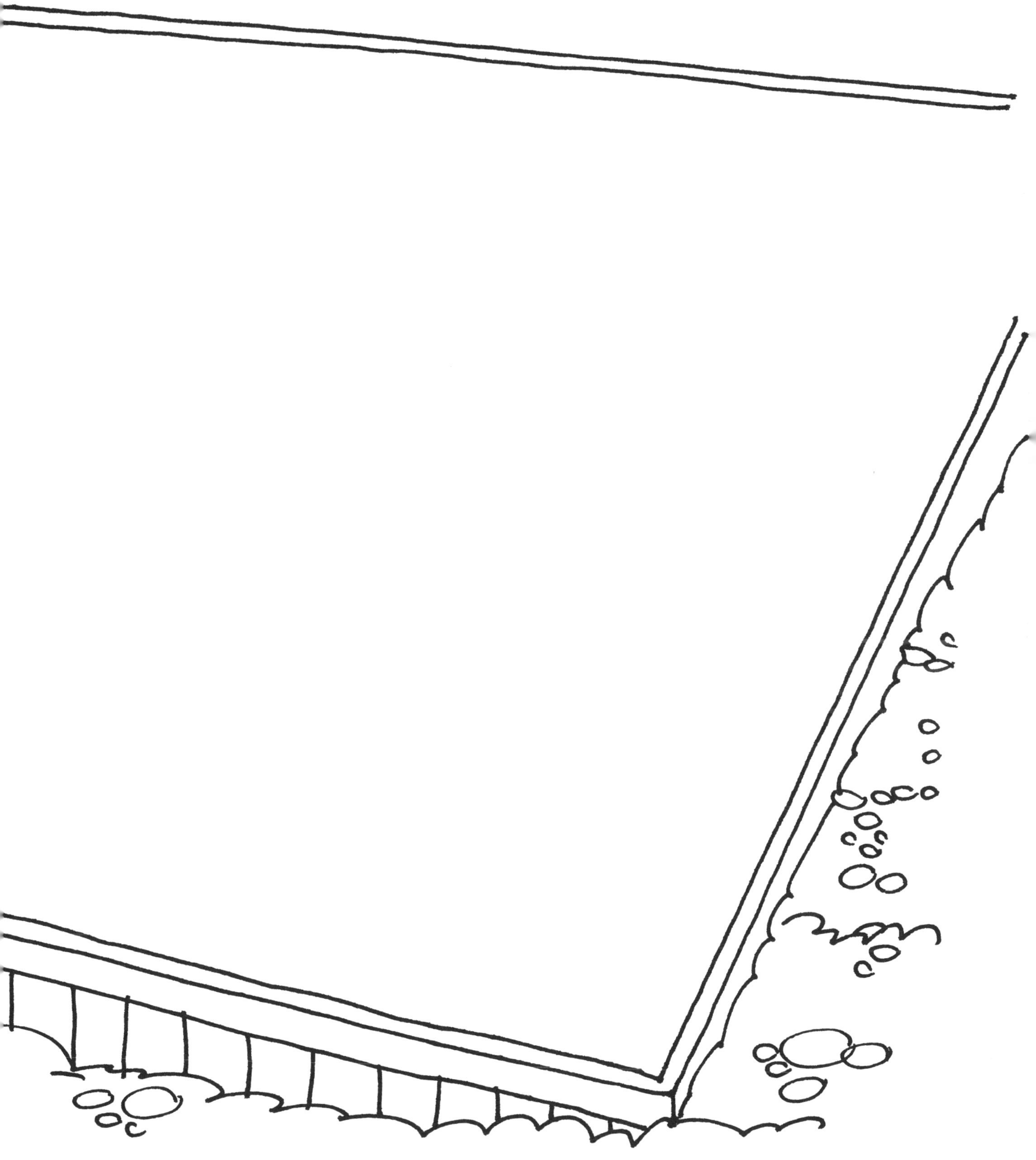

Did the others make the jump?

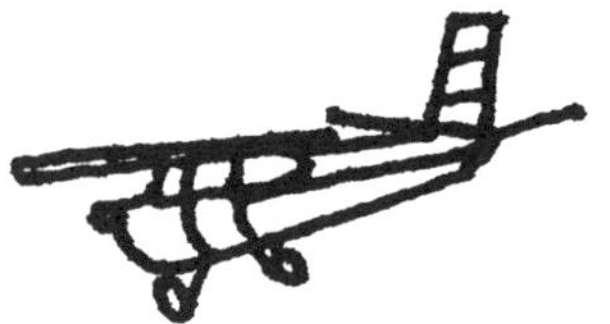

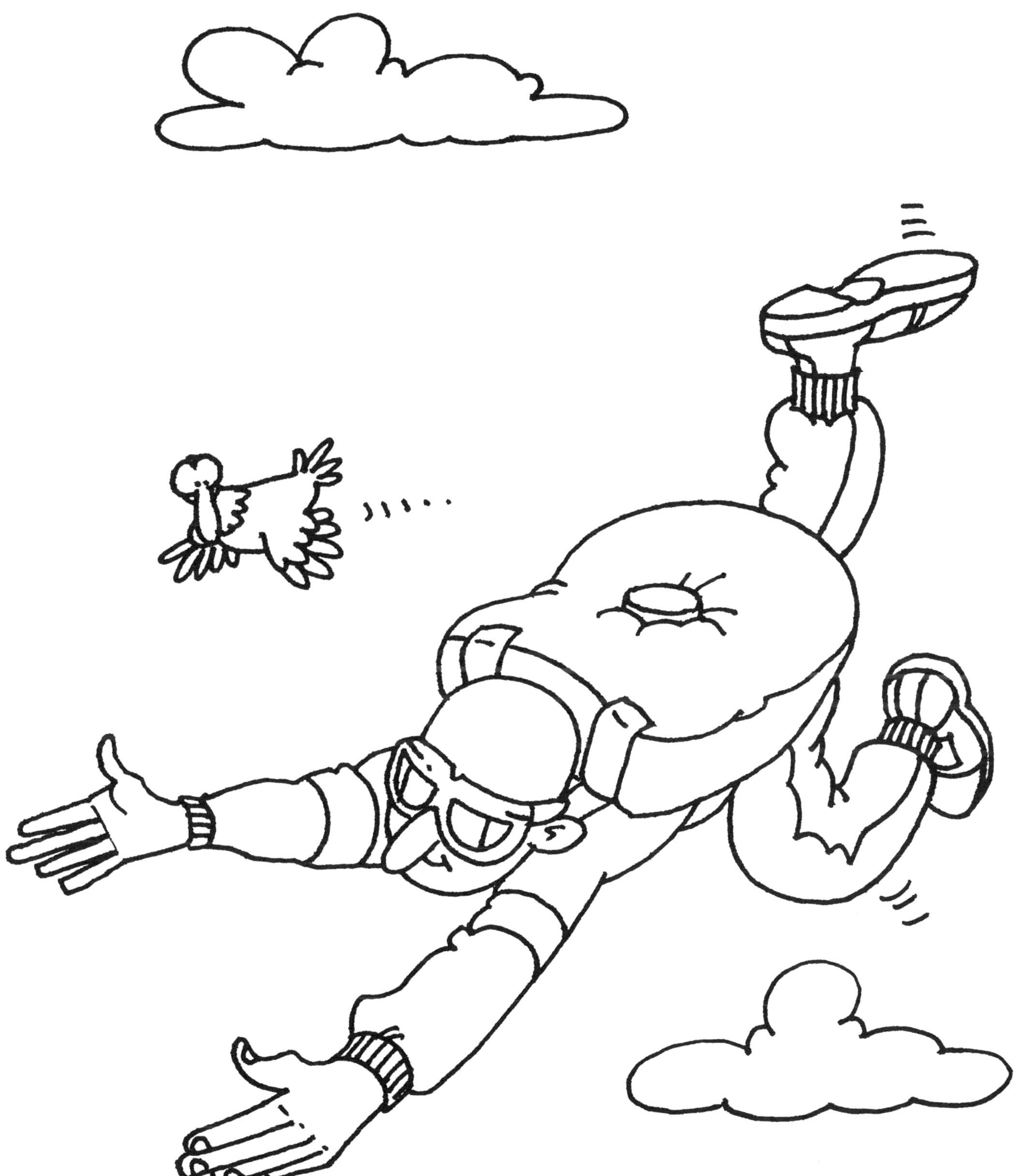

What flavor are the sweets on the witch's house?

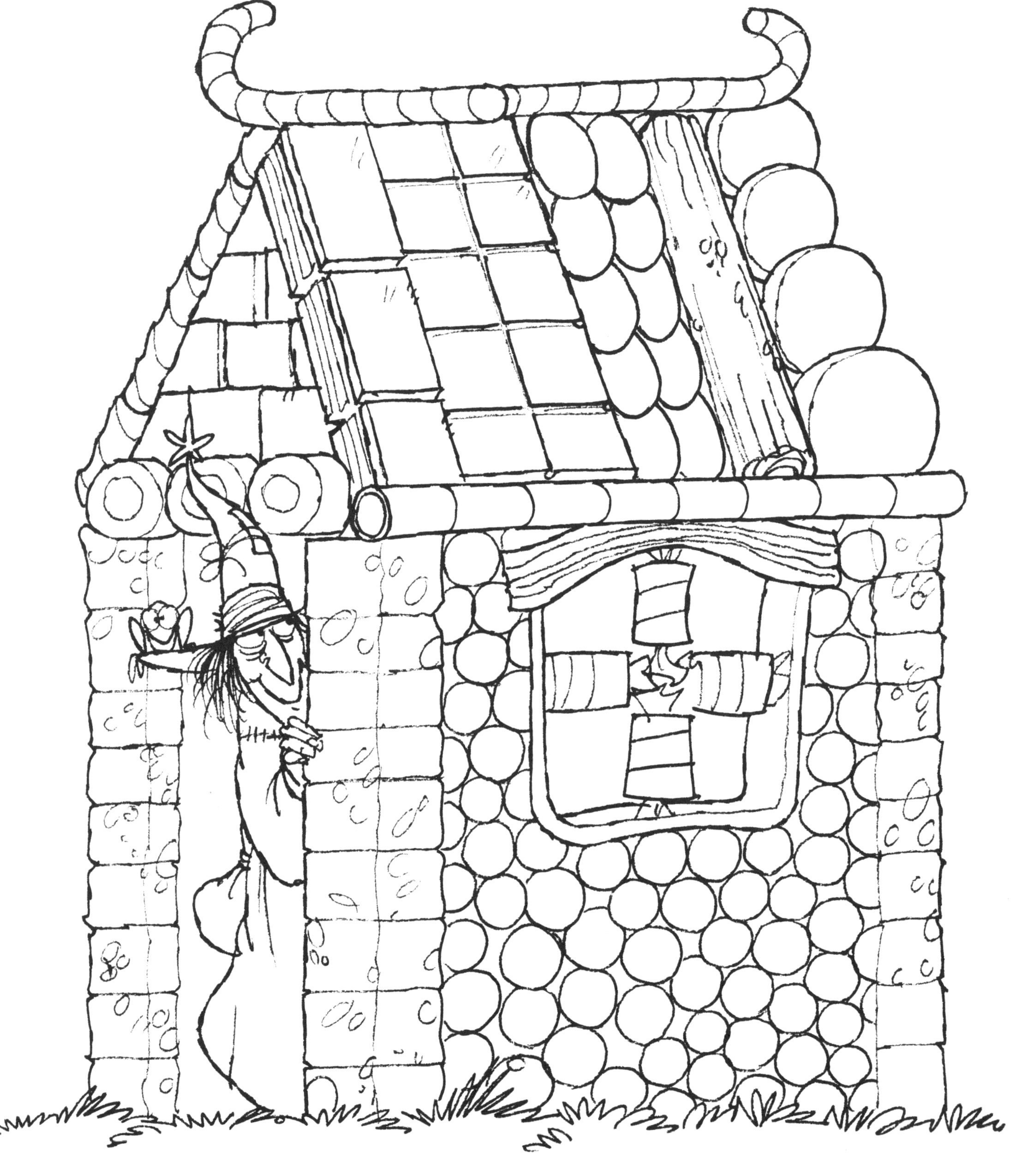

Jim can't resist a certain midnight snack

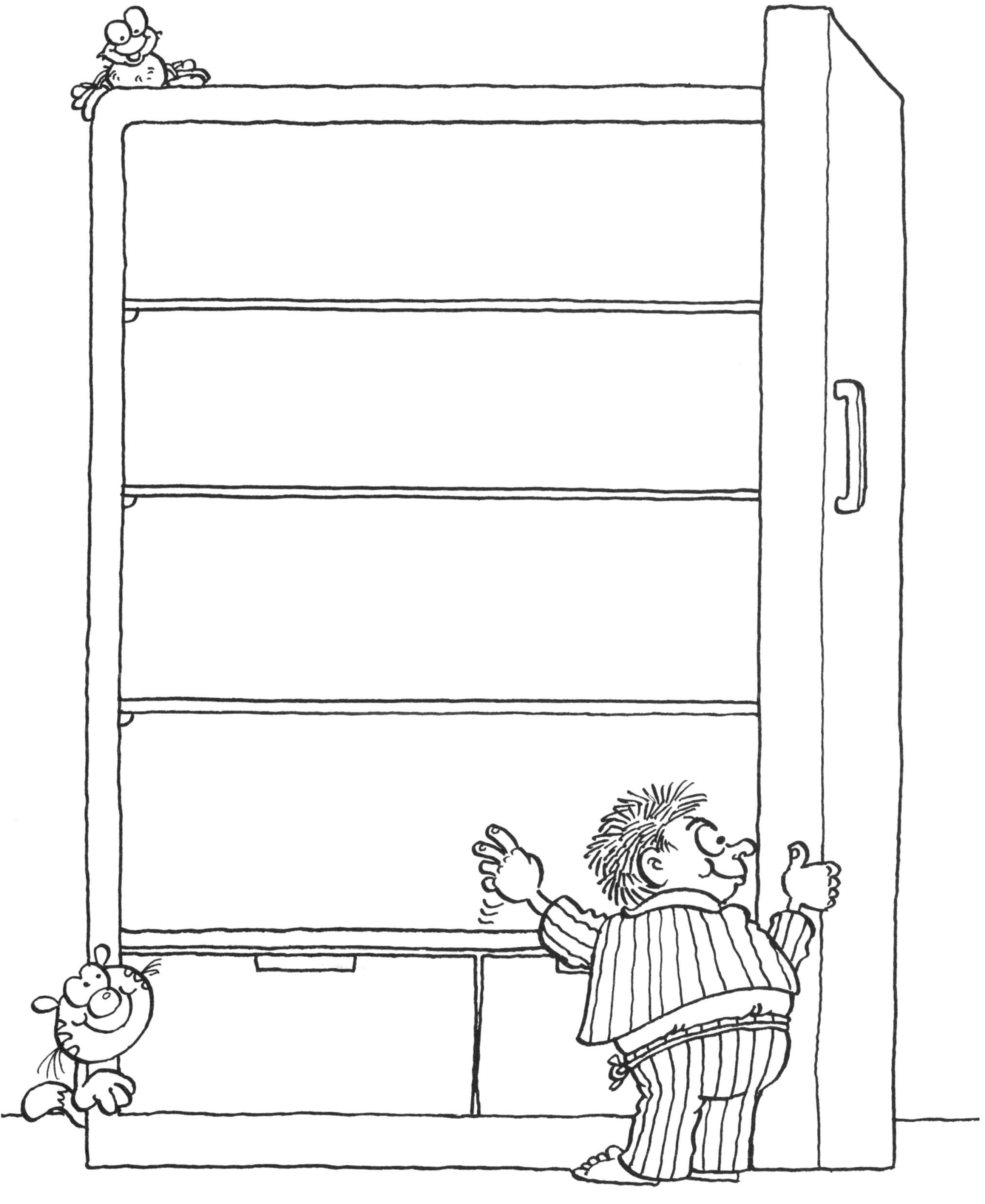

Is it camping weather today?

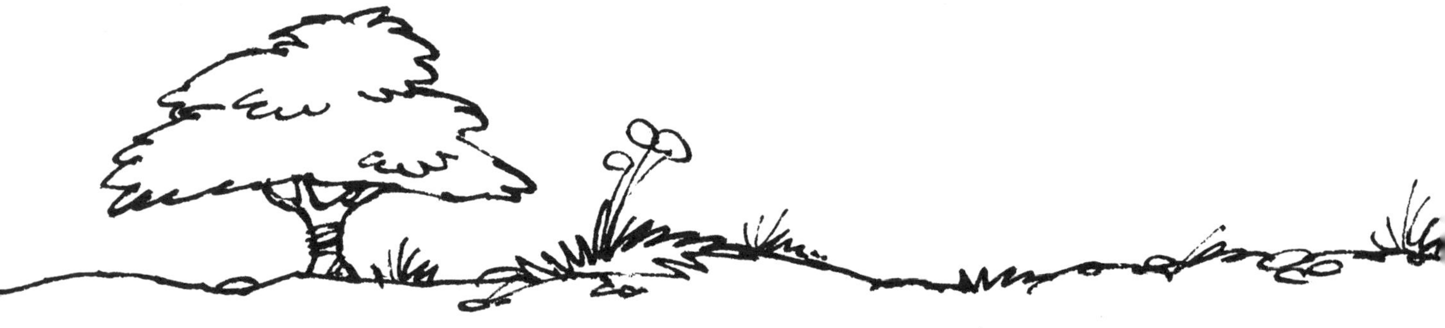

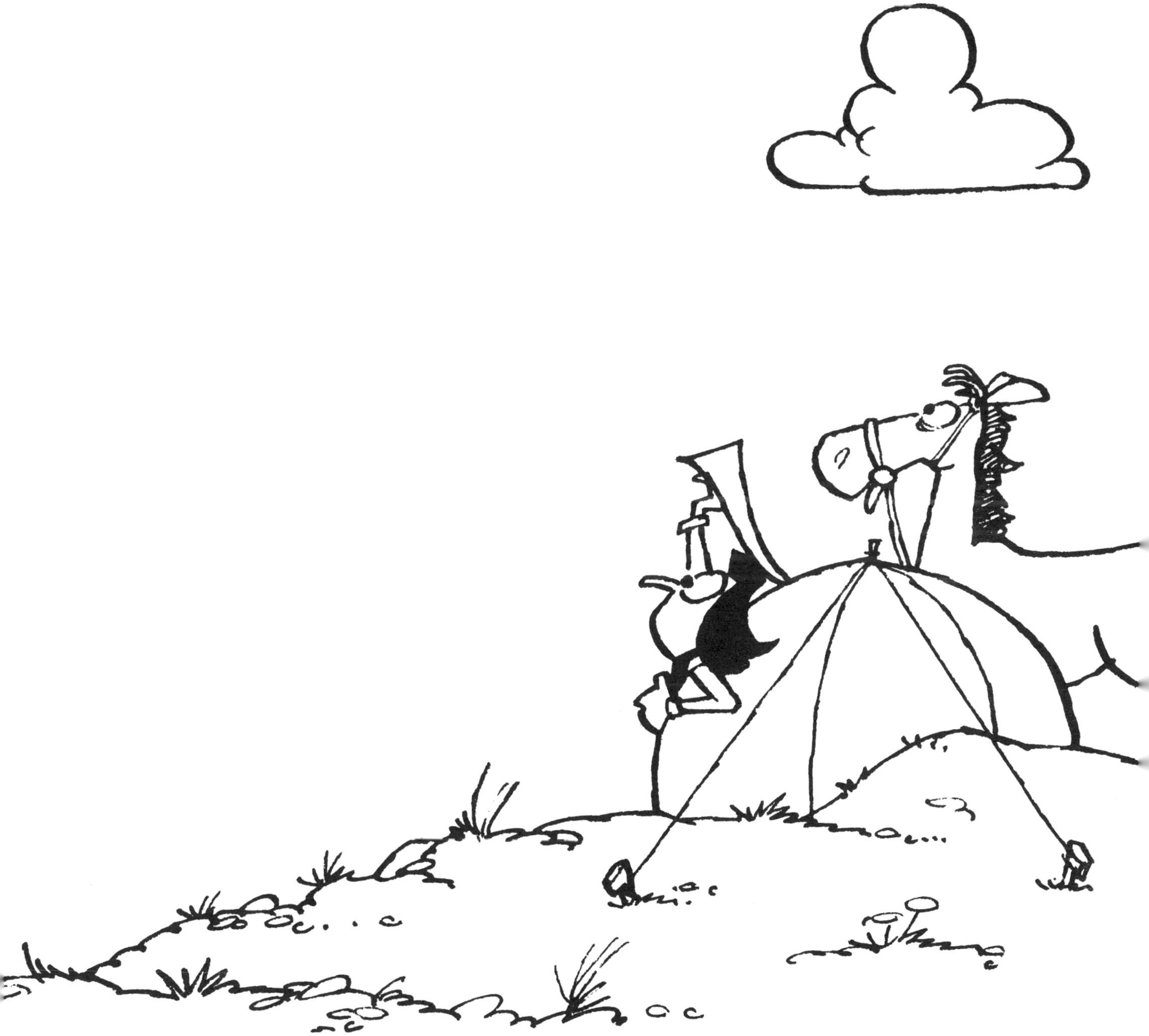

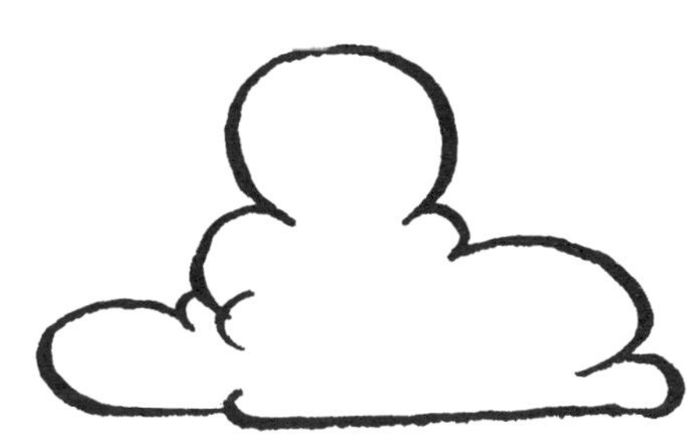

What's lurking at the bottom of the pool?

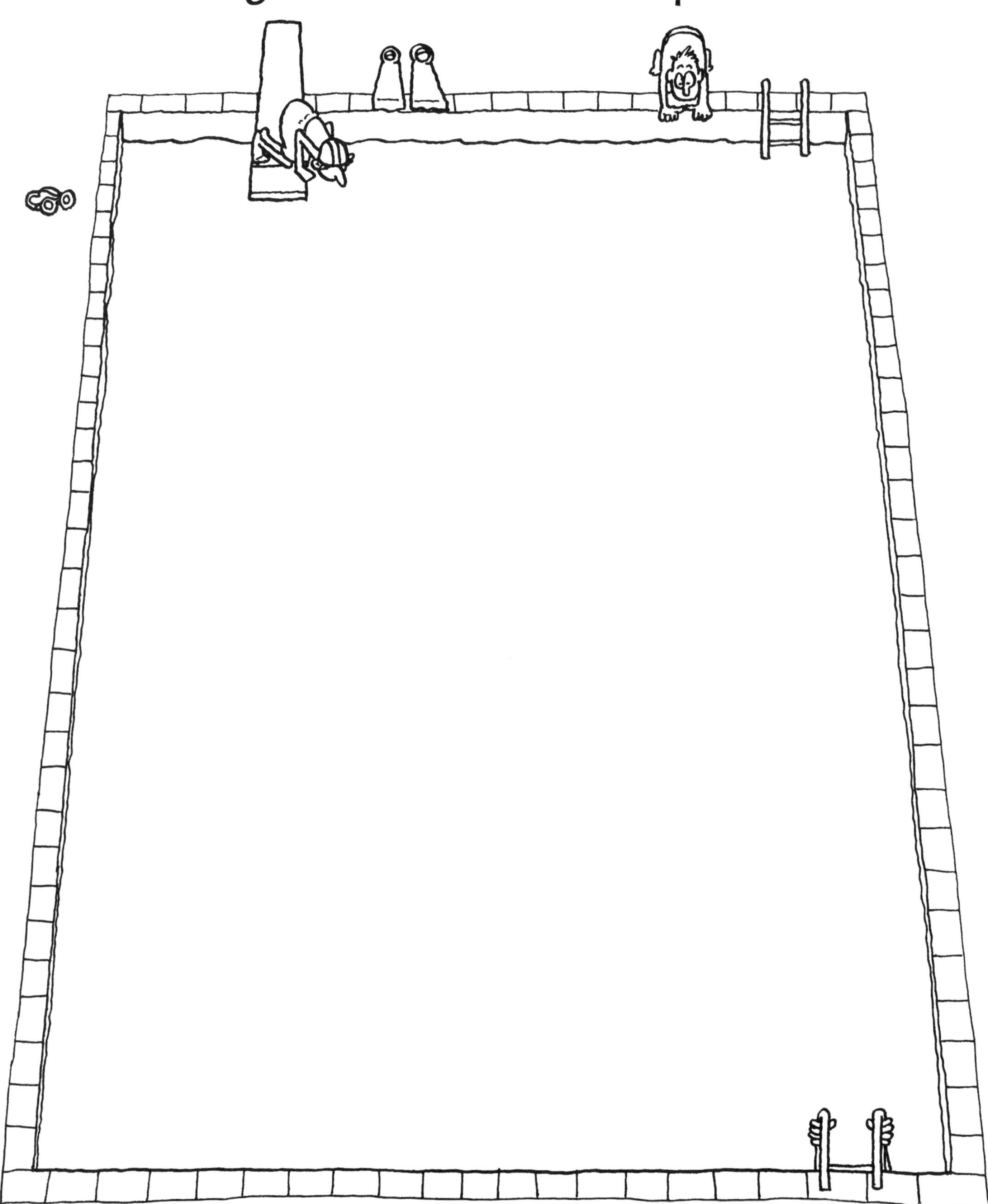

Dress the ugly sisters for the ball

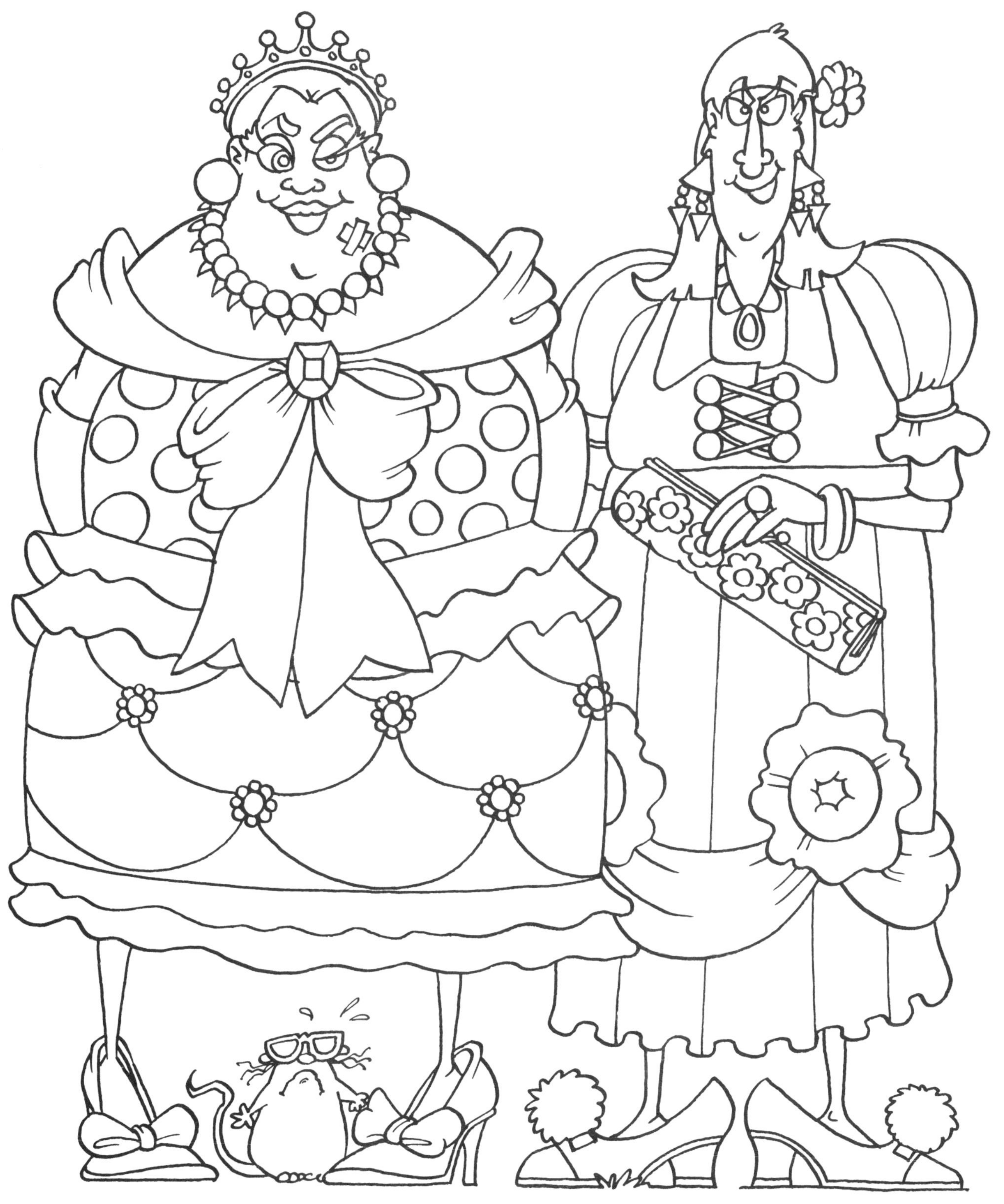

Fantastically brilliant magical stars!

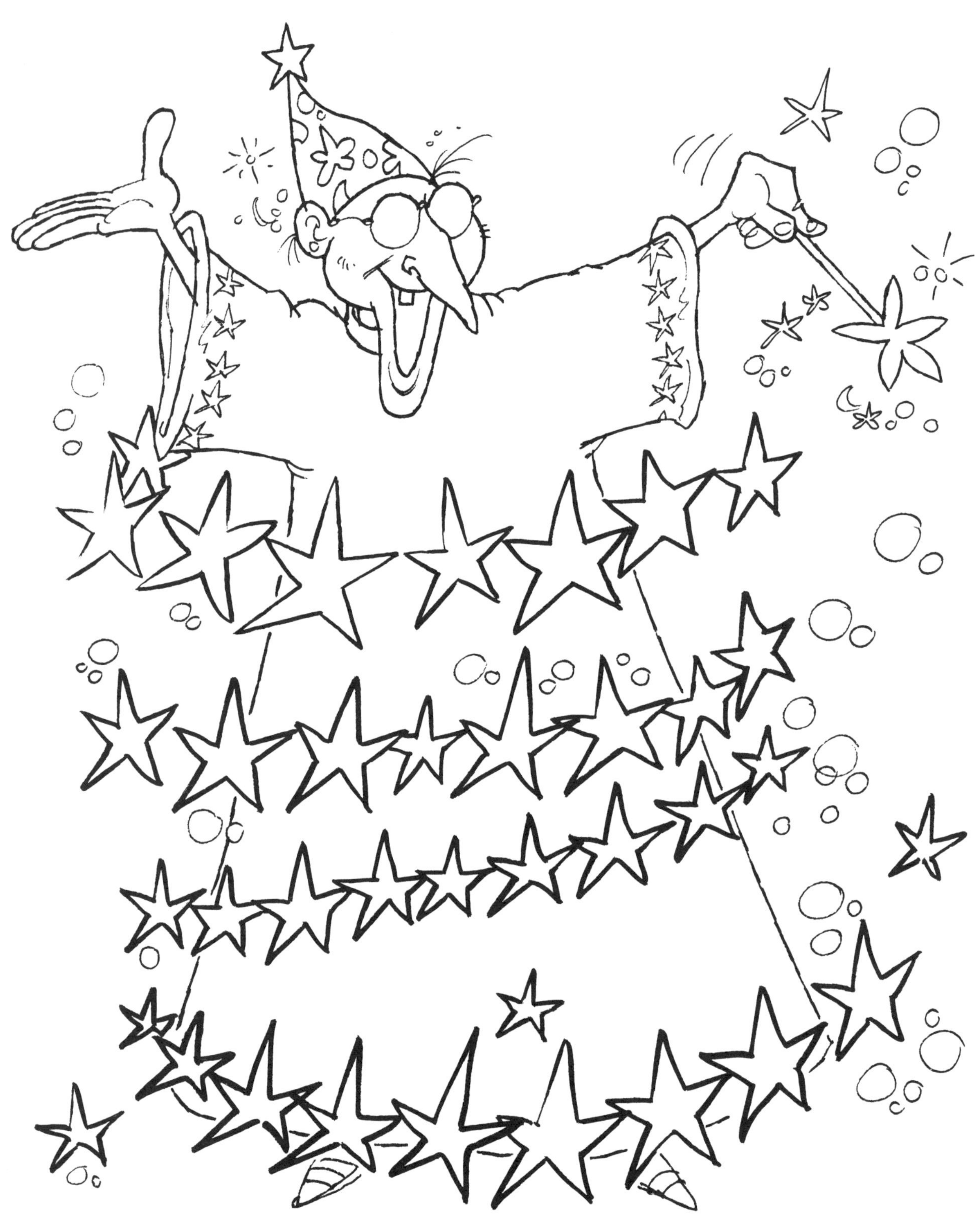

It's the best present ever

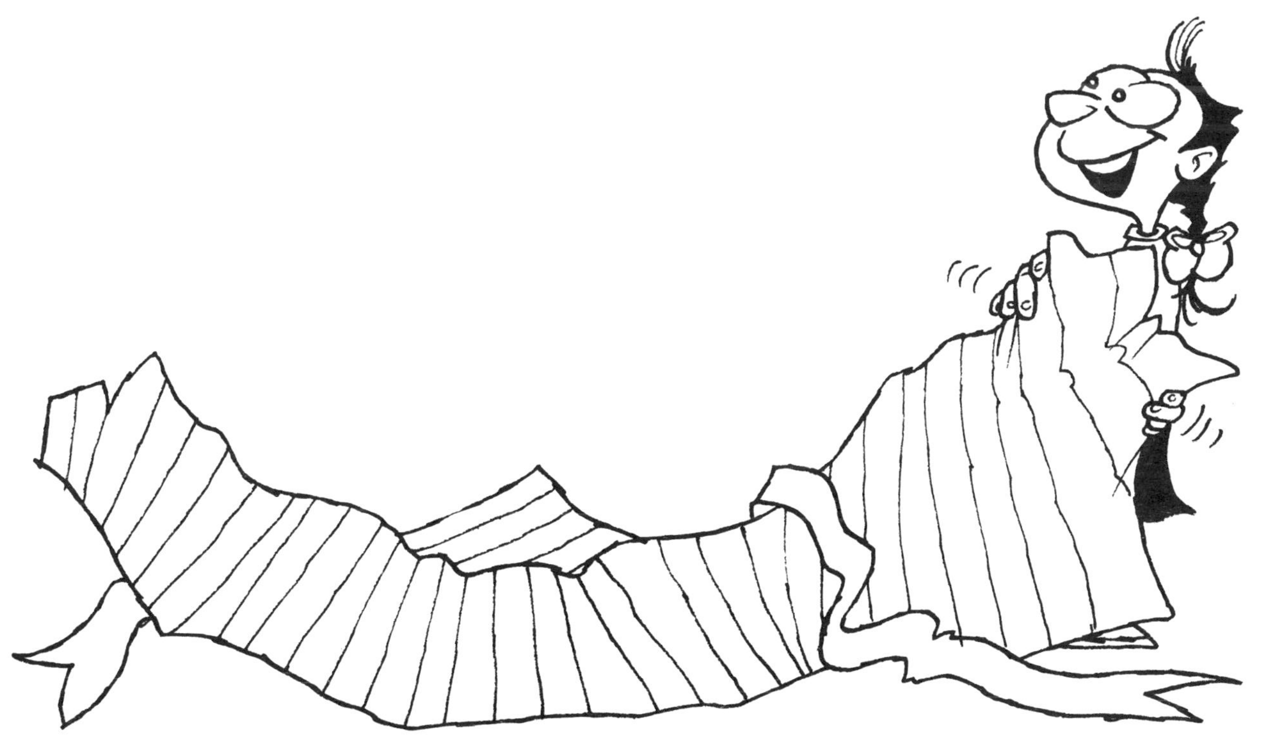

What's knocked Mrs Smith off her bicycle?

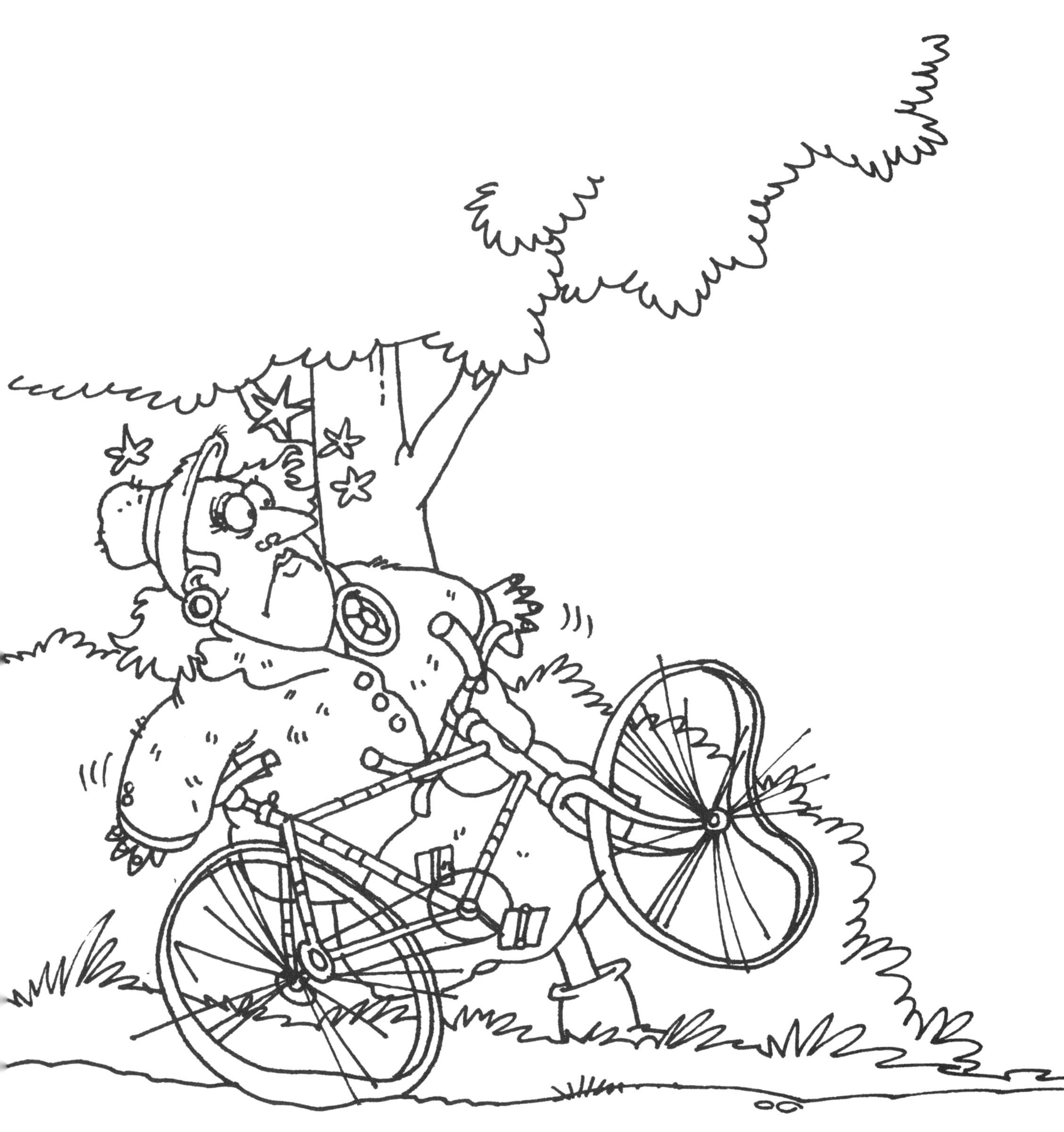

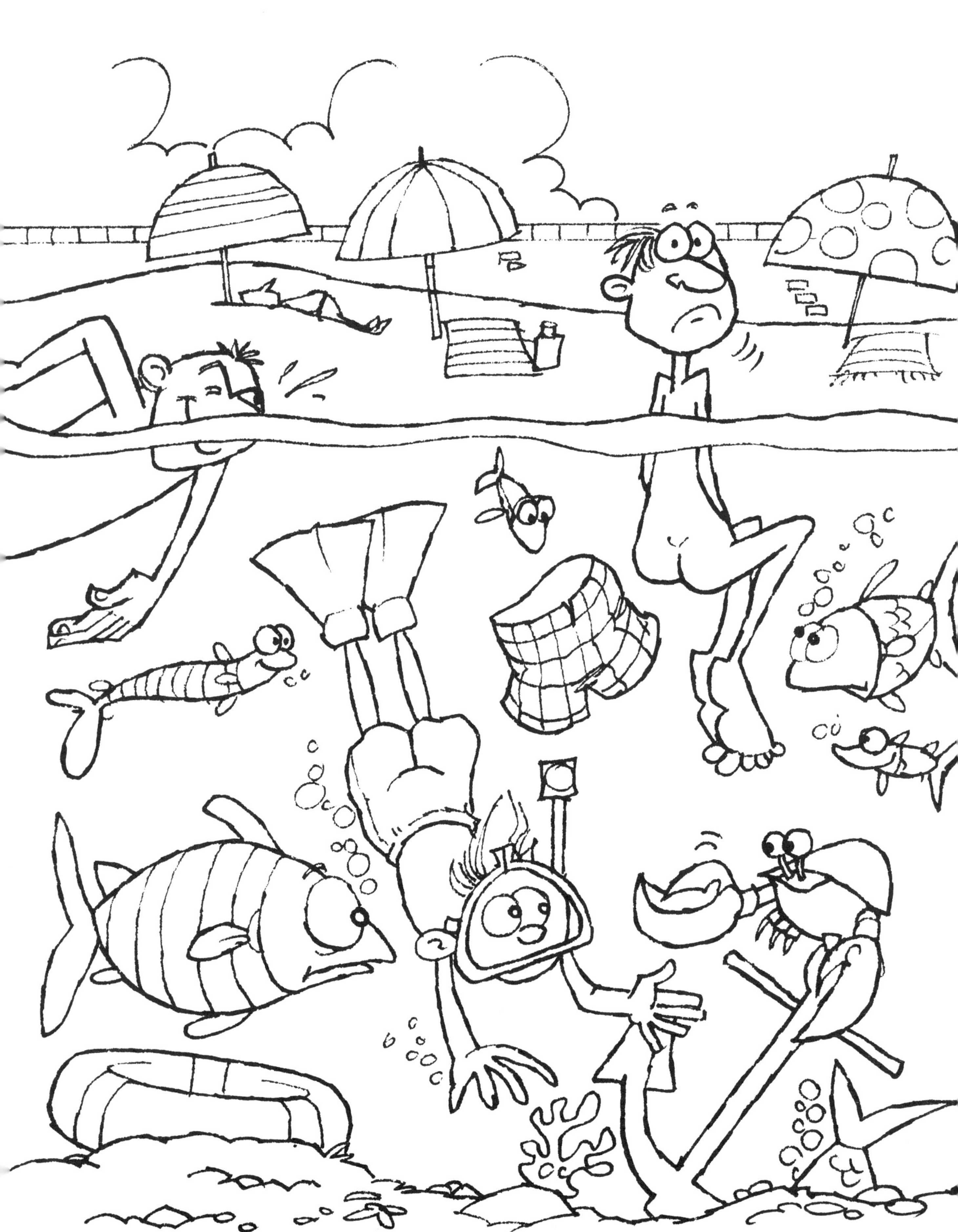

Color in the odd things under the sea

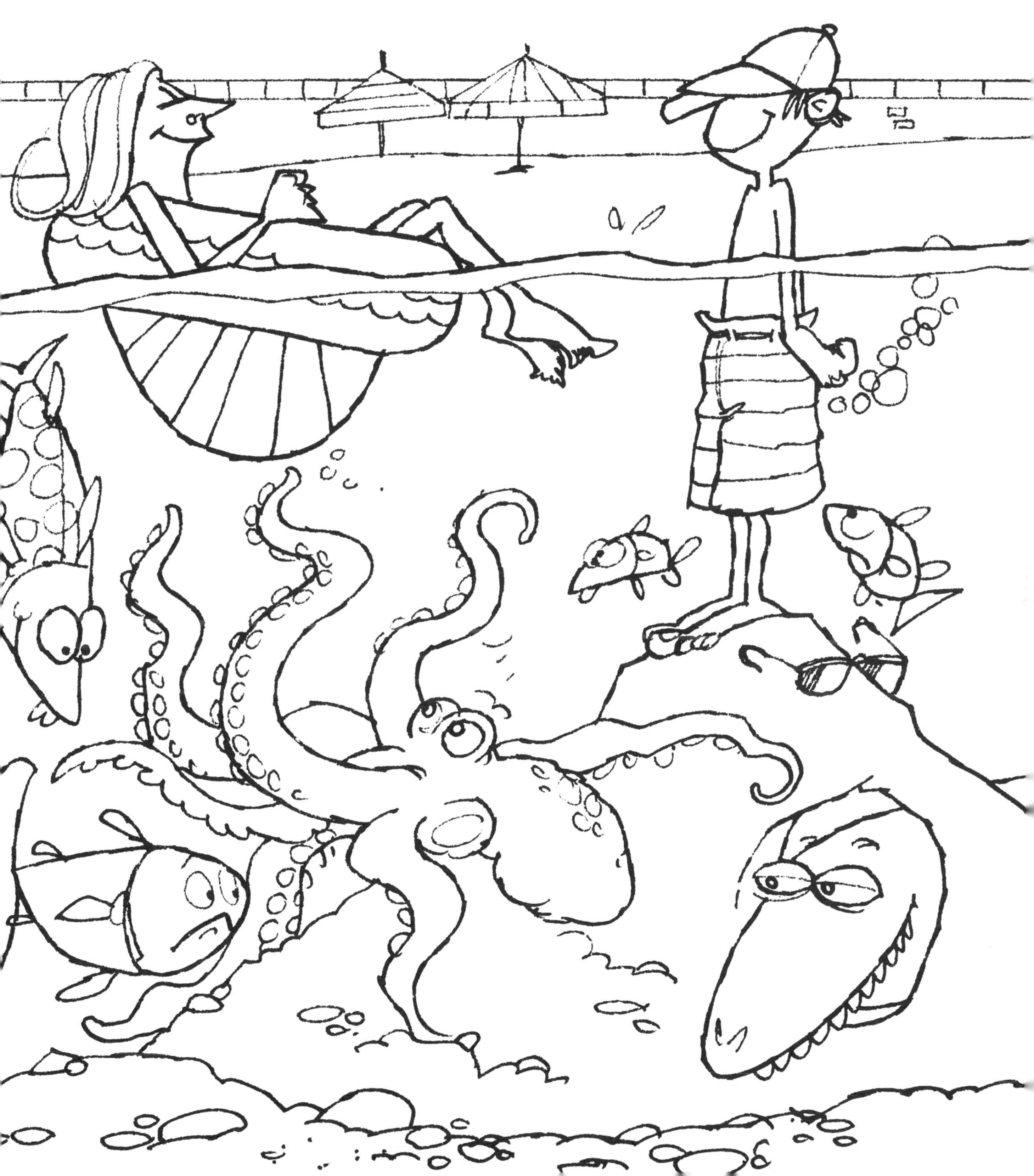

A beautiful castle fit for a princess

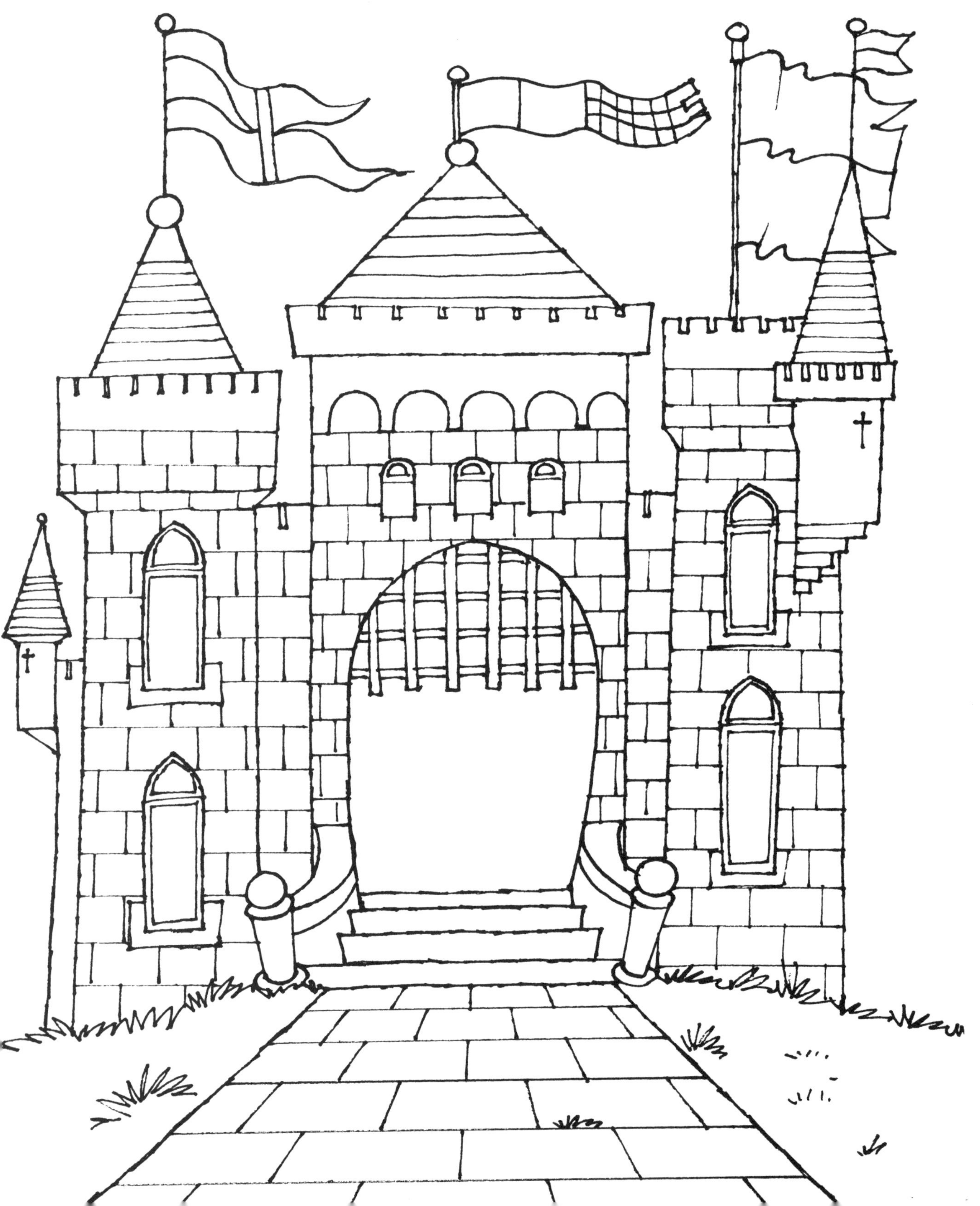

A postcard! Gee, I wish I was there...

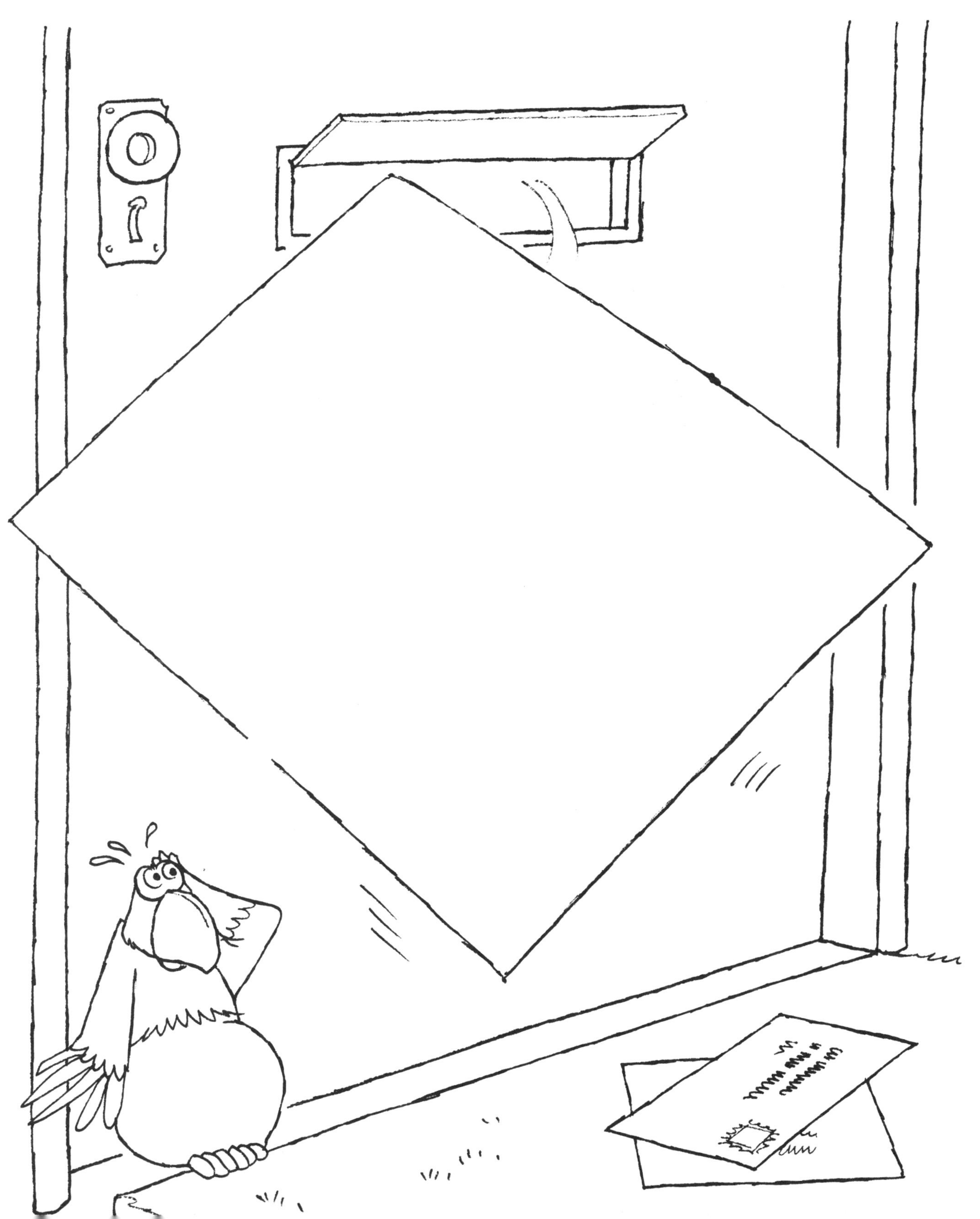

What are the robots making?

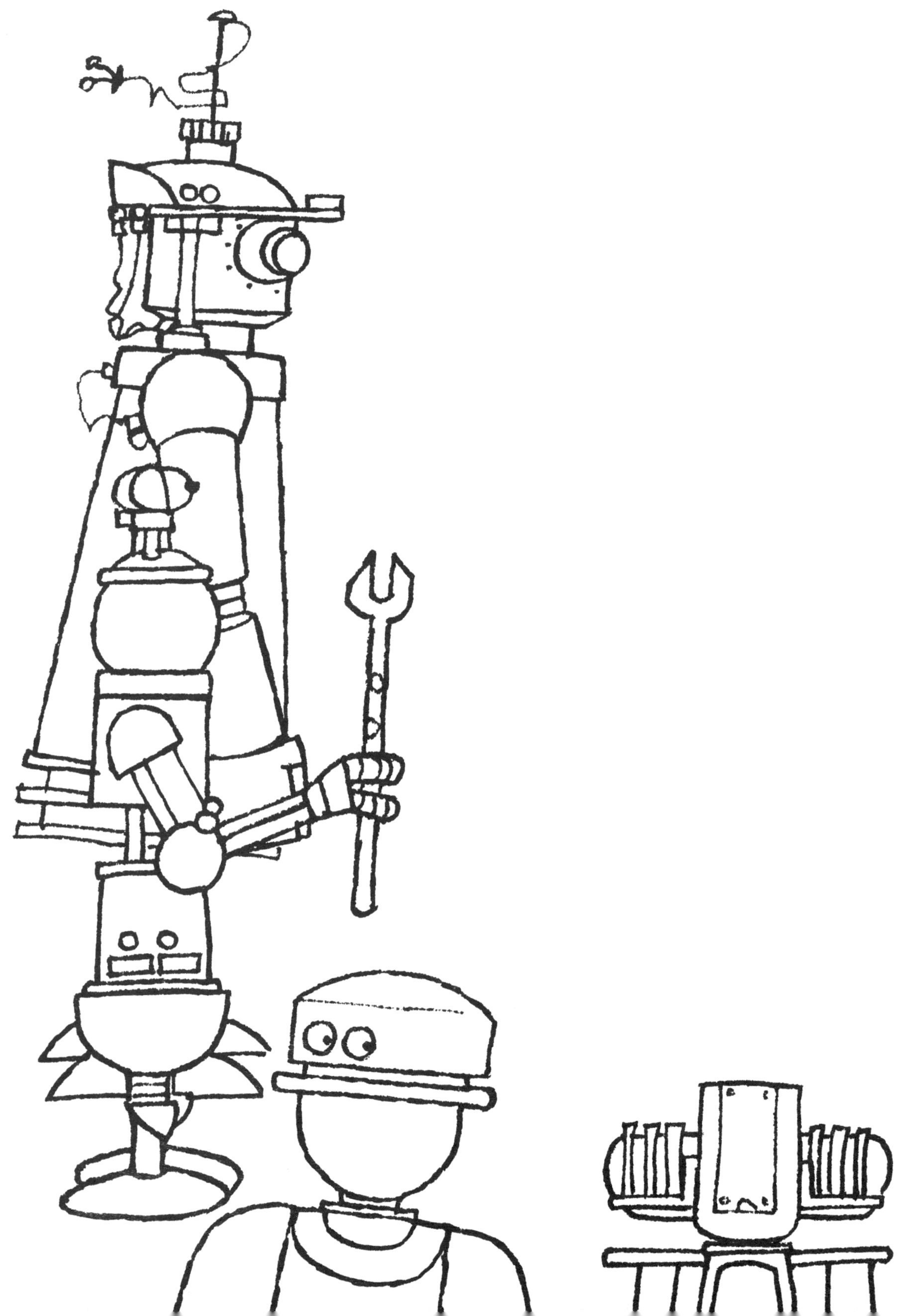

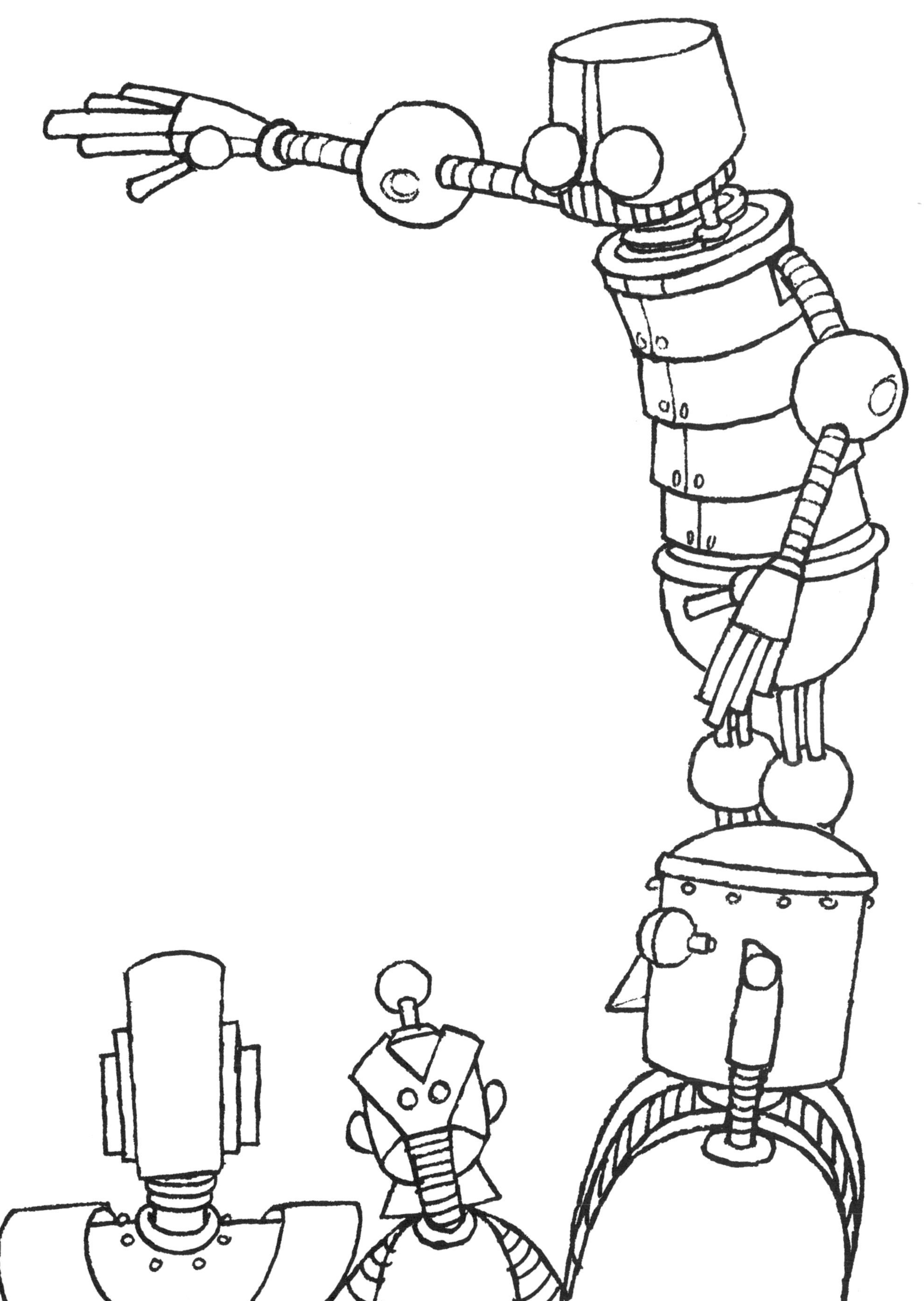

Who is Jane gossiping with?

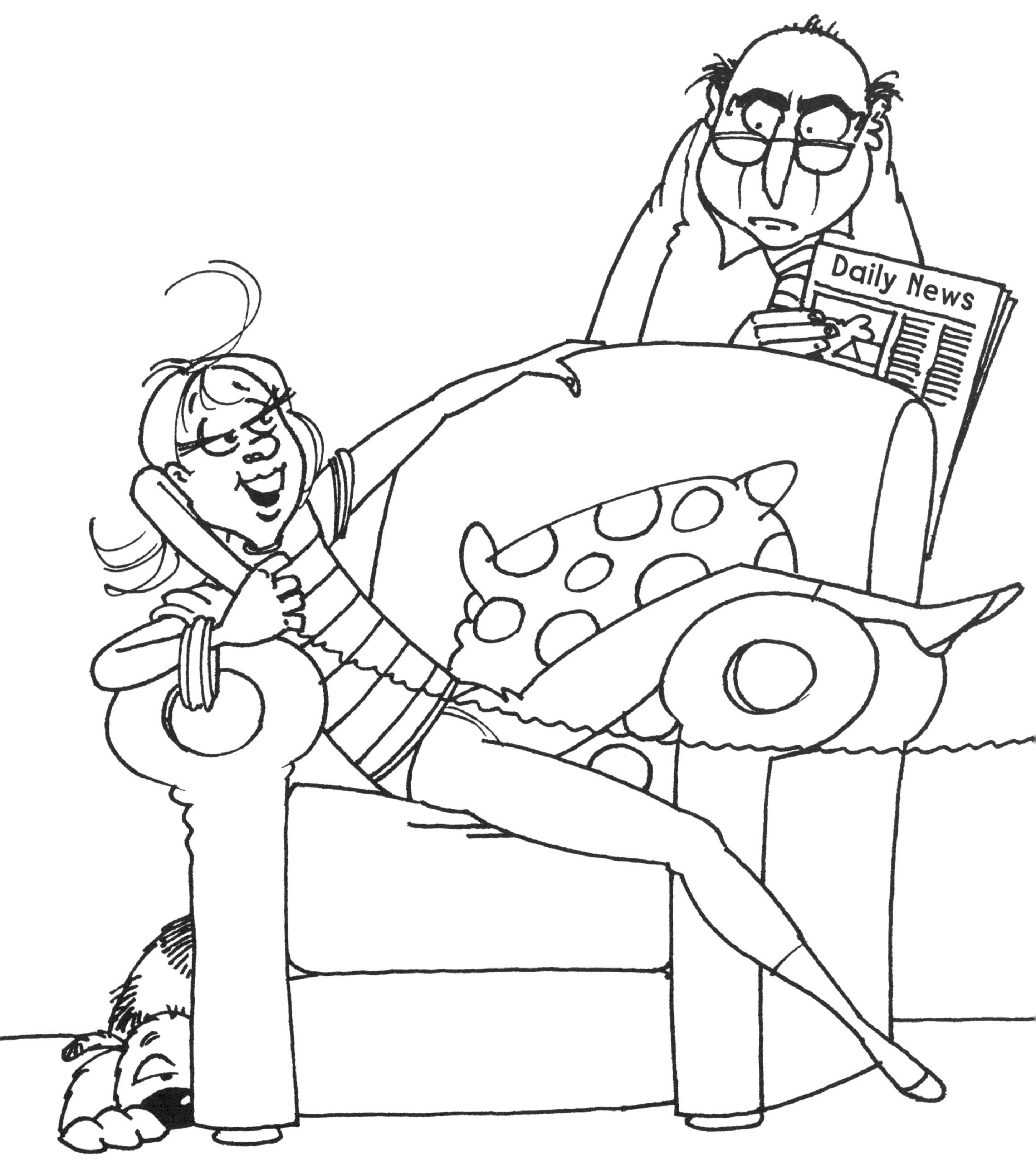

What's about to snap him up for lunch?

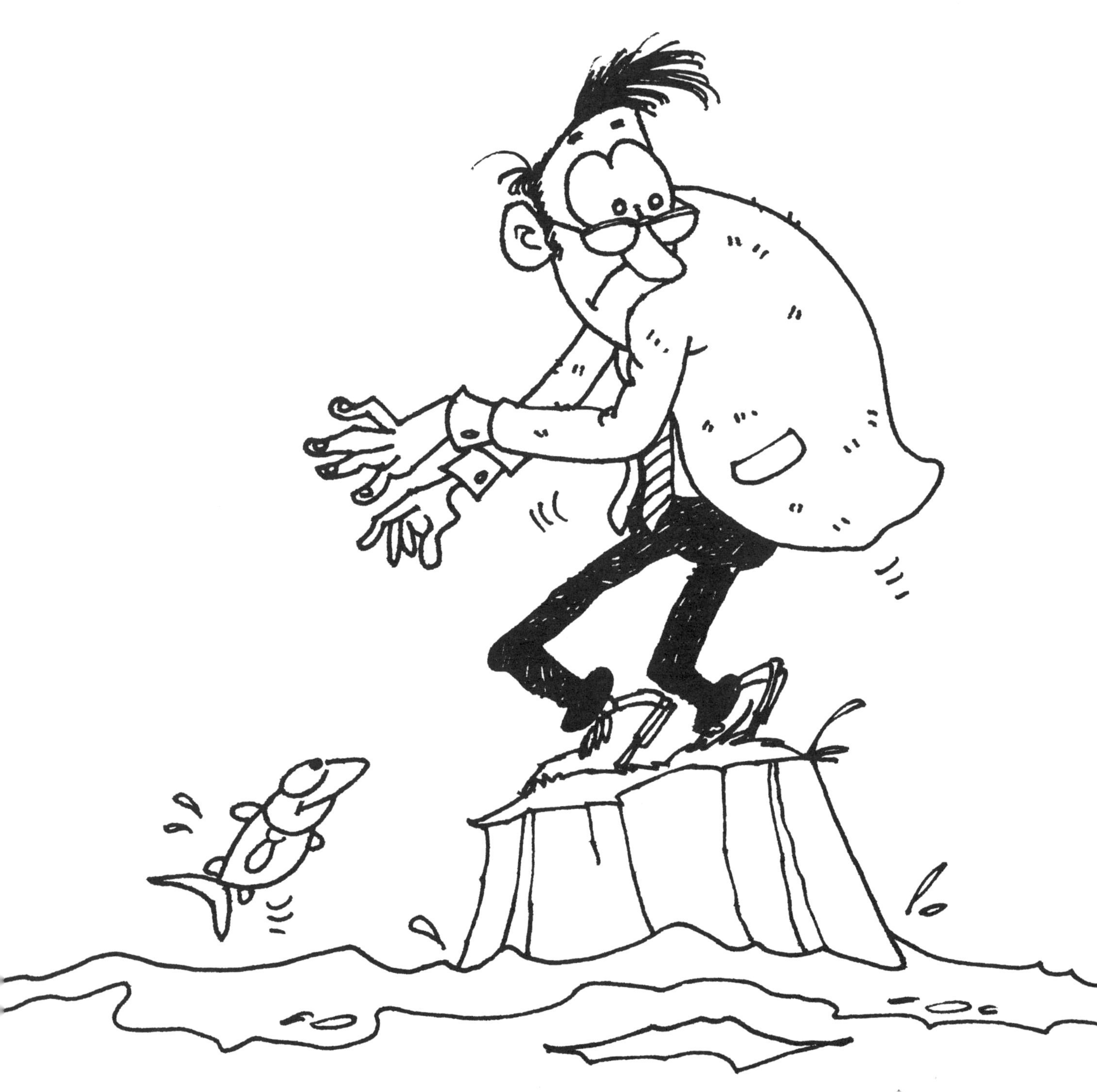

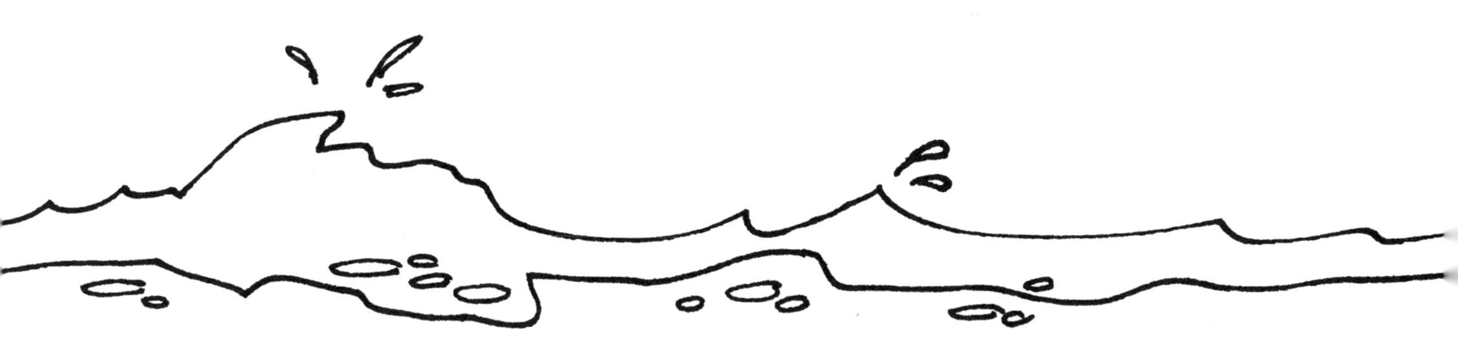

Who are the Romans fighting?

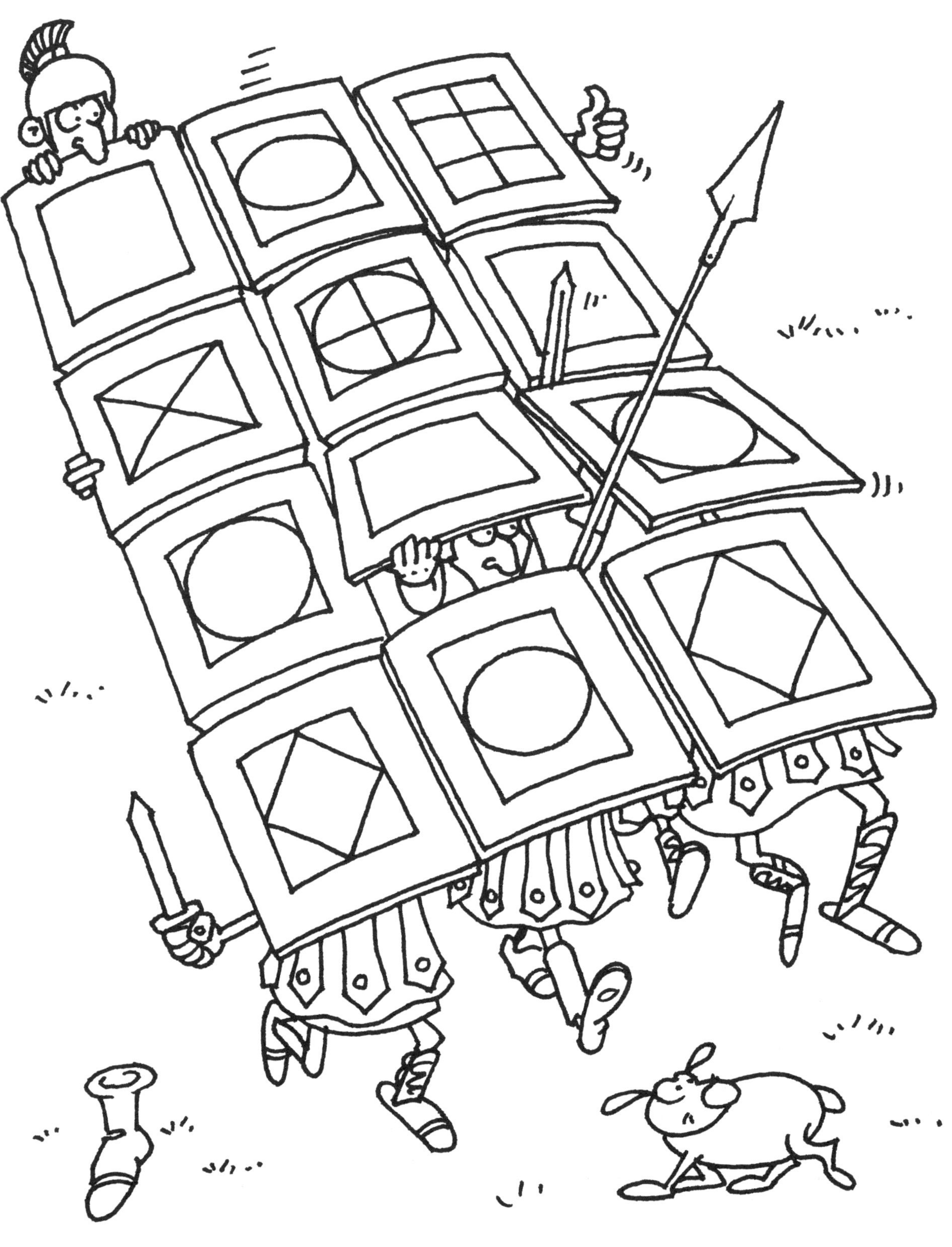

Santa and Rudolf are always cracking jokes

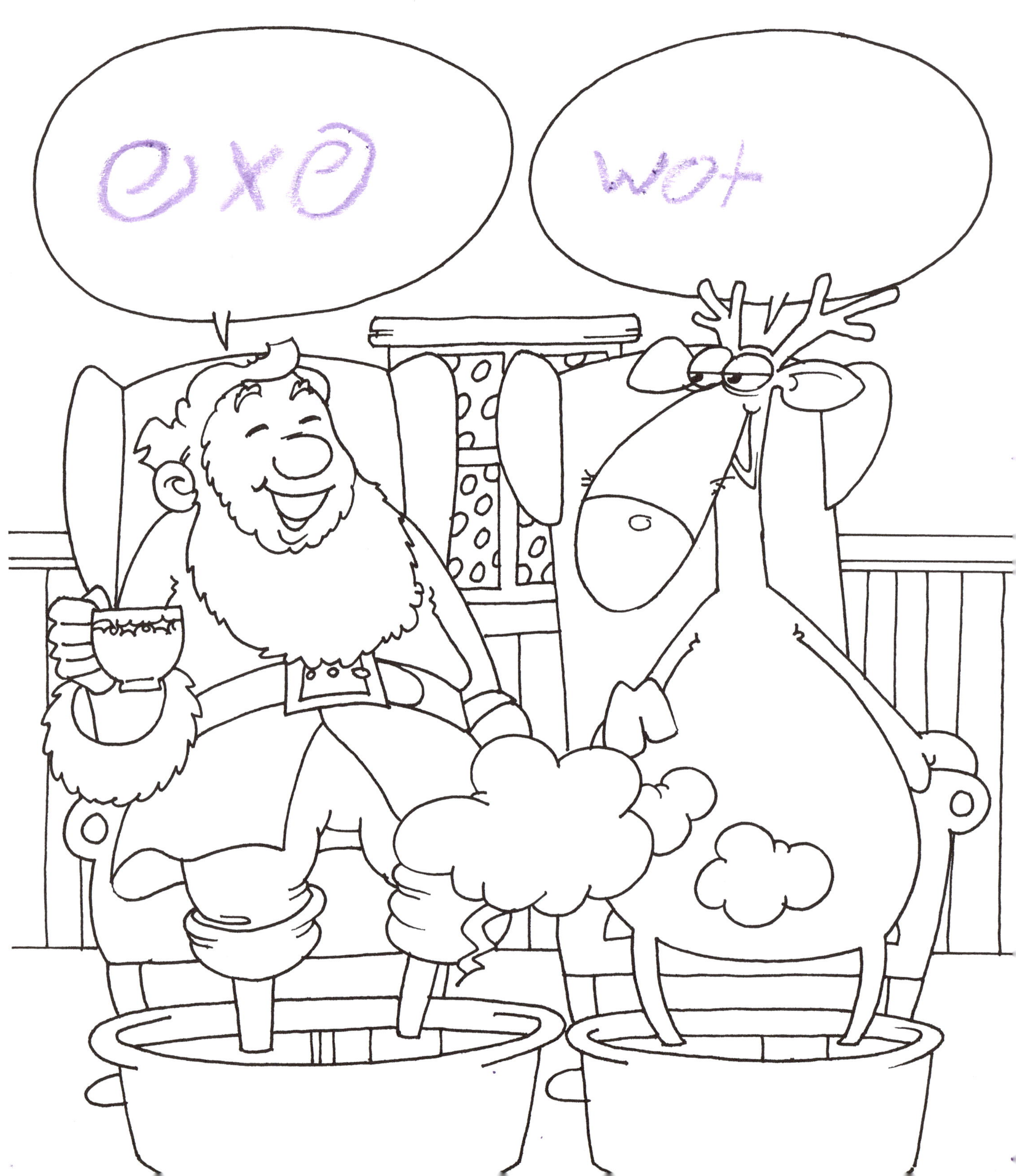

Decorate your schoolbook

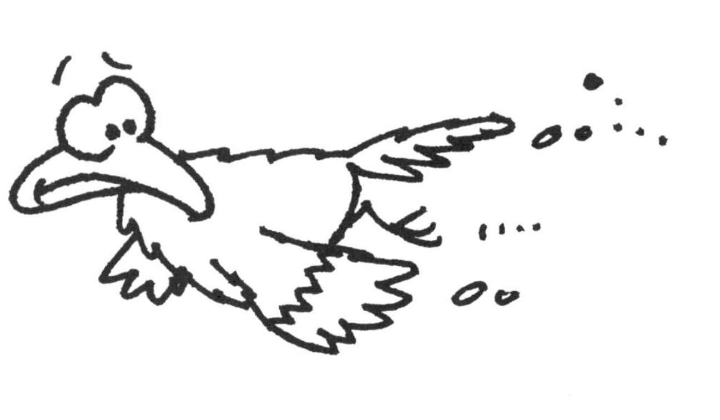

Danger's coming!

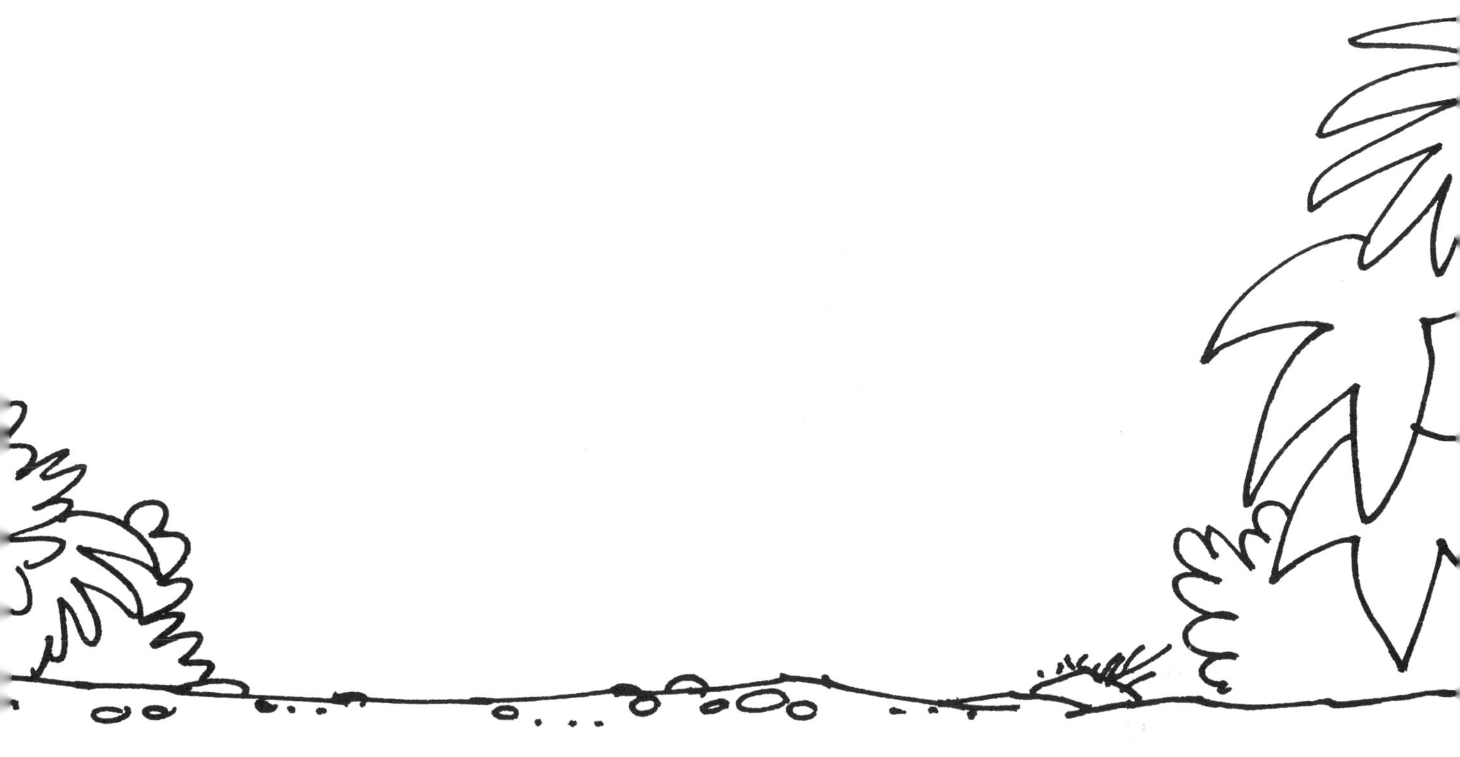

The world's most expensive ring

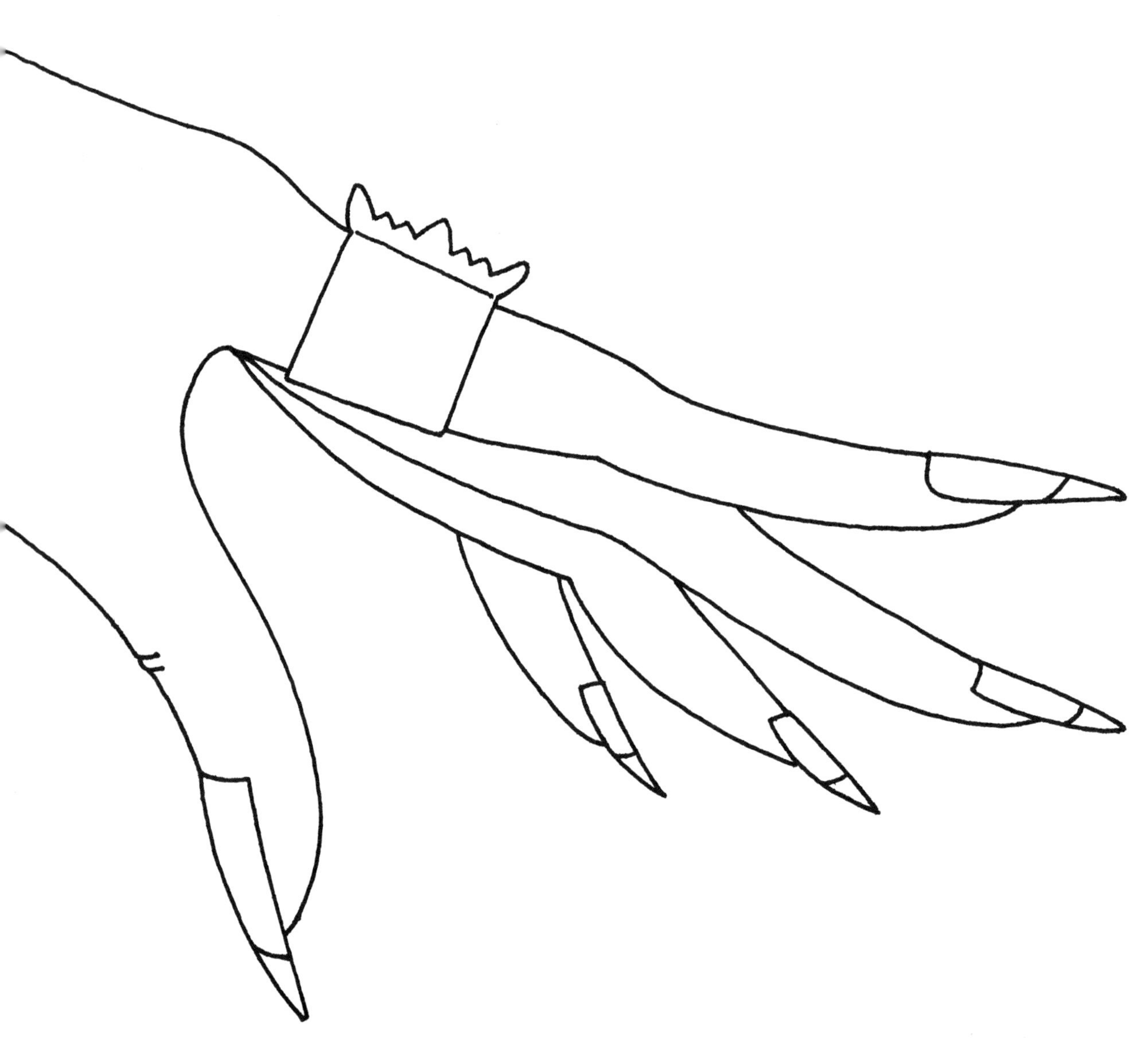

Old Ma's blanket may be warm, but it sure is ugly

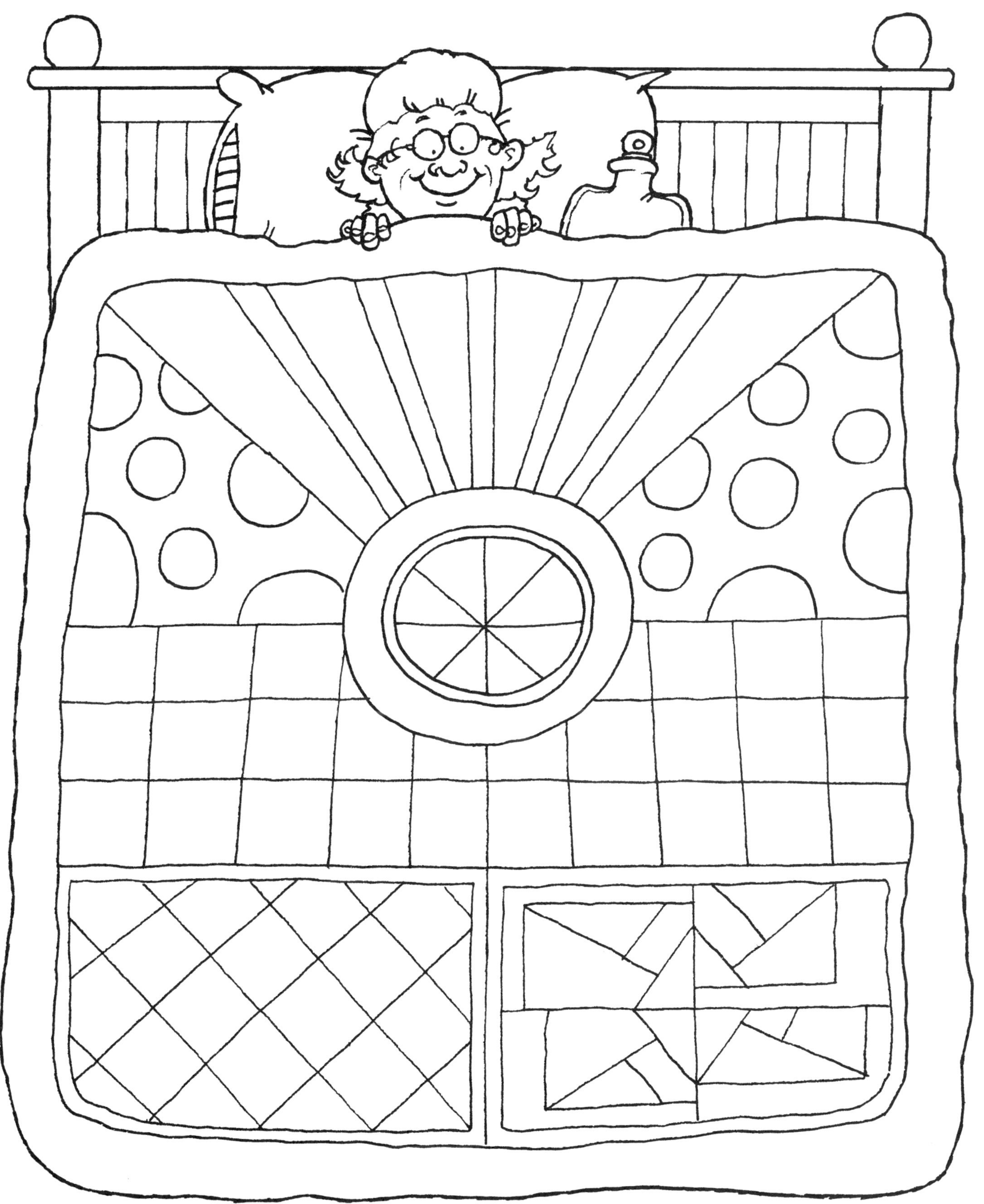

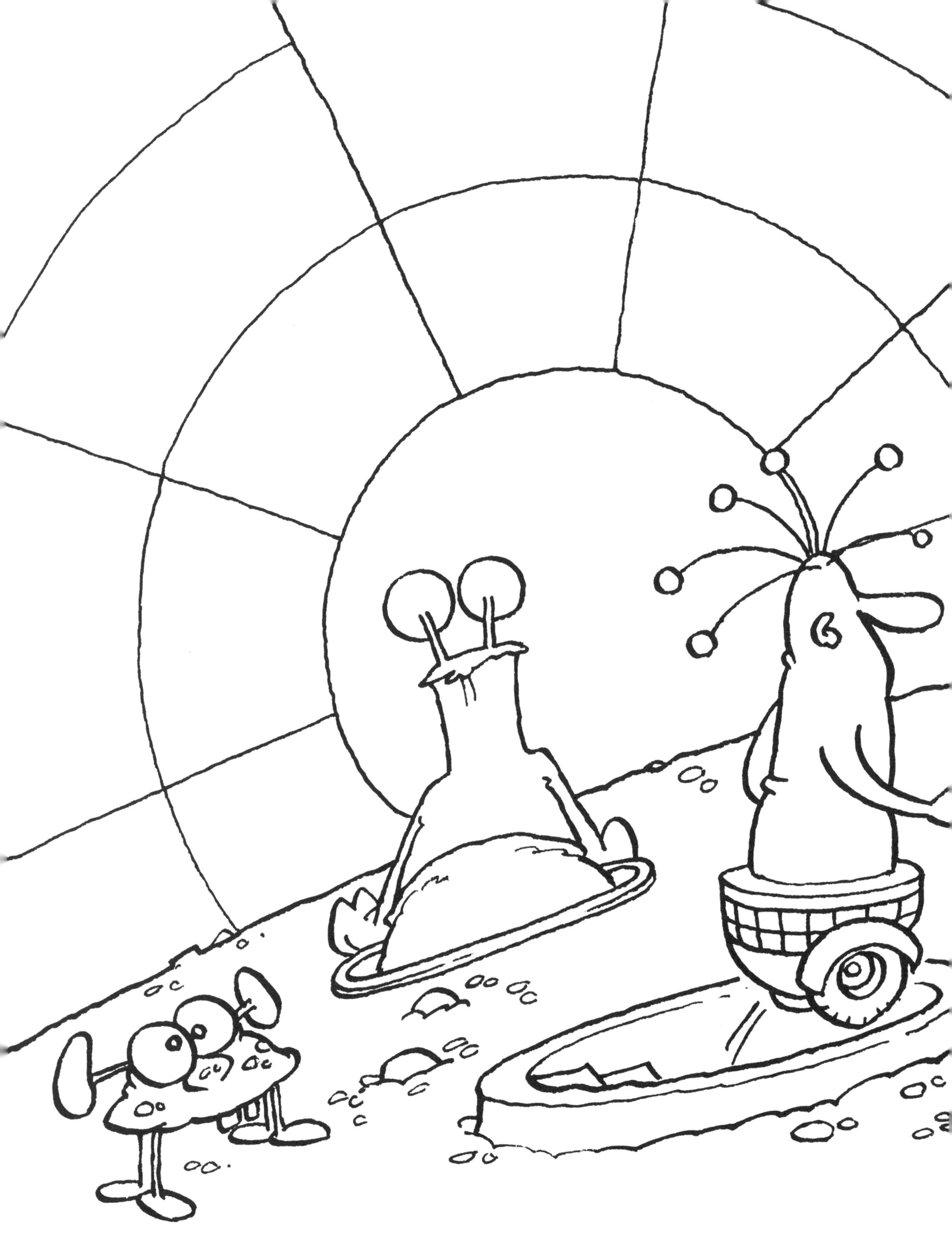

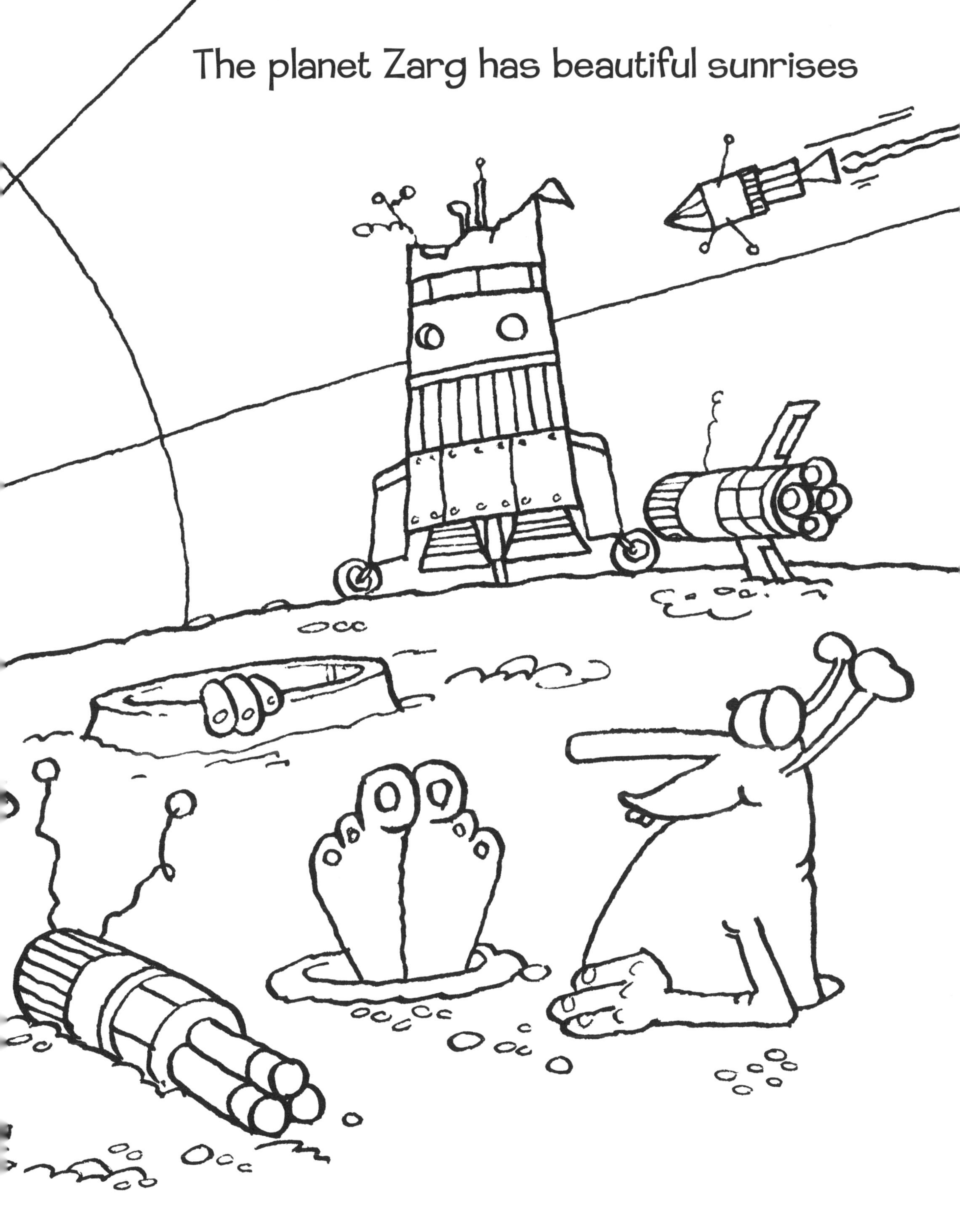
The planet Zarg has beautiful sunrises

Those dancers have
really got the groove

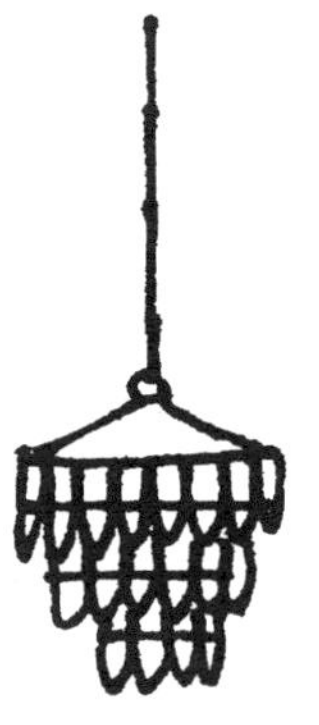

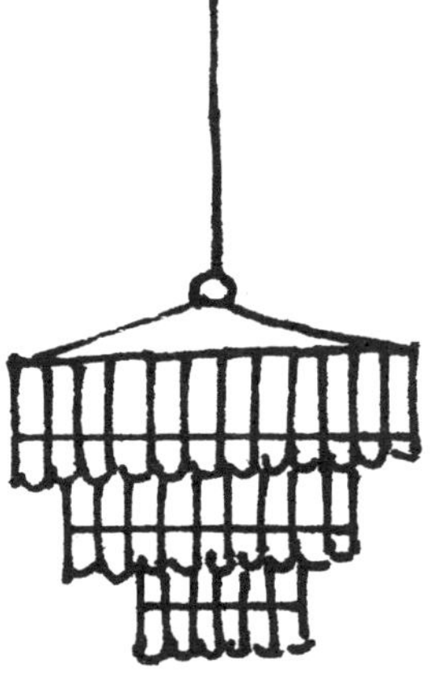

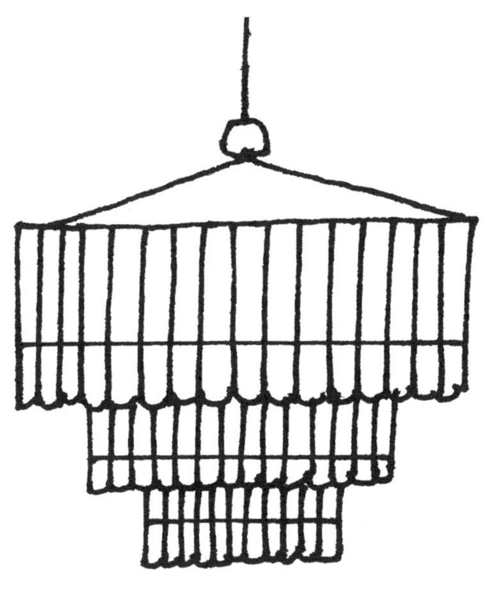
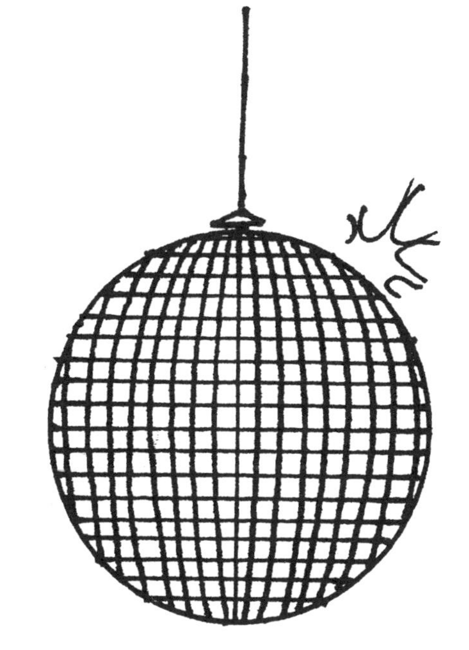
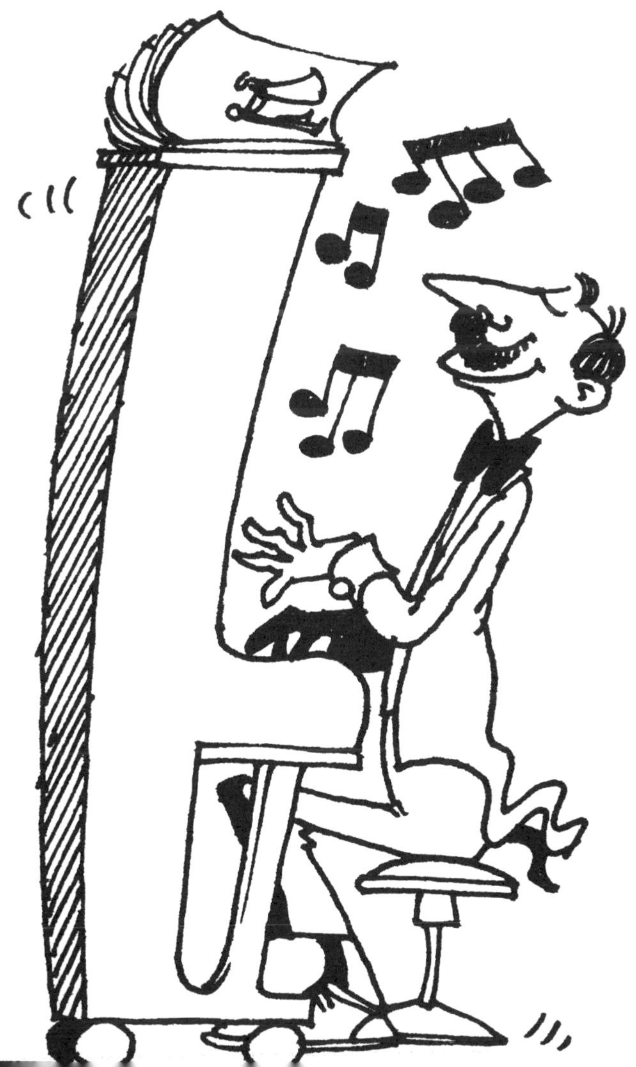

Who is hiding from the mummy?

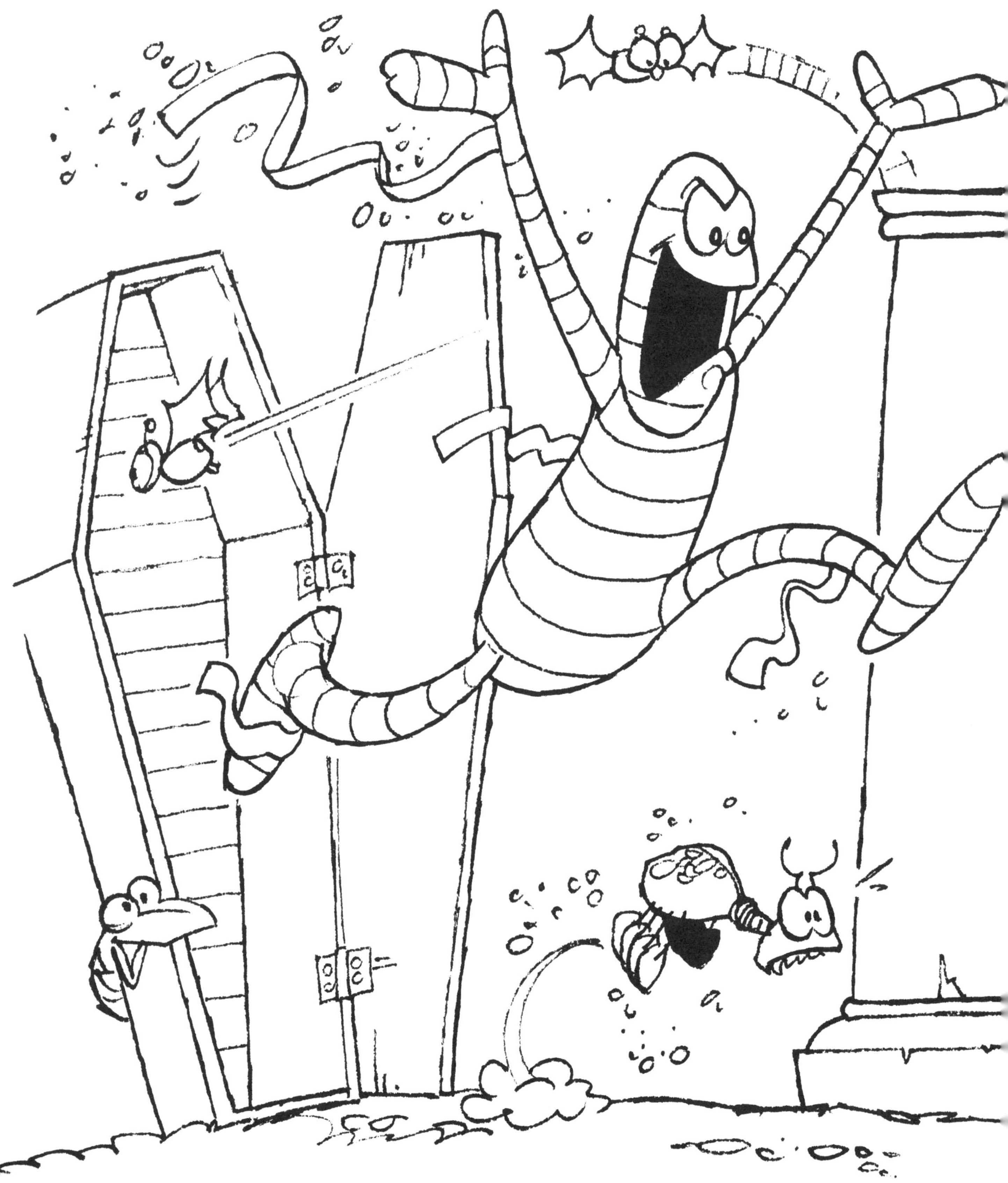

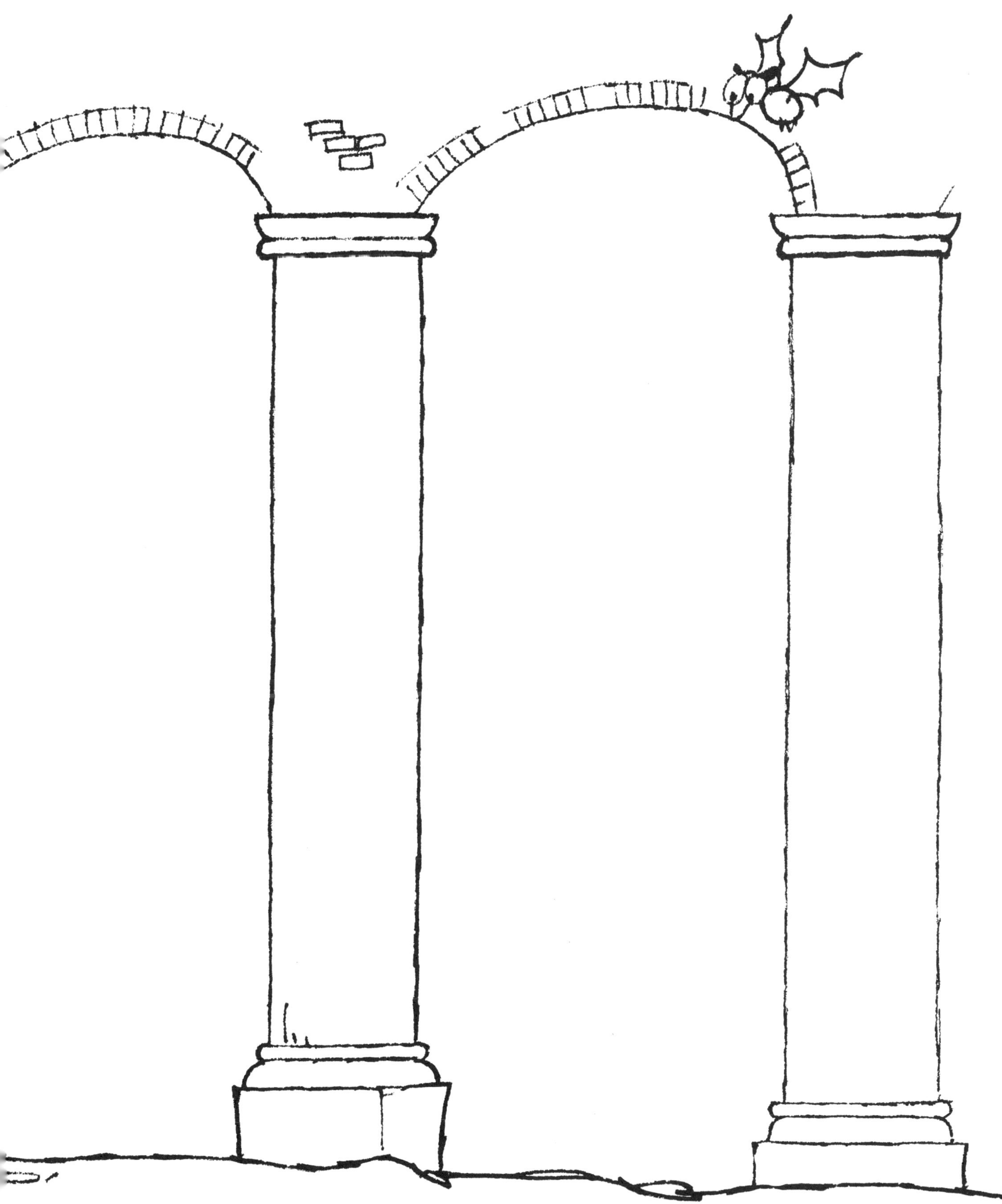

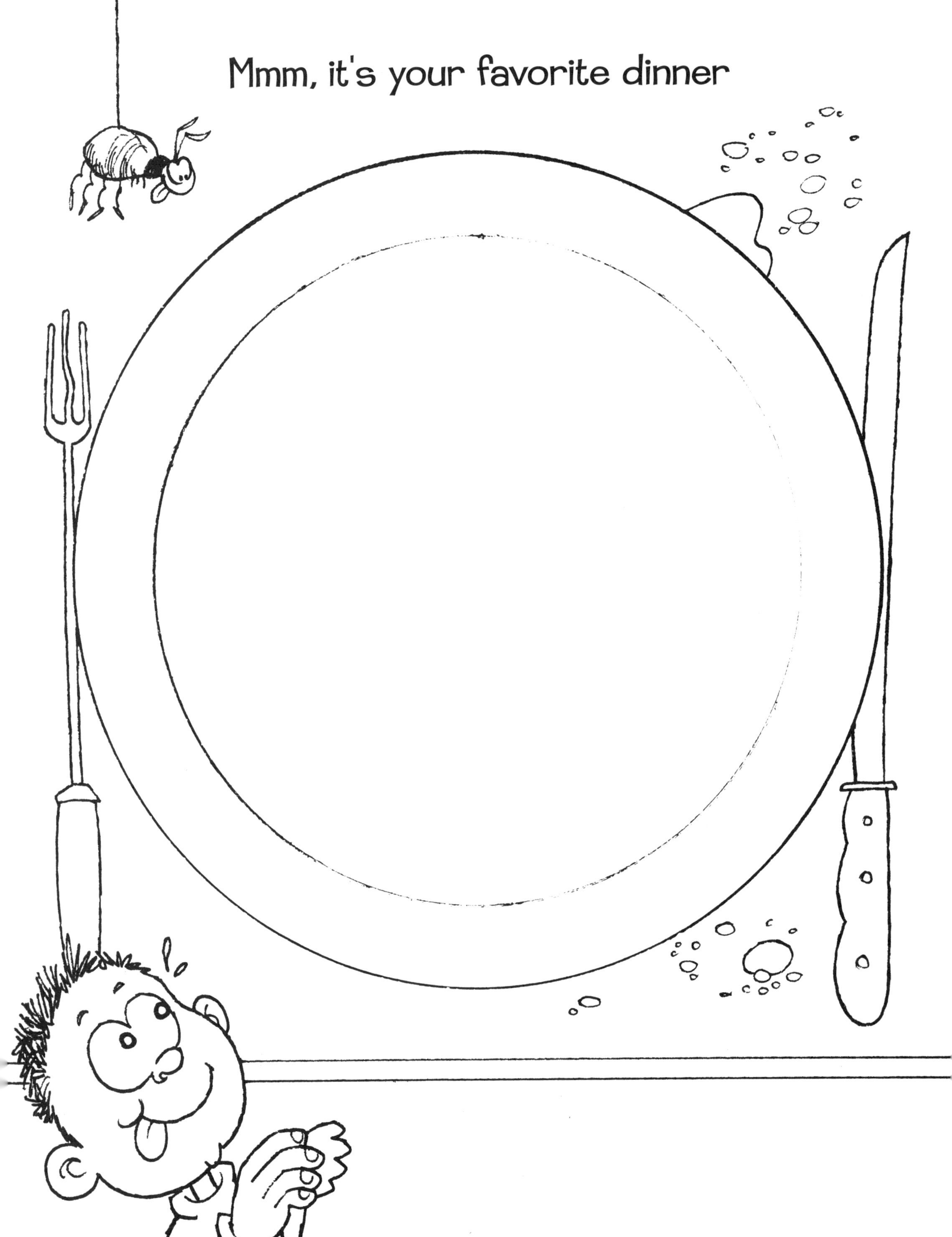
Mmm, it's your favorite dinner

Finish the city's amazing skyline

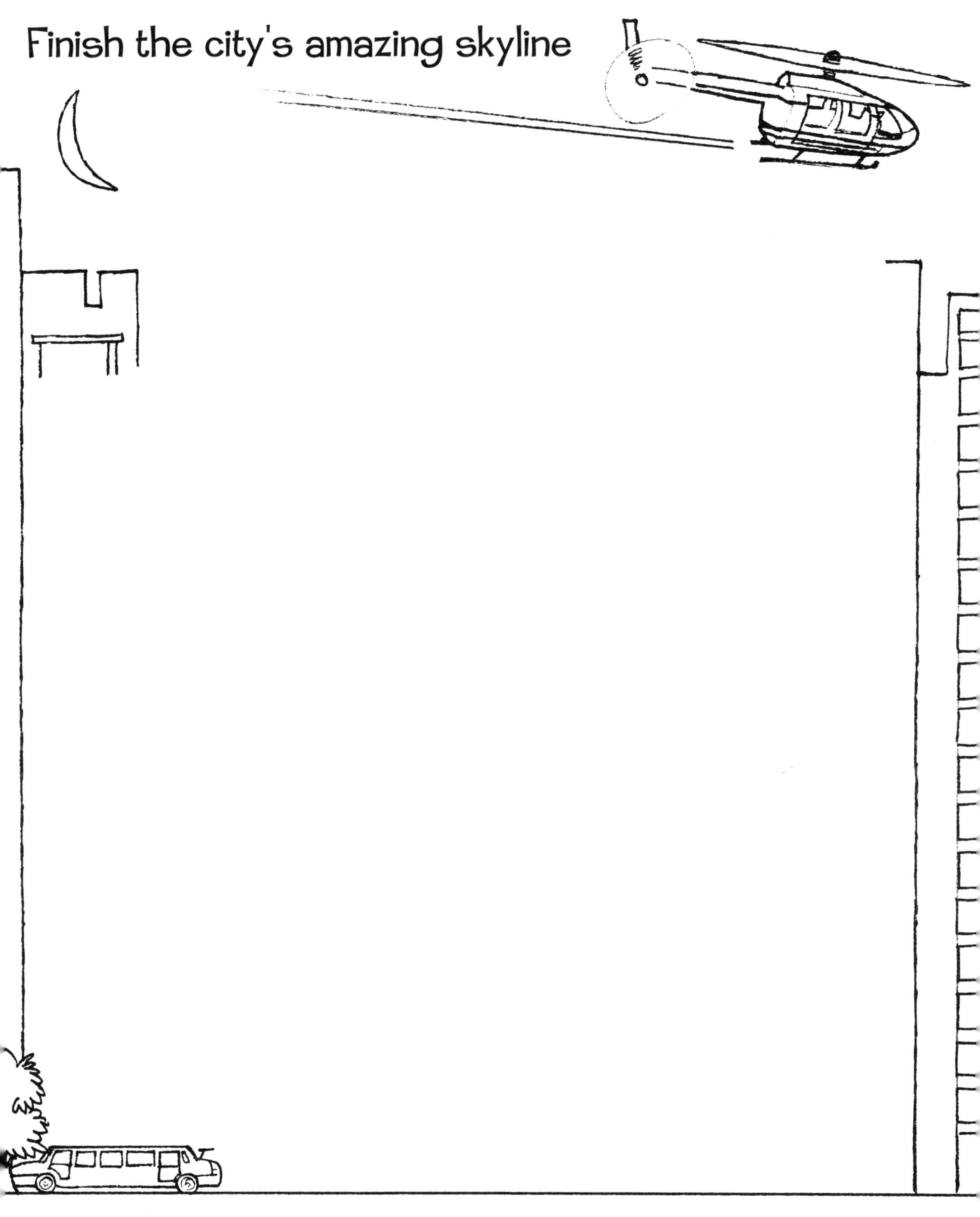

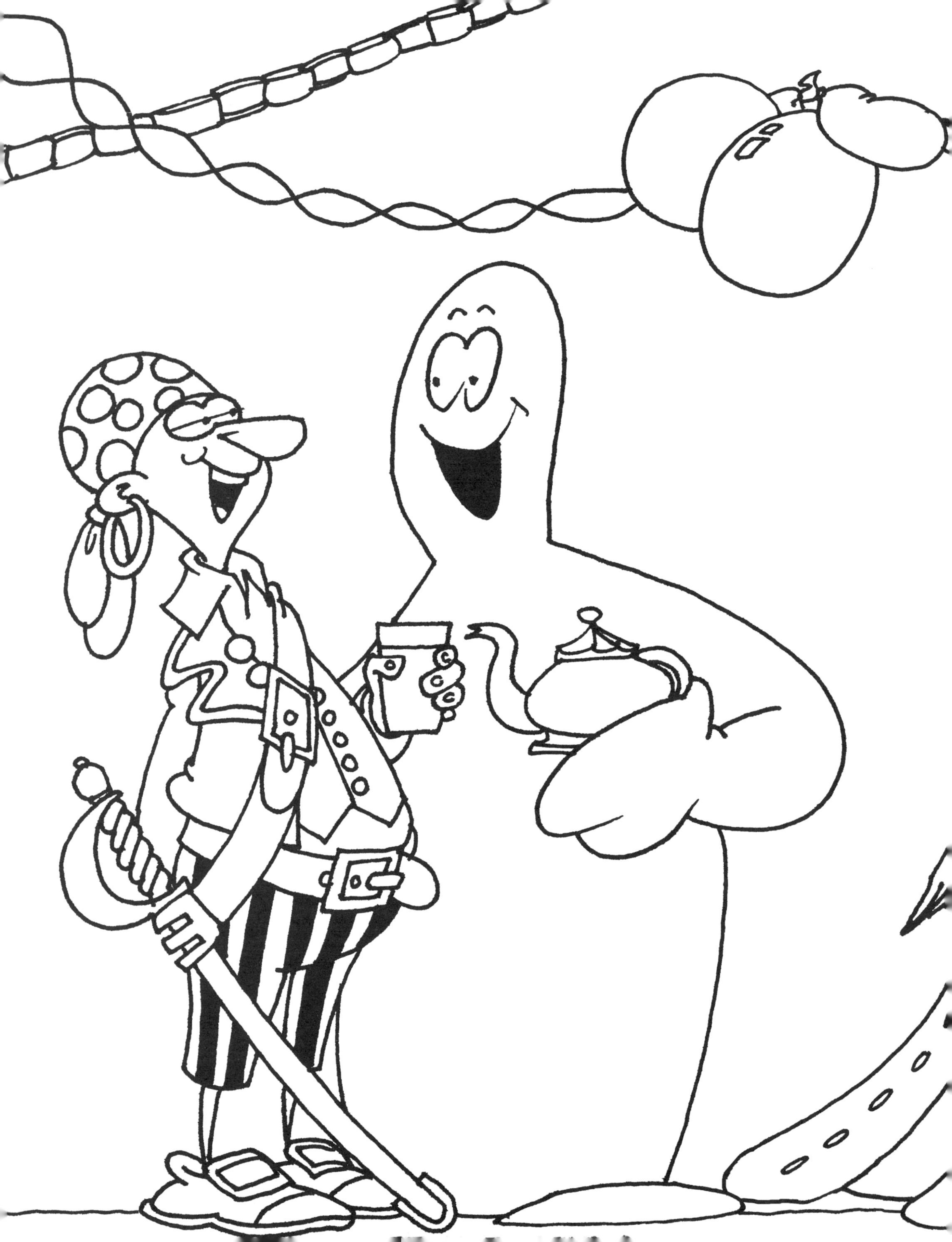

What are you wearing at the costume party?

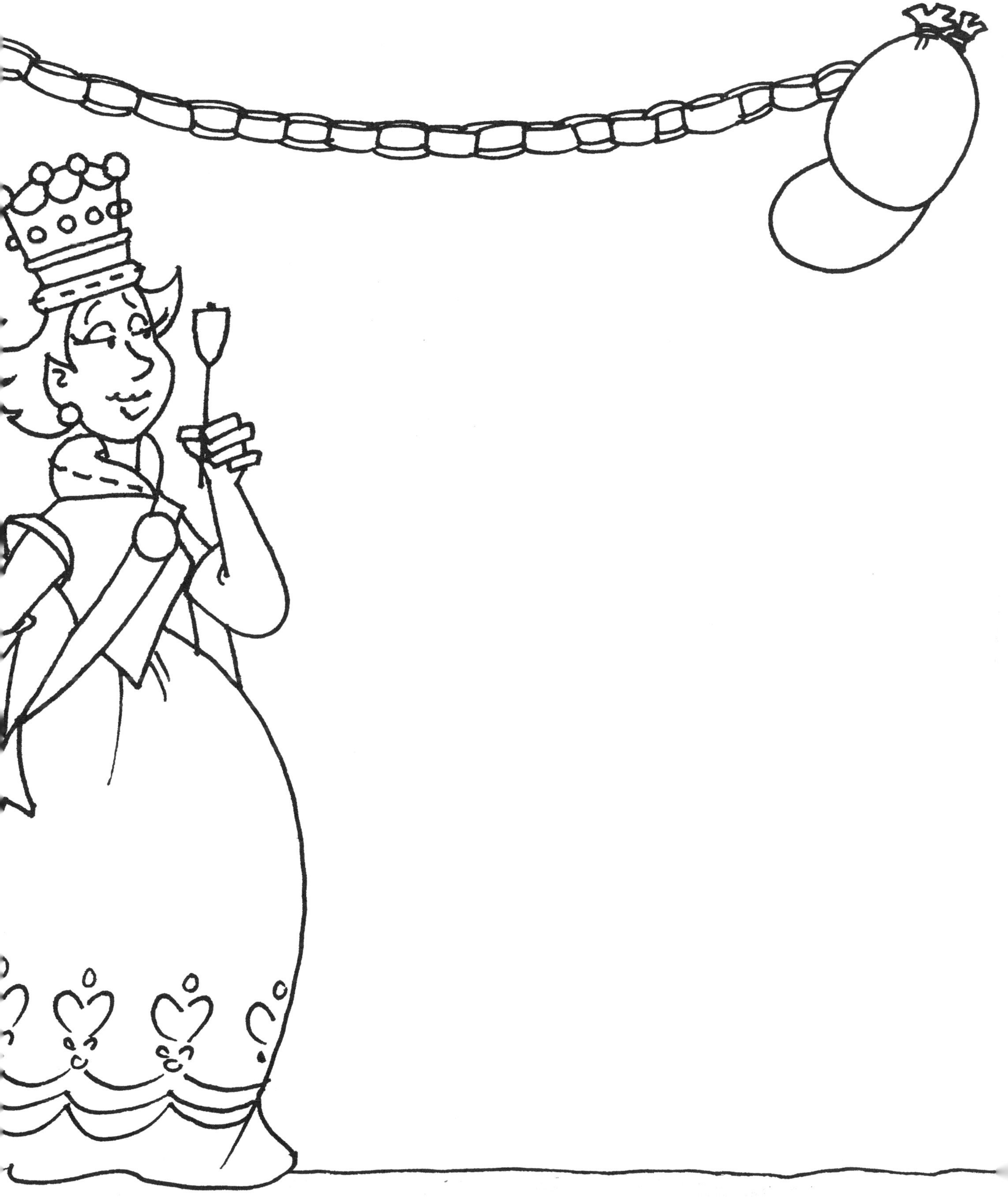

How are you feeling today?

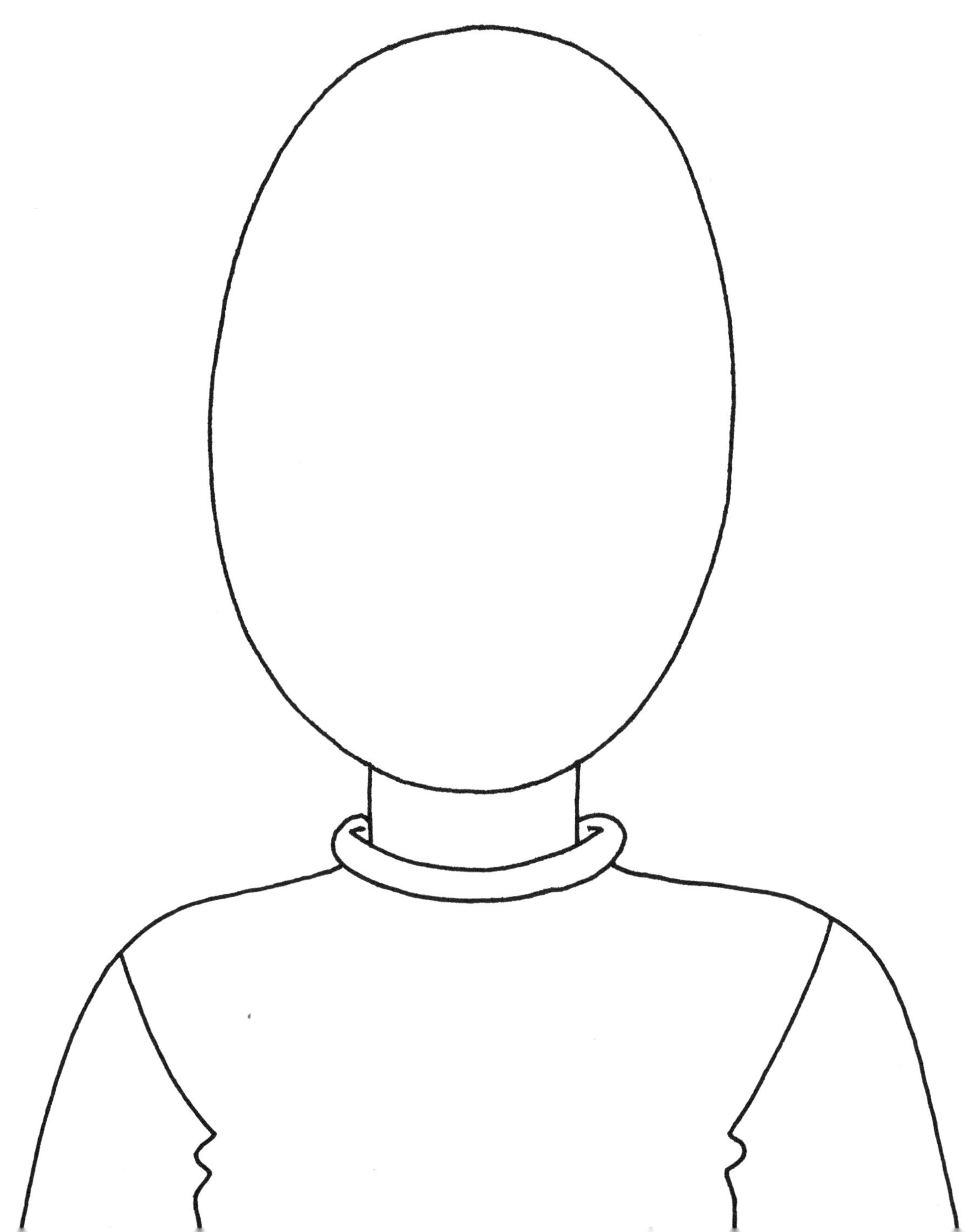

Use your X-ray vision to see what's in the bag

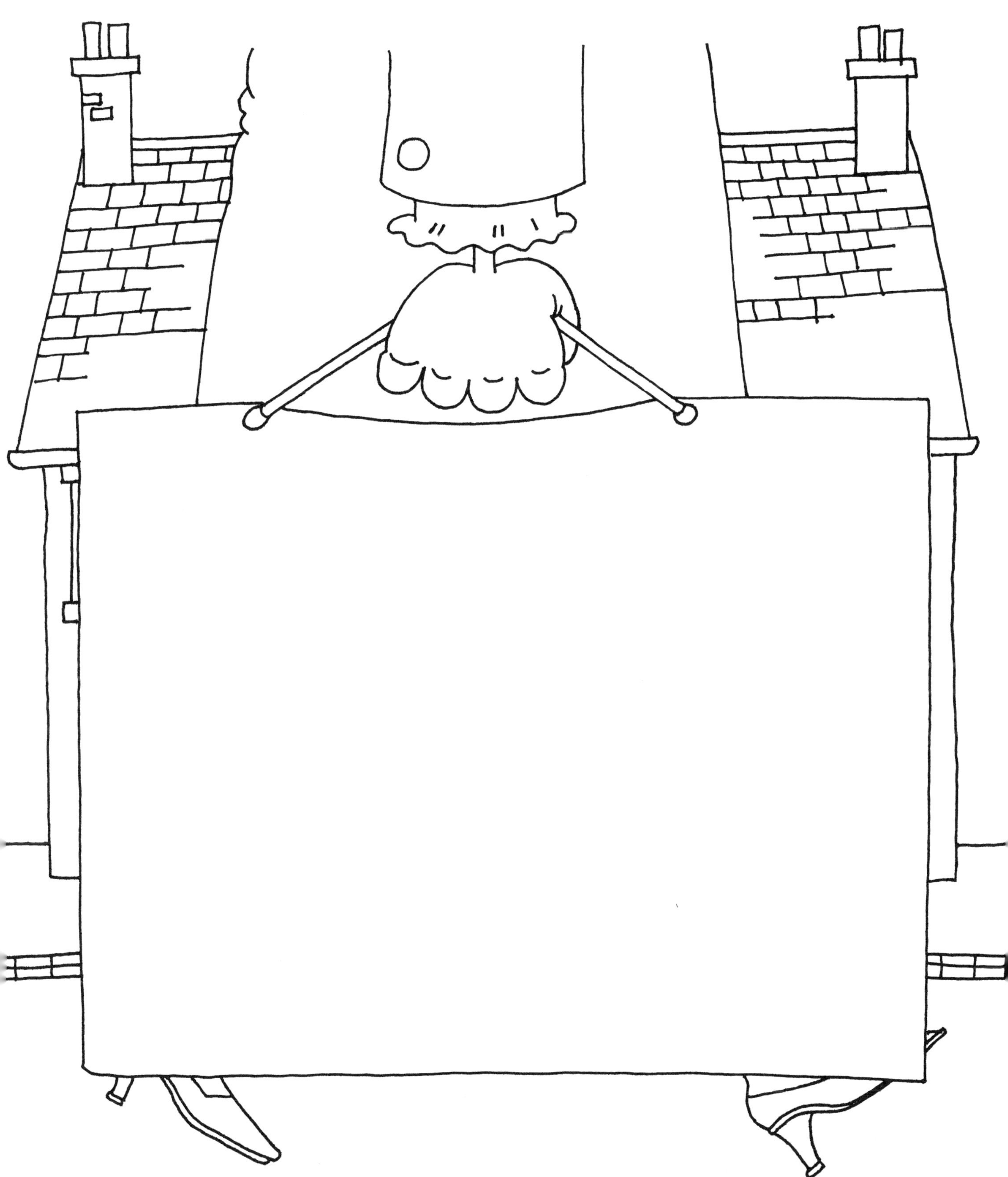

Hammy the hamster needs a cage

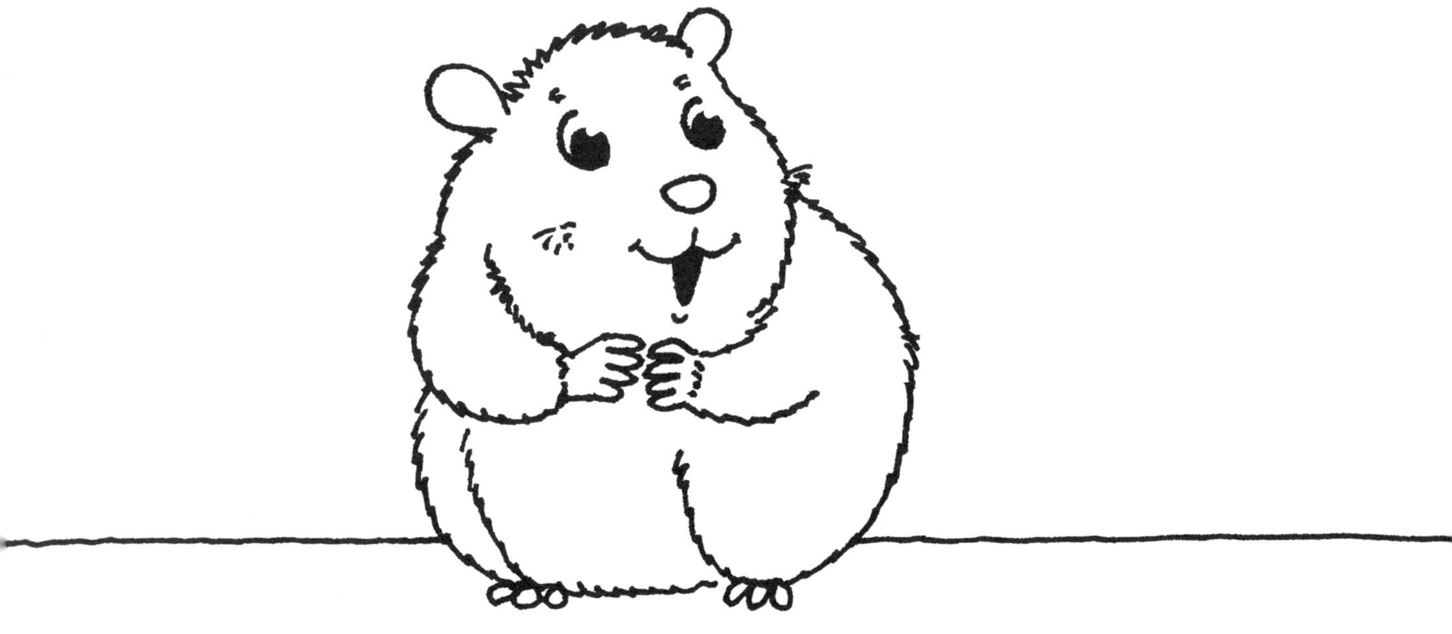

Who are you spying on?

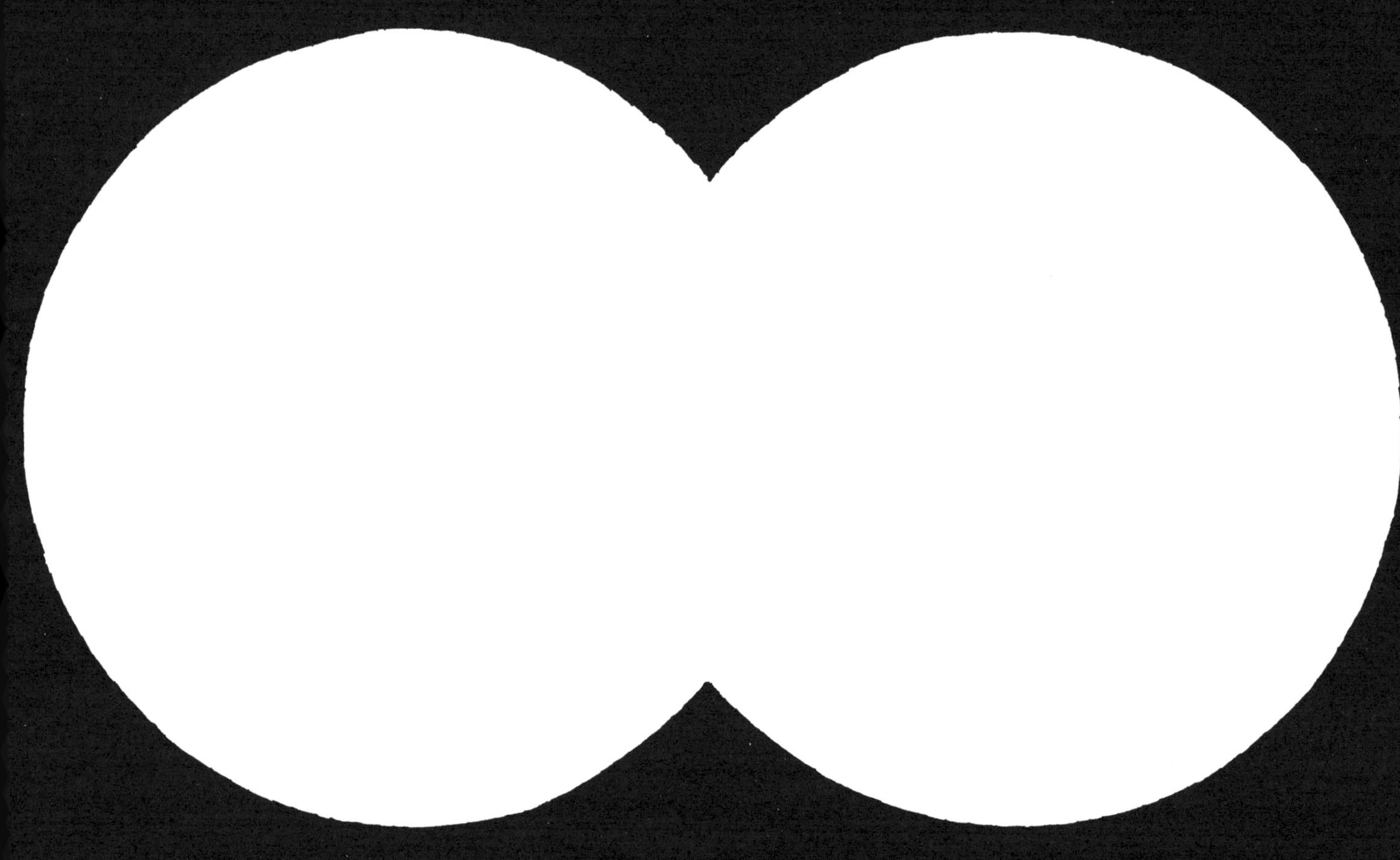

What does the mouse's house look like?

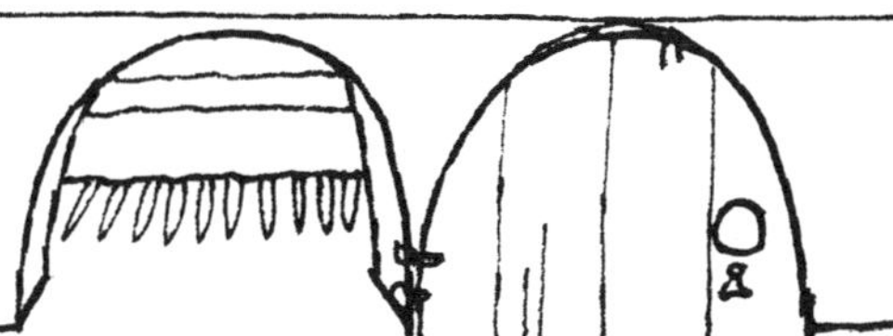

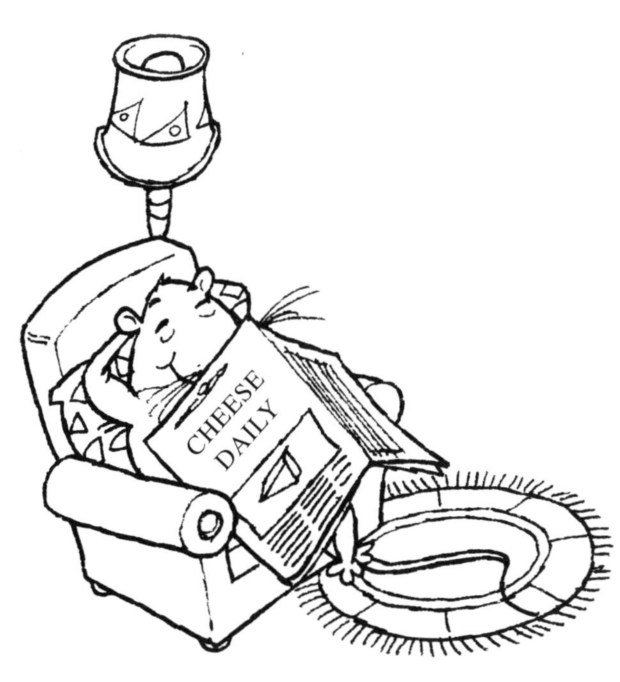

He's ready to skate...

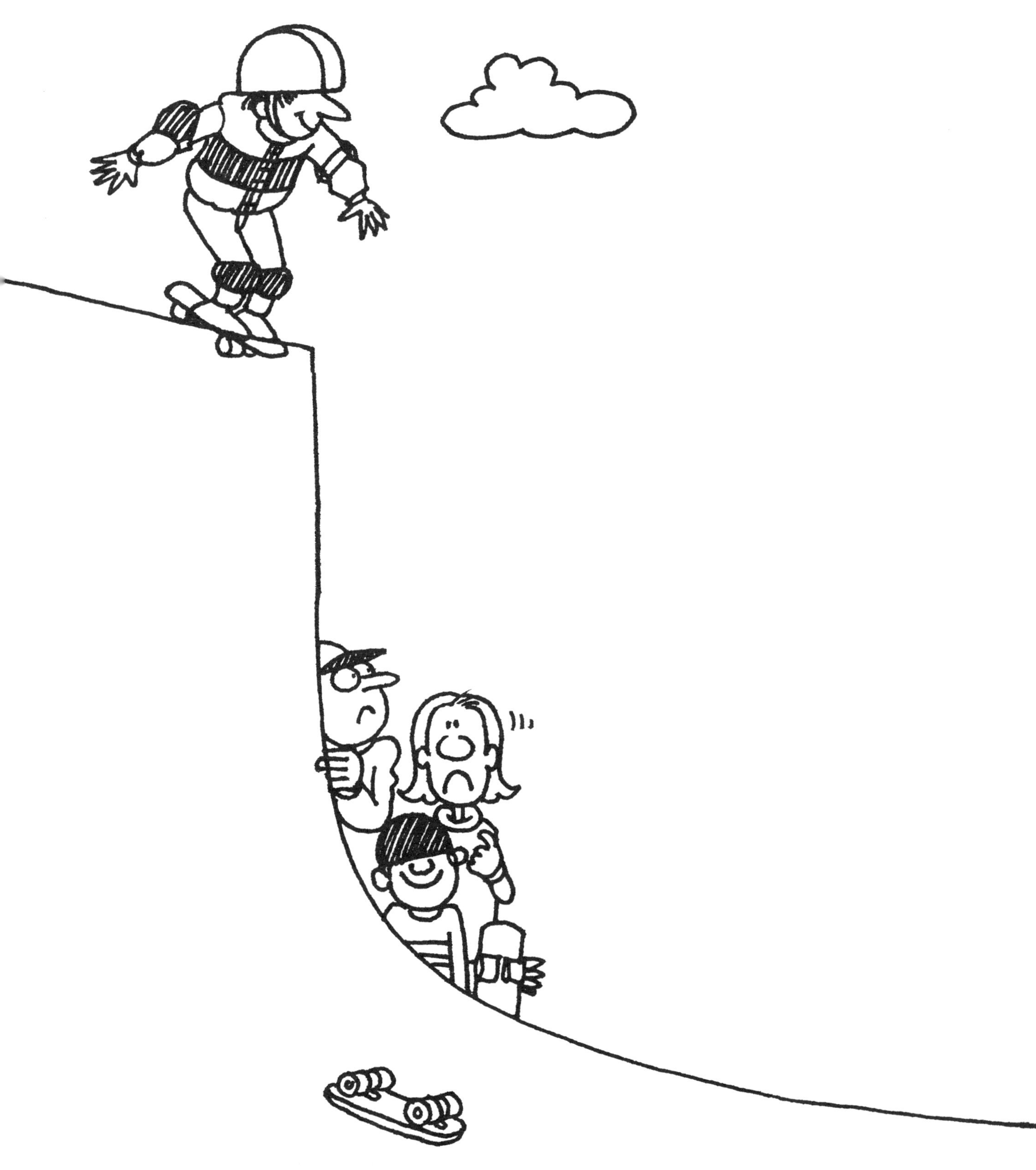

... but what move did he pull?

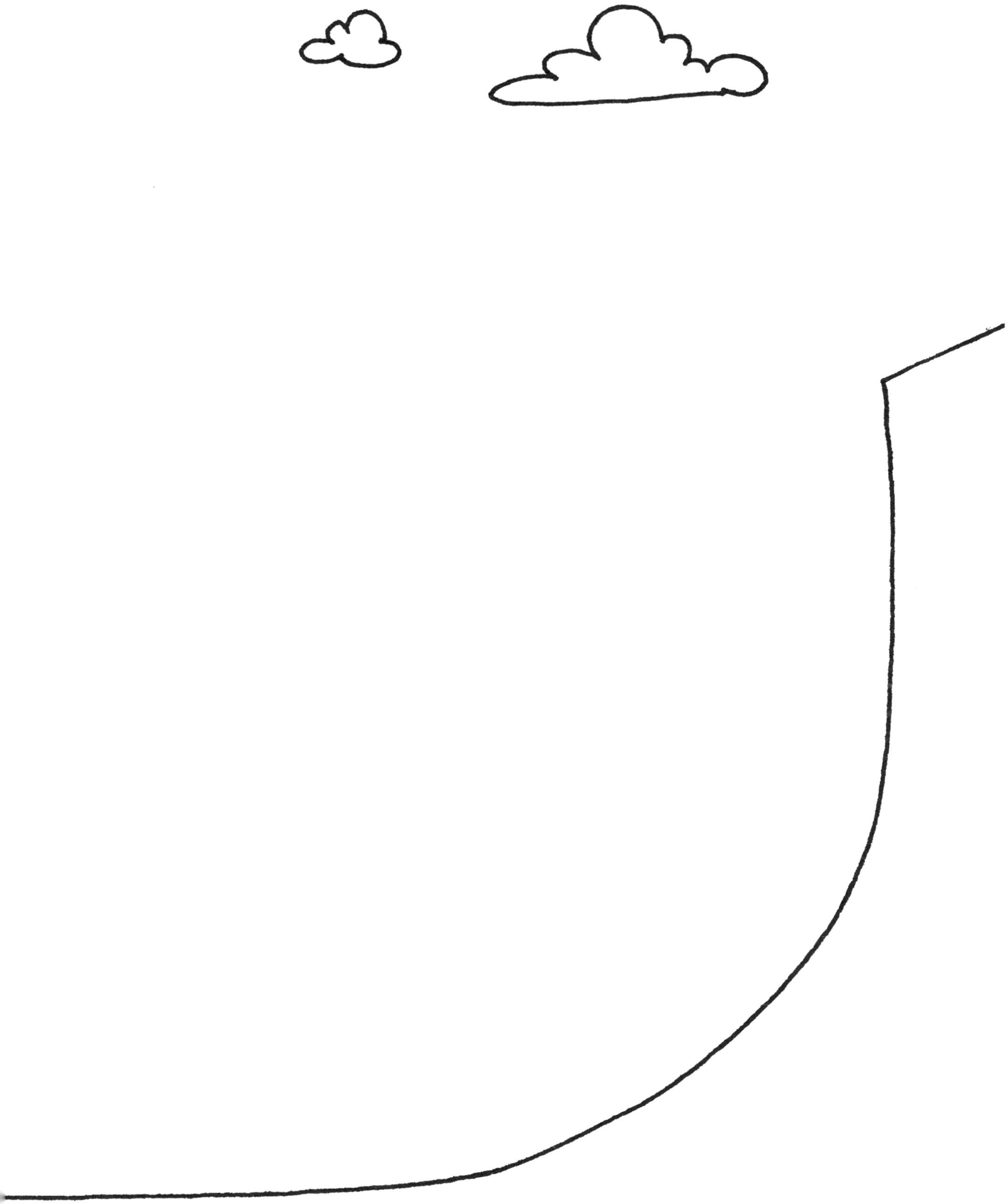

One of his roses is the wrong color

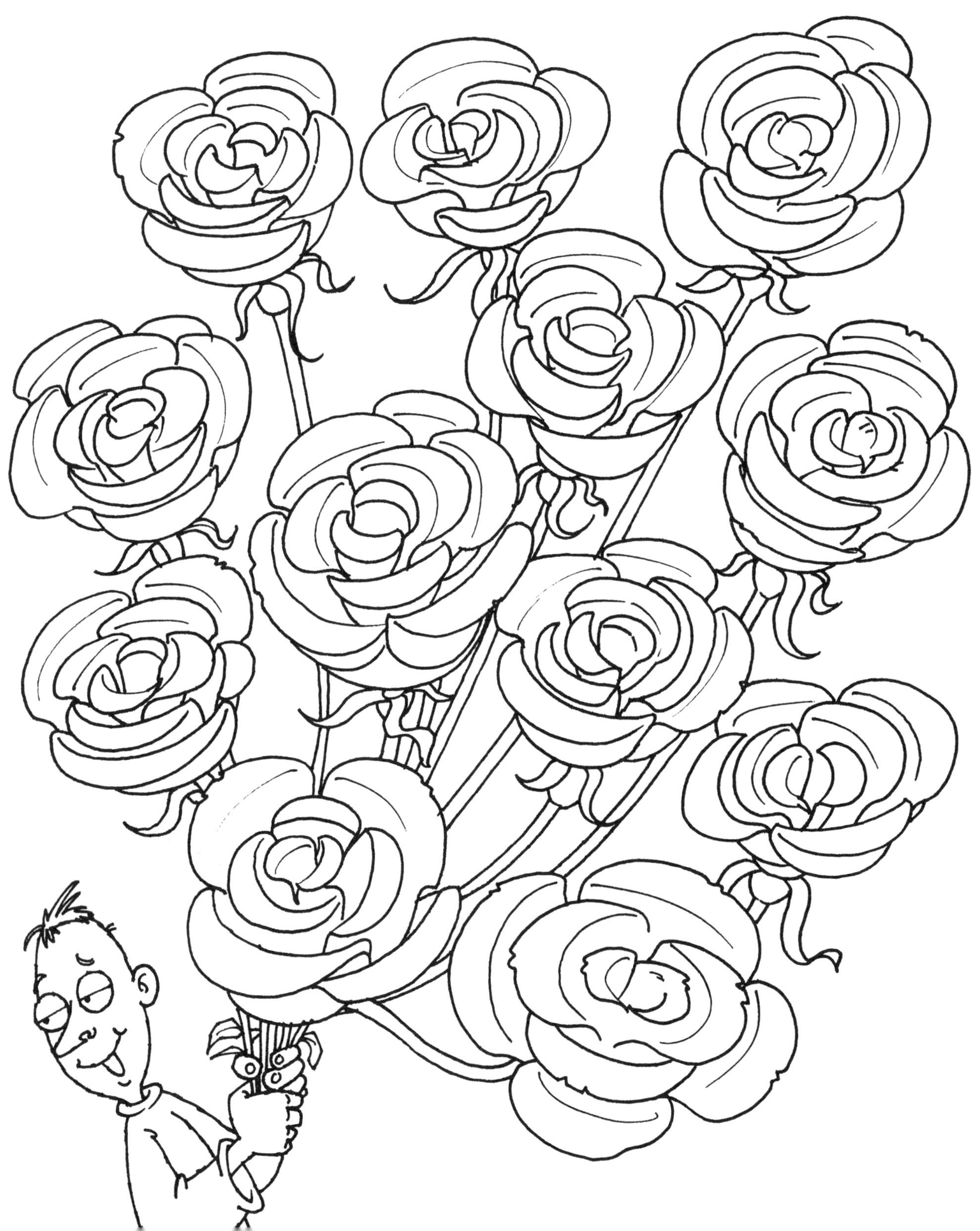

This windmill needs more sails!

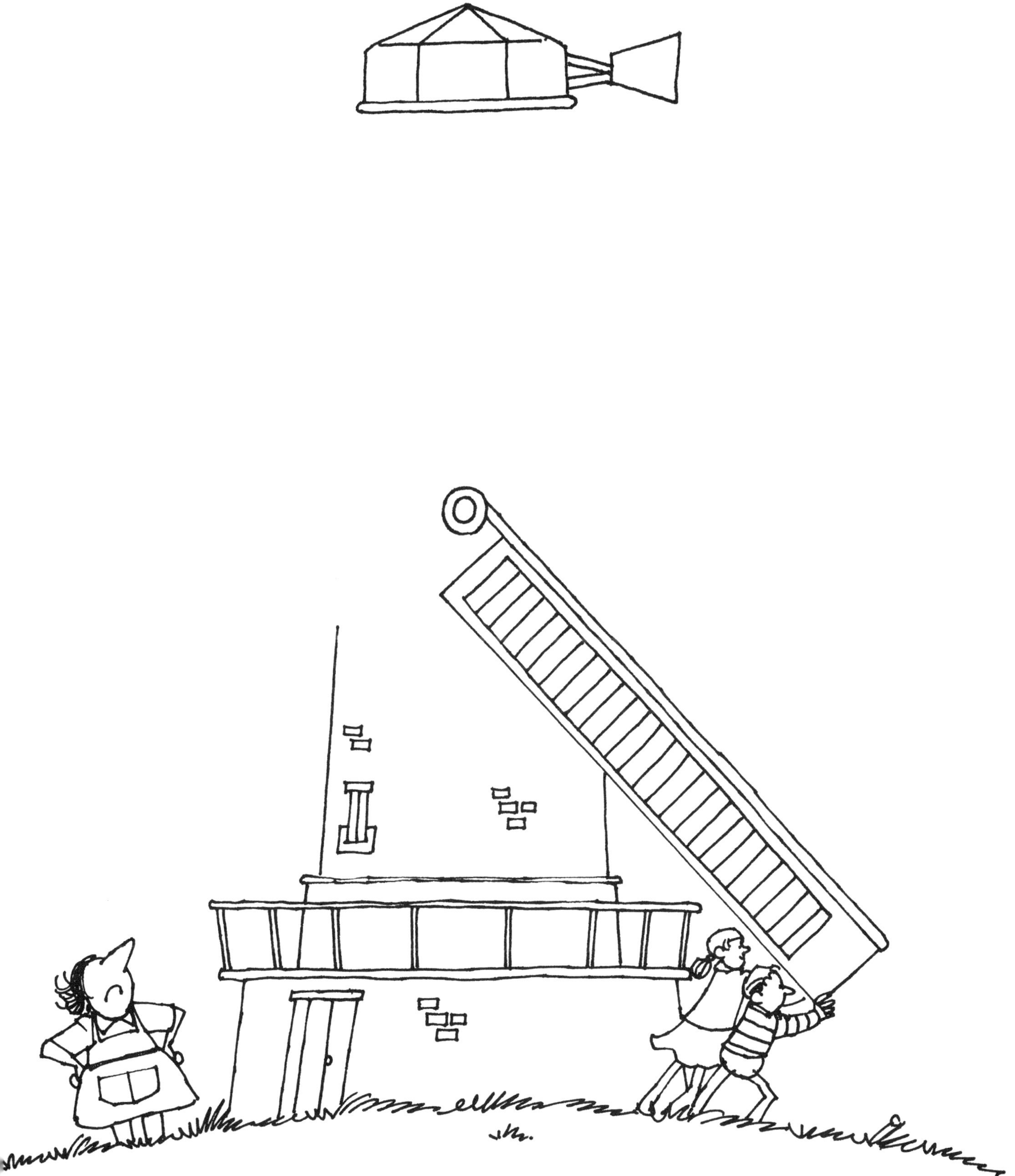

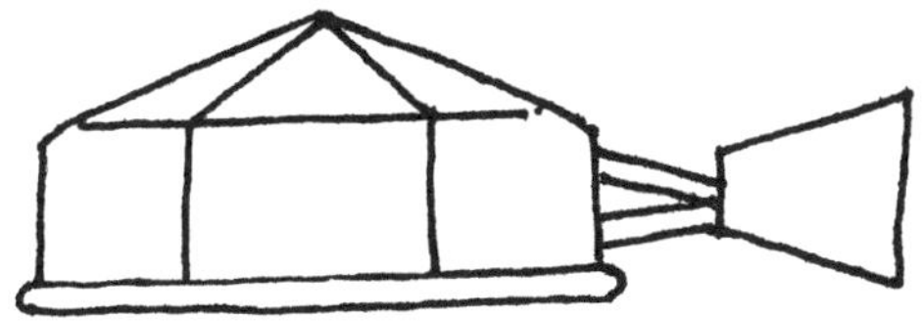

Quick! Give the diver a tank of oxygen!

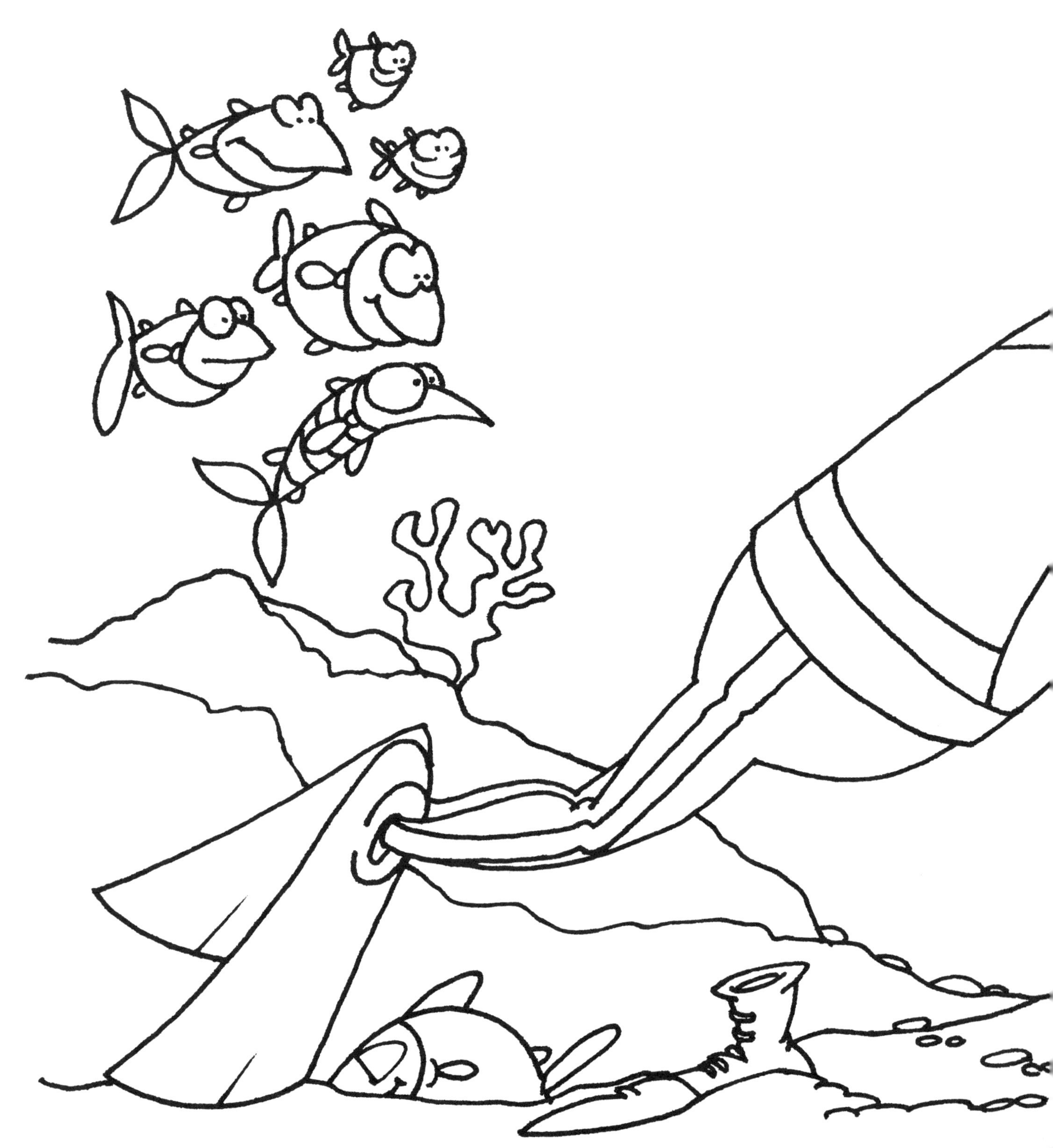

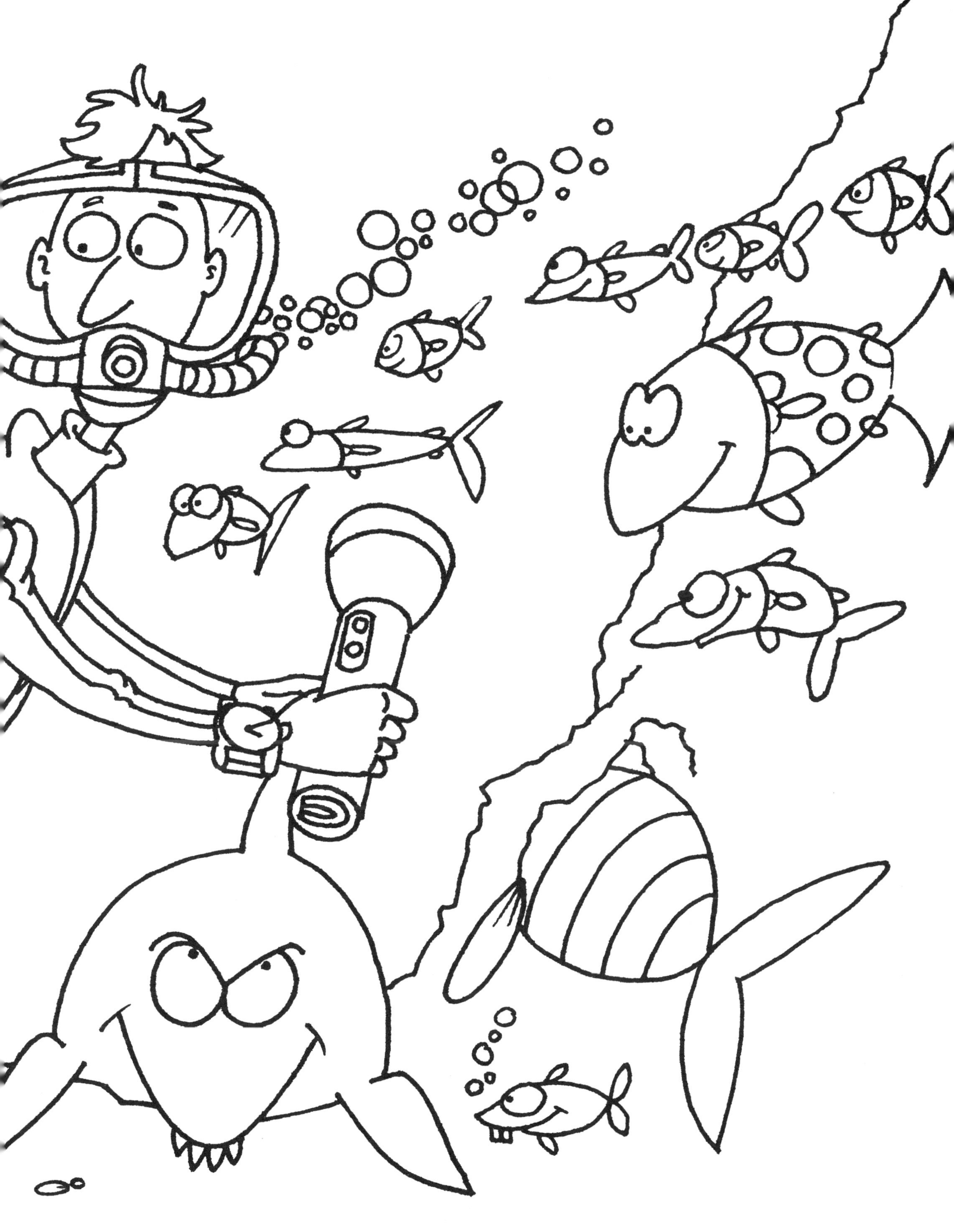

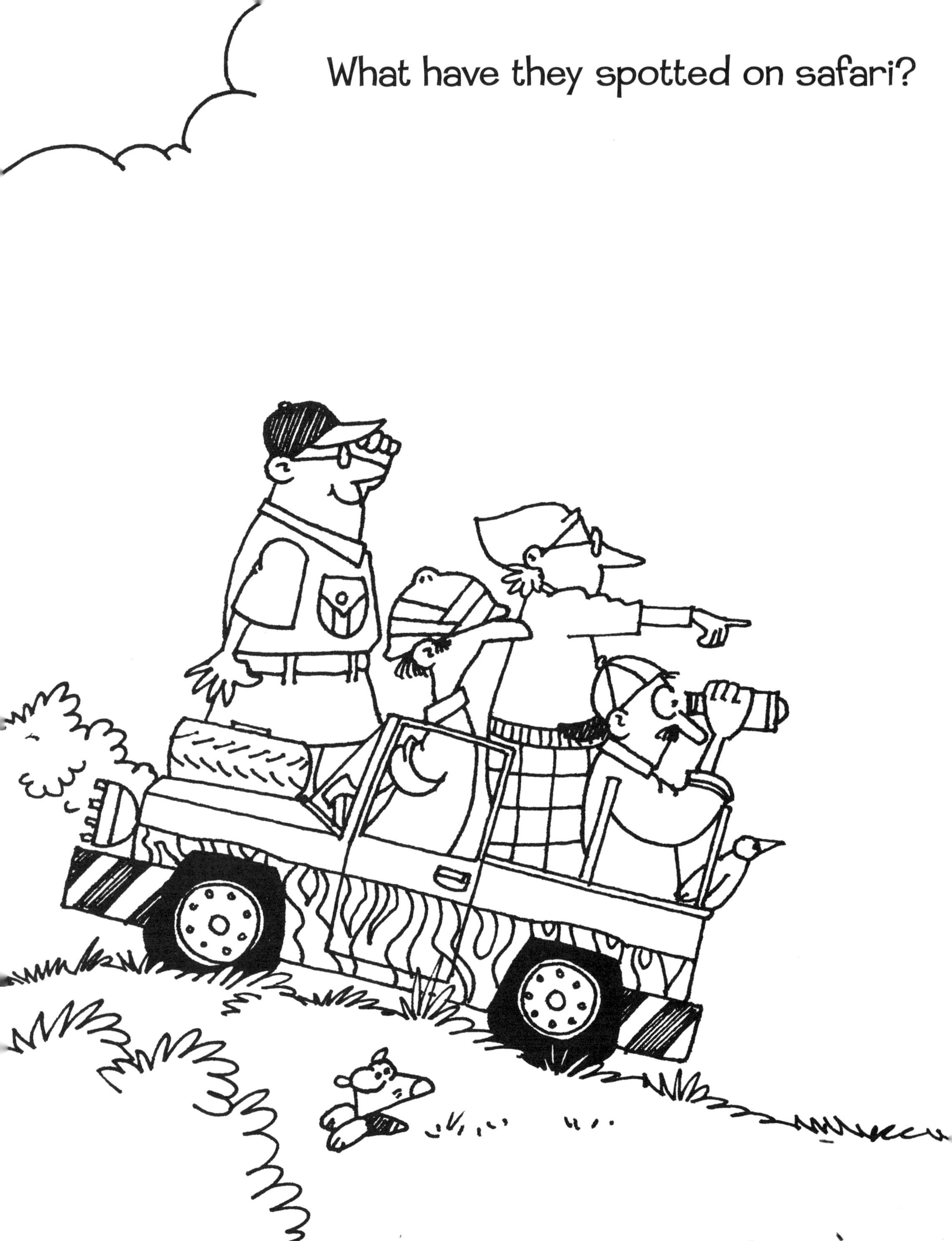
What have they spotted on safari?

He's chosen the wrong garden to dig into here

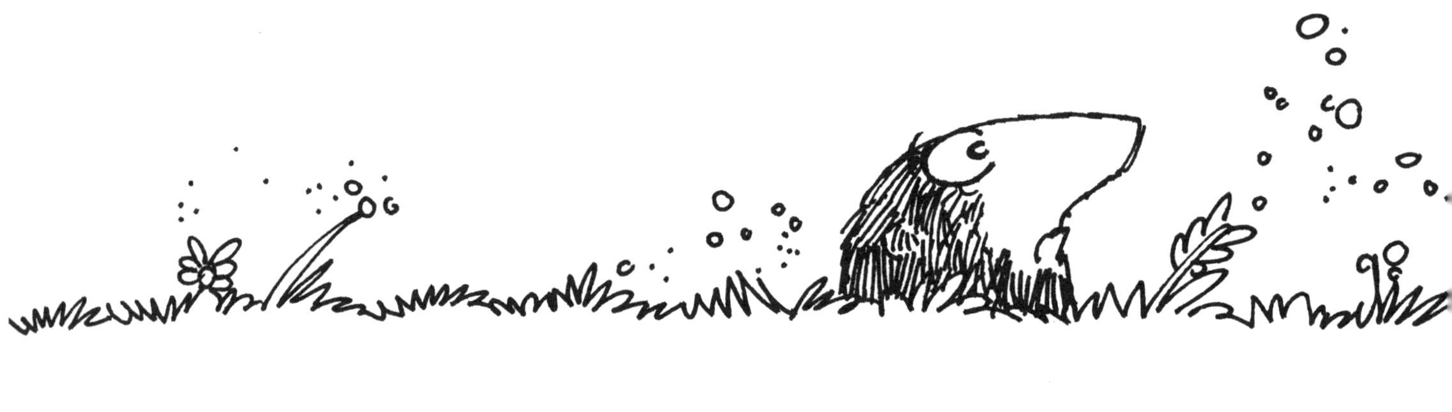

What can you see from the airplane window?

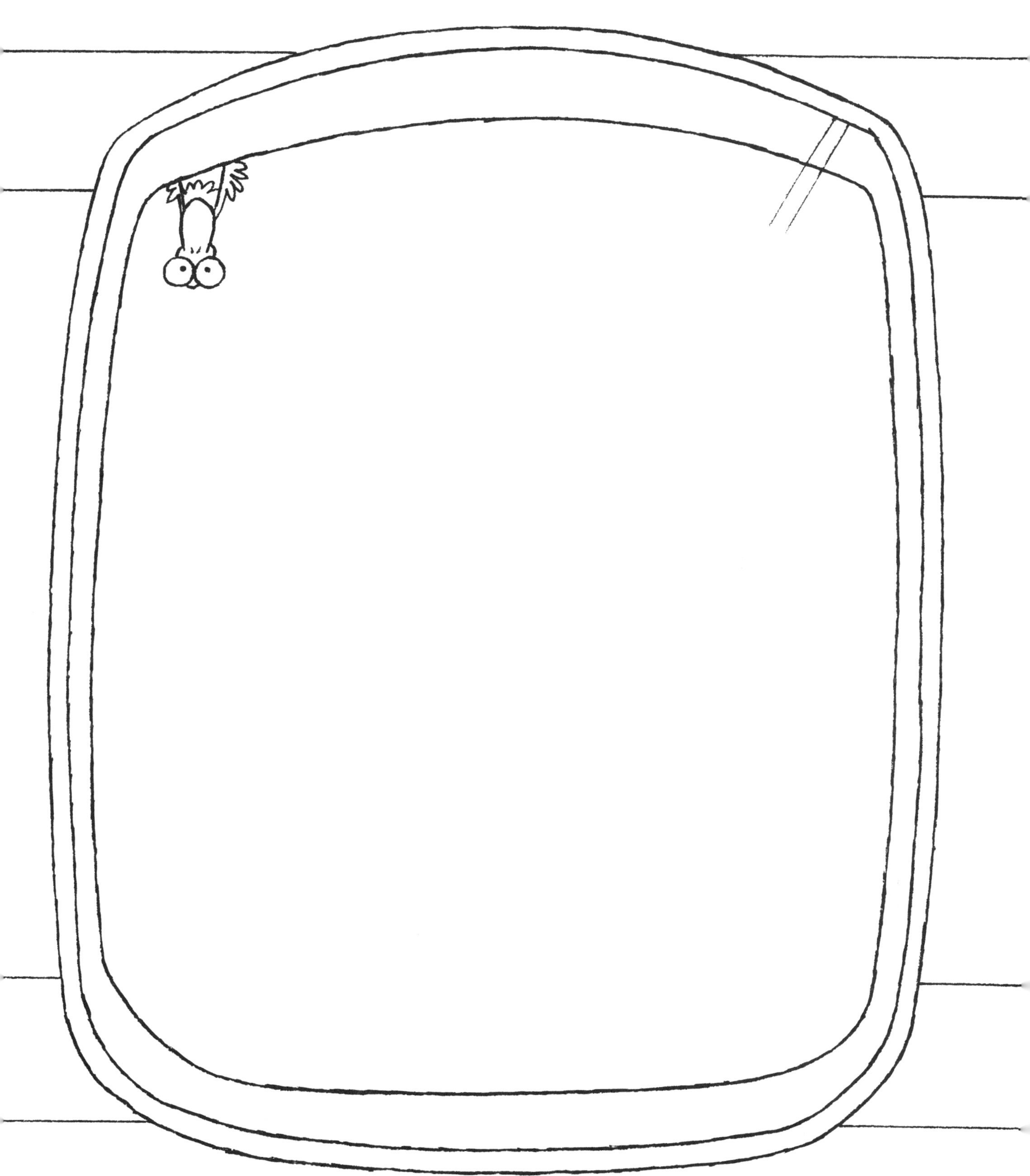

They've all come to see your exhibition

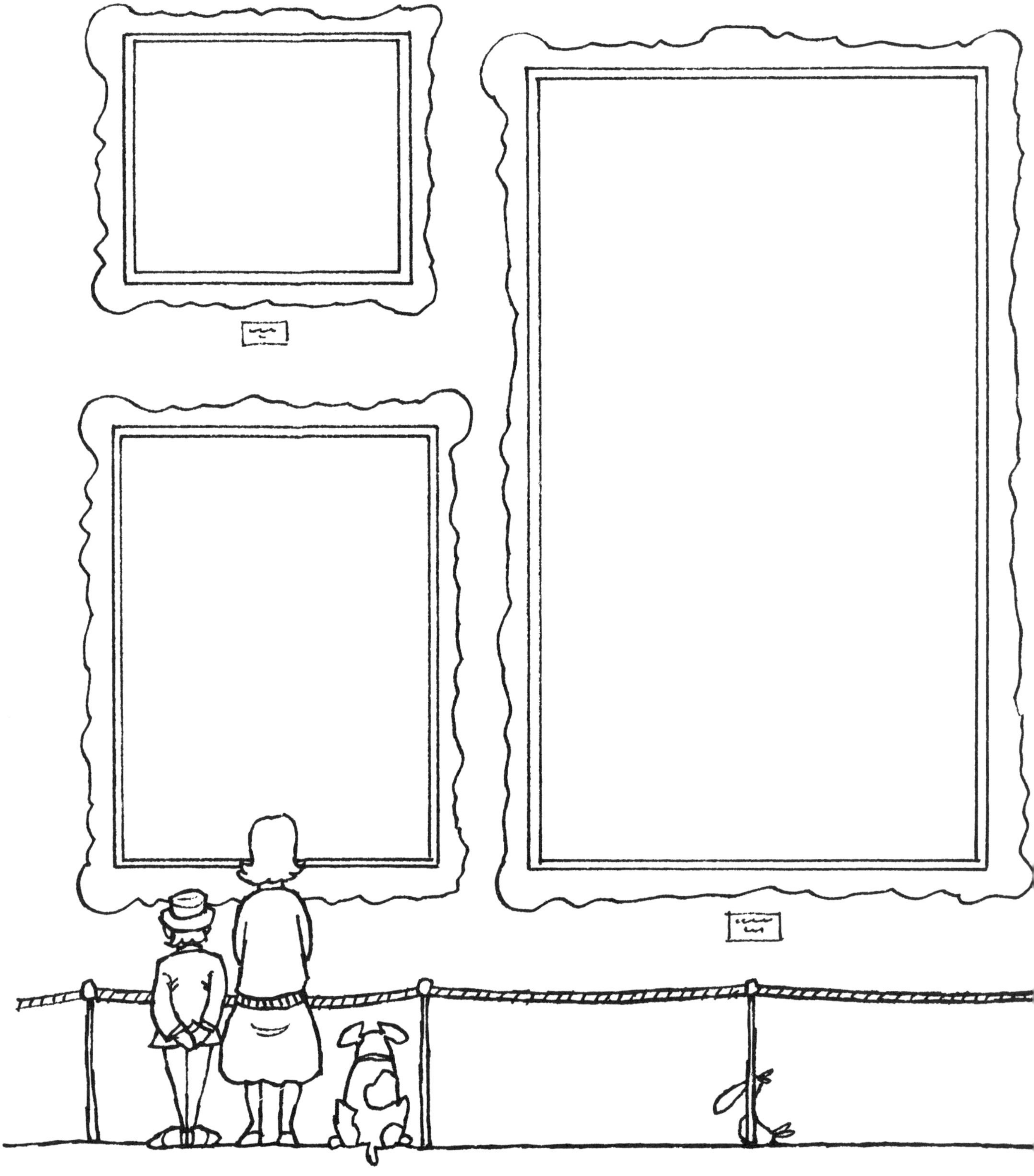

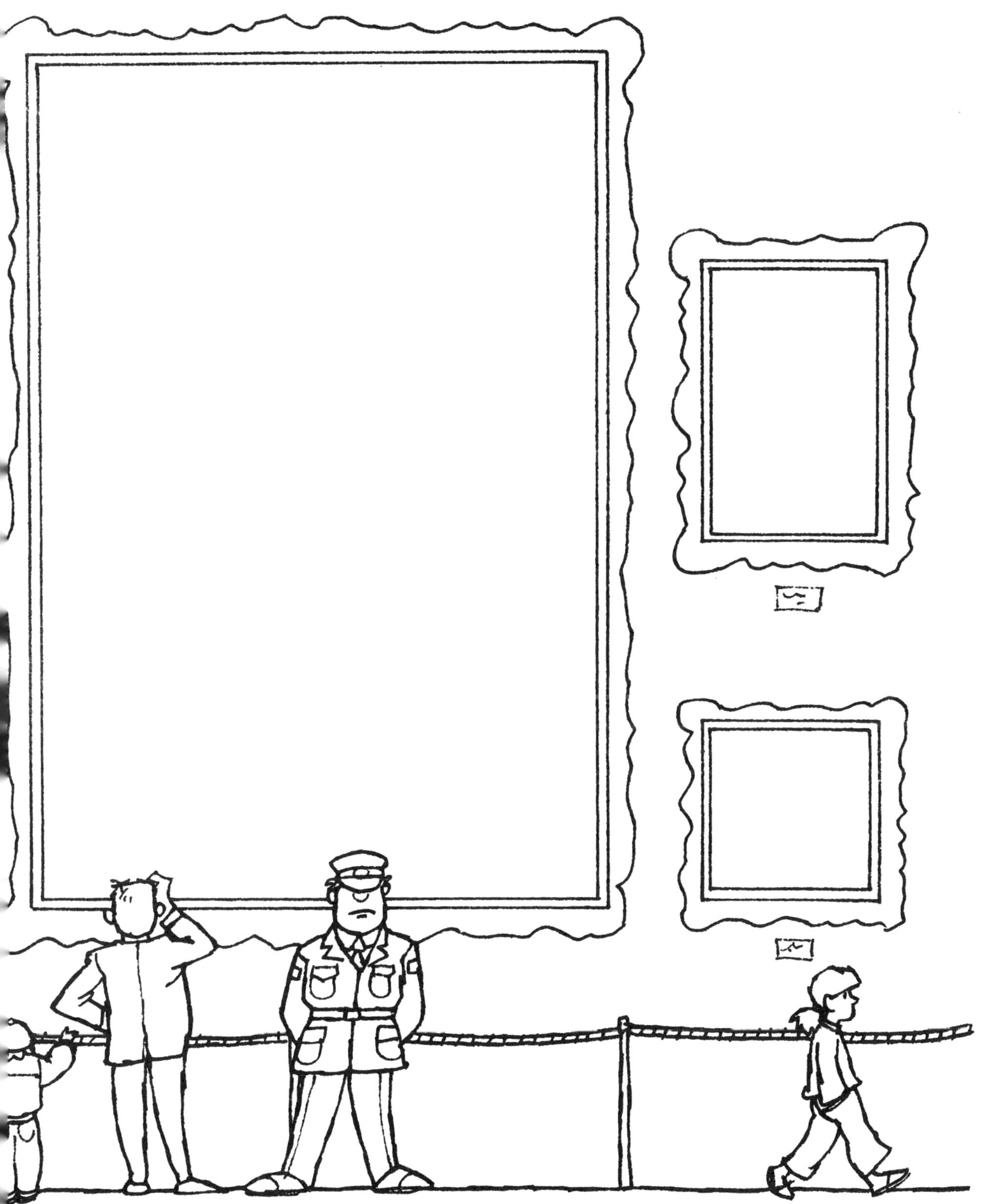

Create a new species of butterfly

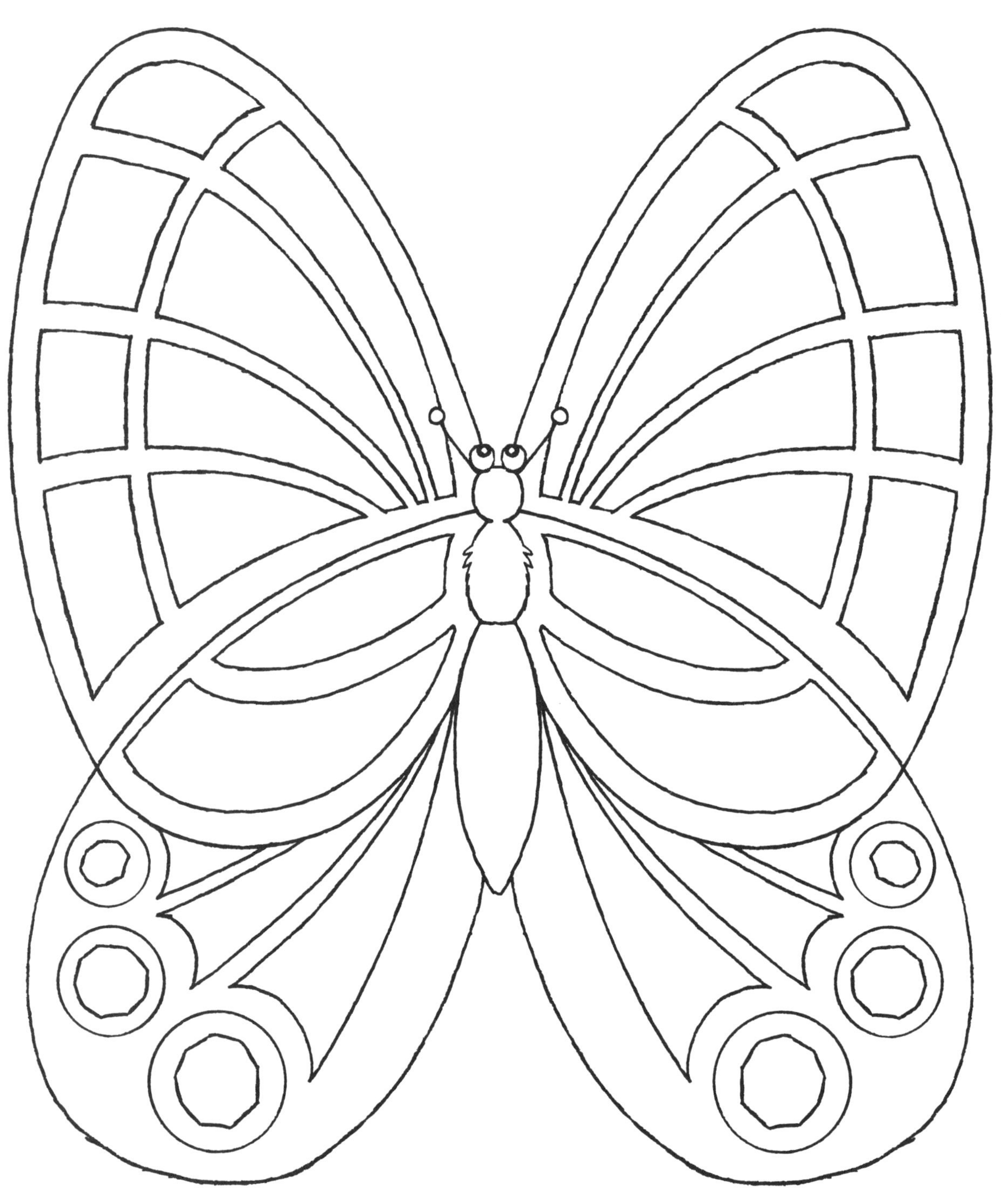

What won the Monster Vegetable Competition?

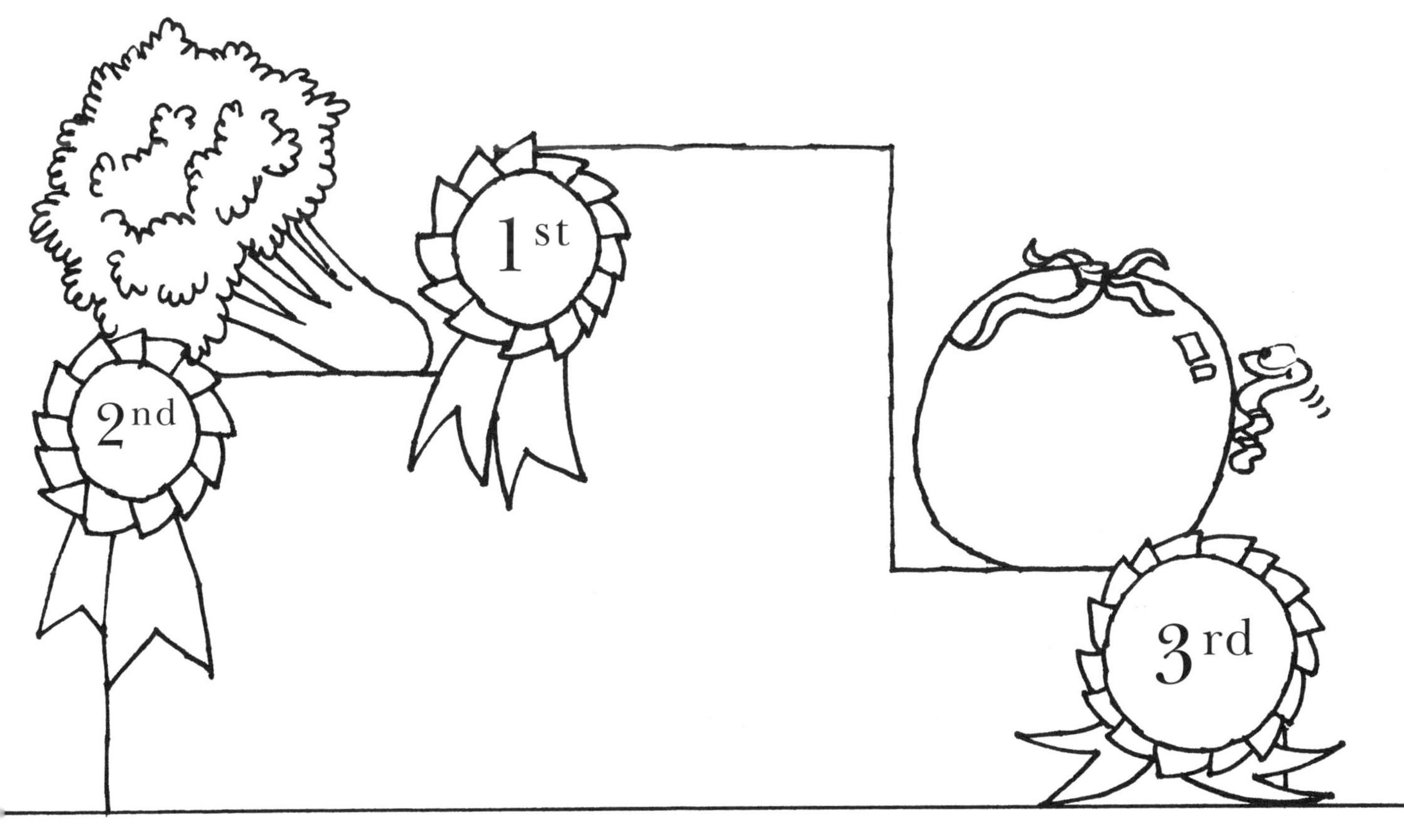

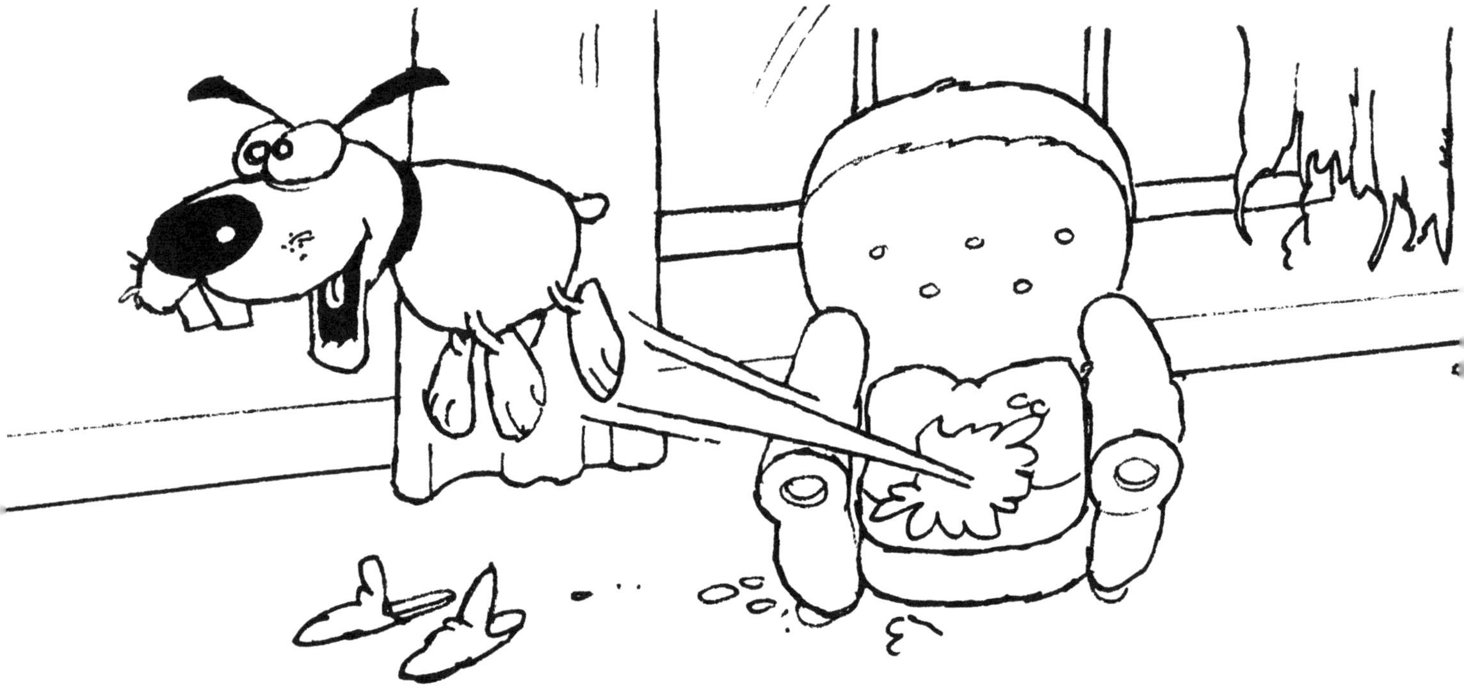

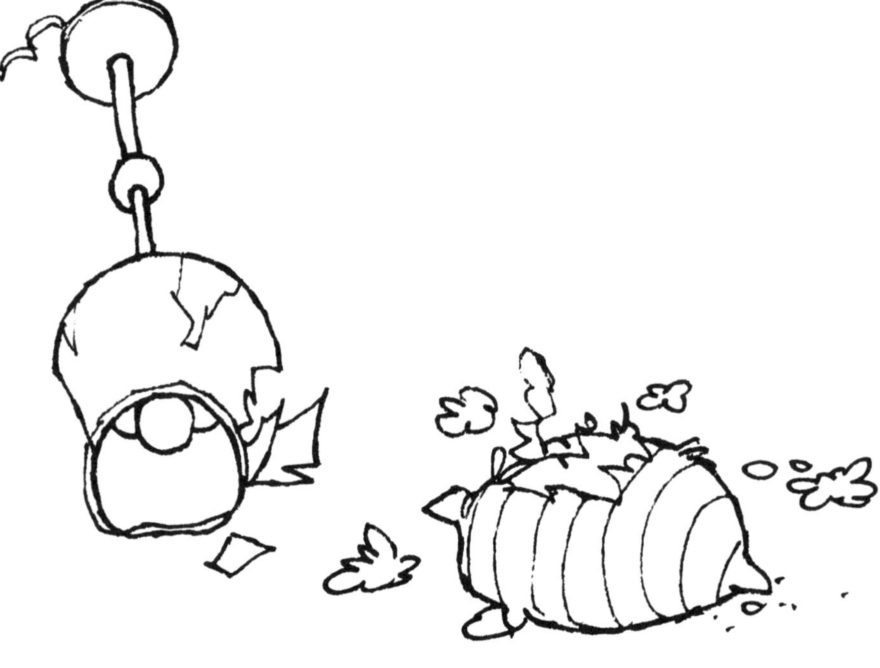

A doggy disaster!

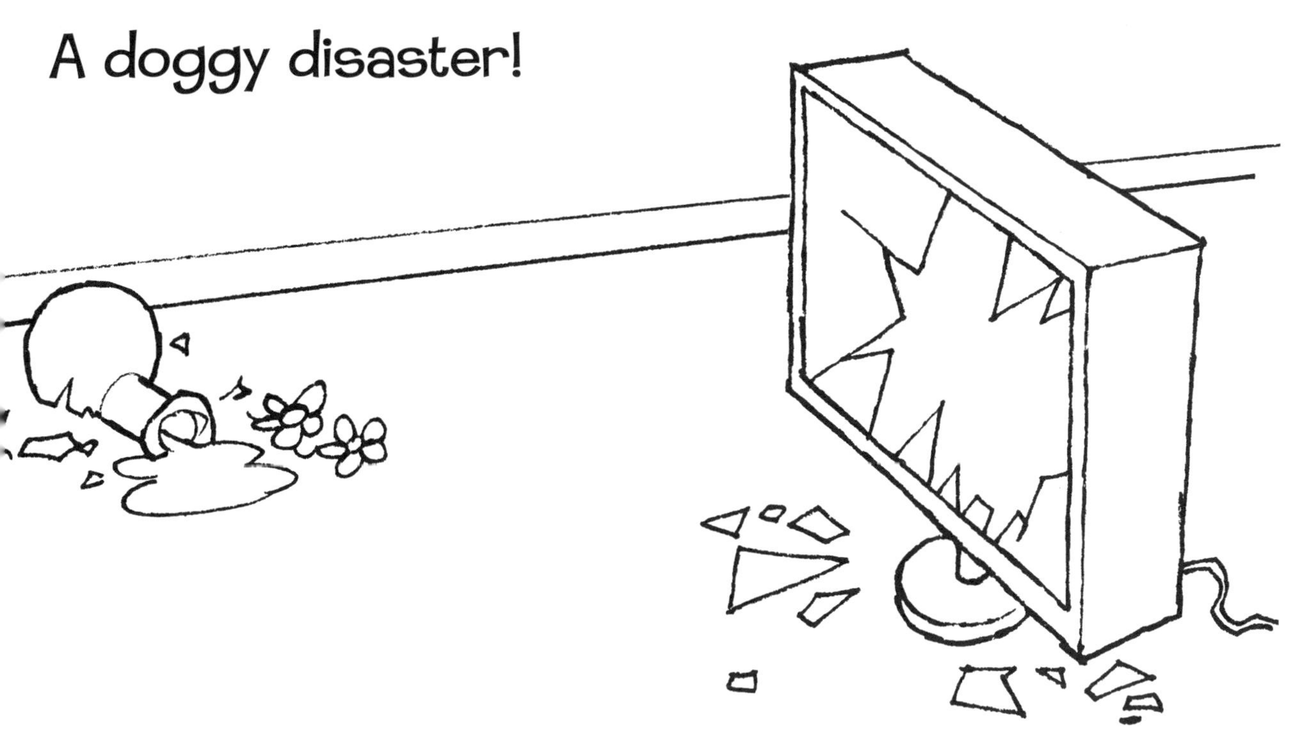

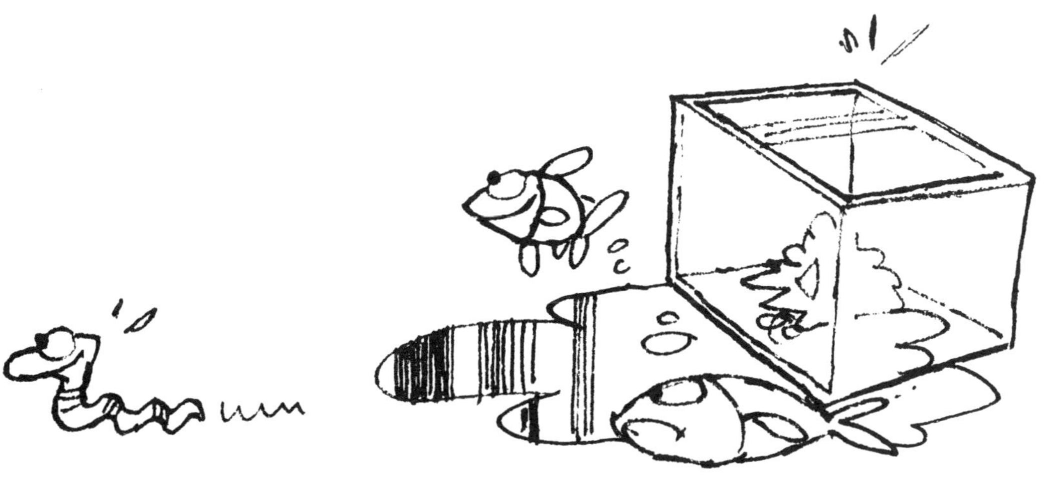

Your dream house

Bees like brightly colored flowers best

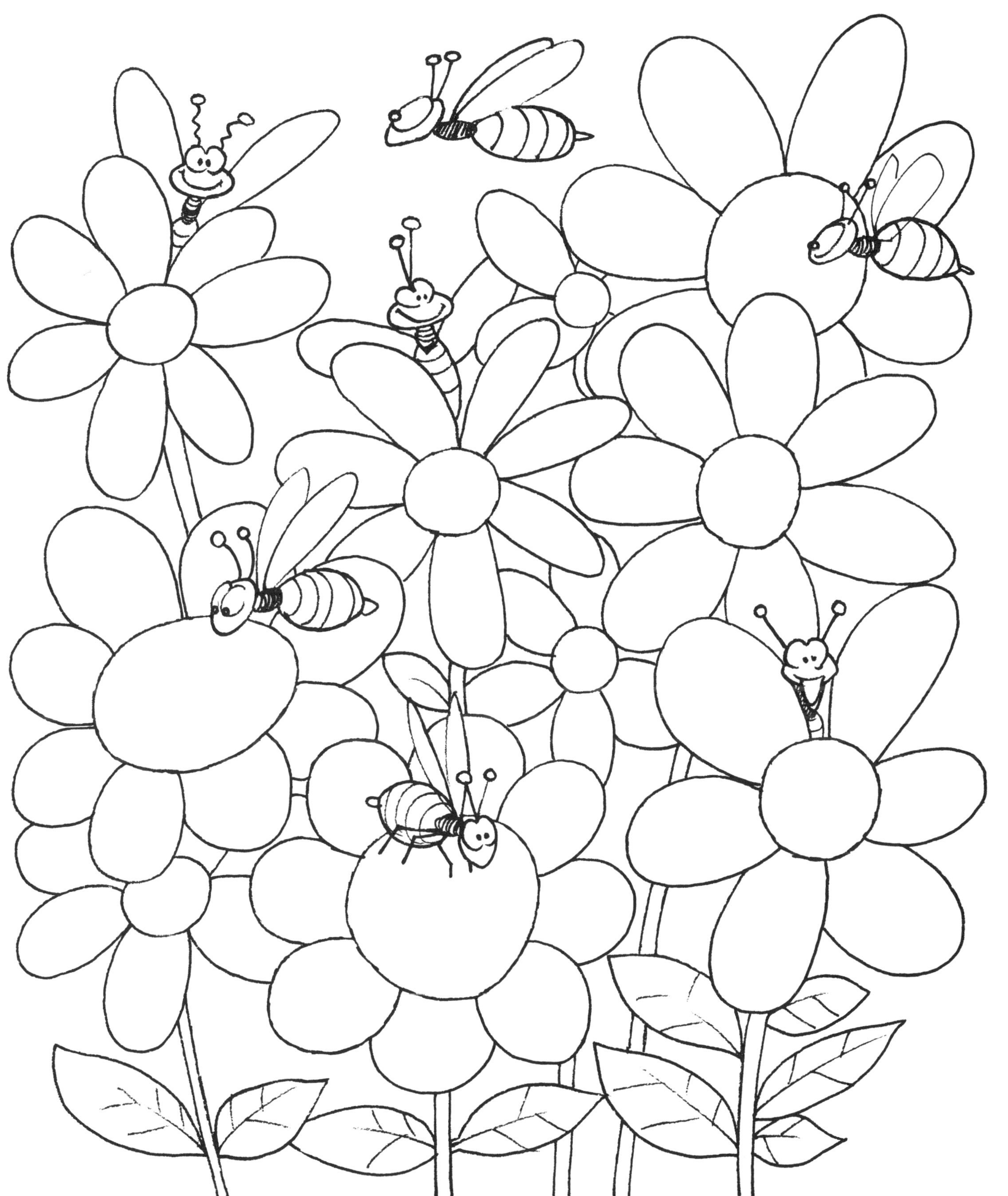

Give the band some rockin' t-shirts

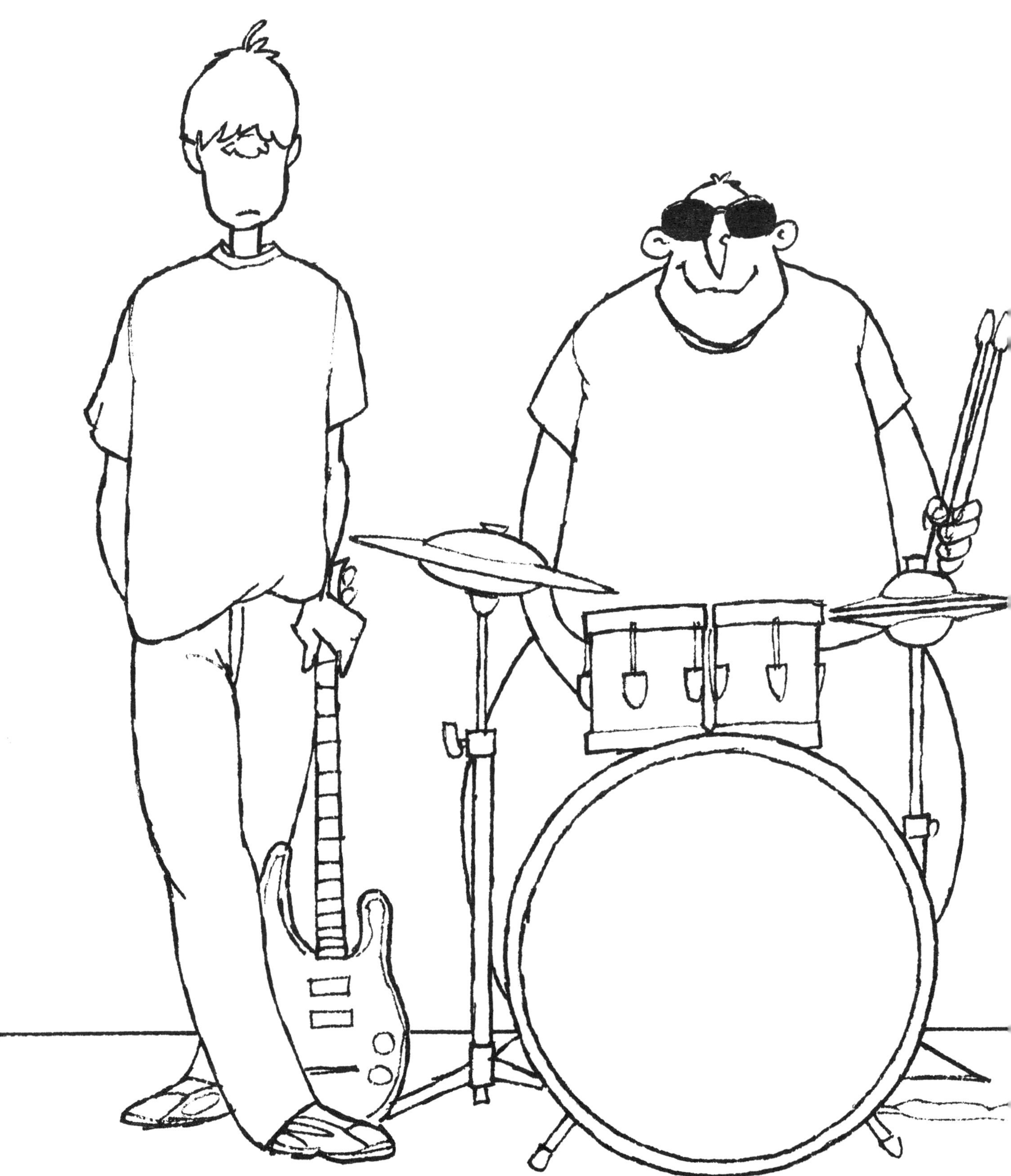

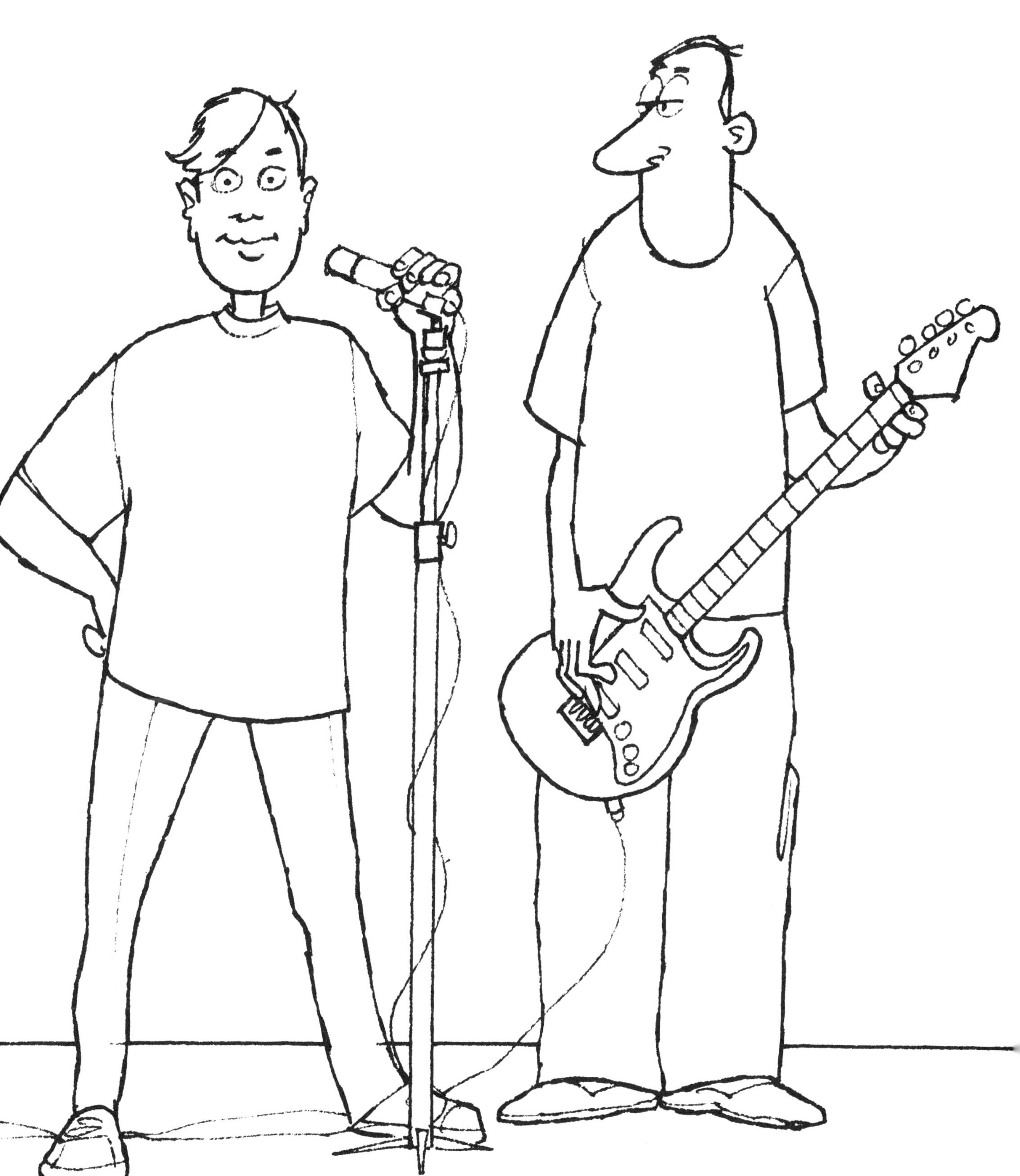

How do dung beetles greet each other?

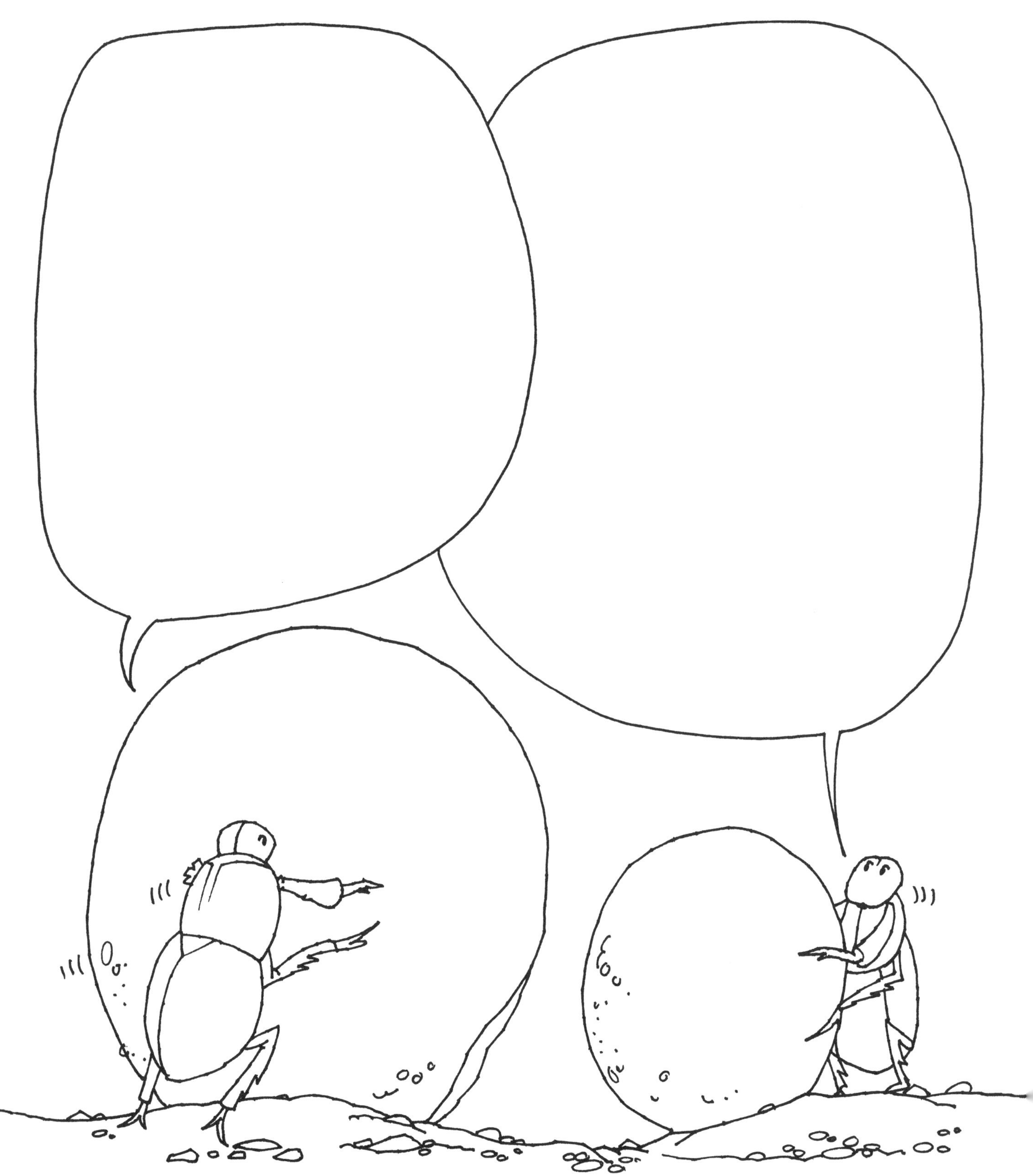

What's the view like from Mars?

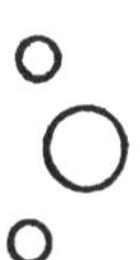

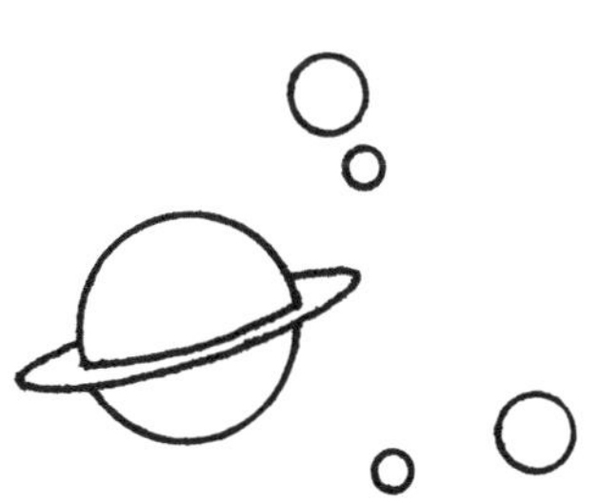

Decorate the eggs in time for Easter

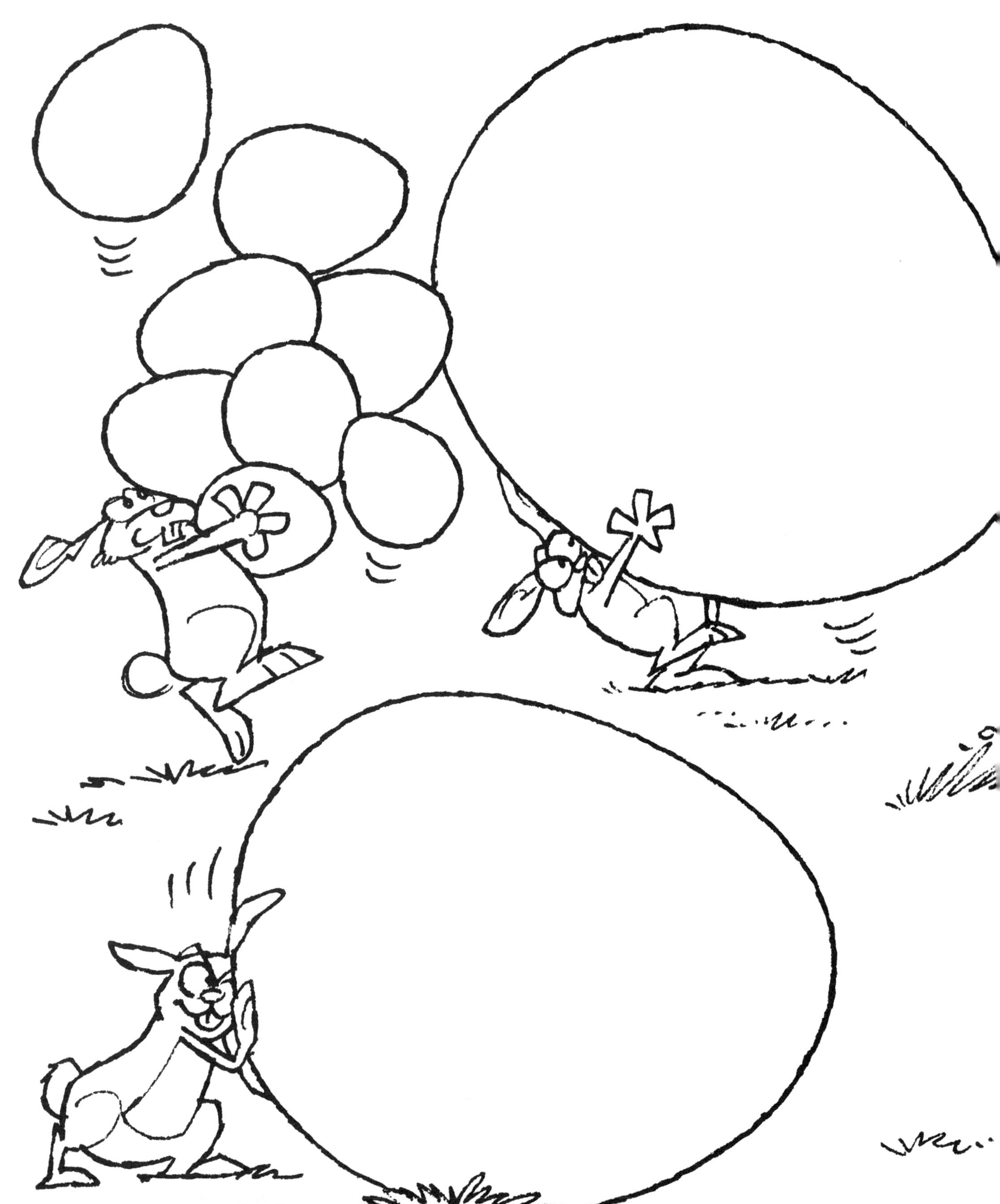

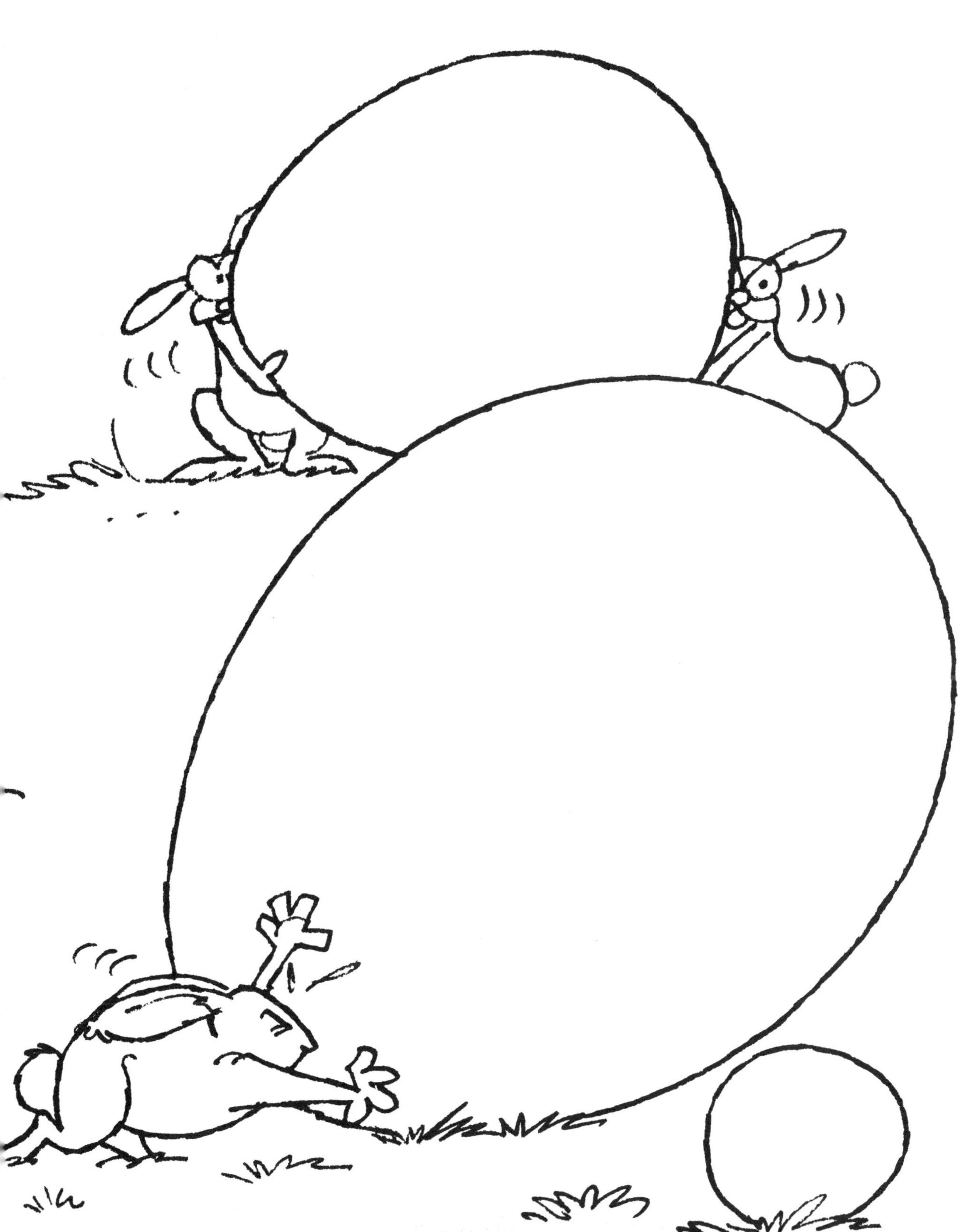

What an excellent hiding place

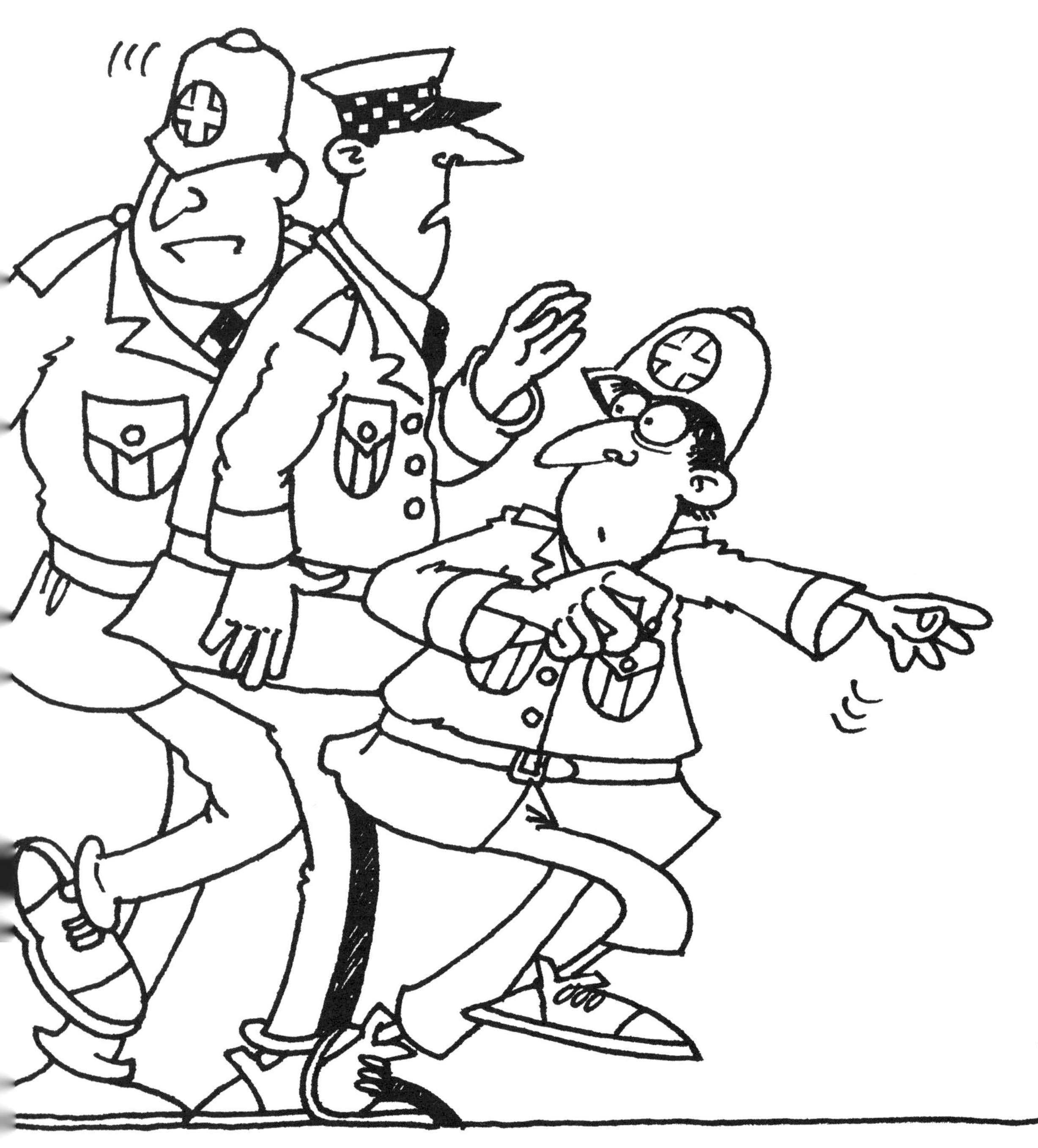

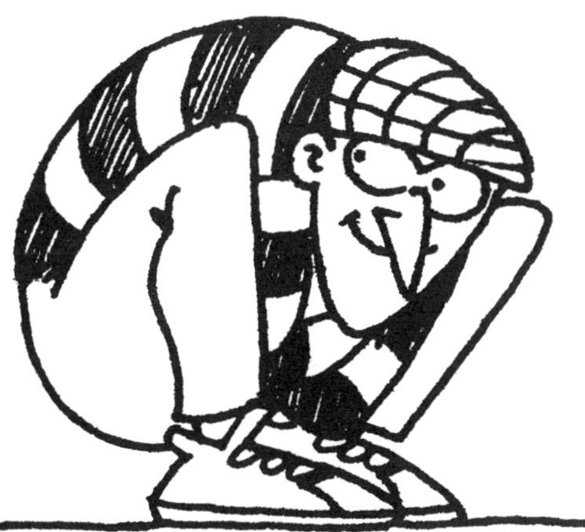

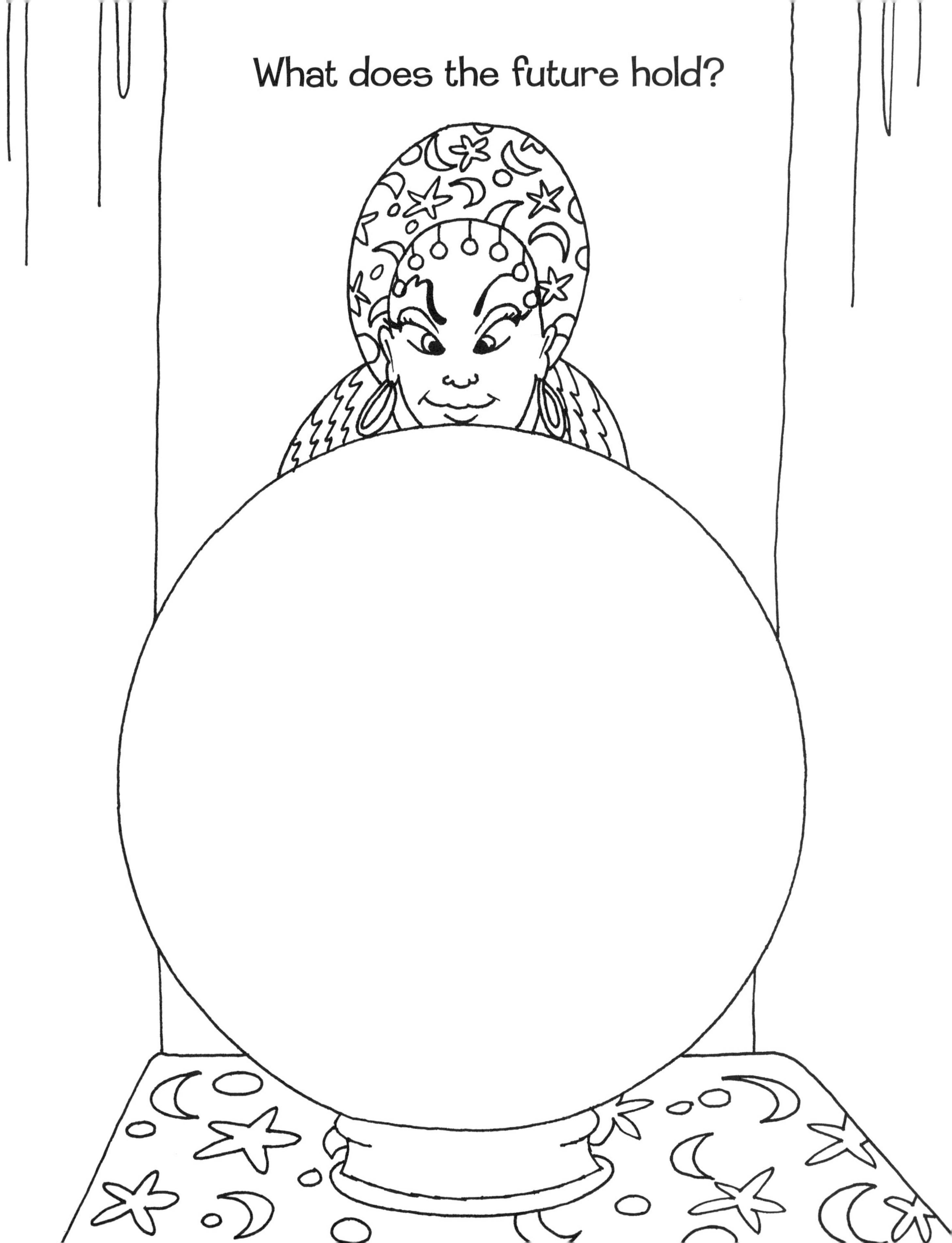
What does the future hold?

Who is he saving from the burning building?

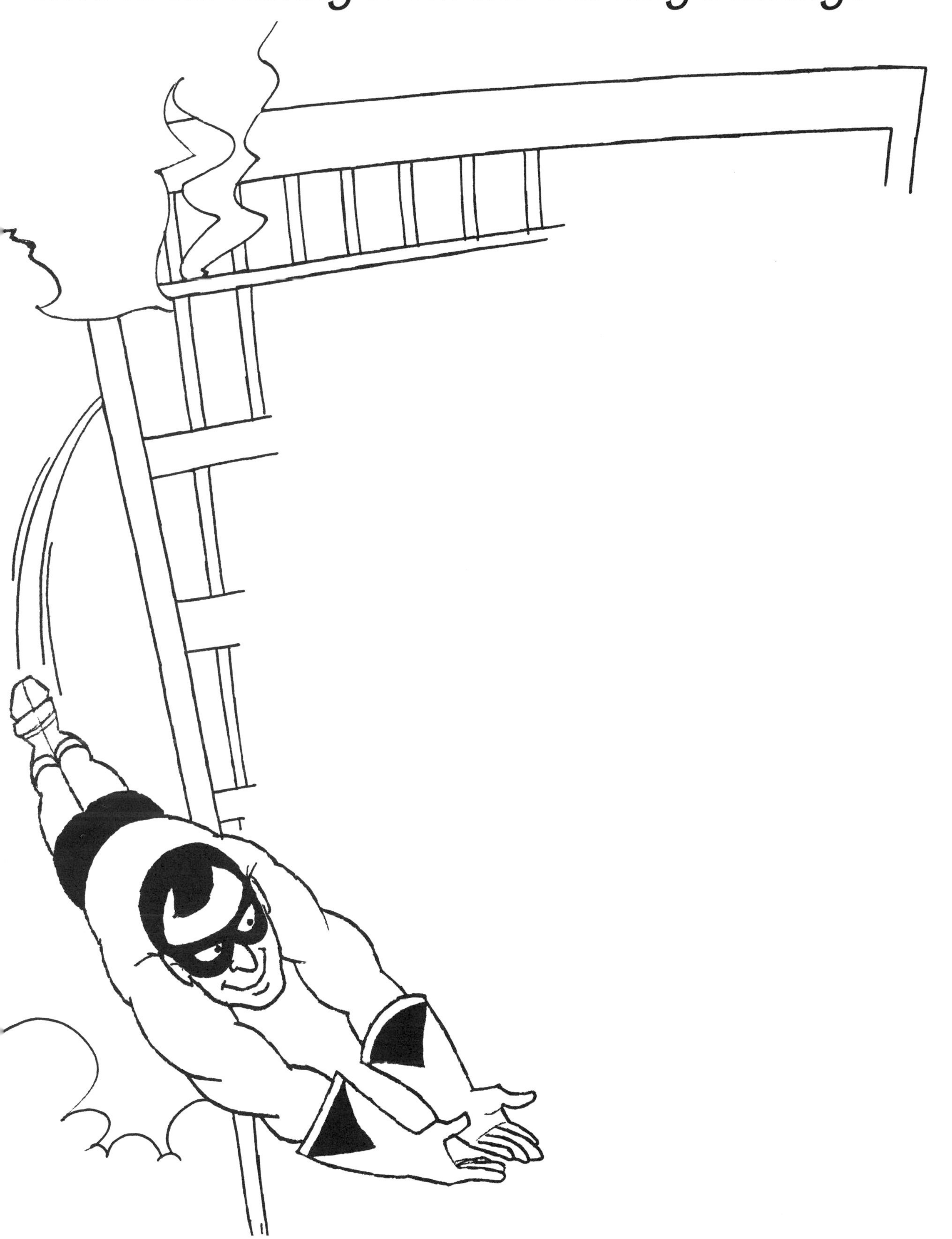

I'd like to buy that car

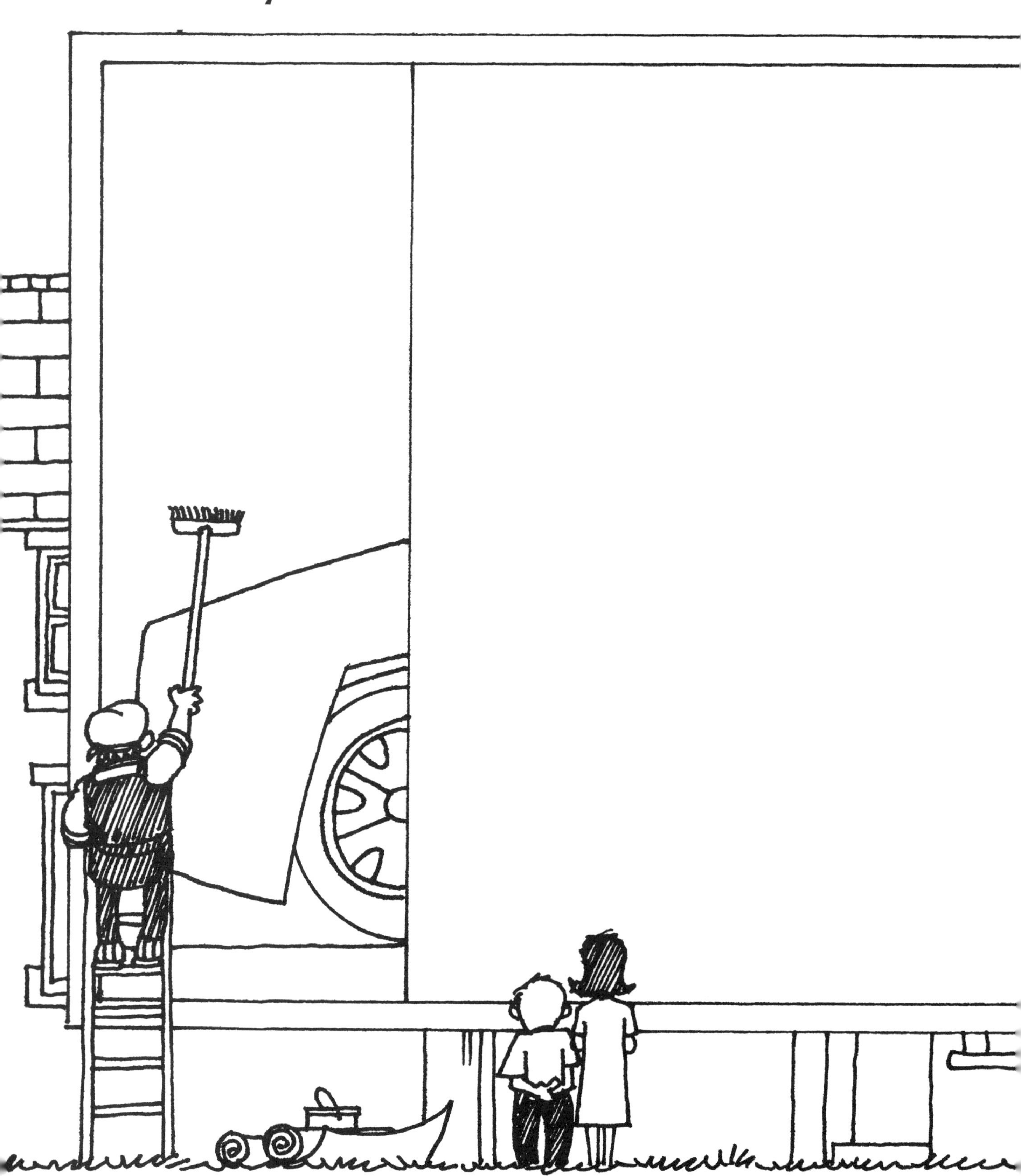

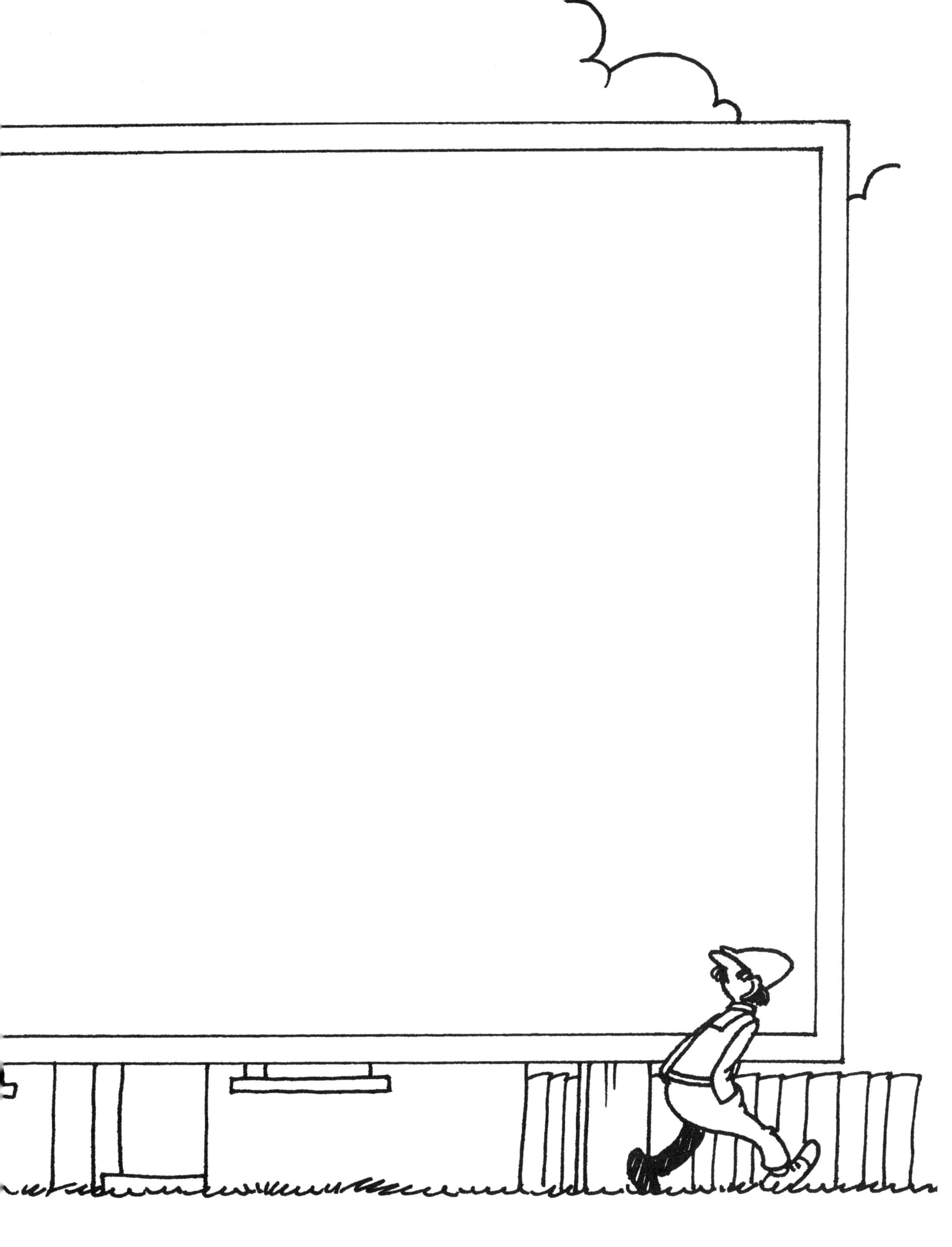

Give the doll's house some furniture

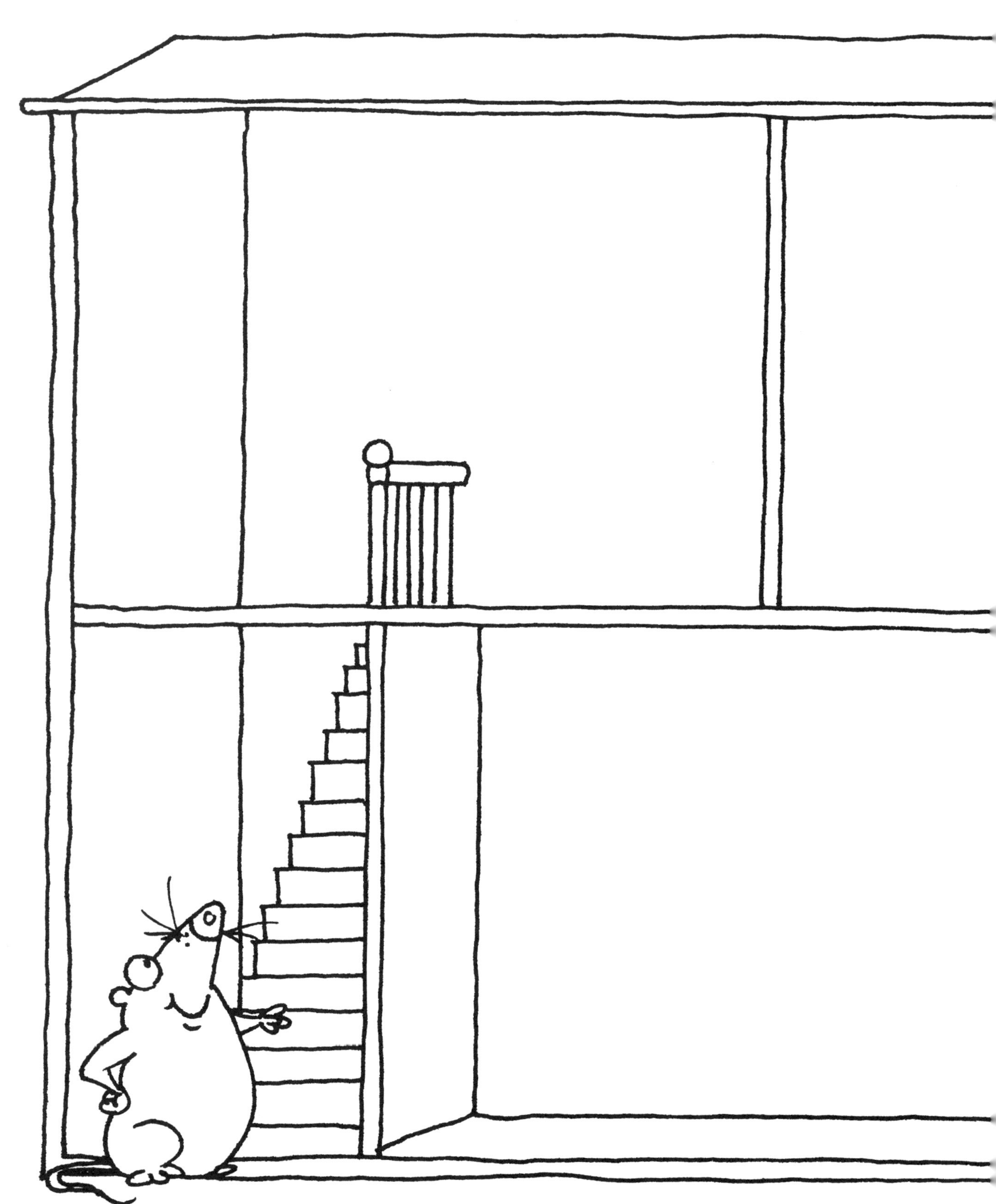

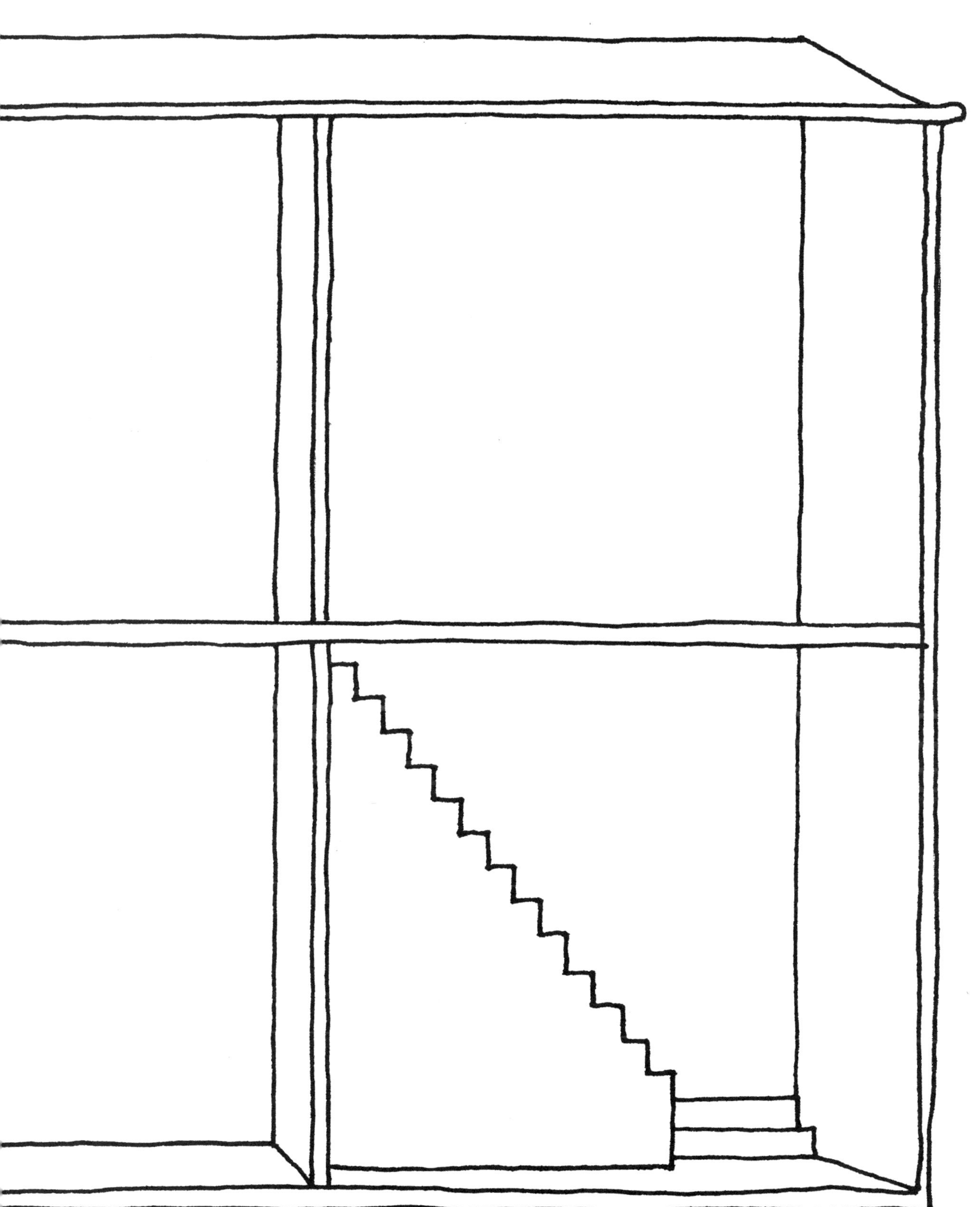

What do you see in the mirror every day?

Finish and color the pile of autumn leaves

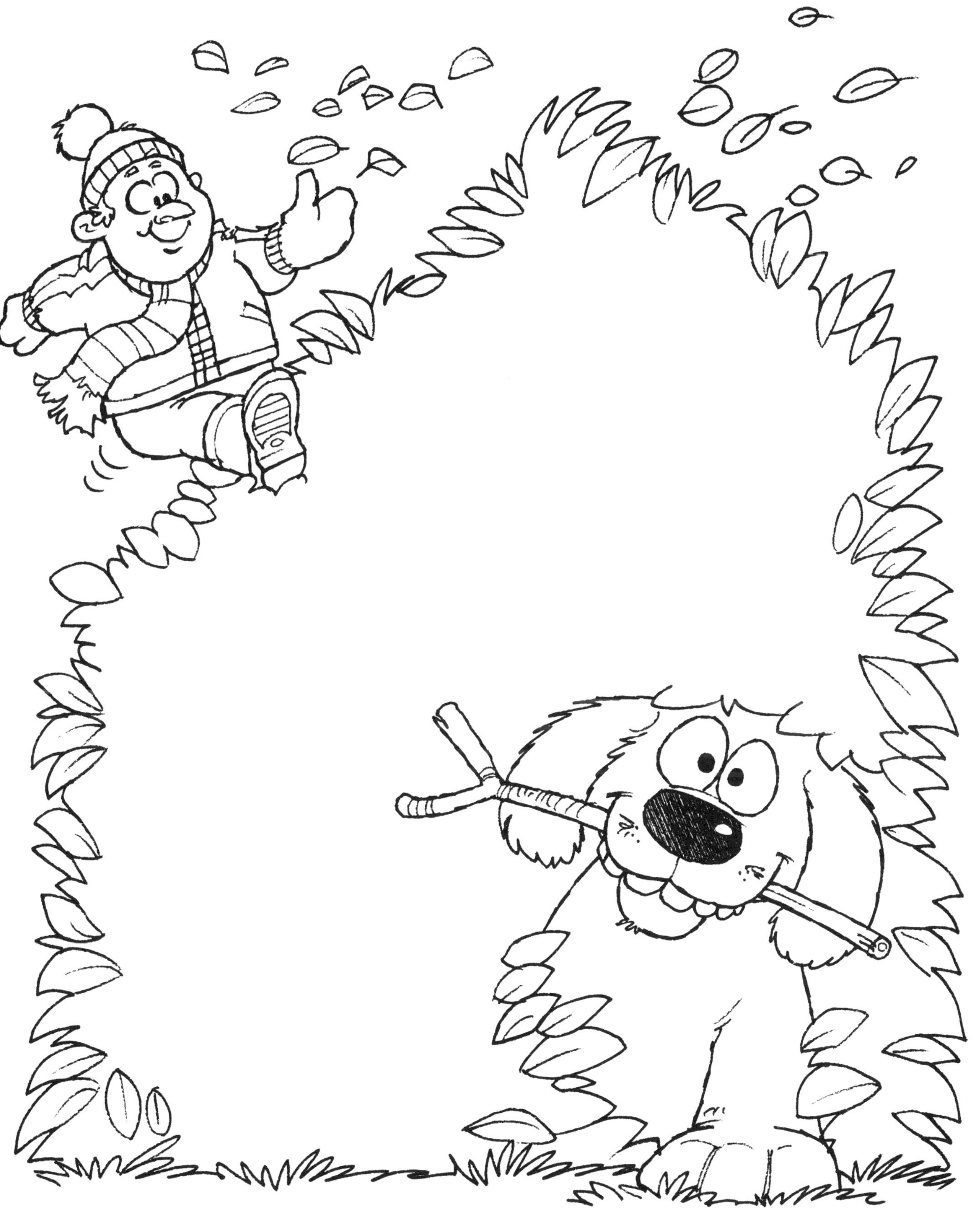

They can see their bright tents from miles away!

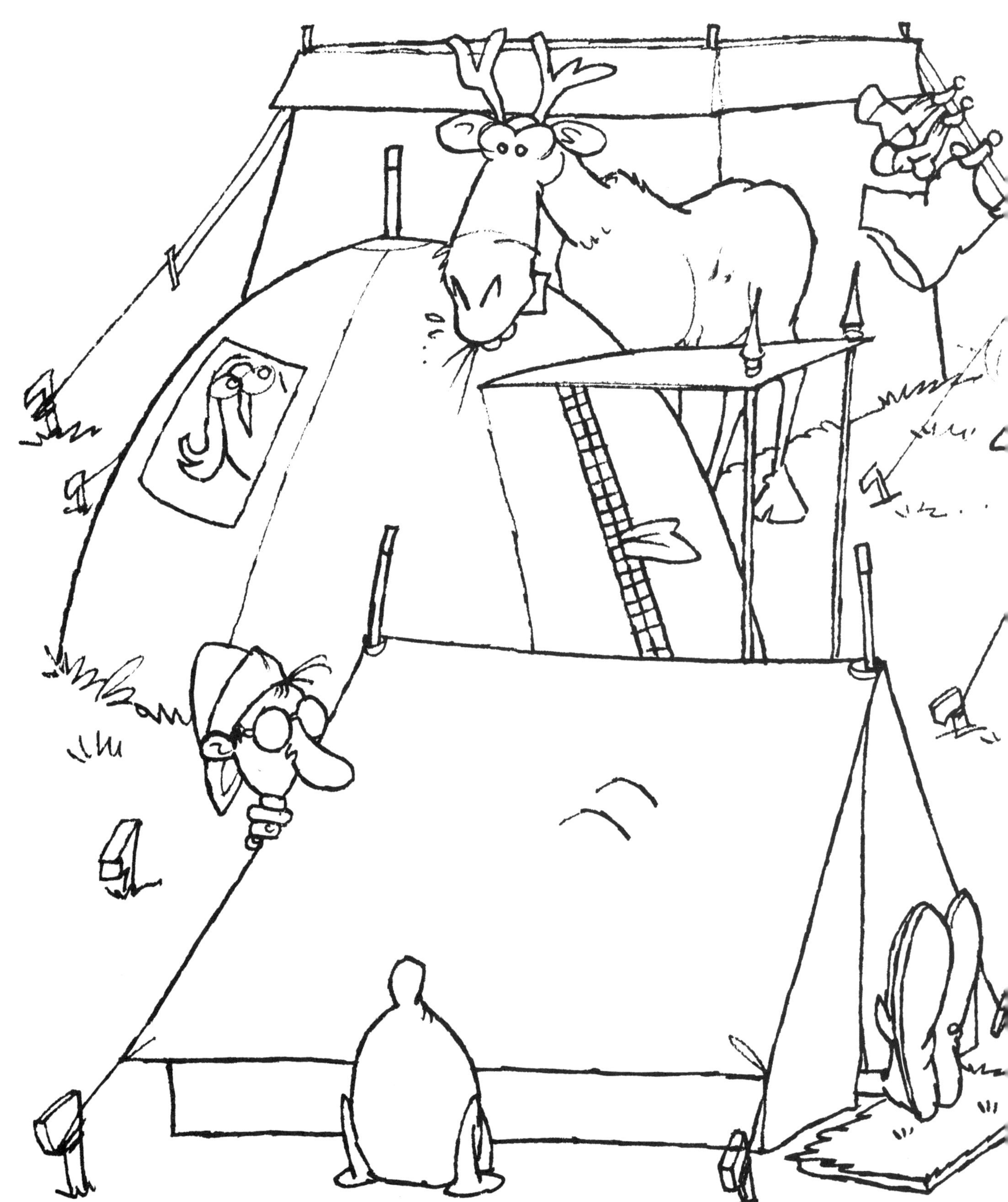

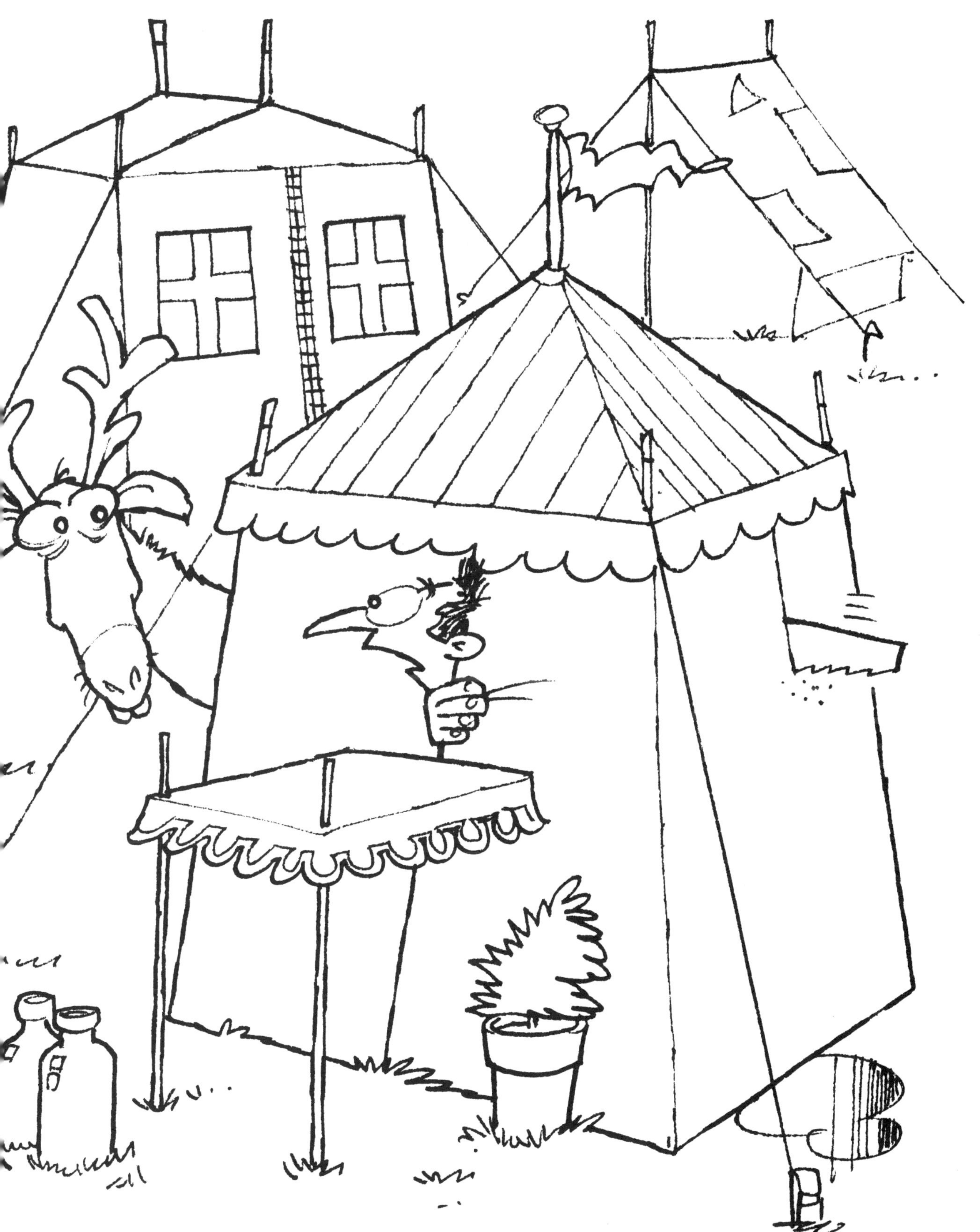

He may look mean, but he's such a silly color

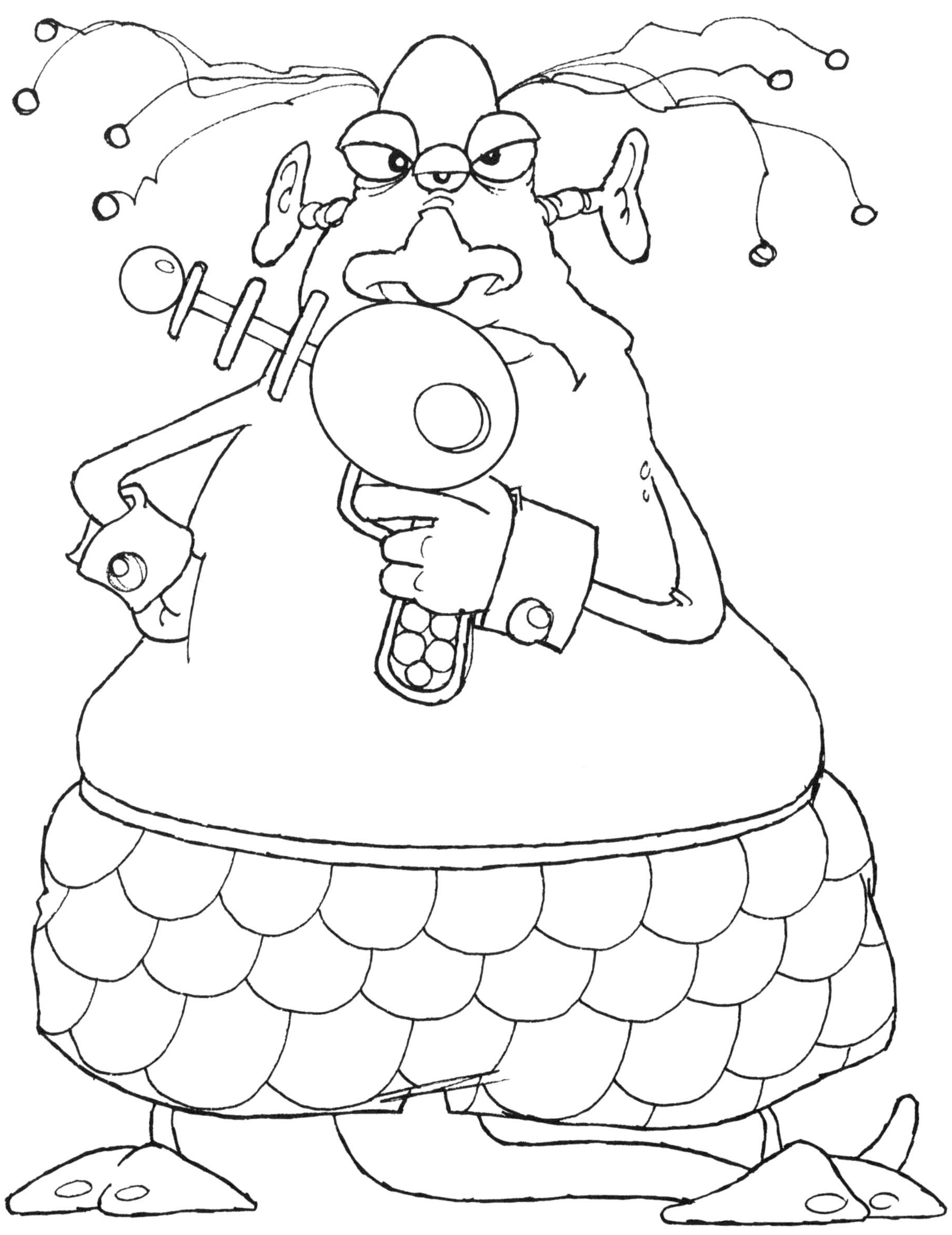

Ouch! What has the crab caught in his pincer?

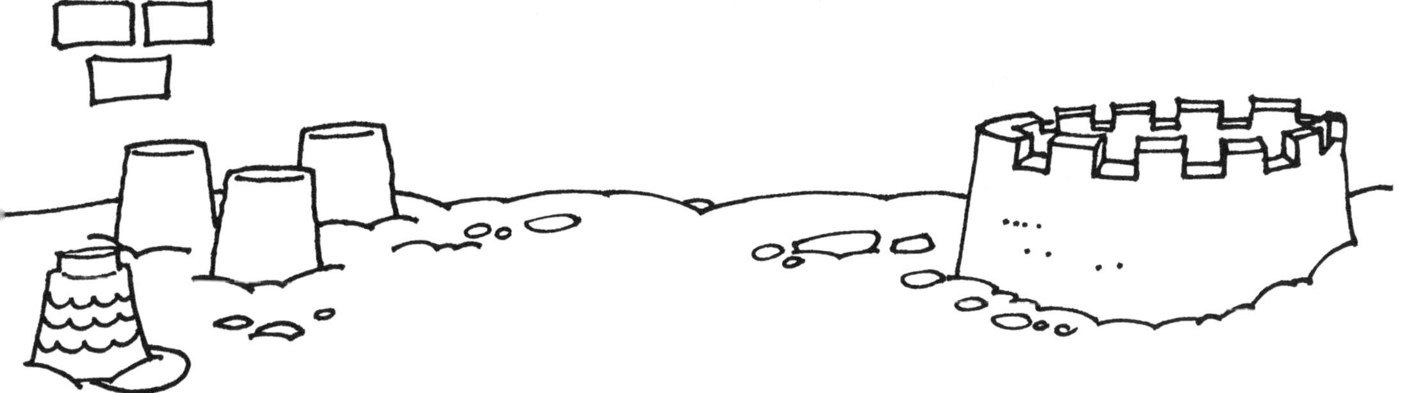

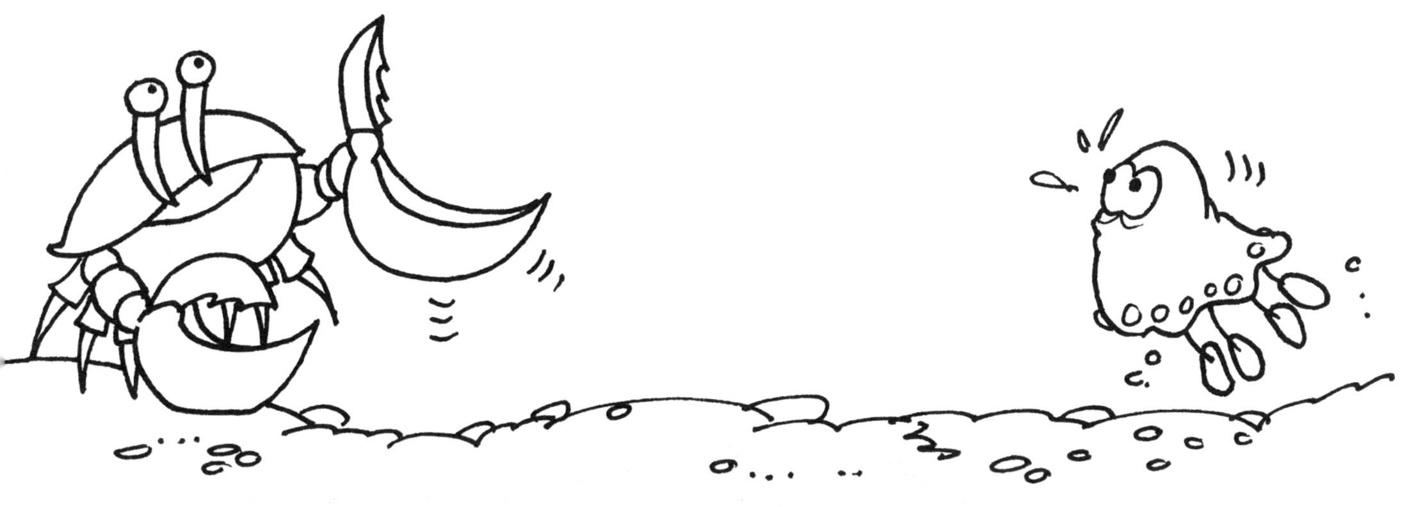

What can you see through the keyhole?

Who's flying on the magic carpet?

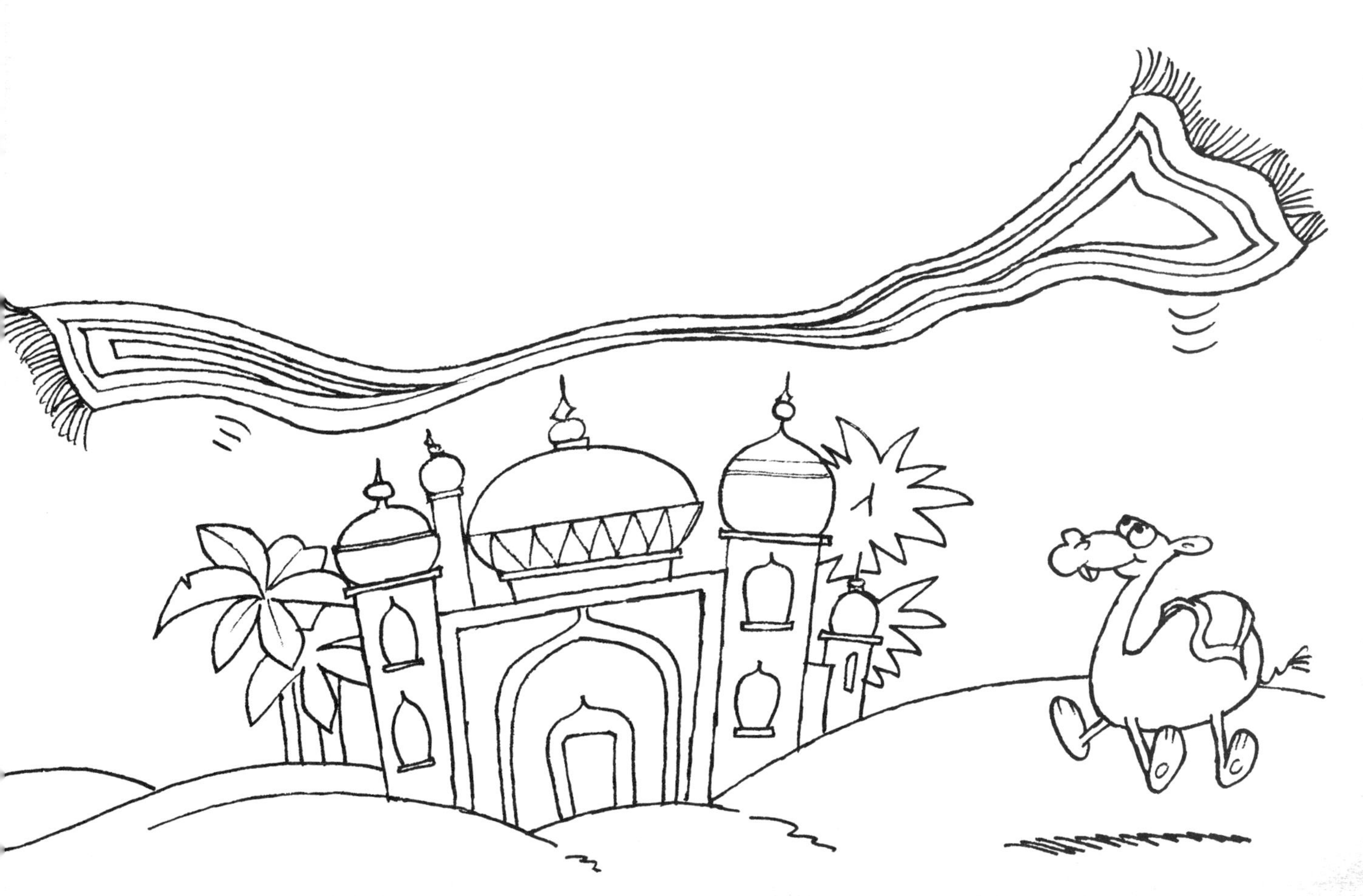

What funny clothes your neighbors wear!

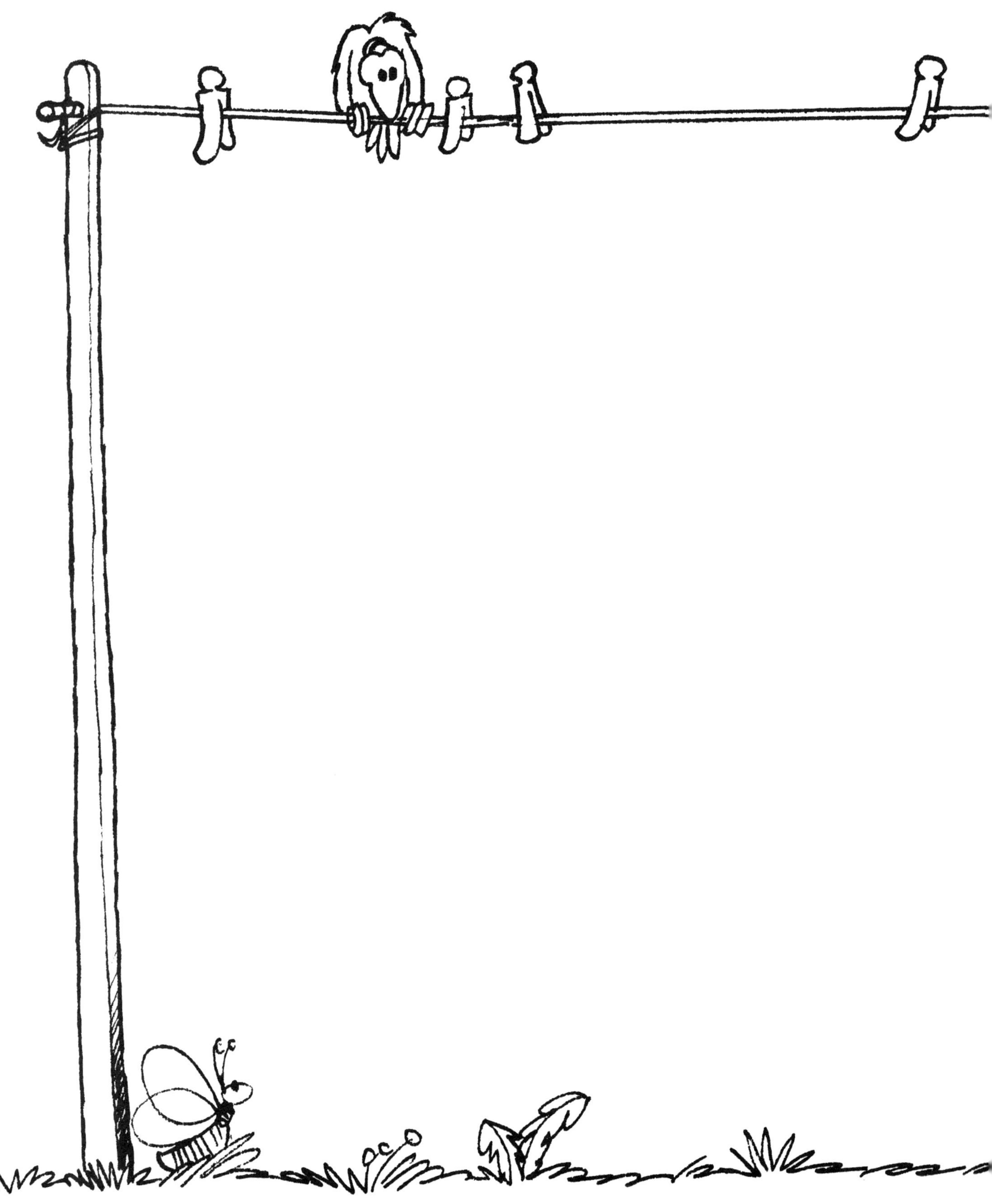

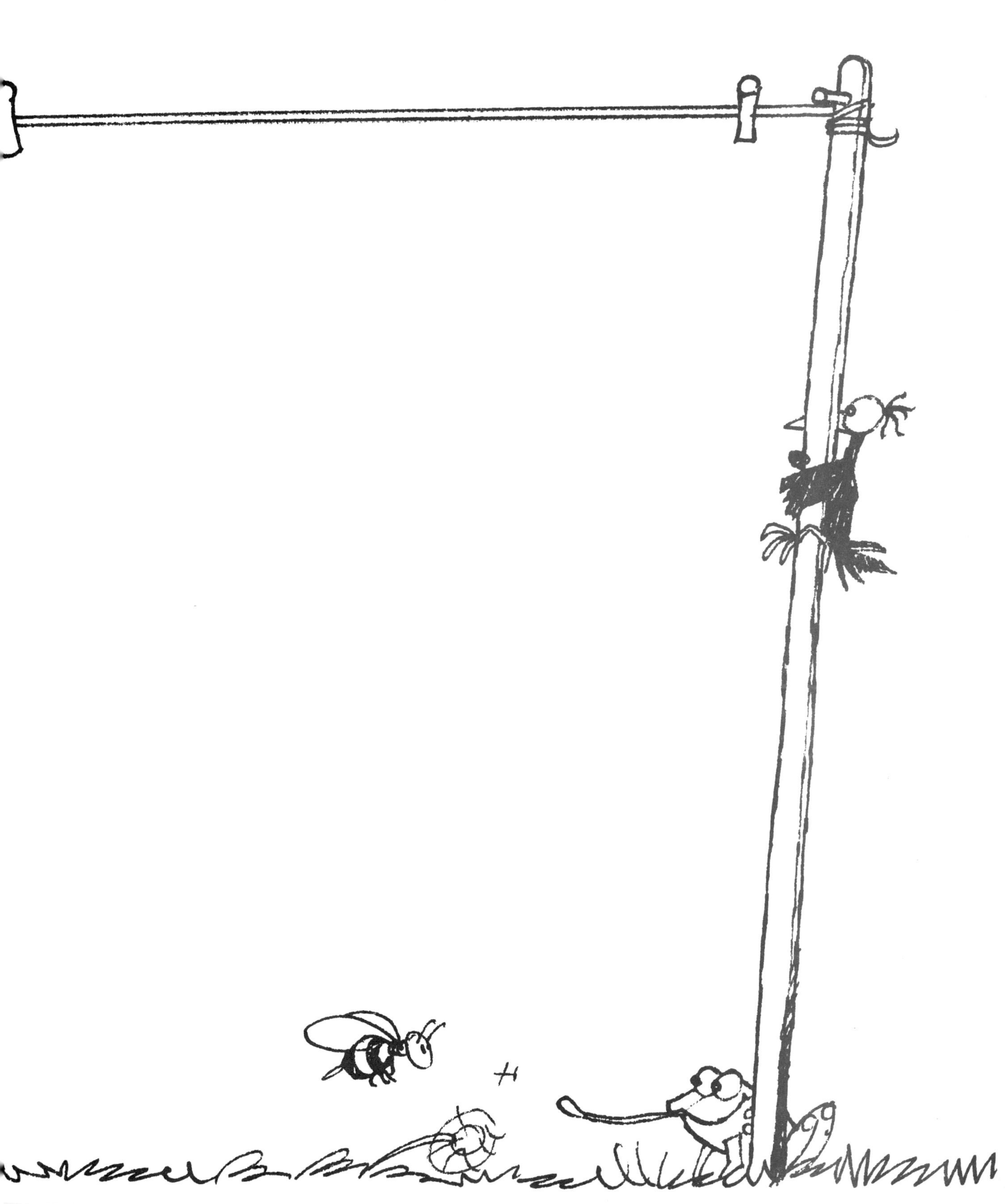

They've stolen the picnic!

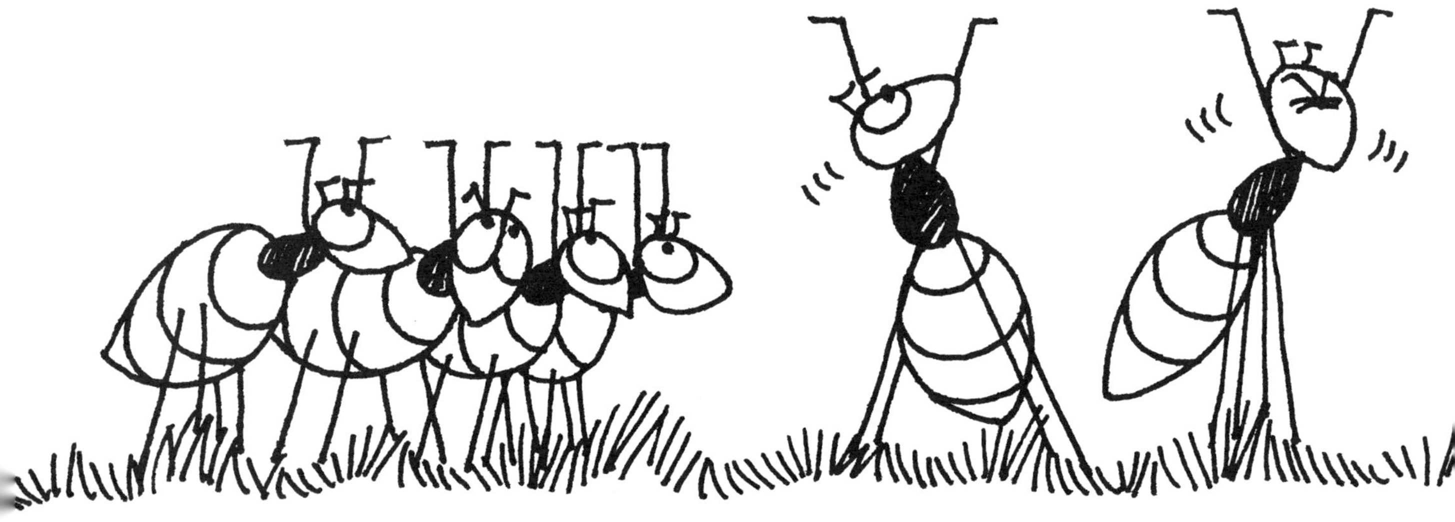

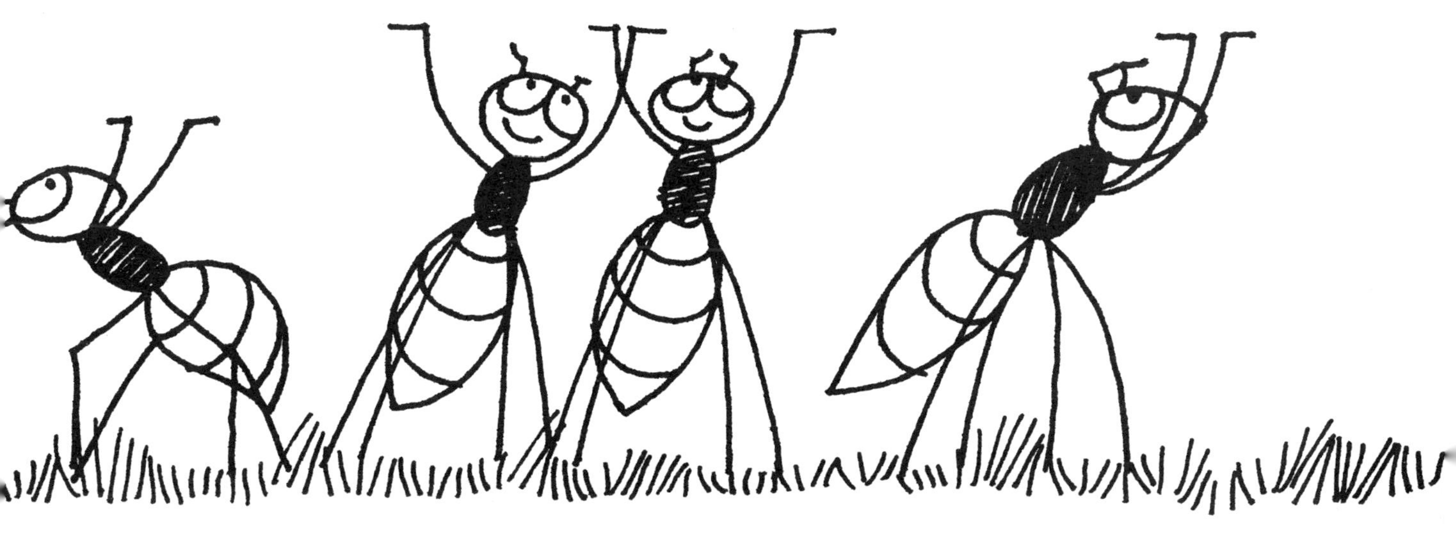

What are you planning?

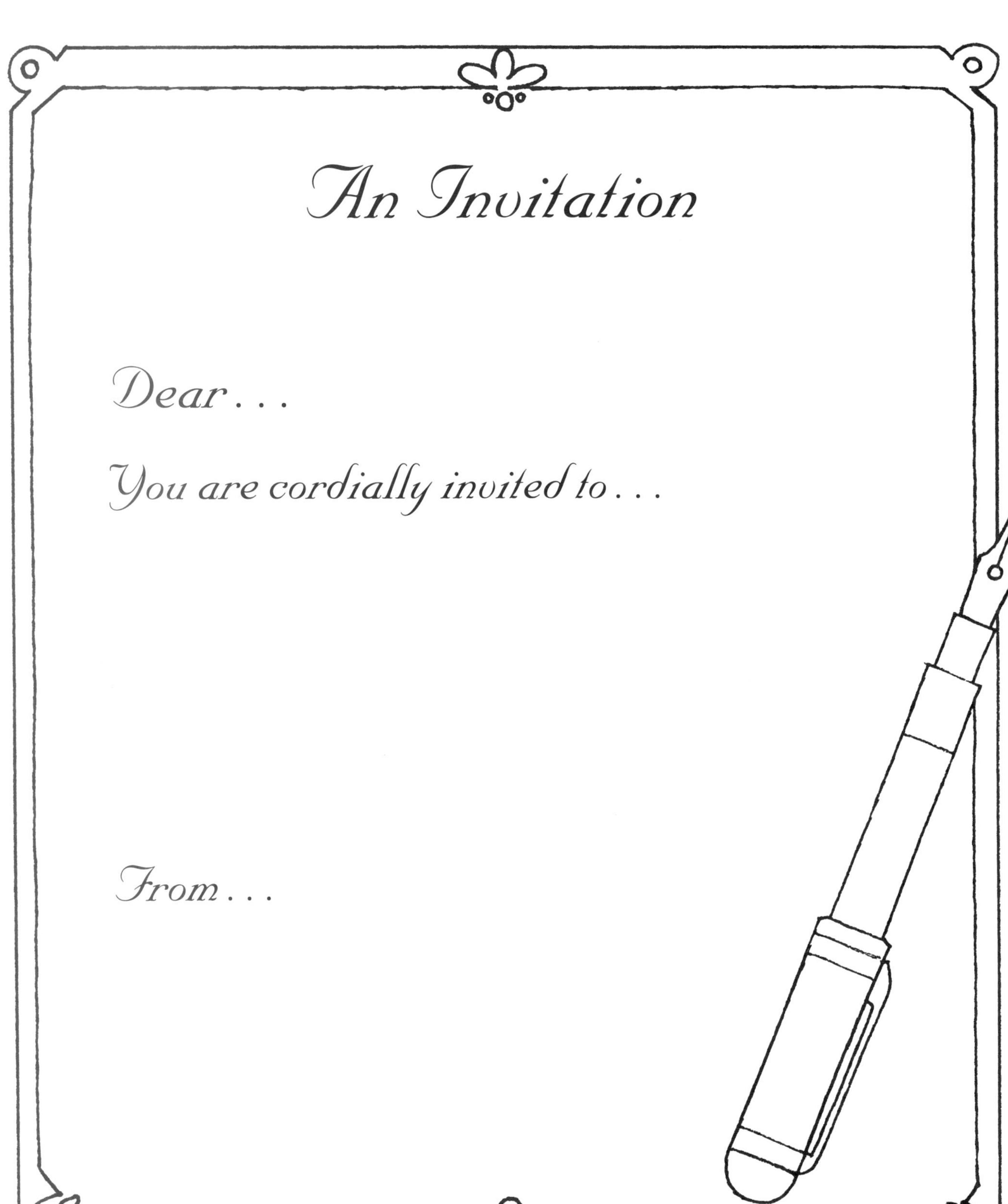

Give her a fabulous hat

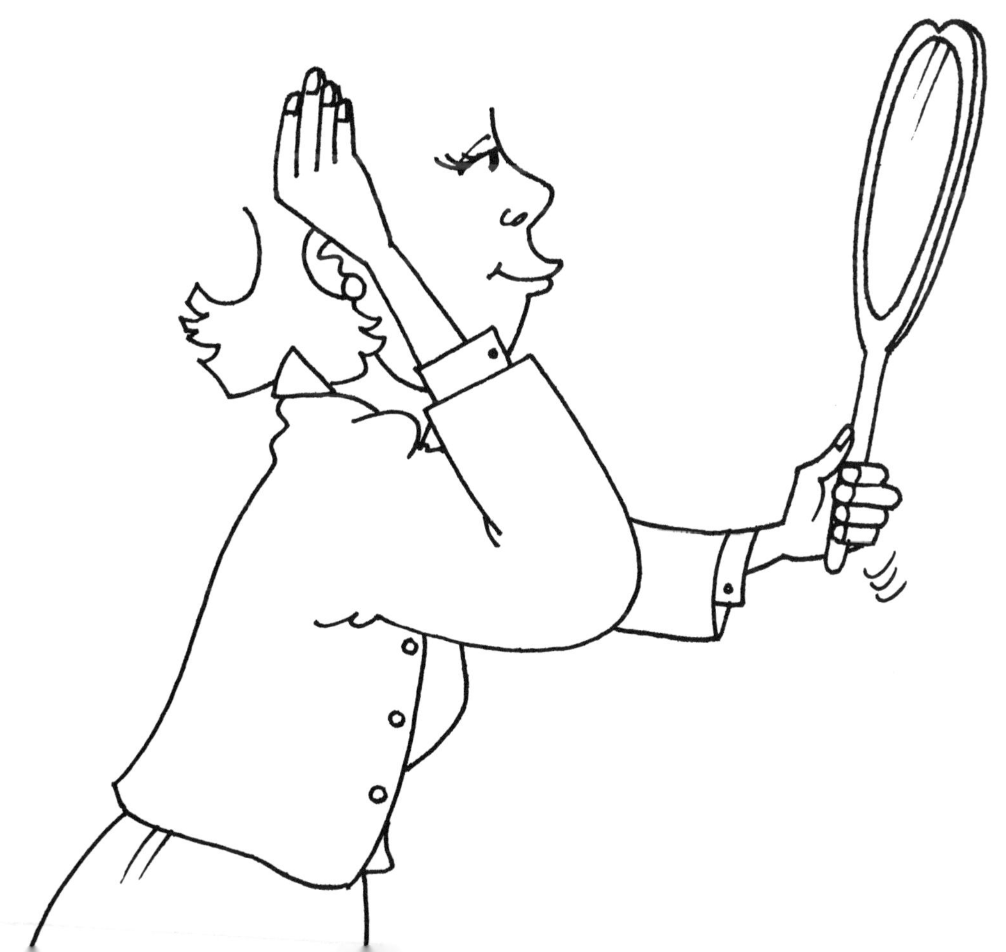

What color are the cheerleaders' outfits?

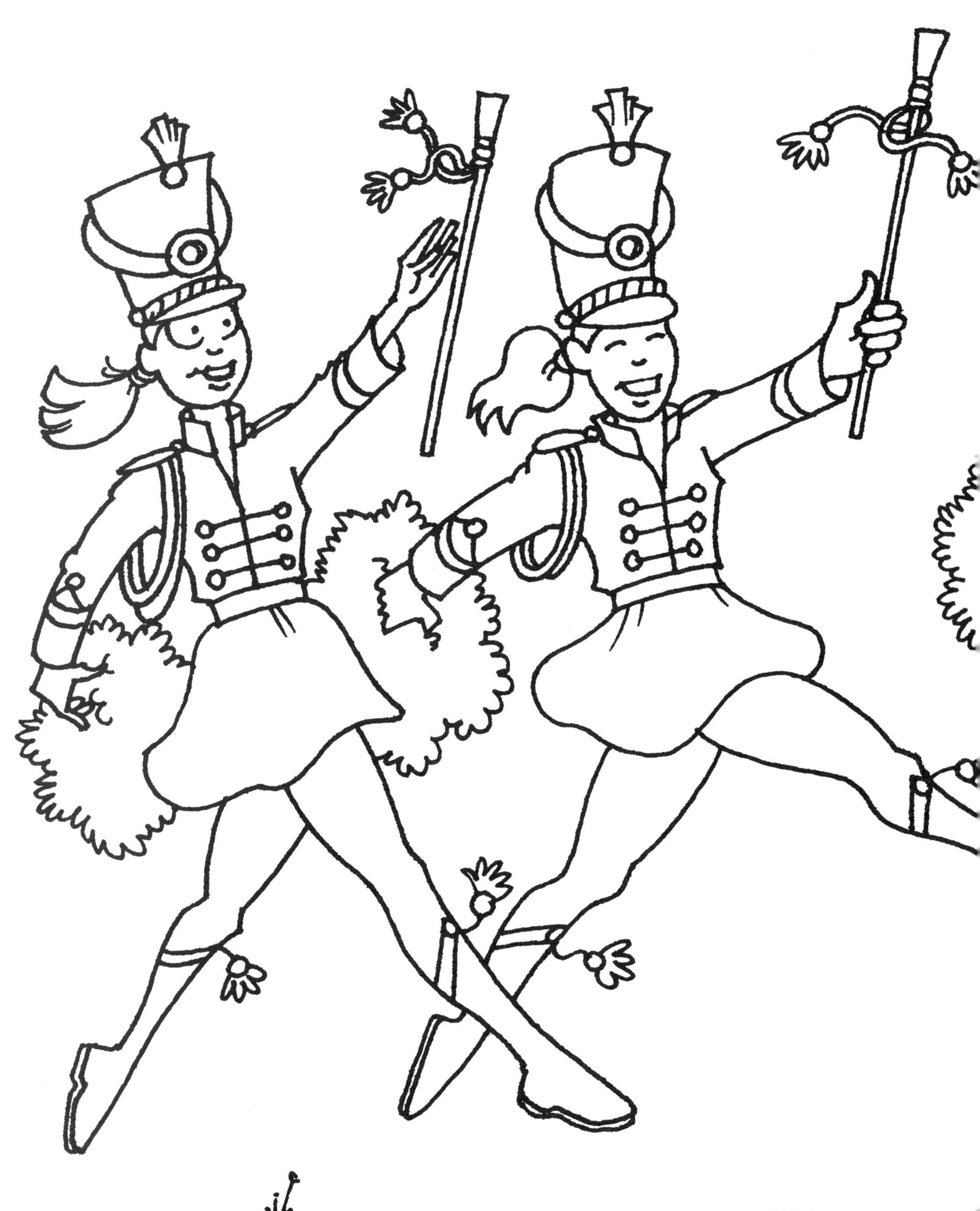

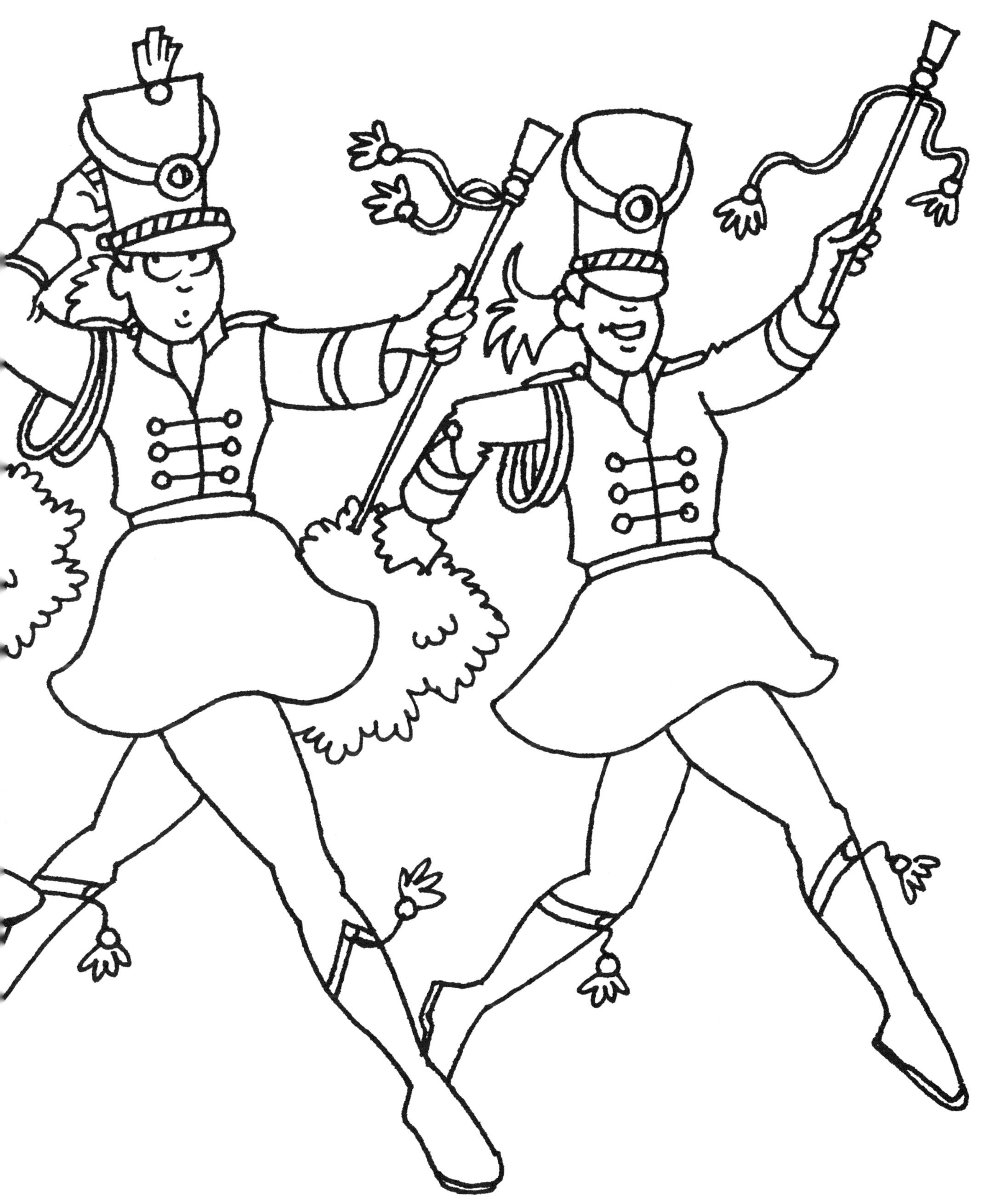

Make the monsters feel whole again

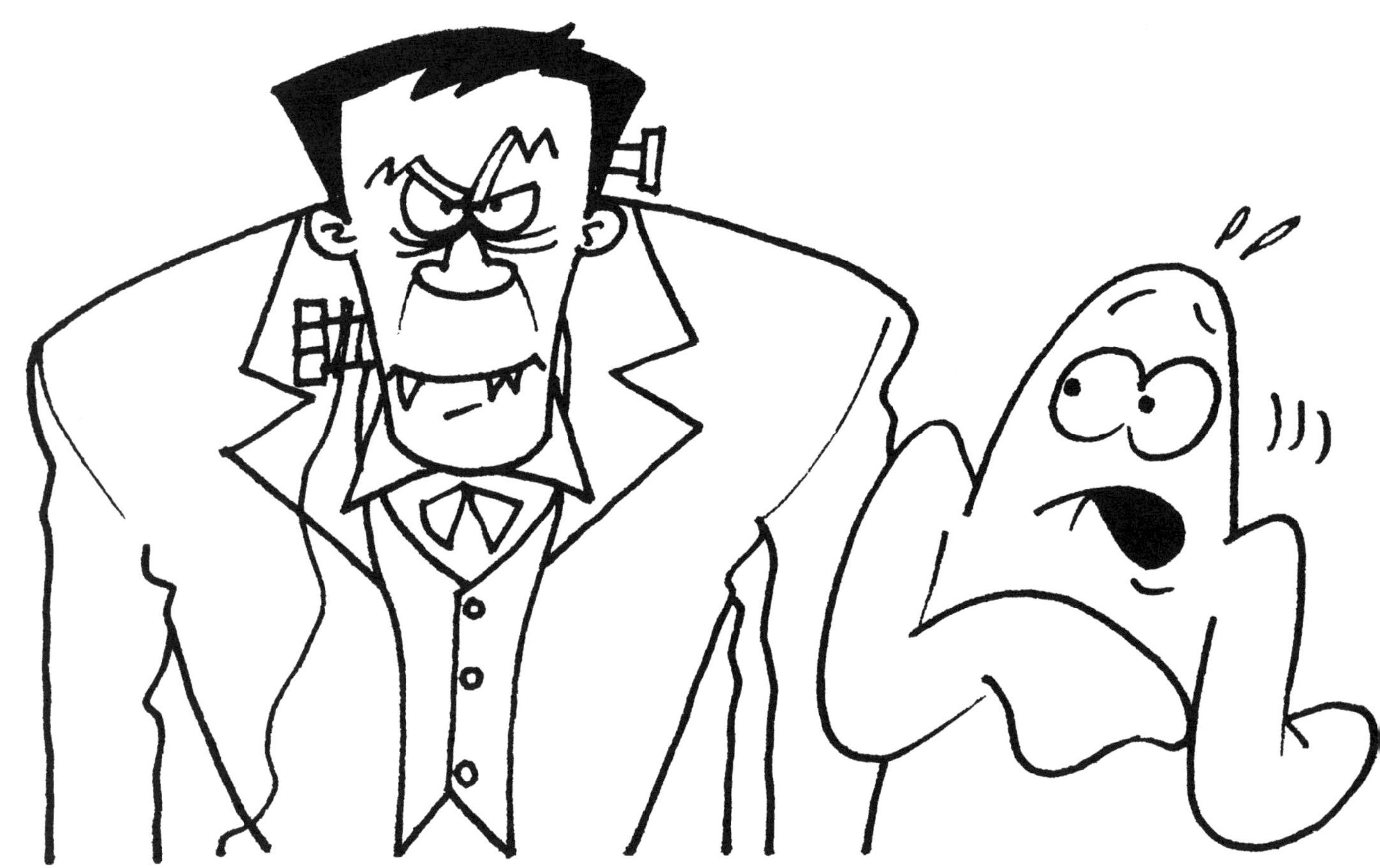

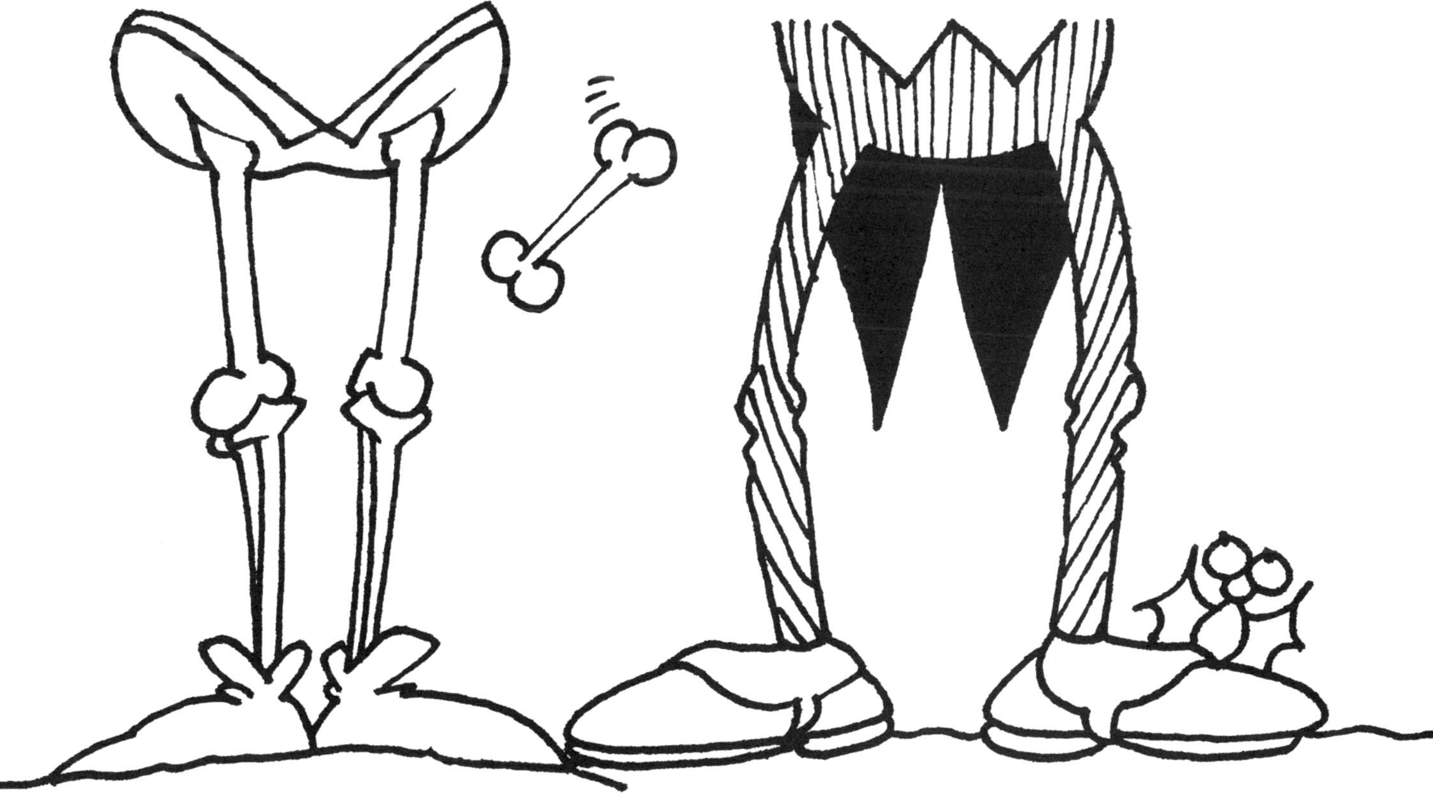

Cool marbles - all different colors!

Draw the champion alley cat

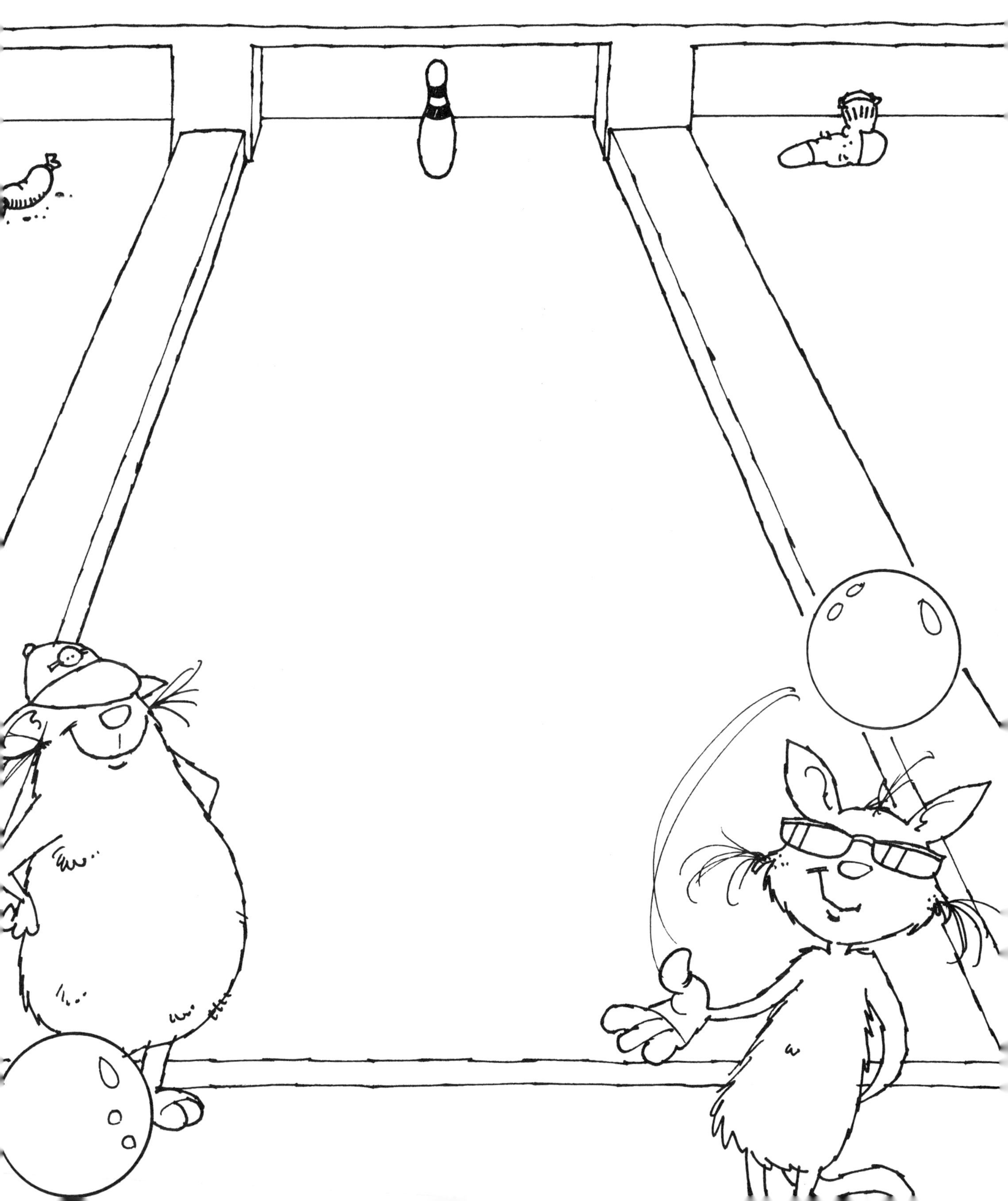

Looks like Ron's discovered something!

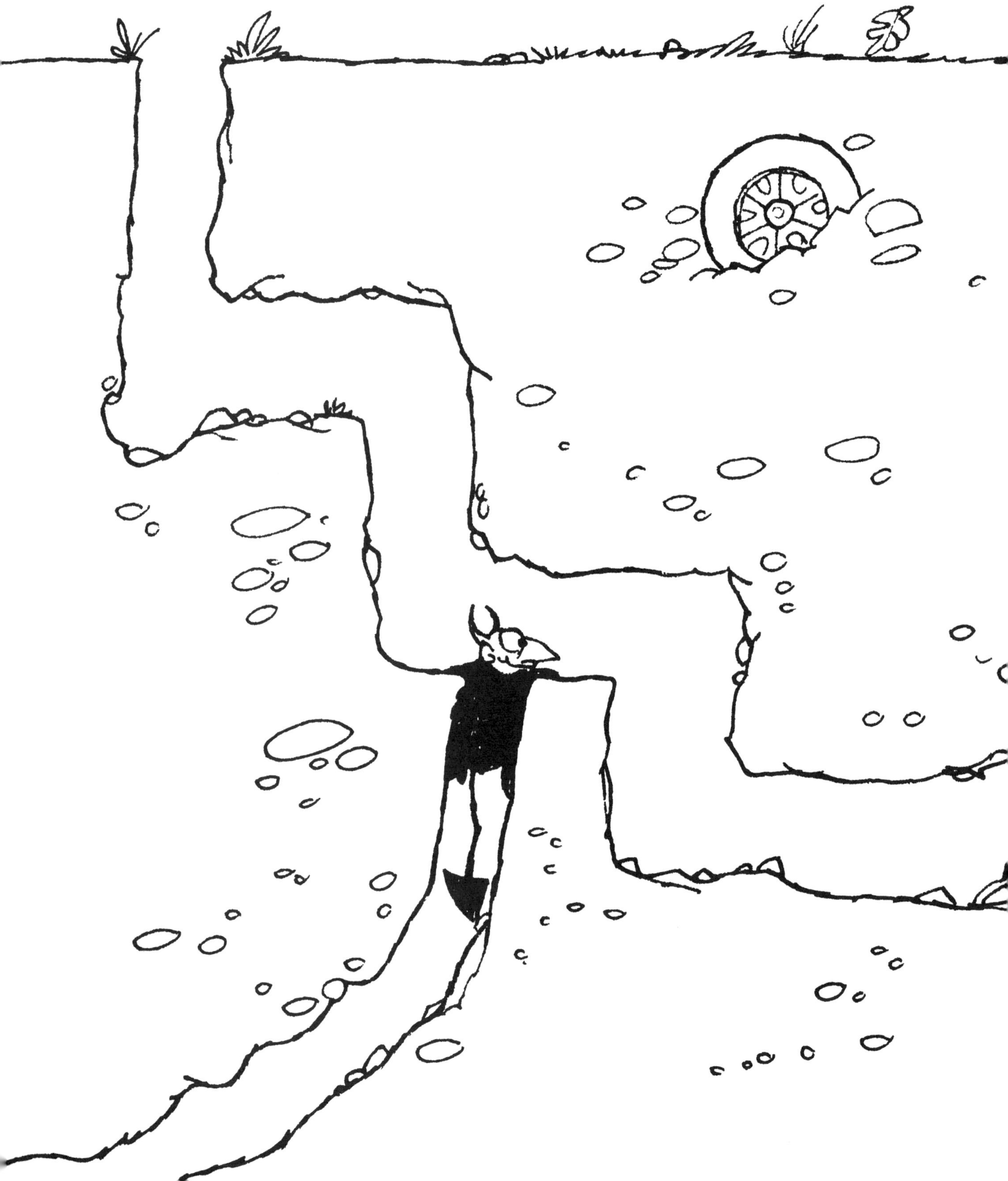

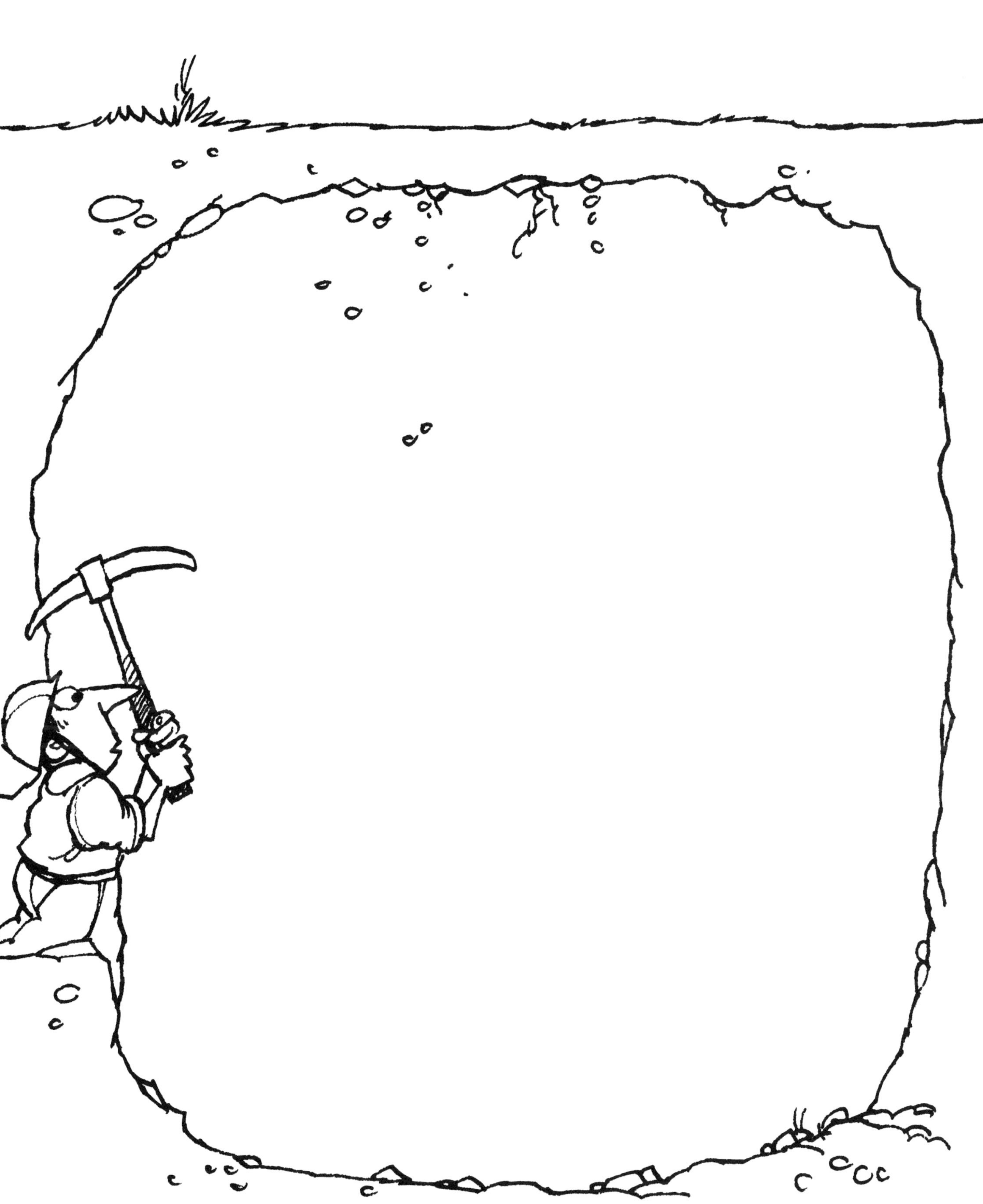

He's a businessman by day...

...but a superhero by night!

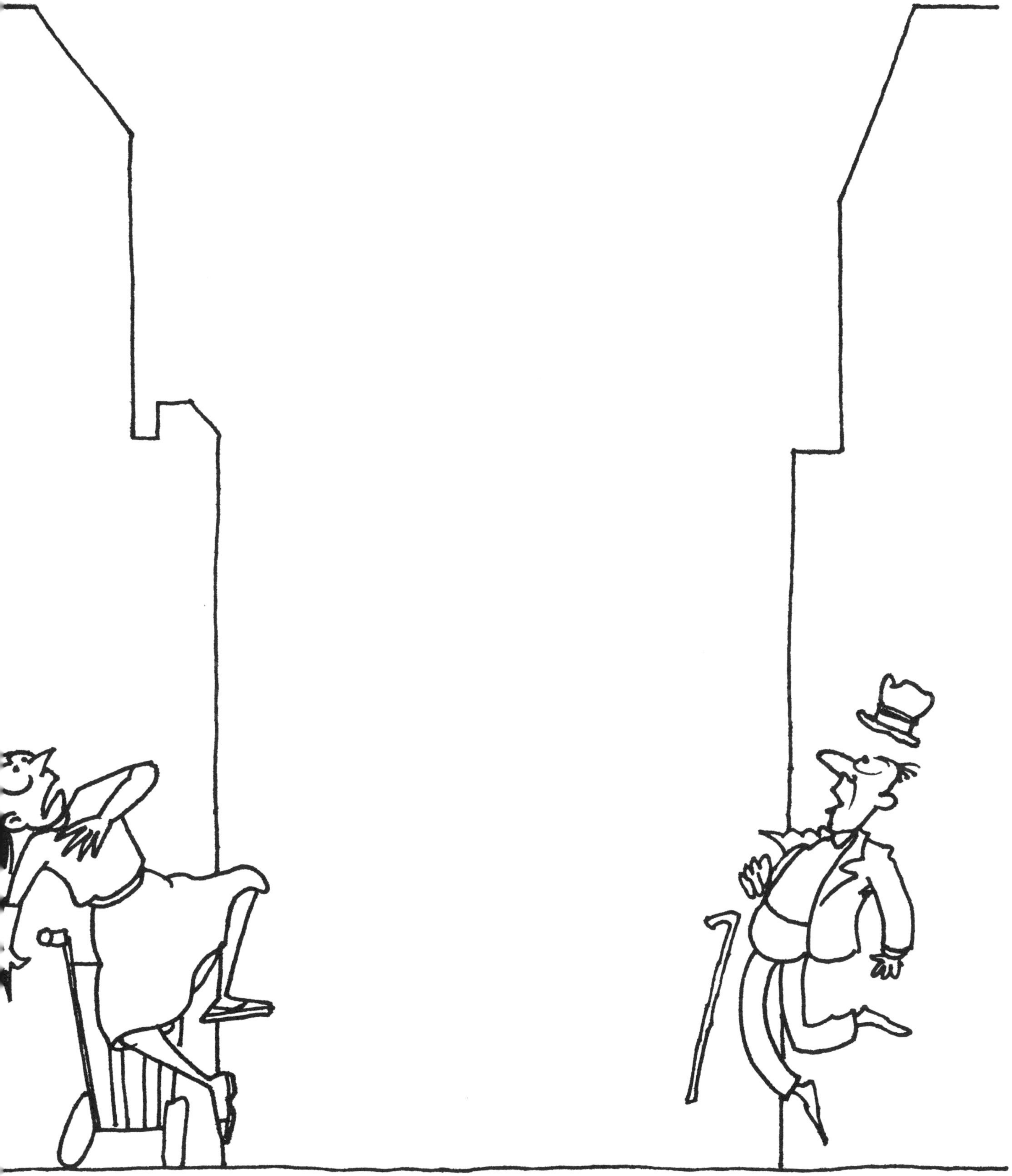

What's caused a commotion on the farm?

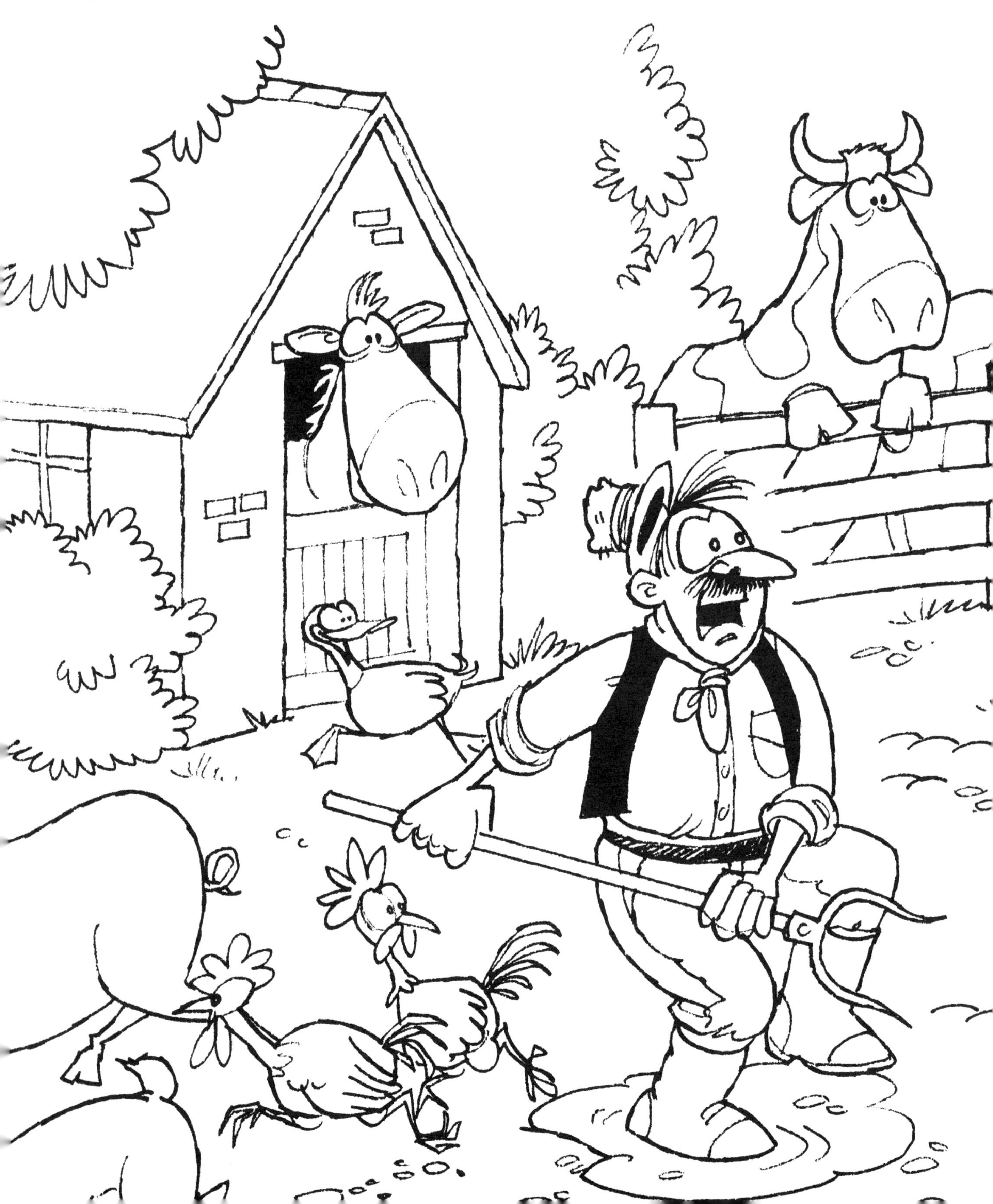

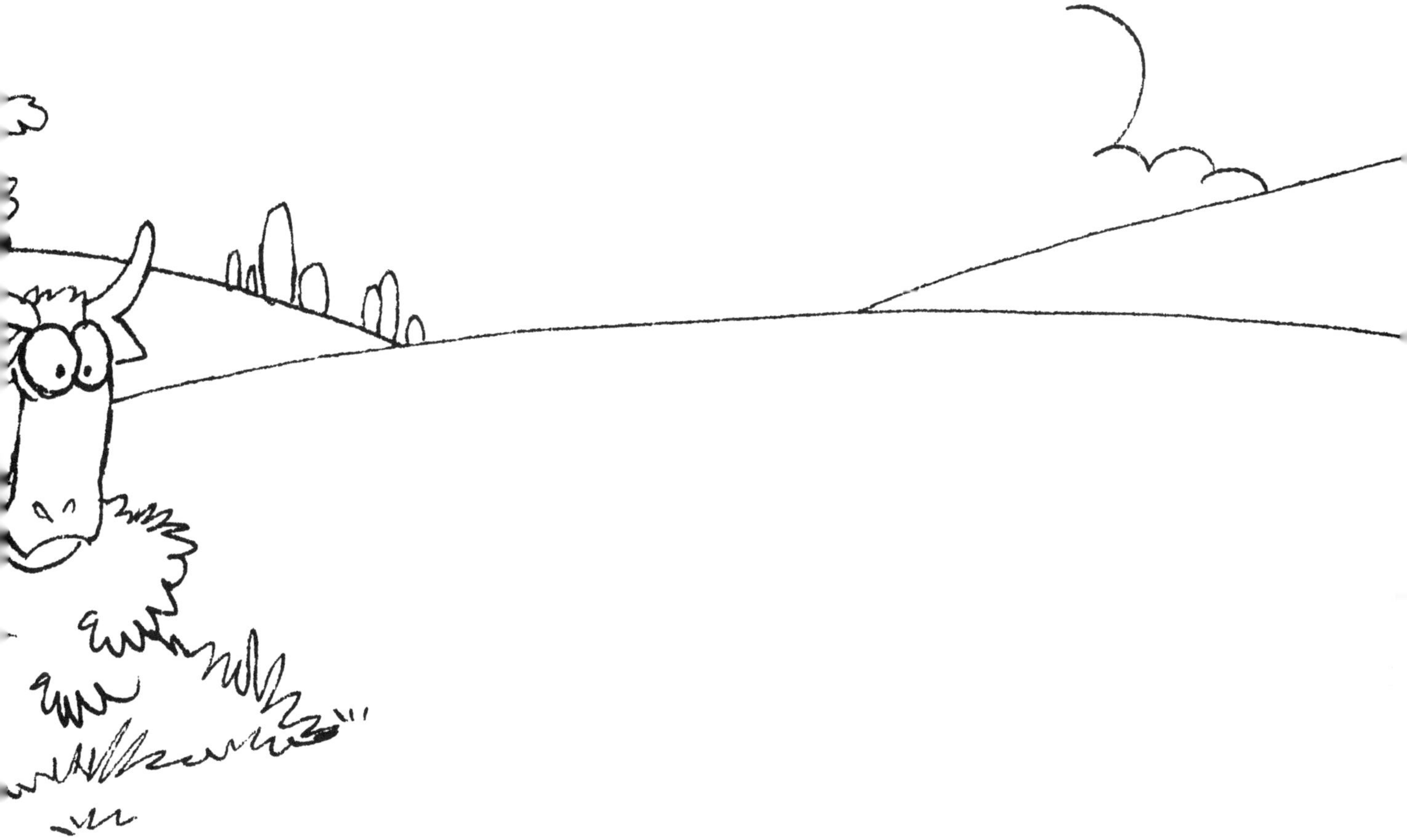

What do dogs really think?

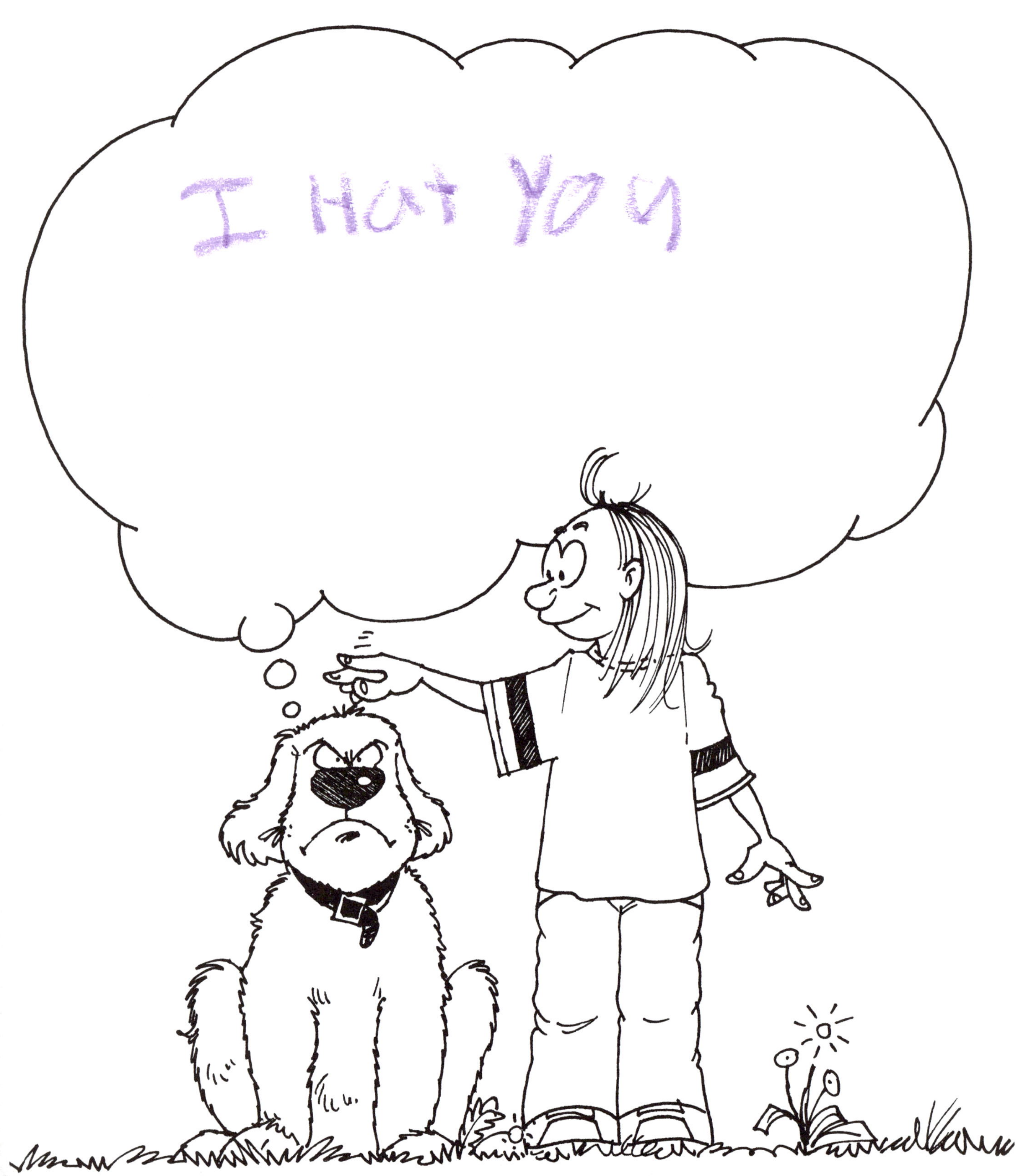

Draw the spooky house on the hill

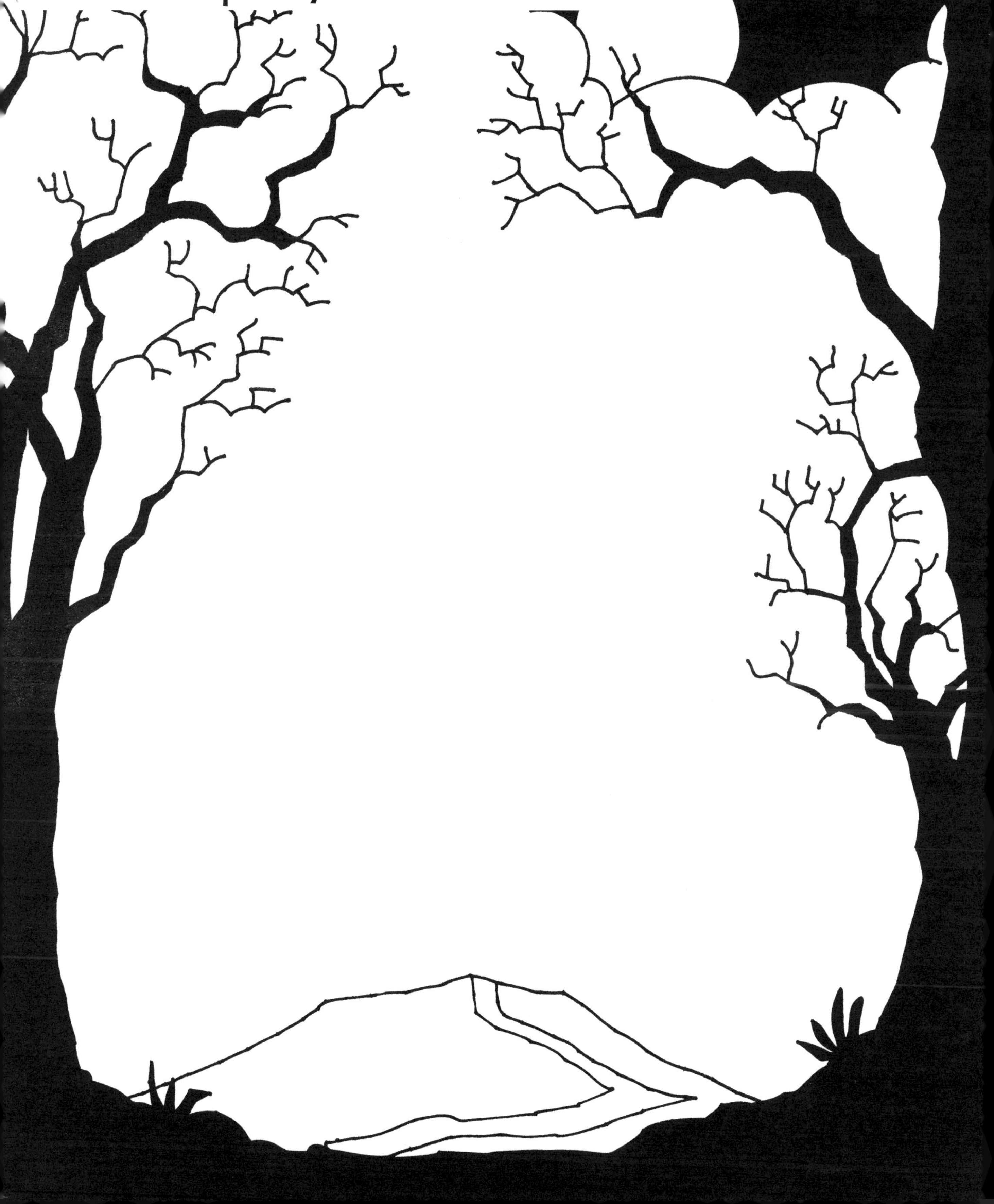

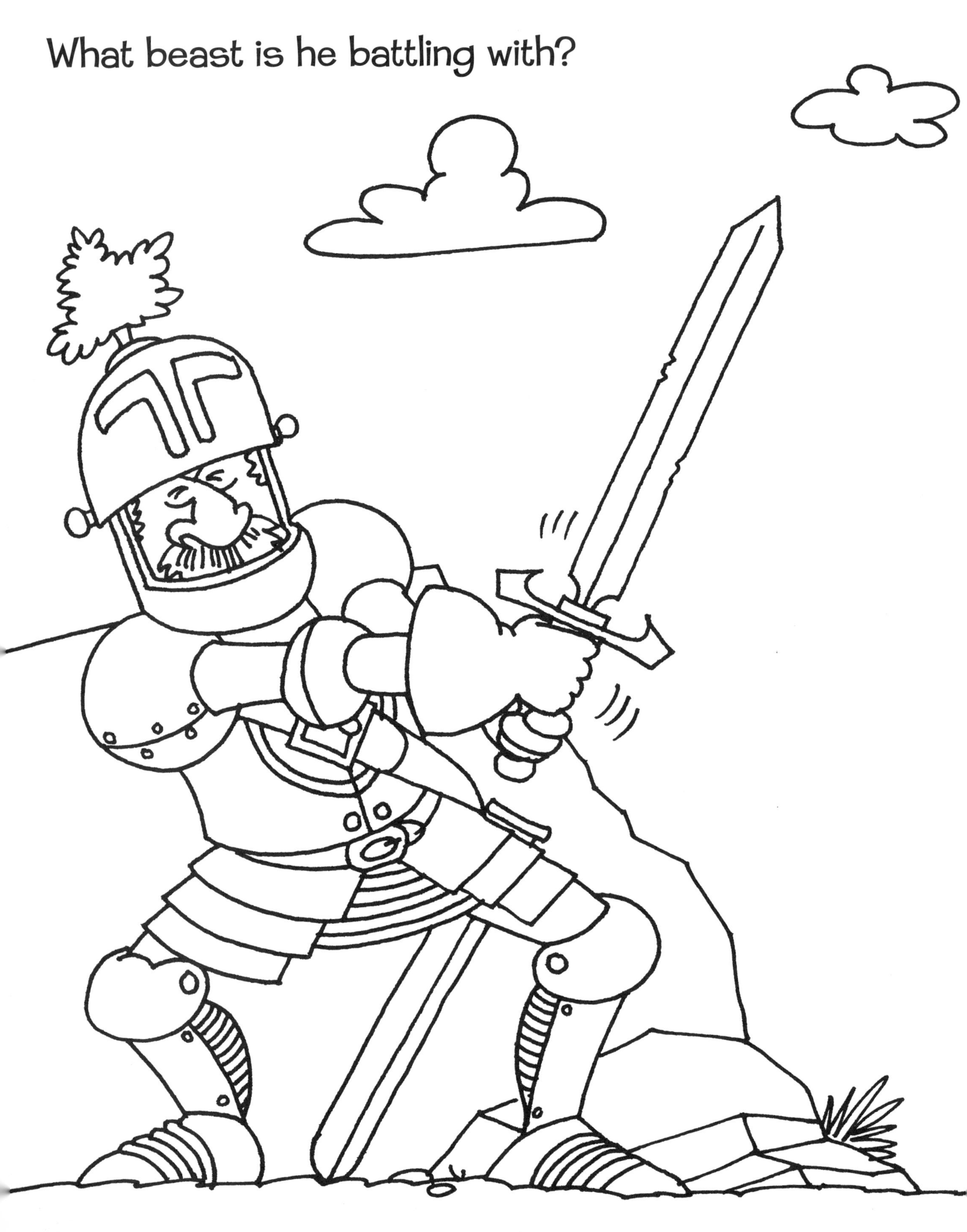
What beast is he battling with?

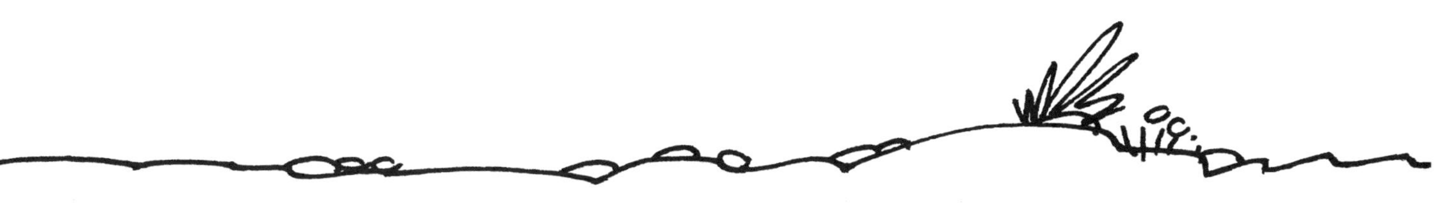

Liven up this boring sitting room

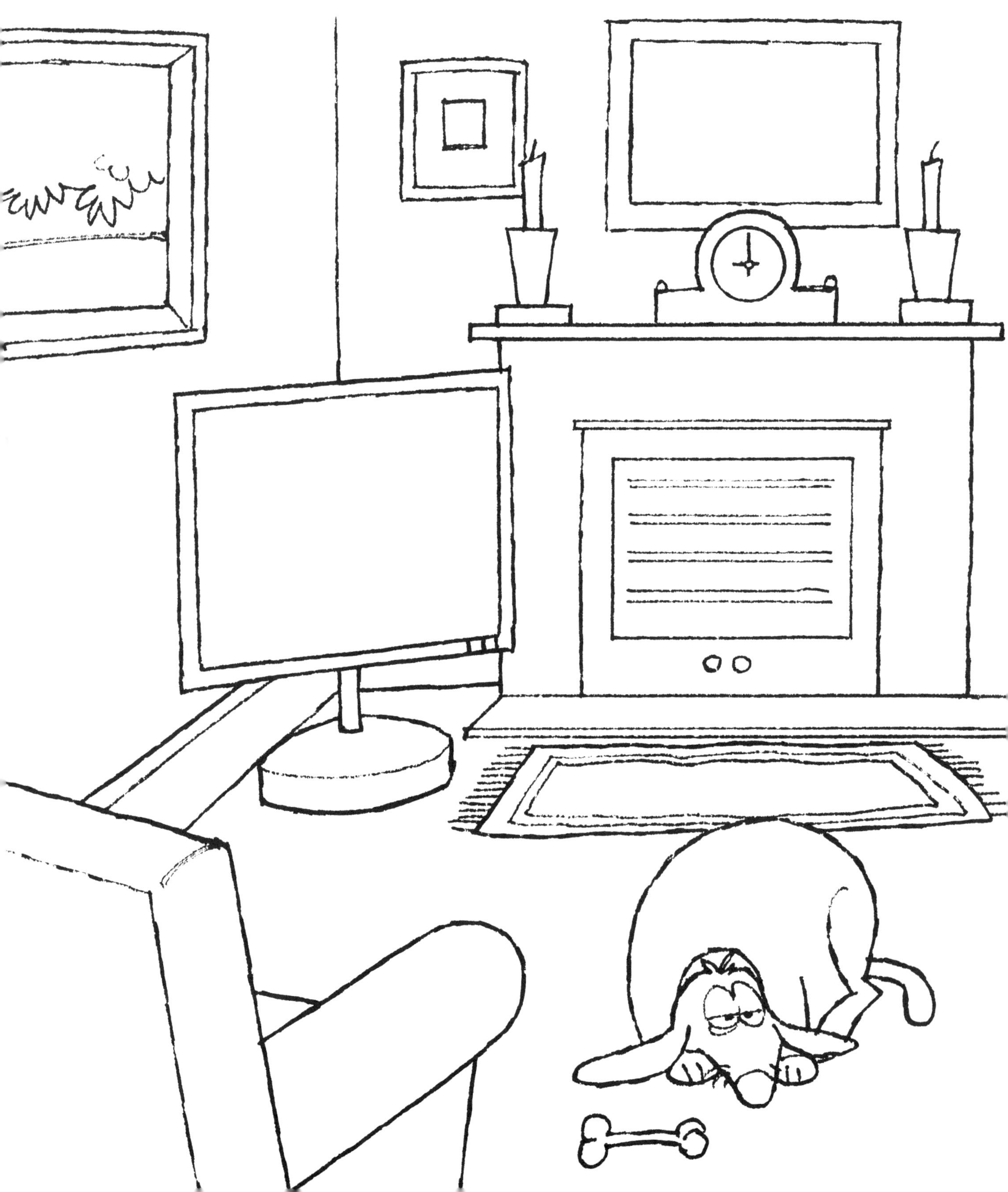

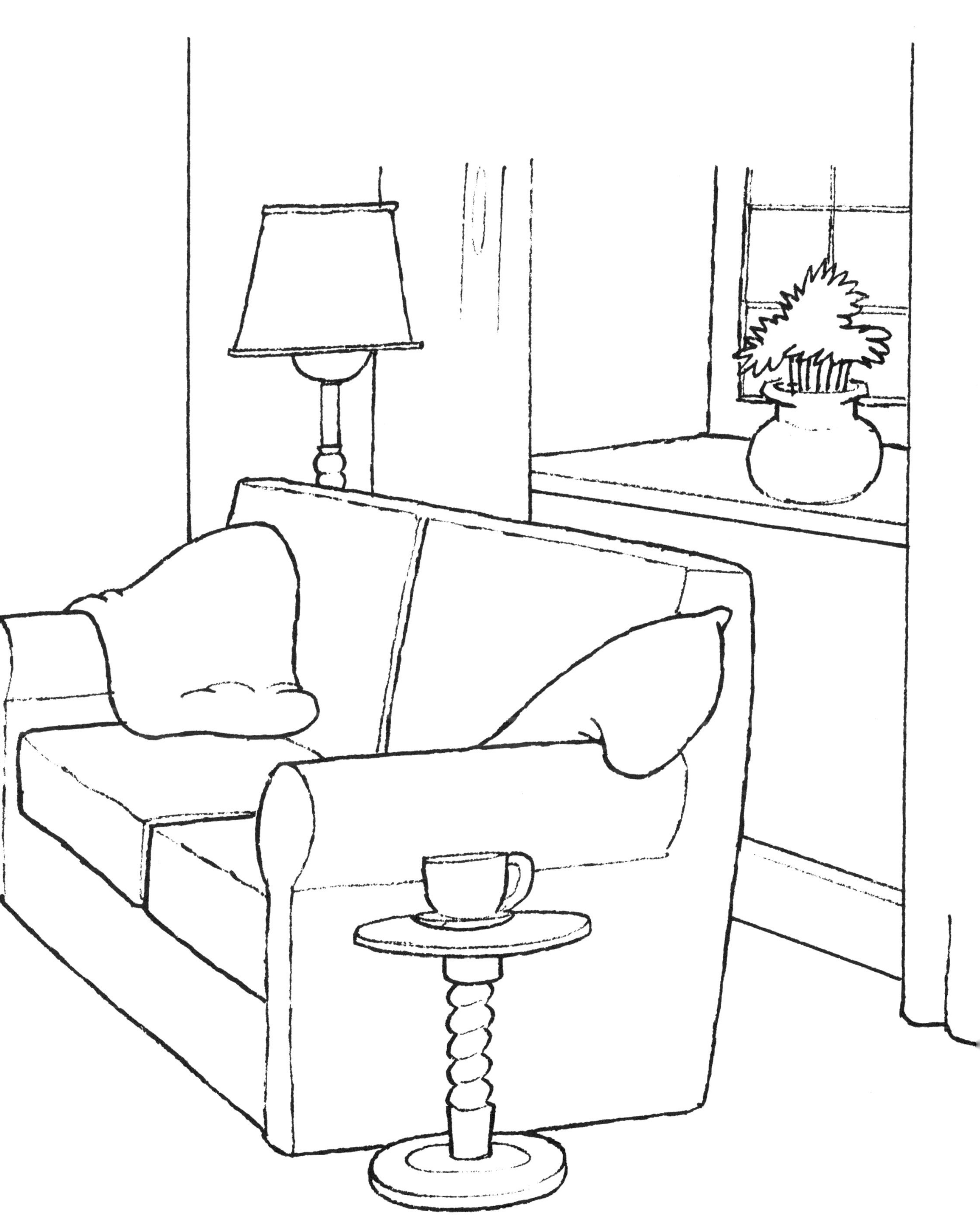

An ugly ducking always turns into...

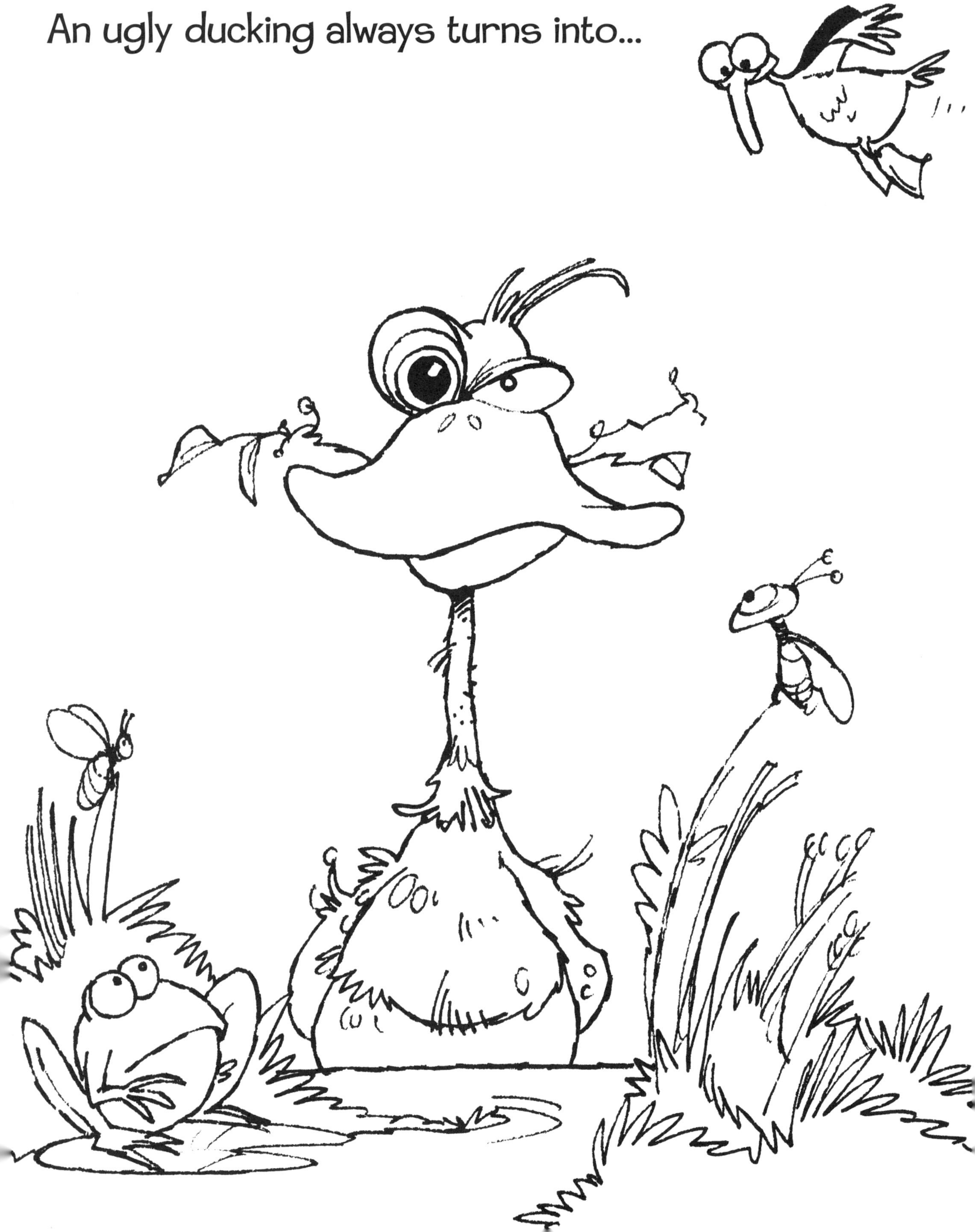

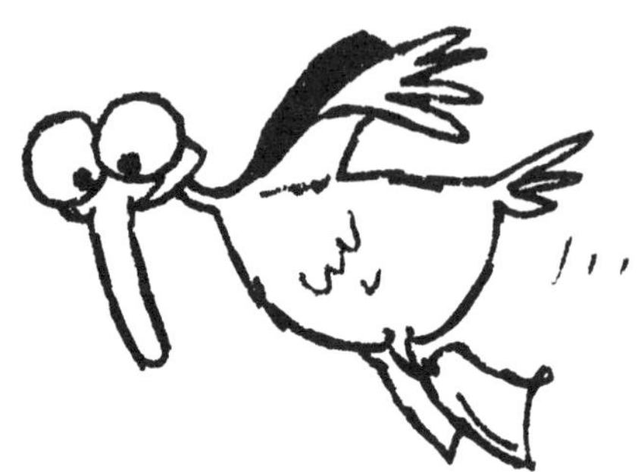

...a beautiful bird!

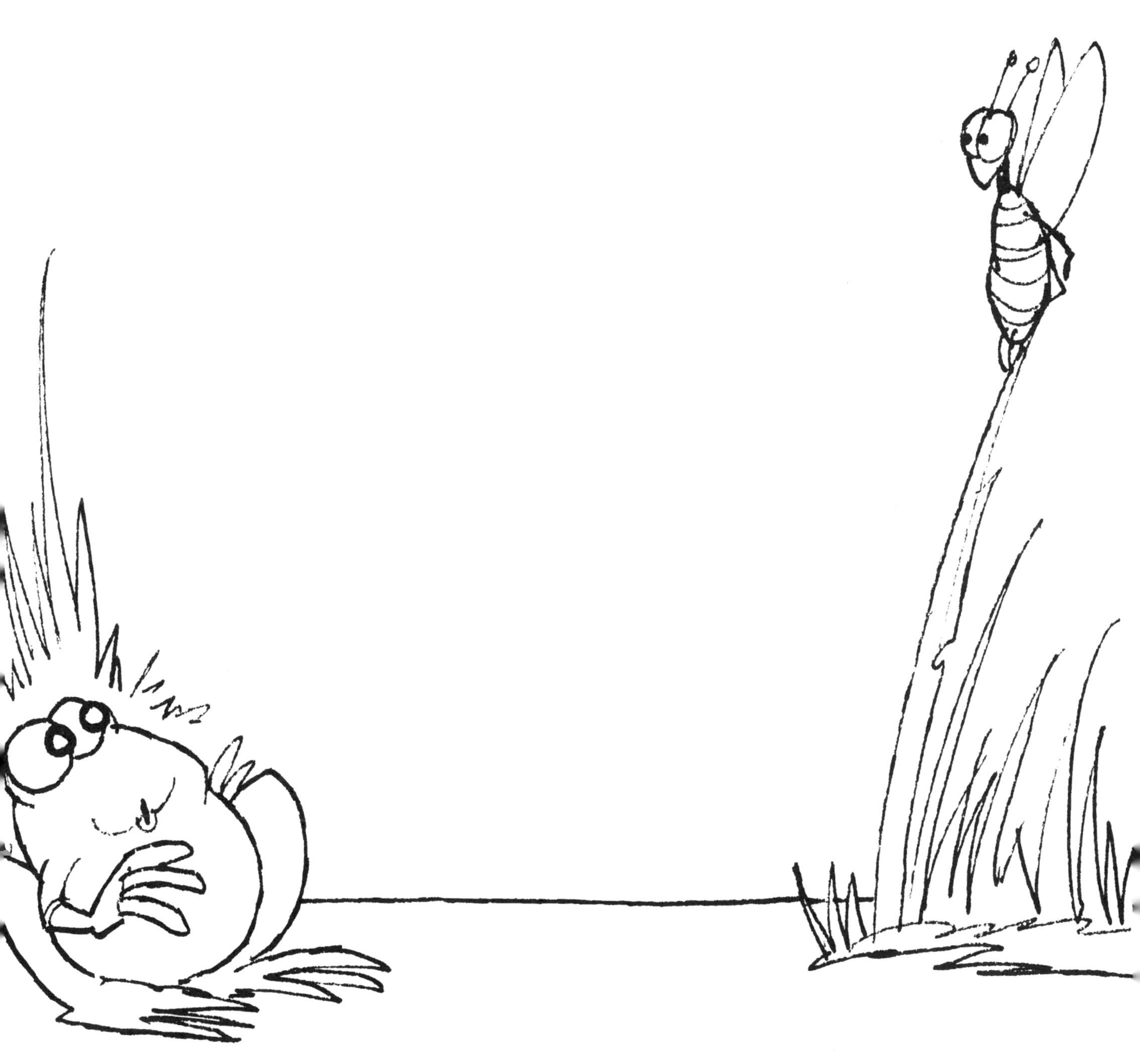

Decorate Sally's camper

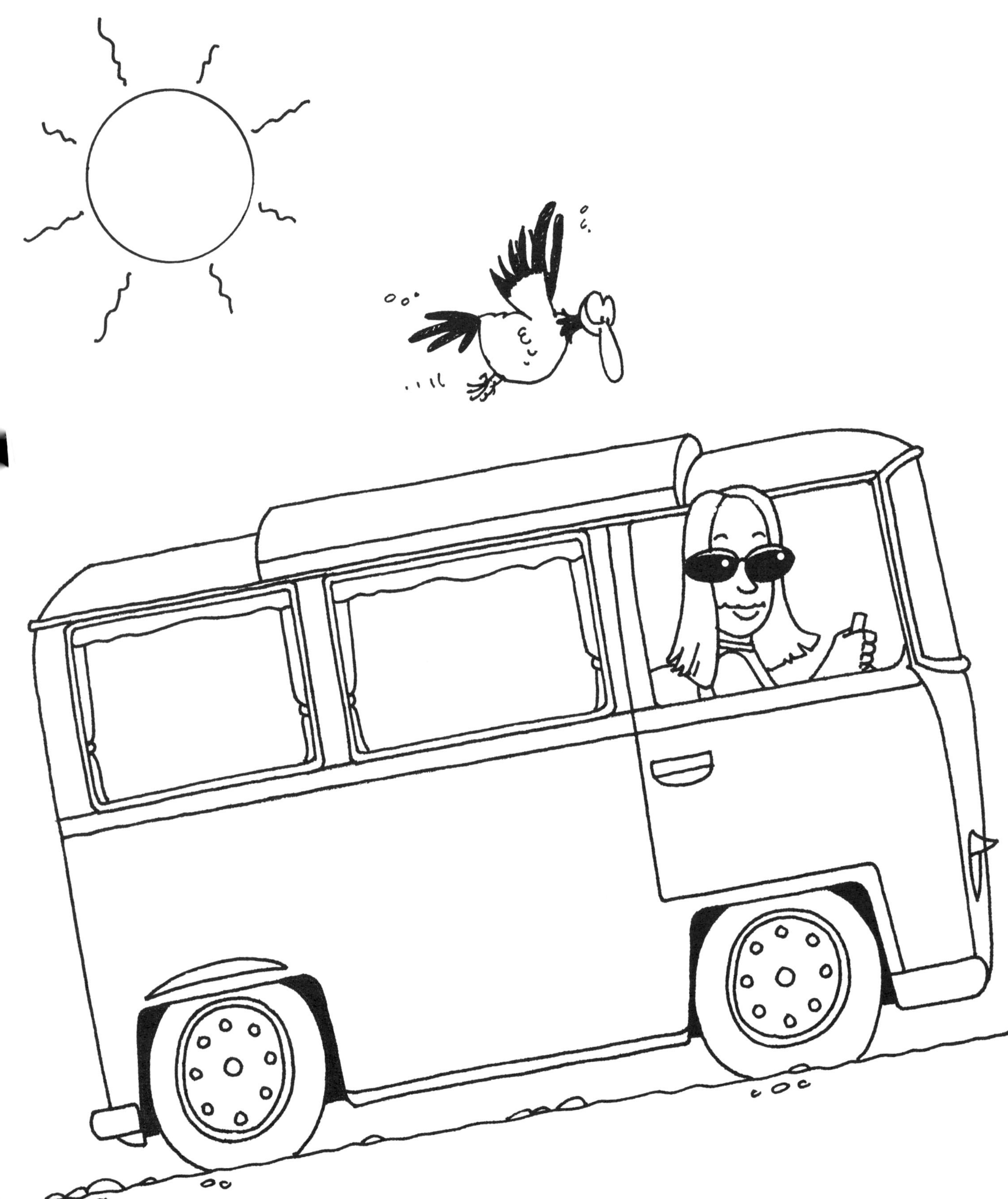

A monster takeout!

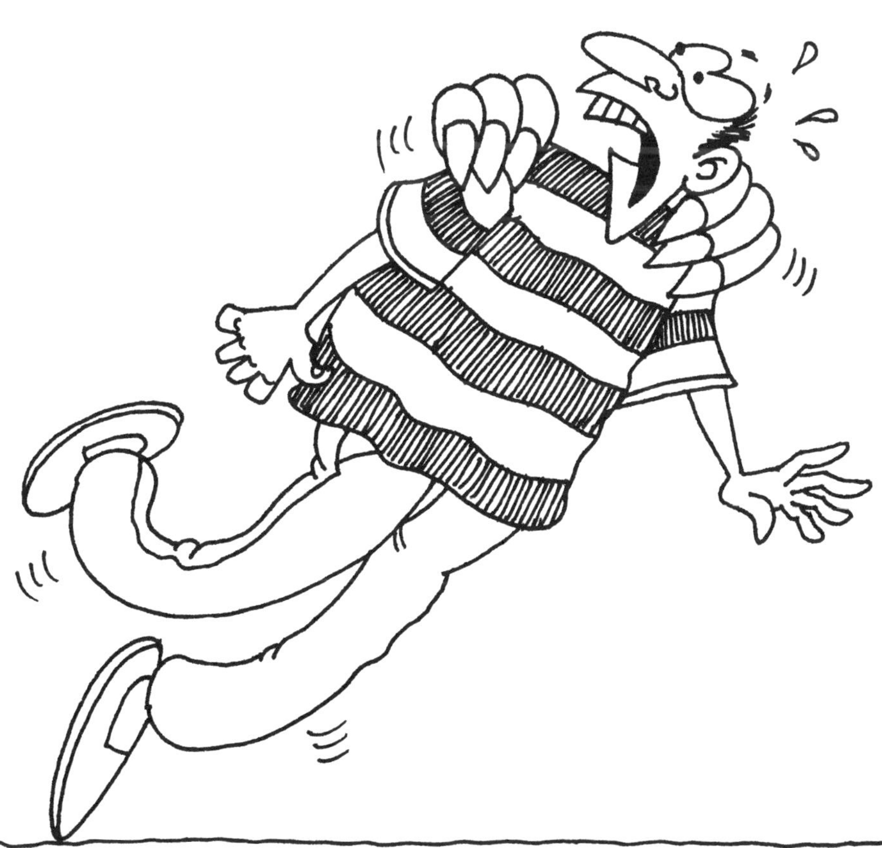

What's lurking underneath your bed?

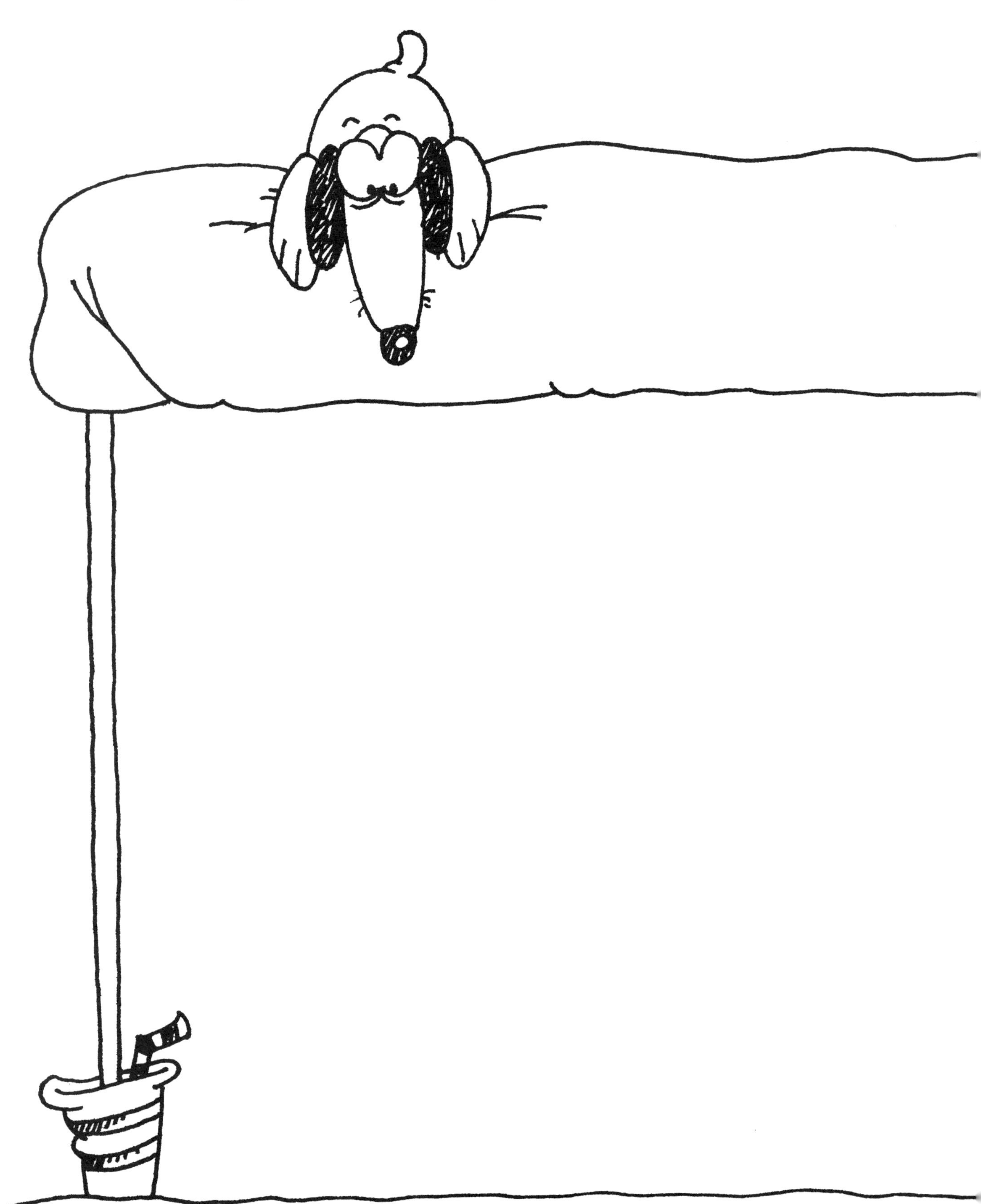

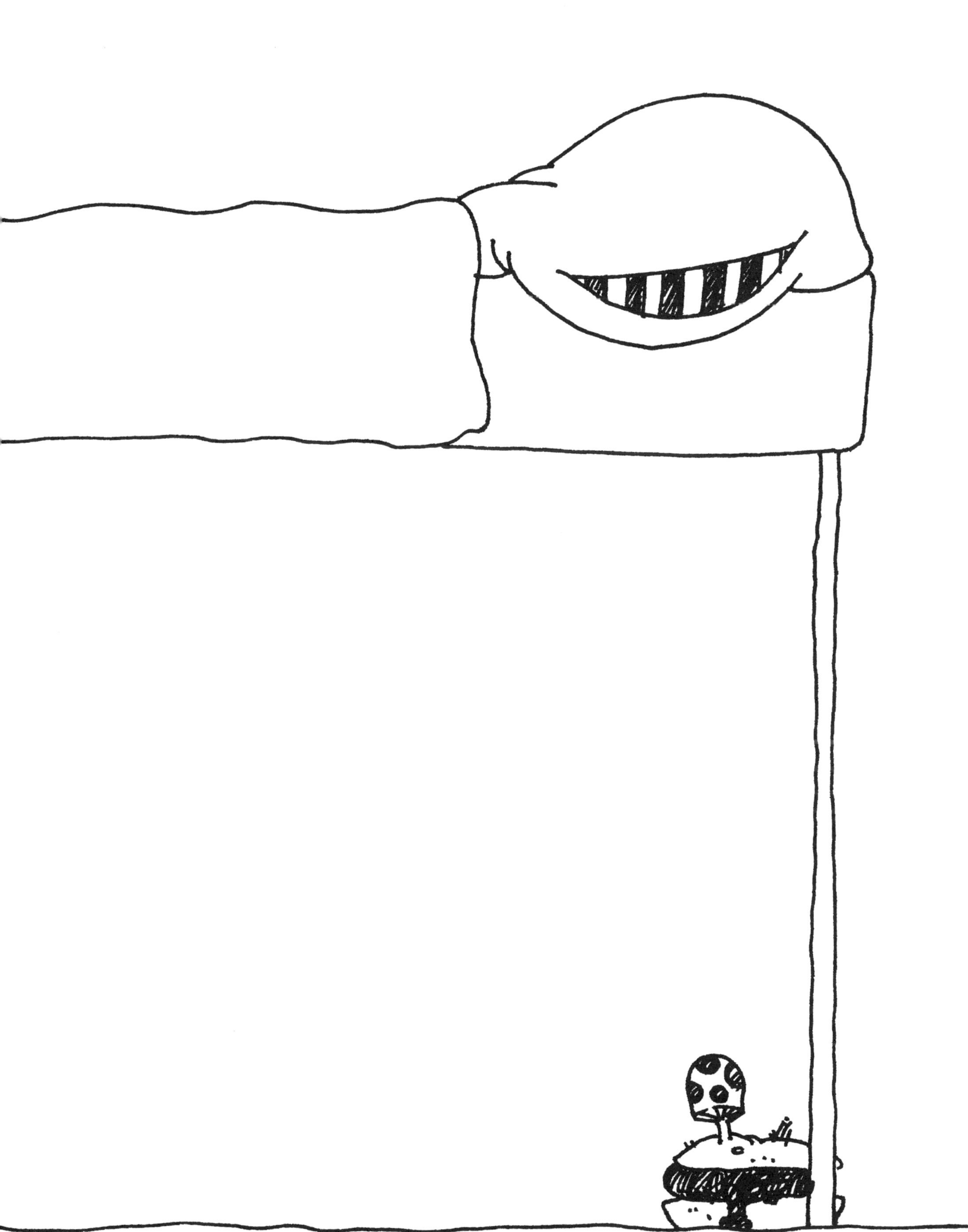

Who's wearing the wrong color team shirt?

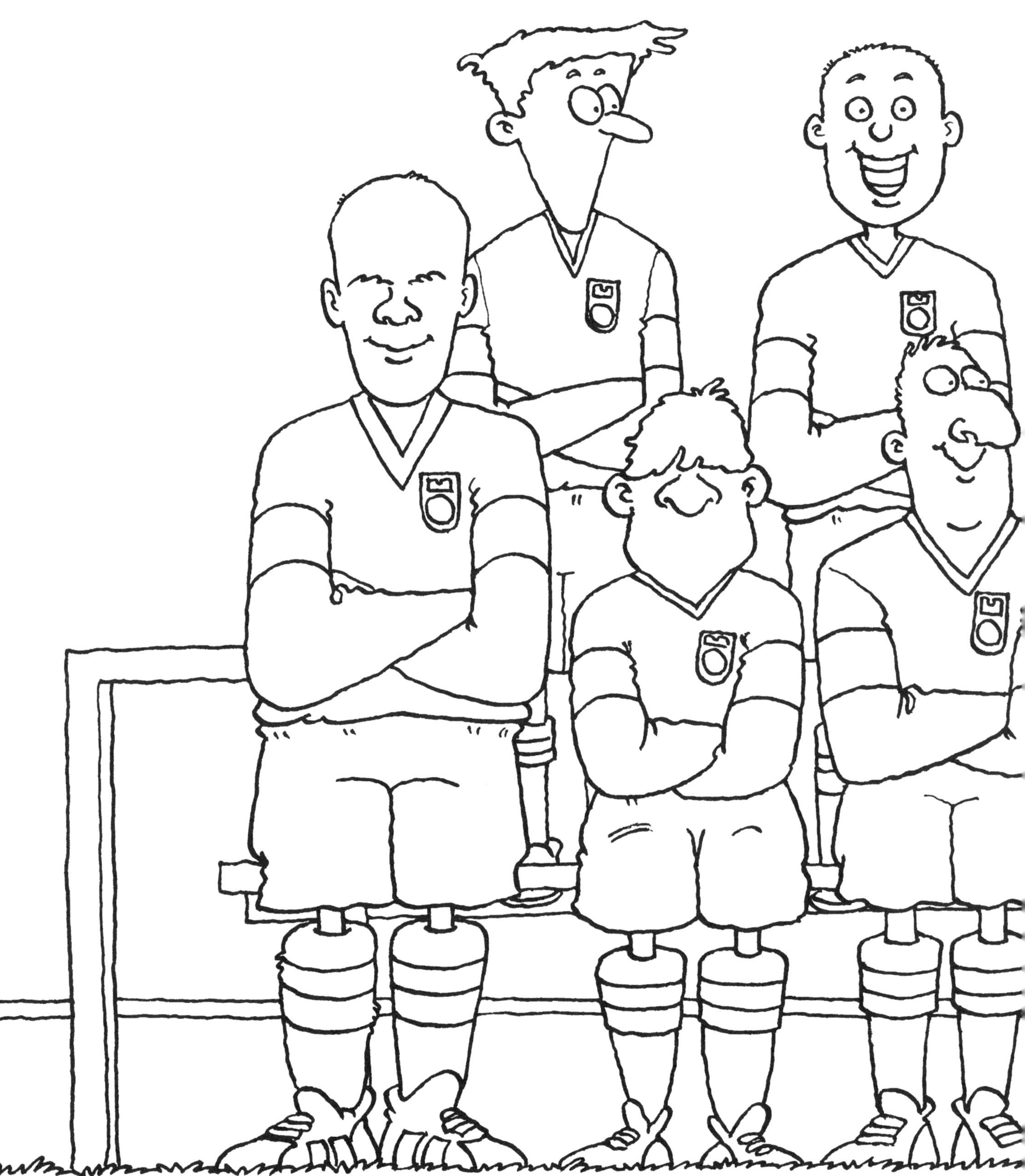

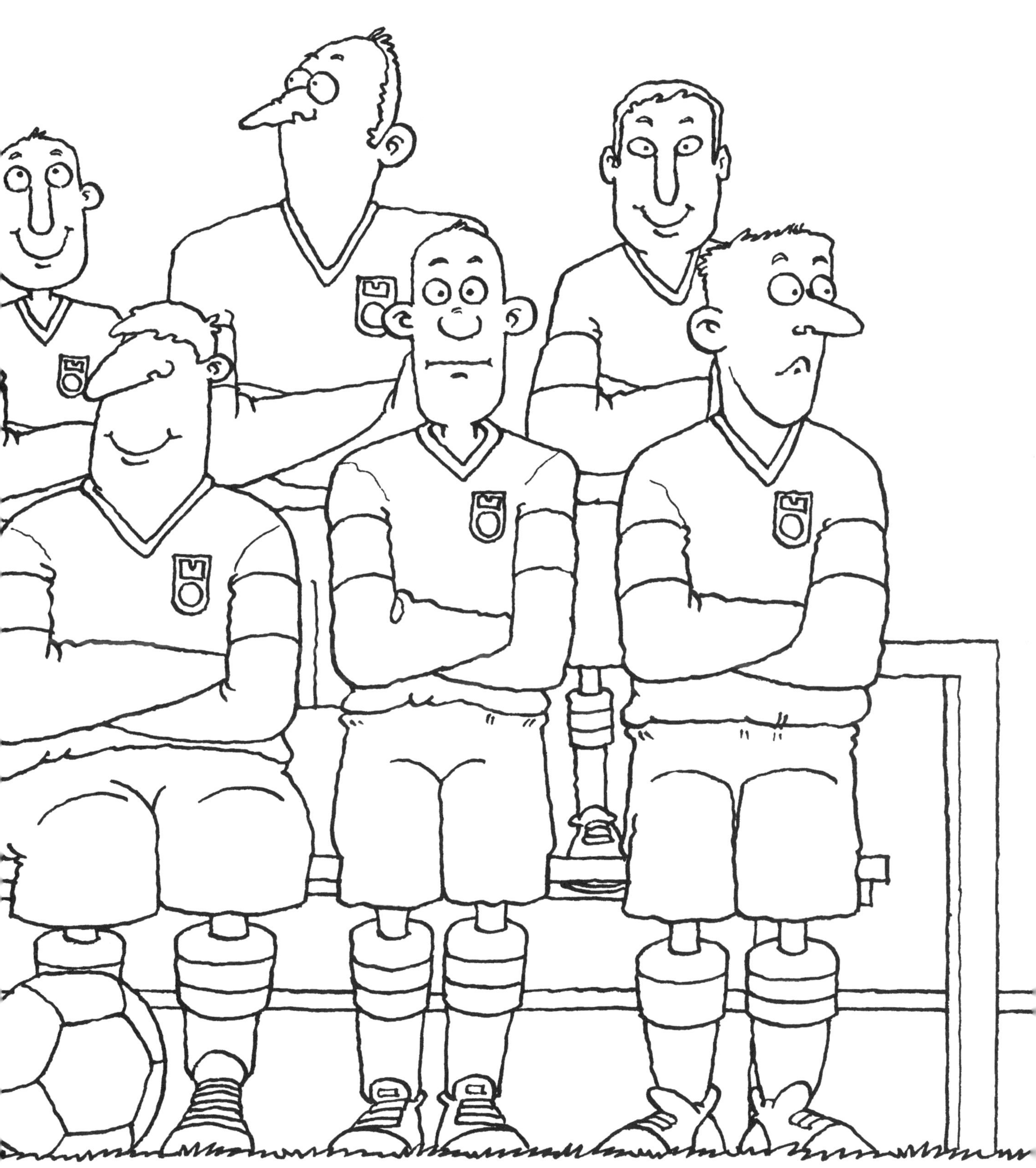

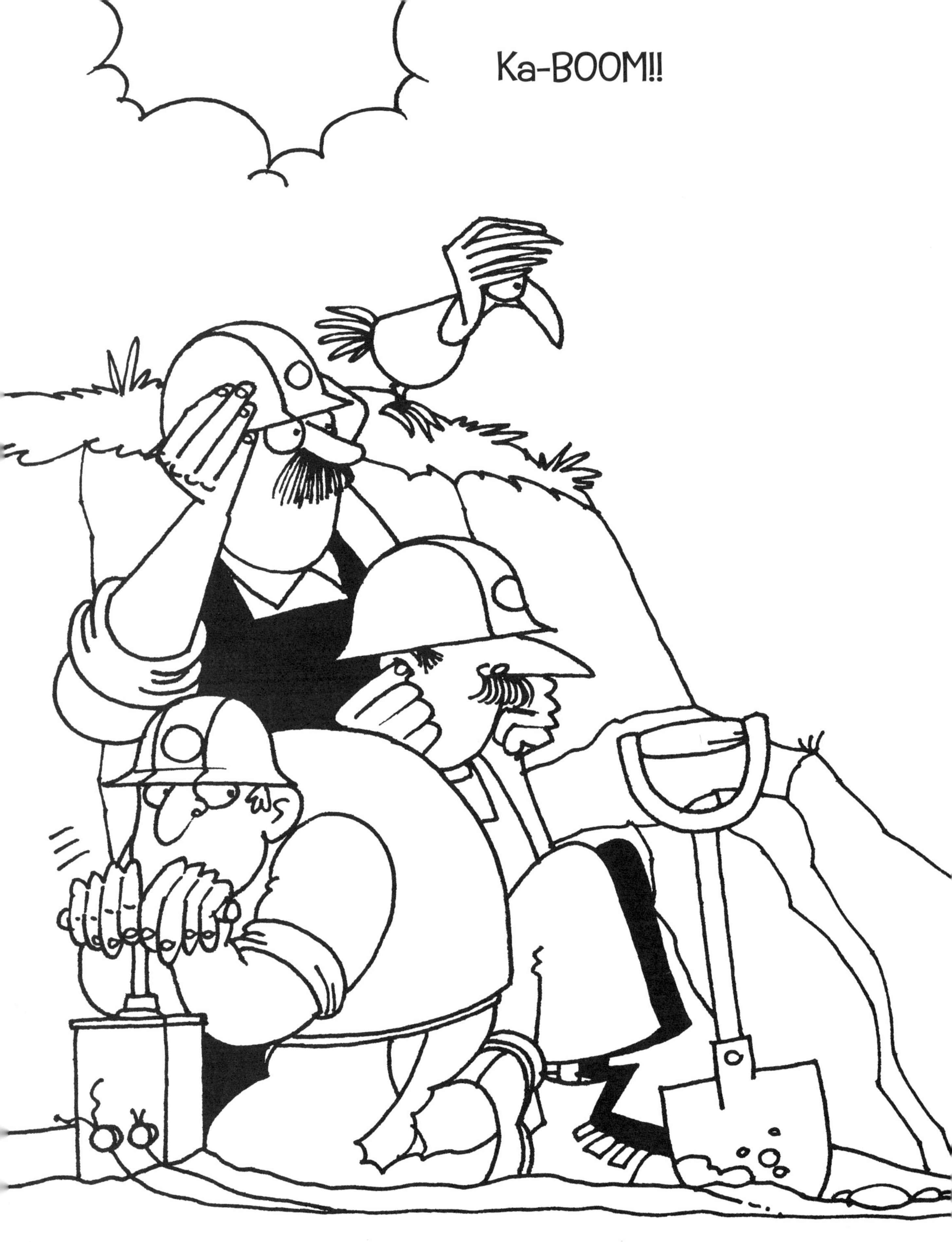
Ka-BOOM!!

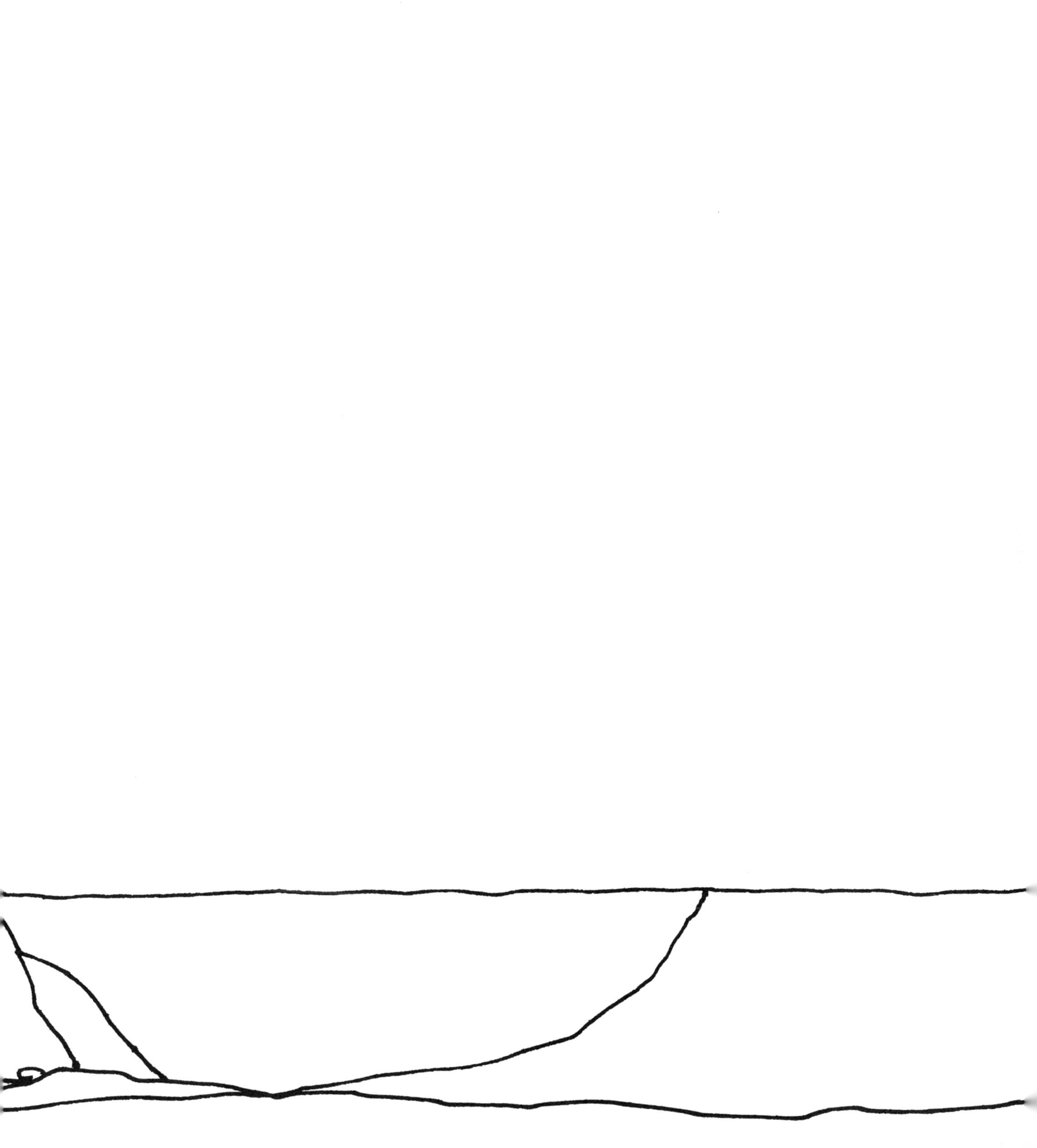

Looks like Derek's in for a bumpy landing

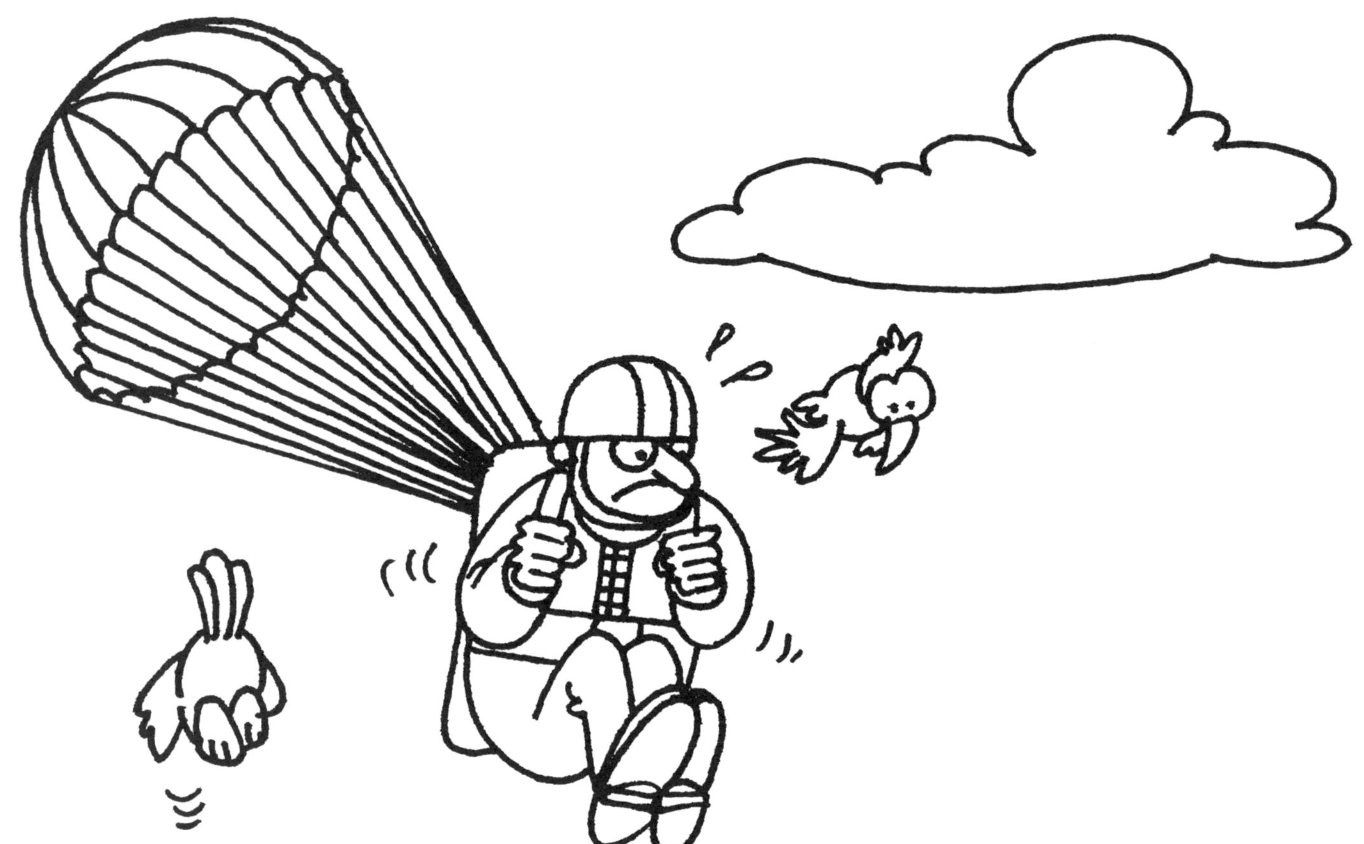

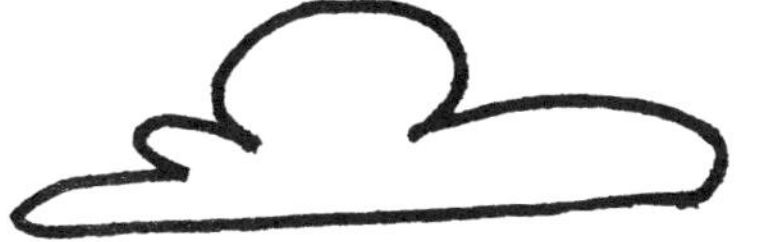

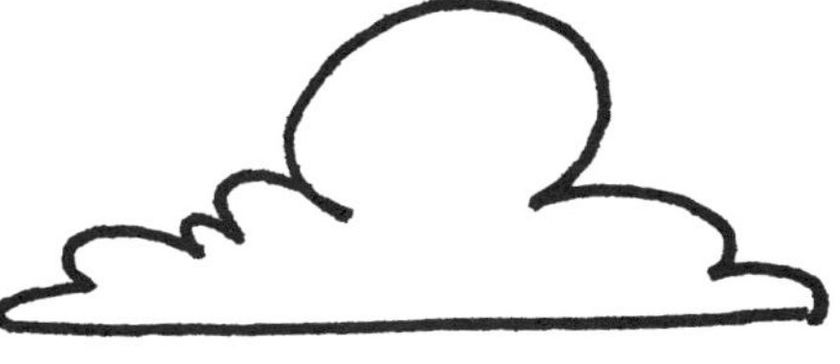

This fish needs some scales

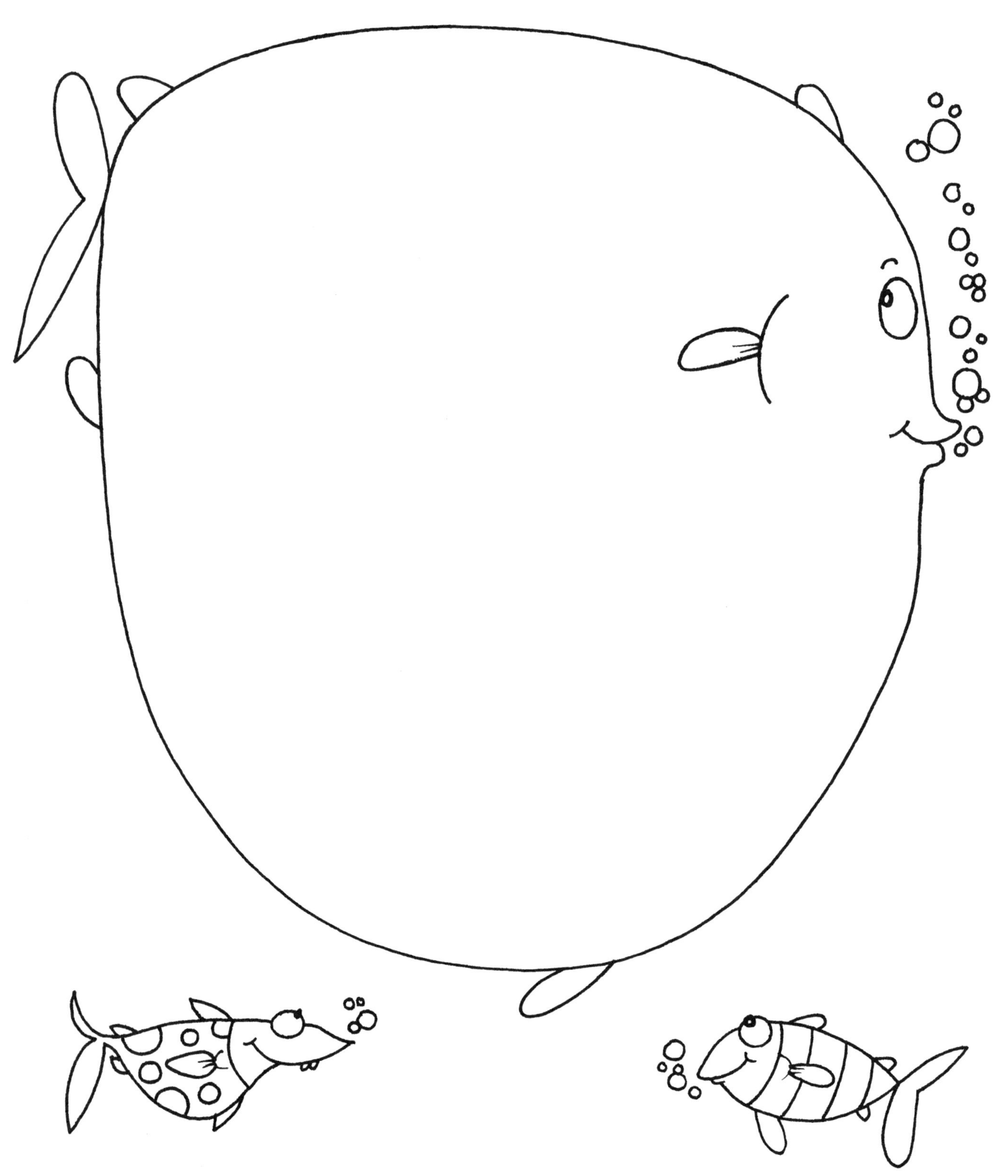

Build a brilliant treehouse

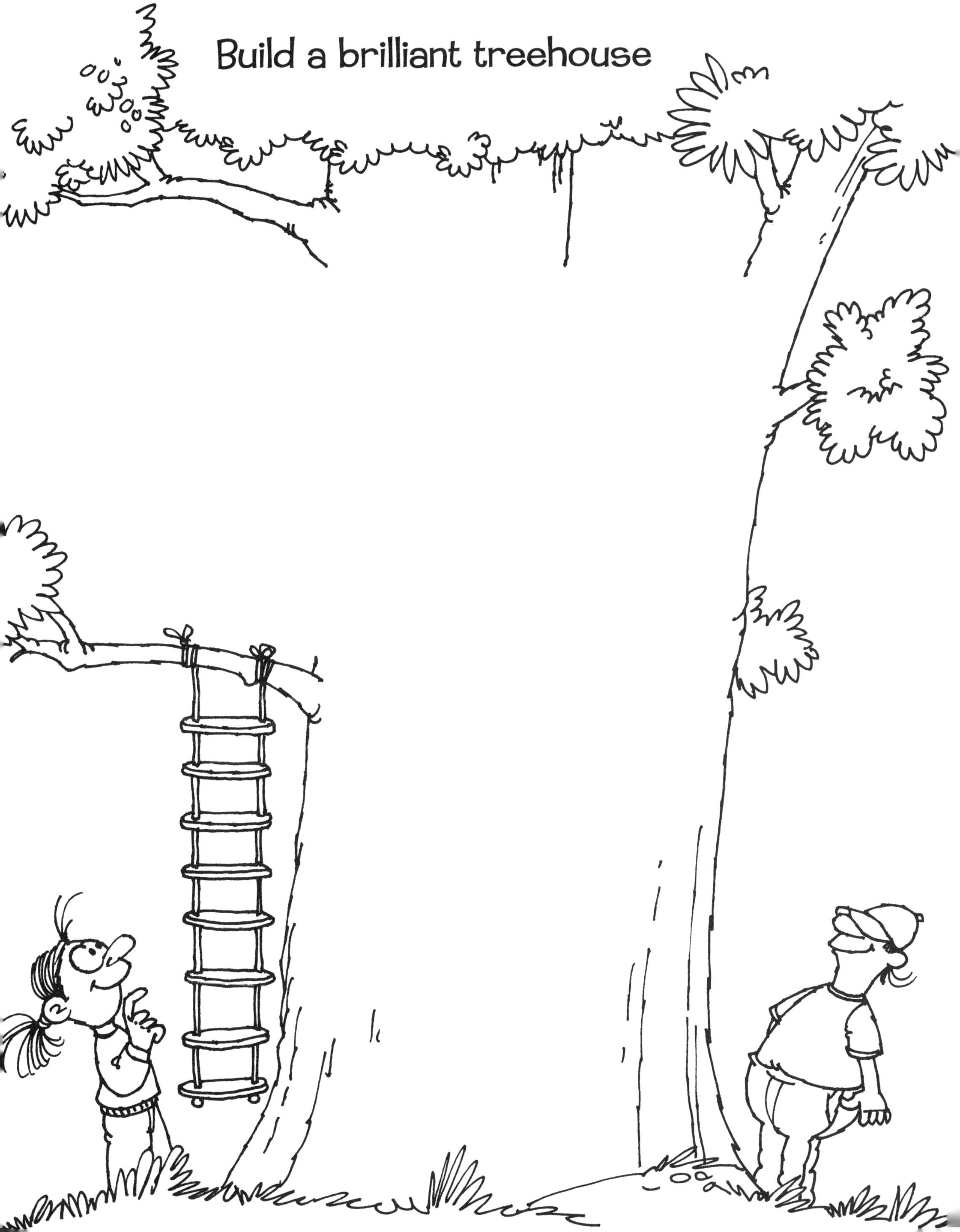

Color in Ice Man's cool set of wheels

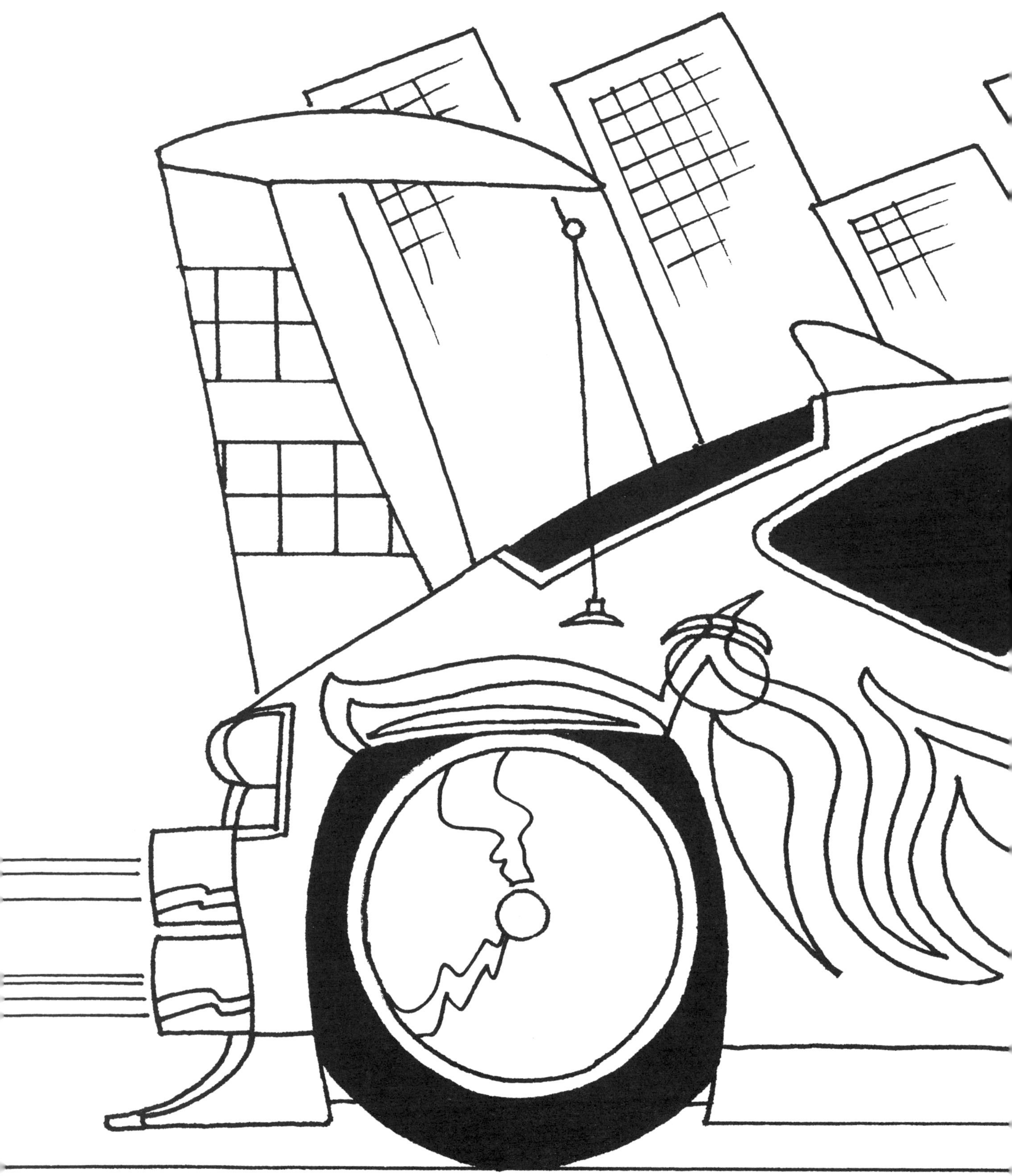

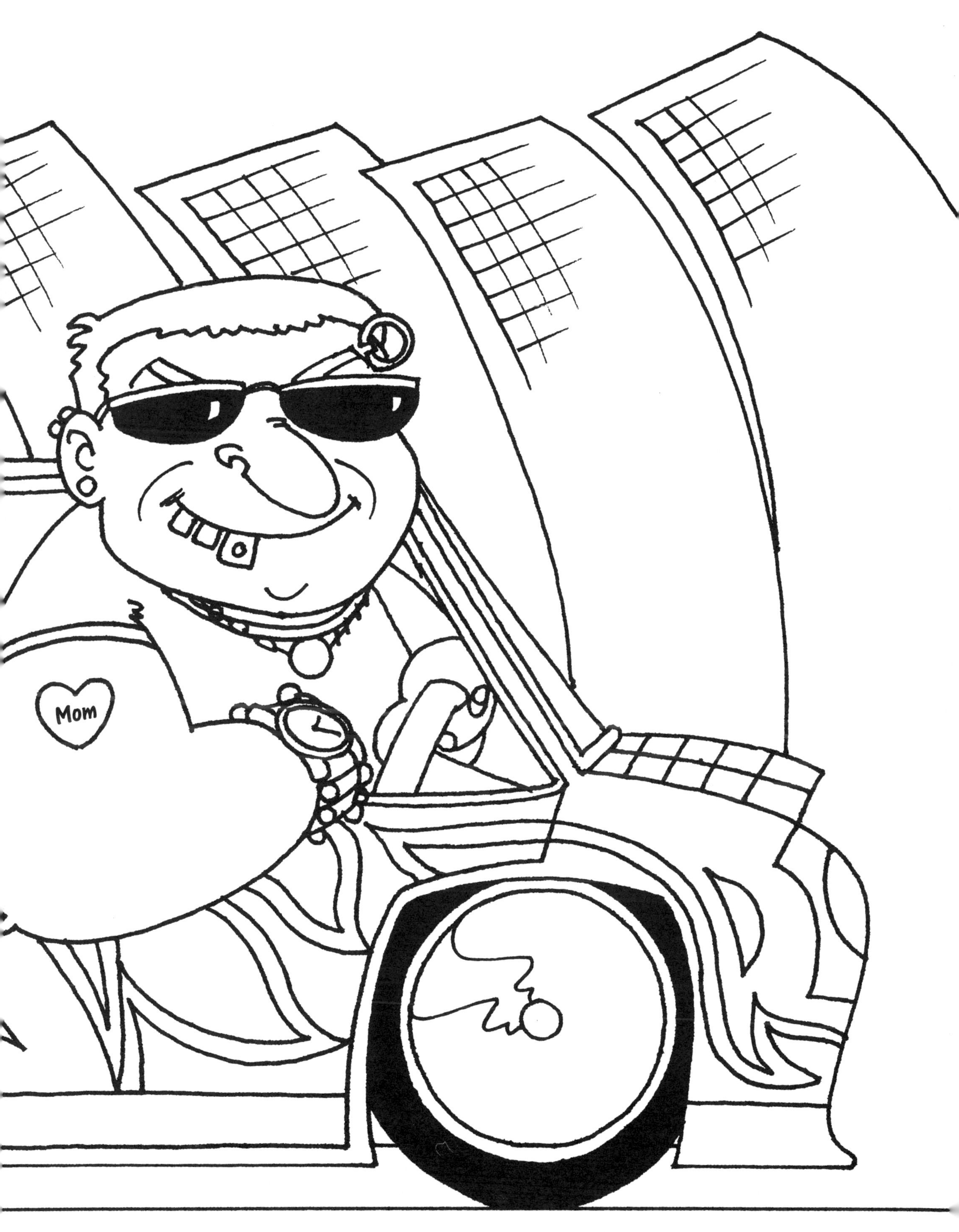
Mom

What are these boys up to?

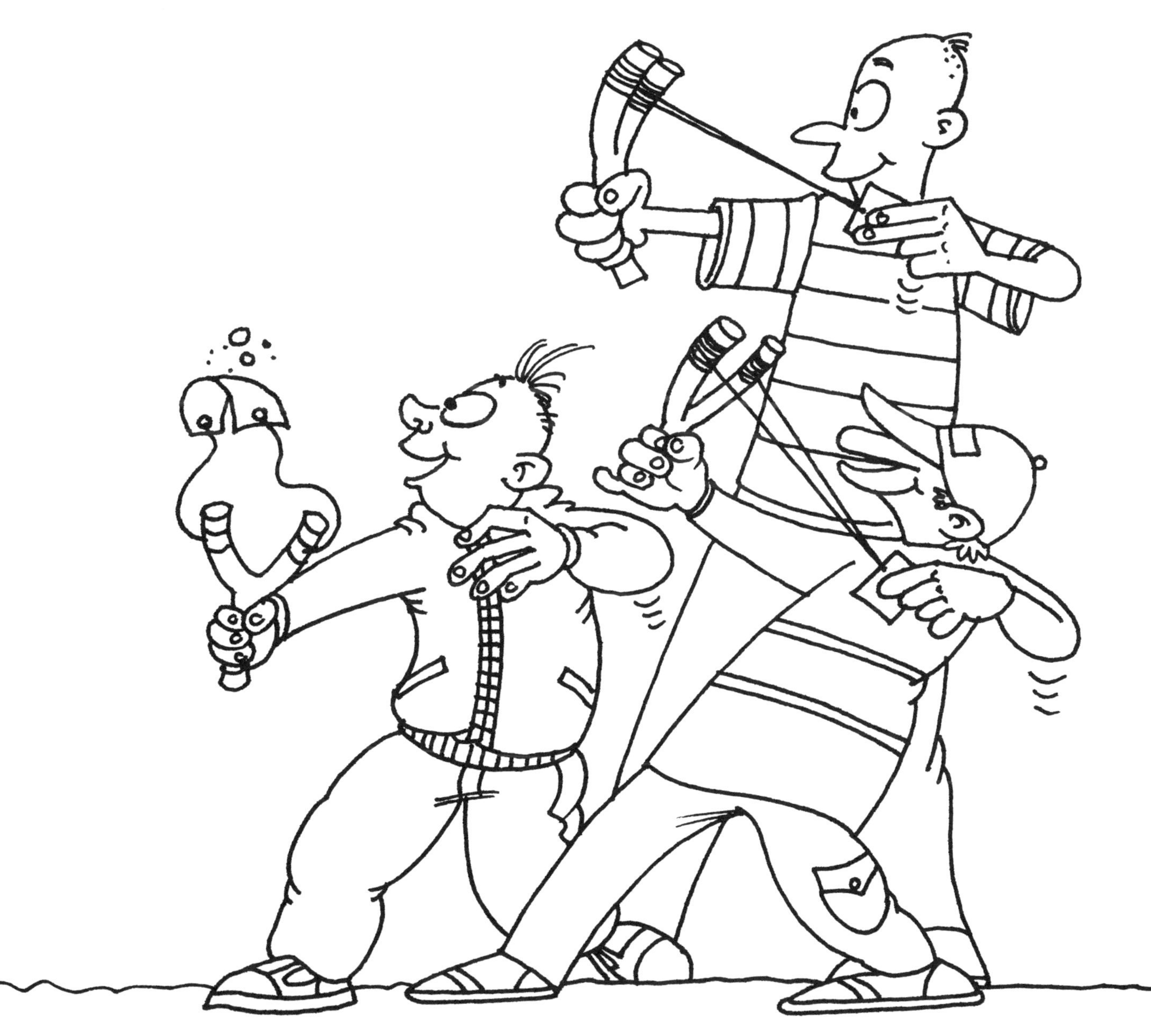

Every trucker needs a truckin' hat

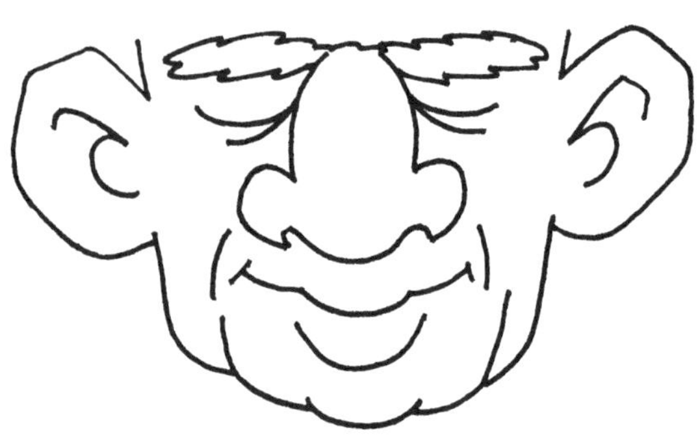

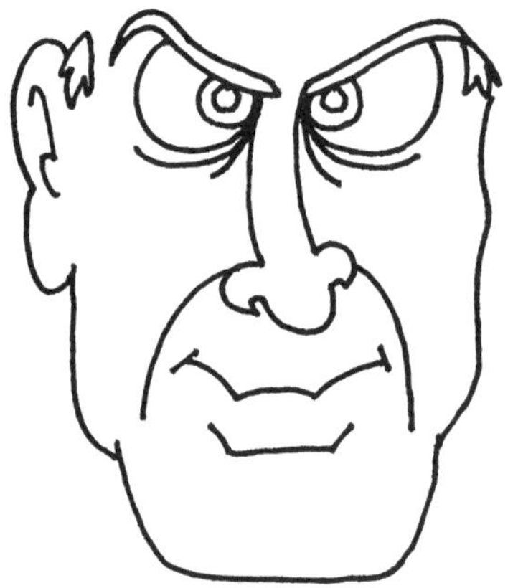

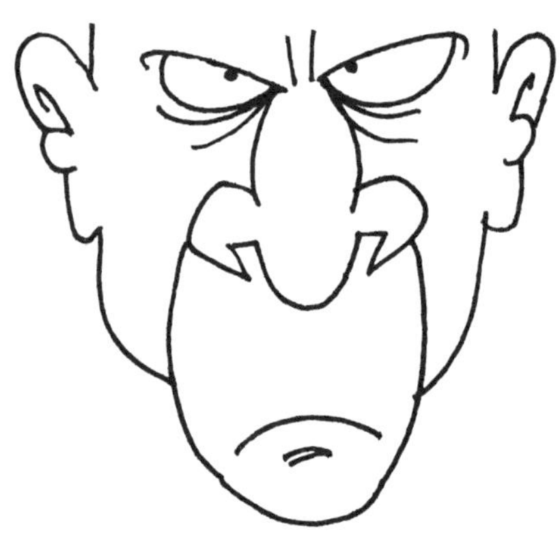

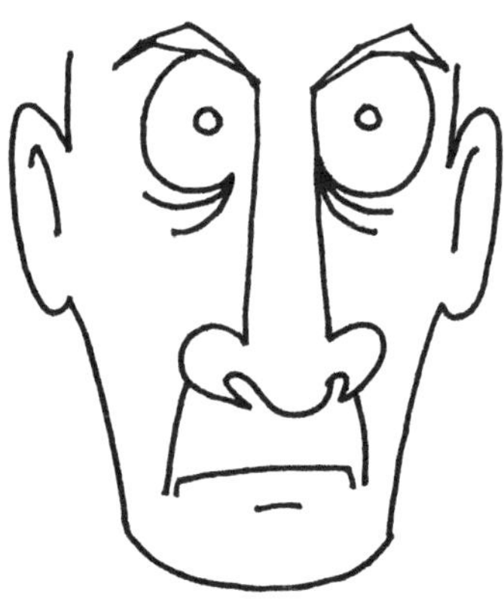

This fruit is all the wrong color!

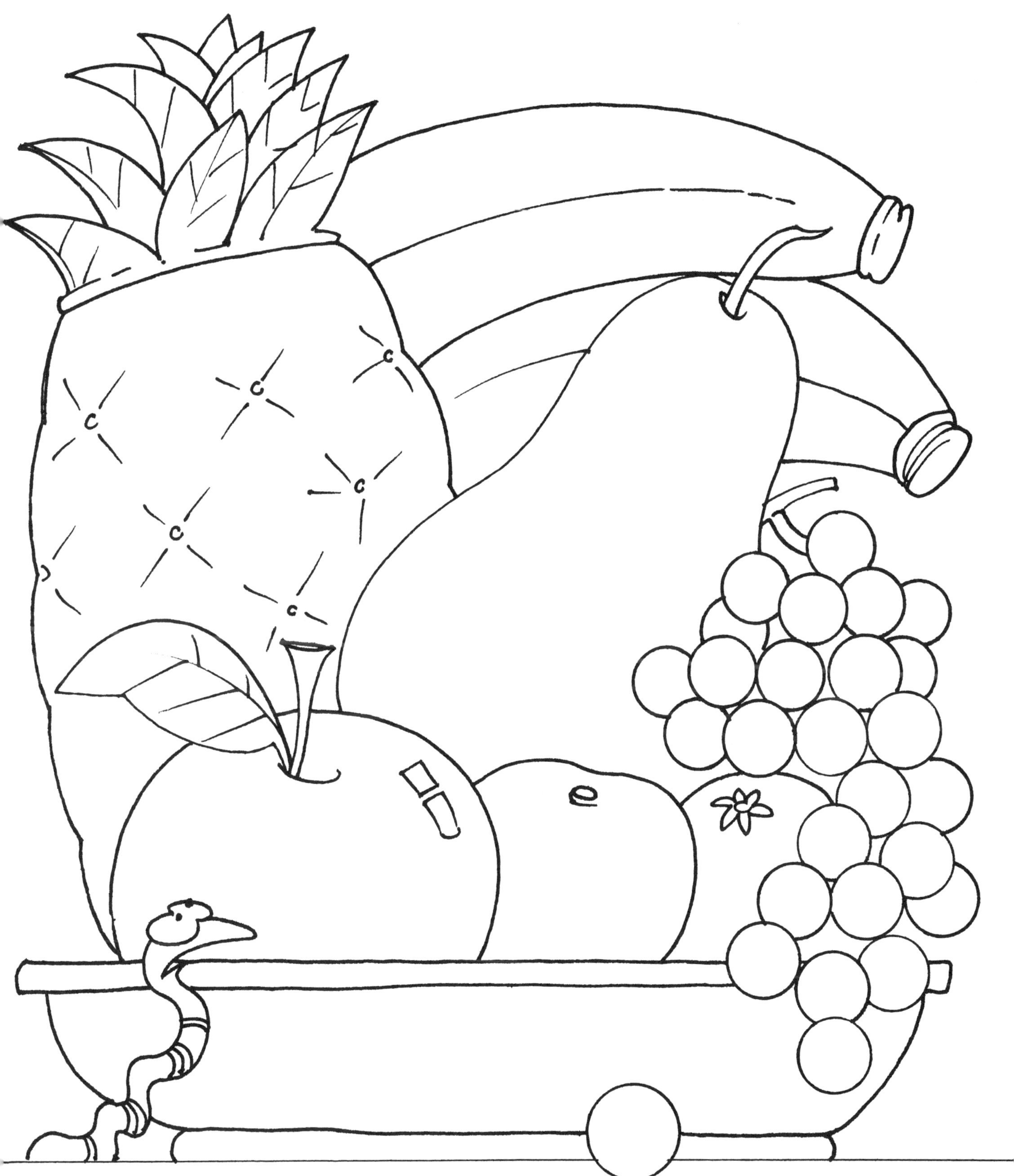

Who's caught the most colorful catch?

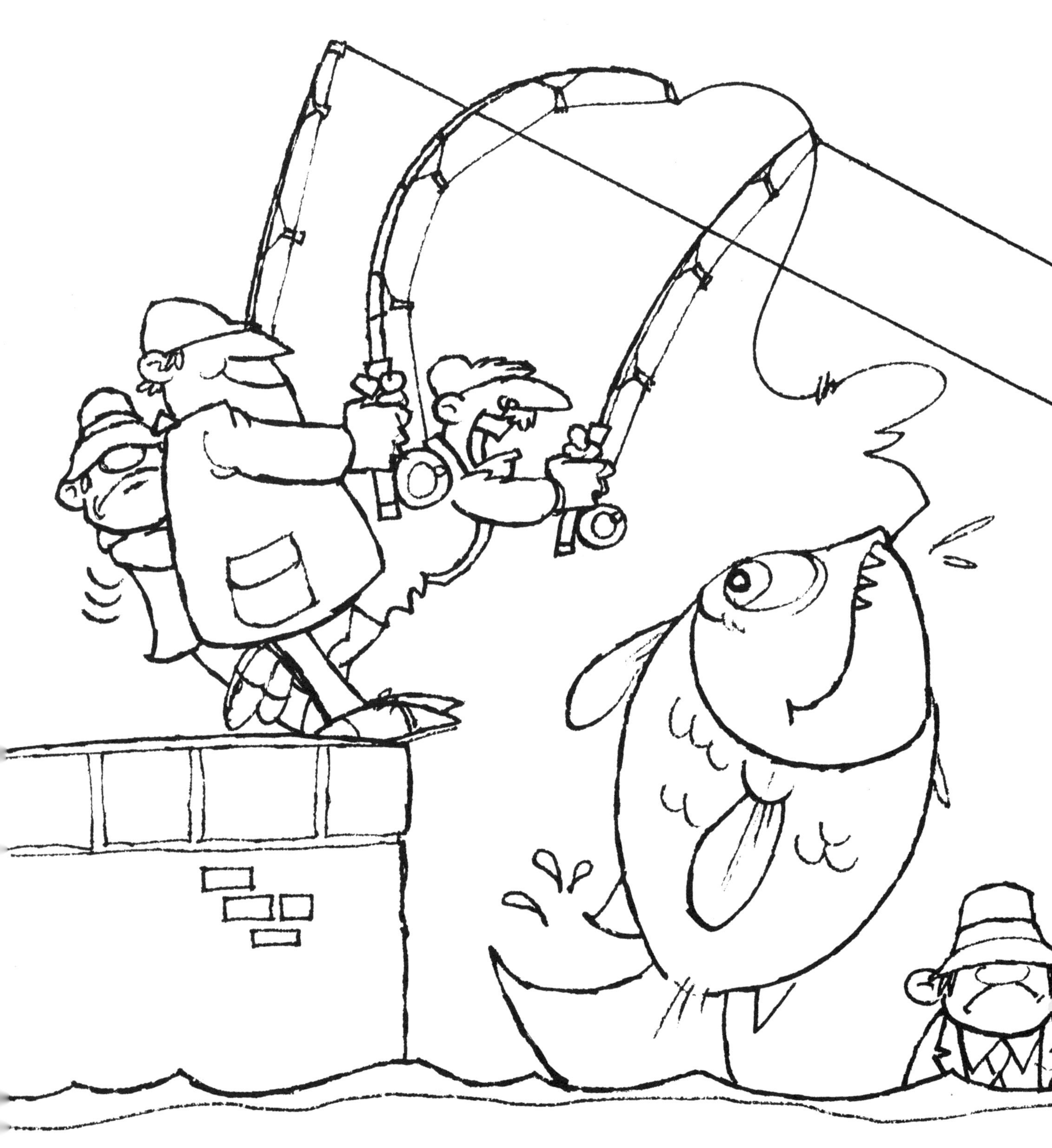

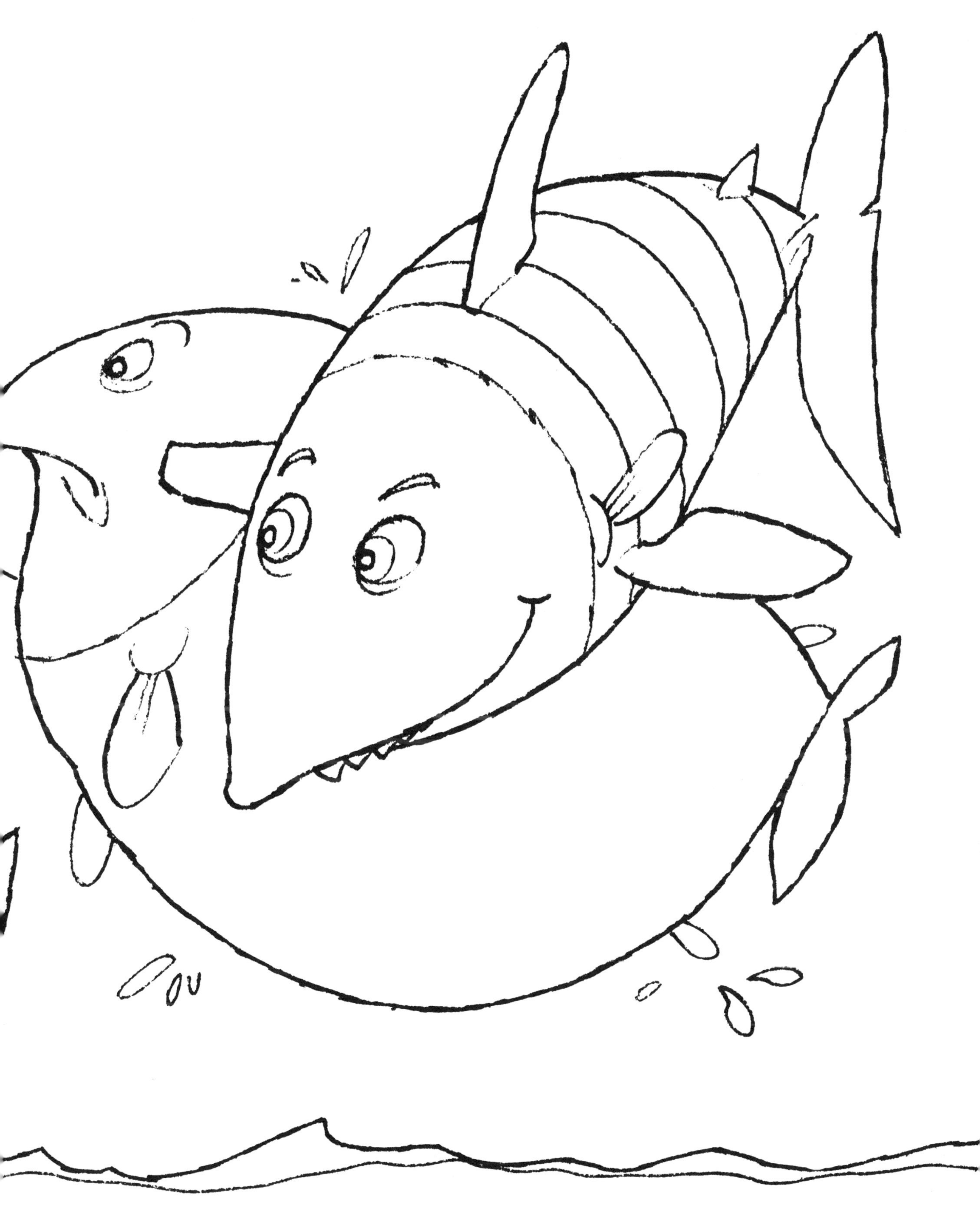

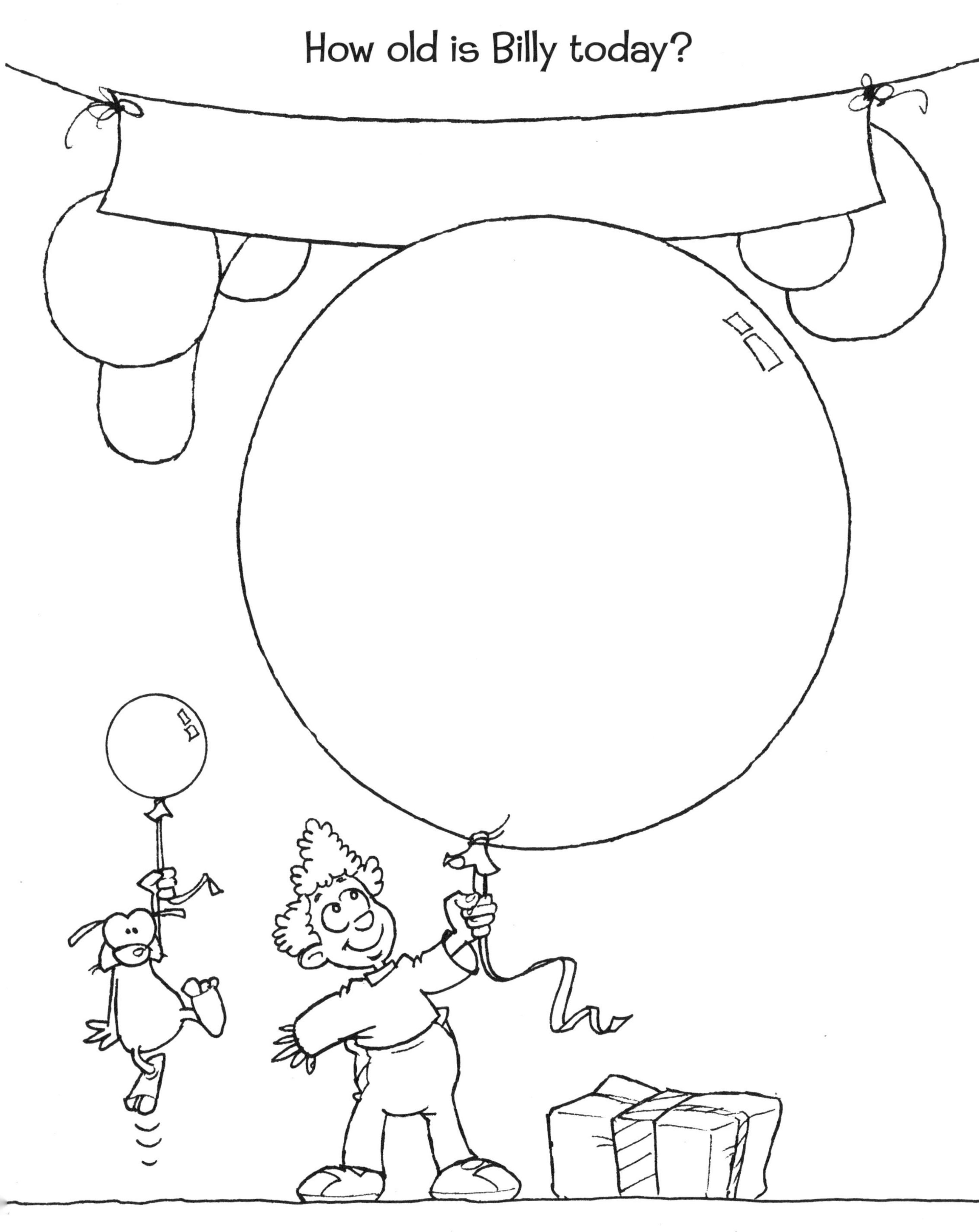
How old is Billy today?